JAMIE O'NEILL

AT SWIM, TWO BOYS

Scribner

First published in Great Britain by Scribner, 2001
An imprint of Simon & Schuster UK Ltd
A Viacom Company

1 3 5 7 9 10 8 6 4 2

Simon & Schuster UK Ltd
Africa House
64–78 Kingsway
London WC2B 6AH

Simon & Schuster Australia
Sydney

A CIP catalogue record for this book is available
from the British Library

Hardback ISBN 0–7432–0712–2
Trade Paperback ISBN 0–7432–0713–0

Designed by Peter Ward

Typeset in Baskerville by
Palimpsest Book Production Limited, Polmont, Stirlingshire
Printed and bound in Great Britain by
The Bath Press, Bath

à Julien
mon ami, mon amour

PART ONE

1915

I will make inseparable cities with their arms about each other's necks;
By the love of comrades.

– WALT WHITMAN

*T*HERE GOES *Mr Mack, cock of the town. One foot up, the other foot down. The hell of a gent. With a tip of his hat here and a top of the morn there, tip-top, everything's dandy. He'd bare his head to a lamppost.*

A Christian customer too. Designate the charity, any bazaar you choose, up sticks the bill in his shop. 'One Shilling per Guinea Spent Here Will Aid the Belgian Refugees'. 'Comforts for the Troops in France'. 'Presentation Missions up the Limpopo'. *Choose me the cause, he's a motto to milk it. See him of a Sunday. Ladies' Mass by the sixpenny-door, stays on for the Stations for his tanner's worth. Oh, on the up, that's Mr Mack, a Christian genteelery grocerly man.*

What's that? A modest quencher, if your honour is asking. Don't care if I do.

A sargentleman even, for yous know he was a soldier of the Queen, me lads. Royal Dublin Fusiliers, Second Battalion, the Old Toughs. Joined up in old God's time. This was down in Tipp. Tipperary, says he – the Yorkshire of Ireland. Not a patriot by any stretch.

> *Some say the devil he lives in Slane*
> *More say he comes from Blarney*
> *But them that tells the truth agree*
> *He joined the British Army.*

Well, I was only a kidger meself them days, with the wandering soles on me feet – nothing would do but a sodger's life for me. Had I known the class of galoot they favoured, I better had stopped in me bed. For no time at all old Macks was made a sergeant of. Quartermaster-Sergeant Mack. A responsible position, quoth he, in charge of the regimental vittles. So now yous know. The relief of Ladysmith was down to bread baked on time.

Here's the boy with the creature comforts. Pardon me parsnips while I do the aqua. May your purse nor your prick never fail you, young sir.

Wait and I tell yous. Small accommodation I asked for one time, old comrades and all that. This was after our sodgering days was done, above in his huckster's emporium was this. Old Macks had me splitting firewood till closing. And meself here with me lungs destroyed and half me guts left bleeding on the kopjeses. Not the Boer War, says he. Incorrect to name a war for the losing party. Nothing'll suit but you calls it the South African Campaign.

Not that Mister-me-friend-Mack saw spit of any fighting. Too cute by a quarter. Stowed for home on HMS Funk with his mawsey hide stamped time-expired. I know him of old or me name's not Doyle, you may take your oath on that, good gentlemen fair.

Cheers now, here's hoping. Where it goes, it goes worth chasing. This is a good one for yous:

> *To be sure did you hear*
> *of the heresy beer*
> *that was made for to poison the Pope?*
> *To hide the blame a sin is*
> *the name is Arthur Guinness*
> *for salvation no turncoat can hope.*

Sure a bird never hopped on one leg. Pint of purge, if your honour is asking. Don't care if I do.

Look at old Macks now, would you run your lamps over that. He's tipped his hat to the milkman's jennet. Carry me out, the tippest-toppest gent ever that loaned you nuppence.

Yous know what I'm going to tell ya, do yous know what I'm going to say? He has this handle round the parish hereabouts. They calls him the General. He don't mind, a nod to his gallanty past. And the magnolious sight of him behind of his counter – purl one, plain one, all day long knitting stockings for the troops. Sure no one has the heart to let on 'tis General short for General Maid.

Whisht now, he's after turning. What's he forgot? Never fear, he wouldn't darken the likes of here. Hardened tea-drinker is his nibs. Now now, where's his corpulence at? Back to the paper stand. Will old bags risk a morning paper? Curse the beggar. He'll be looking for his change next. Old shoes, up again.

Well, would yous believe it. That bangs it. That bangs Banaghan. Is he a lunatic altogether? Does he think he's a Protestant? He's only after taking an Irish Times!

CHAPTER ONE

AT THE CORNER of Adelaide Road, where the paving sparkled in the morning sun, Mr Mack waited by the newspaper stand. A grand day it was, rare and fine. Puff-clouds sailed through a sky of blue. Fair-weather cumulus to give the correct designation: on account they cumulate, so Mr Mack believed. High above the houses a seagull glinted, gliding on a breeze that carried from the sea. Wait now, was it cumulate or accumulate he meant? The breeze sniffed of salt and tide. Make a donkey of yourself, inwardly he cautioned, using words you don't know their meaning. And where's this paper chappie after getting to?

In delicate clutch an *Irish Times* he held. A thruppenny piece, waiting to pay, rolled in his fingers. Every so often his hand queried his elbow – Parcel safe? Under me arm, his hand-pat assured him.

Glasthule, homy old parish, on the lip of Dublin Bay. You could see the bay, a wedge of it, between the walls of a lane, with Howth lying out beyond. The bay was blue as the sky, a tinge deeper, and curiously raised-looking when viewed dead on. The way the sea would be sloping to the land. If this paper chappie don't show up quick, bang goes his sale. Cheek of him leaving customers wait in the street.

A happy dosser was nosing along the lane and Mr Mack watched with lenient disdain. Any old bone. Lick of something out of a can. Dog's life really. When he came to the street Mr Mack touched a finger to his hat, but the happy dosser paid him no regard. He slouched along and Mr Mack saw it puddling after, something he had spilt in the road, his wasted civility. Lips pursed with comment, he pulled, squeezing, one droop of his bush moustache.

'Oh hello, Mrs Conway, grand day it is, grand to be sure, tip-top and yourself keeping dandy?'

Nice class of lady, left foot, but without the airs. Saw me waiting with an *Irish Times*, twice the price of any other paper. They remark such things, the quality do. Glory be, I hope she didn't think – his *Irish Times* dropped by his side – Would she ever have mistook me for the paperman, do you think?

Pages fluttered on the newspaper piles, newsboards creaked in the breeze. Out-of-the-way spot for a paper stand. Had supposed to be above by the railway station. But this thoolamawn has it currently, what does he do only creeps it down, little by little, till now he has it smack outside of Fennelly's—

Mr Mack swivelled on his heels. Fennelly's public house. The corner doors were propped wide where the boy was mopping the steps. Late in the morning to be still at his steps. The gloom inside gave out a hum of amusement, low mouths of male companionship, gathered by the amber glow of the bar. Mr Mack said Aha! with his eyes. He thrust his head inside the door, waved his paper in the dark. ''Scuse now, gents.' He hadn't his hat back on his head before a roar of hilarity, erupting at the bar, hunted him away, likely to shove him, back out in the street.

Well, by the holy. He gave a hard nod to the young bucko leaning on his mop and grinning. What was that about?

Presently, a jerky streak of anatomy distinguished itself in the
door, coughing and spluttering while it came, and shielding its
eyes from the sun. 'Is it yourself, Sergeant?'

'Hello now, Mr Doyle,' said Mr Mack.

'Quartermaster-Sergeant Mack, how are you, how's every
hair's breadth of you, what cheer to see you so spry.' A spit
preceded him to the pavement. 'You weren't kept waiting at
all?' This rather in rebuttal than inquiry. 'Only I was inside
getting of bronze for silver. Paper is it?'

The hades you were, thought Mr Mack, and the smell of drink
something atrocious. 'Fennelly has a crowd in,' he remarked, 'for
the hour.'

'Bagmen,' the paperman replied. 'Go-boys on the make out
of Dublin. And a miselier mischaritable unChristianer crew – '

Ho ho ho, thought Mr Mack. On the cadge, if I know my
man. Them boys inside was too nimble for him.

'Would you believe, Sergeant, they'd mock a man for the
paper he'd read?'

'What's this now?' said Mr Mack.

The paperman chucked his head. 'God be their judge and
a bitter one, say I. And your good self known for a decent skin
with no more side than a margarine.'

Mr Mack could not engage but a rise was being took out of
him. The paperman made play of settling his papers, huffling
and humphing in that irritating consumptive way. He made
play of banging his chest for air. He spat, coughing with the
spittle, a powdery disgruntled cough – 'Choky today,' said he –
and Mr Mack viewed the spittle-drenched sheet he now held in
his hand. This fellow, the curse of an old comrade, try anything
to vex me.

'I'm after picking up,' choosily he said, 'an *Irish Times*, only
I read here—'

'An *Irish Times*, Sergeant? Carry me out and bury me decent, so you have and all. Aren't you swell away with the high-jinkers there?'

Mr Mack plumped his face and a laugh, like a fruit, dropped from his mouth. 'I wouldn't know about any high-jinkers,' he confided. 'Only I read here 'tis twice the price of any other paper. Twice the price,' he repeated, shaking his cautious head. A carillon of coins chinkled in his pocket. 'I don't know now can the expense be justified.'

'Take a risk of it, Sergeant, and damn the begrudgers.' The paperman leant privily forward. 'A gent on the up, likes of yourself, isn't it worth it alone for the shocks and stares?'

Narrowly Mr Mack considered his man. A fling or a fox-paw, he couldn't be certain sure. He clipped his coin on the paper-stack. 'Penny, I believe,' he said.

'Thruppence,' returned Mr Doyle. 'Balance two dee to the General.'

Mr Mack talked small while he waited for his change. 'Grand stretch of weather we're having.'

''Tisn't the worst.'

'Grand I thought for the time of year.'

'Thanks be to God.'

'Oh thanks be to God entirely.'

Mr Mack's face faltered. Had ought to get my thanks in first. This fellow, not a mag to bless himself with, doing me down always. He watched him shambling through the pockets of his coat. And if it was change he was after in Fennelly's it was devilish cunning change for never the jingle of a coin let out. A smile fixed on Mr Mack's face. Barking up the wrong tree with me, my merry old sweat. Two dee owed.

At last the paperman had the change found. Two lustreless pennies, he held them out, the old sort, with the old Queen's hair in a bun. Mr Mack was on the blow of plucking them in his fingers when the paperman coughed – 'Squeeze me' – coughed into his – 'Squeeze me peas, Sergeant' – coughed into his sleeve. Not what you'd call coughing but hacking down the tracts of his throat to catch some breath had gone missing there. His virulence spattered the air between, and Mr Mack thought how true what they say, take your life in your hands every breath you breathe.

He cleared his own throat and said, 'I trust I find you well?'

'Amn't I standing, God be praised?' With a flump then he was down on the butter-box he kept for a seat.

Bulbous, pinkish, bush-moustached, Mr Mack's face lowered. He'd heard it mentioned right enough, that old Doyle, he was none too gaudy this weather. Never had thought to find him this far gone. That box wouldn't know of him sitting on it. He looked down on the dull face, dull as any old copper, with the eyes behind that looked chancy back. Another fit came on, wretched to watch, like something physical had shook hold the man; and Mr Mack reached his hand to his shoulder.

'Are you all right there, Mick?'

'Be right in a minute, Arthur. Catch me breath is all.'

Mr Mack gave a squeeze of his hand, feeling the bones beneath. 'Will I inquire in Fennelly's after a drop of water?'

'I wouldn't want to be bothering Fennelly for water, though.'

Them chancy old eyes. Once upon a time them eyes had danced. Bang goes sixpence, thought Mr Mack, though it was a shilling piece he pulled out of his pocket. 'Will you do yourself a favour, Mick, and get something decent for your dinner.'

'Take that away,' Mr Doyle rebuked him. 'I have my pride yet. I won't take pity.'

'Now where's the pity in a bob, for God's sake?'

'I fought for Queen and Country. There's no man will deny it.'

'There's no man wants to deny it.'

'Twenty-five years with the Colours. I done me bit. I went me pound, God knows if I didn't.'

Here we go, thought Mr Mack.

'I stood me ground. I stood to them Bojers and all.'

Here we go again.

'Admitted you wasn't there. Admitted you was home on the boat to Ireland. But you'll grant me this for an old soldier. That Fusilier Doyle, he done his bit. He stood up to them Bojers, he did.'

'You did of course. You're a good Old Tough, 'tis known in the parish.'

'Begod and I'd do it over was I let. God's oath on that. We'd know the better of Germany then.' He kicked his boot against the newsboard, which told, unusually and misfortunately for his purpose, not of the war at all but of beer and whiskey news, the threat and fear of a hike in the excise. 'I'd soon put manners on those Kaiser lads.'

'No better man,' Mr Mack conceded. Mr Doyle tossed his head, the way his point, being gained, he found it worthless for a gain. Mr Mack had to squeeze the shilling bit into his hand. 'You'll have a lotion on me whatever,' he said, confidentially urging the matter.

The makings of a smile lurked across the paperman's face. 'There was a day, Arthur, and you was pal o' me heart,' said he, 'me fond segotia.' The silver got pocketed. 'May your hand be stretched in friendship, Sergeant, and never your neck.'

Charity done with and the price of a skite secured, they might risk a reasonable natter. 'Tell us,' said Mr Mack, 'is it true what happened the young fellow was here on this patch?'

'Sure carted away. The peelers nabbed him.'

'A recruitment poster I heard.'

'Above on the post office windows. Had it torn away.'

'Shocking,' said Mr Mack. 'Didn't he know that's a serious offence?'

'Be sure he'll know now,' said Mr Doyle. 'Two-monthser he'll get out of that. Hard.'

'And to look at him he only a child.'

'Sure mild as ever on porridge smiled. Shocking.'

Though Mr Mack could not engage it was the offence was referred to and not the deserts. 'Still, you've a good few weeks got out of this work.'

'They'll have the replacement found soon enough.'

'You stuck it this long, they might see their way to making you permanent.'

'Not so, Sergeant. And the breath only in and out of me.' An obliging little hack found its way up his throat. 'There's only the one place I'll be permanent now. I won't be long getting there neither.'

But Mr Mack had heard sufficient of that song. 'Sure we're none of us getting any the rosier.' The parcel shifted under his arm and, the direction coming by chance into view, Mr Doyle's eyes squinted, then saucered, then slyly he opined,

'Knitting.'

'Stockings,' Mr Mack elaborated. 'I'm only on my way to Ballygihen. Something for Madame MacMurrough and the Comforts Fund.'

'Didn't I say you was up with the high-jinkers? Give 'em socks there, Sergeant, give 'em socks.'

Mr Mack received this recommendation with the soldierly good humour with which it was intended. He tipped his hat and the game old tough saluted.

'Good luck to the General.'

'Take care now, Mr Doyle.'

Parcel safe and under his arm, Mr Mack made his way along the parade of shops. At the tramstop he looked into Phillips's ironmongers. 'Any sign of that delivery?'

'Expected' was all the answer he got.

Constable now. Sees me carrying the *Irish Times*. Respectable nod. Little Fenianeen in our midst and I never knew. After hacking at a recruitment poster. Mind, 'tis pranks not politics. Pass a law against khaki, you'd have them queueing up to enlist.

The shops ended and Glasthule Road took on a more dignified, prosperous air. With every step he counted the rateable values rising, ascending on a gradient equivalent to the road's rise to Ballygihen. Well-tended gardens and at every lane a kinder breeze off the sea. In the sun atop a wall a fat cat sat whose head followed wisely his progress.

General, he calls me. Jocular touch that. After the General Stores, of course. Shocks and stares – should send that in the paper. Pay for items catchy like that. Or did I hear it before? Would want to be sure before committing to paper. Make a donkey of yourself else.

A scent drifted by that was utterly familiar yet unspeakably far away. He leant over a garden wall and there it blew, ferny-leaved and tiny-flowered, in its sunny yellow corner. Never had thought it would prosper here. Mum-mim-mom, begins with something mum. Butterfly floating over it, a pale white soul, first I've seen of the year.

Pall of his face back there. They do say they take on worse in the sunshine, your consumptives do. Segotia: is it some class of a flower? I never thought to inquire. Pal of me heart. Well, we're talking twenty thirty years back. Mick and Mack the paddy whacks. We had our day, 'tis true. Boys together and bugles together and bayonets in the ranks. Rang like bells, all we wanted was hanging. But there's no pals except you're equals. I learnt me that after I got my very first stripe.

He looked back down the road at the dwindling man with his lonely stand of papers. A Dublin tram came by. In the clattering of its wheels and its sparking trolley the years dizzied a moment. Scarlet and blue swirled in the dust, till there he stood, flush before him, in the light of bright and other days, the bugler boy was pal of his heart. My old segotia.

Parcel safe? Under me arm.

The paper unfolded in Mr Mack's hands and his eyes glanced over the front page. Hotels, hotels, hotels. Hatches, matches, dispatches. Eye always drawn to 'Loans by Post'. Don't know for why. What's this the difference is between a stock and a share? Have to ask Jim when he gets in from school.

He turned the page. Here we go. Royal Dublin Fusiliers depot. Comforts Fund for the Troops in France. Committee gratefully acknowledges. Here we go. Madame MacMurrough, Ballygihen branch. Socks, woollen, three doz pair.

Gets her name in cosy enough. Madame MacMurrough. Once a month I fetch over the stockings, once a month she has her name in the paper. Handy enough if you can get it.

Nice to know they're delivered, all the same, delivered where they're wanted.

His eyes wandered to the Roll of Honour that ran along the paper's edge. Officers killed, officers wounded, wounded and missing, wounded believed prisoners, correction: officers killed. All officers. Column, column and a half of officers. Then there's only a handful of other ranks. Now that can't be right. How do they choose them? Do you have to – is that what I'd have to do? – submit the name yourself? And do they charge for that? Mind you, nice to have your name in the *Irish Times*. That's what I'll have to do maybe, should Gordie—God forbid, what was he saying? God forbid, not anything happen to Gordie. Touch wood. Not wood, scapular. Where am I?

There, he'd missed his turn. That was foolish. Comes from borrowing trouble. And it was an extravagance in the first place to be purchasing an *Irish Times*. Penny for the paper, a bob for that drunk—Jacobs! I didn't even get me two dee change. One and thruppenny walk in all. Might have waited for the *Evening Mail* and got me news for a ha'penny.

However, his name was Mr Mack, and as everyone knew, or had ought know by now, the Macks was on the up.

The gates to Madame MacMurrough's were open and he peered up the avenue of straggling sycamores to the veiled face of Ballygihen House. A grand lady she was to be sure, though her trees, it had to be said, could do with a clipping.

He did not enter by the gates, but turned down Ballygihen Avenue beside. He had come out in a sweat, beads were trickling down the spine of his shirt, the wet patch stuck where his braces crossed. He mended his pace to catch his breath. At the door in the wall he stopped. Mopped his forehead and neck with his handkerchief, took off his hat and swabbed inside. Carefully stroked its brim where his fingers might have disturbed the nap. Replaced it. Size too small. Would never believe your head would grow. Or had the hat shrunk on him? Dunn's three-and-ninepenny bowler? No, his hat had never shrunk. He brushed both boots against the calves of his trousers. Parcel safe? Then he pushed inside the tradesmen's gate.

Brambly path through shadowy wood. Birds singing on all sides. Mess of nettles, cow-parsley, could take a scythe to them. Light green frilly leaves would put you in mind of, ahem, petticoats. A blackbird scuttled off the path like a schoolboy caught at a caper. Then he was out in the light, and the lawns of Ballygihen House stretched leisurely to the sea. The sea oh the sea, long may it be. What a magnificent house it was, view and vantage them both, for its windows commanded the breadth of Dublin Bay. If he had this house what wouldn't he do but sit upon its sloping lawns while all day long the mailboats to'd and fro'd.

Mr Mack shook his head, but not disconsolately; for the beauty of the scene, briefly borrowed and duly returned, would brighten the sorrow of a saint. He followed the path by the trees, careful of stepping on the grass, till he came into the shadow of the house where the area steps led down to the kitchens.

And who was it only Madame MacMurrough's slavey showing leg at the step. Bit late in the morning to be still at her scrubbing. From Athlone, I believe, a district I know nothing about, save that it lies at the heart of Ireland.

He leant over the railing. 'You're after missing a spot, Nancy.'

The girl looked up. ''Tis you, Mr Mack. And I thought it was the butcher's boy after giving me cheek.'

She thought it was the butcher's—Mr Mack hawked his throat. 'Julian weather we're having.'

She pulled the hair out of her eyes. 'Julian, Mr Mack?'

'Julian. Pertaining to the month of July. It's from the Latin.'

'But 'tis scarce May.'

'Well, I know that, Nancy. I meant 'tis July-like weather. Warm.'

She stood up, skirts covering her shins. Something masonic about her smile. 'Any news from Gordie, Mr Mack?'

Mr Mack peered over her shoulder looking to see was there

anyone of consequence about. 'Gordie?' he repeated. 'You must mean Gordon, my son Gordon.'

'No letters or anything in the post?'

'How kind of you, Nancy. But no, he's away on final training. We don't know the where, we don't know the where to. Submarines, do you see. Troop movements is always secretive in times of war.'

'Ah sure he's most like in England, round about Aldershot with the rest of the boys.'

No cook in evidence, no proper maid. Entire residence has the look of—'Aldershot? Why do you say Aldershot?'

'Do you know the place? Famous military town in Hampshire.'

'You oughtn't be talking such things. Didn't I just warn you about submarines?'

'In Ballygihen, Mr Mack?'

'Matter a damn where.' He felt he had stamped his foot, so he patted his toes on the gravel and muttered, 'Dang. Matter a dang, I meant.'

The breeze reblew the hair in her eyes. Slovenly the way she ties it. Has a simper cute as a cat. 'Is there no person in authority here I might address my business to?'

'Sure we're all alone in the big house together. If you wanted you could nip round the front and pull the bell. I'd let you in for the crack.'

Flighty, divil-may-care minx of a slavey. Pity the man who— He pinched, pulling, one droop of his moustache. 'I haven't the time for your cod-acting now, Nancy. It so happens I'm here on a serious matter not altogether disconnected with the war effort itself. I don't doubt your mistress left word I was due.'

She looked thoughtful a moment. 'I misrecall your name being spoke, but there was mention of some fellow might be bringing socks. I was to dump them in the scullery and give him sixpence out of thank you.'

After the huffing and puffing and wagging his finger, in the end he had to let his parcel into her shiftless hands. She knew better by then to bring up the sixpence. He had tipped his scant farewell and was re-ascending the steps when she let out,

'Still and all, Mr Mack, it's the desperate shame you wouldn't know where your ownest son was stationed at.'

'A shame we all must put up with.'

'Sure wherever it is, he'll be cutting a fine dash of a thing, I wouldn't doubt it.'

Slavey, he thought, proper name for a rough general. 'Don't let me disturb you further from your duty.'

'Good day, Mr Mack. But remember now: all love does ever rightly show humanity our tenderness.'

All love does what? Foolish gigglepot. Should have told her, should have said, he's gone to fight for King and Country and the rights of Catholic Belgium. Cutting a dash is for rakes and dandyprats. All love does ever what?

He sloped back down the road to Glasthule, his heart falling with the declining properties. Could that be true about the sixpence? It was a puzzle to know with rich folk. Maybe I might have held on to the stockings and fetched them over another day. Nothing like a face-to-face in getting to know the worth of a man. Or maybe the lady supposed I'd be too busy myself, would send a boy instead. Jim. She thought it was Jim I'd be sending. Jim, my son James. The sixpence was his consideration. Now that was mighty generous in Madame MacMurrough. Sixpence for that spit of a walk? There's the gentry for you now. That shows the quality.

Quick look-see in the hand-me-down window. Now that's new. Must tell Jim about that. A flute in Ducie's window.

Second thoughts, steer clear. Trouble enough with Gordie and the pledge-shop.

Brewery men at Fennelly's. Mighty clatter they make. On purpose much of the time. Advertise their presence. Fine old Clydesdale eating at his bait-sack. They look after them well, give them that. Now here's a wonder – paper stand deserted. Crowd of loafers holding up the corner.

A nipper-squeak across the road and his heart lifted for it was the boy out of the ironmonger's to say the tram had passed, package ready for collection. He took the delivery, signed the entry-book, patting the boy's head in lieu of gratuity, recrossed the street.

He was turning for home into Adelaide Road, named after – who's this it's named for again? – when Fennelly's corner doors burst open and a ree-raw jollity spilt out in the street. 'Sister Susie's sewing shirts for soldiers,' they were singing. Except in their particular rendition it was socks she was knitting.

'Quare fine day,' said one of the loafers outside. Another had the neck to call out Mr Mack's name.

Mr Mack's forefinger lifted vaguely hatwards. Corner of his eye he saw others making mouths at him. Loafers, chancers, shapers. Where were the authorities at all that they wouldn't take them in charge? Fennelly had no licence for singing. And the Angelus bell not rung.

Package safe? Under me arm. Chickens clucking in the yards, three dogs mooching. What they need do, you see, is raise the dog licence. That would put a stop to all this mooching. Raise the excise while they're about it. Dung in the street and wisps of hay, sparrows everywhere in the quiet way.

The shop was on a corner of a lane that led to a row of humbler dwellings. He armed himself with a breath. The bell clinked when he pushed the door.

Incorrect to say a hush fell on the premises. They always spoke in whispers, Aunt Sawney and her guests. There she sat, behind the counter, Mrs Tansy sat on the customers' chair, they had another fetched in from the kitchen for Mrs Rourke. Now if a customer came, he'd be hard put to make it to the till. Gloomy too. Why wouldn't she leave the door wide? Gas only made it pokier in the daylight. Which was free.

'God bless all here.' He touched the font on the jamb. Dryish. Have to see to that. Blessed himself.

'Hello, Aunt Sawney. Ready whenever to take over the reins. Mrs Rourke, how's this the leg is today? I'm glad to see you about, Mrs Tansy.'

New tin of snuff on the counter. Must remember to mark that down in the book. Impossible to keep tabs else. Straits of Ballambangjan ahead. 'I wonder if I might just . . . pardon me while I . . . if you could maybe.' Manoeuvre safe between. Find harbour in the kitchen. Range stone cold, why wouldn't she keep an eye on it? Poke head back inside an instant. 'Range is out, Aunt Sawney, should your guests require some tea.'

Three snorts came in reply as each woman took a pinch of snuff.

He sat down at the kitchen table, laid the new package in front of him. His eyes gauged its contents, while he reached behind his neck to loosen the back-stud of his collar. He flexed his arms. Let me see, let me see. The boy at the ironmonger's had dangled the package by the twine and he had a deal of difficulty undoing the knot. Keep the torn paper for them on tick.

And finally there they were. Bills, two gross, finest American paper, fine as rashers of wind, in Canon bold proclaiming:

Adelaide General Stores
Quality Goods At Honest Prices

Mr. A. Mack, Esqr.
Will Be Pleased To Assist In All Your Requirements
An Appeal To You!
One Shilling Per Guinea Spent Here
Will Comfort Our Troops In France!

Page was a touch cramped at the base so that the end line, 'Proprietress: Sawney Burke', had to be got in small print. Still, it was the motto that mattered, and that was a topper. Will comfort our troops in France. Appeal to the honour of the house.

Moustache. Touch it. Spot of something in the hairs. Egg, is it? Stuck.

Was I right all the same to leave it to honour only? Nothing about the pocket. How's about this for the hookum?

Pounds, Shillings and Pence!
Why Not Buy Local And Save On Leather?

Appeal to the pocket of the house. Might better have had two orders made up. One for the swells, other for the smells.

Never mind the smells, the Macks is on the up.

Jim. What time is it? Home for his dinner at five after one. Gone twelve now. He could maybe deliver the startings in his dinner-hour, the leavings before his tea.

Have I missed the Angelus so? How's this I missed the Angelus?

Clink. That's the door. Customer? No, exeunt two biddies. She'll be in now, tidy away. Aunt Sawney, I've had these advertising-bills made up . . . ? No, wait till they're delivered first. Fate accomplished. Where's that apron? Better see to the range. 'Aunt Sawney, there you are. Must be puffed out after

22

that stint. I'll do shop now. You read the paper in your chair. We'll soon have a feel of heat.'

'Stay away from that kitchener,' she said.

'The range?' said Mr Mack.

'That kitchener wants blacking.'

'The range?'

She was already on her knees. She had a new tin of Zebra black-lead with her. 'Yc'll have me hands in blisters. I left it go out since yesternight.'

Surely a touch uncivil to name a kitchen range after the hero who avenged Khartoum. 'Did we finish that other tin of Zebra already? Right so, I'll mark that down in the book. It's best to keep tabs.'

''Tis cold plate for dinner. And cold plate for tea.'

'Whatever you think is best, Aunt Sawney. But you're not after forgetting it's his birthday today?'

'I'm not after forgetting this kitchener wants blacking.' She damped a cloth in the black-lead tin, letting out a creak of coughing as she did so.

The door clinked. Customer. 'I'll be with you directly,' he called. Then, thoughtfully: 'Not to trouble yourself, Aunt Sawney. I have a cake above out of Findlater's. Sure what more could his boyship want? But no mention of birthdays till after his tea. We'll have nothing brought off all day else.'

'I suppose and you got him them bills for his treat.'

Well, I'll be sugared. How would she know about the bills? He watched her at her labour for a moment. Wiry woman with hair the colour of ash. The back tresses she wore in a small black cap which hung from her crown like an extra, maidenly, head of hair. Even kneeling she had a bend on her, what's this they used call it, the Grecian bends. If you straightened her now, you'd be feared of her snapping. Cheeks like loose gullets, wag when vexed. When the teeth go, you see, the pouches collapse. Nose beaked, with dewdrop suspending. Not kin, thanks be to God, not I, save through the altar. Gordie and Jim are blood.

She coughed again, sending reverberations down her frame. Brown titus she calls it. Useless to correct her at her age. 'I'll leave the inside door pulled to in case you'd feel a chill from beyond. You're only over the bronchitis.'

'Mrs Tansy says the font wants filling.'

Gently Mr Mack reminded her, 'Mrs Tansy is a ranting Methody.'

'She still has eyes to see.'

Why would anyone look into a font? he wondered as he poured the holy water. Suppose when you are that way, dig with the other foot that is, these things take on an interest, a mystery even, which all too often for ourselves, digging as it were with the right foot, which is to say the proper one, have lost – lost where I was heading for there.

Cheeses, would you look at that motor the way it's pitching up Glasthule. Tearaways they have at the wheel. Take your life in your hands every turn you take. Hold on now, I believe I recognize that motor-car. He blew on his moustache, considering. There's a pucker idea: fonts for trams. Should send that in the paper. Never seen a font in a moving object. Would a bishop have one in his brougham for instance? Or is there maybe an injunction against fonts in anything not stationary? Should check the facts before committing to paper. There's fellows ready to pounce, the least miscalculation.

Nothing much in the street. Far away beyond the fields and the new red-bricked terraces rose the Dublin Mountains. Green grew to grey. Oats by reason the wet climatics. Clever the way the fields know to stop just where the hills begin. Turf then. They were down the other week trying to hock it on account the price of coal. Is there a season for turf, though? Make a donkey of yourself buying the wrong time of year.

Curls of smoke from the cottages nearby. Keeping the home fires burning. Back inside the shop. Clink, it's only me. Font again, no wonder it dries up so. Trade a little slack. Always the same this time of day. Might give that counter a wipe-down. Bits of snuff and goodness knows. Time to finish a stocking before dinner? Wouldn't it be grand now if Gordie would be wearing one of my stockings.

Where's there a place to fix a new shelf? Need a display for maybe a quality range of teas. High-grown, tippy Darjeeling, cans of, please. That would fetch the carriage trade.

What's this that Nancy one was on about, all love does ever what? Damn silly child. Holy show she made of his parade. Marching with Gordie in the ranks to the troopship. Son of mine stepping out with a slavey. Where's the up in that?

Here a shelf, there a shelf? Can smell it now, the wafting scents. Would madam take a seat while I weigh her requirements? None of your one-and-fourpence populars, but Assam and pekoe and souchong, and customers to match, and souchong and oolong and Assam and—

Peeping up at him, her dabs just nipping the counter, a little female bedouin with dirty face and half an apron on.

'Well, little lady? Why aren't we at school today?'

'The ma sent me over for a saucer of jam.'

Beside the door Mr Mack had fixed a makeshift sign. 'One Shilling per Guinea Spent Here is a CREDIT to You!' He might better have saved the paper. 'Ha'penny,' he said to the slum-rat.

The sleek green motor cleared the feeble rise, haughty jerk as it jumped the tramlines, swept through the gates, gravel flittering with road-dust in its wake. Past the lodge, empty these years, least so by day, under the fairy light of arching trees, to emerge at its stabling where it shuddered in quiet triumph before a gauntleted glove that had stroked its wheel reached down to cut the engine.

Silence then, a world at rest. Not the antithesis of dust, of speed, but its complement. The gloved hand ungloved its partner which in turn ungloved its mate. Fingers untied her chiffon and felt for hair under her hat. Strays tidied behind her ears. The chiffon became a scarf, her hands reawoke the wide sloping brim of her hat. Gradually the earth too rewoke. Hedges chirruped to life, a crow bickered above, the sea resumed its reverend tide. Her hat was hopelessly *démodé* but the fashion was too ridiculous: she refused to wear flower-pots, and would have nothing to do with feathery things she had not shot herself.

Eveline MacMurrough slid to the passenger side, shifted her skirt over the low door. One leg, two legs, she steadied on the running-board, then slipped to the ground. The hand that held her gloves patted the coachwork, patted the trim. My Prince Henry. And they had thought to requisition you for an ambulance at the Front. *Les brutes anglaises.*

There was no one to see to her entrance, only the skivvy from the kitchen whom she had scarcely begun to civilize. This skin of jitters received her gloves, her chiffon, hat; Eveline allowed the dustcoat to be eased from her shoulders. *L'idiote.* 'Not through the hall, child,' she said. 'Outside and shake the dust.'

In the stand glass she reviewed her visage. The wind-screen had not been a total success. Then again goggles did leave such hideous lines. Perhaps it must be the veil after all. Though she did so resent the implication of purdah. Toilet water, a good scrub, then hot damp towels.

'Is old Moore about?'

'Would he not be in the garden, mam?'

Peasant insistence on interrogative response. It rather appealed to Eveline. Yes, she rather believed she liked it. 'When you find him, tell him the motor-car wants cleaning. Lamps too, I dare say. Cook?'

'Hasn't she taken the morning to visit her sister in St Michael's that's poorly?'

Defensive really: none of my doing, as though to say. 'Are we to starve so?'

'No, mam. She left a cold dinner prepared.'

'Lunch,' said Eveline.

'Lunch, mam.'

There was a quick call through the staff roll. Bootman repairing a leak in the attic, meaning presumably he was high; parlour maids called back to the registry, replacements not turned up. Really she must see to appointing new people, a housekeeper at the very least. So trying with the war on. Rush to the altar to avail of the separation allowances. It was something her nephew might take in hand. 'And my nephew?'

'I'm not sure, mam' – flush in her cheeks – 'if he hasn't gone bathing.'

Eveline had completed her inspection at the hall stand. The child waited by the pass door, hands by her sides like a board-school girl. Itching to be below stairs out of harm's way. *Pauvre ingénue.* Eveline smiled and ordered hot water and towels to her dressing-room. Even the *imbécile* might manage that.

While she sponged her cheeks with water of roses, she considered her interview with the new curate at St Joseph's, Glasthule. Naturally, it was the canon she had called upon, some invitation to decline, but a young priest had received her, offering regrets at the canon's indisposition. The canon's health was neither here nor there to Eva, her confessor being of the Jesuits at Gardiner Street, but the young man made such parade of hospitality, she had quickly perceived her demurs would serve but to encourage his insistence.

She had accepted tea in best blue china. The curate gave his name – unless she misheard, Father Amen O'Toiler, which sounded a sermon in itself. He fingered her card, then, still fidgeting, stood to make his say. 'I cannot tell you, Madame MacMurrough, what pleasure it is to greet a scion of your famous name.' Her famous name was given its due, which she heard as a type of Cook's tour of Irish history. Bridges taken, fords crossed, the sieges broken, battles lost, long valiant retreats – and not a one but a MacMurrough had been to the fore.

It was a familiar account and she had waited politely, seated at the edge of an aged Biedermeier whose stuffing was gone. Absently she wondered which charity the curate had in mind and what donation might eventually suffice.

The priest had continued his progress round the sunless parlour, chilly yet fuming from an ill-ventilated fire. Every few paces he referred to her card, as though the heads of his argument had been pencilled thereon, as onwards he passed through the dark centuries, the long night of Ireland's woe. Yet night, he averred, not so dark as to blind, for in every generation a light had sparked, betimes no more than a flash on the hillside, moretimes a flame to set the age afire. And not once in all the years but the cry had gone out: MacMurrough! The name was imperishable, ineradicable, sempiternal, a lodestar in the Irish firmament that had blazed to its zenith, as many believed (and not least the curate himself, if he might make so bold), in the brilliant, some might say heliacal, career of Madame MacMurrough's late revered regretted father, Dermot James William MacMurrough, Queen's Counsellor, quondam Lord Mayor and Chief Magistrate of our great metropolis, freeman of the cities of Waterford, Cork, New York and Boston, Chevalier de la Légion d'Honneur, Knight Grand Cross of the Order of St Gregory the Great, Member for the Borough of Ferns.

'And there at the moment of her direst need' – the curate's voice had strained as he came to the crux of his tale – 'when sacred Ireland stood upon the edge, at the very brink of extinction, who stood forth to show the way? Who but your father saw through the genteel broadcloth, the polished suaviloquence, to the degenerate soul within? Who was it saved Ireland from the alien heretical beast?'

Yes, Eveline thought now, before her dressing-table glass, her father had been first to denounce Parnell. Though it had been a close race, so fierce the stampede.

Perfume bottles, phials of scent, Gallé and Lalique; a porcelain shepherdess proffered tiny sugared treats on a tray, offered them twice, for the toilet glass reviewed her, stretching through the bottles, a child sinking through coloured viscous water. Eveline chose a bon-bon, sucked it thoughtfully.

There was more to this curate than at first she had suspected. More than once he had made allusion to the Fenians. His face had pecked in the intervals after, seeking collusion. She had nodded, blinked with charming detachment. Then taking her leave she had felt his high neck bend toward her. That odour of carbolic and abstinence so readily in the mind confused with mastery. The priest whispered in her ear: 'The sword of light is shining still. England's difficulty is Ireland's opportunity.'

The formula was stale, let alone the notion, but it had sounded singular on the lips of a priest. If this now was the teaching of the seminaries, change most certainly was in the air. Poor old Parnell – the Chosen Man, the Chief, the Uncrowned King of Ireland, adulterer, fornicator, the Lost Leader – it would be the supreme irony: to have terrified the Church into Irish Ireland.

She rose now from her dressing-table and approached the garden window. She turned the hasp and the casement opened. She inhaled the breath from the sea. Casement, how very beautiful was the word. She spoke it softly. A decidedly beautiful name, Casement. 'He is far from the land', she softly hummed.

A trundle on the stairs and the child came in with towels and steaming water. At the washstand she ventured to say, 'There was a delivery while you was out, mam.'

Eveline nodded.

'Only stockings, mam. Was I right to leave them in the library like you said?'

Stockings, yes. She must see to them directly her toilet was done.

One more bon-bon from the porcelain shepherdess. It was evident the maids – the few were left her – had been at her supply. 'When you have finished whatever you are doing below, go down to Glasthule. The confectioner's will know my order.'

As she came down to the library she saw through the open door the gardener and the gardener's boy and the gardener's boy's boy all greedily washing her Prince Henry. It was the one chore she might charge them to perform. Her mind drifted to a time late last summer when she had motored over the hills to the old demesne near Ferns. With her had travelled two gentlemen of the press and a representative of the Irish Automobile Club. Her intention had been to astonish the world by ascending and descending Mount Leinster, whose track, winding to the summit, had in parts a gradient steeper than one in three. This feat would prove not only the motor's magnificent pedigree but her own accomplishment, representative of all Irish womanhood's, in handling it.

And indeed she had carried the day. The motor performed superbly, the IAC man figured and stamped in his book, the newspapermen assured her of a prominent notice. She had expected at the least a Johnsonian quip – the wonder being not in her exploit, but in a lady's wish to stage such performance. But the next day's newspapers gave no mention of her. The August bank holiday had passed and while she had been conquering Mount Leinster Great Britain had declared war on Germany.

At her library desk, begloved once more, this time in creamy four-button mochas, she opened the brown-papered parcel of stockings. Plain-knit, rough-textured stuff. Queer specimen down Glasthule had suggested the arrangement. She might not approve of enlistment in the tyrant's yeomanry, but she did not see why Irish soldiers should suffer cold feet. Besides, the soul had grown soft since Parnell, with the English and their ploys, killing home rule with kindness. A reacquaintance with arms might prove useful, indeed requisite, in the coming times.

For she too felt the change in the air. Last August, while she motored home alone through the acetylene-lit gloom, the twilight had forced itself upon her. But this was not the evening twilight of the foolish poets. It was the half-light before dawn, the morning of a new Ireland. For indeed it was true: England's difficulty is Ireland's opportunity. And she, a MacMurrough born to lead, knew well where lay her duty.

Inside the foot of each stocking she inserted a slip of paper. Green paper whose script proclaimed: 'Remember Ireland!'

CHAPTER TWO

T HE GIRLS WERE colloguing outside the confectioner's when
Jim came by.

'Lookat, there's Jim Mack, home for his dinner. Isn't he the
grand swell in his college get-up? Dinky cap and lovely shiny
boots on. Delivered out of a bandbox.'

'And his knickers up to his knees and proper black stockings
on. Wouldn't you love to take him home with you and stick him
on a cake?'

'Ah, but why wouldn't his da put him in longers?'

'On his birthday and all.'

'Big boy he's getting, and handsome with it.'

'Though without the anatomicals yet, would you listen to
me!'

'Are you getting your greens there, Jim?'

'Ah, the wee spurt, little by little.'

'Shush now,' said Nancy, 'leave him be. You'll have him
baked for shame.' She left her companions and beckoned Jim
privately over. 'How's the birthday boy?' she asked and she
planted a smacker on his cheek. 'There you are for luck.'

From a distance his face looked unwashed, but closer to you
saw there were rosebuds on his cheeks, buds that bloomed now

32

to perfect pinks, occasioning a further shrill of laughter from the girls behind.

'Well, Nancy,' he said, brushing a hand against the wet.

'Is that all you have to say for yourself?' She hooked his arm and marched him onward. 'Don't mind them saucepots. Them saucepots is only ignorant.' She chid them over her shoulder, 'Ignorant, so yous are!' He was muttering something, but she held to his arm. Past the butcher O'Brien's where tubs of brine fumed on the pavement and carcasses buzzed with blow-flies above. Past the buttery milky smell of Smelly's marbly dairy. 'Muck for more luck,' said she when he stepped in dried-up dung. Adelaide Road was spilling with children from the national school and there were cries and street-calls all ways. Only when they came to the entry to Adelaide Cottages did she draw him aside.

'You'll never guess.'

'Guess what?'

'I've news from Gordie. Got a letter in the first post.' She watched his eyes close, squeeze, then open wide again. A right scholar he makes. Can't even blink without thinking. 'Has that woken you?'

'He's all right?'

'Flying sure. You know where he's at?' She had the letter out of her apron pocket and she stumped a finger at the top of the page.

'All Love,' he read, 'Does Ever Rightly Show,' he read, 'Humanity Our Tenderness . . . ?' He looked up, querying her face.

'Do you not catch on? Likes of you, a scholarly chap and all.' She danced her finger under each word, spelling it out. 'A-L-D-E-R-S-H-O-T. It's a code, of course.'

'Aldershot! I see it now.'

33

'It's in England. Famous military town. I looked it up in a book in Miss MacMurrough's.'

'We knew he was to go to England,' said Jim, 'only they couldn't say where.'

'Well, now you know.'

'Yes, now we know.'

His head dawdled over the letter. The peak of his cap pointed up at the sky. She couldn't make out the face for his quiff fell over his eyes like the fringe of a show horse. She let him read on, biting her lip, till she knew by the purpling ear-tips that he'd reached the passage she intended. Enough. She snatched the letter away. 'I'd leave you read the news for yourself, only it's a taste mashy inside.'

'Mashy?'

'Oh mashy something desperate.'

He looked up and a smile travelled his face as though unsure where to fit. When she returned the letter to its envelope, the 's.w.a.k.' on the seal caught his eye and he asked, 'Is that the return?'

'The return, would you listen to it!' But the ox-eyed look of him brought the fondness out of her. She laid a hand on his neck, relishing the twitch when she rubbed behind his ear. 'Don't mind that. That's only Gordie trying to land me in scrapes at Miss MacMurrough's. He's a bold particle is your brother. I hope and you don't take after him. You don't, sure you don't, Jim Mack?'

Again the ponderous squeezing blink. 'I think I take after my mother. I'm not sure.'

'Ah sure, God bless you, what more could you ask? Your poor mother and now your poor brother gone and all. Do you miss him? Of course you do. The street isn't the same. But God is good, he'll be home again. Safe and sound, you'll see.'

He was fidgeting with the flap of a pocket. She could feel the hairs on his neck bristling. And the heat off him! She lifted her hand. 'I do declare, if you blush any redder you'll go up in a smoke.'

'I'd better be getting in.'

'Don't let on to your da about the letter. He came by this morning giving such a slice of the ignore, I thought to let him stew.'

At last she had made him smile. His cheeks rose, the dimples came, the lonesome look departed.

'You see?' said she. 'That's found the sunshine in you.'

It was sunshine rarely seen at home. As soon as the shop door clinked closed, his father bustled from the window and said, 'What were you doing talking to hussies in the street? Shop-girls and maids-of-all-work. And you had your college cap on.'

And from in the kitchen, Aunt Sawney called, ''Tis cold plate for dinner and take off them boots when you're stepping inside.'

'"Memorable Scenes at Dardanelles". Now that's a further development. "Race to land before dawn". We'll have to mark that down on the map. "Australasians' Gallantry". Australasians means Australians and New Zealanders, them both. No word of the Dubs, but we know they're out there.'

Dinner was cold bacon and cold cabbage, the cabbage adrift in a murky water. Mr Mack brought his fork as far as his lips. 'Eat up your greens, Jim. World of goodness in cabbage.' He waited while his son obeyed, then back to the news.

'"Fight for Ypres. Use of Stupefying Gases". Now that's shocking. That's beyond the beyonds. "Canadians' Gallantry". Still no mention of the Dubs. Mind you, don't know why we're supposed to be shocked. The German soldier has no tradition of honour. That's the case with Germany. See it with the Kaiser. All Prussian gas and gaskets, but no command of honour. And that's the sad truth.'

He gave the sad truth a moment's commiseration, staring at his fork. From out the shop the Rosary came, Hail Mary low and Holy Mary high. He leant closer over the table. 'I've a small something inside needs seeing to after.'

'I'm finished now, Da.'

Out in the shop Aunt Sawney disremembered her Rosary sufficient to bang her stick and bawl, 'Boys don't speak at table.'

Mr Mack half turned to the open door. A stickler for decorum, no harm in that. 'Have you finished your dinner, Jim?'

'Yes, Da.'

Again the bang of a stick on the floor. Mr Mack frowned. He looked doubtfully at the mess of cabbage. Best thing for it was to say grace and get back in the shop. 'We give Thee thanks, Almighty God, for all Thy gifts, who livest and reignest world without end.'

Over which, as though in competition, Aunt Sawney brayed: 'Holy Mary, Mother of God, pray for us sinners now and at the hour of our death.'

It was a race to Amen, which Aunt Sawney won. Mr Mack rose. The Rosary of course was good and proper, but had she forgotten there was socks needed knitting for the Front? 'I'll take over now, Aunt Sawney. You come back to your chair.' Confidentially to Jim he said, 'Fetch the shop bike out of the yard and meet me inside.'

The boy's face creased and he said, 'But Da, I'm due back at school.'

'Papa,' Mr Mack corrected.

'Papa,' said Jim.

'Better put some juldy in it so. Chop-chop.'

He watched his son as he loafed through the scullery. Keen as mustard a moment since, now he's hanging dogs. Would want to catch on to himself.

'What use is a chair to me?' Aunt Sawney complained as she came in from the shop. 'I'm beckoned hither and beckoned thither like a common shop-miss.'

'Now now, I'm only thinking of your health. You're only over the bronchitis and you needs your rest.'

When she drew level with him, she abruptly jutted her chin in his face. 'I'm still the name on the lease of this shop. And while there's saints in heaven, 'tis stopping that way.'

When his son had fetched the bike, Mr Mack muttered, discreetly closing the inside door, 'Crumbi rumpitita. Latin for cabbage warmed up. Save that wasn't warmed up even.' He thought a moment, recollected himself. 'There's plenty would walk to Dublin for a plate of cold cabbage.'

'What do I need the bike for, Da?'

Mr Mack said Aha! with his eyes, and from under the shelves pulled out an onion box. He lifted it on the counter. 'I want you to deliver some advertising-bills round the local populace. What do you think? They're hot off the printer's press.' He showed one to his son, running his finger along the words at the expected rate of reading. 'It's the modern way of drumming up trade.'

The boy gazed into the box, his face growing longer and plainer. Makes a comical sketch, thought Mr Mack. Eyebrows straight and nose the length of the Shannon. Has a face like a capital T. He thought – did he think that? – the box held his birthday present. All in a rush, he spluttered, 'I've a cake for you after out of Findlater's.'

'What, Da?'

'Deliveries first.' His son flicked through the pile and Mr

Mack had to check himself from cautioning against creasing the sheets. 'Don't crease them now,' he said, defeated by the boy's shiftlessness.

'You want me to distribute these?'

'Deliver them.' Though in point of fact, distribute was probably the more appropriate sentiment in this particular instance. Fair dues. Comes from having a scholarship boy for a son. 'Distribute them if you choose. But you needn't do it all the one go. Do a couple of streets now, the bulk after your school.'

The Capital T was for Tragic on his face, till the boy shrugged. 'All right.'

'Hold your horses, do your buttons up first. Don't you want to know where to deliver them?'

'You said the local populace.'

'But which local populace? Have you not the horse-sense to ask?'

'Which local populace, Da?'

'Well, up Glasthule Road towards Ballygihen. Do you know where I mean?'

'The posh houses.'

'Quality Street,' said Mr Mack. 'We're on the up, Jim, never forget it. Juldy on now. And don't be late for school. And remember, that bicycle is shop property, not something to hare up and down with.'

He had ushered his son to the door, but at the door his son said, 'Papa, do I have to?'

Incomprehension creased Mr Mack's rotund face. 'What does it mean, do I have to?'

'It's just that, some of the boys at school, that's where they live.'

'Some of your schoolfellows?'

'Yes.'

Mr Mack stroked the end of his moustache. 'That tops it,' he said. 'You can ask your schoolfellows to put in a good word for the shop.' He tapped his nose. 'Word of mouth, a personal recommendation. But see they gets the bills first.'

A sudden notion and he jabbed his hand into a jar of Lemon's sweets. He emptied the handful into Jim's jacket pocket. 'Distribute these to your schoolfellows. They'll think the more of you for it.'

'Yes, Da.'

'Papa,' said Mr Mack. 'That's three times, four times you've called me Da.' But Jim was already out of tongueshot, pushing down the road.

Peculiar case, thought Mr Mack. He's not sullen, nor yet very gamesome. Is he cheerfuller in the street? Hangs up his fiddle when he's home, that's for sure. Sixteen: hobbledehoy, neither man nor boy. Might have perhaps wished him a happy birthday. But he'd be looking for his present then, and we'd be Christmas Day in the morning before them bills got delivered.

Now what's this the commotion is up the hill? Something going off whatever it is. And that whiff. Recognize that whiff.

A woman in dark bombazine walked by holding a clean child by the hand. Mr Mack mimed a tweak of his peak, then patted the child's head. 'Open till late,' he said.

Way up Adelaide Road, over the railway bridge, undriven came a low cart. That smell, thought Mr Mack. Then: 'Herrings above! Aunt Sawney, where are you? Get up out of your chair, Aunt Sawney! The dungcart is coming. They'll be here in the hour and we've nothing prepared.'

Jim propped the bike against a garden wall, took a handful of bills and went to the first door of a terrace of villas. He was sliding the

handbill inside the box when the door opened and a boy stepped
out. He wore the same cap as Jim, with the same badge: *Dirige
nos Domine.*

'Who is it?' called a voice within.

'It's a billing-boy from the Glasthule huckster's.'

'What does he want at the front door? Tell him to mind his
manners.'

'Mind your manners,' said the boy who was Jim's school-
fellow, and the door closed in his face.

Some words you could really hate, and one of those was
fellow. They used it all the time at college. His first day at
Presentation, a boy had approached: 'The fellows wanted to
know, is it true you live in a corner-huckster's?' Jim had said
no, it was the Adelaide General Stores and some of these fellows
sniggered. 'Do you sleep at night in a bed?' Jim slept on a
settle-bed made up in the kitchen, so he said yes, but they were
up to that dodge. 'In a bedroom?' He shook his head. Then,
decisively: 'The fellows wanted to know what name do you call
your father?'

'Da,' Jim answered.

Sometimes the jibes spilt over into rough stuff, like shoving
when he queued for the water-fountain or hard scragging at
football. In the end he claimed a fight with the ugliest fellow,
a bullocky lad named Fahy. He could still feel the shock of
the chatterer to his chin, the dizzy sway round the circle of
honour as grassward he fell. But they left out the physicality
after that. Whenever his hand went up in class, they chaffed
him for the Grand Exhibit. When for lack of his own he shared
a schoolbook, they goosed him, chiming, 'For the scholarship
boy is a needy boy.'

He mentioned it once to his father, and his father said, 'What
is it they call their own fathers?'

Jim shrugged. 'Papa, I think.'

'That's easy fixed so. You call me Papa in future, then you'll be equal with your fellows.'

It might have passed but for his father's interfering. He couldn't keep away from the college, but was ever at the gates, offering his services for field days and bazaars. The school wouldn't play a match but his cart rolled up with pop and sweets. Save the souls of piccaninnies! A shilling per guinea to the Presentation Missions.

Ballygihen Avenue ended at the sea and when Jim came there he rested on the sea-wall and stared out across Dublin Bay. The city lay under a haze, but Howth was sunny and clear, a sleeveless, sinewy arm thrown out while Dublin dozed.

For years he had believed that Howth was England until finally his father took him there, him and his brother, on the two tram journeys across Dublin. They made a scratch tea in a heathery field and his father had him speak to a poor fisherwoman to ask was this still Ireland. He remembered the surprise of her answer. 'Not since the Chief passed over, nor yet till he come again.'

'Curious old harp,' his father had said. 'Did you mark how and she grabbed the boy? Would frighten a boy that way.'

'She was a witch,' said Gordie. 'The old woman of the sea.'

'Queer old harp she was.'

But she wasn't old, Jim didn't think. If she loosed her shawl she was young and beautiful, like the photograph-portrait of his mother at home.

The tide was half-way down and he listened to the lazy rush of its waves. Straggling rocks creamed in the sun, melting to tan, to umber in the sea. Dark weeds chained them. He smelt the breezy air that was like ozone through the school latrine. Farther along, towards Kingstown, urchinous boys were scraping for bait. Their cries mingled with the calls of gulls that hungrily wailed above. The sea glistened in the bay, a blue sheet that was hardly blue so sharply it shone, nor yet a sheet so spangled its surface. A calm upset by light alone.

You carry your weather with you, his father was fond of saying. Yet the day was glorious.

Sandycove's beached harbour, the Martello tower on its cliff, its cliff improbably landward. Two figures strolled from the Point, towels slung over their shoulders. Bathers out of the Forty Foot, gentlemen's bathing-place. There was a loneliness in watching them, for they were actors in the day's glory, like the gambolling boys and the boisterous gulls.

His father had a story about that Martello that when the Government decommissioned the towers, after the French scares, its garrison had been overlooked. 'Twenty year and more,' he told, 'they remained at their post, when all this land was back of God speed. They were the lost troop, a sergeant and two swaddies. And yet, at long last when the authorities caught up with themself, it was discovered from the books in all those years not one guard-mount, not one sentry-go had been shirked. There's soldiering for you. That's the spirit of the British Army.' And indeed it was not difficult to see his father there, reveille to Last Post, at spit and polish, jankers and Queen's Regulations, counting in his quartermaster-sergeant's English: boots, leather, pairs of, three.

Forlorn hope is from the Dutch for lost troop. How sad the words and beautiful. All love does ever rightly show humanity our tenderness.

Bills, two gross, local populace, delivery thereto. When he watched the horny hands with veins like rhizomes in the flesh carry up the onion box, he had believed it was his birthday present. His father would often confound surprise with suspense so that, even when faced with the bills, Jim had needed to rummage through to the bottom to be sure there was no mistake. Whatever else, there was no long trousers. Last in his form to be still in breeches with a cake from Findlater's for after. Acme of swell.

The breeze brushed the sweat on his forehead. It would be good to take off his cap, feel wind in his hair. There were other actions he could envisage performing: loosening his tie, slipping out of his boots and stockings, unbuttoning the knees of his breeches. He imagined padding out to the edge, toes bunched against the jag of rocks. The way the weed would slither beside you, sea-lace and thong-weed. The water grew chiller as it climbed. Or he might venture as far as the Forty Foot itself, strip off and plunge headlong to the deep. He had never swum in the Forty Foot, he had never swum in the sea, but he could conjure the charge of the waves all over. Like those two bathers strolling down, he too would have acted. Involvement, not witness, would mark the day.

If you carry the weather with you, then character is determined by the prevailing wind.

In his pocket he found some sweets; Lemon's, he remembered. The crinolined lady on the wrapper looked light and gay with her parasol, very much like Nancy would look if she wore Aunt Sawney's drapes. Nancy made him blush and he believed she always would now. His brother had rarely mentioned her before he left for England, but on the last night at home he said, Nancy's a bit of – jam, he called her. When Jim remonstrated, he grew coarser still. Don't come the green with me. I know the sniff of the glue-pot. Then – Is it Nancy you think of when you fetch yourself off? How could his brother say such a thing? How dared he utter those words. Jim couldn't look at Nancy since

43

without the blood rising, and the blood rose now to his ears as he thought of it.

He crushed the wrapper and let it fall behind.

The breeze died and the heat was suddenly material, like a cloak that dropped on his back. The wall made him conspicuous. What might a watcher suppose was his purpose? He counted the clues to his identity: school cap, shop name on bike, bills in the pannier. His availability to interpretation intimidated him. He saw that his arms were hugged round his knees. He sniffed the muggy flocculent smell, then let go his legs. In his mind a formula impersonally repeated: he has never swum in the Forty Foot, he has never swum in the sea. Of a sudden he leant forward to check for the Muglins, but the rock of course was obscured by the Point.

It was time to be gone, but a murmur of voices cautioned him. The bathers from the Forty Foot had rounded the bend and were nearing the promenade below. The younger was a shock-headed black-haired lad, Jim's age, though bigger-built. He tossed his cap in the air as he walked and as he walked he lurched slightly, weak of one leg. For all he had been swimming, he had a filthy look about him and his towel was a rag of threads. The other, by his tweeds and tone, was of the quality.

Jim believed he recognized the lad. He was not sure but, delaying to see, he left it too late to leave. Movement now would draw their attention.

They halted at the private steps that led to Ballygihen House. The toney man, who had his back to Jim, said, 'I might show you still, if you'd a mind.'

The lad shook his head. 'Due back for work. Already late as it is.'

'Another time, perhaps. I believe you'd take to it. Don't think about the leg. You're quick enough off the mark.'

'Another day maybe.' He had the usual Dublin drawl, but with an open edge, like a kick, at the end of it. Breath of the west, Jim thought.

The man made a sudden motion – 'Here,' he said – and silver spun in the air. A fist shot out and nimbly the lad caught the coin.

'For your trouble,' said the man.

Ivory flashed between thick dirty lips. 'No trouble at all.' The smile, like the face, was familiar. Then the lad's gaze lifted and he saw Jim watching from above. His eyes were dark as night, not dull, but gemmily shining. The smile broadened as though in invitation, as though the rocky shore and the birds and the blue were his to share.

'What cheer, eh?' he called.

Jim found himself smiling back. And long after, while he scorched down Glasthule Road, well late for school, he was smiling still. What curious cheer.

Mr Mack kept a keen eye on the young lad shovelling out his midden. Vile job that. Vile smell. Murder on the lungs, day in day out. Never grow accustomed to a smell like that.

Sturdy fellow, though, beef to the heels. And would want to be. That job won't last long. Way behind the times. Sewers will be here any day soon and no need of all this foostering. Funny that. The modern way means this fellow's out of an employment.

Sucked cheeks dimpled to a smirk. They'll always want a general stores.

Hair as black as the devil's waistcoat. Could do with a scissors while we're about it. Jaunty as muck and in muck he's covered. Only white is in his eyes. Disease, all sorts you get with a job like that. 'Careful with that bucket, now. Don't be swamping it. Can't have slops all over the shop.'

That's a good one. That's a good motto for the contractors. Your business is our business. Might send that in. Bit on the flowery side, all the same. Second thoughts, steer clear.

All the same, why wouldn't they stick to the stated times? Sending the dungcart a day early, the commotion it causes. Poor Aunt Sawney, she's on her last legs without the vexation of middens. Dung-dodgers, she calls them. Do they dodge the dung or what? Goo-wallahs it was in India. Shifting furniture, clearing a gangway, rolling up the oilcloth. Deal of commotion, up and down the street.

Up he weighs now, great brute of a bucket on his shoulder. Fancies himself a taste. Likes to show his brawn. 'Careful now, we don't want any mess.' Is that a limp I see? Bit of a hop there. Tries to bury it, but can't dish an old sergeant. Wait now, that face. Great big grin on him, width of Cheshire. Don't I know that face?

He tramped back into the house after the dungman's lad. Now would you look at that. Heap of mess on the floor, right below the Georgius Rex. Told him about loading that bucket. Straight up to the brim he filled it.

'Here you, young hopeful, I want a word with you.'

'Yes, Mr Mack?'

Mr Mack peered. 'It's young Doyler, isn't it? You're Doyle's eldest.'

'That's right.'

'Well, I'm glad to see you back in the parish. In work and all. Yes, I'm very glad.' Mr Mack stroked the bush of his moustache. 'I was only talking this morning with your father.'

'Is that right, Mr Mack. Mr Mack, could I trouble you for a drink of water?'

46

How germs are spread. Could risk an old jam pot? Unchari-
table. In the end he brought water in his own special cup. The
boy turned back the cuff of his sleeve and wiped his mouth on
the inside. Mr Mack was touched by the gesture, a courtesy he
was sure addressed to him and his cup. 'Thirsty work,' he said.

'A bit all right.'

'How long are you back?'

'Not long yet.'

'Your father is above with the papers now.'

'He is.'

'He might keep at that employment.'

'Hard to keep a job down, Mr Mack, with his lungs the way
they are.'

Mr Mack let a grunt. The bellows, the bronicals, any shift
you choose. If work was in a bed, that man would sleep on the
floor. Consumption, my eye. Of spirituous liquors is what it is.
Sure he'd sell his mother for a tuppenny wet. But that's the
way it goes with some of these fellows. They leaves the army,
they wouldn't know to sneeze without they're ordered to. I'm
glad now to see his son turning out a better class. 'Not long at
this work?'

'Not long,' said Doyler.

Knock the spirit out of you, this work would, give it time.
He had the collar of his waistcoat turned up against the muck,
and the inside of the lapel showed a badge with a red hand in
it. What's this, the Red Hand of Ulster? The Doyles is never
northern folk. The father nobody knows where he hailed, the
mother is out of the west some place. Though father might not be
the appropriate sentiment in this particular case. Doyler Doyle:
had to take the name twice to be sure of it. 'Where was this they
sent you? Clare, was it? Your mother has people that way.'

'Clare, aye.'

It struck Mr Mack he had been wanting this morning in his encounter with Mr Doyle. Never once thought to ask of the family: the wife nor the care. That was amiss now. Quickly he inquired of the mother, who was grand all right, and of his brothers and sisters, though as it turned out he had only sisters, but they too were grand. And were they still down the Banks, his folks?

'Where else would have us?' the boy replied.

Indeed. 'Still, you'll be glad to be back in the parish. In work and all.'

'To be frank, Mr Mack, there's little enough for me here. The contractors has us on short time.'

The advancing sewers, didn't I say?

'Most the men they laid off. Employed a grush of boys in their place. Half the wages and the same blow they proves their loyalty to the Crown.'

'Crown?' said Mr Mack. 'How's this about the Crown?'

'Sure what hope has the men but they list in the army? The contractors is held for a great example.'

This was serious talk and close to, if not beyond of, politics. And Mr Mack was not at all sure it fitted his dignity to be argufying with the dungman's lad. 'Do you not see,' he said, ''tis the sewers is the problem?'

The boy shovelled in silence a while, then said, 'There's sewers in it all right. But the fact remains the men as used be working is soldiering now. Can see them camped on Tivoli Fields. God knows, I'm thankful for the work. But it's hard taking another man's job. Harder still at half the pay. But that's the times that's in it, Mr Mack.'

The times that were in it indeed. He might mention three square meals a day, smart uniform, healthy living, separation money for the women at home, pension at the end of it.

Satisfaction of fighting for King and Country. Glory to be had and to spare. Travel far and wide.

'Though I was thinking of joining the band.'

But down the Banks where this one lodges there's scant notion of glory. Hard-scrabble place, the Banks. Mean cottages, rotten thatch, entire family cramped into—'Joining a band?'

'Flute band.'

'But Brother Polycarp out of the college takes that.'

'The very man. I saw him this morning only. The new curate as found me this employment gave me the word.'

'Curate? You mean the band is not restricted to college boys?'

'So far as I know, Mr Mack.'

'Well, I'll go bail.'

'Have to get me flute back first, though.'

'Don't tell me,' said Mr Mack. 'Ducie's window.'

''Fraid so.'

Mr Mack puckered his lips. Abstractedly, he said, 'I have a son in that band.'

'Jim, is it?'

'James, my son James. James is a college boy now.' His voice had risen above the ordinary, so in token of fellowship, he jerked his head and said, 'Oh, easy street for some, I suppose.'

Doyler set his shovel squarely down. It made a rasping noise on the tin base of the privy. 'Mr Mack, I'd never hold it against a man that he tried to better himself.'

That's right, thought Mr Mack. Comes back to me now. Same time Jim won his exhibition, they had one gave out to young Doyler too. Sure what would that man care for a scholarship? Hunted his son down the country instead. Always grafting. Half-timer at school. Late-to-come and soon-to-go. Wonder he learnt his readamadaisy.

49

Poor lad to fetch up down the Banks. That's where you go when you can't keep up the rent. Demon drink, curse of Ireland.

He watched the boy shovelling muck with his steady muscular rhythm. His dowdy clothes were all in fits, the seat of his pants so often patched it was a puzzle to tell the material. You'd be all day putting that shirt on, avoiding the tears and repairs in the sleeves. Wretched muffler pulled up round his nose. Mr Mack was overcome with pity, at a boy's life stunted by the failings of a father. He waited till he was leaving with the last bucket of filth and thrust a bag of broken biscuits into the crook of his free elbow.

'Take these now and don't say a word.'

'That's kind of you, Mr Mack.'

'Not a word now. And eat them all yourself.'

'I couldn't do that without sharing them.'

'No, of course you couldn't. That wouldn't be Christian at all. But mind you keep your puff up. That's a man's job you're at.'

The gaffer appeared at the shop door. 'Hey you, you little Larkinite. Put some beef into it. You're close to the door as it is.'

Larkinite, Mr Mack pondered. Now why in the world would he call young Doyler a Larkinite? Wasn't that an agitator of the blackest variety? When he came to the kitchen Aunt Sawney was on her knees with soap and scrubbing-brush. 'Would you like me to help with that?' he asked.

'Get away out of my way.'

'I'll tend shop so. There'll be a rush on soap and soda after the dungmen.'

'There will, but 'twill all be on tick with your lordship at the till.'

Under the picture of King George the pile of mess had risen.

Odd how he managed to slop his swill at that place every time. Could almost be on purpose. Wait now, hold on to yourself. Was that young gallows taking a rise out of me? Wasn't there something last year about agitators employing the Red Hand? Business about sharing, was that Christian sharing or red-flag Larkinite? I hope now my Jim won't be falling into bad company at that band.

There was a moral to all this but Mr Mack could not immediately catch wind of it. That evening, while he made out the orders in the shop, he said, 'I met an old accomplice of yours today.'

His son looked down from the steps where he was dusting a stack of jars.

'Remember that Doyle one, was at the national school with you? He's back now and he's the dungman's lad.'

'Doyler?' said Jim.

'What's this the smile's in aid of?'

'Only I saw him myself and I thought I recognized him.'

'Where was this?'

'Down by the sea-wall.'

'And what were you doing by the sea-wall?'

'Delivering bills.'

'To the sea?'

Smile gone and capital T for Tragic in its place. 'Was catching my breath is all.'

In a shake Mr Mack discovered the moral of the day. 'Now that lad's father is a shaper and a hook, and look where his son has fetched up. If now I was to fritter my time catching my breath by the sea, where would that leave you? Not to mention your brother. Not to mention Aunt Sawney. On the ash-pit with young Doyler is where. You want to catch on to yourself. Have you done with them jars yet?'

'Yes, Da.'

'Did you deliver them bills like I told you?'

'The most of them, Da.'

Mr Mack squeezed his moustache. 'Papa,' he said.

When Aunt Sawney called them in for their tea, he stopped by the door, surprised out of himself by the sight. A groaning-board of a feast. Cured ham, the tongue of a sheep, buttered shop-bought bread. And there was more. She was carrying in a jelly now that wobbled alarmingly before her face. 'Glory be,' he said, 'that's a grand spread you're after fixing, Aunt Sawney. I had no notion you was going to such trouble. Did we, Jim?'

''Tis no trouble to me,' said she, 'not to be the clutching hand.'

'Well no, I didn't intend—'

'There's some I know afeared to sneeze, they might give something away.'

'Well yes—'

'There's others too mean to join their hands, leave out to pray for a soul.'

'That's surely true—'

'But there's one I know has two poor boys. The one he hunts away to die, th'other he keeps to slave on his birthday.'

This final turn was accompanied by a thump on the table as she banged his plate in front of him. He looked down and in the heel of the hunt he knew what was her game. The same doling of cabbage and bacon that had outfaced him at dinner. The spread was for the boy alone.

'Bless Thee, Father . . .' But his heart wasn't in it and he quickly signed the cross. He picked up his knife and fork. 'Happy birthday, Jim.'

He could feel her grinning gummily at him. Incorrect to say she was a malicious old witch. The wits aren't your own at her vintage. Besides, she was only over the bronchitis. And the house was her own to do with as she pleased, the house and the shop and God knows, don't we know it. But this new rigmarole about Gordie, hunting him away. As though 'twas I invaded Belgium.

He heard her now, a horse-whisper to his son. 'I have a treat to go with the splash, little man.' And from out the press she produced a parcel.

Mr Mack felt the blow like the homer she intended. Before the boy had the paper unwrapped he could tell it held the finest long black broadcloth trousers a young man could want or wish for.

'Look, Da.'

'Why, I must say, that's handsome in the extreme, Aunt Sawney.'

'Handsome be damned,' she answered, the gullets of her cheeks agitating. 'Is it handsome to keep the little man in breeks all his days? He's been wanting of them a twelvemonth and more but ye, ye're too thick to know and too grasping to get them him.'

Mr Mack grinned delicately. 'Now now, Aunt Sawney.'

'Can I try them on, Da?'

'Say thank you first.'

She lifted her chin and he lipped her skin then, turning his back, slipped out of his breeches and into the longed-for legs.

Aunt Sawney drew her blanket closer round her shoulders; said, 'I'll mind shop now while ye and your lordship has your feed. And don't mind the rule on your birthday, little man. Speak your fill, if there's any worth speaking to.' Out she went and soon enough the Joyful Mysteries came moaning through the door.

'Da, what's wrong?'

'No no, nothing wrong.'

'Papa, you can have some of mine to eat.'

'No no, 'tis your birthday, I wouldn't dream. Well, maybe

one slice of tongue, no more. Go on then. I've a cake if you've space for it after.' In truth he was verging on tears. He took out his handkerchief and dabbed an eye then, disguising the gesture, blew roughly on his nose. 'How are the trousers on you?'

'They're fine.'

'That's the hookum. Bit wide in the waist. I'll put a tuck in them for you after. Could maybe turn them up a patch too.' Why was he so sad? His son was his son no matter his breeks. But he looked so grown-up in his trousers. Had he tried to keep him a boy and why had he tried it? I wasn't being thick, nor mean, he wanted to say. It's not the time for a boy to be a man. Wait till the war was over.

'That's grand to have something best for Sundays, isn't it, Jim?'

'For Sundays, Da?'

'Best take them off now. Don't want them creased.'

Later on, while Jim did his homework, Mr Mack returned to his *Irish Times*. He was still trying to put flesh on the bare bones of the London communiqués. Hard to work out where the Dubs was fighting. Only chance was to glean it from the death notices. Foolish secrecy that wouldn't give out the names of regiments. Headlines full of British gallantry, but did British include Irish? Why wouldn't they be done with it and say Irish gallantry? Do the world of good for recruiting. Gallantry of Royal Dublin Fusiliers. Old Tough's Heroism. World of good 'twould do.

All over the world they were fighting, from the steppes of Russia to the African plains. Well, not America, granted not America. But in the seas around, they were fighting everywhere. From Canada they came to win glory in France, from Australia and New Zealand to knock out the Turk. If you looked at the map you saw the corners folding over, returning the blood of the young dominions to stand in defence of their motherland.

It made you feel grand to be a part of it, this great empire at war, its fighting men sent forth not for gain but for honour, and Dublin its second city.

But one son was enough.

When he looked up, he saw that Jim had arranged the settle-bed and was already lying in it. He heaved up from Aunt Sawney's chair, disremembering having got into it, rubbed his eyes. The only sound was Aunt Sawney above coughing and the low hiss of the gas. 'Have you said your prayers?'

'Yes, Papa.'

'That's not your good shirt, is it?'

'No, Papa.'

'Goodnight so.' He lit a small candle from the Sacred Heart vigil, signing the cross as he did so, then opened the door to the box-stairs. He was preparing to turn off the gas, when Jim said,

'Papa?'

'What is it?'

'I'm worried about Gordie.'

'What are you worried for?'

'If they send him to France. They're using poison in France.'

Mr Mack sat down on the edge of the bed. The candle was wasting, but that didn't signify. 'He's in the army, Jim. And the British Army is the finest-trained and best-rigged army the world over. Look at me sure. Nobody knows what happened my mother and father, may the earth lie gently on them. But the army took me in, fed me, clothed me, made the man I am today. It's a great body of men he's joining. They wouldn't send Gordie in with a damp cloth on his face. There'll be respirators and all sorts, then nothing can harm him. Take my word. He's safer in the army than crossing a road in front of a motor. All right, honour bright?'

'All right, Da.'

In the bluey light he smiled down at his son. He found himself touching his forehead, momentarily checking for temperature, then sifting his fingers through the fall of his hair. How well he looked, how rude in health. Both his sons looked well, for they lacked the pallor of Dublin. They were born down the Cape and their first few years had been spent in the warm. A memory of that sun glowed in their faces, in the high colour and the brownish skin. Or maybe it wasn't that at all, was the Spanish blood rumoured on their mother's side.

Yes, both boys had their mother's face, thanks be to God for that. But Jim positively sang of her. They lose it, you see, age coarsens it from them. But say what they will, I've reared two goodly boys.

On his padded way up the stairs, he said under his breath, You'd be so proud, if you saw them, you'd be so pleased. God rest you in peace everlasting. God rest you in peace, my dear.

In the bedroom, above the bockedy prie-dieu, hung a photograph-portrait of his wife. I'm so so sorry, he told her.

Way up Glasthule Road, through Kingstown and its breezy streets, a smack of industry hits the sleeping town. Outside a black-brick bakery, in the fallen light from a window, a young lad crouches. He looks to be reading, but in fact he's nodded off. The book slips from his hands and slides to the road.

The bakery hand comes out and shakes him. 'Here y'are, son,' he says and drops the broken bread in his lap. 'God save us, I hope 'twas worth the wait. What's that you're after reading?'

He takes up the cheap cardboard cover. '*Socialism Made Easy*, what? By Mr James Connolly. You don't want the polis catch you reading likes of that. No, nor the priests.'

The lad acknowledges him but he's too tired to grin or

say anything. He stuffs the bits of bread in his pockets and homeward treads.

Through George's Street with its shuttered shops, named for the king who named Kingstown, past the railed-in People's Park and down the slope to Glasthule Road. The road must squeeze between chapel and college and he glances up at the gaunt red brick of Presentation where no light shows. No light shows from the church and on he treads without signing the cross. At the lane that leads to the Banks, he halts and sniffs the air. Weedy fishy middeny air that follows where he goes.

The words come to him of the old famine song and softly he sings while he crosses the road and past the public house to Ducie's lamplit window.

O we're down into the dust, over here, over here,
We're down into the dust, over here.
O we're down into the dust, for the Lord in whom we trust
Has surrendered us for lost, over here, over here.

'Flute, is it?'

Cigarette smoke and a glove on his shoulder.

'Band flute, aye.'

'Boxwood, I should say. German. What they used to call a student flute.'

Still Doyler doesn't turn, but gazes dead in the glass. The chatty manner has an edge to it which he feels in the press of the hand on his shoulder.

'How much do they ask for it?'

'Five bob, actually.'

'Tidy sum. For a flute.'

'Worth more.'

'I dare say.'

The grip on his shoulder guides gently him round. The face lights up in the cigarette glow. Guard's moustache under a soft felt hat. The amicable nob from the Forty Foot. Had wanted to learn him a dive. Brim drawn down.

'What's your name?'

'Doyle.'

'MacMurrough.'

Costly smell of the tailor-made smoke.

'Walk with me a while.'

Doyler shrugs, careful of dislodging the hand. 'If you say so.'

'So,' says MacMurrough.

CHAPTER THREE

Brother Polycarp rapped his wand on the easel and the fluting straggled to indefinite desistance. 'Will the man at the back with the grace notes kindly stand forward?'

Feet shuffled, some faces turned, eventually the culprit rose.

'The new man, is it? Tell me, Doyle, where did you learn to play flute at all?'

'Nowhere, sir. Brother, I mean. I mean I learnt meself.'

Brother Polycarp inclined his head while a suspense playfully mounted. 'In this band, Mr Doyle, we are accustomed to a respectable music. A music in the tradition of Kuhlau and Briccialdi and like gentlemen of the transverse mode. We do not slip and slide the like of Phil the Fluter at his ball. Sit you in front in future, boy, and play by the tongue not your maulers.'

In a coarse whisper someone let out, 'Plays be the arse be the smell off him.'

Brother Polycarp chose to disattend the cod. 'Go on now, home with ye. No, stand still till we say a prayer first. Would think the public house was closing on us. Name of the Father, Son and the Holy Ghost.'

He charged through the Our Father versicle, the boys doing a trailing response. Three times in all, then three Hail Marys and an invocation to St Cecilia. In the end, he called over the clatter of benches, 'Now punctual next week. Don't leave me down. The new curate is due this fortnight and we needs must cut a dash for his reverence.'

At the front row, Jim was wedging his flute in its sock, a sewn-up sugar-sack on which his father had stencilled *Master James Mack, Esqr.* There was more chaffing behind which he strained to apprehend. A boy randled metallically, 'I think I think I smell a stink, I think I think I do.'

Fahy, the ugliest of his schoolfellows, added, 'Something fierce in here whatever it is.'

Surreptitiously Jim wiped the wet patch on his breeches where his neighbour's flute had dripped.

'Worse than a cheeser.'

'No,' said Fahy. 'Less than a cheeser, it's the dungman's monkey.'

A hand from behind landed on Jim's shoulder. It stiffened like a vaulter's pole. He had time to glimpse a cloudy, mismatched suit sail by, then a kick in its leg sent Fahy's case scattering.

'Gabh mo leithscéal,' said Doyler when he landed. 'That's excuse me in our native tongue.' He thrust the bits of his flute in his jacket, cocked an eye at Jim, then strode out the passage, lurching once, twice, as he went.

'Class of gouger they're letting in now.'

'A stinker and a cripple.'

And Fahy said flatly, 'That one's not long for this band. No, nor long for this world.'

Jim stared toward the door, moving his lips to the Gaelic phrase. He believed Doyler had uttered something more while he clambered past. It had sounded again like What cheer! The mix of quaint and Gaelic struck him as fantastical in the school commons.

'Mr Mack?'

'Yes, Brother?'

'Close your mouth, boy. You're not in training for a fly-paper. Kindly do the honours and collect me the music. I'll be waiting within.'

A head leant into Jim's ear and uttered the one word, 'Suck.'

'I heard a coarse word and mention of smell this evening,' Brother Polycarp said when they were alone in his monastery room. 'Was it you, Mr Mack?'

'No, Brother.'

One eyebrow drolly lifted. 'Who was it so?'

'I didn't hear, Brother.'

'A vilipendence about the new boy, no doubt.'

Jim's face perked at the word.

'The new curate was very insistent he be let in. Why would you say that was?'

'I wouldn't know, Brother.'

'There's moves afoot. The new curate speaks Erse. Did you know that? An Erse-speaking priest. Wouldn't you think they'd get the Latin right first. The inflexion one sometimes hears is deplorable. All chees and chaws like an ice-cream vendor out of Napoli.'

Jim finished lighting the candles. Grease had spilt on his finger and he rubbed it now with his thumb. Particles fell like dandruff to the floor.

'He's a decent enough mouth on the flute, I'll grant, for all he's not a college boy. Howsoever, there is a certain redolence.' The eyes yellowly closed, whitely opened. There was intimation of humour in the thirsty wax of his face. Muscles strained and opened till a wheezing noise let out. 'The ars musica,' he said with lubricious intonation.

He picked up some music he had been studying, fetched a sigh, replaced it on his table. 'On that subject St Augustine as always is enlightening. Feast Day?'

'August twenty-eight.'

'What he says, inimitably, is: "There are those who can break wind backwards so artfully would they sing." Dates?'

A brief hesitation. 'Three-five-four, four-three-o AD.'

'The anno Domini is unnecessary. A supererogation in the instance of a saint.'

'Yes, Brother.'

The brother was shifting through the folds of his soutane in search of the slip for his pocket. Unbidden otherwise, Jim stood and waited. He could never be sure if Brother Polycarp liked him, or, if he liked him, was it for company or play. It was a trust of sorts to be the audience of these remarks. But was he trusted to share their scandal, or merely not to repeat it? His eyes roamed the scanty room, its whitewashed walls, crucifix over a bed perfectly if thinly made. In the corner, the little grotto to Mary, Our Lady of Presentation. Smell of Macassar from the grey-sleeked head of the brother.

He took Jim for Latin, and on those mornings when he ran a fever and his hands shook with the strain he had Jim stand up and read page after page of Virgil. All morning long the stumbling feet, while the brother nodded and the boys like Virgil's Trojans embraced their arms in weary sleep.

Keep in with the brothers, his father admonished. Mister Suck, said the boys, the Grand Exhibit.

Was that true about saints? He could think of any number that were born before Christ, but had any died BC? St Zachary perhaps, father of John the Baptist. Supererogation. It was an easy word to say once you had heard it spoken. Tomorrow he'd look out vilipendence in the school dick.

The candles at the grotto glimmered and guttered. He wished the brother might hurry that their devotion would begin and be over. Our Lady's downcast eyes.

A silver snuff-box had appeared and the brother made play with settling the top layer of dust. There were stains all down his soutane, a tide of rust, from grains that had rubbed in and soiled. On his sleeves was a shine of chalk-dust. Before he snorted, he blew his nose on a big blue belcher with grubby white spots. The ritual over, he picked up the new sheet of music again. 'What do you make of this, Mr Mack?'

A Nation Once Again, Jim read. The page was white as nip. *Con brio* was crossed out and underneath, in green ink, a phrase in Gaelic had been substituted. Surprising, on account Brother Polycarp wasn't known for his advanced opinions in politics.

'Are we to learn this next?'

'The new curate has asked for it. A particular favourite, evidently. He would appear to be under the impression we are a band of rapparee fifers. Mountain-men musicianers. Fluters with slips and slides.' He watched Jim's face a moment, then brightly said, 'How's your Virgil today?'

'Brother?'

'Vincet amor patriae laudumque immensa cupido: translate.'

Reddening, Jim said, 'Love of fatherland will conquer and the immense cupidity of applause.'

'Applause? Where do you get applause? "The overwhelming greed for praise", says Virgil.' He took the sheet of music. 'We'll give it a blast, I suppose.' Opened a drawer, let it slide within. Before the drawer closed, Jim saw without looking for it the protuberant cork of his whiskey bottle.

'An all-for-Ireland personage,' the brother continued. 'Went out of his way to tell me "God Save the King" is an Irish air the English have purloined on us. Father O'Táighléir he calls himself. Meaning Taylor. In my day it was a pandy on the palm for speaking Erse. O tempora, O mores: now they have you priested for it.'

Another pinch, another snort. He sneezed and spindrift floated through candleshine.

'Take the hair out of your eyes.'

Momentarily, Jim mistook this for a metaphorical injunction, but screwing his eyes he saw the brother's encouraging nod. He fingered the flop off his forehead.

'You might train your hair to keep out of your eyes. You have long lashes for your eyes, Jim, and no need of hair to hide them. I'm surprised your mother didn't tell you that. But I was forgetting. You don't remember your mother.'

Jim was counting the candles. Twelve. He blinked. Six.

'It is a shame, for a vocation is often the easier with a mother in the home.'

The brother shifted from his chair, heaving himself up and round, and Jim closed his eyes as resiny black linen enfolded his neck. The brother's arm wrapped round him, bringing him down, on to his knees, the brother kneeling beside.

'Don't worry you feel confused. It is only natural you feel confused with your mother taken from you.'

A finger rubbed on his cheek, down his chin-bone, to the collar of his shirt. Far out to sea, Jim registered the touch.

'Believe me, Jim, this world without a mother's care is a parlous place indeed. I know this because mine too was taken from me at a tender age. But I found solace in the words of our Lord. Do you know the words I intend, Jim?'

'I do, Brother.'

'When on the cross our Saviour in His passion turned to the disciple He loved. And He said to him, to the disciple whom He loved, Behold thy Mother. Believe me when I say to you now, Behold thy Mother, Jim.'

The statue glittered before them while the finger that had played on his neck ceased its roam. Suddenly the brother called out, 'Mater misericordiae, mater dolorosa, advocata nostra, O clemens, O pia, O dulcis Virgo Maria: ora pro me!'

His arms had swept forward and the shadows shook in the disturbed air.

After a while, he said dully, 'We will pray to Our Lady of Presentation for her continued longanimity. Ever glorious and blessed Mary . . .'

'Ever glorious and blessed Mary . . .'

'Queen of virgins, Mother of mercy . . .'

'Queen of virgins, Mother of mercy . . .'

'Hope and comfort of dejected and desolate souls . . .'

Arm-enfolded they prayed, so close that Jim could trace on the brother's face the imperfect course of his shaving. Each time their heads bowed in honour of Jesus, he sensed the chafe of jowl on his cheek. And when in the prayer's pause silently each made his lawful request, he heard the brother's breath come short and sharp, tingeing the air with a tinct fume of alcohol.

The road squeezed between college and church. Light streamed from the chapel doors where the congregation was leaving after their First Friday. Aunt Sawney would be among them. Jim felt the smother of the coming streets and the coal-smoke from the houses. The memory was with him still of the monastery's candles and the manufactured sting of whiskey and Macassar oil. He pulled up his collar and made for the shore.

Shiny sky with scratchy clouds. Mares' tails, his father called them: they had something to do with storms. Thin stars in misty faces, a frosty breath in the nightfall.

When he turned a corner he came on the sea, the sound of it sudden and as always unexpected; and as always he was struck by its equivocation. He heard the tired roar and felt its casual toil, the fresh breeze that whiffed of decay.

There were ships in the bay, hulks of darkness against the night, waiting the turn of the tide. The fishing-boats were out, he could hear the men, their reboant calls, but he couldn't see them. The lights of Kingstown shone in rows, twice reflected, three times, in the slowly moving mirror, while away on Howth, the Bailey Light flashed welcome and warning. He followed the sea-wall to Sandycove, then up past the Point, where the wind hit him full from the sea. He peered down the dark hole that led to the Forty Foot, gentlemen's bathing-place, then on round the Martello to a thin ledge of grass that gave out on the bay. And there at last it was, the Muglins light, blinking redly, redly blinking. *Ave, Maris Stella.*

Gordie maintained he could remember their mother, but Jim remembered nothing. He was only an infant when she died, on the voyage home from the Cape. They buried her at sea. At home they had a photograph-portrait, but his father kept that in his room. Sometimes Jim saw her drifting in the weeds, not weeds but the floating gardens of the Sargasso. Other times she had washed upon the rocks and there she reposed with seaweed in her hair, while all about the candles danced, bobbing on the waves.

He believed it had been his decision to embark on the Thirty Days' Prayer, though he could not now retrace the steps that had led to his taking it. Over the evenings, in his guidance, the brother had introduced the notion of vocation. But it was unclear to Jim was he to pray for a vocation or only that he hear it should one call. Looking back, he recalled other boys that the brother had taken a fondness to. Had they too prayed thirty nights at his grotto? Each had heard his vocation in the end. Each had disappeared one sudden morning. Seminary, if anyone inquired.

A bat squeaked past. Hush, said a wave. Rush, said its fellow.

Where goes the tide when comes the ebb?
Where goes the night when comes the day?

He was musing on these lines, seeking their provenance, when a patter of feet behind, a tap on the back of his head and his cap tilted forward over his eyes. He turned wildly.

'There you are, pal o' me heart.'

Jim blinked. It was Doyler. Dowdy suit and his cap at a rake. Teeth flashing in the gloom.

'I say,' said Jim and immediately felt foolish for it.

'Say what?' said Doyler, clambering on to the wall beside and clapping his hand on Jim's shoulder. He had a bunch of flowers with him which he waved in front. 'What cheer, eh?'

'Tulips?' said Jim.

'Aren't they brave? They will be brave in the morning, anyhow. They're for the ma. You know there's hordes in the gardens behind.'

'You're after stealing them?'

'Stealing, me arse. Redistribution if you must know.' He leant forward and spat into a rock-pool below. 'What kept you at the brothers'?'

'You were waiting on me?'

'Wanted to say hello was all.'

Jim said, 'Brother Polycarp has me doing a Thirty Days' Devotion.'

'Mary and Joseph,' said Doyler. 'You'd be all year at that.'

Of course they wouldn't, only Mary's month of May, but it was a humorous thing to say. Jim took off his college cap to set it straight, and Doyler said, nodding sideways, 'See you got the scholarship all right.'

'I did. I heard and you got yours and all.'

A moment, then Doyler slapped his hand on the coping. 'Get piles off sitting here. Walk along back with you?'

'All right,' said Jim. He picked up his flute-sock and fell into step.

Peripherally he was aware of a luminescence beside him. Doyler's blue-gone clothes, so thoroughly brushed, shone like the night sky. He sniffed to see if the smell was there that the fellows had complained of at practice. Nothing, unless his smell was same like the shore.

'Still got that blink, then?'

'What blink?'

'They used call you Blinky for it.'

He'd forgotten that. Blinky they used call him at the national school. 'That was years since.'

'Four years,' said Doyler. 'D'you remember them soaps?'

'I do.'

'I never thanked you for that.'

'That's all right.'

'You never split on me. I was thankful for that.'

'Sure, you returned them all.'

'Could have been in bother over that. Himself could have been in bother.'

'You replaced them,' said Jim. 'There was no harm.'

'I'm thankful all the same.'

A tram scooted past, looking for speed for the climb out of Glasthule. Bovril briefly was British beef, then all lay quiet. Save

68

for Doyler's walk. A slip-jig step, crotchet and quaver, crotchet and quaver.

'What happened your leg?'

'The leg? Polis done that.'

'Why would the polis do that to you?'

'Batons came down. I was one in the crowd.' Doyler shrugged. 'Was a lot of that in the Lock-out.'

The Lock-out. It was the word they used for the Larkinite riots of a year or so back. The papers had been full of it, mob rule and baton charges in the streets of Dublin. It never really touched Kingstown, let alone Glasthule, save for a while the trams into town hadn't run on time.

'What were you doing in the Lock-out?'

'Was a newsboy then. The newsboys was the first to go out.'

'Weren't you sent to County Clare?'

'I got about. Are you straight?'

'Straight?' repeated Jim.

'Hold on to these a crack.' He thrust the tulips into Jim's hand and Jim watched astonished as he tore at a poster on a letter-box they were passing. '*When are the other boys coming?*' a strapping Irish soldier inquired, save now his legs were missing. And Doyler was rhyming,

'Full steam ahead! John Redmond said
That everything is well, chum.
Home Rule will come when we are dead
And buried out in Belgium.'

Jim blinked. 'You've turned a right Sinn Feiner,' he said.

'Sinn Feiners, me arse. I'm a socialist, never doubt it.'

This was unchancy ground and Jim was relieved they were approaching the Adelaide turning where the red-brick shops and naphtha flares would prove a civilizing force. Out of the blue, an arm lumped round his shoulder. ''S all right, Jim. Sure no one saw us and Dora's away in the arms of Murphy.'

'Dora who?'

'Go way, you gaum.'

Jim squinted round to get a view of this queer and friendly character. He had a big round grin like a saucer was stuck in his mouth. His Adam's apple jogged above his muffler while he chuckled away to himself. The arm round Jim's neck gave a squeeze.

'Defence of the Realm Act, of course.'

Tramlines glistened under the quietly hissing lamps. The old woman with the widow's stoop that people called Mary Nights was passing through, her pram of belongings behind her.

'How're you, Mary?' called Doyler. 'What way are the nights this weather?'

'The nights is drawing out,' said Mary Nights from her bent old head.

It was coming late now, and the boy was hooking the carcasses from the butcher's shutter. Doyler said, 'Wait for us a crack,' and darted inside. Jim watched him through the window, bargaining for some broken brawn.

His eyes were drawn to a shelf at the back, where above the barrels of corned beef, a cow's head was on display. The butcher had prised its tongue out and curled it over the corner of its mouth, the way it would be licking its lips in anticipation of its own taste. Moony eyes were staring down, contemplating its blood collect on a plate. There was blood on the pavement too where the carcasses had dripped.

'After you with the push!'

A drunk had stumbled backwards out of Fennelly's and knocked into a bunch of fellows. He turned on them with colossal injury.

'Who're ya shoving at? Who d'ya think yous're shoving? Come back to me here and I'll learn yous manners.' He staggered to his feet, cursing and reeling. But he had lost the direction he was travelling and kept peering about as though to find it in the road. 'Who is it wants a puck? If's a puck yous want, need look no farther!'

Jim turned aside and found himself facing the blind lane that led to the Banks. Only a hundred yards from home, yet he had never been inside. There was no call for deliveries to the Banks. Gordie said he saw a naked woman there once. He used go down to buy bait when he was too idle to dig his own. He maintained it was like a party inside, with all sorts being drunk, red spirit even, and indeed you often heard singing in the night hours. Shrieks too, and sometimes, worst of all, that mad laughter that goes on too long and loud.

A marvel to picture tulips in such a place.

The Banks was the worst, but all about there was hardship. The dwellings beyond his father's shop, the courts behind the butcher's. You heard them at times, and if the wind went strange you had to smell them. But if you looked, you need never see more than shops and solid house-fronts. And when he looked up Adelaide Road to his father's shop on its watch upon the lane, he saw it for once not from his schoolfellows' view, as a dowdy and hucksterish stores, but as his customers must see it: the last and least, but still part of the strip of well-to-do that hedged their lives.

> *'Oft in the stilly night,*
> *ere slumber's chain has bo-o-und me —'*

It was the drunk out of Fennelly's who had begun to sing.

> *'Fond memory brings the light*
> *of other days aro-und me —'*

Moore's old melody. Under a gas-lamp he stood, in its puddle of light, lurching a little; his face cadaverous thin, though his voice, for all it rasped, surprising true. He aimed his song above the rooftops to where the night sky shimmered, while he told the tears of his boyhood years, the words of love he had spo-o-ken.

So ardent did he sing, each note might carry a breath of his life. People passing stopped to hear. And seeing them gathered, he stumbled among them with his hat held out. It was easy to credit the truth of his song, that his dim old eyes, they once had shone, that his heart, once cheerful, had been bro-o-o-ken. Two coins chinkled in his hat. And so it was when nights were still and sleep had yet to bind him, round him shone that other light, fondly to remind him.

A creak in his voice, and the spell broke in a raucous cough. He sought to regain his moment, but he could not. People who drifted away he followed with his hat. Those drinkers who had crowded Fennelly's door set in to mock him.

Jim retreated in the butcher's doorway. There was another boy, he saw him in his mind's eye, who when Doyler came out took hold his arm and strolled him away up the other direction. But Jim was not that boy, and now when Doyler emerged with his parcel of brawn, he stood mutely by, sensing the darkened mood.

'Mary and Joseph,' Doyler muttered, 'in the street and all.' In a jerk he had the pieces of his flute whipped out. 'Are you straight, Jim Mack?'

That question again. Jim cautiously nodded.

'Hold on to me flute, will you? I might not catch you before practice again. Will you mind it for me?'

'All right.'

'Next week then. I'll see you there.'

He had been bidden to go. It was so quick, Jim wasn't sure what was happening. 'We could maybe meet before, if and you wanted.'

'Aye maybe'

The drunk was hacking in his sleeve again, and one of the mockers from Fennelly's called, 'Have you a licence to go hawking in the street?'

Doyler spun round. 'Get on, you gobshite. Can't you leave a body in peace?'

'Who said that?' yelled the drunk. 'Who's it calling me a gobshite?'

Jim edged away. 'Is he all right?'

'Is who all right?'

Jim cocked his head. 'Your da.'

'I said I'll see you.' The apple in his throat was leaping now. He swallowed and the voice tempered. 'Look, pal o' me heart, right? If he decks me with the flute he'll have it fecked again.' Still Jim didn't understand. 'For to sell it of course or to pawn it.'

Jim slowly nodded.

'Go on, then, before he catches on you have it.'

In the shadow of an archway Jim watched the encounter of father and son. Mr Doyle shadow-boxed in his circle of lamplight. 'Who called me a gobshite? Was it you called me a gobshite?'

Doyler caught him by the arm. He muttered something while he held out his brawn. In a wild flail his father had it knocked to the road. 'Is it you is blackguarding me? Look at me, mister, when I talk to you! Look at me, I say! Who d'ya think you're looking at? Ladies and gents, do yous know who it is? Do yous know who it is now, ladies and gents?'

Like lazy sparks the tulips had fallen. Doyler bent to retrieve them and the brawn. And when the father raised his arm it seemed to Jim the son had offered his neck for the blow.

'"Thus in the stilly night" – This is the whore's git I has to call me own. And there's a whore inside did bounce him on me.'

*

73

Twelve years old. He was helping his father in the shop when the bell clinked and a fantastical character stopped in the door. Out of a bright check suit, buttoned high at the collar, shone a bright red face that danced with smiles under an orange flame of hair. A handkerchief flowed from his top pocket and a buttonhole bloomed in his lapel. In his hand he held a silver-topped cane, a bunched pair of lemon gloves and the brim of a brown bowler hat.

Jim saw his father standing at gaze; then gradually his mouth came to work. 'Well well well, I'll go to hades and back. What's this blown in of an old Irish morning?'

'Hayfoot, strawfoot, stand and freeze. Fusilier Doyle at the steady.' Click went heels and the character made a humorous salute.

'If it isn't the Queen's bad bargain himself!'

'Let me present arms now, Mr Mack, and if I shake your paw I'll shake the paw of the finest quarterbloke's bloke the Dubs did ever see.'

'Well, if it isn't Mick me old sweat.'

'If it isn't Mack me old heart.'

It made Jim smile himself to see his father so beaming. He had come out from the counter and he had the stranger's hand gripped in both his own. 'I'll go to hades and back,' he said again. 'Haven't seen sight of you, haven't heard wind of you, not since—'

'Pete'n'Marysburg, the Natal Province, October fourteenth, eighteen hundred and ninety-nine.'

'That's about the length of it. The regiment was setting off for Ladysmith, I remember.'

'And your good self, Sergeant Mack, was setting off for home.'

Gordie had come out from the kitchen, and he nudged Jim's

shoulder. A sliver of doubt had crossed their father's face. 'Well well well,' he repeated. 'And you've been prospering since. You'd take the stick on parade yet, so you would.'

The newcomer gave a swank of his clothes. 'Not a greasy button in sight,' said he.

Again that doubt in their father's eyes, his face a margarine smile. 'My my my,' he said. 'And what brings me natty old sweat to the parish by the sea?'

'Amn't I domiciled local now? The dog's lady, the grawls and meself.'

'Married and all?'

'Priest and witnesses.'

'And whereabouts would you be staying so?'

'A handy four walls down a vicinity called the Banks. That's till we finds me feet, of course.'

'You won't be long about that be the cut of you. Mighty prosperous altogether.'

For a season then he was a regular in the shop and the two old comrades would often be jawing over old times. Every now and then a roar would let out of a regimental song: 'Hurrah, hurrah for Ireland! And the Dublin Fu-usiliers!' In the kitchen Gordie would wink at Jim and Aunt Sawney used bang her stick on the floor.

Gordie called him Burlington Burt, and it was curious to see him late of a morning step out from the Banks, his swagger suit alive against the slob and a bloom in his buttonhole if only an old dandelion he plucked on the way. His bowler he tipped at an angle and his cane he carried sloped to the ground. 'It was the Colonel gave him that,' their father explained to them. 'Five times in a row the smartest man in the bat-talion.' He said it with pride, the way he would share in his comrade's splendour. They had never known their father be friendly with anyone. It was inconceivable he would give credit so free.

Then one day Gordie took Jim aside. 'Old Burlington Burt's put the stiffeners on the old fella.'

'What stiffeners?' asked Jim.

'Don't you know the old fella cut and run from the Boers. Scut away out the army the first shot was fired. He's scared of his wits thinking Burlington Burt will blow the gab.'

'The da never scut.'

'Young 'un,' said Gordie and he cuffed Jim's neck.

The pinch of tea and the tins of milk soon proved a burden, till finally Aunt Sawney put her stick unshakably down. 'A double deficit,' his father said sadly. 'For they won't mind what they owe us and what pennies they have they'll spend elsewhere now.'

'Ye're the slatey one,' Aunt Sawney chid him, 'and himself inside of Fennelly's regaling them what a touch ye are.'

The brown bowler hat was presently an item in Ducie's window. The lemon gloves quickly joined it, followed one drab morning by the silver-topped cane. Then one evening Mr Doyle came in the shop with Doyler in tow.

'Cross-patch, draw the latch, sit by the fire and spin. Is the coast clear, Sergeant?'

'She's away at chapel,' Jim's father answered. 'And who's this you have with you? Who's this the grand wee fusilier?'

'Sure you know the eldest. First shake of the bag. Say hello to Mr Mack, son.'

'Hello, Mr Mack,' came the surly voice.

'Though 'twasn't your humble what shook that particular bag, I don't think.'

'Ha ha ha.'

'You and me was sodgering yet when this wee mustard came out the nettlebed.'

'Ha ha ha,' echoed his father's strained voice, and the inside door closed to a crack.

In the kitchen, Jim returned to his books. Doyler he knew from national school. He was the rag-mannered barefoot boy who glowered at the back and never played games in the yard. He was mocked for a baldy peelo, for his hair would often be shaved against the itch, and his cap would slip and slide about his head. Every morning he was hauled for a thrashing because every afternoon he went working in the street. The master's face had been a sketch when he went up for the scholarship. But he sat it and was waiting, like Jim was now, the decision.

Movement by the door caught Jim's attention. Through the crack he saw Doyler's shadow, and the shadow of his hand was darting up and down to a shelf. Soaps. He was stealing soaps.

The grown-up banter continued beyond. Immediately, Jim understood what was going forth. Mr Doyle kept his father occupied while his son helped himself to the shop-goods. He rose from the table, and with that movement Doyler clocked him. He froze in the jar. His coat was open and the torn lining sagged with his haul. Jim made to approach, but a jerk of Doyler's head commanded him wait.

The eyes shifted to where the grown-ups were, shifted slowly back. Dark ovals washed Jim in their gloom, and as though some deep communication had passed the face nodded, nodding assurance. Slow and deliberate, he buttoned his coat.

Jim nodded back, but it was unclear to him what he had assented to. He came to the door and pushed it a gap.

Inside, the hilarity had quickly faded. 'I'm sorry now,' his father was saying, 'I couldn't be more assistance. But as you can see from the books here—'

'Spare your breath, old camerado. The well ever dried for the thirsty.'

There was still that remnant of the swell about Mr Doyle. His face was prinked and scrubbed and his jacket was brushed and buttoned high. But a patch of skin showed between the lapels. His cuffs gleamed their usual white but you could see they were unattached to any shirt.

'Where's that young buzzard after getting to?' he said, looking round for Doyler. He pushed him roughly to the door. 'Sergeant Mack says we're to approach the Benevolent Fund. Say thank you to Sergeant Mack.'

The black look deepened on Doyler's face. Without lifting his eyes from Jim, he said, 'Thank you, Mr Mack.'

'Quartermaster-Sergeant Mack's the brave man for advising, never doubt it. He'd have the gun advised off a Bojer's back. Which is all to the good, for devil the chance he'd fight him for it.'

When the shop door closed his father ushered Jim back into the kitchen. He took a heat from the range. He waited there with his back to Jim. 'Wouldn't mind now what that fellow says. That fellow says the worse thing comes in his head. Terrible man for a dodge. Terrible man for the lend of a loan. Wouldn't mind anything that man says. Do you hear me there?'

The next morning on his way to school, a spit landed at Jim's feet and Doyler dropped from the wall above.

'You won't say nothing about last evening.'

The words came out for a threat. He had that way of looking or talking that expected trouble. 'No good,' Jim answered. 'The da'll soon feel the miss of what was took.'

'Not if you put them back for me.' Out of his coat he pulled six cakes of soap. 'There's one got sold. I'll pay that back, only not till Saturday fortnight. You'll leave me off till then?'

Jim handled the cakes. Monkey Brand. *It won't wash clothes* was the slogan. Costly stuff that they never used at home. Neither did their customers, for they'd gathered dust as long as Jim could remember. Comical to think of Doyler stealing soap. His tousled hair and dirty face were a study for the monkey on the wrapper.

He wasn't just dirty: there were bruises forming round the eyes and his lip was gashed. 'He beat you, didn't he. He beat you, your da did, 'cause you wouldn't hand over the soaps.'

Doyler glared and for a moment Jim feared he might cut up rough. He spat at the wall, a streak of browny phlegm. But when he looked up again, his eyes were shining, and the hint of smile took the ape off his back. 'I didn't want you thinking me a thief.'

'I wouldn't have told.'

'You'd be thinking it all the same.' At a dueller's distance he called back, 'Good luck with the scholarship results.'

'Good luck with yours,' said Jim.

They met a few times after that. They walked up Glenageary once. They walked as far as Ballybrack. He put leaves on Jim's leg after he was stung by nettles. One time he called Jim *cara macree*, which he said was Irish for pal of my heart, and he took a thorn and pricked their palms and smeared their blood together. In the back of Jim's mind an idea was forming that if after all he went to college, it would be better if another from his own streets went with him. They were palling up, on the cusp of being great, when news came of their joint success. That day Doyler wasn't to be found. County Clare, they said.

When Jim came in his father had the Soldier's Friend out and was polishing his medals. The table was a rainbow of ribbons, blues and greens and reds. He looked up, glazed from his painstaking.

'There you are at last. Home from the spit and dribbles. What kept you?'

'I was at the devotion with Brother Polycarp.'

'Oh, keep in with the brothers,' his father said wisely. 'The brothers won't see you down. Is that a new flute we have there?'

Surprised at the ease of it, Jim answered, 'The brother wanted me to try it for him. He wasn't sure with the tone. He said to keep it by me for the time being.'

He climbed on a chair to fetch the cleaning rod from atop the press. When he looked down, his father wore a doubtful look.

'If you say so,' he said. He watched a while, then added, 'No wonder he's worried with the tone. That wood looks cracked away. You'd be all day fetching a tune out of that. Mind now, see what happens when you don't look after your instrument.'

Jim swabbed his flute and Doyler's, then laid them together inside his sock with a piece of precious orange-peel to keep them humid.

'There's bread and jam for those that wants it.'

'Thanks, Papa.'

''Twon't break the bank. Hungry work at the spit and dribbles.'

Under his father's gaze, Jim thinly spread the jam. He wondered vaguely what Doyler would be eating. The brawn had looked pitiful scant. Though they wouldn't be eating brawn of a Friday. A gratitude filled him as he ate for his own home and he regretted having lied about Doyler's flute. Why had he done that? An impulse he could not readily explain. He watched his father the way he worked. His lips moved with his concentration and the wings of his moustache blew up and down each breath he took. He frowned at the medal he was polishing, breathed on it, rubbed. 'Do you know this one, Jim?'

'Khedive's Star.'

'Dull old thing it is. Hard to get a shine off it. Bit of brummagem really, not regular British. Sandstormers, we called them. Khedive gave it us for saving his bacon. There.' He tried it against his chest. 'Will I pass muster? Hangs awkward too. Three rings on the clasp where, correctly placed, one would suffice.'

'I like it, Da.'

Even the ribbon was dull: plain dark blue. Yet it was Jim's favourite. Arab script like the scrawl of time, the exotic symbols, star and crescent, and a rather jolly Sphinx who smiled before the Pyramids. More than any the others, for all their dates and inscriptions, it begged to tell a story. When he had asked what tale that might be, his father had looked nonplussed. 'Sure we all got one. Nothing pass remarkable.'

'Is there some occasion, Da, that you have your medals out?'

'I was thinking about your brother and I thought – never can tell when you needs your medals. There's a war on, don't you know.'

He dabbed the cloth in the Soldier's Friend, chose a fresh medal, then set it down again. 'I'll be up with the owls at this.' Cloth redabbed, medal up, rub. 'That was a turn-up, I don't mind me saying, a son of mine parading through Dublin with my old regiment. It was always a shame to me that I never got to parade with the Dubs in Ireland. Oh, we paraded when we left, right enough, but I was only aetatis a nipper then. That was eighteen, that was eighteen-seventy, that was eighteen-seventy-nine. The barrack rat, they called me. Well, they called all the boys the barrack rat, that was the name they had for us. Barrack rats it was. Chuckaroo in India.'

Medal down, change cloth, medal up, shine.

'But I always regret that I never paraded through Dublin as a man. Of course, we paraded through many a town in our travels from the Rock to India and back, and very pleased they were to have us. Power of cheers we got from the assembled populace, venture wheresomever we may. But to march through Dublin as quartermaster-sergeant, now that had been the cheese. In charge of the stores of the fair city's regiment, marching behind the Colours and the battle honours waving, now that had been the Stilton. But we never came home till after I left the army and I never got my wish.'

Arcot, Condore, Wandiwash, Pondicherry . . . Jim knew the battle honours by heart. Guzerat, Sholinghur, Nundy Droog, Amboyna . . . a rote that in his mind came before the rivers of Ireland, before the kings of England, before his two-times table even. The names were beautiful and told of isolated scenes, little gardens of Eden, where stepping-stones forded spuming streams and cherry-trees hung overhead. Once in a while a cherry dropped in the wash, a burst scarlet cherry.

He was leaning at the table with his head on his palm, lazily watching his father. How meticulous he was, yet disorganized with it. The way he tidied away the medals, each in its place, then each removed, returned, adjusted.

'Why was that, Da?' he asked.

'Why was what is it?'

'We came home to Ireland before the regiment.' He knew, of course. The parish knew. And once at college when Jim muffed at football he heard a brother say to another brother, 'Quakebuttock for a pater.'

'Oh sure don't you know that was your mother.' His father was silent a while then he added, 'Heaven be her bed tonight.'

'Did she not like Africa?'

His father looked him a caution. 'You have your fill of questions tonight.'

'Was wondering only.'

'There's enough of your wondering now.' The box of medals went inside in the press. His hands remained on the open doors and he stared at the interior dark till in a tone of revelation he announced, 'Mimosa.'

'Mimosa, Da?'

'Mum-mim-mom,' he said. 'I had a smell of it the other morning walking up toward Ballygihen. Mimosa it was.'

'What's mimosa?'

'I never thought 'twould prosper in this weather. She'd have been right pleased to know.'

'Do you mean my mother?'

'Who else would I mean? She did always favour the mimosa. We had it in the garden when we were quartered there. Wait-a-bit thorn, the Boers called it. Strange class of people.'

Jim signed the word with his lips. Mimosa. What book at school would he look that out in?

'Whatever about that,' his father said, stretching his back for a heat by the range, ''tis Gordie we must look to now. Deo volenting, he'll come home to Dublin with the regiment and they'll march with the Colours in triumph.' He reflected a moment, his face clouded, then charity found his better side. 'No, fair dues. He signed up, so he did. Upped his age and took the man's part in the end. Albeit behind my back.'

'Aunt Sawney misses him, Da.'

'Aunt Sawney?'

'She came down in the night looking for him. She wanted to know why wasn't he home. I think she thought it was morning.'

'Did she give you a stir?'

'A bit all right.'

'She forgets sure. It's her age. They were very thick together.

Never knew for why, for he was ever on the tease with her. With her and the world and his wife. That's all that boy ever needed, a taste of army discipline. Sure wasn't he first chop the last time he stayed? The changed man. I always said if the army don't drill some sense into that noddle, then the devil's not in Ireland. If only now he hadn't let that drapery miss to spoil his parade.'

Jim couldn't but smile. A week back, they had marched with Gordie's battalion from the barracks, along the quays, up Dame Street, College Green, O'Connell Bridge down to the Custom House, a grand tour of the city's princely centre. And everywhere they passed, the flags were waving and handkerchiefs and hats, and from every window the hurrahs came till the panes rattled with the roar. He could feel his father set to burst with pride. And when the band broke into the regimental song, his voice joined lustily with the ranks:

A credit to the nation
A thousand buccaneers
A terror to creation
Are the Dublin Fusil –
Dublin Fusil –
Dublin Fusiliers!

But the occasion had been marred by the sight that greeted them at the dockside. There was Gordie, fine, manly, with his good-conduct badge and his skill-at-arms badge, and his hands that seemed suddenly as large as his father's, save his hands were wrapped round Nancy from Madame MacMurrough's. Nancy in her Easter bonnet and Sunday finery, 'looking a proper drapery miss,' said his father. And his father made Jim turn away, for she was kissing Gordie in the street.

'Well, Gordon, I trust and you won't let us down.'

'Spectamur agendo, Da,' and he shook his father's hand.

The regimental motto made his father's eyes water, and he

said, muttering and turning aside, 'Thanks son. Thank you, son.'

Then Gordie scuffed Jim one final time on the neck, but his hand lingered there and rested almost gently on his nape. Thick coarse cloth enveloped his face, and Gordie was whispering, 'Look after the old man for me. And look after Aunt Sawney. And look after Nancy too. And look after yourself, young 'un. Remember me.'

He straightened up. 'Mind this fella keeps to his books, Da. He's beggar all use else.'

A final salute to his father, a wink at Jim, and he returned to Nancy. Arm in arm they walked to the gangplank while the gulls above were calling. And it struck Jim that maybe his brother had been on his side all along. Had protected him from his father's ways by all the time bringing damnation on himself. A great remorse rose in him and he wished desperately to speak once more with his brother, to share one more night the narrow bed at home. But the band had faded into 'Come Back to Erin' and the ship pulled out from the quay, and all the hands waving were as wheat that shifted in a wind.

'Has the dustman passed?'

Jim realized he must have yawned.

'Time for Last Post so.' While Jim readied the settle-bed, his father lit his candle from the Sacred Heart lamp. 'I don't seem to find the time these days. What with knitting the socks and polishing the medals and totting up the club-books for the tally fortnights. Tonight was First Friday. We might have found time to go.'

'I had my devotion with Brother Polycarp tonight.'

'But this is something we might do together. Father and son.'

'Yes, Papa.'

'The Sacred Heart has promised great things.'

Jim nodded.

'Or we could find something to do with the Virgin Mary. There's a better class of people goes after the Blessed Virgin. I did always think that.'

'My devotion with Brother Polycarp is to Mary.'

His father blew at the edge of his moustache. 'Perhaps you're right. Keep in with the brothers.'

The gas went down, the stairs door closed, and Jim lay down to sleep.

The glow of the Sacred Heart gained slowly before him. Its flame swayed the shadows on the wall. Once in the night he had put his hand in that flame, but his courage had failed him. He had to pray then that God would not call him for a martyr. For if he failed again, the flames would be for ever and unconsuming.

Gordie used always blow out the lamp, bringing another day's bad luck that only Jim's frantic litanies could abate:

> Jesus, meek and humble of heart,
> Make my heart like unto Thine.
> O sweetest heart of Jesus, we implore,
> That we may love Thee ever more and more.

The flame flickered on the gold crosses of the Sunday beads that hung from a shelf where the missals were kept, whose gold tooling flickered in flame. It played on the statue of the Blessed Virgin, dancing on her starry nimbus, then solemnly stained the golden corpse of the kitchen cross. The campanulate shade of the gas-lamp it found and the brass handles of the bread-box that was the table's centrepiece. On the pans that hung like haloes over the sink and on the winged girandole by the stairs it shone. And just level with his eyes as he lay, it kindled the knob of the box-stairs door.

If you stared long enough at this door, you'd see it opening. Gordie had told him that. He told him Aunt Sawney came down in the night to steal his breath.

'What does she want with my breath?'

'Have you never watched in the day? She daren't breathe at all. Only by night. And it has to be from a boy's babby mouth, else she'll die.'

'Why'll she die?'

''Cause she's a witch in league with Old Horny and she feeds on a young 'un's breath. Be careful, else she'll catch you.'

'She's not a witch.'

'That's all right so. Nothing to fear.'

He told him about the Protestant church by the railway bridge up Adelaide Road that played hymns on its bells on Sundays. 'Folk have got it wrong, you know. You don't have to walk three times round to make the devil appear.'

'No?'

'Not at all. Just bless yourself as you pass and Old Horny'll come.'

That was all right because it was easy not to bless yourself, you could do that just forgetting. The cunning was too soon revealed. The cross was your sole protection, yet by signing there under the shadowy trees you invoked the enemy. The panic of those journeys past the Protestant church was with him still, a blink away.

He stretched his legs to the end of the sheet. How wide the bed, how still without his brother's dominant breath. The face of Our Lord reproached him. I promise you in the unfathomable mercy of My heart . . .

Pal of my heart. Wished I hadn't seen that. Wished I hadn't delayed in the road.

Mice in the shop. Outside he heard a shrill voice calling, Stop Press! Stop Press! Jim thought of a baton coming down on a newsboy's leg. Why would they do that to a newsboy?

Lusitania, he was calling. Another place he had never heard of. Tomorrow they'd mark it down on the map. Soldier in the mud with his legs missing and he turns with Gordie's face to say, When are the other boys coming?

Our Lady clothed with the sun and the moon at her feet and the twelve-starred crown atop the Muglins. No clear idea what a socialist does. Oft in the stilly night.

Upstairs, Aunt Sawney coughed and creaked in her cot. 'She's on her way,' Gordie had said on his last visit, his embarkation leave.

'Her way where?'

'Young 'un,' he said and cuffed Jim's neck.

That night, lying head-and-tails as of old, Gordie had said quietly, 'Do you never think of girls, young 'un?'

'What about them?'

'Nancy's a bit of' – jam, he called her. 'I take her out the odd time. Picture palaces together.'

'What do you see?'

'Matter a damn what you sees.' His toes nudged Jim's ribs. 'Dark as be damned in the picture palace.'

He wished it was dark as be damned in the kitchen. He wished it was dark as he was damned. He shifted on his side and a hand reached under the sheet to the hole he had cut in the ticking and felt its way through the lumps of horsehair till it found the rag he kept stolen there. He shut his eyes from the gaze of Our Lord and the reddening gaze of King George and Sir Redvers Buller, and he crossed out the image of Brother Polycarp's face and squeezed the mimosa from his mind, and he wondered what would it be like to swim in the sea, to swim in the sea off the Forty Foot, while his shirt lifted and the sheet began to move and the smell came up of the glue-pot.

Old horny.

CHAPTER FOUR

'NICE BIT OF skirt.'

    'Ah stuff it, will ya?'

The joke had been aired ten times over and no one was stirred by it any more. And yet it was curious to be wearing a kilt, to be clothed and to feel undressed inside. Four yards of saffron swung from Jim's hips. Creamy stockings, Scotch cap, white shirt from Lee's of George's Street.

A glance beside at Doyler who was tangling with a garter. Dark hairs curled from his stockings, stopping at the knee where the kilt hemmed. He caught Jim's look and saucily swayed, lifting his hands in a Highland manner. The ribbons from his cap dangled down his neck. All about the white shirts glared with newness, giving to everyone a bright and flourishing air.

'What cheer, eh?'

'Grand,' said Jim.

The usual must of the school commons was thickened with the sweat of unclothing. Over the benches lay shirts and gallused trousers, and the chatter and chaff was like many drums and many fifes and many boys and mayhem.

'Are we to be a marching band now, Brother?'

Brother Polycarp was at the blackboard where he was chalking an arrangement of 'A Nation Once Again'. 'Never fear, boy, when we of Presentation march it will be as gentlemen.' He turned. 'Not as an early turn from the palace of varieties.'

'Why the kilts so, Brother?'

'Wouldn't ye think to be merry enough with your Whitsun gauds, not to be moidering me with speculation?' He rapped his stick on the easel. 'Quiet now, men, please. Ye can see the push I'm in. I have this jewel of the Hibernian muse to twist some refinement into it.'

He looked surprised at the effect of his command. Every boy stood stock still. He nodded appreciatively, turned back to the board. Only then did he see the newcomer at the door.

A priest. A young priest, black-suited, with a black felt hat, one hand stiffly in his jacket pocket, thumb hooked outside, the other holding a black breviary, finger keeping the page. So tall, his head had a stoop. Wire-framed spectacles saddled his nose. Oddly, ever so, foreign-looking. Stuck in his lapel, a button with a Celtic cross and words in Gaelic underneath. A young, tall, Irish-speaking priest.

'Dia agus Muire dhaoibh.'

Brother Polycarp was stung into action. 'Father Taylor, we had not looked for you.' He strode the floor, offering his hand. 'Boys, let me introduce the new curate at St Joseph's. Father Taylor has taken a keen interest in our musical diversions. Already he has provided us a costume. It will be a great treat, Father, to hear the boys play uniformis for the nonce.'

The priest smiled generously at the brother while he released his hand from his shake. 'Dia agus Muire dhaoibh,' he said again.

No one answered.

'Did ye not hear me, boys? Dia . . . agus . . . Muire. God and Mary be with ye.'

His nose pecked before him as he spoke, crossways, as though each of his eyes required independent view.

'Have ye no Gaelic?' Silence. 'No boy?' Mounting silence. 'No Gaelic at all in the vaunted college of Presentation?'

At last Doyler spoke. 'Dia 's Muire dhuit 's Pádraigh, a hathair.'

Clap went the priest's hands. 'Did ye hear that, boys? God and Mary and Patrick be with you. Such is the response appropriate to my greeting, indeed the only response for an Irishman. For, as ye know or had ought to know, the Irish tongue may not speak but it utter a prayer. Good man for yourself. Good boy. There's one true Irishman amongst ye, I am pleased to hear. Though, if I am not mistaken, you are not of Presentation?'

'No, Father.'

'It would seem, Brother Polycarp, this is not the unmingled elect you had led us to believe. Sigh síos.'

They followed Doyler's lead and sat down. The priest dusted his hands together. When he smiled starch had cracked. 'Brother Polycarp, I fear we have a way to go yet with the Gaelic. I trust the music is on a firmer footing.'

'For our sins, Father, we persevere.'

'I would not doubt you. Well boys, *pace* the brother, my name is Father Éamonn O'Táighléir. Ye'll know I have recently joined the parish here and I have great hopes for us all. Ye'll be with me in that, boys?'

Yes, Father, they would.

'I hope soon to be coming to know each of ye individually. In a moment we will say a prayer for Ireland and her sequestration from the pagan breaths that on every side assail. In the meanwhile ye might entertain me to a rousing chorus. I believe Brother Polycarp will know the Hibernian jewel to which I refer?'

His head tilted to Brother Polycarp who simpering deflected his glance.

'Though why he should allude to our country by its Latin name, I do not know. Our country which alone withstood the degenerate embrace of the Roman Empire. Perhaps ye can tell me, boys?'

No father, they could not.

'Brother Polycarp, "A Nation Once Again", if you please.'

The brother suffered his smile to remain. He looked to be chewing on leathery gums. Humbly he bowed. 'Welcome though you be, Father, it is unfortunate your visitation should come all precipitate. What with the gimcracks and kickshaws of Mozart and Bach and sundry other euterpean gents, we have not found leisure to give justice to your request.'

'Do you tell me?'

'Another five minutes and we'd have made a fist of it.'

'I believe I take your gist, Brother Polycarp.'

The brother was all condolence till a notion occurred to brighten his guise. 'There is, nonetheless, in our repertoire an old galliard that I have on good authority is a stirring Irish tune.'

The pecks strayed from brother to boys. 'Any music will serve that stirs the patriotic heart.'

'Stand boys, please,' said Brother Polycarp. He raised his stick, wavered a moment. 'Father Taylor, are you sure you would not rather stand with us?'

The priest nodded and stooped to his feet.

'Very well, boys. A rousing rendition for our new curate, please, of "God Save the King".'

'Game for a walk?'

'Where to?'

'Forty Foot.'

Doyler didn't wait for a reply but bounded over the bench. At the door he motioned for Jim to hurry. Furtively Jim was shaking his head, then Brother Polycarp intervened.

'Have you forgotten your *Christian Politeness*, Mr Mack? A gentleman does not beck and twitch. Talk sensibly, boy, and after you're done, collect me the music. I'll be waiting inside.'

'The usual, is it?' asked Doyler.

'Half an hour maybe.'

He made a contemplative mime of a spit. 'I'll be waiting.'

The day was down when Jim came out the monastery gate. A shadow waited on the chapel wall opposite. Vernacular transformed it to Doyler. 'Half an hour, me arse. Them Protestant bells has gone three goes at least. Get on and shift your bob. I've piles waiting.'

Jim felt the creep of eyes on his back, and turning he saw the blind shift in Brother Polycarp's window. The brother had been in purple spirits throughout their devotion, smiling for holiday before their prayers; and during them, in their silences, Jim heard him chortling to himself. 'Nation once again, how are you,' he said afterwards. 'I think we put the kybosh on his Gaelic reverence. He'll know better in future to poke his bake in Presentation. What do you think, Mr Mack? Did we introduce our bootmaker to his tailor there?'

The blind was down now but still Jim made the dark shape behind. The brother's mood had shifted when he spied Doyler outside. Twice the past week they'd met after Jim's devotion. Brother Polycarp wasn't long catching on. Corydon, he called Doyler. 'I see Corydon awaits his Alexis again.' Tonight he added, 'Better alone than bad company, Jim. Lie down with dogs and you'll rise with fleas.' Jim sucked his cheeks. There was nothing in the Cassell's about Corydon. Nothing about Alexis either. He hurried down the lane to catch up.

There was plenty about bad company, however, in most the books they used at Presentation. In particular a manual called *Christian Politeness* which described the proper deportment of a Catholic gentleman. Where the eyes should rest, where the hands; the lips part so when drawing breath; exhaling, a gentleman employs his nose. Doyler might have posed for the thou-shalt-nots. His hands wouldn't settle, but swept along a wall or slapped against any lamppost he passed. He scrunched stones underfoot or scooted them away as though they posed an obstruction. According to *Christian Politeness*, the eyes were the windows of the soul: Doyler's rarely rested: proof of a giddy and unstable character. Occasionally they glanced on Jim's eyes, prompting a confederate grin. Jim might scatter a pebble, but he was conscious of imposturing. The fall of his hair bounced flatly on his forehead under the peak of his cap. He saw himself a study in brown that lumbered ponderously along. Then Doyler's arm would bang on his back. 'Slow as a wet week, so y'are.'

'Watch them go, the cripple and his pooch.'

Under the yard wall of the parochial house, a cigarette glowed in a huddle of forms. 'Fahy,' said Jim.

'Ignore 'em,' said Doyler.

A throat hawked and an oyster of phlegm splashed at their feet. Doyler spun. 'What ails ya, Fahy? Have you something to say or what is it?'

Fahy laughed and one of his cohorts, a clever-shins named Butler, crowed, 'There's that whiff again.'

Doyler grabbed at Butler's coat. 'Any more of that and I'll have ya ate. Ate without salt I'm telling ya.'

Fahy detached from the wall and leant forward the way his

finger pressed on Doyler's chest. 'Now listen to me, my wee sleeveen. You're becoming a pain in the Erse, if you don't mind me saying. Hop away home to your hut in the Banks. And take the pooch with you.'

'Let's go,' said Jim.

Doyler let go Butler, who brushed himself prettily down, and measured Fahy with his eyes. But Fahy was not easily browed. His father owned a slaughterhouse in Dalkey: he fed his sons on steak for breakfast.

Suddenly Doyler was laughing, 'Ah, have a banana.' A thin streak of spit landed expertly on top of Fahy's. 'What ails them fellas?' he asked when they climbed down the steps to the sea-wall and the jeers were left behind. 'Are they that way always? Are they that way at Pres?'

'Mostly.'

'You'd do better to ignore them.'

'I do.'

He stopped Jim with a hand that bolted on his shoulder. 'Do they give you trouble? You'd tell if they laid a hand?'

Eyes burnt and the ridge of brow protruded like horn. The grip was fast through Jim's jacket. He could feel the press of each finger.

'Sure why would they give me trouble?' he said, though in his heart he knew if trouble came it would come on account of Doyler.

'Butler's all mouth, but Fahy's a hard nut.' He spat his bile on the rocks below.

Jim swallowed. The hand had lifted, but the tension it had induced remained. 'Are we really to go to the Forty Foot?'

Doyler looked round as though the rocks would decide him. 'Said you never been. Thought to show you was all.'

'It'll be dark soon.'

A flash of his grin. 'I'll see you won't fall in,' he said and the arm went round Jim's shoulder.

Gently this time, though still the touch shot through Jim's clothes, through his skin even. It was this way whenever their bodies met, if limping he brushed against him or laughing he squeezed his arm. The touch charged through like a sputtering tram-wire until it wasn't Doyler he felt but what Doyler touched, which was himself. This is my shoulder, this my leg. And he did not think he had felt himself before, other than in pain or in sin.

'Are we straight so?'

'Aye we're straight,' said Jim.

'Straight as a rush, so we are.'

The shore lay deserted in the last light of evening. The tide was far out, no sound bar a faint tingling and every now and then a wallow in the deeper pools. Doyler slipped down from the sea-wall to the rocks – 'This is madness with our flutes,' said Jim – and they slid their way across the scalp. Up and down he lurched, making odd heelers when his right foot failed. 'Good for the balance,' he maintained.

They skirted the ladies' bathing-place, that seemed a deep and untouched pool, and climbed instead the brawny ridges that thrust to the sea, over the brash and barnacled boulders to Sandycove Harbour. They rounded the cushiony sand outside then plunged in the mud of the breach. And it was queer to enter the harbour that way. Sea-wrack lay everywhere, a rank and oily flow. Hard above loomed the Martello tower, looking ghostly and portentous on its grassy knoll.

Doyler stopped to peer round. The sand was grey, for colour had departed as evening dropped. Rivulets of silver veined its skin, save where the deep dark crept from the caves of stranded boats. The solemn houses of Sandycove looked inward against the night. In the west the clouds were one with the mountains. All was hushed save a crane behind that whispering flapped away. Then Doyler patted his bad leg and gave out a roar.

'What?' said Jim.

'Run!' he roared.

He charged up the slipway, slithering down and up again, roaring all the while, a wild yahoo of a yell.

For a moment Jim stalled, looking about and behind. His mouth had watered and it surprised him to find he had spat. His spittle pearled in the draining sand. Then his feet were running and the breath came fierce in his lungs, and still he roared while Doyler roared, up to the Point where the wind hit them with a coarse cloth cuff; then round the battery wall, down the sloping winders, on through the shadows and shelters, down into the Forty Foot where their howls exhausted on the hanging rocks. They collapsed at the steps that dropped to the water where wavelets lapped, foamlessly lapping.

'That's me spent.'

'Me too.'

His heart was pounding like a throb in the rock and his ears dinned with stopped sound.

'That was madness with our flutes.'

'That was madness with me leg.'

It was grand though too, thought Jim.

The way they had fallen their bodies were heaped, Doyler's leg thrown over Jim's.

'Why did you run?'

'Why wouldn't I run?'

'You was roaring like billy-o.'

'So was you.'

Yet it hadn't seemed it was they who roared, but the stillness that had raged against them. Jim sat up, scrupulously removing his leg from under. Phosphorescent glimmers showed in the cove. Away on Howth the Bailey swept and the lightship at the Kish responded, mother and daughter, crotchet and quaver. In the corner of his eye, he caught the Muglins winking. He felt flushed and able. Forty Foot at last, gentlemen's bathing-place. He reached his hand to the water.

'Too cold for you?'

'Not at all,' he answered.

'Best spot in Ireland for a dive and a dip. Should try it some time.'

'At school they take us to the baths at Kingstown.'

'What use is a baths at Kingstown? Come down here to the sea. Don't have to be scared. I'll see you right.'

'Not scared,' said Jim judiciously. 'Not a strong swimmer is all.'

'I'll learn you. What you need is the crawl. Best day is Sunday. Half-past ten, we'll have the place to ourself.'

'But Mass is on then.'

'Nail on the head. Swaddlers won't swim on the Lord's day, and the Catholics is hearing the Men's.'

'You mean you'd skip off Mass on a Sunday?'

'Can't you catch another if it bothers you?'

'But do you miss Mass?'

'Ah miss it something dreadful.' He stood up with a muttered, 'Back in a crack,' and wandered off behind the shelters. In the quiet Jim heard the scurry of feet, tiny animal scutterings. It was unfair that he had mentioned the baths in Kingstown. They did not let you in at the baths in Kingstown without you were wearing a collar and tie. Red blinked the Muglins light.

A body brushed behind and Doyler hunched down again. He was still buttoning his trousers and Jim turned aside.

'They do say there's a partition at the baths against the ladies' modesty. Is it true?'

'Some days all right.'

'Well, sure as eggs, there's no ladies at the Forty Foot, nor little modesty neither.'

He had his flute out now and he was screwing the joints. 'Does he never have anything Irish to play at that band,' he asked, 'old Polycarp?'

Jim thought through the repertoire. 'St Patrick's Day. Brian Boru. Garryowen.'

Doyler spat. 'Regimental marches. Shagging polis band does that. I mean real Irish.'

'Would "A Nation Once Again" be Irish?'

'Cod-Irish maybe. Like that priest's cod-Irish name. Father O'Táighléir. Did you ever hear the like? Right cabbage-looking patriot.'

It was a puzzle that he'd make a jeer of a priest of God. A puzzle too how quick the ape would leap on his back and quickly then leap off again.

'Never thought I'd enjoy to give the old Godsave, but I did that time, I tell you. Good on you, Polycarp. Puss on the priest was glorious to behold.'

He leant forward on his sitting bones. His grin adjusted to the fluter's smile and he brought the instrument to his lips. Long opening note that was the breath of music, then he burst into play. Grace-notes galore, slurs and sudden staccatos, octave leaps inside of a triplet. The tune was oddly familiar though it took a while for Jim to place it. 'God Save the King' done into a jig. Brother Polycarp would have been appalled, let alone the new father. But the walls of the Forty Foot rang about them.

In the dim light Jim could just make out the contortions that came over his face. It was like the flute was after surprising him there, he had no notion of that leap coming, fancy a flute putting pass-notes inside of that. The impression was of his cracked old stick having a will its own and Doyler merely following on.

After a time the virtuoso wore off. He slowed to a plainer air whose melancholy mode curled over the rocks and out to sea where waves flapped in mild percussion.

'You're after oiling it for me. Greased it too. I want to thank you for that.'

Jim shrugged. 'I was doing me own sure.'

'Almond oil don't come cheap.' He studied his instrument, toying with the bindings he'd made about the joins.

'Where did you learn to play that way?' Jim asked.

'My uncle knew a tinker out of Sligo who knew a traveller out of Roscommon who had the playing. Try along with me sure. Not difficult if it's slow like. Notes do mostly find themself.'

Jim untied his sock, but not without reservation, for he'd been told often enough against shifts in temperature. Indeed he had only to look at Doyler's flute. But in the end it was Doyler's playing that decided him against, for he feared to disfigure it with his fumbling way. The music was remote and unresolved, wound about with slides and those yearning delays, not notes really, but the lingering between. It was like the harmony of another air whose melody he believed he could catch and maybe, had he the fingering, might one day play. He closed his eyes and it wrapped round him, the dark timbre that was breathy and warm; and he carried to black waters where a wave washed, or maybe two waves washed, under the star of an evening. The music ended, but a haunt of it hung on the air like the last heat of a grey fire.

Jim opened his eyes and realized that Doyler was speaking.

'Cá dtéigheann an taoide nuair thagann an trághadh?
Mar a dtéigheann an oidhche nuair thagann an lá?'

'What was that?'

'Nothing. Just saw the tide had turned. It's an old thing they do say in Clare.'

The tide indeed had turned. Waves sent gentle spume on the steps that divided the cove. Behind, unseen, a spray landed with indignant horsy snort. Doyler unscrewed his flute, whipped the bits in the air to dislodge any moisture. It was all the ceremony he had for its care.

It was time and past to go, but neither shifted. In silence they gazed on the dark mid-main, then Jim said, 'I hadn't expected to find you gone that time.'

And Doyler answered, 'I looked for you to say goodbye but.'

'But what?'

'I was in a stir leaving.'

'All they knew was County Clare and they couldn't say when you'd be back and I kept thinking you'd be coming soon and then the college started and still no news and I knew then you were gone for good.'

'I was down with my mother's people.'

'They told me that all right.'

Jim felt himself sloping like a weight was in his shoulder. His neck bristled when the arm came over and the hair of his skin felt the shock of touch as Doyler's mop brushed against his face.

'Old pal o' me heart,' said Doyler.

And Jim said, 'Cara macree.'

'You remember that?'

'I do.'

'We were good pals that time.'

'We were great.'

'I thought of you down in Clare I did. I'd say you'd like it down that way.'

'I would?'

'We'll go one day, you and me together like. We'll stay on the island with my mother's people. And I'll show you the hut on the shore where we change for Mass. You'd laugh to see us. Traipsing in a grush of paupers, then out we troops in our Sunday majestics. They'd love you and all, with your college capeen.' He tipped the back of Jim's cap so he had to catch it quick before the sea would take it.

'You'll have me murdered,' he said.

'Hung, drawn and quartered,' Doyler agreed. Then he added, 'I wouldn't blame you going to the baths at Kingstown.'

There was a note of absolution in his voice. In like vein Jim answered, 'I'd say the sea would have more of a challenge all the same.'

'There's that all right. There's many afraid they'll drown in the sea. Not Doyler though.'

'Never?'

'Who's born to hang will never drown.'

He had gathered spalls of rock in a heap which delicately now, one by one, he plopped in the water. 'Will I tell you the story how I learnt me to swim?'

'Go on so.'

'Himself pushed against me one time and I fell in.'

Himself was how he called his father. 'What happened?'

'Himself jumped in and rescued me, of course. They learnt him that in the army.'

'And did he teach you after that?'

'Not at all. By the time he had me hauled out a crowd had gathered. They had a collection made, bravery and so on. I tell you, from that day out it was dangerous walking near water with the man. If the thirst was on him and he hadn't the entrance to a house, you was liable any minute to fetch up in the splash.'

'But your da wouldn't do that to you.'

Doyler shrugged. 'That's not the best. I listened to meself and meself was after saying, if it's this world you likes over the next, me bucko, had better learn swimming proper like. So I jumps in on me own one time without himself to rescue me. And I'll tell you what, I did learn. Learnt mighty quick, I don't mind me saying. So the next occasion he took me walking I was wary of his temper and I was waiting on him to make his move. I ducked out the way and what happened but he fell in himself.'

'What did you do?'

'I jumped in after, of course. But wait till I tell you. A fellow rescuing a boy is one thing. But a child of ten delivering his old man? The collection rate was doubled. He had us touring Leinster with that one, so he did.'

He seemed genuinely delighted with his story. His teeth were grinning whitely, showing the chip off the edge of the middle one, his dark face chuckled up and down. Then he tossed the last pebble in the sea and said, 'Do you smell a cigarette? I smell a cigarette smoke.'

He was up again and sniffing the air. Whatever he was looking for, it wasn't there, and presently he flumped back on the steps.

'That priest is out of the League,' he said. 'Wears the badge and all.'

'Which league is that?'

'Gaelic League, you gaum. Mind, there's something afoot if the priests is turning patriot. Them was never known cheer a horse but it was at the winning-post. Do they not have nothing Irish at Pres? No music, no Gaelic – they'll have you turned a right old Bertie.'

'There was a matriculation class all right, but the brother who took it went down of a decline.'

'Decline aye?' He coughed twice, politely, in sympathy.

'Is it the consumption your da has?'

'A bit all right. That and a cough won't shift. Eitinn they calls it in Irish. Bet you wouldn't know that in Latin.'

Jim stared to sea. 'No I wouldn't.'

'Curious, isn't it, with college boys how they learn them Latin but they wouldn't care tuppence for their own native tongue.'

Me care tuppence he means.

'Why,' he asked, 'why would I want,' he demanded, 'what would I want going to Pres for anyway?'

There was no answering that. Jim shrugged thinly his shoulders. 'Was it the Gaelic League you got your Irish?'

'Gaelic League, me arse. I got it off my mother's people. Can see me now, Doyler in his duds, in the Garlic Tweed. I tell you, it's a conspiracy against the working man. If you're at hurling and you curse in English they send you off the field. But they won't teach you to curse in Irish. They think our native tongue is good for nothing but praying in. That's why the priests is for it. They think there's no words in it for, I don't know, anything the priests is against. They'd have us blessing ourself in Gaelic the day long. And what worth is a blessing to a working man? For an ignorant heathen whoring bastard working Irish man?'

The air was blue with his swearing and a tinge of it shivered the skin. He got up, muttering something, and was off away again. Jim watched him climb an outcrop where he balanced on top, skimming stones in the waves. A question repeated in his mind. What is the Latin for consumption? Pulmonia, tuberculosis, phthisis even. It felt wrong to be watching Doyler the way he did. The Muglins was blinking, and within a wink it was himself he watched, a fretful boy who crouched with his arms about his knees. But it wouldn't do. At home they'd wonder about the mud on his boots. There'd be a wigging for the hour too. When Doyler came down, he stood up and said, 'Well, was he here?'

'Was who here?'

'You been agitated looking about you since we came.'

'I have?' He let a horse-laugh. 'I met a toff the other week and he said he does often come this way of an evening.'

'Well?'

'I don't know. Didn't fancy to bump into him tonight is all. Are we fixed for Sunday, so?'

'To swim?'

'Sure why not?'

'I go with Brother Polycarp to the Men's Mass.'

'After Mass then.'

'We do a retreat on Sundays.'

'Has you praying with him day and night, that fellow. Mighty devoted, the pair of yous.'

'He says I have a vocation.'

Doyler puffed a cheek and the air hissily issued. 'And do you?'

'He says my mother would want me to be a brother.'

'Why would she want that?'

Because a brother took vows, and if he kept those vows his mother need never feel shame before the angels. 'Wouldn't any mother?' he said.

On the steps to the path above, Doyler ran his fingers in a lackadaisical way through the posters that lined the battery wall. Strips that came off ruffled to the sea, whence the breeze from Wales laconically returned them. At Ballygihen Avenue, an arm lumped round Jim's shoulder. 'I'm sorry about me cursing back there.'

'That's all right.'

'I wouldn't want upsetting you. You're a college boy and they don't be used to that manner of talking.'

Jim felt most indignant. He combed his stock of expressions while Doyler hummed through a rambling air. 'Don't be a damned fool,' he muttered and the hum beside him warbled with humour.

'When does it end, this devotion of yours?'

'End of the month.'

'What happens then?'

'The Monday is the Queenship of Mary. I'll know then if I'm to be a brother.'

'Do you know what my mother always wanted for me?'

'What's that?'

'She always hoped I'd make a dungman's monkey.' The arm gave a squeeze of his neck. 'And look at me now. Haven't I made her wish?'

Old hunchback on her tramp through Glasthule. Widow's stoop to give the correct designation. Could set your clock by her, eight on the blow, there or thereabouts. Every night the road to Dalkey, never known to pass the other way back. How she gets to Dublin again we don't know. Still, she was a harmless soul. Mr Mack tipped his hat as she passed and said, 'Hello, Mary Days. How's this the days are doing?'

The determined old head didn't lift an oat as onward she trudged.

Odd that now. By rights she'd give out how the days is doing. Half the year they're drawing in, come mid-winter then they're drawing out again. Hold on now. Have I got the right handle at all? Is it Mary Days or Mary Nights is her name?

He called out, 'Mary Nights, Mary Nights, how's this the *nights* is doing?' But she had already passed up the road.

Mr Mack stared after. Made a donkey of that, he told himself. He looked round to see had anyone been watching. 'Good evening, Constable.'

The constable beetled from under his helmet, swivelled on his heels to beat the opposite way.

Mr Mack turned into a lane of cottages. Dark-green moss growing up the walls, yellow-green slime coming down. Smell of – what would you call that smell? Crowd of nippers at mud pies by the pump. Curious how quiet they play. If a poor man's riches is his children, these folk is mighty flush. He began knocking at the half-doors. 'Tell your ma it's Mr Mack for the fortnightly.'

Who has fewer childer feeds them fatter. Truer word. That was the way with his own two. Though he supposed had it turned out to the differ, there'd be other feet at his table now, devouring him out of house and home. Nice to have a little girl though. A little girl would be nice to have. Handy about the house and all.

> Little sisters, you may work,
> Work and help your mothers,
> Darn the stockings, mend the shirts,
> Father's things and brother's.

Yes, a girl would have been dandy. God rest your soul in peace everlasting.

That time with Gordie we went down the Banks. Like Calcutta it was. Well, any place in India, you takes your pick. Never suspected to find it on my doorstep. The fever van had called collecting. Children stood watching, the way they would be waiting their turn. Flies on their faces. I said to Gordie, 'We won't bother with that sum now.' Gordie felt it too for he said, 'We've a poor right coming here looking for payment.'

At the last cottage, a little girl came out and pulled the door after her. 'The ma's away on a message,' she said.

Mr Mack bent down till he was level with her nose. Small as she was she had a smaller child in her arms. 'Well, little lady, we'll have to take the little brother so.'

'Ma, Ma, the General's after going to take the buddy, Ma!'

Mr Mack said Aha! with his eyes and waited while the woman came with her poke.

'Why wouldn't you call of a Saturday like any decent Christian?' she complained while she counted out the coins. 'Wouldn't you know we was depending on his wages tomorrow?'

But how could he collect of a Saturday? Sure Saturday was his busiest night in the shop.

Some of these people, you'd think it was the bailiff after chucking them out the way they'd treat you. The trip-club, the communion-club, the photograph-club, the club for Christmas. Had he any sense he'd charge for a new trousers. Has me pockets near destroyed, the fiddler's change I collect. Wouldn't mind but I charge no commission, I share out the interest, not a penny would come the way of the shop necessarily. I only take the opportunity to remind them of the tick-book. And still they'd give you the cold shoulder of mutton. A thankless task it is, more kicks than ha'pence.

As he wandered along home, he felt the poor people's copper weigh in his pocket. Low in the sky hung watery clouds hovering over the gas-lamps. More rain. There was no up in poor people and the sullen skies dispirited him.

Game of a leg, hop and go quickly. Young Doyler it is with Jim in tow. I was thinking his devotions was taking longer these nights. They've palled up. Arm-and-arm they go. Ten days and they're cup and can together.

He made faces to himself while he considered the implications. Already he had caught Jim out in a lie and that lie was nailed now as he saw the flute passed over for safe-keeping. Wouldn't mind, but the age he spends cleaning it for him. Almond oil and cork grease, they don't come cheap. No cop-on, that boy. Got a load of almond oil in when he joined the band, thinking he'd let on to his schoolfellows where to buy it local. Shy of his shadow. Gave up in the end sending him down with the tins. Would weary you, the mortification on his face. Gathering dust now, along with everything else in the shop that can't be sold be ha'pennies.

He watched the boys as they made their farewells. Palled up great so they have. Those chats you have in the green of youth. All the time in the world and all the plans to make for it. But little the future is in it. No friendship without your equals. They learnt me that in the army. And Jim's a college boy now. Jim. My son James.

He had backed into a doorway not to be seen. Now he found himself reading the poster in the window. *An Inquiry From the Front*, the banner said. Inside a giant question-mark, a soldier asked: *When are the other boys coming?*

His hand went to his moustache, explored the comb of its hairs.

Now that's the damnedest thing. See here his cap badge? That's the Leinster Regiment, that is. The 109th Foot as was, the old Brass Heads. But look at this, would you. If them buttons isn't pewter on his tunic, I'm a grenadier. Class of thoolamawn they have doing these posters. Any wonder there's no rush to enlist. Sure any guffoon'd tell you, the Leinster Regiment has brass for its buttons and always has since 1858.

And would you look-see here. This poster's not up to scratch at all. Coming away at the edge already. Some young tearaway now, who knows but he has a sup taken, and he's wending his way merrily along. He sees this corner fluttering in the wind, what care he if 'tis Government property? No sooner seen than done, his hand goes out and bang! Out comes the constable, the boy's before the beak, and there's another young life broken. No wonder there's posters gets defaced. Very sloppy work altogether. Asking for trouble, so it is.

If I could maybe – all it needs is a drop of wet behind – if I could pull it back a touch more, get my finger in. Lick of spit and the job's good as new. Let me see now. Gently does it.

Cheese and crusts, would you look at that. Hames I've made of it now. Whacking great strip come off in me hands. Must be mighty inferior paper they use. Should write that down and send it in. A better class of paper and the posters might stay longer up.

He felt the hand upon his shoulder. He turned and saw the dark blue cape. 'Good evening, Constable,' said Mr Mack.

All along the road to Kingstown, over the bridge and past the railway station, all along the shuttering shops of George's Street lower, then the parade of doctors' and dentists' and lawyers', on their easy tramp through the fashionable township, Mr Mack tipped his hat to all he passed. In a low voice he explained, over and over again, that the glue-merchants and paper-manufacturers were all to blame and truth be told were in league with the Kaiser. Till, with a sense almost of surprise, they entered the doors of the police station and the desk sergeant said, 'Well?'

'Posters,' said the constable.

'If you'll allow me explain,' began Mr Mack.

'Red-handed?' asked the sergeant.

The constable waved the torn strip. 'Scarlet at it.'

CHAPTER FIVE

N ANCY KNOCKED ON the dressing-room door. 'Mam, there's a visitor to see you, mam.'

'Well? Who is it?'

'It's a priest, mam.'

Eveline caught the girl's look of awe in her table glass. 'Did he mention his business?'

'I didn't dare for to ask, mam.'

'Where is he now?'

'Isn't he in in the hall?'

Idiot child. 'Is the fire lighting in the small drawing-room?'

'It is, mam.'

'Show him to the big one so. And make tea, child. Is there cake?'

'Wasn't there Madeira, only Cook said—'

Eveline cut short the elaboration of excuses. 'Bring what you may find.'

'Only Cook says, mam, to ask will he be staying for dinner?'

'No. Neither will he stay for lunch. Now, will you make haste.'

Perfunctory curtsy, then her tread on the clumsy stairs.

Eveline studied the presentiment in her glass. Not the pearls after all, not the studs, nor the jet. It would have to be the emerald eardrops now. She chose a tea-gown of bold and cloqué roses: cerise, chartreuse, grenadine. *Eau de damas* for scent. Her hair was not unparagoned, wisps strayed beyond her ears. Not *en négligé*, but as though stirred by a Celtic breeze.

Father Amen O'Toiler, direct from his first sermon to the parish. She could not remember had she engaged to attend. She would congratulate him nevertheless. Magnificent blow for Ireland. At last a leader has come among us. Feet now. The button boots or the Gibson laces? Gibsons to show her shins.

The Gibsons had not been brushed nor the laces ironed and she cursed her idle people. And the gown, she realized, was a shade perhaps French in its reach. Still she had exquisite shins, and should the priest pretend to look askance she would say the gown had been run up in Donegal. Yes, splendid relict contrives them. One sits at her hearth while she spins and sews and regales with tales of the old times. I suppose they do sew in Donegal?

She viewed the ensemble in the body-glass. A nation's muse, *la belle Irlande*. A celebrated lady poet. Lionizing hostess. Her shoulders sank. Judge at the Glasthule Charity Bazaar. Some fallal or other. Choker with the cameo brooch? In the end she chose an amber pendant with a fly caught inside. She sang to herself, 'Around thee shall glisten the loveliest amber That ever the sorrowing sea-bird hath wept.' They gave it to Mother when Father was returned the third time. Grateful constituents. Oil of palm, she expected.

En grande tenue, she descended the stairs. Forgive me, Father, for I have sinned. Stop it, now, one must be sober.

'Forgive me, Father, for keeping you waiting. The butler has run off to sea, the parlour maids have married their soldiers, which leaves me only the girl from the kitchen and she, God help us, is touched.'

She approached with her hand held out and the young man rose in jerks from the sofa. He fumbled in a farouche way, confused as to whether to kiss her hand or to shake it. At the last moment she glided past and pulled the bell-rope that hung by the hearth.

Nancy came rushing to the door. 'Mam?'

'Be a good child and bring tea. Would tea be all right for you, Father?'

'Tea would be grand, Madame MacMurrough.'

'Isn't the kettle only waiting, mam?'

'Very good. Make haste. Father O'Toiler, do sit down and tell me, do, how are things in the four green fields of Erin?'

She perched upon a fiddle-back and the priest returned to the sofa. He had chosen the centre cushion and she watched as he sank lower and lower till his knees rose to be level with his chin. Whatever it is they teach in Maynooth these days, she considered, it is never command of furniture.

She saw his fingers fidget with the cardboard cover of his breviary. Would a leather breviary be a fitting gift?

The priest hemmed. 'Things are growing apace, Madame MacMurrough. It is my fear, however, that in the parish of the Stream of O'Toole we are lagging somewhat.'

'The Stream of O'Toole, father?'

'It is the translation of Glasthule from the Gaelic.'

'How inspiriting. You cannot conceive how proud I am to hear the ancient tongue spoken once more in my father's house.'

He looked perplexed a moment, then graciously nodding, said, 'Go raibh maith agat.'

She gave an enchanted clap. 'Bravo, Father, bravo. Tell me now, do, what was that you said?'

'It was the Irish for thank you.' Again he nodded.

'Too long have we waited for a lead in this parish. And now you have come in answer to a prayer.'

His smile sucked on sherbet. He leant cannily forward. 'So you heard my sermon?'

'Splendid show.'

'I thought it went very well.'

'A magnificent blow for Ireland.'

'And for the Church.'

'And for the Church, of course.'

'The two are inseparable. And you do not think my hopes too extravagant?'

'In what way extravagant now?'

'No, Madame MacMurrough, I see you stand foursquare beside me. For the past twenty years the Gael has been crying aloud for help to beat back the Anglicization that drags its slimy length along. The immoral literature, the smutty postcards, the lewd plays and suggestive songs were bad, yet they were merely puffs from the foul breath of a paganized society. Even today I saw ye, many of ye here this morning, on your very way to Mass, I saw ye stoop to purchase—'

'I'm sorry, Father?'

'No, Madame MacMurrough, I quote from my sermon, you will recall. It was at that point I mentioned the *News of the World* and there was tremendous shuffling of feet and coughing throughout the congregation.'

'Yes, of course.'

'For we know now that should we continue travelling in this same direction, condemning the sports that were practised by our forefathers, effacing our national features as though we were ashamed of them, contemning indeed our own native tongue that cannot speak but it praise God, and putting on, with England's stuff and broadcloths, her masher habits and feminine follies, we had better at once!'

'At once, Father?'

'And publicly, abjure our nationality, clap hands for joy at the Union Jack, and declare unto a disbelieving world that Ireland! – she has lost her faith of old.'

'I see.'

'It was all in the sermon and I believe it went tremendous well.'

The girl came in with the tray, *délivrance*, and rattled it on to a table. 'Leave us, child. I shall serve the father myself.'

She measured tea into the teapot, poured the water. To her surprise she saw the child had remained.

'Mam, there's a poor woman come to the kitchen door, mam.'

'Well?'

'She's looking to take in washing, mam.'

'Why are you telling me this?'

'Only Cook said—'

'Cook?'

'Didn't she say to tell you—'

'Enough. Show the woman to the pass door. I shall interview her there.'

'Thank you, mam.'

'Go raibh maith agat,' said the priest.

Curtsying cheeses, Nancy left.

'Sugar?'

'I do.'

'Cream?'

'A taste only.'

'Your tea, Father.'

'Go raibh maith agat.'

A gracious language, if somewhat limited of expression. 'You'll excuse me, Father O'Toiler, if I abandon you a moment.'

'A domestic crisis ensues,' he said, rising. But Eveline had already left.

The clock clicked, tock-tick. Over the hearth hung a heavy frame, carved in blackening shamrock lace. It leant ponderously forward as though the likeness within had been listening the while and now intended to intrude. An advocate perhaps, a politician certainly, last scion of a dispossessed clan. The large, square, low-fronted head was quarter-turned, as if to catch from the shadowy plane the ceaseless cries of an oppressed people. The gleam of the eyes showed humour, but the mouth had thinned with scorn as, blow for blow through the midless years, it had turned a conqueror's jibes. In ageing *morbidezza*, the character of their race.

The priest heard the door close and knew that Eveline stood behind him. 'My father,' she said after a time.

His face, which had lifted, lowered. 'A great man.'

'He was that.' A pier glass gave gaze of her profile. I am my father's seed.

'Not a day but he worked in Ireland's cause.'

'He lived for his country.'

'He was a great man and a good. Any number of windows I have seen, painted windows in chapels wheresoever in the province, with his name in dedication.'

Yes, she idly thought, her father had been scrupulous in providing for the Church. The rate of one glass window per bastard born, if she did not mistake.

The priest leant forward now. 'Is it true, Madame Mac-Murrough, he had the ear of the Fenians?'

'He was always very close on that subject, Father. But it was his strong conviction that England never moved but she was pushed.'

'A man of uplifting oratory and acuity of vision. Some say, and I have said it myself, he died for Ireland.'

'So soon he left us.'

'Happy the man who dies for his country.'

'We will not see his like again.'

'Do not say so!' Cup banged on saucer. 'Madame, forgive me, but such thoughts have too long been the bane of our land!'

She was startled by the priest's ardour and could not immediately recall which commonplace had provoked it. She saw he had spilt tea on his trouser leg. 'I'm afraid we have no cake, Father O'Toiler, but the child evidently has brought biscuits. May I tempt you? Or is it too soon before lunch?'

'A biscuit would be grand.'

'They are Irish-manufactured.'

'Proven by their taste.'

She smiled acknowledgment. The smile moued on her face while the priest discoursed, detailing apparently the clubs and classes he intended for the parish and the moral tone that should prevail. She eyed her tea – the girl had brought Indian not China – with a wintry discontent, though it was the service which the more displeased. Accursed child had laid out the Minton. Minton for a bishop at the very least, any old Davenport for a curate.

At one point the priest made to fetch another biscuit, and she quickly brought the plate to him lest he should feel free to roam her drawing-room. She wondered what childhood illness had rendered his face so blemished, for it was pocked and pitted miraculously. What in France they would call *un joli laid*, whose ugliness presented the chief attraction. This dash of a Roman collar – how it gleamed against the black, the white gloss of

Maynooth. How it checked the ride of the apple in the throat. She was minded of those boys, that circle of young manhood – cat's-paws, panderers, fawners, wheedlers, henchmen, conjuror's assistants – that had orbited, till his dying end, her father's star. Some had thought to fawn to her, some to wheedle past her. Some, God help us, had thought to make love to her. As though she, her father's seed, should forsake his side for the side of a gangling weed.

The drawing-room gave out to the garden room which in turn gave out to the lawns, where sycamores waved in the sea-breeze. The may was waving, the bluebells hazed, and she wondered when the strawberries would come.

'However, Madame MacMurrough, intentions are all very well, but without organization, I hear you say, how far will our intentions advance?'

Not for the first time she wondered what she wanted with this priest. Of course, it was her name that he was after, that illustrious and priceless name, on the headed notepaper of one more committee, her gloved hand opening yet another bazaar. How tedious it all could be. One yearned for the grinding of pikes on a stone, but the reality for a woman was tea parties, muffin fights, hearts sunk in raising lucre.

She glanced upon his poking face, the spectacles that slid on his glistening nose. Every morning he brings down God to the altar. God has called him to do this. It was extraordinary and in some way very humbling. She leant forward and said, 'Father, what may I do to help?'

'Help, Madame MacMurrough? Your very presence in the parish is an inspiration. Your name alone is worth its weight in gold.'

Oh lah, here come the bazaars. She felt her pendant with its trapped and prehistoric fly. And I have dressed the part. She decided she would motor in the afternoon. And I shall wear green tweed, the Redfern probably, and my father's guns on the seat beside as over the hills I go. My name is MacMurrough. My father had the ear of the Fenians. I too hear the ceaseless cries.

She rose from her chair that the priest should rise and interrupt his homily. Adjusting a piece on the *étagère*, she said, 'Tell me, Father, did the kilts arrive? A band, I believe. Young men of the parish.'

'They arrived in perfect order. And it is in part my excuse for imposing upon you this morning, to express the gratitude of the parish for your kind benevolence. Madame MacMurrough,' he said, standing and taking off his spectacles, 'go raibh maith agat.'

She was sure she had never known so obliging a tongue.

The priest returned his spectacles, resat, spilling the merest skim of tea. 'Already the boys are wearing them. I fear, however, the man in charge is not of our timber. A weak character of intemperate habit, unsuited to the charge of boys.'

'A Presentation brother, I believe.'

'There is the smell of drink off him. Worse even, he is Englified beyond redemption. All I had requested was a simple Irish tune. He had them play the Saxon anthem.'

'Oh lah,' said Eveline.

'Alas, it is the nature of these Presentationers. What are they but trumped-up Christian Brothers? The Christian Brothers have the virtue at least of knowing their place in a parish. But these shoneen men of Presentation are Englified to the core, if such could be said to have a core. Rugby they play and cricket in season: a college for Castle Catholics is all it is. And this flute band he gives. What does he teach only bits out of old operas, *The Magic Flute* even, that monstrous farrago of masonic falsehood.'

'Oh lah,' she repeated, but she was thinking of her nephew.

There were strings connecting that troublesome boy with the instrument in question. Had he not played flute as a child? She recalled a silver article that came with his luggage from England.

'However, the bird that can sing but won't must be made sing.' The curate scoured his hands. With devious jerks of his head he proceeded, 'There is a Gaelic-speaking lad in the parish. A poor boy who came looking to me for an intro-duction for work. Well, I introduced him to the band for good measure. In consequence, that band is the legitimate concern of the parish clergy. We have, so to speak, our ticket of entry.'

'Bravo, Father.'

'It will be no simple contrivance to prise the brother away. They can be stubborn, these modern orders. In the meantime, we must be upon the look-out for his replacement. He need not be any tremendous musician, provided only he be amenable to our aims.'

'I wonder,' Eveline began, but she trailed off, seeking in her mind the passages her wonder should take her. This coincidence of the flute and her nephew: mightn't two birds be made sing with the one stone? If she might show her nephew to public advantage. A garden party perhaps. Select gathering of advanced opinion. The local youth he leads in song. This is my nephew, whom the English have traduced. With prudent handling, he might, God help us, be regarded a catch.

It did not present a very likely prospect. Troublesome boy, where was he, anyhow? Bathing at the Forty Foot, if she was not deceived.

The priest cocked a kindly query. 'Madame?'

'I was wondering where we should find such a person.'

'We must be vigilant. I am thinking also of a military man

who might drill the boys in marching. There is nothing to stir the patriotic heart as young men who march in step.'

A military man, a type of sergeant-major or *chef de fanfare*. No, she was the commandant, marching at the head of her heroes. 'Let vigilance be our watch-word.'

'It is not that the parish lacks spirit, Madame MacMurrough. In every street, the deceptions of our oppressors are confronted, defied, deposed. It is a tremendous sight to see.'

'In Glasthule?'

'I refer to the torn recruitment posters. But these hidden hands are profitless without we make a public display. Particularly now that, thanks to your good self, the boys have kilts to parade in. And in regard to those self-same vestments, if I might once more impose' – unhooking his spectacles and obtruding them in the air so that four eyes now poked at her, and again rising from his seat – 'Go raibh maith agat.' Spectacled, sinking once more, he added, 'If there is any way, any thing at all you can think of—'

'Well, perhaps—'

'Any little thing whatever we can do to show our appreciation—'

'I had thought of a little . . . a fête champêtre.'

'I believe I don't know—'

'In the garden here. A party.'

'Party, Madame?'

A darker ardour charged his face and briefly she heard his shuffling, coughing congregation. Nothing would do but she must utter the dread word. 'Bazaar.'

'I don't see.'

'For the raising of subscriptions. The Irish classes you mentioned, the hockey clubs. The band would provide a musical interlude.'

'A feis!' exclaimed the priest. 'I see it now. Music from the band, Irish singing, poetry even, the local schoolchildren will play-act scenes from our heroic past. A most marvellous suggestion. And you would suffer your home to be prevailed upon for this exhibition?'

She had countenanced a band of uniformed boys, not national schoolchildren trampling her lawns. She saw herself presiding over the usual banquet of suburbandom. Madame MacMurrough will now present the prizes . . . 'I should be honoured.'

'While we have your good self to the fore, good lady, your father has not entirely left us.'

She believed she'd had her fill of this priest for the present. She pulled the hearth bell. 'Thank you, Father, it has been a most encouraging interview.'

'No no, Madame, thank you, thank you. Go raibh maith agat go leoir.'

'Galore,' she repeated, pouncing on recognized syllables. 'Galore to you too, Father O'Toiler. Isn't it glorious to be speaking the old tongue together?'

He was still wittering when the child came to show him out. 'The Glasthule Feis, yes indeed. I don't know how I can thank you sufficiently. A display of Gaelic crafts we could have. Athletics. Did you know the long jump and the triple jump were Irish creations? Is there space I wonder for a hurling contest? A committee. We must form a committee of interested persons. You will of course grace us at the chair?'

'Your hat, Father.'

'Go raibh maith agat, Madame.'

She waited till she heard the door close, then she dropped into a cushioned chair.

Nancy stopped in the hall and said, 'Dinner is waiting, mam.'

'Lunch.'

'Yes, mam.'

'Have you seen my nephew?'

'Wasn't he out in the garden a moment back?'

'Call him for me. And tell Cook that lunch is to be delayed.'

'But isn't dinner waiting, mam?'

'Lunch.'

'Yes, mam.'

'Just tell Cook I said so. And call my nephew.'

'Yes, mam.'

'Do it, child.'

Minutes later she heard his step on the gravel and the garden doors opened in the garden room. Fresh air preceded him as he came up behind and she felt his breath then his kiss on her temple. 'Aunt Eva,' he said in disapproving tone.

'Did the child complain to you?'

'I understand Cook is throwing pans at the kitchen wall.'

'Why are people so trying?'

He was at the side table. She heard the comforting chink of glass, but still she kept her eyes closed.

'It's their Sunday out. Of course they want lunch to be done with.'

'And my head aches so.'

'Sherry.'

She opened her eyes to receive the glass in her hand. He stood before her, young, relaxed, proficient. Tennisy clothes hung casually from him. Moustache thin as ink. Bored, she thought.

'Did the priest bring on your migraine?'

'You saw him, then?'

'Just in time. I was returning after my bathe, but I scarpered down the garden. Really, Aunt Eva, the parish clergy.

Could you not find a Jesuit to play with? He looked an ugly stick.'

'You oughtn't to talk that way of a priest.'

'I'm sure his soul is very handsome.'

Just as your soul, my handsome young nephew, is damned. 'Are you going to smoke?'

He turned as the match struck. 'Do you object?'

'No. But I should like to be asked.'

'May I?'

Her fingers lifted in acquiescence. Smoke curled from his mouth. She wondered as she watched just how indifferent he could be. 'Am I too strict with you?' she asked.

'On the contrary, dear Aunt. You are the soul of compassion. My presence here confirms it.'

Not entirely indifferent. He does so preen himself upon his disgrace.

Through the garden doors she heard a singing and she turned to see the new washerwoman make her way down the lawn. She had a fantastical and placid motion, carrying her basket on top of her head. Another basket looped through her arm. She remembered the woman's face from her interview that was proud and undaunted. An infant slumbered inside her shawl. Its tiny hand had slipped out. It had looked so delicate, like china against the rough stuff cloth, that Eveline had bade the bootman fetch milk. But the woman refused, saying, 'The blessing of God on you, mam, but I'm looking to keep her at nurse a while longer.' It was that had decided her to employ the woman. Though she had references too from Mrs King whose husband worked at the Castle and from some dissenting clergyman with lilac notepaper.

How proud she walked and softly sang. The air carried over the listening lawns. Beyond the lawns the sea glistened and her song had the breezy yawn of the sea as softly she sang to her slumbering child and her humble burden she carried.

'She takes away the stains of the world,' she heard her nephew say. And when the washerwoman stumbled, Eveline felt a tiny start inside. A start, as though she would reach out herself to help the woman.

At that moment she knew where she would motor in the afternoon. She would take the mountain road to High Kinsella, she would drive through the dark if need be, and she would sit in the room he had slept in there, when convalescent he came and she had nursed him, Casement. And she would pray for his return, for his soon and safe and conquering return, to the Ireland that he loved. And if God willed it, and God send He did, to her.

She turned from the garden doors. Curtly she said, 'I shall be away this afternoon. I may well be away the night. Shall you dine out or should I ask Cook to leave a cold plate?'

'May I ask where you're going?'

'You might, if you chose to be impertinent. However, there is no mystery. High Kinsella,' she said.

He gave the appearance of a smile. 'Emeralds in the country, my gracious. And will he be collecting you?'

His jaded games. 'As always, dear boy, I shall motor myself.'

'You know, Aunt Eva, you'll bring scandal on our name if you insist on tooling up and down the lanes. A lady motorist could be thought dashing to the point of fast. Why don't you advertise for a chauffeur-mechanic?'

Her charming, handsome, damned nephew. For all his sins, a MacMurrough. She rose to ready for lunch. 'Shall you change? Or do you intend dining dirty?'

'To please you I shall change.'

'It would please me.'

'If only for lunch.' The line of his moustache was unmoved by the smirk.

At the door, she asked, 'Usen't you to play a musical instrument?'

'Why do you ask?'

'Which was it?'

'Flute.'

His humourless eyes. It was pitiful to see the affliction behind. There were times he was not handsome at all, her nephew – he but wore that mask. And now when she looked, he was not lean and agile as a glance told, but thin, gruelled, his clothes another's. Yes, there was a deal of work to be done with her nephew.

Her gaze wandered over the portrait of her father, wandered back to his face. Chauffeur-mechanic indeed. 'As for scandal,' she said, 'I believe you have the edge on all of us there.'

CHAPTER SIX

'P APA?'
    'Are you holding tight there?'

'There's been something on my mind.'

'There always is when you calls me papa.' Mr Mack took a grip of the shelf and looked down at his son's upward face. Sallow skin on him. One or two spots coming. Trouble in his eyes. Oh begod, Gordie gone now, oughtn't I – kipping on his own now, oughtn't I – would they not learn him against that at the college? 'Don't do it,' he let out.

'Do what?'

'Say a prayer instead. It does go away, the urge will.' His son was mouthing words so he quickly added, 'Say no more about it now.' He thought a moment. 'Sleep with your hands like so.' He crossed his breast with his arms and the steps tilted under him. 'Didn't I tell you to hold tight?' He regained his balance. 'Let the word Jesus be the last on your lips. Or Mary. A prayer to the Blessed Virgin would often be most affectatious. We'll say no more now. Save it'll leave you insane in the end.'

'What will leave me insane?'

He scratched his head, then felt his moustache. The boy's

eyes, having deeply blinked, were doubly troubled. 'How old is this you are?'

'I'm turned sixteen.'

A cheek dimpled in calculation. 'Show me up them candles like a good boy. I was older than you at your age.'

'Da, it's about socialism.'

'Socialism?'

'It's been on my mind to know what it is.'

'Socialism is it?' He was putting the new candles at the back and bringing the old ones forward. He had already dusted the old ones and now, truth to tell, it was hard knowing the other from which. 'Did you hand me up them dips like I told you?'

'You stacked them sure.'

'Are you holding on to that steps?'

'Da, it's all right if you wouldn't know.'

'Wouldn't know what?' he said, climbing down. 'Ho ho ho, running away with ourself now. Not that I wouldn't know at all. Wouldn't know where to begin is all. Socialism, well well.' He rubbed his hands. 'What it is primarily is, what it is is wrong.'

'But why's it wrong?'

'Do they not teach you these things at the college?'

'No.'

'Well it's, basically it's, what it is is greed. Oh yes, there's greed there. Greed and envy. A heap of envy involved. Then there's pride. Greed, envy, pride – sloth. Sloth there, too. Oh, all the sins. Every man-jack of them. The entire boiling, the hopping-pot, the whole kit and caboodle. I know what it is,' he added wisely. 'You was listening to the sermon last Sunday. Well, 'twas all there. Three-quarters an hour the father spoke on the subject and you can't ask fairer than that.'

'But what does it stand for?'

'It stands for what's wrong, isn't that plain as your nose?'

He pulled out the till drawer. 'What did I tell you? Herself is going dark as well as cranky. Coins all over the place, in the wrong place, you'd be all day grubbing for the correct change.'

With delighted hands he set about the till's rearrangement. 'Socialism means Larkinism and Larkinism means all ballyhooly let loose. Do you not remember them strikes we had and oratating in the street? Bully-boy tactics is all them fellows knows. And trying to send poor Catholic children to Protestant homes in England? That was beyond the beyonds.'

'Only so's they'd be fed.'

'What's that?'

'They had no food, Da. The children didn't.'

'If they had no food why wouldn't they go back to work? Stands to reason.'

'They were locked out sure.'

'Who told you that?'

'The employers locked them out so's to starve them into lower wages.'

'Who's this been spreading notions?'

'It's well known.'

'I asked you a question.'

'Doyler told me.'

The till slammed home. 'Now, lookat here, young fellow-me-lad. Amn't I in trouble enough without you palling up with agitating corner boys? Is it him spreading them notions in you? Lord save us, you haven't the sense you was born with. I'm your father. Your father's in peril of a prison term. Your father's name is muck in the street. My name is in the paper sure. Piece of blackguardism in letters high as your hand. That's talking about your father, that is. And you want to be trumpeting Larkinism? This is where you want it.'

He tapped his son's head, not intending to strike, but the tap

130

in the event came out a blow. The lad recoiled. 'That's where you want it,' he said. Consistency required he drive the blow home. 'And that's where you'll get it if I hear another word.'

'I only wanted to know.'

'You'll know better in future.' The hunted look on the childlike face had him wavering toward conciliation. But the boy had no call to look hunted. The boy had no call to vex him so. 'What are you standing for? Haven't you sweeping to do?'

His fingers agitated the thighs of his trousers. If he stopped any longer he'd know how to clatter that look off the boy's face. He went to the door. 'And you can take that flute back to him and all. Aye aye, you needn't look so startled. Think I'm green as I'm cabbage-looking. Cork grease and almond oil. I don't know where you gets it at all. Let you earn your living for once. Let you have that floor spotless by the time I have my sup of tea. Cut of this shop. 'Tis muck to the street so it is.'

He thrust into the kitchen, staying the door at the moment of its slam. His anger urged a clattering and clanging, but Aunt Sawney was nodding in her chair, and the last thing he needed was herself at her jibes. He had to creep making the tea, filling the kettle with a squeak of water, settling it scrapeless on the range. At the sink he stared through the streaky glass at the yard outside, that blank space he could never make up his mind what do with it. In consequence it harboured old crates, old sacks, broken yokes that one day he'd get round to. His passion shrank with the quietness, returned to the tight ball that lodged in his chest, losing none of its intensity, but changing by degrees from anger through resentment to pity. He sank into a chair at the table and soaped his face in his sweating hands.

It had started with the constable and there was no downfacing that twister. Same at the station where they only played the jack at his explanations. It was a great stroke to have him caught red-handed. They bailed him for the police court and the police magistrate without benefit of reflection pronounced his act a piece of blackguardism. The papers made a banner out of that. 'Piece of Blackguardism', letters high as your hand. Calculated and likely to prejudice recruiting. Respectably dressed man giving his name as Arthur Mack, Glasthule, County Dublin. Regulations in pursuance of Defence of the Realm Acts. And the way the papers would distort the facts. 'Was there the

SMELL OF DRINK

off him?'

Twenty-two years with the Colours, he told the beak.

'Which makes it all the more disgraceful you should appear before me tonight. Bind him over.'

Case adjourned to a later hearing.

The only hope to be had was the parish priest. If the canon would put in the good word. If that the canon would tell them what's what and who's who. The canon would show them the error of their ways. He'd get off with a fine if the canon would speak. A fine? Sure they'd thank him. Stirling act of civic duty.

The kettle was coming on to boil and before it would whistle he snook it off the hob. Water dolloped on the oilcloth as he carried it to the sink. Herself is mighty dozy. She'd need that store of sleep to keep up the vexations.

He listened at the shop door. Mouse sweeping inside. The way he'd make a broom to maunder. Mind, takings is up. Any number of gongoozlers coming in to gloat. Ounce of cut Cavendish while they're about it.

He peeped the door. 'Jim?'

'What?'

'Not what, yes.'

'Yes.'

'Papa.'

132

'Yes, Papa.'

'Will you take a cup of tea?'

'All right.'

'No no, finish up what you're at first. If a job's worth doing. Sweep it out in the road, can't you? The road is where it belongs. Arrah, give it here to me.'

At last he could let go. He swept away, scraping and scrubbing the floor, scratching the boards with the bristles of his broom, his side tugging with the jerks, till a cloud of dust had risen to envelop him. Then out the door with it, out out in the road where it came from, out in the street where the muck belonged. He closed the door on the returning dust while the remaining dust settled about him. 'If a job's worth doing,' he said, ''tis poor Brother Ass had better see it done.'

While he was pouring the tea Aunt Sawney stirred and her rosary slipped to the floor. She rose in an anguish. 'I heard his name. I heard ye say it. What news of me good boy? What news are ye hiding?'

Mr Mack swapped eyes with his son. 'Now now, Aunt Sawney. Was you dreaming in your sleep? There's no news from Gordie. Wouldn't we tell you was there any news?'

'Where did ye send me good boy? Ye hunted him away on me.' She saw Jim at the table and her face cleared. ''Tis the little man here ye'll be hunting next.'

'Will you be quiet, woman, and take your tea. There's no one hunting nobody.'

She ignored the tea he offered and made her way to the stairs door. On the first step she turned.

'They're out to make a brother of him. Aye, ye didn't know that, did ye, Mr A. Mack, Esquire? They'll have the little man taken on us, them at the college will. If ye wasn't so dosed in yourself ye'd know it. If ye wasn't so keen on scandalizing the street, vandalizing the cruitie posters, bringing disgrace and dishonour on my poor house – aye, ye might twig the better your own flesh and blood.'

'Is it true?' he asked when she was safely upstairs.

'Brother Polycarp says I have a vocation.'

'Holy farmer above, what nonsense is this?'

'I thought you'd be pleased if I was to be a brother.'

'And what about the shop?' The look on the boy's face you'd swear it came as news to him it was a shop they lived in at all. 'What about me slaving day in day out for to pay your way? Is that the price of a college education? I don't understand you, Jim. You're not cosmos mentis at all.'

'Maybe my mother would want it.'

'And now you want to bring your mother into it? Lord have mercy.'

'Why wouldn't I? Isn't she my mother?'

'How would you know what your mother would want?'

'I mightn't have a photograph to look at at night, but I still think of her.'

'You don't know snap about your mother.'

'Whose fault is that then?'

He could scarce believe he was hearing this. 'Holy Jesus but you're heart-set on provoking me this night. If 'tis a leathering you're after, you're heading the right direction.' His chair scraped under him as he straddled his legs from under the table.

'Wasn't it you told me keep in with the brothers?'

'This is lip only. Any more of this and I'll settle your hash for you.' He was half-rising in his seat. He had his arm held up and it shaking, the way he felt the threat of it himself. He brought his hands down to his belt where his fingers pulled at the leather. 'I'll hit you such a clatter, young man, you won't know if 'tis Monday or doomsday.'

But instead of looking sheepish and capital T for Tragic, the boy got up and went to the press.

'What are you – where are you – what do you think you're up to now?'

'It isn't Monday nor doomsday, but Friday,' he said. 'And I have band practice on Friday.'

The neck of him. The bold brass monsterpiece of a neck. He saw him take down his flute. He saw him take down that larrikin's flute. 'You're the heartscald to me, Jim. I never thought to say it.'

The boy waited at the door. His thin face had the look of being wedged in the jar. 'Look, Da, if I'm not to be a brother, what am I to be?'

'You're to follow me in the shop of course. There's your vocation. To learn to be a better shop-keeper.'

It surprised what the boy said then. It surprised the way he said it.

'Well it may so be a vocation isn't like that. It may so be a vocation is like a friend you might make. You don't choose a friend. A friend would come to you. And you don't turn him out, no matter what others would say. You're only too thankful if you found him.'

'He does not appear to be watching this evening.'

'Brother?'

'Our Corydon. Tonight he has forsaken his Alexis. Alexis,' the brother repeated, 'delicias Domini.' He turned from the casement and the blind resumed its untelling face. In lighter tone he remarked, 'Mayhap it is a Gaelic feast. Rapparee Friday. Our swain has stepped off his wall and inside the chapel for the nonce. The new curate will be giving the Stations in

Erse.' Such drollery demanded its encore. 'Stations in Erse, I ask you.'

Their devotion had ended a while since but still the brother bade Jim remain on his knees. He tweezed a pinch of snuff and said, 'Hocus pocus.'

'Brother?'

'It is what the Protestants make of the sacrament of our Mass. Hocus pocus filiocus. Did you ever think of the priesthood, Jim?'

Jim shook his head.

'There's many still believes a priest could make a toad of you. All it would take was a twistical squint off his eyes. You wouldn't fall for that blatherumskite, would you, Jim?'

'No, Brother.'

The snort came and the brother winced. His face shook till the eyes cleared, settling on Jim.

'Were you thinking any more on what we spoke last evening?'

'I did, Brother.'

'And are the intentions of Our Lady any the clearer to you now?'

'Not entirely.'

'The vicissitudes of home engross your thoughts.' But it seemed the brother's thoughts too were preoccupied. 'I had him in again this evening,' he said, 'his Gaelic reverence, an Soggarth Aroon. Cut of him – cloth suit and his felt hat. The old biretta and cassock wouldn't be swank enough. The very model of a modern vicar-general. Drill he's talking of now. Left turn, right turn – it lends a whole new twist to holy orders. Spalpeen to be interrupting my tea.'

Jim closed his ears to the rambling, unseemly talk. He was thinking of the words he had said to his father. Was friendship truly to be compared to a vocation? He had a tract from a

Dominican retreat that had a prayer for the blessing of a friend of the heart. The very words: friend of the heart. There was surely something devotional about it, something might be holy even.

'Don't be tempted into the priesthood, Jim. They say the brothers have not the consolation of the Mass. But we have other consolations. Humility is its own reward. Would it bother you if I knelt beside and we had a stim of talk together?'

But Doyler had gave up waiting. The falling damps and the chill off the wall that he complained would give him the piles. He had gone home.

Swish morendo of linen descending. Hand perdendo upon his neck. 'Does it bother you, my hand?'

A shrug moved Jim's shoulder. The hand lifted, dropped. 'No, Brother.'

'At my age 'tis the bolster of the young I look for.' A pause while the finger-tips began their roam. 'Did I mention to you ever about my own vocation, Jim?'

'You did, Brother.' Along his neck, in under the collar of his shirt, the brother's fingers.

'I was your age then. Some might think sixteen old for a vocation. Believe me, Jim, only the riff-raff joins at fourteen. Their parents answer an advertisement in the newspapers. This they call a vocation.'

His collar pulled and his tie strained against the intrusion. He blinked. He was irresistibly aware of the oddness of moving things.

'At that time I had discovered in myself a certain sin. It is not necessary I tell what sin that was, save that it was a solitary vice.'

Thumb-grope and finger-creep. How oddly things moved and strangely unmoved him, they fumbling over the chain of his medal, they playing with the medal on its chain on his chest.

'As fouler I grew and deeper in my misery, the temptation rose to share that vice with others.'

Out over his windpipe, along his throat, pressuring his apple, which made Jim gulp and swallow. The physicality of that reflex surprised him from abstraction. He felt a blush rising, mottling his cheeks.

'Who those others were it is not necessary to tell, save that my schoolfellows were shocked and repelled by my solicitations.'

The hand held now in its span the round of his neck.

'Do you understand solicitation?'

'I think I do.'

'Would you make solicitation to another boy?'

'No, Brother.'

'Would you accept solicitation was it made you?'

'Brother, your hand is hurting.'

A fetch of a sigh while he loosed his grip. 'That priest has me in the megrims. I have not the strength of it this night.' He laboured to rise, unbalancing Jim's shoulders, and Jim at last unblinked his eyes.

A scratching at the door. The feeling of the door ajar. Abruptly his master's voice:

'What is the meaning of this?'

'Nothing, Brother—'

'How long have you been standing in my door?'

'—I was waiting, brother—'

'Waiting for what? You have no business in Presentation.'

'Waiting for Jim,' said Doyler.

The fool had come looking for him, looking as far as the brother's room.

'Out with you. In the road where you belong.'

Already Polycarp was shoving Doyler down the passage. Jim hurried to the door. Other brothers and servants were gathering, roused by the ruction. He heard Doyler explaining stupidly, then Polycarp hit on something inside his collar.

'What, pray, is this? What get-up is this to come to a monastery wearing?'

'These are my clothes.'

'Never mind your togs. What about this?' He flicked his hand at Doyler's lapel. 'You think it hilarious to parade your extremism before me? Does your precious priest know of this?'

Doyler's hand went to his badge and he fingered it, the embossed red hand. 'I do always wear it.'

'Take it off.'

'Why would I?' The brother reached out and Doyler stepped back. 'What has my badge to do with anything?'

'I will not have agitation in my band.'

'This is the parish of St Joseph's, Brother. Patron of the working man.'

Polycarp roasted him. 'Little born-in-the-gutter.' He shot round to Jim. 'Is this vulgarian to do with you?'

Jim felt the burning on his face. 'He's my friend, Brother. You know that already.'

'Pal o' me heart,' said Doyler.

Jim saw himself weighed in the balance, then bitterly Brother Polycarp said, 'And the half of your soul that is damned. Out of my sight, the both of ye.'

Jim let a low whistle in the road outside. 'What was that about?'

'Don't think I'm long for that band.'

'All because of a badge? That's cracked.'

'Not any badge. The Red Hand of Liberty, emblem of the Citizen Army. Sword and shield of the working man, the red-flag socialists of Liberty Hall.'

'It's not as if you're a member.'

Doyler threw him a sneering look that told him not to quibble, then he swerved into the road to take a kick at a stone. Graceful approach, arms wide for balance; the stone scooned along raising puffs of dust. But his leg failed and he blundered after. 'Shagging pins. Come on, Forty Foot.'

They skirted round the back of the chapel towards Newtown-smith and the sea. Some young ones had fixed a rope to a lamppost and Doyler heeled over to take a swing of it.

'Get off, y' ugly brute ya!'

'Honours easy,' said Doyler and swung the rope back.

When he came up with Jim, he clapped a hand on his shoulder and said, 'She's after calling me ugly.' The hand dropped. 'Does he pray that way with you always?'

'We were at our devotion,' said Jim. 'You oughtn't have come in.'

'Curious all the same the way he has you in a hugger-mugger to pray.'

Even now Jim felt the remnants of his blush. On his neck and under his collar he felt a lurk of wet where the brother's hand had passed.

Doyler kicked at a few stones and beat his palm on the coping of a wall. Thoughtfully he said, 'Like a crow he looked from behind. An old rook with a sparrow under his wing.'

At the Forty Foot they lay side by side on the hard stone while the cold of the stone seeped through their jackets and chilled the sweat of their shoolering. Above them glimmered the Great Bear, *an Céacht Cam* in Gaelic, the Crooked Plough. 'Plough and the Stars,' said Doyler, and Jim nodded for he knew that too now, the banner of the men of Liberty Hall, not red but blue. And if you leant your head far back you saw *an Cúpla*, the Twins, glistening just above the battery wall. Then Doyler said, 'Brothers.'

And Jim knew he did not intend Castor and Pollux.

'Curious things are brothers. Neither hay nor grass. They wear the uniform, but they're sergeants really, not officer class.'

Jim smiled. Was this scandalous talk? With scandalous talk you did not argue but, silently invoking the aid of Mary, politely took your leave. 'Matter of vocations, I should think.'

'Vocations me arse.'

Yes, definitely scandalous.

'Sure who'd have a vocation to be a sergeant only? You want to be the officer in charge. Not as though old Polycarp'll get promoted. Once a brother, die a brother.'

'You don't have a vocation to be promoted. The vocation is to serve.'

'Damn all respect he gets for it. You saw the way the priest was down on him. All the vows and none of the glory.'

'I respect him.'

'Do you?'

'Everybody respects the brothers. Why wouldn't they?'

Doyler leant up, looking to see some place to spit. 'Well he don't respect me. And if he don't respect the working man, the Reverend Brother Polycarp can go spit.' And flit went the phlegm through the slit of his teeth.

Jim said nothing, just watched the circling sky. Unseemly talk and scandalous notions, the working man and brothers and priests. Politics was a puzzle at the best of times. Gordie had joined the Irish Volunteers that drilled to fight the Ulster Volunteers that drilled to fight Home Rule. But then the war came and they all joined up and were drilling together now to fight the Hun. All save a few of the all-for-Ireland boys that Aunt Sawney cursed for Fenians whenever they marched down Adelaide Road, which they did the odd Saturday afternoon, hurleys upon their shoulders. And his father shook his head at the door, saying, 'Hogs in armour, hogs in armour.' His father stood for Home Rule, because it was only square after South Africa and Canada and Australia and that, the English had done their job, Ireland was ready to take her place, stand among the dominions. Or so he said to his customers, but Jim doubted he ever brought himself to vote for the nationalists at Westminster. The memory of Parnell was too strong with him.

Politics was always a puzzle but now there were new ingredients to bother the brew: the working man and Gaelic-talking priests and the Red Hand badge that Doyler hid inside his lapel.

'I believe Brother Polycarp thought you were to do with the new father,' Jim ventured after a while. 'I think that's what got his rag out so.'

'Me with the priest? Codding me.'

'Speaking Gaelic and all that.'

'Where was the priests when we called on them? Where was the priests when they locked out the workers? At the pulpit is where, damning to hell the working man. They have a saying down Clare way, the four cautions: Beware a woman in front of you, beware a horse behind of you, beware a cart beside of you, and beware a priest every which way.' He turned his head on the stone and looked cheekily out from under his cap. 'Am I wicked or what?'

'I don't know what you are,' Jim answered, for he hadn't the heart to let on he wasn't near so scandalous as the Reverend Brother Polycarp in his cups.

'Past praying for, anyways.'

And even that was not quite so, for though he gave no names Jim made a prayer at night for the blessing of friends, as told in the Dominican tract he had kept, that they might be granted to meet in the joy of that everlasting home, amen.

'I can't delay long tonight,' Jim said.

'The da, is it?'

'He's on the rare old ree-raw at home.'

'Hold on a short while. There's something I want to show you.'

'Well?'

'You'll see.'

On a sudden notion Jim asked, 'What would you think would leave you insane?'

Doyler pulled a face. 'Is it a riddle or something?'

'I don't think so.' Jim considered the question. Something would leave you insane. The urge to something. Only a prayer would stop it. You'd have to sleep with your hands like so. A prayer to Our Lady.

A shudder passed through him and the muscles of his stomach clenched. But no, it was not that thing. He had thought a moment back in the shop it might be that thing. But no, it could never be. A father wouldn't ever remark such a thing to his son. It was insane considering it even.

'I have it,' said Doyler. 'Your da. Sure he'd have anyone away with the fairies.' There was truth in that, whatever. 'How's he bearing up anyways?'

'Fit to be tied still.'

'They had a bad right to nab him that way. And the paper and all. Thought I'd die reading it.'

'He's to see the canon on Sunday.'

'Sound move. Priest is a good friend at court. How's he to plead, does he know yet?'

'They say to switch to guilty and have done.'

'And will he?'

'I don't know. He's been on the perpetual polishing his medals ever since.'

His poor da. He did not think he would ever live it down, the shame of his name in the paper. Of course it was the sport of the parish. Rumour soon had him flootered to the eyeballs, cursing melia murder and clawing at posters till his nails were raw and his fingers raddled with blood. Six peelers it took and a superintendent to hold him down, frog's march to the station and him bawling roaratorious and abusing the poor polis, seed, breed and generation of them, for Castle whores as sold their soul to England.

'He'll be fine,' said Doyler, 'depend on it. Your da is known for a Britisher true and blue. No one'd credit he was ripping at posters.'

He should not have provoked his father that way. It was unfair provoking him with the court hanging over. Would he truly have belted him? Jim wondered. It was a long time since his father had chastised him that way. His clumsy feet and the chair all wobbly, looking liable to collapse from under him. The lour of his face and the intimidation of his hand raised to strike. Then his great thick fingers on the scrawny strip of leather. The way he made a menace of uncoupling the buckle. He had looked foolish; and in a cold way Jim had felt ashamed of him. He remembered the time Gordie stole Aunt Sawney's pipe. His father bate him with a ha'penny cane from out the shop. The cane broke, but only because he kept missing Gordie and striking the table leg by mistake. What brutality he had in him he could not purpose. Impulse alone gave it vent.

He was pleased the way he had formed that. That was an acute way of thinking. He repeated it to himself, moving his lips to the words. What brutality he has in him he cannot purpose. Impulse alone gives it vent.

Doyler had his flute out, but he wasn't playing it exactly, just running his fingers up and down the holes, making a kind of breath music. Jim would have to sneak the flute indoors somehow. Fix the parts down the sleeves of his jacket, walking in like a scarecrow. Where would he hide it? The only place for certain sure was inside the horsehair of his settle-bed. Would it be safe there? He would have to be careful sleeping. Might have to bring it out at night for fear of it crushing. Might have to sleep that way with it in his arms. It would be like sharing the bed, holding something of Doyler's while he slept.

He glimpsed the dart of a meteor, a soul released from purgatory, so his father told. The constellations gleamed in their dome and all about the sea moaned. Doyler's leg lay hard against his and his arm rubbed up and down with his whispery playing. Below Jim felt a familiar stir. Dispassionately he wondered was he an especially evil person.

Solitary vice he knew from confession. He would look out solicitation tomorrow in the school dick.

A scud of cloud approached from the west. One by one Jim watched the lights go out of the Crooked Plough till in the end there was just the gangling leg sticking out from under the covers.

'Listen,' said Doyler.

Then he heard it, thinly over the water, faint and faintly out of tune, a faraway band playing 'Come Back to Erin'.

Come back to Erin, mavourneen, mavourneen, and the grand resonant mournful horn of the mailboat in reply.

'I knew they'd be playing tonight,' said Doyler. 'I saw them earlier, the troops, marching in formation. I knew then there'd be a send-off.'

He got up and Jim followed to the Peak Rock, a granite outcrop where they could watch the mailboat inch its way. For this once the boat was illumined like it used be, lanterns rollicking in coloured waves; the pier too was decked with lamps, and up here with the wind the band came full and clear. Five minutes and it was over. The music ceased, the lights went down, dark was on the sea again. 'I wish if they wouldn't go,' said Doyler. 'But if go they must let them have their show. U-boats be damned. They're Irish soldiers as deserve their farewell.'

Jim felt the change in Doyler's tone. A fear came on him suddenly and he said, 'You're not thinking of leaving again?'

'Me?' said Doyler. 'You're the one what's leaving.'

Jim was shocked. 'I'm going nowhere.'

Doyler snorted. 'You really don't catch on what's happening, sure you don't, old pal?'

Nothing was happening. I'm straight, Jim wanted to say. We're straight together. Straight as a rush.

'Your devotion ends Sunday week, right? What happens next? Come the Monday they'll have you whisked away. Seminary down the bog we won't know the where of it. Nothing heard of again till we reads in the *Missionary Annals* you was made a weedy soup of. Godforsaken tribe of heathens with more sense than taste. You're the one what's leaving, Jim.'

'I never thought I'd be leaving,' he said.

'I'd say you didn't and all.'

Red infused his eye's periphery. Jim turned from the wind and faced directly the Muglins light. Its period matched his blinking so that each time his eyes unblinked the radiance was there to meet them. Its light had ought to be blue like Our Lady's but the Muglins had always flashed red for hazard. A mother would know your secretest thoughts like an angel would see your hiddenest deeds. Yet he knew so little of his mother, so grudging his father of her memory.

The radiance dimmed and a familiar detachment came over him. He was sensible of this detachment in Brother Polycarp's room when the brother would roam his hand on his skin: he

146

did not feel but he saw himself felt. His mind's eye watched a boy. It watched him at home and it watched him at school and it was watching him now at the Forty Foot. And looking back, it seemed to Jim that he had never prayed for himself at all but for this other boy that his mind's eye watched, a rawney-looking molly of a boy, the son of a quakebuttock, a coward himself, praying that he should hear his calling and join the brothers like Our Lady wished and not to be so inconsiderate. Did the boy not understand it was what his mother wanted?

He said again, 'I never thought I'd be leaving.'

'Come swimming with me,' said Doyler.

'Swimming?' It was the last thing on his mind.

'Forget your baths, come swimming in the sea. It's different in the sea, don't ask me why, but you don't find the same anywheres else. There's a freedom I can't explain, like your troubles was left in your pile of clothes. There's how many waves to wash you, sure they wash right through your head. Will you come?'

'Sunday?'

'It's the Whitsun weekend, but they have me working tomorrow, working on Monday. Sunday's the only day I have to meself.'

Jim saw the crowds that would throng the seaside. Spectating men and expert swimmers. Advice they would give out. Case of the slows. Seen iron swim better. The way they would jostle you, might snap you behind with the wet of their towels.

But Doyler had that misgiving read off his face. 'Miss Mass this once. We'll have the place to ourself. Give up on Polycarp just this once and come swimming with me instead. Will you do that? Out of friendship only?'

Jim shook his head.

'No?'

147

'I don't know.'
'Sunday. I'll be waiting.'

'Is it true, Mack? He called you that?'

Boots resounded on wooden boards and more boys trampled into the study. With a thud Jim closed the dictionary.

'Did you hear what old Ponycart called Mack?'

'The rebel shoneen?'

'The Fenianeen?'

'The croppy boyo?'

And Butler took up the song:

'Good people who live in peace and joy,
   Breathe a prayer, shed a tear for the Soppy Boy.'

'He was after letting a royal curse at him.'

'What did he call him then?'

Fahy came in and said, 'Whom called what which?'

'You wouldn't suppose what Ponycart was after saying to Mack. Ask Mack, he'll tell you. Did you look it out in the dick yet, Mack?'

Jim sensed the brawn of Fahy above. The room had begun to hum with the mushroomy smell of damp tweed. Rain drummed on the window-panes and sistled the fire when it spilt down the chimney. Fahy's breath blew on his hair and his arm leant like a buttress on his desk. 'The get of a blackguard, was it?'

'No, nothing about in the newspapers. This was a different kettle.'

'What did he call you so? Tell.'

'In the yard. There are witnesses. Mack was playing at handball. It's true, Mack, it is.'

Jim looked at the pocky face, filling and draining with its breathless news. Courtney.

'Well?' Fahy's finger toying with the ink-well.

'He asked for the ball,' said Jim.

'And Mack said, Which one, Brother?'

'What did he mean, which one?'

'I had two balls on me,' said Jim, beginning to explain.

'And had they dropped yet?'

'Leave him tell, will you, Butler?'

'But the brother didn't know that. And the screw he gave out of his whites. Would annihilate you. He thought Mack was being coarse, don't you see.'

'But what did he say?'

'Go on, Mack, tell us.'

'He said I was supercilious.'

'Super-what-is-it?'

'No, he didn't. Not at all. He called him a supercilious corner-boy fecker.'

The room hushed. They heard the tread of Brother Polycarp in the hall, heavy to allow his ample warning. Fahy moved back an edge. 'He called you that?'

'Isn't that a royal wallop for a brother to let out?'

'Brother Polycarp said that to you, did he?'

'Did you look it out in the dick yet? Fecker we know, but what does the jaw-cracker mean?'

The boys proceeded to their places. 'We'll ask him,' said Courtney. 'If he's the right colour, we'll ask him. A right cod it will be.'

The brother came in blessing himself, and all rose for prayers. 'Virgil,' he announced, sitting down. 'Book Two. Line? Line, Mr Mack?'

'Forty.'

'Begin . . . Ahern.'

Jupiter Pluvius lashing at the windows. It splattered into

puddles on the sill. So thick it hardly seemed to fall at all, a suspension of glistening threads. The lowering clouds, the sudden chill, the tonant rumour from the hills.

He thought of all the people who would be caught by the pelt. Shopkeepers fussing with their wares, the rails of suits, battered blooms, his father with the Spanish onions, hurrying the crate into the dry. Crowded porches and awnings with the sudden, democratic talk. Flags out for Empire Day, sodden. In the street the dust returns to muck and a horse slithers in the way. The gongs clang and a motor slides on the tram-lines. There he is, clinging to the tailboard of the cart, looking about for a cardboard or an old sack. What cheer, he says. Antiphrasis.

Ireland. O begob, says his father, sure Ireland is England's umbrella.

Then he thought of the rain in the country, far up on the mountains, not raining really, an elemental wet, below and above and all about, and the sound of the wet in the streams that gushed and the sucky squelch of the turf. A bedraggled sheep who watches, a lone bird in the near sky.

In a dreamy way he saw the sea and the way the sea was brighter than the sky when it rained. How the drops leapt on the surface like a myriad hungry fish. And a boy swimming at the Forty Foot, or maybe two boys swimming, the only figures in all the scene while all round the rain fell and the church bells tolled for Mass.

Angelus soon, then home.

'The horse do not ye credit, O Trojans.'

'Credit? What does credit mean? Can you not speak the King's English, boy?'

That time in Dalkey when the pig was squealing. They had it hoisted from a beam and the buckets were waiting below to collect the blood. When the bells came they laid off the slaughter to say the Angelus. All through the bells the squealing and the thrashing legs, on and on, while the men prayed. How it riled his father and he said to the men no God would sanction such cruelty to his creatures. The men laughed, wiping their blades on the bloody cloths, and his father told him afterwards that we are a race immured to cruelty. He had meant inured.

'Quidquid id est, timeo Danaos et dona ferentis.' The brother's eyes roved the room. 'Construe . . . Courtney.'

That old saw – is it from there it comes? Really they had it wrong. Beware of gifts bearing Greeks, it should be.

Supercilious. But why would he think I was being coarse? Did he truly believe I meant my own . . . ? No one would say such a thing to a brother. It made no sense. Courtney is thrilled by it. He thinks it means something else vulgar. Ignorant fool.

After the Angelus, home for Saturday dinner. Coddle in the big stew pan. Aunt Sawney's day for visitors in the parlour. Mrs Tansy, Mrs Rourke. Their fill of gossip over the cream crackers and Wincarnis. Later it was his duty to bring the tea, lump sugar and the sugar-tongues out. Curious implements you found in that room. A grape-scissors though never known grapes in the house. A quirl for scraping butter. Longish spoon with holes in it that was called a mote-skimmer: used for straining the strangers off your tea. All laid out on the pier-table, its cloth so starched it might stand on its own. Tub this afternoon behind the scullery door, then Confession, then shop, then devotion. Mass in the morning. Entire parish in their Whitsun best, the priests' vestments abruptly red. *Veni, sancte Spiritus.*

Pleasant to swim in the rain, they say. It would be too. The sea would lower your temperature already so the rain wouldn't feel so cold. It would be hard getting in, you'd have to push yourself, but were you in already, that would be pleasant. That would be a freedom, to be out in the rain and not to trouble. Your trouble in your pile of clothes.

Confess a sin, is it possible, before committed? Would it be a true confession, anyway, in the knowledge you intended to trespass later? What contrition would it involve, perfect or imperfect? And if imperfect, not contrition at all but merely attrition. What absolution could be given and what satisfaction performed for a sin not of commission, not of omission, but of intention only?

He yawned through these abstract considerations, enjoying very slightly the assonance of the words. It was ridiculous to suppose he might skip Mass tomorrow. It was ridiculous to suppose he might learn the crawl.

'Mr Mack?'

'Yes, Brother?'

'Do we detain you?'

'No, Brother.'

'The phrase fidus Achates. You were asked to decline it.'

Effortlessly he did so. But he did not look at the brother. And he sat down afterwards before being told.

'Achates,' said the brother. 'The friend of Aeneas. Virgil has given him the epithet fidus and the phrase has come down to us as the paradigm of friendship. A bosom companion, one might say. A friend of one's heart even. Animae dimidium meae, says Horace of Virgil, meaning the half of his soul. Such a companion would lead not his friend astray. Teach not his friend the vulgar ways of the mob. He would not put corner-boy notions in the mouth of his so-called pal.'

The brother was watching him, but Jim would not look back. This was a jaw, a pi directed at him. It was mean of the brother to do this before the class. He had not been coarse. It was the brother who had used a coarse expression, not he. 'Such friendships are rare, and it behoves us to guard against their counterfeit, which is a cheap and tawdry lie.'

Then somebody was asking a question and Brother Polycarp answered, 'Where's your Latin, boy? Can't you work it out for yourself? Super-scilious. What does super mean?'

'Above, brother.'

'Scio, scire, scivi, scitum?'

'To know.'

'Put it together. Super-scire.'

'To know above?'

'To think oneself above the ordinary. To be insolent to one's betters. In common parlance, to have side.'

The faces that turned were crinkled with glee. But Jim didn't mind that. His eyebrows rose and he met the brother's stare determined he would not flinch. What a fool the brother had made of himself. What an ignorant fool he was.

The bells came, and suddenly they were all standing and nodding their heads and signing the cross on bending knees.

'Angelus Domini nuntiavit Mariae.'

'Et concepit de Spiritu Sancto.'

In his mind the bells were no longer the Angelus, but the tocsin calling for Mass. By the chapel wall he pauses where the lane leads astray, and all the people throng him by, and the sky is clear after the Saturday rains, and the pavement glistens under the sun. The lane leads to the sea, the beckoning, sparkling, reckless sea.

CHAPTER SEVEN

J IM STALLED IN the giddy wind of the Point. 'Get a move on,' called Doyler. 'Slow as a wet week, so y'are.'

Jim laughed out loud. Then he plunged down the steps into the gentlemen's bathing-place. He certainly did feel giddy. They weren't half-way undressed and he was laughing again and saying, 'I suppose they insist on you wearing some manner of a costume here?'

'What's that?' said Doyler.

'This manner of a place, there'd be rules here and regulations. Regarding what you might wear and all manner of a thing.'

'Are you right there?'

'Don't you feel it a bit public?'

'You've took a right rare colour.'

'Bit public all the same, wouldn't you say?'

Doyler skitted and laughed. Jim's towel had unrolled, showing his father's cut-down drawers that Jim wore at the baths. 'Put them away,' said Doyler, 'and give us here your hand.'

'My hand?'

He took Jim's hand and rubbed it between his palms. 'Stay easy, old chap. There's only the both of us. Didn't I tell you we'd have the place to ourself?'

Jim nodded.

Doyler's clothes dropped effortlessly in their pile. 'Weren't you never out for an easy dip?' he asked.

'At school they take us—'

'I don't mean the baths, I mean with a pal. For a lark like.'

Songbird which sings on the high wing. Exaltation the collective noun. Jim looked straight in the laky black eyes. 'I don't suppose I ever had much of a friend.'

Doyler's brow creased, like ripples in a sand. 'You're a queer one, Jim Mack, I don't mind me saying. Get on out of your shirt and let's get busy.'

When he pulled up his shirt, there was Doyler's face, tunnelled by the collar, then the white cloth seeming never-ending till its tail slipped over his head, and Doyler's face again, a lop-sided grin, appraising him. He'd be all right if Doyler wouldn't be watching the while.

'You know, you don't look half so scrawny in your pelt. Couple of mornings here and we'll soon have you in sorts.'

Somewhere in the heat Jim perceived a smile brought out of him.

'And don't mind about your lad below. That's only the nerves makes him poke up. Nothing to be shy about. Can you jump in?'

'If I hold my nose.'

'Be sure, now, it's your nose you hold.' On the bold grin, he grabbed Jim's wrist. 'Steady – go!'

They raced to the ledge, Doyler letting out his yahoo of a yell. Father, Son, the Holy Ghost: Jim lifted, dropped, splattered.

A freezer of a sea, punching the breath from out of him. Ears filled with the roaring quiet. Falling like in sleep, in green and opaque dream. Then the pumping in his ears grew fierce and the lungs were like a paper bag you could bang with a clap, and he fluttered his hands to begin the ascent, unintentionally frantically by the end. At last he broke surface and dear joy! there really is air. A hand slaps on his shoulder and up pops Doyler. 'What cheer, eh?' says he.

The weight sent Jim under again and he came up spluttering foam and thrashing.

'Are you trying to run a footrace or what? That's no way to tread water. Lookat here, go slow, be easy.'

'I don't know,' said Jim, 'I don't know to—'

'Bicycle steady like,' said Doyler, demonstrating. 'You'll be pumped before we're started else.'

Jim was going to say something but a wave came and found his mouth. He was coughing and sinking and suddenly an arm had caught him under the shoulders, guided him to the iron ladder up. 'You all right?'

'Fine. I swallowed some water is all.'

Doyler frowned. 'You sure about this?'

'Honest, I'm grand.'

The water trickled in and out of Doyler's mouth. He looked uneasy and Jim didn't wish to be the cause of this coddling.

'See the raft beyond?' Fifty yards out a platform was moored. 'Calm now and slow, any old stroke you know, do you think you can make that?'

'I can try.'

'I'll tell you one thing,' said Doyler. 'You're a plucky devil, I'd say.'

'Plucky?'

'Them times in the Kingstown Baths. Was you ever out of your depth?'

'Once or twice.'

A wry look. 'Once, maybe.'

'By mistake, actually.'

'Mary and Joseph, no shortage of guts in this skinamalink. And you after leaping in like it was no bother on you.'

He would have swum to Howth and back, and drownded twice, to bask in such praise. 'Are we straight so?' he asked.

Doyler laughed and splashed a hand through a wave. 'Straight as a rush,' he answered.

It was actually easier outside of the cove. The waves were against him but consistently so, rather than bobbing round bewilderingly. His instinct was to exert his strength, push to the limit, but he heard Doyler's voice calling, 'Steady on, be easy,' and felt his calm purposeful foamless form at his side. It was a punisher all right, and he was knocked up by the time he gripped the looping rope of the raft. But it was grand to look back on the undulant sea and trace the progress of his triumph.

'Pooped?'

'Destroyed.'

'Rest a while. There's no hurry.'

Doyler climbed on the raft, sending it seesawing up and down, and sat with his arms about his knees. Water spilt from him, tracing the hairs of his legs, puddling on to the planks. On his chest a medal caught the sunlight as he heaved. Steam rose from his shoulders.

'Hand up?'

'No, I'm fine.'

Jim pulled himself up and sat beside, gazing back on the stretch of coast. The mountains swooned with shadowy blue, but the nearer hills were bracken-green and bracken-gold. In the vivid air nowhere seemed farther than an hour's walk. It came to him that the smell he usually took for the sea was actually of the land. Here in the waves the breeze was clean.

'Rain,' said Doyler. 'Not for a while yet, but rain is on its way.'

He nodded over his right shoulder, north toward Kingstown, and said, 'See the pier there?'

Long graceful arm, one of a cradling pair, reaching out in the bay.

'Here's a handy trick to remember. Where the elbow is, if the foam is breaking on that, it's definitely too rough to swim. Easy enough getting in, but the devil's own job getting out again. The swell, do you see.'

Jim followed the line of the shore. Kingstown with its three spires, Protestant, Catholic, municipal; the parade of grand houses, palely painted, that led to the sea-wall; the rocks and outcrops and huddled spills of sand that carried his gaze to the Forty Foot.

'Odd the way you lived all your life a spit from the sea and you never swam there. Bet you never went fishing neither.'

'Gordie used sometimes fish,' said Jim, 'but he never seemed to catch much.'

'Stingoes and horny cobblers – little enough you can eat. There's pollack over by the baths there, and bream off Kelly Shore. Mullet sometimes on a calm day. See where the sand is white? – dabs there. Unreliable though. All right if you had the leisure, but if you was hungry you'd be surer minding a carter's horse or flogging firewood up the villas. I caught a conger once. Thing near took a chunk out of me hand, it did. But no one would buy it. Said an eel was food for the devil only. After all me toiling and moiling.

'Crabs was always the best. Over by Bullock after a good tide. Could sell them, you see. The la-di-das would go for the crabs. Never tasted it meself. Squealing'd put you off. Mighty squealing they let out when the pan goes on the fire. Made up me mind to sell them after that. Let the la-di-das to suffer the screams. I bought bread with the money instead.

'Mackerel too. Was on a boat once, out from Bullock, middle of the night this was. I tell you we dropped the lines, a minute later we hauled them in and there was five, six of the fishes there. Marvellous it was. Didn't need do nothing, only drop the lines and wait a crack. Lashings, I tell you, they was tumbling over themself to get in inside of the boat. Over there by the Muglins. What it was, we'd hit a shoal. Four times we turned back to load them off. Four times out again. All the one night.

'The chap was so delighted he let me take a bucket or two home. Well, there was mackerel with everything the next few days. Then after a time, didn't they start going off. You wouldn't credit the stink. Couldn't give them away after that. In the end I had to dump a bucket back in the sea. I was glad to be rid of them, but I was sad too. For a day or so we'd had our full and plenty and that was grand.'

While he spoke, Jim watched the places he indicated, Kelly Shore, the tumbling creamy rocks by Bullock Harbour, Muglins Sound with its deeper ominous green. It awed him that Doyler was not bemeaned by his life as Jim felt bemeaned by his. The lithe and wind-tanned body awed him too, so that he dared only glance at it obliquely. Glance and blink, squeezing his eyes.

'What changed your mind?'

'My mind about what?'

'Coming swimming, you gaum.'

Jim shrugged. That the brother had got it wrong about the root of supercilious did not seem adequate cause to miss Mass, skip his devotion and give over most likely a vocation to the brotherhood. 'The day was sunny,' he said.

''Tis sunny right enough.' He frowned concentrating on the shore, like he was searching for some particular spot. 'What you said back there.' He shrugged. 'Don't suppose I never had much of a friend neither. Saving that time we was twelve together.' A long wait, then an arm went round Jim's neck. Again that shock of touch – it near jumped Jim from his skin. 'Look at the pair of us. Mother-naked on a plank in the sea. Are you straight for your first lesson?'

'The crawl?'

'The crawl it is.' He was about to slip off, but then he paused. He nodded out to sea.

'There's the Muglins out beyond. Couple of weeks back, Easter time, I got to the raft here and I thought to meself, why not? Now there's a stretch would leave you pooped. Destroyed you'd be with the best of them. The tide, see, in the sound gets up a fierce current. Near missed me landing too, had me scrambling like sixty to gain any go of it. It's all of it rock there, no grass, no nothing. But I found me a dip that was out of the wind where the stone was smooth and mossy. So there I lay in the skin I was born in. Whoever it was had fixed a trough, don't ask me why, that had sweet water when I tasted it. And there's this other stone that rocked with the waves, only slow like, and let out a moan when the waves went in under. I reckoned no one would know that place. But it was handsome to stretch with the moss through me fingers and I followed the clouds that tumbled by. I felt my ease that day. The only company was an old gander – I thought he must be lost – that watched an hour or more, stood on a leg and his nose in his feathers. And do you know what I reckon?'

Jim's lips framed a whispering what.

'I reckon if we worked at it hard, every morning, say, we worked on your stroke, before I went to work, before you went to college, out to the raft here and back while the raft is out, every day we'd do it, rain or shine, till you find your feet, or your fins I should say, I reckon come Easter next we'd swim out there together, and I'll show you the place and you'd know, I don't know, what I meant like.'

Jim saw the Muglins, little more than a rock to hold the light that told the rock's existence. He saw the green where the current flowed and the crested horse that broke from it. He saw the storms that would come and the dark mornings and the bitter wind out of the north and the east. 'A year?'

'Could likely do it sooner. That's if you don't turn brother on me.'

The very idea was cracked. 'Why would I do that?'

Doyler laughed and tossed some speck in the sea.

'But it wouldn't be the same if it wasn't Easter,' said Jim.

'Indeed and it wouldn't. Are we straight, so?'

'We're straight as a rush.'

Doyler spat on his hand and Jim did likewise and their palms rubbed in the smear.

'The crawl it is,' said Doyler and he slipped from the raft. Before he joined him and the sea would wash it away, Jim sniffed his wetting palm. A private smell. Like leather, bodily, raw.

Through the window of the parochial waiting-room, Mr Mack the parochial garden viewed.

Cabbages were coming along nicely, he was pleased to note. Potatoes too. See the way they have a carnation there at the end of each drill? That'd be for the chapel flowers. Rhubarb too. We have rhubarb at home sure. Give it away, the most of it, out of luck. All the same, not much in the way of a view. I thought now there'd be a better view from the parochial house. What am I saying? A priest wouldn't have leisure for gongoozling out of windows.

He turned from the idle scene. Is it a canonical hour, I wonder? How long is this they kept me waiting?

Handsome room, a taste Spartan. Deal of deal about. Floor-
boards, mantelshelf. For a long while I thought there was a deal
tree, but in fact 'tis pine it comes from. Norway Spruce to give
the correct designation. He tapped the floor with his toe, desisted.
Need to know these things. Make a donkey of yourself else.
Black hair-cloth chairs. Uncomfortable-looking yokes. Would be
desperate now to wear a shirt of same. Begod, if the canon don't
come up with a recommendation, 'tis oakum I'll be itching with.
Three months' hard and me character destroyed.

Pius X looked down at him from the fireplace. Saintly man,
though they were way behind the times. Now there's a good
opening for a smart young chap. Quick as the puff goes out the
Vatican, out with the pictures of the new Pope.

Did I send in my Easter dues? I did of course.

I hope now the canon isn't out on a sick-call. I hope he
wouldn't be rushing back on my account. I'll say that when
he comes. I hope, your reverence, you didn't rush back on my
account. Not at all, Mr Mack, glad of the excuse. How can I be
of help?

The door opened sharply and a young priest strode in.
Mr Mack, turning quickly, fumbled his hat and it slipped to
the floor.

'Oh, hello, Father,' he said. 'I was expecting – I hadn't
thought – '

The priest swept into the chair behind the desk. He muttered
something which Mr Mack did not quite catch.

'I beg your reverence's pardon?'

'You are evidently not an Irish-speaker.' The young father
had a way of looking that had Mr Mack wondering was his
buttons undone. But no, it was the grand array of his medals
the priest intended, for he said, 'By the trinkets at your chest,
one would wonder where you hailed from at all.'

'Oh sure that's easy, your reverence. Tipperary born and bred. The Yorkshire of Ireland, as they say.'

'Mr Mack, I believe.'

Mr Mack retrieved his hat. 'Only I was expecting the canon.'

'The canon is indisposed.' Already he was busy at a sheaf of papers which briskly he thumbed. 'Had you paid attention at this morning's Mass you might have heard prayers offered for his speedy recovery.'

'Only I thought . . .'

The priest looked up above the rims of his spectacles. 'I am a busy man, Mr Mack. May I make bold to suggest you come to the purpose of your visit?'

Already the hair-cloth chairs looked a heap more inviting. Mr Mack felt a sweat inside his good collar and all down the spine of his back. 'Father, it's about my court case, Father.'

'Court case?'

'I was hoping for a recommendation.'

'I recommend, Mr Mack, you keep away from the courts. Will there be anything else?'

The smile dwindled on his face while he took the gauge of the priest's response. 'I meant a character. I hoped the canon would do me a character in my defence.'

'You mean a witness.'

'A witness, yes, to my good character.'

The priest scratched rapidly on his papers. Whatever it was he was writing, Mr Mack misbelieved it had much to do with himself. 'And this character of yours, do we know it well in the parish of St Joseph?'

'I have been domiciled local these fifteen year.'

'And you are a regular attender at Mass, I make no doubt.'

'Every Sunday without fail. In sickness and in health. Holy days, too, of obligation and every morning in Lent.'

'Regular if not attentive. And to which sodality do you belong?' In the pause, the priest looked up. 'No sodality?'

'As it happens, Father, it's been on my mind a while now to enrol in one.'

'Other confraternities of a religious nature?'

'Well, I had asked a year or so since to join the Hibernians. They said they'd be sure to let me know.'

'And have they?'

'Not yet they haven't, your honour. But any time now I'm expecting to hear.'

'Anything else? The Foresters? Penny Dinners? Third Order?'

Mr Mack shook his head in what he conceived was not too negative a fashion.

'St Anthony's Bread?' the priest continued. 'Society for the Dissemination of St Francis's Cord? The Perpetual Lamp Association of Our Lady of Mount Carmel? Nothing?'

'Not those ones, your reverence, not presently.'

Then pointedly, with a reference to the papers before him, 'The St Vincent de Paul perhaps?'

Mr Mack's face crumpled. 'Ah no, Father, I can explain about the Vincent de Paul. That was a misunderstanding entirely. I'm surprised now the canon left that in his books. I have that cleared up a long time since.'

The priest's hands prayed at his nose then adjusted finely his spectacles. 'I read here that you refused the St Vincent de Paul when called upon to assist in their charitable endeavours. You said it was no business of yours to report who among your customers had more funds than he pretended. I have it here to the letter. Spying, you called it.'

Things were not looking the best. The canon was known for a crotchety damnator and had always the shortest queue at confession. It occurred to Mr Mack this new father might have a shorter queue yet. 'Father, I allow I was wrong in that particular, and if they'll only suffer me to I'll make good my mistake.'

'It is gratifying to hear it.'

'In any case, your reverence, I am very much involved in helping the people myself. Any number of clubs I run for them, the photograph club, the communion club to help with the new communions and that, the Christmas club, any number of things I do in a self-help sort of a way. And I make no stipulations, they can spend the money where and how they choose, I charge no interest and what interest accrues goes straight in the kitty to be shared out one and all. Which is more than can be said for some of these sharpers that go by the name of tallyman. I won't pretend it is not sometimes a trial knocking on the doors come rain or shine, but in the end there is a great satisfaction to be got from helping the people look out for themself.' There was no immediate acknowledgment from the priest, so in clinch to his argument Mr Mack concluded, 'For isn't it a wise teaching that tells us, Father, that God helps those that helps themself?'

'That is an adage, Mr Mack. It is no teaching of Catholic orthodoxy. Indeed there is the smack of Larkinism in its constant utterance. In future you would do wise to charge an honest rate for an honest toil. Leave charity, or spying as you call it, to those the Church has appointed to that task.'

The mountain had laboured and brought forth a rat. The priest stood and on soft soles glided to the window.

'So far I have heard nothing that would persuade me to act in your defence. And much that would encourage to a contraposition. These medals you carry on your chest.' He scratched the windowpane where a smudge had lodged. 'Ribbons, gongs, stars. There is a species of ant in the tropical forests – you may have read it in the *Missionary Annals* – that captures the eggs of a rival nest to rear them as soldiers of its own. These soldiers are renowned for their curious loyalty.'

Mr Mack detected a firmer footing and warmly he said, 'It is the *Irish Catholic* we gets at home, Father, and we reads it every Friday by the fire together. Prior, that is, to saying the Rosary. That and the *Messenger of the Sacred Heart*. But if your reverence would recommend the *Missionary Annals* I'll be happy to subscribe.'

'No doubt.' The priest sniffed. 'However, as regards the present business I do not see how I may be of assistance. The Church has many sons and many daughters, each of whom she cherishes. It is an article of our faith, nonetheless, that the law, even the inequitable laws of the foreigner, is to be observed.'

'But the world will know me for a law-abiding man.'

'Evidently there are those who would disagree.'

He had been bidden to go. Bowing backwards out and twisting his hat, Mr Mack opened the door behind him. 'Father, may I say one more thing, Father?'

'Say away.'

'Only this, Father. There is such a thing as natural justice. And natural justice requires that a man ought not be condemned where no crime was intended. The poster was torn, I allow, but it was no crime on my part that I tore it. In fact I will go the further and say—'

The heels squeaked on the deal. 'Which poster is this?'

'The recruitment poster. I wrote the canon explaining the case.'

The priest was at the desk, reading rapidly. 'Are you the man responsible for the posters?'

He was poised to pounce. Mr Mack said forlornly, 'Father, I fear I am. But 'twas no crime on my part.'

Before he knew enough, his hand was being pumped in a

fast eager grip. 'No crime at all. Let me shake the hand of an Irishman. Mr Mack, is it? Dia dhuit, Mr Mack. Dia agus Muire dhuit. Let me shake the hand that would shame this parish to its senses.'

Morning had dawned innubilious and still while Brother Polycarp paced the street, impatient for Men's Mass, the rose window of the parish church reflected a perfect blue.

'Hello, men.' 'Hello, Brother.' 'Fine day.' 'Fine day it is, Brother.' 'You won't miss Mass?' 'We won't.' 'Don't waste your earnings, boys.' 'We won't, Brother.'

Lads of the village at toss-school. Small sheepish smiles from them and a fumbling away of the makes and the stick. Brother Polycarp saw the gathering strength of their bodies and wondered at how meekly they stood. As though they knew, even they, that She watched them, Mother of meekness.

In Kingstown or in Dublin they would sometimes mistake him for a priest. If a woman or child brushed past, a haunt came in their eyes when they saw the collar. 'Forgive me, Father.' Lucky is the touch of a priest. At such moments his heart filled with joy and Her humble mantle invested his soul. 'No, my child, good woman, my fellow man – I am but a brother of Presentation.'

A family passed, decked out in their Whitsun flaunty. How wide the street on Sunday without the awnings out. Bacon, cabbage and potatoes. Like an incense it came from every door. The very air gloried in the smell. Every wife and daughter in the land must be knelt before a cooking-fire. And Brother Polycarp thought of Her Whose sufferance had made holy the work of women. Under this cerulean sky all womanly things bore Her witness: the diligence of elbows, the charity of hands, the chaste blush of a lowered face.

A sudden clanging and the Protestant tram scooted past, ferrying the lavender-glove and prayer-book brigade to their service in Kingstown. You have stolen the bricks and mortar of our faith but you have never touched our soul! Yet even they who had spurned Her were not entirely abandoned. For was not the vaunted sobriety of Protestants but a dull reflection of Her perfect temperance? He prayed for the Protestant brethren and their deliverance from error, as ineluctably, step by step, his feet carried to Fennelly's public house.

Ora pro me Maria; pro me Maria ora!

She heard his prayer at the last and at the last his steps veered. With joy he discovered he had passed Fennelly's. Fennelly's was behind and all the world lay onward and sunny. With heaven-sent joy he looked back on his triumph, and who was it turning the corner but Jim Mack on his walk to Mass.

Jim Mack, Jim Mack, his heart sang a canticle of songs. How beautiful he was and comely in delights! His checks were as the turtle dove's, his neck as of ivory, his throat most sweet. Such is my beloved, and he is my friend.

The boy enraptured him. What joy it was to pray with him, to hear the delicate pant of his soul as heavenward it soared. There She reigned, resplendent with miracles, fair as the moon, bright as the sun, but terrible as an army set in array. In the blue and stelliferous light he could not bide, but the innocent soul of the boy thrilled to Her presence. Next week your feast, O Queen of Heaven. I have vowed to you my darling.

For the flesh is weak and the blood unruly and how else to atone the sins of the heart than dedicate to Her the heart's desire? Receive my gift, love him as I would I would, pray for my wrung and twisted soul.

He hurried along to join the boy. But the boy turned and down a lane he went, a lane that turned from the chapel to the sea. The other boy came and his arm was on his shoulder.

Brother Polycarp dizzied, and leaning on a wall he smelt the overwhelming stench of the sea. He turned to the streets which stranged and narrowed. The gluttony that coursed from each doorway sickened him. Bells were ringing and angrily he cursed their conceited clangour. He cursed the intemperate streets and the blowsy women with their lips of Eve. A ha'penny spun in the air like a sun that would plunge to the earth and he saw the narrow covetous eyes of corner-boys. In the branches of trees, in the eaves of houses, in the hunched backs of the hills he saw it, the dangling slothful vicious arm about the neck he loved.

It was moments later, though hours had passed. He was sensible of a pain in his hand. Opening his fingers he found a pin there whose shield was the Sacred Heart. Its point had pierced his palm and the blood blobbed pathetically. His temperance pin, he realized. It surprised when he looked about to discover he was seated in Fennelly's select.

'What will it be, Brother?'

'A tot of . . . a small tot of . . .'

'Same again, is it, Brother?'

'Tot of Irish.'

Words were floating through his mind like leaves on a water, and like leaves on a water they sometimes gathered, connected into phrases. Was he praying? *Corydon ardebat Alexim.* That was not prayer. *Delicias domini.* Was that prayer? Suddenly, unmeditated, words burst from him: 'Heu heu, quid volui misero mihi!'

'What's that, Brother?'

'I don't recall . . .'

'There you go, Brother. We'll make this the last. Well after closing and was the knock to come there's never a hope you'd be bona fide. Knock that back now and we'll show you out the yard door. Are you with us at all there, Brother?'

Hands guided him through the dark, the dim and the dark to the light that shone without. Our Lady's Litany trembled on his tongue:

> Queen of Angels, pray for us.
> Queen of Patriarchs, pray for us.
> Empress of India, pray for us.

'Brother! I say, Brother Polycarp! No, this way, Brother!'

Somebody calling his name. How bright it was. He had not expected such light. Such light he could not bide and he trembled for the dark once more.

'Brother Polycarp! Will you watch out for yourself!'

Calling him back. But he was going now, out into the light. The mighty roar of trumpets greeted him. A screech as if the gates of hell had opened. The gates crashed against him closed and he was floating, floating in the light, in the blue and stelliferous bright.

Her face was just as he always had known it would be, noble and wise and pained with care. He closed his eyes. 'Mater,' he said. 'Mater misericordiae.'

Mr Mack was already beside him. 'Brother Polycarp, are you hit?'

'Is he all right?' a woman's voice called.

'There's no blood,' said Mr Mack. 'I think 'tis only bruises. Are you current at all there, Brother? He's dazed yet.'

The woman climbed down from the motor-car. 'Simply stepped in front,' she was saying. 'He gave no sign.'

'Don't trouble yourself, mam. He was clearly in the wrong. Is it Madame MacMurrough it is?'

'Is there anything broken?'

'Not at all. A few scratches is all. You'll know me, Madame MacMurrough. I'm the man with the stockings.'

'Stockings? Is there a constable about?'

'Sure there's never a constable when you wants one, mam. Flapdoodlers is all they are.'

The brother let out a groan and Eveline said, 'Don't stand there wittering, man. Take his shoulders while I take his legs. We must get this fellow to a hospital.'

'In your motor-car, mam?'

'Hurry now.'

While they bundled the brother to the back seat, Mr Mack said, 'Yes, stockings for the troops at the Front. I knits them at home, then you boxes them off. I was thinking of sending the boy up later for I have another parcel made up to go.'

She looked at him slant-eyed, then shook her head. The brother moaned and she bent down. 'Don't fret. You'll be safe soon.'

Mr Mack saw the brother's eyes open. There was disbelief there and his fingers trembled to touch the lady's face.

'My poor man,' she said and held his hand. An incomparable beatitude formed on his yellow smile. 'What does he say?'

'I can't quite catch the wind of it.'

'Is it Latin?'

'I have it,' said Mr Mack. 'The Mater. 'Tis a hospital away in Dublin.'

'There's no time for that. We must try for St Michael's.'

Some young gurriers had gathered and Mr Mack had the honour of scooting them clear of the coachwork. Others jumped up and down to glimpse the injured party. 'Is there bleeding, mister?' they wanted to know. 'Is the brother kilt at all?' Mr

Mack appropriated his handkerchief for a screen against their uncouth snitches.

Eveline loosened the brother's collar. His eyes had closed again but she whispered in his ear, 'Hold still now.' To Mr Mack she said, 'You had better sit with him. Try and make him comfortable.'

Mr Mack would be delighted to assist in any way he could, and he hadn't his seat hardly taken before the vehicle juddered into motion. He held the brother's head in his lap. 'I must say, Madame MacMurrough, it is a great delight to be in a motor-car. It is a Vauxhall design, I believe. A Prince Henry.' She seemed not to hear him over the wind, so more loudly he said, 'I was in a doctor's runabout once. This was after I assisted to change the wheel.'

'Yes.'

'But this is a Prince Henry, I do believe. It is a Vauxhall manufacture.'

He leant his elbow on the furled hood. His fingers patted the trim. He desisted for fear of smudges and he tried once more with the lady in front.

'I do hear the Duke of Westminster has had his many Rolls-Royces armour-plated.' No response. 'The Army Motor Reserve,' he explained. 'For to harry the Uhlans.'

But he had no luck in this wind, so he sat back in the leathery den and checked on Brother Polycarp instead. Dazed is right. Oiled to the eyes if you go to that of it. Atrocious smell of drink off him. I had no notion he was so far gone. I hope now my Jim won't be getting any bad habits. You'd think they'd be safe in the college. But the demon drink, it has the key to every door.

It was the new father had told him that. Fierce down that father has on the brother. Can understand for why now. He was in the right of it too: Polycarp is not an Irish name. Mind, that father is fierce all ways. I had no notion it was Erse he was talking. Dee's mirror git. To which the correct reply is Dee's mirror git is Patrick.

But small the harm in Erse and I'll be happy for Jim to take classes. So long as it wouldn't interfere with the Latin.

'I must say, Madame MacMurrough, I have always wanted to congratulate you on the sterling work you do put in for the war effort.'

'What?' called Eveline over the wind.

He leant forward, holding on to his hat, and shouted, 'The stockings you do collect.'

'What about them?'

'Well done, I wanted to say.'

'Look here, there's a rug in the box. See if you can't wrap it about him.' She checked over her shoulder. 'You say he's a brother?'

'From the Presentation College, mam.' He waited a moment, then said, 'He takes my son for Latin.'

'You have a son there?'

'I do indeed. Latin and music. He gives a flute band out of hours.' The engine faltered and Mr Mack leant forward again. 'Are we doing all right?'

'An obstruction in the road. Gone now.'

'As a matter of fact, the new father is after appointing me drill sergeant. I'm to teach the boys marching.'

'You?'

'Oh, murder above!'

'What is it?'

'I've only now recollected. If the brother's for the sick-ward we'll have no band at all. Oh, holy murder above.'

Silent amid the roaring world, Eveline wove through the trams and jarveys and the May processions of girls and boys.

At the People's Park she swerved to the right, then left along the seafront. The wind confused the groans of her passengers while the road ahead showed clear and sure.

Doyler had been right: the rain came in the evening, and it was still pouring when Jim pushed with the shop bike up Ballygihen hill. The shiny asphalt, the mop of trees, the chimney teeth with a chip off the middle, the squeaks of the wheels which seemed to complain of piles and the falling damps, the mudguard spitting wet: the world conspired with his thoughts and everywhere he looked was Doyler's presence. Ahead lay Killiney Hill, its obelisk stark against the last cloudy light.

He turned under the arch into Ballygihen Avenue, then pushed against the tradesmen's gate to Ballygihen House.

Tyre-grooves in the gravel, but no sign of any motor. A light showed in a bedroom and he saw a figure at the window looking out on the bay. There was an area with a steps down and another light showed there. He propped the bike at the railings, took the parcel in its waxed canvas, went down to the kitchen door.

It was a man who answered and he had not expected this. He was in his shirtsleeves but still there was an air of quality about him. 'I've come with the stockings,' said Jim.

The man lifted an eyebrow in what Jim, an authority now, identified for superciliousness. 'Stockings?'

'They're for Madame MacMurrough.'

'Is my aunt in need of stockings?'

Jim felt the reddening of his cheeks. 'They're comforts for the troops. My father sent me with them.'

The man had an easy and leisured manner that unsettled Jim, the way his eyes felt free to ramble over him. He said, 'Best bring them in so.' But he didn't move from the doorway and Jim had to squeeze past. In the jar he brushed his trousers inadvertently by the man's hand and he felt the breath go puff out of his mouth. 'I'm sorry,' he said.

The man only laughed.

Jim waited with his back to the door, staring at the table. 'Is Nancy here?'

'I believe it's her evening with her relative. Were you looking for her?'

He shook his head. 'Will I put the stockings down?'

'On the table, I suppose. Someone will see to it tomorrow.'

There was a tray with cold meats on the table with two bottles of double-X stout. Still the man's eyes upon him when he glanced round.

On the flag floor a red thing showed. Jim frowned. He blinked and it was still there. Still shining on the flags, a Red Hand badge.

The man saw what had caught his attention and smartly he picked it up. He fiddled with it in his hands. 'Do you need a receipt? Am I required to sign anything?'

'I beg your pardon?'

'Is there something else?'

'No, that's all.'

'I'll tell my aunt they arrived safely.'

Charming, thought MacMurrough as the boy fled past, a streak of wet vermilion which vanished up the steps. He heard the scrape of bicycle wheels on the gravel, then closed the door against the night.

He collected the tray and ascended the backstairs, extinguishing lights as he went. 'A boy about stockings,' he said when he came to the bedroom. 'Now, there's a comfort for the troops.'

Doyler turned from the window. 'If ever you lays a hand on that one you're dead.'

MacMurrough grinned and tossed him his badge. 'I believe you may have mislaid this. Careless, very.'

'Dead meat, you got that?'

CHAPTER EIGHT

MacMurrough woke at the peep of day with the boy's body beside him. He watched it form in the greying light while the voices came in his head. Scrotes as usual remained above the fray but Dick and the chaplain went at it like cats.

– There's an eyeful for you, Dick was saying. A sore sight for hornified eyes.

– Direct not the eyes at naked flesh, the chaplain admonished. The horned beast himself is among us.

– Horny beast is right.

– Is there no conscience in this house of hell?

– A standing dick, sir, hath no conscience.

A kinder voice intervened, Nanny Tremble, to calm the crossness. Now men, leave off the argufying, she said. We have a guest staying and the poor boy is at his slumbers yet. Little lamb, he must be worn away.

But Dick was incorrigible. He'll be shagged away soon enough, I warrant.

The chaplain embarked on his hellfire-jaw and sodom-talk, and *we will all go down for habitual degenerates!* And Nanny Tremble said, Dear dear. Well, I never.

Lazily MacMurrough thought to catch Scrotes's attention.

Scrotes? Are you there, Scrotes? But the old shade was not easily conjured. Often the most he would rouse was a snort, which might be of contempt, might be of exasperation. At times like this, MacMurrough conceived a fusty don in a turret room, bent upon some musty text, absent-mindedly cold, huffing every now and then and scowling over the affray below. A crusty old friend, a ghost in the attic.

Scrotes? Nothing.

MacMurrough turned to his sleeping mate. The boy lay with his back to him, his head steeply inclined, so that his body culminated in the knobbly top of his spine. The knob there recalled to MacMurrough the apple in the boy's throat, which had bobbed up and down last evening. Up and down it had bobbed as he took his turn on MacMurrough's stand. Uncommonly decent of him, really, for MacMurrough had not asked or expected it. Just at one point, the boy had pushed him away and gone down himself between MacMurrough's legs. There was a speculative look on his face while he contemplated his purpose. He closed his eyes and brought the shaft to his lips, but it took a time to appreciate the lips would better be opened.

Not a perfect pleasure because MacMurrough had a suspicion of authority undermined. The boy flushed when he opened his eyes and saw he was watched, as though to have forgotten there was company present. And that was thoughtful of him. But proportion was only duely returned when MacMurrough pressed his hand on the boy's head and forced his measure upon him.

Then he fetched in the boy's mouth and prettily it dribbled till the boy swallowed, popping his apple. 'Gluggary,' said he, 'like egg gone off.'

That had made MacMurrough laugh. He might have sent

him away then, in the decent obscurity of the dead of night. But his gameness was amusing and his smile beguiled that smelt of MacMurrough's comings. He stroked his skin while good-humouredly the boy defended his honour. 'Course I never done it before. Never said I liked it or not. Sure you's the one as asked me here. They talked till he nodded and his eyes closed on the pillow and MacMurrough had watched while the yawning curtains moved in the breeze.

– That blackguard would need a good thrashing, ordained the chaplain. And MacMurrough smiled when Dick volunteered his rod for the task.

Scrotes? Still no Scrotes.

The boy stirred and made grumpy moan. An arm shrugged the covers away. Poor lamb, said Nanny Tremble, he wouldn't be used to the woolly warmth.

MacMurrough ran his hand through the hair, which was scraggy from sea-water. A faint salt dusted his skin that he could feel when he stroked his neck. He smelt of sea-water too, and tasted of it, like an oyster in the mouth. Extraordinary eyes, MacMurrough recalled. No eyes are truly black, but this boy's seemed to be. Like rain on a laid road, rain on a road in the moonlight. Swimmer's body, tight, lithe, all of a piece. It really is the best exercise and might be encouraged more among the lower orders as it costs nothing and the effects are wholly benign. Listen to me, sounding off like the chaplain.

– But we must remember with the Keating's Powder, said Nanny Tremble; and MacMurrough sighed because this was very sound advice.

His hand, which had ranged over the boy's shoulders, traced now through its finger-tips the descent of his spine. And when it came to the flat bone that marked its end – Coccyx, said Dick; Os sacrum, said the chaplain – it splayed its five fingers and cupped the rounding cheeks of his bum. Ripe fruity firm: the peach he had been so careful with last evening.

Funny how they all undress with their tail to you, saving till the last moment the flourish of their manhood. Comes as a shock to discover you're as keen on their behind as their front. Back-scuttler, bum-jumper, arse king, gentleman of the back door, shit-hunter, gut-fucker, stern-chaser who navigates the windward passage: as though all their street expressions were ultimately without meaning for them.

How shy they go then, like a girl with her cherry, the boy with his peach. Buxom seat of unmanhood. Get thee before me, Satan.

Appropriately, it was MacMurrough's ring finger that crept into the crease now, discovering hair, a dampness, a hairyless wetness, dry spot; on to the perineum where a tiny pulse gave him to wonder was the boy awake. He worked his hand through the thighs, clutched in rather a how-are-yc way the tightening balls till, proud as the morning, he found what he sought. Pulled once or twice, just to get the strength of it, then back through the plush and the silky skin to the stone-dry ring. In a bit. Knotted. A Mary-hole.

It would mean a further five bob, but he determined on buggery.

He withdrew his hand from the parting – such sweet sorrow – spat on it, wet himself. He seized the boy's shoulder and as he turned him, mounted him. Not savagely, as Dick would have it, but with patient steady mastery so that Nanny Tremble need fear for neither's posterity.

The boy gasped and battled out of his fox-sleep, but by the time he had marshalled awareness of his surroundings the worst was done. Colour washed from his cheeks and the eyes fixed in their corners, but the pain diminished as resistance fell. His gape unfroze and the fists unfroze that had gripped the sheet. The mouth puffed and little grunts came out, hardly of pleasure, but of pain contained.

It was safe now to leave Dick in charge and MacMurrough felt himself depart. In his mind he climbed spiral stone stairs till he entered a draughty turret room. Scrotes looked up from his text.

– I see you have taken to rape now.

– Is it rape? asked MacMurrough.

– Do you need to ask? Or do you need to be told?

As though from on high, MacMurrough viewed his work. He had tugged the boy sideways again and was fetching him off by hand. Clumsy motion that counter-rhymed with the mounting thrusts behind. The boy too had found an action of sorts and he was bumping his bottom pudently along – more hindermate than help, for Dick went at it like a beast of the wild. At one point, his childlike hand reached behind and pressed the thigh he found. The touch shot a pang through MacMurrough. As though the boy would share what Dick knew might only be taken.

In boyish throes he spurted. MacMurrough would follow, but just as he did he leant over and kissed the boy's lips. It surprised that they parted and his unready tongue was met by another.

He slipped off the boy and collapsed on his back. His head fell on the pillow and, sinking through the down, he heard the pounding of his heart; and every pound was a footstep, as down the iron-railed hall the warder clanged, calling out the numbers of the cells and the cell doors slammed as he called them rebounding, and the bawling and banging and hounding steps came closer till his door was resoundingly next.

– C.3.4, called the warder.

Slam. This cannot be. Prison. But it is.

Songbirds released him. Ballygihen, smell of lawns and the

sea. He forced his eyes to open. His breath returned and the pounding ceased. Sandycovely safe.

He needed a cigarette then, and he got up to find his carton. He drew on the darkly fragrant Abdulla. At the open window he watched the sea and he saw himself a snail at its shore who carries not his home but his prison with him. They only let you out: they never let you go.

'Who's Scrotes?' said the boy, watching him.

'Scrotes?'

'You was calling him out.'

'When?'

'Just then, while you was . . .'

'Really?' You hear that, Scrotes? I call out your name. In the throes of my passion I call for you.

'Friend, is it?'

MacMurrough flicked the match with his nail on its tip, flipped it in the grate. 'Someone I used to know. Dead now.' Hear that, Scrotes? You're dead.

Distantly he heard the rustle of sere pages.

He pulled on his drawers, sat down on the bed. 'Are you recovered?'

'I won't be sitting cosy for a while.'

'Rather a rude awakening, I suppose.' Though he looked comfortable enough. Hands behind his head, showing mohairs under the arms. Less boyish now, as if a dick up the arse really could make a man of you. Rather pleased with himself, actually. Suppose it is a hurdle to be over. Accomplished without need of decision. Put like that, I've done him a favour. Your honour, I was asleep at the time. Something else too. When you use them for pleasure they're more at home in the big house. Breaks the ice, so to speak.

He touched the depression of the boy's chest, running his

finger through half a dozen fledgling hairs to a leather string where clung a cheap tin medal.

'Stay the night, says you. Promise I won't jump you.'

'Hard to resist when you turn your back like that.'

The boy shifted his legs. ''S all right anyway. Don't be sitting much in my line of work.'

A bitter tone which reminded MacMurrough of their first meeting at the Forty Foot. He came from the latrine with his dress unadjusted. In a casual way MacMurrough said, 'Do you need any help with that?' The boy shrugged. 'They works me like a horse. Might as well hang out like one.' At the time, he'd taken it for no more than a chase-me. Not so sure now. Chip on his shoulder. My proud Hibernian boy.

'Seems early yet. What time is it at all?'

MacMurrough leant over for his wrist-watch.

– He will have that item, warned the chaplain. If we are not vigilant, he will.

– Ah no, said Nanny Tremble, and he looks such a nice young man.

– He is not nice nor honest, the chaplain retorted, who will permit what that vulgarian has submitted to.

'Four,' said MacMurrough. 'Twenty after. Rotten bind, I know, but I'm afraid . . .'

Moments later the boy was at the washstand soaping himself. How it gladdened Nanny Tremble's heart to find him so mindful of the daily rinse. Today he would shovel shit smelling of *violette de Parme*. Skin flowed translucently over ribs as he stretched to pull on his trousers. Nacreous or in some way like the sea, rippled. Each bone was defined, perhaps a touch too defined.

– Oh, and he was so hungry last evening, said Nanny Tremble. Remember and he sent you down for the cold meats?

We thought he'd never have his nough. But you can never give a boy too much to eat.

– And he lapped up all his milk, added Dick, stirring in his drawers.

No sign of injury though the limp is there. And that, too, had attracted at the Forty Foot. Youth, poverty, minor impairment: had a lot in his favour. Walked along the sea-wall with him that first time, tried to interest him in diving. Well, anything to keep a conversation up. Knowing grin he had. Convinced all along he was fly to the game. Tossed him a coin. The magic effect of half a crown, deposit on a bit of brown.

Found him that night outside the hand-me-down shop. I remember geese barking in the yards while we chatted on the sea-steps. I bent down and took him in my mouth.

Afterwards he had bread which he was happy to share. Boland's. They don't use foreign flour, he chose to tell me. I paid him, the full pledge, his flute for his flute. His smile was collusive then. And I thought of those lines from Blake: Stolen joys are sweet, and bread eaten in secret pleasant.

And very pleasant it has been. He found his notecase. 'I hope you don't mind paper,' he said, 'as I haven't sufficient coin.'

The boy took the red ten-shilling note. A week's, two weeks' wages, MacMurrough calculated. Not so very long ago and the least smile should have earned a sovereign. He watched him read the note like a morning paper, turn it over and read the back page. Soap shone on his face, and he gave his regular godless oath.

'Mary and Joseph, are you always so free with your bunce?'

'It wouldn't do to defraud a labourer of his wages,' MacMurrough responded and kissed his forehead. 'That sin cries to heaven for vengeance.'

'You're a regular pagan,' said the boy.

'You're not so bad yourself.'

He took him down the backstairs to the kitchen where no one yet stirred though MacMurrough knew the girl, and most probably Cook too, and whoever else in the turnover of staff, would be ears against the walls. He opened the kitchen door and paced up the area steps, suppressing in the open an urge to sneak. The boy felt this, for he asked, 'Are you never worried you'll be catched?'

– We will be caught, said the chaplain. We will go down for habitual degenerates and it will be that young blackguard's blame.

MacMurrough said, 'Actually, I was caught.'

The boy stopped on the gravel. 'You was?'

MacMurrough ambled on. 'It's all right. They never catch you twice.'

'Why wouldn't they?'

'They never release you the first time.'

Down the path to the end of the garden where opened a private gate to the sea-wall. Mist out on Howth and a chill breeze; dew on the lawns where a blackbird practised its range. Distant doves cooed with argumentative insistence. A magpie's rattling gun. He believed he saw a rabbit. He believed he saw a fox. Hare and hyena, he told Scrotes: supporters of our chivalry.

'Good luck so,' said Doyler.

'Yes, good luck.'

The chaplain and Dick proffered their conflicting counsel as MacMurrough watched him tread his way. A sadness and tenderness descended as he saw how beautiful was the world. The clearing sky was beautiful, the leaping dew, the breeze that blew like mint upon his face. His seed was inside a darling boy who limped through this imperial morn in his raggedy-daggledy clothes. Lamb dressed up as mutton. How sad that made him feel, and tender. Tender and sad and cold.

MacMurrough climbed back into bed. He closed his eyes and wandered up spiral stairs till he came to Scrotes's turret room. The old fellow was beavering away at his table. MacMurrough leant at his shoulder to over-read, piecing together with difficulty the vermiculate letters. *Omnis natura*, he read, *in quantum natura est, bonum est.* Aquinas? It sounded like Aquinas.

– Augustine, snapped Scrotes.

MacMurrough wandered about the room, opened a book, closed it again, flicked through the Latin dictionary of Lewis and Short. Scrotes certainly was in a mood, which was inconvenient rather, for he felt a wish to speak with the fellow.

– Why is it always so cold in this turret? he ventured after a time. Never a fire in the grate.

Scrotes tapped his quill in its well.

– I shall tell you why it is cold, he replied. It is cold because you fancy it so. You fancy I wear a skull-cap when I work. You fancy me in threadbare wool. The temperature descends to suit. Industry in your mind is associated with old clothes and ice. Sometimes as I write, droplets freeze on my mittens. It is all most disturbing. A memory of your schooldays no doubt, when they penny-pinched on coals.

MacMurrough yawned. He said, rhyming schoolboy-quick: Amo, amas, I loved a lass, for she was soft and tender; amas, amat, she laid me flat, and tickled my masculine gender.

– He has gone then, your young friend? said Scrotes sighing.

– Yes, I led him down the garden path.

The porcupine quill was wiped with the pen-wiper, the page was blotted, and Scrotes said, You wish to speak with me.

– Do you always eavesdrop on my thoughts?

– You forget: I am your thoughts.

– A portion of them, MacMurrough advised.

Scrotes fleered in deference. The loftier portion, one hopes.

MacMurrough hesitated. It's about that boy.

– Well?

– While Dick was at him—

– Dick? By which you intend your membrum virile and the wayward cerebrations that command it?

MacMurrough sighed. Very well, while I was sodomising the kid, I felt an odd poignancy. The oddness remained while we said our goodbye. It was my desire that had occasioned our intercourse, it was by my leave that we walked through the garden. Yet he chose – I do not know by what expediency – to behave as if this were not the case.

– And this explains your sadness? This explains the tenderness you avowed?

– One is not so foolish as to attribute such sentiments to anything more elevated than selfish interest. I was sad for myself; I desired the world should know me for a sad and tender soul.

– And the boy?

– One pities him, naturally. It would be absurd to say one cared.

– Was it pity you felt last evening? – when he spoke of his friend.

His friend, yes, the comfort for the troops who had brought stockings. They planned to swim at the Forty Foot together, every morning, rain or shine. Dick was thrilled by it all and spent much of the night romancing the two into all sorts of performances. Not sure why, now, possibly to humiliate, probably to goad, I asked did he love his friend. Well, no boy loves his chum, or no boy says he does. But he answered, I do.

I do, he answered as in some preposterous dissenting nuptial. And MacMurrough remembered how touching it was that a young fellow in a stranger's bed should say that he loved his friend. The strangeness of the bed assisted, of course. But still, it was . . . charming.

– But did you pity him? Scrotes would be deferred no longer.

– No, I did not. I thought him naif. Charming, but naif.

– And this morning when you parted, why did you feel sad?

– I have already explained it was an egoistical affectation.

– Your egoism is not in doubt, MacMurrough. What is in doubt is your humanity.

– You never used to hector so.

– You never used to be so cold.

It was cold, and bare with it. Winter prevailed in the dim-lit room. And chancing on the glass that Scrotes kept by his table, MacMurrough caught his face and it seemed to him a fresh and alarming thing, a hanging fruit among the withered leaves. Such a fruit as the ancients described as having a colour as though fit to eat: but if plucked it crumpled in your hands into ashes. *And where they grow by the Dead Sea these fruits are called the apple of Sodom.*

MacMurrough cast an eye on the spiral stairs down. He yearned for Nanny Tremble to come and cosset him. But Scrotes leant forward with eyes of December.

– Answer the truth. Did you not look upon the world this morning and imagine it as the boy might see it? And did you not recognize the mist and the dew and the birdsong as elements not of a place or a time but of a spirit? And did you not envy the boy his spirit? For you know there can be no power over him who freely gives what another would take. Such a one has the capacity to love. Freely, naively, to say, I do.

Coldly MacMurrough answered, You forget yourself, Dr Scrotes: I loved you. Heartily I loved you. Two years hard I spent loving you. They had me watch you die.

– So must you kill everything now in revenge?

'Snapdragons,' said Eveline. 'I'm never sure if they're not too tawdry. Are they tawdry? Or are they merely vulgar?'

'Tawdry,' chose MacMurrough. 'Vulgar when called antirrhinums.'

Her hand squeezed his containing elbow. 'How very Wildean,' she said.

A momentary lapse which sundered them. She covered with tulips. 'They're one's favourites, of course, but he won't grow them, old Moore won't. Or at least he will, but only among the snapdragons and whatever these are, green things. Whereas with tulips what one prizes is their uniformity. Nothing to break a prospect so well as a parade of unvarying turbans.'

Old Moore preceded their progress down the garden path. His hands snapped dead things off, boots slid dead things under the shrubberies. Aunt Eva looked to left and right, but graciously not ahead.

'One argues with him, naturally, but in the end one must give way. Too odd to care too much about a garden, don't you agree?'

MacMurrough did agree and their arms entwined once more. She spoke of tulip-beds she had known at Versailles and in the Tuileries and he thought of Wilde's that had *flamed like throbbing rings of fire*. He was struck still by her allusion.

Squilde. Don't let 'im catch yer bending, mate. We got ourself an arse-fackin-Squilde on us-fackin-wing.

'Whereas here in poor old Ireland all is a galimafrée.' She

strode ahead to quiz the gardener, who shuffled his feet, bowing his head. MacMurrough imagined the mumbling response, his seeking to stumble his words lest expertise should offend.

Green old rambling garden. MacMurrough knew it, of course, from his holidays as a boy. Screen of twisted pines, the sycamores to the road with their clouds of flies. Dark shrubberies scattered about like mounds over warrior-kings. Exciting places for a child to grub in, somewhere to show your bottom to the gardener's lad. Wonderful meadow lawn, quite hidden from the house, where he had liked to lie in the long grass while the ponies came up and nudged him. And always at the end, the sea.

And Aunt Eva. How romantic she looked in her saffron wrap. Her hair was a glossy black after some preparation or other. A pale maquillage. White flowing unfashionable dress whose trail was stained with grass. Not quite the Irish colleen, but whatever it is colleen is the diminutive of.

His gaze took in the run of the house. She called it Georgian, but Georgian here meant anything up to the 'fifties. His grand-father had taken it as convenient for the Mail. The stone was rendered grey, but not sombrely so, lightly grey, *grisaille*, his aunt would say, faded of salt and wind. Canted wings, one grown over with ivy, the other so bare as to be bald, lending the façade a tilted aspect. No turret, nor room for one, which was surprising really, considering the hours MacMurrough spent there with Scrotes. Balustrade bounding the balcony whereon his aunt took tea in the morning. Below the balcony the garden room, whose French windows, open to the day, drew the garden paths together.

'Defney I never seeyan dis many tings in a roowam befroor.' Thus the boy of MacMurrough's bedroom. Shaving-stand, wash-stand, shuttered secretaire, his leafy Saraband rug: it had seemed bare enough to MacMurrough. The house was far less fussy than he recalled. The heavy mahoganies remained, but were islands of furniture against faded walls. Gone the sand pictures, the featherwork scenes, pictures without paint that so had charmed his childish mind: all that jumble of ornament and garnish that marked the high reign of the old Queen. Wandering through the house he felt how light were these rooms and large now, when his memories crowded them with riding-booted feet, gruff voices of visiting gentry, the incommunicado of footmen. Hearths gaped without their screens, pole-screens, cheval-screens, screens against the draught, the light – where had all the screens gone? Yet, for all its airiness, there was a mood of want and disrepair, as though the modern style had fallen by accident, by unreplaced breakage, loss.

And the garden, too, with its wilderness sides and combed lawns – a type of Jekyll and hide. Even here the modern style seemed hit upon by negligence. Or perhaps not negligence but nonchalance, a supremacy over style born of conviction. His aunt was certain of her standing, in history and in place. Anything she touched, ergo, was . . . *à la mode*.

However, she owned a curious inability to keep people. The place was run on the very minimum of staff. Half the rooms she kept shut. He had noticed a certain manoeuvring of the apostles, robbing Peter to pay Paul, with the tradesmen. Was Aunt Eva feeling the pinch? She still topped it the *grande dame* of course – to the extent of keeping a dispensary, what she was pleased to term her Wednesday *levée*, when from the front steps of the house she doled out blue butter and castor oil to the needy sick of the parish. But still, to remain here among the retired majors and advancing suburbandom of Sandycove: a florist's bizarre in the borders.

Our estate is over the mountains, she told him when he asked. But he remembered the family home, High Kinsella, which sat upon a vast heatherless roadless mire: one of those blank Irish houses, with staring windows, and the misgiving as you approached of the roof fallen in. She had taken recently to motoring there of a long weekend.

How interesting if Aunt Eva should be poor. How well they should get on.

Something crawled inside his collar. Impassively, he plucked the gentle seed. Lousy little renter. Nanny Tremble had been right about the Keating's Powder. The grey thing crushed with a tactile crunch and his fingers stained with blood. Had better check for crab-lice too. His shoulders hunched with incipient formication.

In Wandsworth they used water from boiling potatoes. Rubbing it into Scrotes's back that time in the infirmary. Horrid warts he had. Old man's warts. Old lag's lice.

– And only this morning we were treated to proclamations of undying love.

– For your soul, great heart, for your soul.

'He claims it is a July garden,' Aunt Eva said returning. 'Have you ever heard such a thing? A July garden indeed. It was never a July garden when I was a child. Why, I don't remember any Julys here. We always travelled to Paris in anticipation of the recess.'

'This is Ireland. Everything comes later here.'

She sighed. 'Yes, this is poor old sold-out Ireland.'

Even the late blooming of flowers, apparently, could be laid at the union with England. They passed under an arch that come July, politics permitting, would ramble with rose. Low hedges separated the path from the vegetable rows. Cabbage, cabbage, potato, cabbage; potato, potato, cabbage, cabbage. And just there, by the sea-steps, I took him in my mouth.

Aunt Eva stopped. 'Well, it is useless to go on. At the least no one need starve. We can feed them all colcannon.'

They turned, old Moore remaining to potter about in his darling rows.

'If he can grow cabbages that way, why can't he plant tulips in beds? I sometimes despair of my race and its lack of an aesthetic. Of course it comes from the famine. If a thing can't be eaten, one must throw it away. But what am I to do? Dispose my guests among the praties?'

'Wait until July.'

'It looks as though we shall have to.'

They came to a seat and she sat down. The heavy scent of wallflowers hung, members too, MacMurrough recalled, of the cabbage family. He stood over her, smoking.

'Did I mention we are to have a boys' band playing?'

'What sort of boys' band?'

'Local boys. Poor ones, I presume. I arranged for kilts for them to wear.' She looked up suddenly, as if she had caught Dick's murmur of hands wandering up skirted thighs. 'I'm sure I remember you playing an instrument. Didn't you, Anthony?'

'Yes, I played concert flute. I told you.'

'The man in charge is not to be trusted.'

'Trusted with what?'

She looked aggrieved at his interrogation. 'The care of young minds.' Her fingers, which had stroked a stem, now pinched it till it severed. She brought the spray to her nose, sniffed. Before she would toss it aside she said, 'He is not patriotic.'

MacMurrough laughed, a single ejaculated breath.

'There is no occasion for scoffing. Father O'Toiler and I intend the boys to be an inspiration to the parish. It has become too Englified and reminds one of your recreant father.'

His father, yes. Advocate, of course, not brilliant but reliable. For the prosecution, hence the knighthood. Sir John MacMurrough, Knight of St Patrick. Dubbed at Dublin Castle, hence the recreancy. Twins, she the elder by half an hour, he the winner by the unalterable right of male succession.

'As it happens this current teacher is indisposed. An unfortunate mishap on the road. The man to replace him need not be so proficient. He need only be . . . bien disposé.'

'Aunt Eva, you're not suggesting . . . ?' Apparently she was. 'Does your priest know about this? Does he know anything of my situation?'

Sternly she said, 'What is there to know? Other than that you are a MacMurrough and as such bear a name inseparable from our country's cause.' She sought to hold his eyes. Some appeal there he thought might be gratified by his flinching. He did so and she said, eirenically, 'As for your contretemps with the British courts, we must never forget your grandfather himself was imprisoned. Kilmainham Gaol. They have ballads about it still.'

So that was it. They were to play the green card. Wily old bird is offering me a way out. Would anybody fall for it? Even for Ireland it seemed too extravagant to equate his plight with the humdrum consequences of nationalist agitation. And yet he was Irish – as much as he was anything much. His gaze lowered from the sycamores through which the sky still showed. He flicked his cigarette in the flowers. 'Two years with hard labour, hard fare and a hard bed is hardly a contretemps.'

'I am afraid they have coarsened you. However, you will find that in this country incarceration is not quite the disgrace our conquerors would make of it. Why, I myself received a one month's detention.'

'Darling Aunt Eva, even in Wandsworth I had news of your escapades. Eggs at Asquith, gracious me. However, three-quarters of an hour in the cells below till they cat-and-moused you out scarcely amounts to a martyrdom.'

'And what of that?' she snapped. 'If our masters have grown too cunning to permit of martyrs, is the cause to be any the lessened?'

Yes, he thought, she had hoped for prison. Hunger-striking, he did not doubt. How it must have riled her, her brother's intercession. He remembered she had crossed to London for the Coronation demonstration of 1911. His father, invited of course to the Coronation itself, refused her his house. She camped outside in a borrowed motor, festooned with garlands and bannerets. In the procession itself she reclined upon a float, fingering a giant harp, the Dark Rosaleen of Erin, at the head of a mildly discomfited contingent from the Irishwomen's Suffrage Federation. He watched her pass from a balcony in Piccadilly, one remarkable woman in a mass of thousands, each chanting for her vote.

He did not know whence she produced them, for she did not seem to carry anything with her beyond her parasol, but some salts had appeared which now she inhaled. Such a feminine creature. Impossible to imagine her a man. When he posited this, she answered he was impertinent.

'I do not intend to be.'

'Thoughtlessness is small excuse.'

'I merely meant that in some ways you are better fitted to be head of the family, *The* MacMurrough. In place of my – as you call him, recreant – father.'

'One does not wish oneself changed. One wishes the world changed to accommodate one. Such is suffragism. Such is all emancipation. You may wonder where a pipsqueak priest and his poor boys' band may enter in such a scheme. But you will find, dear boy, that all roads lead to the same end. Which end is that? Why, the future of course. It is our task to ensure the future shall be glorious – if not in its state, then in its memory.

We can do no more. And I,' she continued, 'a woman alone, can do little at all, unless my nephew help me.'

She held out her hand, which he took in anticipation of guiding her to her feet. But instead she kept his hand in hers and he felt her searching through the kid of her glove the calluses of his fingers. 'Let us dismiss your embarras with the English. A small clarification is all that is required. How the English, to traduce your grandfather's memory, concocted the charges against you. You will find society only too willing for so happy an éclaircissement. The world of affairs awaits you, my boy. I intend you shall enter it and prosper.'

'I was not aware you had any intentions for me.'

'We shall begin with the garden fête. Don't glower so, Anthony dear. You know perfectly well one cannot have one's nephew staying without an announcement. It would not do.'

'Would not do for whom?'

'For a MacMurrough. Whatever has happened, we are still MacMurroughs, and I will not have you shut in your room the day or flâneuring along to the Forty Foot. The garden fête will mark your return. I shall invite all the leading families. The nationalist ones, naturally. They will see a bright likely young man leading local youth in patriotic song and everyone shall be charmed. For you are a charming boy when you wish to be. You have élan, you have éclat, you have breeding. And you shall marry.'

'Marriage now?'

'Of course you shall marry. Did you think I would allow our name to die on account of some foolishness in London? I have never heard such a thing.'

She was in earnest but he could not bring himself to take seriously her designs. 'Why stop at a garden fête? Why not an advertisement in the *Irish Times*?'

'I do not follow.'

'I might telephone to them myself. Anthony MacMurrough, surviving son of Sir John MacMurrough, and grandson of the late regretted Dermot James William MacMurrough, QC, MP, so forth and so fifth, has returned from His Majesty's Wandsworth where lately he served two years' hard for gross indecency with a chauffeur-mechanic. July Jamboree in Glasthule. Apply Ballygihen House.'

He said this looking her in the face, while her face hardened, but he looked away after and it was from her voice he learnt how deeply he disappointed his aunt.

'Yes, they have coarsened you. They have made – I mean the English have made – a braggart of my nephew. No doubt you believe I interfere. But you are fortunate to have anyone take an interest at all.'

'I should survive without you, Aunt Eva.'

'Yes, you would,' she agreed, 'if only to spite us.' She stood up, a deliberate lean upon her parasol. 'You hold yourself a very proud young man. But I see no pride, only a wallowing in fanfaronade. One day I wish you may have something to be proud of.' Her elbow angled, expectant of his arm. 'I am afraid this chamaillerie has quite exhausted my humour. You may walk me to the house.'

He took her arm but held it stiffly. *Contretemps, embarras, chamaillerie.* The worst crime in the calendar he could live with. Foolishness was too unkind.

'As it happens, I do not flâneur nor shut myself in. I have my work.'

'Yes, a book that you write.'

'I am preparing a manuscript for publication.'

'Some unfortunate you took pity on when you were' – her fingers waved – 'indisposé.'

'He took pity on me, actually.'

'And in return you undertake the publication of his – what is it?'

'It is a scholarly work, Aunt Eva, whose subject is the nature of nature.'

'No less.'

'*De natura naturae*. It was Scrotes's life's work.'

'Scrotes being the author of this exercise.'

'Dr Scrotes, in fact.'

'Indeed. And how did Dr Scrotes come to find himself in your' – again the waving fingers – 'bonne compagnie?'

'On account of some foolishness, as you put it. But not in London. In Oxford.'

'Well, it is very interesting and I make no doubt the nature of nature is a topic we all shall thrill to in due course. In the meantime, we have your future to consider. Cannot Dr Scrotes prepare his manuscript for himself?'

His voice, when he heard it, surprised by its evenness. 'Scrotes is dead. He died in Wandsworth. In a prison corner he died while picking the shreds from hawser ropes. Have you ever seen a hawser rope, Aunt Eva? It is the thickness of my leg. They allow you your fingers to pick it with, and you may not cease till your day's tally has been picked. In the night you smell the bonfire on which they burn the day's work. For the world has no use for oakum any more, only for the labour that will produce it. A scholar, Aunt Eva, a gentleman of sixty-seven years of age, worked to death. On account of some foolishness. In Oxford.'

'How terrible.'

He believed she meant it. 'Aunt Eva, can you truly believe any society would want me now?'

'I want you. I am society.'

They had reached the French windows and she turned to

take one last view of the garden. Gossamer floated over the lawns as though, when she sighed, blown by that breath. 'Sometimes I think the only course is to dig it all up and start afresh. Away with the shrubberies, a fountain that works.'

'Tulip-beds.'

'Yes, tulips too. But do you know, there is a surprising complication with tulips. Every now and then, nobody seems to know why, a perfectly decent yellow will break into the most alarming variegation. There are people who become very excited by it. They take a pride in the display. For myself, however, I find it spoils the effect. As I say, it is their conformity one prizes.'

From Scrotes's turret room MacMurrough watched the waves. Howth was a grey mist and the sea was grey and the gloomy pines that marshalled his view bent to the easterly wind: December descending.

The close scratch of Scrotes's pen. Flick of pages when he searched a reference. *Veni Karthaginem. Et circumstrepebat me undique sartago flagitiosorum amorum.* A little August to shine on our winter. The book snapped shut.

– If we are not to work, Scrotes said, let us rather talk. I cannot abide these wintry broodings. Speak. You are dismayed by your aunt.

Petulantly MacMurrough re-found the page.

– What had you supposed? Scrotes persisted. That you should stay in this fine house with its fine views without charge? One had thought you would enjoy teaching flute to young men.

– You begin to sound like Dick.

– I beginneth as I endeth, Scrotes retorted, sounding as you.

MacMurrough stared again through the window. Dull imperative waves. Like a child, they commanded attention, imparting nothing. Can you see me as Erin's bandleader? he said. Married off to the first Hibernian hoyden with a father sufficiently green? It's too absurd.

– And this absurdity upsets you?

– I might go along with her, I suppose. But I could never bring myself to believe any of it.

– And she requires you believe?

– The worst of it is, she doesn't. All she requires is that I should conform. Which is show, a denial of my beliefs.

– Remind me, said Scrotes: which are these lofty principles you quake to disavow? The world I'm sure trembles to hear.

MacMurrough smirked. Very clever, Scrotes. And it may be true that I don't believe in anything much. But I believe I ought to believe, which is something.

– It is a very modern something.

– You say this while we trudge through Augustine's *Confessions*?

Scrotes raised his eyes in monkish supplication. Da mihi, he prayed, sed noli modo.

– Tee hee hee, rallied MacMurrough, and he jounced his shoulders in pantomime of the other's crow.

Scrotes settled the papers before him, the papers restoring his donnish air. By tradition, he said, those of your station have been more than happy to conform, in public. In private they debauched to their hearts' content. What scruples arose they retained chaplains to resolve. Doubtless it is the way of all great families, all low families, too, in fine. The one to sink, the other to rise, and all to meet in the embracing middle. In time all will throb to the *Daily Mail* and all hands be raised in horror at hypocrisy.

It was a pleasing fancy, but MacMurrough shook his head. I doubt I could rise to hypocrisy any more. Don't you see, old man, I can't persuade myself. I can't pretend with the sniff of oakum in my nostrils. This is what I've come to. It is true. I am this.

– What is this that you are?

– I can tell you what I wanted to be. I wanted to be the queer bugger who lives in that house. See that man? That's the man we don't talk about. I thought I'd come here to Ireland and somehow I'd stop here, literally stop. See that man? He isn't there. But she's not going to let me, is she. She must have it all begin again, this time with fanfares and fêtes. She thinks I have no pride. But I have.

– I wonder, said Scrotes.

– Indeed, said MacMurrough.

– Is it pride you have, or fear?

– Let us say it is a certain reluctance to give delight to these people. An Oscar Wilde in Ireland – whatever next? It's true I hold myself proud. Even my aunt admitted me that.

– Your aunt, a benevolent and admirable lady—

Here MacMurrough raised his finger in interruption. Two pounds a week she allows me, Scrotes. That is not benevolent nor admirable. That is four fucks and no fags.

– Your aunt, Scrotes persisted, after the merest sniff, has remarked what she calls your fanfaronade. An appellation not wholly ill-advised, for you are that strange beast who prides himself yet has no pride. You blush for your nature, yet will freely speak of chauffeur-mechanics, the efficient cause of its detection. You congratulate yourself on a capacity to prostitute impoverished youths, yet are ashamed of the desire that draws you to them. You fear discovery, yet will flippantly bring a boy into your aunt's home.

– Yes, you're right, of course, said MacMurrough. I'll rape him on a rug down the meadow lawn in future.

– Listen to me, MacMurrough. You have survived an imprisonment of two years with hard labour, a sentence which is judged
the maximum a man may suffer and still hope to live. You have
survived it well, with every prospect of recovery. Are you proud
of the fortitude, the determination, the character this proves?
Not a bit of it. You warble a wish to stop, to cease to be.
Even more remarkable, you commingle these sentiments to the
one comprehension. You despise yourself, and are proud of the
despisal, regarding it a virtue. It is an arrogance of disgust –
Scrotes signed the papers before him – venerable as Augustine
and as vain.

– After you have finished this tirade against me, Scrotes, my
treasure, do you intend saying anything nice?

– As a matter of fact, I do. Solvitur ambulando. Come, fetch
my coat, fetch my hat. We shall venture without where the sun
yet shines.

– I rather think not, said MacMurrough. I've already beat
the bounds once today.

But Scrotes was having none of it. While he trussed his neck
with a muffler, his banter carried on.

– A remarkable aspect of this prison you have contrived is
the circumambulance of its walls. Wherever you go, the walls go
with you. It is a kindly improvement on the traditional practice,
allowing for ample exercise and the variation of views. We
shall visit to the celebrated Pavilion Gardens and take tea like
gentlemen.

– The Pavilion? I'll be the talk of the tea-room.

– Gammon, said Scrotes. I hesitate to disappoint my illustrious young friend, but between his incarceration and his release
there has broken out the greatest war mankind has known.
Only last year this country was on the brink of its own civil
war. The people have other concerns. It is the Whitsun bank

holiday. Society rejoices. August brings the Horse Show. Why, next month is the Regatta.

– Next month is Aunt bloody Eva's fête.

Scrotes held the door. MacMurrough pressed his nib on the paper. The dull paper grey as the sea. *Veni Dublinum*. And seethed all about me the noisy stew of infamous loves. The pen pitched from his hold.

– Not the tradesmen's gate, said Scrotes when they were outside. Let us walk with the trees and nod good-day to the neighbours.

– Nod to the neighbours? repeated MacMurrough. Hello and Gomorrha to you. Hello and Gomorrha.

But they met no one at the gates and no one of consequence till past Glasthule. Crossing to Kingstown it was a surprise after the broken paving to hear his shoes clip on the Aberdeen setts. George's Street was striped with awnings. Straw hats, postcards, trinkets, an excursionist's treasury dangled in the sunshine. Those few buildings that were not new and red-bricked had scaffolding on their fronts, properly ashamed amid the town's gay prosperity. A crazy jam of traffic, horsecart and tramcar. Six priests, four monks, seven nuns MacMurrough counted in the space between two public houses.

'Herrody May! Even Herrody May!'

– What can they mean? asked Scrotes.

– *Herald* or *Mail*, answered MacMurrough as the newsboys darted past. I don't know how I know, but I do.

Austrian veal butcher's festooned with Union flags. Indeed, the red-white-and-blue waved high and low.

– Empire Day, said Scrotes.

– Yes, Empire Day, agreed MacMurrough. I had forgotten. And he was not alone, it seemed. Some dismal procession was wedging its way between the tramlines and horsemuck. Men with hockey-sticks, or hurleys as they called them, at a shambling march, their green armbands a scandalous sedition of the chromatic propriety. Jeers from the jarveys, cold stares from gentlemen, ragamuffin boys mocked their step. Even the dogs of the street joined in, yelping and wagging their furious tails: that uncanny sense in the canine that recognizes preponderant disdain. Then a biddy from a fruit-stall stepped out to lead them. She walked backwards in front, waving her skirts and jigging her feet in hilarious burlesque. And how the crowd loved her, cheering her on, and her hawker sisters called ribaldly after. But by degrees that could be measured in the granite setts, her face hardened and her mockery slowed, till all of a heap was revealed in their midst – Mother Erin. Erin go bragh, she sobbed till she stumbled in a gutter. Her sisters came with the bottle and the shambling men marched on.

Then a boy stopped his bicycle outside a shop selling wool and he made to climb off. The way his leg stretched it was like time stood still. MacMurrough could feel the abrasion of his breeches, could catch the sweat of his crotch, taste the ink on his fingers, even. The curve of the leg as it hung in the air had a Palladian perfection. He blinked in an odd way when he saw he was watched. MacMurrough smiled and the boy half smiled before the colour rose and he turned away. The boy with the stockings, the comfort for the troops.

– You know, he said to Scrotes, if Ireland might be a boy instead of a blowsy old cow, I'd be all for Ireland, I would.

At last they turned into Marine Road, quietly sedately hotelled, guest-housed. Matrons in thick-starch double-blue frocks rustled by. Squadron of schoolboys done up as sailors, Nanny Tremble in charge with fob dangling. At the cab-stand, the blinkered blood-eyed nags. He stopped by the entrance booth to a walled and landscaped garden whence drifted the oompah of a brass band.

– So this is the famous Pavilion Gardens, said Scrotes. Has the aspect, you'll forgive me, of an ice-cream factory.

– It's intended to resemble a ship on the sea.

– No, definitely an ice-cream manufactory.

Through the bars of the gate he glimpsed ladies with parasols and gentlemen with cigars who strolled the snow-white palace of iron, of glass and iron and floating belvederes. Behind him, when he looked, two giant constables kept watch from the courthouse steps. He heard the stall-women at the railway station. He smelt the shit of the horses at the hazards.

– I have forgotten my cane, he said to Scrotes.

– You have forgotten nothing, Scrotes returned.

It was true. Only a gentleman might carry a sword. He pitched a coin at the man in the booth and swung through the turnstile.

Waiting to be seated, he felt his fists gripping. He would have preferred his back to the wall, but he had come this far, so he ordered a middle table. He was conscious of little noises, tea-spoons, tea-cups, against a background of refined chatter. His chair scraped when pulled and faces turned. That first meal in Wandsworth. Thanked the old hand who brought it to the door. He shook his head, signalling silence. The warder saw and cuffed him.

The girl came to take his order. 'Sticky buns and a pot of tea,' she repeated. 'Are you here on your furlough, sir?'

MacMurrough nodded.

– She takes me for an officer.

– Naturally. Your upright bearing and eleven-a-side moustache.

A laughter rose from a party two tables away. Fashionable

eyes wreathed in glee. He edged his chair so that he no longer faced them. I don't feel very upright, he said.

He took out his case but, choosing a cigarette, he saw the calluses on his hands. Cuticle: such a dainty word for shredded skin, blisters. Hello, dear, have we been picking oakum lately? He felt his hands retreat up their sleeves.

– A course of manicure, suggested Scrotes.

– And the earth returns to its orbit.

The strains of the band carried through the garden doors. MacMurrough read the programme. *In tribute to our new and glorious allies, an admired selection of Italian overtures.* At the bottom, it informed, *The members of this band have been exempted from Military Service.* He saw now that the saloon and terraces were dotted with khaki.

One of these khakis, a young lieutenant, was shown to the table opposite. He nodded to MacMurrough, who nodded back. Blond mop atop a gentle high-coloured face. Tennis sort of build. He caught MacMurrough watching and smiled, playing with his swagger-stick on the table. MacMurrough raised an eyebrow in return. Barely out of school. Cadet corps and third fifteen. Would let you fuck but really he preferred to hold hands.

Which brought MacMurrough to old Brother Benedict. That last day they walked through the school cloisters while the other boys were at chapel. No alternative, immodest acts, influence on others, disappointment we all felt, shame your mother must feel, under the circumstances, consideration given to father's position, your mother has begged, one last chance, if truly repentant, bright future ahead, knuckle down, I'm afraid not possible. *Deo optimo maximo. Datur omnibus mori.*

– Can't help wondering if they get much, he said to Scrotes. Officers, I mean. Get to choose your batman. Clean hands and eager-to-please nature. Be like setting up house. Pull me off, Atkins, I'm feeling wotten weawy.

– I am happy to find you relax somewhat.

MacMurrough laughed and lit a cigarette, careless at last of his hands. You know, he said, I had a friend who was set to marry but they were in some terrible train disaster. He found himself in a hospital and the nurse told him his intended had died. He was devastated, of course, but devastated the more to find he was attracted to the nurse. Every time she passed he went stiff under the sheets. But dicks are like that. Callous they may be, but they never lie. He was alive. He had survived. His dick told him.

The girl came with the buns and tea. 'Will there be anything else, sir?'

'No, that's all.'

'I hope and you enjoy your holidays.'

'Yes,' said MacMurrough.

'Oh let me do that and your poor hands and all.' She poured the tea. 'Is it home from the Front you are? Don't mind me asking, sir, only I have a man in Flanders. Sure it's never as bad as they say, sure it isn't, sir?'

MacMurrough eyed the empty chair beside as if Scrotes might actually be found there. 'No,' he answered. 'It's never so bad as they say.'

'Thank you, sir,' and she bobbed away.

– Worst of it is I should be an officer now. I mean, all one's contemporaries are.

– You might still volunteer.

– You think they'd have me?

– One suspects the authorities have grown less particular of late.

– Well I haven't. What do I care about this war? Whoever the victor, they'll still despise me.

– It is not their despising that concerns us. It is your own.

– Why this harping on my despising myself, Scrotes? It really is tiresome in you.

– My friend, we wish to be rid of something. How to be rid without finding it first?

MacMurrough pushed the tepid tea aside. He left a tip for the ladlorn waitress. I give without loss as I buy without gain.

He walked afterwards along the pier where another band was playing, a military band this time, and listened a while until the recruiting-sergeants grew too insistent. Then he passed through a gap in the wall to the seaward side, where the wind hit with the blast of guns. There were slum children on a Sunshine Trip clambering over the rocks and MacMurrough watched their ragged antics and listened to their bootless cries. At the pier's end he waited within the spray of the waves as the mailboat came in. It recalled his own arrivals here as a child and the expectation that rose when his father changed his watch to Irish time.

– You know, I used to enjoy those holidays at Aunt Eva's. As a boy, I mean. It was always a friendly, idle sort of house. She used to tease my father for sliding into an Englishman, and to prove her wrong he would take punch and sing songs into the night. The children were let run free. It's odd, considering the interminable political plight, but Ireland for me has always signified freedom. A lazy freedom which you don't really know what to do with.

– What did your mother make of the place?

– She, being English, put up and smiled. Aunt Eva terrified her. One begins to see why now.

– Does she terrify you?

– All this rot about flutes and fêtes. It's absurd, but I mayn't deny it's tempting, too. To see society return. Once more to dine at a club. Unghost my father with posterity till again he shines on his son. It's terrifying to be tempted into happiness.

   – Do you not wish for happiness?

   – I don't wish always to hope knowing there can be none. Even Aunt Eva cannot scratch time.

The mailboat had entered between the piers and he saw the passengers crowding the decks. He saw the excited face of a boy with his father beside who pointed out the places. The boy gulped the air, gulping in the sights and sounds, electrified by the strangeness and the strange familiarity. Holidays, that unbelievable future, had arrived.

Yes, he had enjoyed those holidays at Aunt Eva's. Enjoyed them and mostly forgotten them. Until out of the blue his aunt wrote him in Wandsworth Gaol.

   – I remember, said Scrotes. You wept when they showed the envelope.

   – Did I cry? I'm not sure.

   – You wept. They were induced to call the chaplain.

   – Her green notepaper and the Irish postmark in my cell. It was like all of Ballygihen spilt out of it. There was the boy with his glass jar and his collecting-net and the waves washing as he played on the sea-wall. I felt he stopped suddenly and a recognition came over his face which turned to horror when he met my eyes. I think for the first time I felt – I realized the enormity of what had happened in my life.

   – What did you feel?

   – You know what I felt.

   – Say it.

   – I don't need to.

   – You do.

   – Disgust. I despised myself.

He felt Scrotes's hand in his pocket and his handkerchief

unfolded before him. So brilliantly washed and ironed, the cloth seemed a thousand miles away.

– It really isn't fair, you know. If it weren't for this rotten war I might have gone to France or Italy where you're supposed to go when they find you out. What on earth brought me to Ireland? What on earth am I to do here?

– There there, said Nanny Tremble, but it wasn't Nanny Tremble, it was Scrotes, who only said, We shall see.

The washerwoman was coming down the garden when he returned to Ballygihen. Her feet were the colour of boots and her shawl was black, but her skirt beneath showed a rich red which surprised, though he could not say why. The infant that snuggled inside her shawl seemed too large to be carried. Its wide unwondering eyes hinted at simplicity. She had her wicker load as usual on her head. How could a burden lend such poise, he wondered, for she appeared to glide along, as though the dirt on her feet were one with the grass. Her face was stern, probably older than her years. She was singing, but only when she passed did he catch words from her song.

MacMurrough shut his eyes. Her song was of a swan on a lake but her singing held the sadness of Ireland, the lost lonely wastes of sadness. He saw the black water and the declining sun and the swan dipping down, its white wings flashing, and slowing and slowing till silver ripples carried it home. It was a scene which seemed the heart of this land. The lowing sun and the one star waking, white wings on a black water, and the smell of rain, and the long lane fading where a voice comes in the falling night.

– Ireland, said Scrotes.

– Yes, this is Ireland.

CHAPTER NINE

THROUGH THE HALF-DOOR of the cabin the sun came and tickled his face. It dazzled his eyes when they opened. There was a scent on the air that called him to Clare, to Coney Island with his mother's people. Chickens clucked in the lane and the milk cow lowed for her milking. In a shake he was up and sitting, listening for his uncle and the surly stamp of the ass.

The pallet was strange. A motor honked, sounding nothing like the geese that honked on the Fergus. Nothing like the tide's rush were the rasps that came from the shadows. A Dublin-bound tramp blew in the bay, lonely and cow-like and wanting.

He was home, but not on the island. Down the Banks, down in Glasthule. Yet something in the air had called him to Clare.

He rubbed the seeds from his eyes and sights and sounds adjusted. Torn loaf on the butter-box. Himself's suit in a crumple on the floor. He looked to the bed where came the rasping breath. The mouth hung open and fingers picked at the bedding. No sign of the ma, and Missy gone too. Where would she be so up and early?

The girls all were sleeping still on their shakedown in the corner. Like the leaves of a cabbage they lay, each leaf enfolding the next one down. Eleven, nine, seven, five: the same face told in tripping years. Red hair same like himself in the bed. Another had come and gone while he was away in Clare, and it disturbed him now that he could not recall her name. What name had they gave her, the little one with the tiny stone above in Deansgrange? He could not recall and it ailed him so to disremember.

Turf, that was it. Ship-coal had grown too costly in the war and now they were burning turf in Glasthule. He wondered how he didn't notice it before. The whiff alone would heat you.

Burn everything English excepting their coal. Well, it was partly coming true.

He raked the fire that had a glow in the ashes yet. Then he pulled on his trousers and took the kettle to fill it. He felt in turns the dusty warm and shadowy cold as he padded between the cottages. All was still save a scrawny old bantam that pecked in the gutter. No birds, for they had no trees for birds to sing from, but he caught the hum of a woman's voice, and coming to the yard where the pump stood he found his ma with her tub beside her, hushoing to Missy while she worked.

'Well, son.'

It was like she knew him from his shadow or the fall of his feet, for she did not look up to greet him, only kept at her work. It made him smile that she took such pains with her scrubbing, for it was form's sake really. The stains she shifted with the hard of her stare.

'Is breagh an maidin é.'

Now she turned, humoured by his Irish. ''Tis a fine morning all right, son, God's blessing on the day.'

'Give us here little Missy,' he said. The shawl unwound and he took the bundle in his arms. 'What way is she today?'

'Bright as the morning, thanks be to God.'

The fingers stretched and there was trouble in the eyes that only settled when the shawl was about her again. He too could smell his mother in the wool. 'Did I tell you I can get milk for her, Ma?' he said. 'I know a place sells Peamount milk.'

'Did you hear that, Missy? Your brother will get you milk. Isn't he the fine and able man to be getting you milk, now?'

'Peamount milk is best. They do keep out the microbes at Peamount.'

The dirty water rinsed in the tub. 'She has her plenty of milk, son.'

He chucked his head. She'd rarely admit any help, his ma. He humped the child in his arms, surprised at the weight. 'All the same, she's a deal heavy to be carrying. Wouldn't you think to have one of the shrimpses mind her?'

'The girls has their schooling.'

She was searching the sheet for any patch of dirt remaining. He fetched the pump for her, one-handed, and said, 'I was working at their age.'

'And did I ask you did?' There, she'd found a stain. The soda sprinkled and her scrubbing began over. 'Age eight, could neither lead nor drive you. Age twelve, there was no talking.'

'Age twelve, I was walking the road to Clare.'

He had spoken softly, not wishing her to hear, but unable to leave the words unsaid. She looked up from the washboard.

'Not on your own, son. Not a fall of your foot but my prayer was under it. I had the stones on the road counted each night for you.'

He frowned, avoiding her face. He could see her all right, in the cabin at night, with the shrimpses about her and her fingers numbering her beads in the dark. It was a long road that had no blessing to begin it. It was a long road to Clare all right, and him with a limp like Baccoch the Shooler.

He humped the child again. Already the wisps of hair were colouring. Red, to be sure. He saw the blue veins in the nose that had the neighbours whispering in corners. God love her for an angel, they shook their heads and said. Has she come to stay at all?

'She's quiet to the world, Ma. Has she no words yet?'

'What words would she want?'

'I could bring her to the dispensary.'

'We have no call on the dispensary.'

'I can get money for a doctor. I know to get money for a half-crown doctor.'

'Listen with me, son. Your sister is grand. She's slow only. Why wouldn't your sister be slow? She has all God's time.'

He felt the wide infant eyes upon him. Slow eyes that only his worry would trouble. His mother rinsed her sheet and left it on the washing-stone. Already the stone gleamed with whites. Before she would pour out the dirty tub, she muttered under her breath, 'Beware the water.' It was a caution to the good people. The way the good people had followed from Clare to dance in the Banks about her daily.

'What has you up so bright?'

'I heard the cock-crow and I thought to take the morning's breath.'

'Aye did you. And you tripped over some washing on the way. Whose is it?'

'Out of the houses over. Only the linens, but there's plenty that.'

'Have they no copper at all?'

'They have an old monster in a shed all right, would have you shaking to fire it.'

He grinned. His mother would never use hot water if there was cold to be had first. 'They have their share of sheets at any rate.'

'There's every chance it wasn't sheets you had in Clare.'

'Never in life. It was the hay below and a sack above and the pet pig to keep me cosy.'

'I had the pet boneen myself, I remember it.'

He bit his lip. 'Ah no, Ma, I wanted to come home. I missed you, I did. I want to change things now. Change things for the better like.'

She said nothing, only concentrated on her work. But her face had softened and she was looking at them like she'd find them lovely, these strangers' sheets.

'Why do you smile, Ma? I only mean the best for us.'

'And what would prevent me? Isn't it my son here, the strong able boy would carry the world? And all the woes of the world would not be too many for him. It's God's morning to be smiling.'

He chucked his head. He didn't mind her getting a pull of his leg. He was home then and sure of it. He felt a tug on his buttons. The tiny fingers had reached inside his shirt. 'Lookat, Ma, she's found me medal.'

'She likes her handsome brother.'

'Am I handsome?'

''Tis the handsome man and him with a child. I did always think that.'

'Was I ever this little, Ma?'

'A fine thing and you was not.'

'But do you remember when I was little?'

'I do surely.' She turned from the tub. 'Is there something troubling you, son?'

'Nothing, Ma. Was wondering only.'

'Let me look on you.' He stood up straight for her scrutiny and the sun met his eyes so that he squinted in its shine. There was an awkwardness he felt before his mother, and though he never intended it, he heard his speech come stilted at times, the way he would ape the men of the island with their slow and considered words. And the way he stood, too, like the men of the island when they poled their boats to the jetty – though all the world heaved, they alone stood firm. He would put her in mind of those island men, the men of her girlhood, but that distance was between them, his mother and himself: the road to Clare and the hard words of his taking it.

Now she said, 'My black-headed black-eyed boy. I remember every day of you. How would I forget?' She wiped her hands on her smock, greying the white with prints of wet. 'Give Missy here to me now and let you get on with your day.' She crooked her elbow and the bundle fell home. In God's pocket, they called that, snug inside of the shawl.

He said, 'You was hurt me leaving.'

'I wasn't laughing,' she told him.

The water sloshed and the washboard jolted. Only her arm was steady where Missy slept. He scratched his head, wishing now if he'd taken a rake to his hair. 'What choice did I have?' he said. 'It was all I could do to go to Clare.'

'It wasn't you going to Clare upset me but the way you went at it. I was proud of your scholarship and so was himself.'

'Aye was he proud. And if he was, it was mighty curious pride.'

'That was his way, as well you knew. We would have the money been found but there was no waiting with you. You were away off without a look behind. You had the face of your father that day.'

Which father is that? He didn't ask but he knew she read the question in his eyes.

'Wisha, you're back now. For a time whatever.'

'For good, Ma.'

'For good or ill. Not but it's done you well, I can see that,

216

your stay away. But you weren't sent, son. Don't say you was sent.' She withdrew from the pump. 'Let you have your wash now. The houses are rising and I have my load to finish.'

He took the handle and worked it hard, punishing his muscles. The water drew and still he pumped. 'You know, Ma, I woke up thinking I was back on the island.'

'And did that take the temper off you?'

'Which temper is that?'

'You was murdering rough on himself last night. I heard him begging of you to hang his coat for him.'

'He was drunk at it. If you seen him in the street.'

'He's outgrown his strength. But he's no stranger yet.'

He splashed water on his face and shaking the wet from his hands he said, 'You know what he says, don't you, Ma? When he's away on the tear with his butties. He says he saved you out of the workhouse. An opportunity wouldn't pass but he gets in that cut. And he has worse than that to say.'

'I know what he says.'

'And do you mind him?'

'Sinn féin,' she said, 'sinn féin anseo.'

Her wish for peace had her resort to her Irish. We're ourselves here: no quarrels. 'Do you know, Ma, you're the true Sinn Feiner. The right patriot for peace, you are.'

She cocked her head at his humour. 'In with you and shift your shirt. Leave that one out for me to wash it.'

'Ah, Ma, I've no call to be wearing a clean shirt to work. It doesn't last two minutes on me.'

'You might take a leaf from himself inside. While you have it to wear, be thankful of a clean cloth to your back.'

'Have it to pawn is better.'

'Son –'

'Aye?'

'Come back to me now.' He came back and she said, 'Don't be bitter, son. There's bitterness enough in the world.' She touched his chin as she spoke. The hard of her face was in the soda of her fingers. 'I'll be in to fix your bite to eat.'

'Ah no, Ma. Sure you have the seven cares of the mountain with them sheets. You'll share a sup of tea?'

'Don't wake himself.'

'Why would I do that?' He made tea and brought out two jars of it. He hunched beside her with a heel of a loaf that he dipped inside. 'What house is it at all needs all them sheets?'

'Ballygihen House it is. Up Sandycove way.'

'Ballygihen?'

'They have any number of help and still they wouldn't cope.'

'Not MacMurrough is it?'

'Miss MacMurrough,' she answered. 'Spinster of the parish.'

In a confused way he watched the sheet she was scrubbing.

'The slavey says 'tis a nephew from England they have staying and he's the jack and all for clean sheets. Please God, he'll stay a while yet. 'Tis the dirty linen of them above us will keep us body and soul together.'

'Ma, let me do that.'

'Away now. Haven't you your swimming?'

'No, ma, I'll do them sheets.'

He had his hand out and was tugging at the washboard till she let go and said, 'What ails you, son? You look on me like I was the washer at the ford itself. Is it something you have to tell me?'

'I don't know if it is, Ma.' Missy was watching him. The eyes looked suddenly knowing, wide-awake and gauging him. 'You know me flute, Ma?'

'I do.'

'Did you never worry where the money came to get it back out of Ducie's?'

'I did wonder. Was I better to worry?'

'I didn't steal it.'

'I know you wouldn't steal it.'

'Honest I didn't.'

'Tell me what's troubling you.'

'I can't, Ma.'

She shook her head. He saw the white of the sheet and the grey splashes on her smock and he thought of the washer at the ford that when you passed she held up her washing and it was your shroud she held with the marks of your sins upon it. The grey washer at the ford.

'I know my son and whatever it is troubles him he won't stray far.'

'Do you know that for sure, Ma?'

'Aren't you my black-headed boy? I know it well.'

He nodded at his mother. He tightly bit his lips and nodded.

That morning he brushed himself's shoes and the two pair boots his sisters shared, and he even brushed his own that his ma wouldn't be ashamed of him leaving. He dusted down himself's suit and hung it on the wall. The eldest girl was awake and he gave her money to fetch things for breakfast. She looked at the sixpence and said, 'Danny, will you be bringing the flute with you tonight? It was great when you used play for us.'

'Go on to the shop. And get some relish for your da.'

'But the flute, Danny?'

'Do your schoolwork and I'll play for you. That's the deal.'

'You'll help me, so?'

'Get on out of that and I'll see. And mind them boots.'

On his way to the lane he stopped a moment to watch his

mother in the yard. The half-doors were open in the cottages and the caged birds sang from the windows. His mother cronawned to Missy – shoheen lo is shoheen la-lo – while the child dozed and the stains washed away.

Then he came by the sea-wall to the Forty Foot and the worried narrow face was waiting for him there.

'Thought something might have happened.'

'Not at all,' said Doyler. He clapped his arm on the elfin shoulder. 'Pal o' me heart,' he said.

'Muglins,' said Doyler. He tossed his head backward out to sea. 'Did you ever hear tell of the patriots Gidley and MacKinley?'

'I didn't,' said Jim lazily, for the raft was warm to the skin and it was pleasant to stretch on your belly while the boards pitched amiably in the swell.

'They was on a ship out of Spain that was bound for Ireland, carrying armament and store, what have you. This was way in the penal days. The captain took fright or turned traitor. I don't know which, but he turned the ship for England. Well, the bold Gidley and MacKinley was having none of that. They knocked him on the head, the captain, and they set their sails for Waterford. I don't know but there was a storm and they was tossed up near Duncannon. The British took them and strung them up in St Stephen's Green. It was there they was left to rot, save the good citizens of Dublin what took their promenade in the Green found the sight disagreeable. So the poor bodies was taken out in boats and chained beyond on the Muglins. People said there would be howls heard in storms and big weather off the ghosts that rattled in their chains. Howls that called on Irishmen for vengeance on their murder.'

Jim squinted at the spill of rocks. He had a foreboding of his dreams that night. 'Penal times?' he said.

'Long while ago, right enough. But do you know what it is? When we swim out there we'll bring us a flag to raise. We'll raise the Green and claim the Muglins for Ireland. Then finally the ghosts of Gidley and MacKinley, bold patriots them both, will go to rest.'

'How'll we carry a flag?' asked Jim.

'Mary and Joseph, but you're the practical fellow. I'll string it round me neck, will that do for you?' He slipped into the water. 'Ready for the back?'

'Ready enough.'

'You want to try a kick in your legs this time.'

To this Jim did object. 'Sure you never kick.'

'See me kicking and 'tis round in circles I go. But give a kick yourself. Don't break the surface, mind. You'll find you get the pull of a push off it. Are we straight so? Great guns you're going.'

And Jim was back inside the water, where his thoughts tumbled in the spill.

He had feared he might grow used to the mornings, but over the weeks the adventure had not diminished. First thing on waking, he moved the blind to test the sky. Not that it made any difference what weather it was. A spat handshake was copper-bottomed. He had told his father that and his father had to agree. 'Though 'tis a shame you wouldn't ask at home before entering into commitments.' All the same it was better if the day promised bright. Better on the raft or after their swim when they would dry in the sun; for swimming it made no difference. The sea was a freezer, rain or shine.

He skipped breakfast for fear of the cramps, only he brought bread to share afterwards. Jitter bread, Doyler called it, for it stopped the teeth from chattering. Doyler would fetch an onion out of his pocket that he rubbed along the surface. 'There's relish for you.'

Jim was always early at the Forty Foot and he waited outside the entrance whilst the regulars came past. The regulars were all sorts, Protestant and Catholic, clerks and clerics, all kinds of accents you'd hear. At first he tried to look inconspicuous, like he hadn't a friend to be waiting for, and if a friend arrived it was only the off-chance they thought to go swimming. But these men soon grew accustomed to him. 'Begod 'tis fresh this morning,' they'd say coming out. It surprised him how open they were, that they wouldn't mind him intruding on their spot. 'He's behind himself this morning – no, speak of the devil, hopping along the front there.' A cheery wave the regulars would give and Doyler waved in return. 'Sure we're regulars ourself now,' he said.

And down they'd descend the winders into the gentlemen's bathing-place, still raw and long-shadowed. A quick strip and a mad dash to the water. That instant before he jumped when he did not quite believe he would dare. Water up his nose, sensation close to nausea, and the swell all round, till he rose with his bubbles to the surface. The crazy wafting horizons, the floundering rocks. That marbly numbness below and the way his thing floated free, near alive in the water. It was special to swim naked. The way nature intended, so Doyler claimed. Nobody minded at the Forty Foot, though in the day you was supposed to wear costumes. Then off to the raft and Doyler saying, Great guns you're going, as beside and a little behind his smooth and inconsistent form made its kickless stroke.

Jim's father had changed his mind about Doyler. Doyler wasn't a bad hat after all. Doyler was a bit of a black diamond in fact. 'You might stick in with that one. The new father has a great wish for him. See if you can't pick up any of the

Erse while you're at it. Mighty fond of his dee gits is our new father.'

Father O'Táighléir seemed everywhere at once. If he wasn't opening a new class he was raising subscriptions for one. He had the Gaelic League in the parish hall, and Miss Biggs the newsagent, though a notorious Orangewoman, did a power of trade in the thin little O'Growney primers. To the envy of Jim's father, who searched his head for something Irish a general stores might sell. Language classes, singing-classes, dancing-classes (no skipping, no battering, girls Friday, boys Saturday). The curate had his eye on a plot of the Castlepark Fields where hurling and Gaelic football would be played. In the meantime collections were made for jerseys and boots, hurleys and balls. In the court outside the parish church he had the Irish Volunteers out of Dalkey parade, and they marched up and down each Sunday after Men's Mass. His influence pervaded where his presence could not. The Protestants grew less assured of their ascendancy and the Union flag on their churches and schools flew rather in defiance than in dominion. The Salvation Army hall was window-boarded and silent. More and more the recruitment posters were torn.

Band practice was now three evenings a week, held in a summerhouse in Madame MacMurrough's garden. Her nephew took them, but he was a reserved man, had rarely anything to say. It was clear he was under the eye of the priest or his aunt. Reserved, but not unkind. He would smile at times and the injured look depart his face. Once or twice, if the priest or his aunt was called away, he entertained them with his own flute. This was a grander instrument altogether, no finger-holes at all but keys all down the side and along the top, and the sound was grander too, sweetly so, that made the boys' music rough and unready in compare. His eyebrows would sometimes lift in Doyler's direction. Jim understood an intelligence passed between them. He was a little green of this friendship, but he was a little glad too. He seemed a lonely man to Jim, and a way sad.

Those boys who were not thought likely enough at the flute were given drums to bang instead. So now they were a flute and drum band that Jim's father drilled after practice.

Doyler thought it hilarious and it was funny, Jim supposed, in the usual way with his father. They paraded as instructed, two rows of boys on Madame MacMurrough's lawn: heels in a line, touching, feet turned out to a V; knees straight but not stiff; body erect but inclining a touch; shoulders square; arms hanging what his father called natural: elbows in, palms turned a little to the front, little finger resting on the side pleat of the kilt. Up and down his father paced, correcting each boy's stance. Then would come the words of command.

'Young piggy heart!'

And of course they would fall out in sniggles of laughter. The priest had insisted the commands should be gave in Gaelic and his poor father could never get his tongue round the alien sounds. Quick march came out: Gum on my shawl! Right turn was: Arrest young piggy! Shower of gigglers, his father complained. Jack-acting and jig-acting in the ranks. But if he called a boy out, he must call him at the double, and that dread command off his father's tongue was: Erse sodder! And his father's tongue would taste his moustache in puzzlement at the scurrility it spoke.

But little by little progress came and they learnt to slope, port and shoulder their flutes. Up and down Glenageary they marched, sometimes fluting, moretimes with their flutes like toy rifles to their shoulders. His father marched in front, twirling his cane. In his Sunday suit and bowler hat he looked the picture of an Orangeman on parade. Save the sash he wore was green.

Their first public showing was the second Sunday in June,

a high day in the patriotic calendar, for it marked the annual commemoration at the grave of Wolfe Tone. The evening before, Father O'Táighléir gave a lesson on Tone and the United Irishmen, that was the fraternity he set up. He told of his noble ideals and how the tale that he destroyed himself was a scandal put about by the English. He warned the boys it was a Protestant grave they would be visiting, in the grounds of a Protestant church; but that, though born a heretic, Tone had served for many years as secretary to the Catholic Committee. It was too late now to prove or disprove them, but rumours persisted of his deathbed conversion. The boys were at liberty to believe as they chose; for his part the father knew where he stood and where stood every true-hearted Irishman. With a nod then to Madame MacMurrough, he spoke of the '98, of the boys of Wexford and their heroic stand, how their priests had led them, how the yeomanry hunted them, till the last lad with his harp on his shoulder was butchered while he knelt to pray.

Doyler was well pleased. 'What cheer, eh?' he said after the talk. Which meant Tone was all right. Wolfe Tone was some way pro the working man. 'Are you straight?'

'Straight as a rush,' Jim answered automatically.

'No, you gaum. I mean that's where it comes from. It was their test for to join. Are you straight, they asked. I am, says you. How straight so? Straight as a rush. Go on then, says they. In truth, in trust, in unity and liberty, says you. That was the United Irishmen. Don't mind that priest what he said about Tone. That priest would have them all voteens did nothing but count their beads. Wolfe Tone was a free-thinking man.'

'Is it true he did destroy himself?'

'They had the gallows built outside of his cell. What hope would he have? He cheated the English of their show. He brung the French, so he did. But the French was too late coming. Too late for the boys of Wexford.'

The boys of Wexford, the croppy boys. Dimly Jim saw them from out their cabins creep. It's the dark before the moon's rise and their eyes are wide and faces narrow. In the smoky light of spits and fangles, new-forged pikes give a steely glow. It's the cleanest sight they might ever have seen, these creeping crop-haired boys. The black-frocked priest leaps up on the rock. Arm, arm! he cries, I've come to lead you! By heart and hand they will fight for Ireland and by morning they have the militia beat. Wexford falls, Enniscorthy falls, only New Ross bars the way. But the drink is their downfall. The crazy fiddle and the lawless dancing, wretched whiskey and looted wine. Through Protestant blood they wade for a last stand at Vinegar Hill. Death comes merciful with a yeoman's blade or blazes with pitch upon their heads, made candles of by the English. The ruction, the ignorant had called it, meaning insurrection. Another word, like bother and boycott, given the English language.

'Do you know what it is?' said Doyler. 'When we come to Bodenstown we'll lie down on his grave.'

'Why'll we do that?'

'Don't you know the song?

'I lay on the sod that lies over Wolfe Tone

And thought how he perished in prison alone.

'It's traditional, lying on his grave. That's what you do sure.'

Jim shrugged. He didn't suppose he very much minded lying on a grave. 'I thought it was something your own,' he said. 'Are you straight, I mean.'

'Well, 'tis ours now. For you and me,' and his arm came over Jim's shoulder, 'aren't we straight as a rush together?'

The Sunday, then, they piled into a charabanc that took them to Bodenstown, over the hills in County Kildare. It was a bleary day with a drizzle falling. They waited their time in a pasture field, under the watch of cows, while the grass soaked into their boots. The different bands tuned their instruments – peeping, brattling, droning, thudding – all flat in the sodden air. Everything sagged, banners and flags, their flapping kilts, the boughs of the trees. In a rainy way the fields foretold the bogs, and Jim thought of the vast Bog of Allen over the horizon and he felt it for a sinking thing in the heart of the land.

Their time came and they marched past a wall, without ever a sight of a grave, letting out 'A Nation Once Again', till they halted at the tail of the assembly. A man was set to give a speech from a steps. A tall man with a pale face. He was dressed in the smart green of an Irish Volunteer. 'We have come,' he said, 'to the holiest place in the land.' And if it is holy, thought Jim, it's the damp miserable holiness of Ireland.

Yet the man had a pleasing way of talking, with none of the preachment of Father O'Táighléir. He spoke the way he had known Wolfe Tone for a friend. His brother in blood, he called him. He said they were none of them strangers here, if they loved Wolfe Tone. And in spite of himself Jim found he strained to catch more.

The soldier-speaker spoke of Tone, of his vision and his spirit, of his love for the common people. He was saying things out of history books, but still he made it sound like it was his friend he was talking of. His friend had been a great man; he had died for his love of Ireland: they stood now at his grave. That must be hard, Jim thought, to be talking at the graveside of your friend. Death, it was a dark and empty falling when Jim thought of it, before the thought had blinked away. Such is the destiny of heroes, the man said in his slow and melodious way – to follow the far, faint call that leads to battle or the gallows tree.

Was it the wind in the grass or the whirring rain, but Jim heard it somewhere, the whisper of a flute.

Slow and affecting, the soldier-speaker went on. Did ever a man, he asked, have more of heroic stuff in him than Wolfe Tone? Did ever a man go more gaily and gallantly about a great deed? Did ever a man love so well? Was ever a man so beloved? 'For myself,' he said, speaking slow and a little shyly, 'I would rather have known Wolfe Tone than any man of whom I have ever heard or ever read.'

Jim knew this man's heart was deep and true, for he made Jim wish for an equal love and an equal truth in his heart. He was swept by a great desire to take hold Doyler's hand and tell him in his ear, That's how I think of you, that's exactly how I think of you.

Jim sensed the crowd was edging forward. He was conscious of a fellowship growing with those about him, with the boys in kilts and the men in suits and uniforms, some with rifles and swords, and the stockinged girls and women under their umbrellas. The drizzle had lightened a touch. Away on a hillside the sun was seeking a path through the clouds. Its shaft was like a beam from heaven, like God searched his creation. And Jim thought, if that light should find them here, what wouldn't the gaze of God dispose?

Slow the soldier-speaker continued, slow and now suddenly stirring. For war at last has come and Tone is on the sea. The French fleet ploughs the waves. A shift in the drizzle – there is no rain but ocean spray – and Jim is there too. With Tone he stands at the prow of the ship. Beyond lies the beloved land. They come so close, they can see the houses and the people on the shore. They could toss a biscuit. But the coward French fear to land. Jim turns to Wolfe Tone. So proud his face, and generous. A tear falls on his cheek. His eyes are strangely bright and black.

Now swoop the English, a fleet entire upon Tone's one ship. How slow and proud he spoke of his friend, this soldier-speaker who stood by his grave. Six hours the battle rages. What a glorious six hours for Tone! And Jim is there, too. The fire of battle is on his face. A wish of ferocious courage charges his heart. Oh, who would not follow Wolfe Tone to the grave? Oh, who would not love Wolfe Tone?

Slow and determined the soldier-speaker closed his tale. A battered hulk, the vessel strikes. The French are fêted while Tone, that spirit, that ardent flame, the English drag in chains to Dublin, there to be condemned to a traitor's death. Jim feels his pulse is racing. His glands are hurting with the choke of emotion. This is wrong. This is not fair. What is it with the English? Did ever a nation hate liberty more?

The soldier-speaker paused. Straight and austere he stood, a man very far apart in that crowd. It crossed Jim's mind how awful it would be in any way to disappoint this man. When he resumed, his voice had a fiercer strength. Men come to a graveside to pray, he told them, and each of us prays here in his heart. But we do not pray for Tone. Men who die to free their people have no need of prayer. We pray for Ireland that she may be free. We pray for ourselves that we may free her.

A moment – then all of a glow the sun is on Jim's face. He looks up where the clouds have parted. The sun shines and bathes the world, and the land trembles at the touch. How green are the fields, how lush the grass. Each blade of grass glistens, and the leaves of the trees and hedges glisten with a silvery light all their own. The crows above cease their mockery. The fat contented cows look up in wonder. How rich is this land. It is a rich and a rare land. Why wouldn't it be rare, fed on the martyred dead? And who could doubt but this place is holy? Aren't the bones of Tone interred below?

Will we pledge ourselves? asked the soldier-speaker. But of course they would pledge, how could he doubt them? Pledge themselves to follow in the steps of Tone,

Never to rest, by day or by night,
Deeming it the proudest of privileges
To fight for freedom,
To fight, not in despondency, but in great joy,
Never lowering our ideal,
Never bartering one jot or title of our birthright,
Holding faith to the memory and inspiration of Tone,
And accounting ourselves base
As long as we endure
The evil thing against which he testified
With His Blood?

What is that evil thing? That evil thing is the English in Ireland!

We will! they roared. The kilted boys, and youths and men in suits and soldier green, even the women under their umbrellas and the white-frocked black-stockinged girls. Round after round they cheered and Jim, too, roared with the full of his lungs. Save, looking round, he saw that few stirred, that few cheered. Were they deaf? Were they stunned? Like herded beasts they waited. Till he understood he too was stunned, and it was his blood pounding, not his throat roaring, that clamoured his ears.

He turned to find Doyler. Doyler was behind, looking away. Following his gaze, Jim saw a straggle of men arrayed by a hedge. Their green was duller than the smart Volunteers, and their cloth had a cheapness about it. Working men that even in a uniform looked jumbled together. A Red Hand badge was pinned to their hats.

'Citizen Army,' said Doyler. He was whispering in Jim's ear. 'The Citizen Army is here.'

Jim's father had not attended that day, and it was strange listening to his cheerful chatter at supper that evening. He had a vocabulary all his own. The insurgents of '98 were not the Croppy Boys or the brave United Men, but he called them Babes in the Wood. And the cruel militia and crueller yeomanry were Blaney's Bloodhounds. 'The 89th Foot as became, Royal Irish Fusiliers, 2nd Battalion, as is. The Rollickers they calls themself. Fierce fellows altogether. Though not to be confused with the 1st Battalion, for them is the Faugh-a-Ballagh boys. The Old Fogs. Faugh a ballagh! Clear the way! There's Ersc for you. Bird-catchers, on account they took the French eagle down the Peninsular Wars.'

Jim couldn't tell were his father's loyalties shifting or if he saw at all the direction the band was heading. His sentiments, to all seeming, remained the same. His old regiment first and foremost, then any of the Irish regiments, then the generals who won the Boer War for the British – Roberts, French, Kitchener, Kelly-Kenny and Mahon – 'not a one but he was an Irishman.'

Only Aunt Sawney was steadfast. Saturday afternoons when the Irish Volunteers marched by, she was quick sticks out the door, waving her ashplant and lashing her tongue, scourging them to hell and back for idle Fenians. And when Father O'Táighléir chanced by one time, collecting for the Chinese missions, he said, 'A word missus,' and was off explaining how the Volunteers were decent honest Catholic sons of Ireland and of the Church, whose leaders in the tradition of this sainted isle were poets as much as gentlemen.

'No, Father,' Aunt Sawney corrected him. 'Them is the Fenians. Idle blaspheming rebels is all. The canon was certain.'

But the canon was convalescing in Mayo. Jim's father had to dash out with a half-crown donation to the cause of buying Chinese children to convert them to the Cross.

'And ye,' Aunt Sawney blasted him afterwards, 'ye'd sell your soul for the twopenny-door.'

And maybe that was the truth of it. For his father had been given the tuppenny collections at chapel on Sunday. 'A responsible position,' he maintained, 'in charge of the parish comings-in.' He had been enrolled in a respectable sodality; was a member now of the Mary Immaculate Traders' Guild of Glasthule. 'Only last week Phillips ironmongers stopped me in the street, asked my opinion of the Corpus Christi. Sure the up isn't up enough for us now. The Macks is on the ascent.'

The great event to which all energies were directed was the Glasthule Feis, due to be held the last Saturday in July at Ballygihen House. Tamasha, his father called it, rubbing his hands at the prospect. 'You know what's this we'll do, Jim? We'll fetch the old cart out of the yard, splash it over with a paint of green. How's this for a slogan? Saint Patrick spoke Erse! Shilling per guinea spent here will aid our kiddies to the same!'

When Jim would practise at home his father sometimes reached for the cutlery drawer and he'd rattle along on the spoons beside. Aunt Sawney would soon be banging her stick. The Rebels' Medley, she called it. For their repertoire now was wholly patriotic. 'Memory of the Dead', 'Wearing of the Green', 'Rising of the Moon', 'Boys of Wexford', and of course 'A Nation' not Once but a thousand times Again.

It was this last that occasioned his father's second misunder-standing with the Dublin Metropolitan Police.

*

He was still not very clever at seeing where he was swimming, but Jim knew by the slither of seaweed that he was coming into the Forty Foot cove. A last heave carried him to the steps. His arms were leaden coming out the water, he could scarce pull himself up. His mouth wouldn't close and his teeth chattered convulsively.

'Mary and Joseph, you're like an ape at his prayers. Round in the sun while I fetch the tats.'

Jim scooted off to the boys' end, where the sun was shining, while Doyler collected their clothes from the shelters. When he came over, he was whistling 'The Peeler and the Goat' in a low but taunting way. 'Visitors,' he said. 'Bevy of polis.'

Jim peeked round the battery wall, which already was warm from the sun. Burly men in shadowy blue disrobing. 'Come for a dip is all.'

'I wish if they'd dip to the bottom.' He held out Jim's towel. 'After you with the Baden-Powell.'

Jim rubbed himself roughly, then passed the towel back. He delayed a while, flapping uselessly in the breeze, before he pulled his shirt on. Even so the cloth glued to his back. Doyler had no shyness at all. He took great pains over every inch of his body, leg up on a rock, while each crevice between his toes was investigated, wiped, and investigated again. Jim liked to watch him then, when the morning light hazed about him, fuzzing with gold the hairs of his outline. Behind loomed the battery walls and beyond stretched the craggy rocks. It seemed a glorious place in the morning, an extraordinary grace to be allowed there, where man and nature mixed and lost each other, one in the other like the land in the sea.

Doyler's shirt was sewn and resewn that special military way Jim's father called sank-work and which all old soldiers must do for their sons. When he had it on, he hunched on the ledge with his knees pulled up and said, 'Have we breakfast or what?' And Jim fished out the bread and scrape from his jacket pocket.

There were new recruitment posters on the battery walls. Mother Erin, looking troubled and wan, wondered had they no womenfolk worth defending. Some wag was after adding Kitchener moustaches to her face. A dig at England or Ireland, you wouldn't know. Mackled mimeographed bills had been overpasted. *Get a gun and do your bit – Join the Irish Volunteers!*

'Get a gun, me arse,' said Doyler. 'Get a shagging prayer-book more like. Sure the Volunteers is in league with the priests and the priests is in league with the bosses and they're all agin the working man. No better than horneys is the Volunteers. They were agin us in the Lock-out and we'll never forget them that.'

Shin Feiners, Leaguers, Volunteers. They stood for Ireland, that much was clear, Ireland her own. Doyler was a socialist. Jim liked the way he pronounced the word, without the expected *sh* sound, but he still had only the muzziest idea what it stood for. Doyler himself was small help. His talk was names and slogans. Citizen Army. Liberty Hall. Nor King nor Kaiser.

A haze was rising and the sun strained to shine through. Over by Ringsend the towers smoked, needles in the sky that Jim's father once had told him were there to make the clouds. 'For without the clouds there'd be no rain, and without the rain there'd be no grass. And no milk in your tea without the green grass, so they has to be sure of the clouds.'

'I liked the man at the Wolfe Tone,' Jim said.

'Which man was that?'

'He gave the speech.'

'Aye aye,' said Doyler. 'I seen that look on your face. Good luck to any Saxon was there that day. You had pikes in your eye, so you did. Poetry, what?'

'Is that what he is, a poet?'

'How would I know? Quid to a bloater he don't be shovelling shit.'

He spat now, the same way he'd spat that day after they
snuck back in the churchyard looking for Wolfe Tone's grave.
A conspiracy against the common man, he'd called it then. For
there was no lying on that sod. It had all been railed in, top and
sides, with rusting iron bars. 'There's poetry for you,' he said to
Jim. 'They've made a prison of Wolfe Tone's grave.'

Doyler rubbed his bread with onion, then he lay on his belly
at the turn of the battery wall. He was watching the peelers
at their swim. 'Old breaststroke they're using,' he commented.
'The crawl is best for speed right enough. But the breast has its
uses. You're head up with the breast, can always see your way,
even when the water would be littered. Muck or wreckage, never
know what would be in the water. See the way them horneys
does the breast? Only way to swim if you're under a heavy pack
or you has your rifle you need to keep it dry. Soundless too if
it's sneaking up you want. Don't knock the breaststroke, for in
war it has its uses. Speed's not everything in war.'

'Who's talking about war?' said Jim.

A cock of disbelief in Doyler's face. 'Is there anyone who
isn't?' He dribbled a spit over the ledge, then turned from the
cove. 'You know why they calls this the Forty Foot?'

'Forty feet deep?'

'Not nearly. Twenty at most. Touched bottom once. Conger
was down there. Wouldn't see me for bubbles the way I scut out
of that.'

'Why's it called it so?'

'The Fortieth Foot regiment was stationed at the battery
once. They gave their number in the line to the best spot for
bathing in Dublin.'

It was the sort of thing Jim's father would tell. 'That all?'

'I'll tell you what all. We live in a country where nothing is named but for an occupying power. Look about you. Battery here, the Martello towers, all them castles in Dalkey. There's nothing lasts but was made for to subjugate the people. Even the cove we swim in is only a hole they left after blasting the granite for Kingstown piers. Kingstown named for an English king, the piers to bring his soldiers quick and safe. That bread's good.'

'Aunt Sawney bakes it.'

'She bakes good bread.' He sat up and glared at the policemen's bobbing heads. 'You'd wonder what manner of a country this is where nothing is safe but the paid hands of empire barge in and they fling your clothes to the floor.'

'The polis done that?'

'On the wet floor they flung them. Straight in me face. And me shirt only clean on. But sure why wouldn't they? Aren't they the polis? Aren't they paid to keep the working man down? It's them would make a cripple of you.'

He finished the bread and pulled his cap down on his eyes. 'Back to the old slog.' Then he laughed and in the usual shake the ape was off him. 'Would you look at the cut of you. Like a gurrier out of the Banks with your shirt to the wind. Come here till I see you straight.'

All of a heap, Jim was being bundled round and his collar adjusted and his tie reknotted too tight and his shirt-tail tucked in his waistband.

'Leave it off, Doyler, I'm all right.'

'How would you go home like that? Your da would have a fit. And I'm the one he'd blame. Doyler's the one would land on the mat.'

He spat on his hand and smarmed it on Jim's hair, saying, 'Gob-oil. If you knew me ma you'd know all about gob-oil, you would. All your share of hair ever needs is a spit of gob-oil on it.' He turned him round again. 'Let me look at you now. I suppose you'll pass muster.'

The grin went lop-sided. 'I never remarked the length of your nose. I might have really, for they say 'tis a sign of what's below.'

'Shut up, Doyler. You know that's not true.'

'A long nose is a lady's fancy.'

This was coarse talk, and with coarse talk you did not argue.

'Serious, though,' said Doyler, 'was you ever sweet on a girl?'

Jim realized he must have looked very blank, for Doyler in a laughing undertone bent to his ear and gave him to understand that girls were the ones without the lad below. He could think of no answer beyond, 'Was you?'

And Doyler answered, 'Can't say I was. Particular like.'

'I don't believe I know any girls,' said Jim. 'Saving Nancy out of MacMurrough's.'

He felt himself blushing and really he couldn't think why, because he didn't look on Nancy that way and it was wrong of Gordie when he said those things about her. Jam, he called her. And then he asked, was it Nancy he thought of when he did that thing to himself?

'I suppose, then, the time being, we'll just have to make do with each other.'

'I suppose we will,' agreed Jim in a resigned tone that had Doyler chuckling again.

'Come here. No, come here to me.'

He had ducked back down on the ledge and he held his arm out for Jim to join him. Jim slunk in under the arm, which pulled round his neck. 'Do you mind me going on the while?' he asked.

'I don't follow you the half of it.'

'Thing is you're a decent skin, Jim Mack. I know I wouldn't go far wrong if you was along with me.'

'Along with what sure?'

Pinch went the fingers and pain went his neck. 'Ireland, you gaum.' But the fingers stayed there and stroked the sting. They stroked his neck and Jim felt the waking of each of his hairs as they passed. They seemed very much alone suddenly. Jim could hear the peelers in the cove, but they sounded a long way off, in a different sea almost. He was aware of other parts of his body waking too. How odd this moving thing that woke in his breeches. How very odd it was. Jim's mouth opened and a little cough came out. It sounded amazingly polite in the sea-quiet.

'Funny to think we was swimming a minute back,' Doyler said, 'naked and all.'

His face was very close to Jim's. His tongue obtruded its tip and Jim felt the strangest wish to touch it with his own. 'Yes,' he said.

'Is it hard still? Bet you anything it's hard still.'

'But it's getting easier.'

'What is?'

'Swimming.'

'Gaum you.' He pulled Jim closer round the shoulders and his other hand reached to Jim's knee. It just rested there, the thumb stroking the weave of the cloth, just very softly the warp and the weft.

Away in the Southern Ocean, Jim heard the policemen chaffing. He was convinced the hand would move. It would travel up his leg. It would find him there, this moving thing. 'It would be great if you'd kiss me,' he said. But he didn't say that at all. He jumped to his feet, shrugging the arm from his neck. 'We could pay them out.'

A spall of distrust in Doyler's eyes. 'Pay who, is it?'

'The polis. Pay them out, so we could.'

'With what?'

Jim's heart was racing, but not so quick as his tongue. 'We could nip in the shelters, they'd never see us, we'd take their uniforms, how'd they catch on it was us? Even and they did, they'd never find us, away up the hill before ever they was out the water. And how'd they chase us anyway if we had their clothes? We could throw them in under any old hedge.'

The spall stayed in Doyler's eyes but he let a low cackle. 'A bevy of horneys in the buff.'

'And everyone gawking.'

'Oh, what a blow for Ireland.' He took off his cap and wiped his forehead. 'It's a shame, though, you wouldn't think of that earlier.'

'What shame?'

'You've been doing the swell in your college capeen this quarter of an hour. They'll have you decked for certain. First pop and they're knocking at your school. Second pop they're down at your door. And you know the reputation your father is getting.'

'I'm sure they didn't see me.'

'It was bravely thought, old pal. Another time we might risk it even. Get on now and I'll walk you up the road. They'll have me morgued at work and I'm another day late.'

All along the road Jim felt the limp exaggerated beside him. Doyler kept stiffly apart and their long thin shadows were parallel lines that never in this world would meet.

'Till tonight so,' Jim said at the junction.

'Practice, aye. I'll be keeping me flute after.'

'But what about your da?'

'Don't mind himself. And don't mind me. I came on the back of the wind. With the heat of the sun I came.'

It felt a punishment in some way, and Jim asked, 'Is it to play with Mr MacMurrough?'

'What'd you say?'

'To play flute with Mr MacMurrough.'

'What're you allegating now?'

'Nothing,' said Jim. 'Nothing. He's your friend, I thought.'

'What d'you mean by that?'

'Only I thought he's your friend.'

'How dare you. How dare you. To me face and all.' He was looking blue murder.

'I didn't know,' said Jim. 'Only I thought—'

'Did you know me ma does their washing?'

'Oh.' There was no sense to any of this, but Jim just wanted it to be all right. 'It's all right, Doyler.' He nodded his head, nodding agreement, conciliation, anything at all.

'She washes their sheets for them.'

'All right.'

'I only found out. She washes his sheets, she does. You follow me?'

'I do.'

'No, you don't. You're no more than a kid, Jim Mack. You don't follow nothing.'

He was aware of a great misunderstanding between them. It was not his college cap and it was not the policemen. It was not the mother having to take in washing. Why had he done that with Doyler's arm? Shrugging it away as if it was nothing to him. All that day if another touched him or bumped into him he was wildly angered. His father laughed, saying how precious he was become. And he was precious, too, and it was fanciful to imagine he would ever swim well, let alone against the stream to the Muglins.

*

Lonesome look of him, all down the dumps, young Doyler Doyle retires to the Banks. Depend on it, the country is a wholesome place but already that flush is fading. Would do that for you, the Banks, so it would. Soon enough now our Doyler'll be down with the odds and sods of the rest of them.

Mr Mack frowned. Go bail now, he's been up the shop all evening. Hanging about the till. Hop and go lightly.

Goes swimming with my son. Jim, my son James. Learning him the crawl. A new stroke, he calls it, but there's nothing new about the crawl. That's only the old trudgen dressed up with a modern name. I swam the trudgen myself down the Cape. In the Indian Ocean I swam it. Beat that, young larrikin.

A horror returned of a dark morning and the grey sea. The boy's body they found on the rocks. The people shake their heads and usher the man away. You must be brave, they tell him.

Sure, why would I mind if my son goes swimming? Power of good in the sea. He sucked his cheek, chewed what he found. The way I'd have any say in the matter. Crossed the road.

Lone nipper now with his sheaf of final *Mail*s. Mr Mack stopped. 'What's the latest?' he asked.

'Munittens,' said the boy.

'Munitions,' Mr Mack corrected. He already had an afternoon edition but he toyed with the idea of purchasing another for no better reason than the boy would be earlier to bed this night. 'There's a deal of shortage there,' he said by way of conversation.

The boy screwed his face, eyeing him cautiously. He leaned closer and on his tippy-toes he asked, 'Is it you is the General?'

'Well, I have the general stores above.'

'Is it you is the General of the Fenians?'

'What's this?'

'The da has you for the General of the Fenians. The A1 of Glasthule parish.'

'Why – where would he get such nonsense?'

'Wasn't it you the man tore down the British posters?'

'I did nothing of the sort.'

'Wasn't it you got 'rested for patriotic singing?'

'That was only the flute band marching.'

'Outside where the Orangemen was giving a Godsave?'

'I had no notion the Protestants was—' But Mr Mack took hold himself. He had not this minute left St Joseph's sacristy, where his views had been sought on scapulars – their trade, retail and donative values – to chop logic with newsboys in the street. 'Enough of that,' he said. 'I have never in my life heard such old-fashioned sauce.'

'But you know what, mister?'

Again the boy inclined his head-sending Mr Mack his baleful halitosis. 'Well?'

'I amn't much, but I'm ready whenever. Me and me pals is with you. Only say the word and we're out, Mr Mack. A Nation Once Again.'

Mr Mack viewed the nearly four feet of him. Bootless gurrier with his nose on tap. The snot sniffed back inside the nostril, then he did a thing never heard of before. Never known to pass in Glasthule parish or any parish in the barony, nor ever in the four fields of Erin, go to that of it. He pulled out a paper and gave it gratis for nothing. 'The Sword of Light is shining still,' said he, then he crossed the road to Fennelly's. 'Final Buff!' came his high-pitched quaver before the doors swung shut behind.

Mr Mack stared after. The scrawl of him to give such scandal. He stroked his moustache, attempting to trace in its hairs the series of events that had led to his being the darling of newsboys. Sclanderous. And all I had wanted was a little respectability.

He came to the shop, but before he would clink the bell he looked in through the window. There he was, nose dug in a book, hand on the counter with cloth at the ready. Mr Mack pushed the door, the door clinked, the hand was set in motion. 'I see you have that counter nicely polished,' he said.

'I was only—'

'Never mind your only.' He took off his jacket. 'Is your Aunt Sawney inside?'

'She was at her beads.'

'You might fix a cup of cocoa for her.'

'We're out of cocoa but.'

'Take some from the shelf, can't you? No no no, the shell cocoa. Are we made of money? In the book, now. How am I supposed to keep tabs if you won't write it down?' He watched the boy jot the item in his careful, elegant and not altogether satisfactory hand. 'Have a cup yourself while you're about it.'

'Do you want some, Da?'

'Oh sure, if you're making it, why not? Go on with you so. Make it with milk sure. We're not in the poorhouse yet.'

He sat down behind the counter. Let me see, let me see. His fingers tapped on the greasy till. It was beyond him why he stayed open these hours. Mug's game for the most part. Irrah, what option would a man have? Inside at the range with herself at her cuts. Direct, indirect, cuts sublime and infernal. Sclanderous altogether.

What was he about at all, he didn't know. In his mind's eye he saw the curate and the queer twistical look he'd have. And if ever you raised a kick, might just be you said yea or nay the wrong tone of voice, the screw he'd give out at you. And the coins jingling in his pocket like tuppences would rattle in the collection box.

Where was he going and where would it take him? He did not

know. Looking down he saw on the shelf below a stocking he had
started how many weeks back. The needles were still attached.
Hadn't found the time since. Footless stocking with a hole in it.
What the Connacht men shot at. Nothing.

But there was small use complaining, you got nothing for
it. And the father says if 'tis a fine I get, they'll raise another
subscription. Can't ask fairer than that.

He looked about the shop. What about them dips? Did he
dust them dips like I told him to? Heck as like. Talking to meself.
He took out the steps and was busy with the top shelf when his
son returned. 'Did you fix that cocoa?'

'I have it here.'

'Hold on to them steps while I see to these dips.'

'I already done them, Da.'

'You did?' He felt angered by the boy, he could not tell
why. Climbing down again, he said, 'Wouldn't you think to
do something proper for once? Just once in your life to have
a job done well and the next fellow comes along will see 'tis so.'
He took the cocoa. 'Is she asleep inside?'

'Yes.'

'We might risk a heat from the range so.' He had been saving
it for a treat for God knows when, but the cast of the boy was
so weeshy-deeshy, he decided to let on immediately. 'We had a
missive in the late post.'

'From Gordie?'

''Tis on the shelf.'

While his son raced through the letter, Mr Mack recounted
the news. 'Reviewed by the King, no less. Their Majesties King
George and Queen Mary, no less. Royal salute, followed by a
march-past. Entire division in column of platoons. Band playing
the music. Duty band that didn't have the scores for the Irish
regiments. Had to be playing at the British Grenadiers. With

a tow-row-row for the British Grenadiers. The Grinning Dears, we used call them. They didn't like that.'

Gordie had included a photograph with the letter. Very likely he stood with his chest out and his shoulders back. You could be proud of a son that way. He had a cigarette in his hand and underneath he'd written, I trust the cigarette does not offend. That too would stand you proud. Sign's on, it was farewell to the old Gordie. It wasn't any old slavey would do for him now.

He felt her before he heard her, the friction of her eyes on his neck. 'Ye're back,' she said.

'Hello, Aunt Sawney, are you awake so?'

'Don't tell me, ye was away vandalizing the posters.' And she was off. He was away scandalizing the street, she made no doubt. Wasn't he at St Joseph's, he told her. And if he was, she said, it wasn't to pray he went. The price of him to be tooting his Fenian songs outside of a church. In vain Mr Mack protested he had no notion about the Protestant church. Outside of a church, she went on, where a poor soldier laddie was having his last respects. In vain he protested he had no notion there was a funeral in progress. Might be his own son one of these days, she said. But what would he mind with his fond priesteen and his rebels' medley?

'Will you give it a rest, woman?'

'So long as ye have your twopenny door, the world can go stand on its head.'

But Mr Mack was saved by the bell. Clink. Customer. This time of night and all. 'I'll be with you directly.' But he wasn't out of his chair before the inside door opened and think of the devil, the horns is there.

'Hello, Mr Mack, and how are you at all? Is that a letter you're after reading, Jim? Who's it from, don't tell me. Is it Gordie? Oh, Mr Mack, I'm pleased he's wrote at long last, for it wasn't fair leaving you out in the cold like that. Hello, Miss Burke, is it well you're keeping? Did you get a snap, Jim? I got a lovely snap.'

'Nancy, this is the private quarters. You know that well.'

'Fierce handsome he looks in his racoon-skin cap.'

'Thank you, Nancy,' said Mr Mack ushering her into the shop and closing the door behind.

'And the plumes sticking out on the side.'

'Hackles.'

'What's that?'

'Not plumes, Nancy. Hackles.'

'Hackles, Mr Mack?'

'As it happens, Nancy, the shop is closed, only Jim forgot the gas. Howsomever, as you're here already.'

''Tis only I was thinking he won't be sporting a racoon-skin hat where he'll be headed. Will he now, Mr Mack?'

'I don't know what nonsense you're talking, Nancy, but if you'd care to purchase anything you need only ask.'

'I was only saying if it's out East he's going, it's the pith helmet he'll want. Sure you'd go demented with a racoon on your head in all that sunshine.'

'East? My son is going East?'

'Did he not let on? Oh yes, they was issued with sun-hats. Weeks ago, this was. I'm surprised now how it slipped his mind to tell you.'

Mr Mack had to sit down. My son is going East, he kept telling himself. Thanks be to God almighty and all the saints. Our Lady of Ransom, pray for us. Out loud he said, 'I was a good while out East myself.' Out East in the sun where it's safe. Safe bar the sun and the Punjab head and the Doolally tap and the dhobi itch and the Billy Stink and the rest. But safe from the trenches. The Lord between us and harm, and he was.

'I'll be with you directly, Nancy, I must just—' He snuck his head inside the kitchen door. 'Jim, Jim!'

'Da?'

'He's going out East.'

'Gordie is?'

'Isn't it great?' He waited to be sure his son understood the significance, then back inside the shop.

'I know what it is,' said Nancy. 'He must be worried there's agents about the premises.'

'What agents is these?'

''Tis well known, Mr Mack, the Fenians do be in league with the Kaiser.'

Sternly he told her, 'There are no Fenians here.'

'And after the newspapers and all?'

'The newspapers is lies. You might listen what the priest says on Sunday.'

'You'll be getting a fierce name for yourself, Mr Mack. Second mention in as many months. Breach of the peace, wasn't it, this time? Likely to occasion? Mind you, that was unfortunate that the poor dead soldier was the son of a superintendent.'

'Lookat, Nancy, once and for all I had no notion about the funeral.'

'Oh, Mr Mack, I wouldn't doubt you a minute. I stick up for you desperate in the street, so I do. I let them know that Mr Mack is a gentleman. He wouldn't break the peace if he dropped it.' She was scamandering about, touching articles with her fingers. 'They say the Fenians has a telegraph and they do tap out instructions to the German U-boats. That's why troop movements is secret in times of war. Did you know that, Mr Mack?'

Her long fingers touching his wares. Unholy the way she moved, making play with her hips. He recollected his station and stood by the till. 'Was it something in particular you was after?'

'Was wondering had you any of them gurkhas left?'

'Haven't I told you already 'tis gherkins you mean. Gurkhas is Indian troops. Is it Madame MacMurrough sent you?'

'Not at all. I have a great fancy for them these days. Have you tried one ever yourself?'

'Nancy, I got these gherkins in for special customers. They're not to be thrun about idly.'

'Sure they're above gathering dust since I can remember.'

Grumbling, he fetched down a jar. 'Scattering your earnings on nipperty-tips. Have you no bottom drawer to be seeing to?' This was sailing too close to the wind, so he quickly humphed and changed the subject. 'They'll leave you ill if you eats too many of them.'

'Maybe you're right,' she said. 'For I do be getting the gicks something rotten of a morning.'

'Now, didn't I tell you?' He took her money and was counting her change. Already she had the jar open and she dipped her fingers, spilling brine on the counter. More Jeyes Fluid. He looked at her face while she crunched the green thing. Grown-up she looked and clean and spotless. Ladyfied almost, under the gas. In a way it was a shame she was only a slavey. Her face was radiant in fact. Never mind the gick, she looked the pink of health. 'There you are, Nancy.'

'Thanks now, Mr Mack.'

Big blue bow on her blouse and a petersham round her boater. He held the door for her leaving. 'Do they let you out this late at Madame MacMurrough's?'

'Not at all. Amn't I only back from my aunt's at Blackrock? She's poorly sure.'

'I'm sorry to hear that.'

'She's old, Mr Mack.'

'May God keep her.'

'Your mouth to God's ears.'

'Go careful now, Nancy.'

'Why wouldn't I?'

A thought struck as he bolted the door. He shuddered, then quickly cast it out. Through the ha'penny canes that hung at the glass he watched her cross the spill of light. The saunter of her, the way she'd crack nuts with her tail.

Abruptly, down the lane, a voice broke into a clear musical whistle. He pulled a damning face. That'll be Gordie now, making a mockery of us in the street.

The thought died on him. No, that's not Gordie at all. No, that won't be Gordie, not for a long while yet.

CHAPTER TEN

A̲UNT E̲VA WAS in the garden room, on a bentwood rocker, a tickled surmise on her face. She was perusing through a spy glass a rough sheet called the *Irish Volunteer*. The wicker table presented similar matter. *The Gael*, the *Gaelic American*, *Eire*, *United Irishwoman*, *The Leader*, *Spark*; along with the Irish Automobile Club newsletter and yesterday's London *Times*. 'At last,' she said when MacMurrough joined her. Her head flicked in irritation, a mannerism from her girlhood, he believed, when her trailing locks she tossed behind, a forbidding come-hither to his grandfather's cronies.

She offered her hand and he guided her up and into the dining-room. He pulled her chair and sat her, but before he might sit himself, she remarked, unfolding her napkin, 'I recollect it was the previous King who instituted that curious fashion. Whether through negligence or corpulence, we are not told.'

His unclosed waistcoat button. Friday lunch: the routine fish to break the flesh routine; food to be served tepid and dolloped on plates; but the service pristine, plates boasting the family crest, all form obeyed. He slipped the last button through its loop in his waistcoat and sat. A maid came, unknown face and manner, only the white Berlin gloves familiar.

Soup. God knew what of.

'I remember to have been in Paris one time when that gentleman visited. This was after the débâcle with the Boers. He was hooted through the streets. At the Comédie Française the gallery hissed when he took his box. Within three days he had the mob eating from his hand. It was "ce bon vieux Eddie!" all over again. There is much to be said for personal charm and uncomplicated indulgence in fun. Though it must be added the late King was never known be unpunctual in his life. And I doubt he went promenading with kitchen maids.'

How did she know? MacMurrough had never yet seen his aunt condescend to talk with a neighbour. He had been on his way to the little bench by the Martello tower where he liked to sit of a morning and watch the boys at their swim. He had found the kitchen girl at the Forty Foot wall, retching.

'Cook tells me she is not so well these days,' his aunt remarked, 'these mornings, I should say.'

Yes, retching quite severely. 'I thought her flourishing,' MacMurrough said.

'Well, that is a very good news, as I should hate anything to happen to the child, la pauvre, la petite innocente.'

The dining-room reflected his aunt's Parisian sojourns. Side table, Directoire, with Phrygian-cap motif; large casolettes, pair, ormolu, on top. On shelves above, row upon row of painted glazed plates. Souvenir china, he should have thought, but his aunt, who valued such things, reckoned them *faïence patriotique*. Their patriotism was not in doubt: the untrammelled cock crowed from each: *Vivre libre ou mourir!* or suchlike.

They reminded him of the children's dishes he ate off as a boy. The virtues they advanced. 'If little girls and boys were wise, they should always be polite. For sweet behaviour in a child is such a delightful sight.'

'What a particular thing to say,' said his aunt.

'I was remembering when I was a child.'

'Yes,' she said, and she regarded the plates as though for her, too, they brought memories of his boyhood. 'You were a happy child. A delightful child, one might say, if not noticeably polite.'

'I was?'

'Mischievous, of course, but happy with it. You would insist on playing carpet bowls in the hall. You had the maids in terror of tumbling. You were a great encouragement to the footmen we had then. But it was impossible to be annoyed with you, annoyed for very long. Such a sweet smile you had in those days. Your eyes smiled with your face.'

A type of soldier's blessing: fond memory that wrapped a current disapproval.

'One wonders at times if the wind didn't change and the good people took you from us.'

Fish replaced the soup. Plausibly mullet.

'I do hope the weather will improve,' Aunt Eva continued. 'So unpleasant motoring with the hood up. They call it an English hood. I cannot conceive why. The Delage I had previous had the same équipage. Nobody thought to call that an English hood. It was simply la capote.'

'Have it dyed green. An Irish hood.'

'Such a notion. Still it would not temper the downpour.'

'When do you intend motoring?'

'Tomorrow.'

'High Kinsella again?'

'What an inquisitive boy you are.'

'But what if something should happen to the car? The roads must be dreadful.'

'The car, as you call it, is a Prince Henry. My Prince Henry has never faltered a stroke.'

'But what do you find to do up there in the mountains? You must see that mystery provokes curiosity.'

'The mountains,' she answered, 'yes. Whence the O'Byrnes and O'Tooles, our tributaries, harried the Dane, and Art MacMurrough Kavanagh, of undying fame, descended on the Palesmen. Whither the boy O'Donnell fled from his Castle captors, where Fiach Mac Hugh swore his word. They held out longest there, the insurgents of '98. They hid him there, poor Robert Emmett. There Parnell first looked upon the land of Ireland, there the Fenians blundered in the fog. Over the mountains I go, over the military road.'

It was futile his pursuing the matter. And perhaps she let on more than she knew. Her tryst might truly be with history. He saw her on some dolmenned moor, sipping a Chablis on a picnic rug, defying through the smokes of Dublin the castle-turreted foe. He remarked, 'It seems a signally busy road.'

To which witticism she deferred with a smile. 'Did you know,' she inquired after an interval, 'that a Fenian has died?'

'I did not know there were any Fenians left.'

'No. Well, there you are. Dead ones, leastways. This was in America, which continent, I am persuaded, will ever produce novelties. He was of your grandfather's time, this particular Fenian. Something of the dynamitard, if I recall. The remains are to be returned to Ireland. There will be a public demonstration of grief, which naturally I shall attend. If I am not deceived, my nephew will offer to accompany me.'

'Should you like me to accompany you, Aunt Eva?'

'That would be most acceptable. It is just what the country needs. To electrify the soul, galvanize the sinews, march the patriotic heart: a glorious grand monumental funeral!'

'Cometh the hour,' MacMurrough murmured, 'cometh the corpse.'

'In the meantime we have the garden party to consider. Really, Anthony, you might show more interest. Caterers,' she offered by way of example. 'Where to rope off, where for the canaille. We are to have a play performed. Won't that fascinate? An enterprising young man of Father O'Toiler's acquaintance keeps a school for Gaelic youths. He has composed a drama which his boys will enact.'

'I had not thought the drama a subject to move our priest.'

'I have read the résumé. All quite wholesome, what I could make of it. Father O'Toiler assures me it is a mystical chef d'oeuvre. Whatever, it has diverted his mind from this hockey bout. Really, hockey on one's lawns. I had suggested croquet at a shilling a mallet, but this apparently was not the thing. So difficult when one entertains outside one's circle.'

'How many are expected?' he asked.

She glanced up, then glanced down again, having perceived in his eyes the root of his query. 'Absurd boy. That a garden party should dismay a MacMurrough. I have never heard such a thing.'

'One can't help wondering if one isn't to be paraded as a fairground attraction.'

'How little you know of the world.'

'If one were to be blunt, one might posit a similar nescience in one's aunt.'

'Really Anthony, you would have me believe that a term of imprisonment and a bent for slumming are to be reckoned an education. The naivety of the young never fails to amaze. Nor their impertinence to offend, no matter how iffed.' She rang the little bell at the table's centre. 'The world does not hang upon your misdemeanours. The world is no longer interested.'

'Oh, but it is, Aunt Eva. To the tune of Church, Parliament, press, the mob, the courts, police, the prisons. It is that I should take an interest that is objected to.'

She stared at the door a moment in expectation of the maid. No maid forthcoming, she said, 'I can form no idea of the occasion, but suppose I had thieved at one time. Do I hold myself a thief for ever? Do I attempt a philosophy of my thieving? I do not. I have blasphemed. A saint would blaspheme with such a nephew. Am I nothing ever more than a blasphemer?'

'There is no equivalence.'

'The laws are unjust, that I will grant. But not as you would have it. It is girls and young women they prejudice. Men who rake hell in the customary manner, in them the courts discover no wrong, the law propounds no remedy against them. Yet how many young women have they ruined? And you think to right this wrong by having chauffeur-mechanics for ever at your disposal? My nephew will not persist in this. I think better of him than to suppose it.'

She had shifted into French, but still this was pretty strong stuff, and MacMurrough couldn't but feel impressed. At home, he hadn't dared say Stomach for fear of his mother reaching for the smelling-salts.

'No more of this Job and Jeremiah now. It is over, it is done with.' But not quite done with, for she added, with a haughty lift of her chin, 'As though to say twelve men in London, whom the law humorously describes as your peers, should decide the fate of a MacMurrough. Why, were I to heed the opinion of the street, I should think myself insane.'

'Is it the opinion of the street that you are insane, Aunt Eva?'

'One seeks the deliverance of one's country from subjection. One's country does not wish its deliverance. One's countrymen would settle for a Home Rule that would shame a county council.

Its leaders harangue its manhood to fight in the tyrant's cause. These are the sane ones, these the nation's respectability. At present one is clearly in the wrong. One is pernicious or malign, one is mad. One does not despair, however. One knows that should sufficient change their minds, one will be a good and honoured prophetess. One therefore decides those minds shall change.'

MacMurrough grinned at her. 'I had not thought you so sophistical,' he said. 'That the good and the true should obtain in the opinion of others. You make a democracy of virtue.'

'If it is to be anything, it is to be an aristocracy,' she replied. 'For some have the say of thousands, whereas many have no say at all. And let me tell you, it is the best who will join us. How shall we know them for the best? By virtue of their joining us, of course.'

'Then why must we trouble with the mob at all? I mean, this jamboree, why have them here?'

'Dear boy, with all your papers and manuscripts, have you never thought to inquire into the nature of your birthright? Ours is not to lord, but to lead. That is why you teach flute to boys. That is why my guests will be charmed.' Again she rang the bell, irritating it in her fingers. 'You do remember you have the band this evening?'

'How should I forget?'

'Father O'Toiler is very pleased with your progress. Tremendous, to quote him. At the garden party you and your boys will present the grand finale. There will be fireworks.'

That was then. Now there was only the French ticking clock while they awaited the maid's pleasure. Soon MacMurrough gave up and reached for the potatoes himself.

'Don't be impetuous, Anthony. One so dislikes stretching at table.'

They waited, both glancing at the brass lady at the table's centre whose legs were clappers to her crinolined bell. Eventually, Eveline patted her lips on her napkin, those darned and redarned cloths cut from her grandmother's trousseau. She brought the potatoes and served him herself.

'Stretching is so disagreeable, don't you find?'

Damnation once again. Rataplan of snares, thubadub of drum, breathless flutes. MacMurrough beat time with his baton in front, beat rather the boys' time than his own ordained. Keep things simple. His eyes strayed their hundredth time across the score; their hundredth time they scanned the words.

> When boyhood's fire was in my blood,
> I read of ancient freemen,
> For Greece and Rome who bravely stood
> Three hundred men and three men.

Always something bathetic about a double rhyme. Besides, precious little to do with Ireland.

— It is a reference.

— Scrotes! All hail! You join us!

— A reference, if I am not mistaken, to the first Battle of Thermopylae, when the Spartan three hundred under Leonidas, their king, fell in honourable combat against the Persians.

— Fancy.

— The three, then, would be Horatius the one-eyed and his two companions who, in the brave days of old, defended the Sublician bridge.

— Well I never.

And then I prayed I yet might see
Our fetters rent in twain,
And Ireland, long a province, be
A Nation Once Again.

– Stirring stuff. True, too. When boyhood's fire was in my blood, I did dream of ancient Greeks. Though I'm not sure three hundred and three lusty spearmen isn't coming it a bit high.

The last rasp of the snare was like Scrotes's snort of disdain. Then the priest stepped forward, pattering bar-bar, and launched the band into prayer. Bar-bar done, he clapped his hands, commanding kilts. Subdued voices while the boys shifted from jackets and trousers. Careful boys, chary with their charms. Smell that would always carry to school. One by one they metamorphosed till before him ranked the heroes of Erin's past – if heroes they were who dazzled with shirts and golden-pleated cloth. They sat with their legs apart, a droop of skirt between their knees. How touching was their vulnerability then. Half-girl faces on man-size bodies. Till their caps cocked and a braggartness stiffened their chatter. The breached masculinity of the unbreeched.

He thought of the monstrous urges of that age and the incommensurate imagination. It was astonishing that his aunt should flaunt such game before him. She distinctly did not take him seriously at all.

I should become a master at a small public school. And yet boys are tiresome after a time. I should visit down the back of the pier and find me out a sergeant-major. Pretend temples there that give out on the sea. Might have been built for the purpose.

His aunt had been raised to a type of honorary male, for she remained in the summerhouse while the boys changed, albeit with her back to them, talking now with her priest and the queer card who taught the boys drill. In keeping with this status she had dressed in sober worsted. He thought of her wardrobe: billowy Lucilles in surprising neighbourhood to frumpy reforms. And those Poiret pyjamas she relaxed into of an evening. Aunt Eva in trousers and boys in skirts. What an interesting nation it will be.

It was Scrotes he had a mind to speak with, but Dick was nudging him, and at last he allowed his eyes to settle on the front row. Master Doyle, how are ye. How he leapt for joy, did Dick, to know, of a couple dozen fresh-faced lads, one already had drunk his spunk.

Has an out-of-the-way face, our young friend. Not unlovely, but as if the features had yet to take root. Jug-eared and mop-haired, lips slapped on with a raddle-brush. Reminds me of a game Nanny used to play: you got a potato and fixed it with buttons and pegs and shards of old crockery till you'd made a little man. A face of scraps and hand-me-downs where nothing as yet quite fits. All save the eyes, darkly avoiding me.

Yes, he avoided him now. MacMurrough did not know what, but something had passed between them: the boy was no longer agreeable. Young chap beside most like, little comfort for the troops. The merest glance and that one's blood came flooding. What secret shame doth rose thy Ganymede cheek? Entirely desirable. I have Master Doyle's word on it that should ever I lay a hand to that one, I'm deh meah. Yet my cup runneth over shouldst thou bear it to me. Watching, MacMurrough felt his fingers for claws.

He could hear this boy's father prattling to Aunt Eva and her priest about some detail of apparel. An officer's sash goes opposite ways to a non-com's. Well, most fathers are hard to conceive. Who would suspect the stiff-necked widow-peaked raven in London for my progenitor? Certainly the progenitor had his doubts.

Something in the comfort's manner, like homage. Holds Doyle's flute for him while Doyle attends his stockings. Quickly shines it with his cloth. Doyle takes it back, breathes a silent tune, Dryden's soft complaining flute. My hero.

– Ah, said Nanny Tremble, it's the lovely sight to see the two maneens together. When friends meet the heart warms.

It was true there was an attraction in their friendship. How many mornings have I gone down the sea? Charge myself to join in their swim. Well, God knows, might even be of some help. Dick is certain he could teach a stroke or two. End up on the bench by the Martello instead. Like the tramp in the V&A who marvels at beauty: he wants to touch but, should he touch, the marble is sullied. Lured and stopped by the same desire.

– The Victoria and Albert, Scrotes observed, is justly famed for its divers wonders. Not the least of which, from a tramp's consideration, is a roof which shelters from the elements.

– Good old Scrotes, always to hand for a bring-me-down. I feared you had deserted us.

– It is not for the scabrid knees I have delayed. I wished to regard the two boys in question. Do you think they may be lovers?

MacMurrough conjured Arcadian groves where lover and beloved, ephebes both, reclined upon the coarse grass. Cicadas sang in the boughs above, where olives swelled in the sun. Or it was later in the palaestra when, weary of wrestling, lover draws down the tender blade to scrape the beloved's sweat. Of serious things they speak.

Back in the summerhouse, he saw Doyle pull off the comfort's cap and search inside. He made play of finding a morsel therein, a louse indeed. Plucks it, plops it in his mouth.

Delicious, grins his face. Giggling, reddening, the comfort turns aside.

– Not in any Greek sense, MacMurrough answered.

– Lovers none the less?

– It is not impossible. They have youth.

– Would age forbid them?

– Rather youth permits. The not knowing and the slowness of days. Lack of imagination may move mountains.

– Quaere: did you love at their age?

– Oh well, said MacMurrough, thinking back. There was a boy at school, I suppose. We became quite regular. One time, we'd been at it, and I turned round and held him. Is this love? I asked. I suppose it is, he answered. And we both sat back, not touching, thinking the same I suppose, the vacuity of it. We stopped soon after. He smelt of oranges.

The priest clapped his hands again, the detail of sashes apparently decided, and the boys trooped out to the garden. In the evening light MacMurrough watched their parade. The antics of their instructor had amused at first, until he had discovered in the man's eagerness an innocence childlike as the boys'. In profile he saw the faces of his aunt and her priest. A dusk of midges danced above but their features were set like grim tutelaries. It struck him how little pleasure they gained of the boys and of their callow willingness to please. How little shame they felt of their exactions. The glances of the boys cut him and he foresaw in an inkling the thousand uses their willingness would be put to, until their faces changed, until they too were set.

He ambled towards the sea. He asked Scrotes what he had made of his aunt's disquisition over lunch. Scrotes replied saying, O thou stranger woman, thou sayest well! Which brought knowing smiles to their bookish faces.

The sun on a stone wall – yellow, gold, bronze, red-metal

– shaded through and was gone in moments. He smoked with his ear to the waves and he thought of a ten-year-old boy whose rollicking kingdom this shore had been. Truly, he was a happy child.

– What did your aunt intend, Scrotes asked, when she spoke of the good people taking you away?

– The fairies, MacMurrough answered. They take the beautiful boy and leave a changeling brute in his place.

He looked back up the lawns to where the boys still paraded. In their golden kilts they looked like tulips, tulips which glowed and marched in the dusk.

– We're gods, he said. And these our playthings.

– There are many gods, returned Scrotes. Many to whom even you are but a whim.

– Ah yes, scaly-eyed Themis, guardian of law.

– One was thinking of Eros, whose arrows pierce and bring life.

Grey morning dulled the bay. Banks of clouds, Howth just one more bank, rolled to sea, where other Howths grumbled to greet them. Swollen spumeless tide. Heads that bobbed like floating gulls and gulls that floating bobbed like heads. Two heads. At swim, two boys.

And yet not boys but youth itself. Distance detached them, water unformed them, particularities washed away. Nasal whine, feet that smelt, these were accidents of their mundane selves. The sea proposed an ideal, unindividuate, sublime. Above on my perch I sit and watch. Alone one man.

– Not entirely alone, said Scrotes.

– No, MacMurrough conceded. One is never alone with the ghost of a friend.

He took up his towel as though to make room, patted it on his lap. In return Scrotes heaved a sigh, his weary limbs to ease, as if. Side by side they sat, chatting of this and that. With the boys swimming below, it was only natural their conversation should turn to friendship; and Scrotes remarked that the ancients had considered friendship a stimulus to virtue. The Philosopher, he further observed, went so far as to raise friendship to a virtue of itself. MacMurrough wondered was that still so, and Scrotes thought no, that its role had been subsumed in the family.

– Why should that be?

Scrotes did not immediately say, and MacMurrough conjectured that the family was more easily governed. Certainly friendship had its political implications and Scrotes was able to advance instances of friends who had effected risings and revolts against despots and bullies. Tyrants, so Plato said, stand in awe of friends. The question then arose: was friendship incidental or essential to these actions? MacMurrough inclined to the latter view; for friendship, he maintained, tending to the good of both friends, by extension might seek the good of all. Scrotes wondered might the same not be said of families? From this proposition MacMurrough dissented, discovering as he spoke what seemed to him the differentia of those two institutions: the one, being generative, must seek its interest against the competitive generation of others; the other, owning no posterity, was free of such claims. Might we then say, asked Scrotes, that the virtues advanced by two such differing institutions should themselves be different?

– It seems we very well might, MacMurrough replied.

And it was pleasant to speak of such things while on their windy prominence they sat. Below, the boys thithered and thenced to the raft and back. Three times, four times, five times, six. Like mating ducks they swam: parallel but one slightly ahead.

– And if it be the case that the one has subsumed the other, Scrotes continued, might we not then infer that the virtues advanced by the one are more in kilter with the times than the virtues advanced by the other?

– It seems inevitable that we should, said MacMurrough.

– What, then, are the virtues advanced by friendship?

MacMurrough replied that they were surely divers and legion; but that the cardinal virtue of friendship must be selflessness. That quality, he maintained, was exampled in all the heroic friendships, but for its cynosure he chose Castor and Pollux, opining that greater love hath no man than this, that Pollux laid down his immortality for his friend. He touched on the loyalty of Damon and Pythias and lightly glanced on Sergius and Bacchus and other couplings of the Christian calendar who had found in their friendship the fortitude to accept their martyrs' crowns. Of the Sacred Band of Thebes he spoke, which at Chaeronea fell, each friend by his lover's side, and told how Philip of Macedon had wept for such valour, pledging through his candid tears, 'Woe unto them who think evil of such men.' Of Achilles and Patroclus he naturally spoke, of Pylades and Orestes (*nomina fama tenet*), of Theseus and Pirithous, of Nisus and Euryalus. Nor, in passing to the modern era, did Summoner and Pardoner, Colin and Hobbinol, the two kings of Brentford, Sir Symphony and Sir Foeminine Fanviles, Chapman and Keats, Burke and Hare, Fortnum and Mason, Gilbert and Sullivan, Hook and Snivey, Karl Marx and Friedrich Engels escape his survey, but all were mentioned, and the virtue exemplified by each particular friendship was granted its due regard.

– What, then, are the virtues advanced by family? asked Scrotes.

But MacMurrough was becoming bored with this now. Down below, the boys had touched the raft their seventh time and now they clung to the ropes. On kindlier mornings they would climb aboard, but the wind was too chill today. They rested in the water, chatting, he supposed, catching their breath, friends.

– You know, he said to Scrotes, I remember at my school the monks discouraged particular friendships. Particular friendships they condemned as occasions, if not of sin, gravid with its potential.

– Friendship tending to love may tend to desire, said Scrotes.

– Yes, but desire was there anyway. We all desired. We were riven with it. The monks policed friendship but all they effected was a sexual abandon. Instead of fumbling with love, we fumbled in the dark.

MacMurrough then descanted on desire's having itself been the cause of friendship's fall. For whereas desire (by which, he informed Scrotes, he intended carnal desire) was for the pantheists unproblematical (Scrotes raised his eyebrows at this), in the teleological universe of the theists (by which, he informed Scrotes, he intended the Christian world-view) the gratification of that desire being fruitless (excepting the pleasure it afforded), it was therefore purposeless, and what was purposeless was of itself contrary to a purposeful god's will, therefore sinful.

Scrotes thought this rather a long-winded way of saying Christians disapproved of schoolboys jumping into each other's beds and MacMurrough had to laugh at his gentle teasing.

Scrotes allowed, nevertheless, there was something in what MacMurrough had said and by way of illustrating this allowance he quoted from Augustine who had *polluted the vein of friendship with the filth of desire* – a phrase, Scrotes remarked, which would mean nothing to the Greeks, for whom friendship and desire were congenial (if MacMurrough would forgive the paronomasia) bedfellows. And yet, Scrotes continued, even for the Christians, friendship was not irremediably flawed for, as Augustine later confessed, it was his love for his friend that brought him closer to his God – a notion, said Scrotes, worthy of the Athenian Bee himself.

Such gentlemanly discussion, so affably did they speak, MacMurrough felt a rising gratitude for his old friend. He was a decent sort was Scrotes. True, he had taken to haranguing of late; but this morning it was like old times again, when they had had leisure in the sick-ward at Wandsworth to converse. Not conversation by any civilized standard, but a kind of a mussitation, the prisoner's half-mime half-whisper, under the nodding eye of an orderly. Funny old man with his donnish ways. His courtesy had affronted the warders whose satisfaction lay in black looks and oaths unuttered. At first MacMurrough had conceived it a kindness on his part that he should take an interest in the fellow. Months passed before he understood it was the odd old fellow who had taken him in charge. Their friendship became his refuge; their talks his reprieve. That old man's nidorous whispered breath had entered into MacMurrough's heart an insufflation of – of what, exactly?

MacMurrough could not exactly say. He sniffed now, and sniffing caught the smell of hearthstone and heartbreak that had tenanted those echoing halls, those echoing halls, those echoing, those.

Whatever about that, he was sure this morning they were getting along famously. Indeed, he was coming to the opinion they had their subject nicely wrapped; when Scrotes of a sudden smacked his palm on the flat of his forehead and exclaimed,

– First principles!

MacMurrough queried the void beside and repeated the curious ejaculation.

– Here we are discussing the media, Scrotes elaborated, through which virtue may be advanced, without firstly having decided what virtue may be.

It was a grievous fault and they immediately set about its rectification. Scrotes, as was his use, delved to the root of the word and expounded its meaning as that which befits a man. As such, he said, virtue in its original was unavailable to women. Whereupon MacMurrough introduced a lighter note, to whit: nowadays the reverse held true, virtue being most commonly construed an instinct, proper in girls, to preserve their virginity, and in women to nurture the results of its loss.

Between these extremes, they had stoics at the door, epicureans to dinner, they had cynics snapping at their heels. Doctors they examined, angelic, subtle and invincible. They passed from the sophists' virtue of the interest of the strong over the weak to its happier sibling, latterly denominated enlightened self-interest, but whose epitome they found in Matthew 7:12. Of mechanicalists they spoke, of rites and taboos; of revelationists, of ultimate goodness, of the soul. Of *himeros*, the desire that strikes the spirit through the eyes; of *pothos*, the soul's yearning for its separated love. Injunctions detained them: *Gnosce teipsum*; *Cogita ut sis*. Nor did the utilitarian ethic of the greatest happiness of the greatest number escape their attention. Did they speak of the hedonic calculus and the is/ought problem? Most assuredly. As also of imperatives, categorical and hypothetical; of eudemonia and pandemonium. *Tabulae rasae* – these were not omitted. Neither were hedonics, aesthetics, the Balmorality of good Queen Vic, the Ibsenity of the drama.

Was any science or branch of science, pertinent to their inquiry, omitted? Yes; axiology. On what account? MacMurrough's having forgotten for the moment what axiology meant. When reference was made to mechanical religion, did they happen to mention that taboos in the main are topographical, alimentary, bodily? To be sure. What rough-hewn witticism did MacMurrough thereupon interject? He postulated the most unvirtuous man of all, who fetched off in chapel while eating sweets. Did they laugh? They did.

Was MacMurrough satisfied with the course of their inquiry? Immediately, yes; ultimately, no. On what account was he ultimately dissatisfied? On account of his remembering that Scrotes was no longer with him. To what may be attributed Scrotes's absence? His being dead. Was this a sad fact? Without the least shadow of a doubt. What logical implicative was employed by MacMurrough, the unforeseen consequence of which was his realization of Scrotes's unbeing? If . . . then. State the protasis. If Scrotes had really been there on the bench. And the apodosis? Then he had reminded MacMurrough the meaning of axiology. All together now in *oratio recta*. 'If you really were Scrotes, you'd bloody well know what axiology meant.'

Was MacMurrough brought up sharp by this iteration? He was, figuratively. How did it affect him? Coldly, literally. Name three emotions of similar character that MacMurrough felt. Grief, loss, regret. Of which the greatest was? Loss. What did MacMurrough say? He said: 'You left me the writing, old man, but not the cipher. You left me the words without their meaning. They dance on pins for me now, but with you I had the glimmering of answers. You are gone and I but know enough to mock.' What quality, hitherto unmentioned, did MacMurrough thereupon ascribe to friendship? Kindness. Please to elaborate. His friendship with Scrotes had given him to feel kinder to the world; their parting had left him kindless.

What of the boys swimming? They let go the raft's ropes

and swam their final length to the cove. The walls secreted them as they left the water like the earth would clothe whose nakedness belonged in the sea.

What does axiology mean? MacMurrough no longer cared. What did he do?

He got up and left the bench. At half-past eleven he saw his aunt off on her motoring spree to the mountains. He followed the car up the drive and peered inside the lodge. Derelict, roofless, yet someone made his home there. The kitchen maid found him and asked about his lunch. He told her he would chop at the Pavilion Gardens. Then he told her to take the afternoon off. He told Cook to take the afternoon off. His munificence might have extended to the gardener and the gardener's lad and to the gardener's lad's lad, save he came not across them. To the bootman he gave a three-quarter bottle of dry sherry wine.

But this was not kindness, merely the hunter's preparations. At half-past one he spied his prey, kicking its heels along the sea-wall. Dawdling thither, he sprang.

'Afternoon off, is it?'

'Could say that. Short time they has us on.'

MacMurrough curtailed a smirk: he was well aware of the boy's working arrangements. 'Anything special in mind?'

'Home.'

The boy kicked stones. MacMurrough clicked the coins in his sovereign-purse. 'Wouldn't fancy a spot of lunch, I suppose?'

'Lunch, would you listen. Where would I get lunch?'

'Anywhere, I should have thought. I was thinking of the Pavilion Gardens, if you wanted to join me.'

'Get in off the grass. Doyler in the Pavvo. That'll be the day.'

'Serious. Come, my treat.'

'Thanks all the same but.'

'Why ever not? No strings, company only. My word of honour.'

That raised a smile. The face plained immediately after. 'Need only look at the state of me.'

It had to be admitted he was in rather a muck. Funny, really. After those months inside, forgotten how my nose would turn up. Perhaps we should all spend a term in quod. Debt the leveller. 'Walk with me anyway. Bored talking with myself.'

They passed the fellows who fished along the sea-wall and the boy spat derisively after them. 'Too much larking for real fishing.'

'What do they catch?'

'Pollack if they're lucky. Cook it as whitebait. Dabs, I suppose. Mostly all that lot'd catch is cold.'

Father tickling trout. Why did he bring me along? Tedium of those hours not allowed to speak. Struggle of the fish against the line, end always so flat. The pity of it served up at supper. Test of a true hunter. Do you eat your catch?

Doyler. I wonder what a doyler does. He doyles of course. But what is doyling? 'Have you really nothing to change into?'

'I have a shirt all right.'

'No more?'

'You don't want to know very much, do you, Mr MacMurrough?'

'I didn't intend . . . I don't wish to pry.'

''S all right. I know what you meant. This is where I turn.'

High wall by a mud lane which MacMurrough had always supposed led nowhere. So that's where the smell comes from.

'So now you know where I live. And it's me ma as cleans

your dirty sheets, Mr MacMurrough. So don't be thinking I'll be coming with you, you understand that now?'

'Wait a minute, can't you?'

'Wait for what?'

'Just talk. Can't we talk?'

The boy squinted up the lane then back at MacMurrough. 'Talk so.'

'About lunch—'

'I already told you about that.'

'What if I were to arrange a suit of clothes?'

He snorted. 'You kidding me on?'

'We could go up George's Street. What's it called, Lee's. Just something made-up.'

'You'd really buy me a suit? Where's the sell? You want your jeer at me in the Pavilion, is it?'

'Forget the Pavilion.'

'Why, then?'

'Does it matter why?'

'Matters to me.'

MacMurrough felt an anger rising, which really he might have contained. But, feeling liberal, he let the lid off a squeeze and said, 'If you don't recognize friendship when it's offered, that's your misfortune.' And he strode purposefully off. He had gone a dozen yards and had quite despaired of human nature, when the boy called after.

'No strings at all?'

'I told you, none.'

Some further jittering but MacMurrough in victory could be a patient soul. At length the boy smiled, in what MacMurrough was pleased to decide was a doyling way and, having doyled deliciously, he said, 'Wait for us, then. Be back in a crack.' And the loveable legs went gamely tripping.

– Nicely tickled, said Dick.

And the chaplain said, That guttersnipe is out for anything
he may get.

But Nanny Tremble thought he'd look dandy in a nice clean
suit. Tweed, she proposed, out of Donegal. For I'm sure it looks
awful damp where he stays.

MacMurrough glanced at the sky, whose lowering clouds
were edged in sun. He smiled at the fishing men who, too,
unhungrily hunted. He looked up the lane, feeling in his pocket
his sovereign-purse, pondering wise old saws upon muck and
brass and how amiably they got along, those commodities.

A boy was scampering over the far rocks. MacMurrough
watched him. An unkempt but well-dressed boy, ten years
old, maybe younger, lost in a private world with his glass jar
and collecting-net. Through his feet and his scrambling hands,
MacMurrough had a sense of the stones and sand and barnacles
and wet. And breathing his air, he savoured the lazy freedom
of holidays. The boy stopped suddenly, as though something
had struck him. He stood poised on a slip of rock, attending
as if he heard a whisper in the faraway or glimpsed a shadow
in the deep of his eye.

MacMurrough was seized with a certainty he would turn.
The boy would turn and he would see MacMurrough and a
horror of recognition would come on his face.

He stepped back till the wall stopped him. But the boy did
not turn. His head shook the disturbance clear. Then, dipping
behind an outcrop, he was gone.

Hobbling feet told Doyler's return. 'You changed your mind,'
he said immediately he saw MacMurrough's face.

MacMurrough looked down on the soap-bright phiz. His
hair was smarmed and a new shirt blossomed, collarless but
clean, inside his new-brushed serge. Really he had ought to

send him packing. 'Not changed my mind at all,' he said. He dropped the stub of a cigarette, unmindful of having smoked it. His eyes peeked along the shore where the little boy had been. Gone. 'Are we ready?'

'No strings,' Doyler repeated in a tone that would admonish himself more than MacMurrough.

MacMurrough's hand patted his bum. 'Not that a little feel would go astray.'

His face washed and his mind made up, Doyler could laugh. 'Mary and Joseph, but you're the heathenest case I did ever meet.'

A Man Of Moderate Means Finds True Economy In A Suit! A Suit Will Give A Man Ease, Spirit, Confidence! A Suit Will Make A Man Know His Worth!

The boy read the notices as they passed down the aisle. He snorted and MacMurrough said, 'Just think what an overcoat would achieve.'

It took the name of Ballygihen House to get decent ministration and MacMurrough was happy to give it. The mask in charge became a face with a welcome. Man and boy he had served the MacMurroughs of Ballygihen. 'And let me see, you must be . . . ?'

'Nephew,' said MacMurrough.

'The nephew,' he repeated. 'Over from England if I do not mistake. I hope now and you're enjoying your stay with us?'

The tone was familiar, a custom of the Irish servantry which at times MacMurrough found charming. Today, however, it was crack service he required and he rapped on a glass-topped case.

'Is there anyone in charge who can see to me? My friend here needs a suit.'

'I was thinking the very same thought myself,' said the man.

He could feel Doyler flustering beside him. The Irish assurance with which he'd entered the store leaked away under the sidelong stares. MacMurrough sighed. 'Can't you just find us something? We have a meeting this afternoon with my nephew's solicitor.'

'The young gentleman's solicitor, no less. Well sir, you have come to the appropriate shop. A suit bought at Lee's of Kingstown will give ease, spirit, confidence to any man or youth that wears it. Matthew! Matthew!' he called. 'Where are these fellows when you need them? Always on the gallivant, what? On the gay galoot, I don't doubt it. Matthew, will you show the young gentleman to the fitting-room and take his measurements for him. Have you given any thought to the cloth you'd be thinking of? Tweed, we have found, is a rough hard-wearing fabric and will often show to the best in difficult weathers.'

'He's not going ratting. We want something smart.'

'No, I like tweed,' piped Doyler.

'The young gentleman has a mind his own. Let you go with Matthew till he gets the measure of you, and Mr MacMurrough and myself will decide what is proper.'

Doyler hung behind, looking doubtful. Though he didn't feel like it, MacMurrough winked and nodded for him to follow the boy. 'Where may I sit?'

'Take the weight off your legs, please do, Mr MacMurrough. Is it Anthony now it is?'

'Do I know you?'

'Not at all. Though I have served the MacMurroughs, man and gorsoon, these forty years, I wouldn't doubt it. Over from

London. Your aunt will be mighty glad to have you on her hands. Is it for the recuperation you have come? I dare say it is never the local sights that has you brought this way out from Piccadilly.'

It seeped into MacMurrough like the grease off his tongue. Newspaper reports, of course. And one had begun to forget. Had begun to imagine nobody would care. Aunt Eva, damned seductrix. He smoked while the walker extolled his cloths, slipping his head between the rails of ready-mades and his palter inside his patter. Terrible shortage of young men this season. Due to the war, he wouldn't doubt it. The trouble in finding a willing boy. No sooner found than he was off to enlist. One had to take them as one found them these days. Had he noticed a similar shortage in England? Of clerks, he meant.

There was more to it than newspapers. Something stickier in his ointment. 'He'll need shoes too.'

'Boots or shoes? Will we settle for high-lows? That way they may be serviceable to the young gentleman after his meeting with the solicitor.'

MacMurrough waved a hand. 'And a shirt. Tie, collar.'

'One of each will be ample. One pair cuffs, one pair holders, one pair studs. Will the young gentleman be wanting a nether integuments with his outfit?'

'What?'

The walker bent to whisper. 'A drawers, I was meaning.'

It had gone beyond a joke. MacMurrough rose. 'Do you pretend to practise upon me?' But his searing eyes caught the man's urgency which betrayed little nastier than a wish to engage. Good grief, he's a sod. All it is. Damn fellow's one of us. He laughed out loud. 'A drawers? No, my nephew doesn't wear them. Most unhealthy.'

'I quite agree,' said the walker. 'A needless encumbrance on the young.'

MacMurrough chuckled on so that he had to leave the gentlemen's outfitting and wander about the store. He touched things, silk and satin, then went out in the street, sniffed the breezy air. They change the sky not their soul who run across the sea. But he could think of unpleasanter ports of refuge. His boy was in good hands, if not auspiciously safe ones. He took a turn round the town.

Outside the Catholic church he read the news bills. He looked at the flowers and considered a buttonhole. A chap sat on the steps in whose eyes he saw Dick's as they followed the Saturday skirt. Wintry face of the flower-seller.

How delightful it was to spend money. There was a thrill in providing for another that was close to, if not actually, sexual. A thrill that very nearly, though not quite, sufficed.

A wedding left the church and, meeting a funeral, walked three steps with the dead. Three girls like miniature nuns, their shawls pulled over their heads, passed a little tramp who fed his dog with little crumbs of bread. He tossed his butt in the gutter and a boy retrieved it whose magic blows reglowed its end. Under a barber's pole old men stooped. The church bells rang, signifying something. With holiday ears MacMurrough heard, with holiday eyes he watched.

He came upon an old man on a bench, and feeling the sulter of weather and fumes, he thought to share a while the shade and the old man's air of being at ease with the world. He nodded, sitting down, and the gentleman tipped his hat. His old lips smacked and made gummy calculations; then he coughed, and coughing became Scrotes, who presently leant forward and inquired of MacMurrough,

– Who are we?

– I'm sorry, old man?

– The gentleman in the haberdashery. You mentioned he was one of us. Who are we?

– Sinners, old man, said MacMurrough laughing. Habitual degenerates in the making.

Doyle was emerging from the fitting-room when MacMurrough returned to the store. He had chosen his own cloth in the end, a bright brown tweed with gas-pipe trousers. The man and his boy fussed with the turn-up. Doyler wore a look of mortification.

'It is only a temporary stitch we had opportunity to put in, but the young gentleman believes there is at home a practised hand who will make it the more durable for him. Else I would tap my toes and insist on Lee's quality alterations.'

'How do I look?'

'See for yourself.' MacMurrough led him to a body-glass and the boy turned this way and that.

'Don't hardly recognize meself.'

'Do you know what you look like?' MacMurrough was about to say an apprentice chauffeur-mechanic. But he stopped himself. He might be a boy from his schooldays. He might be any mother's son.

'What do I look like?'

'Gilbert the filbert.'

'The knut with a K?'

'The pride of Piccadilly, the blasé roué.'

As a last touch MacMurrough pulled a cap from a stand and landed it on his head. It was a wide flat cap which childed his face and made his eyes look deeper than ever.

'Are you sure you're sure about this?'

'Quite certain.'

'For free?'

'Free – but you might come to the Pavilion with me.'

He grinned. And with ease, spirit, confidence, said, 'Never mind the Pavvo. Go to the shagging Flower Ball in this rig-out.'

MacMurrough signed at the desk, and in his ears the chaplain's words of doom: Your aunt will know of this. The account will be queried, questions will be asked. All for a grin and a foolish will to win.

They were wrapping Doyler's tats in a parcel. Sparing his gloves, the clerk used expendable hands. Doyler broke in and said, 'Hold on a crack,' and he rummaged through the mess of his jacket. He found the pin on the inside of his lapel and quickly transferred it to its new concealment.

'Well, then, are you sorted?'

'Right I am.'

'Pavvo beware,' blarnied MacMurrough.

'Listen to you. It's you is supposed to rub off on me.'

– If there is any god, said Dick.

'Sticky buns?'

'All right.'

'And an assortment of buns,' MacMurrough told the waitress. He tilted his chair and stretched his legs on the paving. 'Touch crowded this afternoon.'

'Saturday, aye.'

'Shame about lunch.'

'Cakes is fine but.'

They were seated in a portico giving on the gardens. The band had removed temporarily for their teas and the air sustained a patter as though the trees received a dry adumbration of drizzle. Waitresses in white forked aprons swept past for all the world like mobile Ys. The boy hunched with a stiff neck. Only his eyes roamed and, roaming, gleamed.

'Not a bad spot, I suppose,' MacMurrough conceded.

'Slap-up so it is.'

'Told you you'd enjoy it.'

'Sure I been before,' said Doyler. 'Many's the time I snook in the Pavvo.'

'I see.' Rather a disappointment.

'Hawking the newspapers, of course. Could always reckon on ten minutes to get a sheaf of them sold. If you was quick like and handy with the makes. Then they catched on to you and it was out on your ear with a boot up the b-t-m. They had a down on newsboys, thinking us thiefs. But the takings was good while it lasted. Makes,' he added, having considered his eloquence, 'is ha'pennies you do give for change.'

The tea arrived with the sticky buns. Nanny Tremble fretted about manners and the chaplain complained of sulphurous breaths. But toggery maketh gentle man: almond-eyed Doyler viewed the stand; morsure at a time, he chewed like a choirboy.

He leant forward over the table carnations. 'You see the one what brung the tray?'

'What about her?'

'She's after dropping her scent in the tea-pot.'

MacMurrough conspired in his smile and said, 'You might have a soda, if you preferred.'

'No, tea is grand.'

Behaving as though I really did have a nephew.

The boy supped, swallowed, said, 'Tea is quite satisfactory, I thank you.'

Which jollied the occasion no end. They chatted a time,

then the boy looked hole-and-corner about him. Again he leant closer. 'Do you mind me asking?'

'Ask away.'

'Is there many about that likes what you do?'

A long draw on his Abdulla. He stubbed it out. 'I don't know, actually. Common enough for there to be laws against it.'

'Wouldn't mind the law.'

Antinomian little buggeree.

'Only the young fellow in Lee's what measured me up, he said to me was you my gent. Said he had a gent and all. Said the walker there does look after him nicely. Then do you know what he did?'

Yes, thought MacMurrough, though his brows rose in candid query.

'Damn fellow had a squeeze at me flowers and frolics.' He sat back in consternation. 'What would he want doing a thing like that?'

He was genuinely mystified. MacMurrough said, 'Perhaps he liked you.'

'Liked me? Sure he wasn't rich.'

This leap of logic required another cigarette. MacMurrough lit one slowly, then flicked the match. 'Does one need to be rich to enjoy the company of a handsome young man?'

'Am I handsome?'

MacMurrough pulled deeply and savoured the smoke, smiling, his eyes on the boy's face. 'Yes.'

'And you're rich. Rich as crazes, you are.'

'My family might be. Myself, I haven't a bean.'

'How bad you are. Wasting away, I can tell.'

Little brat is teasing me now. 'Money is irrelevant to desire. Only it helps to overcome another's shyness. That's all.'

'No, it's not all.'

'Explain.'

'You think any fellow would want another fellow?'

Scrotes. Where was bloody Scrotes when you needed him? 'I don't see why not. I don't say every fellow. But look at the clerk in Lee's.'

'That's me point sure. If it wasn't for the walker as led him into it, he wouldn't think to do that. If it wasn't for meeting you I wouldn't be . . .'

'Wouldn't be what?'

'I wouldn't be sitting here, that's all.'

Comfort for the troops. He wants his friend. He actually wants his friend. Briefly MacMurrough glimpsed balmy waters where ephebes naked bathed. And on his bench, in pallium draped, their tutor kindly watches. Pulling on an Abdulla.

'He means a lot to you.'

'Who does?'

'Your friend.'

The eyes flared and, sneering, he said, 'Don't think I don't cop you getting your eyeful of us swimming.'

Coolly MacMurrough replied, 'Not watching so much as waiting my turn. Wouldn't seem right, somehow, disturbing your lessons.'

The sneer curled the corner of his mouth while he considered this. The lustre dulled in his eyes; his head bent. In its stead reared Mammon's nummular nob.

'They do say money is the root of all evil.'

'I thought that was supposed to be the love of money.'

'There's neat for you. 'Tis them without that loves it best. That puts Doyler in his place. Doyler and all his kind.'

Nanny Tremble thought another sticky bun and a refreshment of the cups was in order and MacMurrough did the honours. 'Look here, do we have to talk about money?'

'Talk what you like. It's you what's paying.'

'I thought we'd got past all this.'

'Oh well, damn the thing anyway.' He seized a bun and took a munch of it, dominoes flashing between spittled dough. 'You can have the suit back if you wants it.'

Was this good humour returning? MacMurrough searched till he found a little doyle that with coaxing might grow to a doyling full grin. 'Would you let me watch you take it off?'

'Go away, you – I don't what you are. A bad lot for sure.'

Friends again and honours easy. Time for a change of subject. 'That badge you're so careful about. I've noticed before. Some religious attachment?'

Quick dart of his eyes. 'Religion, me arse. I'm a socialist.'

'An agitator, no less. In the Pavilion Gardens.'

He liked that. 'Never know where we'd be.' He turned the lapel and screwed his eyes to view it. 'Badge of the Citizen Army. Nor King nor Kaiser we serve, but Ireland. Meaning the working man.'

'Why do you hide it?'

'Don't hide it.'

Very well. 'Why do you wear it where no one can see?'

He let go the lapel and fussily patted it down. 'They have them banned at work. Door to the street if they catched you wearing your badge. I suppose and you could say I have it hidden. Hard to know what's for the best. You know why I got this job?'

'Good worker? Hard worker? Honest?'

'The owner was after letting the men go for to encourage them to list. Great plaudits he got for that day's work. Then he employs us boys at half the rate. He has the union banned. What can you do? Half the rate means half a loaf but nix means nothing on the table. They don't like you to

282

have ideals. Ideals is for likes of you. For your aunt and the father.'

'Yet you still have ideals.'

'Aye do I. I have the words of them. I have a badge I don't dare to show.'

It was a tale of woe which was just verging on the tedious. 'Can be hard to believe in something when the world's against it.'

'Aye aye, and what do you believe in, Mr MacMurrough?'

A wasp buzzed about him and he felt, or apprehended, the small breeze of its wings. The terrace sloped to trees at the bottom and there beyond the railway began the harbour, whose arms reached to cuddle a calm. Swifts or swallows darted low in the air. An Irish summer: half-hour's sunshine between the showers. God help the rain if it thought to pour on Aunt Eva's fête. 'Believe that I exist,' he said.

'Aren't you the bold one.'

'Bolder than you might think. I have a friend, or rather I had one, he's dead now; but he believed that I existed.'

A compursion of the boy's face. 'Does it mean something I don't understand?'

'That we existed, he and I, and others like us.' MacMurrough shifted in his chair. A voice was wondering why he bothered with this; an innominate voice which was plausibly his own. 'You asked me earlier were there many of us about. The question for my friend was, were there any of us at all. The world would say that we did not exist, that only our actions, our habits, were real, which the world called our crimes or our sins. But Scrotes began to think that we did indeed exist. That we had a nature our own, which was not another's perverted or turned to sin. Our actions could not be crimes, he believed, because they were the expression of a nature, of an existence even. Which came

283

first, he asked, the deed or the doer? And he began to answer that, for some, it was the doer.' MacMurrough smiled, seeing the boy's concentrating face. 'I don't follow much of it myself,' he said.

'You think I should wear my badge with pride?'

He had forgotten about the badge. I have spilt my soul and he bothers with baubles. 'I shouldn't risk losing my job over it. But in the Pavilion Gardens I don't see why not.'

In one of his cracks he had the badge pinned openly. Red hand supinate on a tinny metal. In this he believes.

He made to stand up. 'Have to go round the corner.'

'You'll need some change.'

'They makes you pay?'

'A tip. There'll be a woman outside. Just drop it in her saucer. It's expected.'

He shot his cuffs, in a gesture unbecomingly spontaneous, and swanked through the tables. Thruppenny masher I've made of him, thought MacMurrough. Already his neck was reddening where it wasn't accustomed to a collar. Howling check he chose. On their way from Lee's he had called at the railway station where he plastered his hair with tap water.

Shit-shoveller and comfort for the troops, *Arcades ambo*. Naturally he blames me. And I suppose I have cast that apple before him.

– That apple, the chaplain trumpeted, which, once he taste of it, shall rot in his mouth to the apple of Sodom.

Yes yes, we know all that. Besides he's already taken a tolerable bite. But did my giving it him to taste beget his desire or waken it? That is the question. Or is that the question? Mayn't they find a half-hour's happiness in each other's arms? God knows, there's little enough joy in the world, and precious little for free.

I wonder does he frig himself thinking of his friend. Don't suppose he finds much privacy where he sleeps. I should like to hold him while he frigged. Yes, that would be pleasant. To stroke his hair and hold him close while he thought of his friend and frigged in my bed. His flowers and his frolics to fondle and lovingly Dick to lunge, while the name of his friend to the pillow he moaned.

Test of a true hunter. Do you fuck your catch? Pater, O pater, behold thy son.

Doyler returned. Sheepishly showed his hand, the coins still there. 'Do you mind?'

MacMurrough shook his head. 'She does little to earn it more than ask for it.'

They walked back through George's Street, then through the People's Park, which pleased the boy immoderately. No, he had never been before, never in his puff. A right cheek they had calling it the People's Park, then the keepers chasing you out without you was wearing a collar and tie. And vaguely MacMurrough agreed.

'You know, Scrotes had many friends in the socialist movement.'

'Scrotes? Your friend, is it?'

'Some people in Sheffield. I was supposed to visit with them. But I didn't. I came here instead.'

'Maybe you was better going with the socialists.'

'England is bloody at the moment. This war has got into everything.'

'There'll be war here soon enough.'

'They're always saying that about Ireland.'

'Sure as tomorrow's rain, there'll be fighting in the streets.'

'Yes, and the Russians are on the Tyne and the angels are at Mons.'

'Ah well, you being a visitor, you'd know better than me.'
MacMurrough laughed in good grace.

'Tell us about them socialists anyway.'

'Fellow called Carpenter. Written books, apparently. Talks about comrade love.'

'Aye does he.'

'No, seriously. Believes it's a way of bridging the social divides.'

'Likely story. If that was the case, every time a nob took a tart they'd end up talking socialism.'

The import of what he had said gradually dawned. Mac-Murrough raised a brow in curiosity. But the boy, too, had a good grace.

'Ah sure well,' he said, having spat on the wall, 'that makes me the tart.'

They slowed their pace, yet still they came to the lane where he lived. They watched the fishing men a while. MacMurrough put out his palm, feeling wet. He looked up at the sky. Drizzling again.

'Suppose you're going to ask me to go on with you now.'

'Would you – if I asked?'

'No.'

'That's plainly said.'

'Not if you asked. Different if I offered.'

This was a new adventure. And though Dick wasn't particular what machinations were employed, MacMurrough was not so sure the rest of him felt so agreeable.

'And do you intend to offer?'

Twisted lips which pursed to the embouchure of a kiss. 'You'll have to wait while I find the ma. She'll be looking for me wages packet.'

There was a shout from behind. One of the fellows on the

rocks had caught a fish. MacMurrough saw the exultant face and the limp thing held up. Then he heard the dog-patter of slippered feet as down the spiral stairs, step at a time, step at a time, Scrotes descended from his turret retreat. A breath of cold preceded him till round the bend his face appeared. And which are you his eyes inquired.

– Fisher or fish? he asked.

But it wasn't Scrotes who held MacMurrough's attention. Out of the very corner of his eye he saw the small boy who earlier had scampered over the rocks. He held his nanny's hand now and was walking with her home along the sea-wall. He looked over his tiny shoulder. Even from this distance, his eyes shone blue as once MacMurrough's had shone. And it seemed to MacMurrough that a recognition came on his face. That he smiled. That he waved his tiny hand and smiled.

CHAPTER ELEVEN

'Anthony, dear, if I am to knot your tie you shall have to stand still. Cannot you bend your knees? How tall you must be.'

'Six feet to the inch.'

'Don't say so too loudly. Only Our Lord was six feet exactly. Some of these people can be very touchy on these subjects.'

'Ought I to be shorter or taller?'

'For the moment you might consider being shorter. It is an age since I bowed a man's tie. Not since your grandfather. Let me see. No, that won't do at all. We want you looking your best for our guests. Young ladies, and more pertinently their mothers, have an eye for a well-bowed tie.'

'It being the first serious step in life.'

'How whimsical you are.'

Wilde, of course; though he did not say so. There had been disappointment already. 'Turn-ups in your trouser legs. Really, Anthony, I cannot think what your tailor intended. A turn-up is a slight on a gentleman's carriage.' And his socks. 'Lavender, indeed. I have never known morning so colourful. Is it the last cry of St Germain? Perhaps we might utilize that.

My nephew has been abroad. Yes, la Légion étrangère. So happy to have him home.'

'Surely they will have heard where I've been?'

'They will have heard what the English have said. Truth is quite another matter.'

Now, while she pulled at his throat, he said, 'Hadn't I ought to be told who's coming?'

'Few that you would know. Though you ought to know them. It is absurd that a MacMurrough should be so ill informed of his country's society.' While her fingers fretted, her tongue spilt names. 'The usual foule en fête. Old Mrs Houlihan has long arrived. Ensconced in the garden room with her invalid wine and wafers. Really it was only a charity that I invited her at all as the family has fallen considerably. The estates are encumbered and her sons have flitted about the globe squandering what fortune remained. One fears the daughters may suffer the same trait. Still, she was quite a figure in her day and one had to invite her, if only as a point de départ.

'Then whom have we? Lady O'Brien, to whom we all pay tribute for her remarkable triumph at Crufts. Her Great Danes were judged best of breed, and I might add myself they are the friendliest tamest beasts, quite belying their grisly appearance. She is to present her daughter, wild young thing, gap-toothed, alas, and rather quarrelsome, one hears.

'Madame O'Connor with her crony that Breifne woman. Such memories these people have. I doubt if we'll ever be forgiven the incident with your grandfather. He invited the woman to share his compartment and such a fuss she made afterwards, protesting she had no notion the train was travelling to Ferns. In the end her husband had to come fetch her and there might well have been a scene had not your grandfather prudently dispatched to Bristol for the season.

'Then there's poor Lady Geraldine. Did I get the simnel cake? Did I enjoy it? Isn't it the king of cakes? She is quite touched, I find. We are told the family line was saved by a monkey. I do hope not in Mr Huxley's sense. O'Neills, O'Donnells, Maguires, unmanageable fillies out of the north. It is the fathers I blame. Cook's tours of the Continent and the poor children left to mind for themselves. Miss Butler with her darling spaniels and picture-hat. Quite the cavalier.

'Charming couple from Lucan I met in Paris with their daughter Ruth. I'm sure that child's not all together. Something alarming the way her head lolls. It seems Limerick has evacuated for the season, for not a solitary reply has returned from that quarter. The Misses French insist on coming by yacht. I cannot think how they may hope to debark in this tide. The Bridges will be here, Grattan and Butt, but they of course are Protestant.

'Still, there is nothing like a Protestant to raise the tone. Hence poor Miss Emmet, though I fear she has waited too long and now must be written off entirely. Numerous dreamy blue-stockings who write poetry for the press. I say poetry. I say press. And that poor old tired old thistlewhipper out of Kerry. She also was at Crufts. But her Irish terriers were found thin and straggling in the end. They have been bought as a job lot by the Ministry for War and will work as fetchers and sentinels in the trenches, the creatures. And in fine Miss Ivy Day, about whom least said, soonest mended. I believe the only hope for that child now is a convent's laundry.'

MacMurrough said, 'It sounds a tolerably uninspiring lot.'

Tightly she tensed a temporary knot. 'Do not mock the Irish womanhood,' she commanded. 'It was not the monks or the chiefs who civilized the Dane, but the Irish slavewomen who nursed his sons. It was not the great kings nor the petty kings who had the Normans more Irish than the Irish themselves, but the daughters of kings whom they took to wife. And it was their Irish wives who kept the Old English to their faith. Who knows, but that the gentlemen took flight, their women might have made something of the planters who replaced them. But the men deserted her, and their dark Rosaleen they beggared to the hillside.'

He watched her reflected view in the glass. An emerald glittered in her hair and fine pearls lustred below. The rest was long and black, as though her shadow and she might be one. 'Beggared?' he asked.

'As good as, for all the gentlemen recked of her.'

A last tug and she withdrew. 'Still, beggars may not be choosers, and I am sure we shall find many a suitress in the months ahead. That, after all, is what young ladies and gentlemen are for. Now, let you turn round.' His neck reprieved, his hair was next arraigned. 'Oh lah, Anthony, you might have visited a barber. You look every inch a banjoist.'

'An't I supposed to be a musician?'

'You are supposed to be what you are: a MacMurrough leading the young to their duty. Nobody has asked you to be artistic about it. Please don't smoke.'

He closed the carton lid.

She glanced about the room in a withering way. Huckaback towels rumpled on the shaving stand. Unslopped Minton slop-pail. His papers at his desk. Her hands hugged her arms. 'Is it very chilly in here? Does the child lay a fire for you?'

'I forget to keep it sometimes.' Her dress, he saw, was not entirely black. A fine embroidery greened its neck. She looked a very elegant, very tragic relict. 'And you, Aunt Eva, what are you supposed to be?'

'I am my father's daughter.'

'Yet you never married.'

The withering look advanced, narrowing on its way, glinting towards him. Then it passed and settled on the view through the window. 'Do hurry, Anthony. I shall need you to organize your boys. The guests will be arriving any time and I had thought how thrilling if our golden heroes served the bonnes-bouches.'

Coming down the stairs MacMurrough halted at the half-pace glass. Momentarily a blue-eyed boy in Fontleroy lace quizzed him. He winked and the glass returned the boy grown up. And such an elegant gentleman he was. Sleek fell of hair, his thread of a 'tache, eyes the colour of a blue-fox fur. Morning-coat and grey slip showing, pearl pin, pale gardenia, choker of a collar to keep his chin up. In his hand a slip of gloves, silk topper, his grandfather's best malacca. His front-creased pants, pearl-grey spats, his bals, buttoned, patent. An aubade in black and dirty white.

He felt an itching in his nose which, if Nanny Tremble were to be believed, boded a stranger to meet. Or perhaps he was already looking at him. He satisfied the itch, then lodged the cane in the half-pace corner, sloped the gloves above. *Légion étrangère*, my aunt. I'm Gilbert the filbert. He topped the silk, tipped it to an angle. *L'incroyable*. Tapped down the stairs.

His aunt's voice came loudly from the garden room, surdity now having apparently been loaded upon old Mrs Houlihan's other misfortunes. He thought a livener might be in order but there was a gentleman in uniform by the library door.

'Ah, MacMurrough,' this officer called. 'Don't suppose you'll remember me.'

His hand was out for a shake. MacMurrough gestured a brief delay and darted through the pass door. Kitchens like

Piccadilly Circus. Child in the corner weeping to herself while the trays passed overhead.

'Is everything all right, Nancy?'

She looked up through reddened eyes. 'Oh, Mr MacMurrough, I'm a good girl, really I am.'

'Yes, I'm sure.' Though somebody evidently thought otherwise.

He came out on the area, then up the steps to the side terrace. Family groups knotted about, each with its attendant cleric; magnificent matrons in powder and mink, maidens pale beside. Threading between, black-tailed waiters and exotic-liveried youths.

Now that he'd thought about a drink, he couldn't get the notion off his mind. Who was that fellow in uniform? Should have lifted a glass while I was down the kitchen. Interesting specimen against the wall there. Glass tilting out of his hand. Very louche he looks. Lounge suit inside the enclosure, sound the alarm. One of the Houlihan sons who have frittered their wealth. Or is it? Good grief, it's bloody Doyle.

'Well, Mr MacMurrough, grand isn't it?'

'Shouldn't you be in your kilt? Shouldn't you be serving the guests?'

'Thought I'd swank it a while in me suit of clothes.'

'Did you indeed.'

'Besides, there's the division of labour involved. I'm here for to play music not to be kowtowing to the la-di-das.'

'You're looking rather la-di-da yourself. Is that champagne you're drinking?'

'Don't rightly know what it is. Was standing here, just looking, like, and a young thing comes and offers me the tray of it. Sure why not? says I. Is that what it is, champagne? Wait till I tells them at home.'

'Fetch me a glass, will you? Fetch two glasses. I need to keep clear of the house for a time.'

They stepped over the rope that enclosed the high lawns from the mud-show proper. Stalls were still setting up as they wandered down the paths. Banners fluttered with looping Celtic letters. Rinuccini's ice cream. Keogh's saddlery. Catering by Allen, Larkin and O'Brien. Clod-hopper who taught the boys to march trundling his barrow to its station. Through sombre umbrage of trees shadow-tailed squirrels flickered.

'Queue a mile long at the gates,' Doyler said. 'What time's it due opening at?'

'Whenever the refreshments are finished, I suppose. We don't want feeding the hungry, do we?'

'Wouldn't do at all, that wouldn't.'

Makeshift stage where later his boys would perform, where now hob-nailed labourers thumped the boards. Behind and in the wings, national schoolteachers led their charges in final rehearsal. Communion-frocked girls sang hymns to Our Lady, crop-haired boys peeped *Hibernia irredenta*. In equal doses, Home Rule and the BVM. Horrisonant call of somebody's warpipe.

'Let's cut to the vegetable garden. Private there.'

It had rained overnight but morning in its discretion had seen better sense. It might even prove a summer's day. They passed the cracked sundial, overgrown with briars, whose gnomon shadow zigged and zagged to find some time to tell. The paths were streaked with slime where snails had passed. Why do snails travel in the rain? MacMurrough did not know but he watched Doyler step carefully aside to rescue those that had lost their way. They sat where old Moore liked to sit, amid the dilapidated cucumber-frames, with his half a loaf and can of tea.

'Good garden of potatoes there,' Doyler said. 'What they calls a broo, with the cabbages in between.'

'You're welcome to help yourself, you know.'

'Serious?'

'Don't suppose anyone would notice.'

'Aren't you the grand nob, Mr MacMurrough. But you don't know gardeners very well.'

He hadn't thought of old Moore, it was true. 'Must you keep on with this Mr MacMurrough? We know each other better than that.'

'Aye do we. First off you're asking why amn't I serving your guests. Next you're offering me spuds to steal.'

'You're sharp enough to know what I meant.'

'Aye, you meant charity.'

Out in the bay MacMurrough saw what he presumed was the Misses French's motor-yacht. Its jolly-boat had moored by Kelly shore. There were toy poodles inside. He heard their yapping and he could just make out their crimped heads as up and down they leapt, will-they-won't-they spring to land.

The best amongst the poor are never grateful. They are ungrateful, discontented, disobedient, and rebellious. Wilde again; his observation concluding: *They are quite right to be so.* Wilde, too, had provided his boys with suits of clothes. At the trial Carson produced one in evidence. We picture the scene, the lawyer's flourish, almost the prestidigitation, Do you deny, sir, that you provided this boy with this suit of blue serge? It was said the lad in question, paperboy off Worthing pier, was to be found that afternoon outside the Old Bailey with the other renters, winking and nodding at likely customers. Oh, to have bought them all that day, the luxury, and only a few quid the lot, glorious.

Were Wilde's panthers grateful or rebellious? Eventually, of course, one prefers a rebellious bedfellow. But it requires a degree of gratitude to get him to bed in the first place.

While he watched the poodles and mused on charity and

rent, his hand descended on Doyler's thigh. He could wish Doyler had chosen blue serge instead of this agony in check. A shave of the rough cloth and his hand was brushed aside.

'Do you never give over?'

'Beg pardon, I'm sure.'

'Wouldn't you let a body be himself?'

Rather a lacuna then, fit of the magnificents. MacMurrough inclined his head to search through the glowers. 'Aren't we friendly today?'

'I have me friend.'

'I could help.'

'Help with what? He don't need clothes.' He stood up. He took a swig of his champagne. The sulky look was disturbed by surprise as a hiccough escaped his throat. 'Champagne, what?'

'Boy, they call it.'

'Who calls it boy?'

'Them what drinks it.'

Doyler laughed, expectorated. The cap came off and returned dégagé and a hand lunged in his pocket. 'Lookat, I'm thankful I met you but.'

You're all right, Doyler, MacMurrough thought. You'll do fine, my sputative disputative boy. 'Come here,' he said.

'What is it?'

MacMurrough felt for the pin inside the boy's lapel, unpinned it, fixed it flagrantly on the outside. Doyler looked gaugingly at him. MacMurrough said, 'I hereby grant you the freedom of my garden to wear your badge with pride.' Then he kissed him on the cheek and muttered in his ear, 'I'll bring a blanket down the meadow garden. Tonight at ten.'

'Get on with you,' he answered, pulling away. He wiped his cheek, the action too impulsive to be thought discourteous. 'What if they catched you?'

'This is my garden. I refuse to be cowed in my own garden.'

'Aye aye. Why're you avoiding them above so?'

Damn me, if he isn't sharp enough to slice himself. MacMurrough quaffed the last of his wine, tossed the glass in the briars. 'Shall I let you into a secret? You know what the good cause is here? For which every family in the parish has prinked and spruced and scraped its pennies? The marriage of a MacMurrough. My aunt is to find me an Irish colleen.'

'So?'

'You don't find that deceitful?'

'Running away with yourself. Do likes of this, there'll be any number of weddings after it.'

The troubled trebles of schoolboys greeted them as up the path they returned. A nation once again, a nation once again, a nation, a nation, a nation. And rather a latration of yaps and yowls as a harum-scarum of dogs swept past. Then, out of the agitation, a nation rising yet again.

'You know those Greeks the song refers to?'

'Ancient freemen? Did often wonder about that.'

'They were from Sparta. One of the Greek cities. Rather militaristic, actually.'

'Well?'

'It was considered among the soldiers – and the soldiery was every citizen in Sparta—'

'Sound enough.'

'Considered disreputable if a soldier among them did not have his lover.'

'His lover, aye?'

'Friend. Comrade, if you like. Another man.'

'What're you saying to me?'

'Just pointing out the history.' The boy is interested. Scrotes,

I take my hat off to you. Bloody papers have a use after all. 'It was an Irishman who first made this point. In print, I mean. Chap name of Mahaffy, in his Greek history. Not sure about now, but he was often to be seen beetling under the clock at Trinity. Mind you, that was the first edition. Scrotes tells me, told me, in the later editions the subject was purged. He taught Wilde.'

'Is it Oscar Wilde?'

'Yes.'

'He was a very bad fellow, they say.'

'Yes, they do.'

'They'd say anything against an Irishman, the English would.'

'They might tell the truth, too.'

'Aye, they might. They say he used be very famous at one time.'

'He was. He stayed here, you know.'

'In this house?'

'Walked these very paths. It's whispered some of his poems were, if not written, contemplated here.'

'Is that where you . . . ?'

MacMurrough laughed. 'I wasn't thought of at the time. Or if I was, I was only an infant in your mother's shawl.'

That took the queries off his face, dimpled his face to smiliness. 'You seen the ma and the missy so?'

'She made a difference to me, your mother did. I came across her one time and I heard her singing.'

'She does always be singing, all right.'

'I felt I might belong. I might, God help me, be' – irrational, irrepressible, irresponsible, iron-brained, irascible, irksome, entirely irresistible – 'might be Irish,' he said.

'There you are, Anthony. I have been searching aux quatre vents.'

*

'Aunt Eva, I was coming to see to the gates.'

'The gates are long opened. Really, Anthony, you might be more considerate. Est-ce que je connais ce jeune voyou?'

'Doyle. He's from the band.'

'Quel insigne intéressant il porte. La Main rouge. You are from the band,' she said, enunciating clearly for the dull ears of the low. 'Scurry along, young man, and change into the costume provided. There's all to do and each to his task.'

She took MacMurrough's arm and wheeled him round. He had a glimpse of a black devil beshadowing the path, and Doyler was gone. 'Did you need to be quite so direct?'

'I have annoyed you. Oh lah, que je can be brusque. It was his vesture. Such colourful taste. Is your friend by any chance a bookie's runner?'

Suit. She knows, of course. Does she know? Of course she knows.

'But of course he is not your friend. He is, as you say, a boy from the band. Now do come along. I have a most interesting young man I wish you to meet.'

'I thought I was to be wed.'

'All in God's time. Today we display the goods. To their best advantage, one hopes. Good day, Mrs O'Donnell. Good day to you, Mrs O'Neill. Splendid show, I agree. Yes yes, Erin go breagh! O'Donnell aboo! Sassenachs à bas! Presently now.'

She directed him to a tangential path. 'Ulster folk, a contumelious breed. I discovered them earlier arguing the name of a flower. It is a sweet william. Not at all, it is a stinking billy. They do pout so. Dear dear, Anthony, and you have scuffed your shoes. Lead me to a seat and we shall sit a moment. You have a mouchois?'

'I have a handkerchief.'

'Now, this young man, Father O'Toiler has brought him along, he is a schoolteacher. His pupils will enact a drama. Something of a lisp and all the gaucherie of youth, but he has such stirring ideas. You recall my mentioning a Fenian had died?'

'The dynamiter.'

'The funeral is tomorrow. This young man is to give the panegyric at his graveside. He was tempting us with little morceaux choisis on the terrace. How we thrilled. Les fous, les fous, les fous! Meaning the British. The lisp is unfortunate and he has small grasp of oratory, but the words had us all a-tingle.'

'Is the speech to be given in French?'

'Don't tease. One translates for dramatic effect.'

Her oh-lah French and her oh-lah ways. He was nettled still by her sharpness with Doyle. But of course it wasn't her sharpness, it was his own pusillanimity. What a dumb dog I am, forever consulting my safety. Not even my safety. My *menus plaisirs* – two quid a week.

She was mentioning now some school in Rathfarnham where everything was taught through Irish. Wasn't that a marvel? An Irish school was just what Glasthule needed.

'And will you run down the entire Presentation College to have your way?'

'You have a very diseased imagination. Where is that priest?'

'Who is the fellow in the library? Officer of some sort.'

'Oh, that's just Tom. Tom Kettle. His father and your grandfather were sparring-partners of old.'

'Tom-tom Kettle-drum,' said MacMurrough.

'You know him, then?'

'He was above me at school. That dreadful year I schooled in Ireland. After you ragged father into sending me here.'

'For all the good it did you.'

'Why's he in British uniform?'

'Tom Kettle is a very teasing man. But he is a Member of Parliament. And, more to the point, he is married to a Sheehy. The Sheehy girls are all mad or married to madmen. One of them, after all, has fetched up with that dwarfish oaf in knickerbockers. But they will have many befitting acquaintances, any of whom should be delighted to meet a MacMurrough.'

'Don't you feel any shame at all?'

'Shame?' she repeated and her fingers tapped on her parasol.

'The duplicity of it all. Charging a shilling a head of the poor, just so's you can see me wed.'

They had come to a bench and she waited while he took her hand and led her to sit. She said, 'Balmorals,' and he took out his handkerchief, began wiping his bals.

'How very little you know of the poor, Anthony, dear. No doubt you would deck them all in screaming tweeds. But they are poor people: they are not garden pets. They will take what they wish from this entertainment. Fear not, they will have their shilling's worth. And should a wedding come of it, that too will entertain. They will queue outside the church, praising the fine clothes and the grand procession, and the talk for weeks to come will be of you and your bride. They expect these things. They do not expect one to perambulate in their muck. The duplicity you remark has given employment to fifty men. That is fifty tables with dinner tonight.'

He looked up from his shoes with surprised admiration. A surprise that was becoming ever more customary. He had never supposed she had considered the subject.

'I am sure that does not surprise me,' she said. 'You suppose very little in your elders beyond fatuity. Where has that priest got to?' Her gaze glinted east and west but nothing she found dulled its edge. It glanced off MacMurrough's eyes, grazed his chin, then settled on the pearl pin of his neck-tie. 'Perhaps this is not the moment to speak of it,' she said. 'I wonder.' The wonder flittered across her face. Dismissed, it fluttered down her sleeve, to butterfly away in her fingers. 'We have something of a scène de ménage on our hands. It requires attending.'

'We have?'

'The kitchen girl. She is with child.'

'You are sure?'

'Cook is certain. It's not . . . ? No, of course it is not.'

'Aunt Eva!'

'One is a woman of the world. Such entanglements occur in a big house. Your grandfather was a great man, but he was not renowned for a saintly conduct. And no one would have expected it of him. Least of all I.'

'Why not you?'

'I have told you many times. I am his daughter. You are his grandson. It is not ours to concern ourselves with the petty inadequacies of human nature. There is the confessional for that. Our role is to lead, if not by example, by force of will. Where is that damned priest?'

She leant on her parasol, half standing, so that MacMurrough had to rise and take her elbow. 'I saw him earlier at an ice-cream stall. He seemed in his element.'

'I know what you think,' she replied, sitting again. 'A cockalorum of the walk. What they would call here a Puncheous Pilate. But a spinster of the parish, of whatever means or dignity, has little sway without a priest at her side. The old canon was a dotard, and one can only hope for his speedy deliverance from the sufferings of this world. Father O'Toiler is a godsend to us all. Until one's nephew come into his inheritance.'

'Aunt Eva, what do you propose doing about the girl?'

She sighed. 'Yes, la pauvre. In the country parts they call it tinning. They tin the girl out of the parish. I have never witnessed the procedure, but one presumes the rowdies and roisterers of the village, the men in plainer words, follow the girl, banging sticks on tin drums, until she has passed beyond the parish bounds. She will not return.'

'What becomes of her?'

'The poorhouse, possibly. In the bigger towns they have convents for such unfortunates. With luck she may arrange her affairs as far as Liverpool. She will need more luck there, of course. The fever may overcome her. It is rumoured many have fallen by the hedge.'

'But you're surely not intending to do any of these things?'

'What can you be thinking? I shall do nothing of the sort. Indeed, I shall do nothing at all beyond sending her home. It is her people who will cast her out. You think me very harsh. But let me tell you, were she my niece I should manage the affair differently. I should look after her and arrange, one way or another, her return into society. And the child should be for ever grateful. She would not fall so publicly again. Would she?'

'No, Aunt Eva, I dare say she would not.'

'Had she any sense. But one despairs of discovering sense in the young. And now, here at last is Father O'Toiler. Father O'Toiler, how do you do? I have been telling my nephew of the schoolmaster you have brought along. Tell us, do, where is the young man now? My nephew is most anxious to make an acquaintance.'

*

MacMurrough splashed soda in Kettle's glass. 'I was surprised to find you in British uniform.'

'There's quite a war on, you know.'

'Only it jars with the nation-once-again crowd outside.'

He handed Kettle his tumbler. Kettle said, 'Where it goes,' and knocked it back and MacMurrough raised his glass in reply.

'Your aunt has grown advanced with the years. But good old Eveline, she keeps a finger in most pies. Last I heard she was collecting comforts for the troops.' The glass was at his lips before he remembered it was dry. 'Will I help you to a refresher? Not a sportsman for it. Well, you're not long back.'

'Don't they worry you?' said MacMurrough.

'The boys from Sinn Féin?' He turned cunningly from the tray. 'They have me shivering in me socks.' He had spoken with the accent of a street-hawker and there was something in his look of the Dublin blowsy. He raised his glass, 'Gaudeamus,' and decorum returned. 'Why should they worry me? There were ever out-and-outers in Ireland. But these upstarts of your aunt's represent the past. Home Rule is on the books now. The people know that, they know whom to thank: the Parliamentary Party. Once this war is over we'll have our separate legislature. We have one final hedge to leap and that is to rout the Germans. Then it's consummatum est. Consummatum for the Sinn Feiners, anyway. Let them keep their kilts and Gaelic. No harm in that. In a way they've done us a service. I'm quite an O'Growneyite myself, you'll find. But politically they're dead as mutton.'

The flushed boyish face moved away. MacMurrough remembered that from school. The muscular mouth-breather who bobbed into your face then bobbed back again to utter a little laugh at what had been said. Kettle. Now here's a man whose name is a household word. It was the school taunt.

He had another mannerism, which was to scratch quickly behind his ear then examine his fingers to see what had they unearthed. His smile now told it was something charming. Liberal to a fault, he flicked the charm away. The library shelves diverted him.

'I see your aunt has the entire *Thesaurus palaeohibernicus*. Isn't that Eveline to a tittle? The rest of us must make do with O'Growney's Irish primers while your aunt has the collected glosses of Dark Age Gaelic. Has she opened them at all?'

'I shouldn't think so.'

'No. Still, she keeps a good Home Rule.' He meant, apparently, her Irish whiskey. At the drinks tray again, with his back to MacMurrough, he said, 'Look here, I was sorry to hear about your trouble.' A pause, then the phrases came magpie quick. 'In England. Your aunt has clarified all. One had no idea. An abominable slander. That the terriers should go to such lengths. Besmirch your grandfather's name. It is intolerable. Look here,' he said again, and this time turned, 'I have influence with a publication. We might write you up. As I'm a Member of Parliament it would be my duty to assist. The truth ought to be told.'

'I don't know what my aunt would say.'

He looked blankly a moment from glazing eyes, then scratched his ear. Another charm he found there. 'Perhaps you're right. Sleeping dogs lie and all that. But the offer stands. We cannot have the terriers and their Orange whelps carry off every slander they choose. Speaking of whelps, I wonder what Carson makes of your aunt's to-do.'

'Carson? He's never here.'

'Here in the garden? Not while grass is green, he's not. But he takes one of the villas over. A lot of bad blood between Eveline and our Orange friend. He always complained your sycamores interrupted his view to the sea. Who knows, perhaps it's that which has advanced Eveline's opinions. There was rumour of a court case.'

Carson. Sir Edward Carson, Wilde's prosecutor, his persecutor, next door. Why, sir, did you mention this boy was ugly? Why, why, why? Until the poetry was beaten from him and he was just a fat blustering man. Squilde. It is the worst case I have ever tried. Two years' hard. Next.

MacMurrough knocked back his glass. 'To our enemy's enemies,' he said.

'May we die in Ireland,' Kettle returned. Then he was off. 'They've done a blundering stupid thing bringing Carson into the Government. More we work with the English now, less the country will work with us. We finally make a peace with them and they go and ditch us like that. Carson – leader of the Orangists, an avowed law-beaker, Attorney-General they make him. Tell me about the English. All the sensitivity of a pin-cushion. Sense of justice, fair play and all that. Play up, play up and play the game. Lauded game of cricket. Load of rot. Never did understand the Irish. Never will, until we look them in the eye from our own legislature. Home Rule,' he said, raising his glass in toast.

MacMurrough shifted his gaze from the thick spittle-wet mouth and stared instead through the garden windows. What a dreary drunk he was. He recalled the Spartan custom of inebriating slaves that young men should see how contemptible was drunkenness. Nowadays we leave it to our leshishlashors. And one had idolized him at school. Tom-tom Kettle-drum in his cricket whites. Tom-tom Kettle-drum come to say goodnight. How sad to recollect in the dull-eyed face the rose-white boy.

Aunt Eva deep in conversation with her priest. What is she hatching now? Two golden boys eloped toward the sea. The way their heads inclined, the way an arm embraced: like a capital A they walked.

'Meanwhile I'm up and down the land, making a sacrifice of my throat, getting the buggers to enlist. What a hope. All down to Kitchener, of course. Gives the Ulstermen their own division. Catholic Irish get kicked about in any old sod's brigade. But as I say, this is no time for nationalist quibbling. I ask you, have we that luxury when German steel is skewering the maidenhead of Belgium?'

'Shall I fix a drink?' said MacMurrough.

'Well, why not? Nunc est bibendum, what?'

Skiagrams, silhouettes, pictures of shadows which turned their faces from him: MacMurrough's gaze roamed the library pictures. Family crest in the unlaid hearth: lion rampant, rather a boxing pose actually, a shadow-boxer, argent on a bloody field. On the library shelves, bound volumes of the saints and scholars. *Acta sanctorum Hiberniae. Navigatio sancti Brandani abbatis. Book of Moling. Annals of the Kingdom of Ireland.* Bunting, Moore, Lecky. Novels, various, in the love her and leave her vein. *The Love Songs of Connaught.*

Above the hearth hung a print of Maclise's *Marriage of Strongbow and Eva* – 'Courtesy of the House of Commons', ran the tag. Kettle remarked it now, saying, 'And yet she never did marry, did she, our particular Eva. After her father, no mortal man would answer. Though they say she made quite a run at Casement when he was here.'

MacMurrough turned. 'Casement?'

'Don't start me on that blackguard. An Irishman, a Protestant even, prancing about Deutschland tempting our men to turn traitor. Our brave Irish prisoners of war, wants to turn them into renegades. Man's a blackguard, a cad.'

A name at last. Casement. 'In Germany, you say?'

'I say, am I being indiscreet?'

'Not at all,' said MacMurrough.

'Bloody Sinn Feiners. Mark my words, they'll get their come-uppance. The country don't know them, don't wish to know them, too citified by half. Gaelic League, the Gaelic Athletics, our friends from Irish Freedom, all that rag-bag and bobtail. Could say they've done us a service. We in the Parliamentary Party, we were so occupied dealing with the English, we had forgotten to be Irish. We've admitted that criticism now and our policies are clear. Our land, our learning and our legislation. The three Ls, I like to call them, after the three Fs of your grandfather's and my father's time.'

MacMurrough could remember something of those three Fs. Feast, a fuck and a footrace, wasn't it? Alarmingly the face wobbled directly in front.

'I'm pleased you remembered me,' it said. 'Lot of water gone under since school.'

'How should I forget? Your name is a household word.'

'That old clench. Of course, it was one of Parnell's. Said it of my father. No, there's a drop in that glass. I'll just – there you go. May his shadow never grow less. It was witty, no doubt, but also the man to a dot. He needed us. There's no purpose to a locomotive except it pull a train. But the engine is sui generis. Never liked us. I believe it was only the English he disliked more. We owe a lot to him naturally. One worries we owe too much. His shadow stalks the land. You find that amusing?'

'I was thinking: Parnell and Wilde, the two great scandals of the age: both Irish. It's good to know Ireland can lead the world in something.'

Something less charming he found behind his ear this time. 'Morbid thing to say.'

'You know, what my aunt said – about the charges being trumped up against me.'

'Water under the bridge.'

'Not exactly.' MacMurrough wondered was he going to say what was on his mind, and after a while discovered that he very possibly was. 'When we were at school together that year, I quite admired you.'

'One had an equal regard for yourself, be assured.'

'You were brash and outspoken and you saw no harm in friendships and acted on that impulse.'

'Don't know if I'm sure what you mean.'

'It's quite true. I was guilty as charged.'

Kettle swayed on the soles of his feet. He appeared to waver between outburst and conciliation. An indignant compromise prevailed. 'You can't imagine I didn't know? God's sake, man, I took silk years back. I am informed you have since – how to say? – put away the things of a child.'

MacMurrough's eyebrows lifted. 'Truth, for instance?'

'You are telling me that there is a flaw in your character?'

'I am telling you that I do not think it is a flaw.'

The empty glass went down on the table. 'There's nothing more to be said.' But there was just the tiniest drop at the bottom of the glass. He lifted it, bottomed it, banged it down. 'Damn it all, MacMurrough, are you telling me you are an unspeakable of the Oscar Wilde sort?'

'If you mean am I Irish, the answer is yes.'

'Where we going?'

'Out of this crush for a breather.'

By private paths Doyler led away from the lawns, across a vegetable garden, past the gate to the sea-wall, and up narrow overgrown steps where their kilts snagged on the briers. They came out on a sunny corner, quite hidden from the house, and near enough level with the sea-wall so that the view gave out directly on the sea.

'How'd you know this place?' asked Jim.

'Maybe I been before,' said Doyler, slumping down in the grass. The grass was long and meadowy, quite wild. Jim sat down beside, though he had to hitch up again to arrange the kilt properly under. He believed he knew better now than to ask was it Mr MacMurrough had taken Doyler here.

'Did you ever in your puff see such a crop of la-di-das?'

'It's a let-out all right,' Jim agreed.

'And that old witch Madame Mac-shagging-Murrough. I'll tell her next time, I will. Came to play the flute is all. If it's a flunkey she wants she can re-im-bloody-burse me.'

'What's up with you?'

'Nothing up with me. Have me pride is all.'

Doyler was in his band kilt at last. It was a relief to Jim because he couldn't see that strange suit but he was searching for blood stains on it. Some young fellow had died in that suit and his mother, unable to bide the memory, had given it away out of charity. The stains wouldn't shift, inside maybe, where you wouldn't see, but you'd know they were there, reminding.

Doyler picked his nose. He twiddled with what he found, watching Jim the while. He flicked it over Jim's shoulder. Jim scowled at the indignity. Doyler leered.

'Your da's doing a roaring trade. Bet you was up all night painting them bottles green.'

'We was.'

'Were, Jim. Were, not was. You're a college boy. Speak the King's English sure.'

'What's wrong with you, Doyler?'

'Nothing, I told you.'

He hawked his throat and spat. Jim watched the gobshell jelly down the stalk of a grass. 'Is it something I said?'

The flash smile aged on Doyler's face. 'Not at all.' He looked mean with his smile that had no humour in it. 'Them high-sniffing nobs eye-glassing you would have any man out of sorts.'

He lay back, chewing on a grass. The way he lounged he had his knees up and wide apart. They were grazed and grassy from the athletics earlier. His kilt had slipped back. Jim shredded the seeds of a grass in his fingers. The shadows of the trees reached out. They wouldn't be long here in the sun.

'Did you see your man from the Wolfe Tone above? He'll be giving a speech I suppose. You'd like that, wouldn't you, Jim? A speech from your man.'

Jim shrugged. 'I wouldn't mind it.'

'I seen you bring him the tray of tea. Big wide eyes on you same like a cow. I'd say you've took a fancy to that man. Sounded to me you was coughing up Gaelic at him.'

'What and I was?' The man had smiled at Jim, in a way that wasn't at all uncomfortable. It was hard to think this was the same soldier-speaker who had thundered of war and Ireland and death. But Jim had liked him all the more for his gentle manner. 'He was pleased if I tried to speak Irish with him.'

'God and Mary with you,' Doyler said in a peenging voice. 'And God and Mary and Patrick with you, your honour.'

'Shut up,' said Jim.

'Shut up yourself.'

A kick poked his boot, and Jim clambered his feet to give a kick back, but the way Doyler reclined he could see right up his kilt. It flustered Jim to look there and he quickly turned away.

Doyler said, 'What you blushing for?'

'Who said I was blushing?'

'Even your ears is gone purple.'

'I'm not blushing for you anyway.'

'There's nothing down there you not seen it before. Seen it a hundred times swimming. Aye, and looked for it and all.'

'Are you going to talk dirty?'

'Little molly, you.'

Jim got up. He went to sit on the wall. A courting couple passed on the promenade below. Away up the lawns, a band played something jolly, something nice, something way out of tune. He looked at his boots with his stockings down at his ankles. He didn't feel shame, but rather looked at it. He looked at a boy who sat on a wall, carefully pulling his stockings up. A shameful sight, quite wretched really.

'U-boat scare,' said Doyler. He had come up beside, and he nodded to the plume of the mailboat as it hurried in from a strange direction.

'Yes,' said Jim.

'The *Helga* now'll be out on a sweep.'

'It will.' Jim knew he had only to wait and the arm would come round his shoulder. He would be mollified then. Mollified, that's what he'd be. He sat stiffly apart. He stared at the bay. The houses on Howth looked brilliantly clear. They reminded him of pictures he'd seen of Italy or the Aegean Isles. The sea was deeply blue, save far out where waves broke, like fallen sails, in flashes of white.

'Lookat, are we pals or what are we?' said Doyler.

'Of course we're pals. Only you're not very pally today.'

'Don't you see it's that MacMurrough woman? Was I a college boy, now, she wouldn't treat me that way.'

His hand was slapping on the curve of the wall. Jim counted the white spots on the fingernails. A gift, a friend, a foe; tidings to come, a journey to go. Doyler's hand had all five. 'She treats us all the same,' Jim said. 'What would she care who's a college boy?'

Doyler aimed a spit right across the promenade to the rocks beyond. Jim watched the propulsive lob, the curl in the air, the splash on the stone's tip, the way the saliva seemed to cling to the granite. Truly, he was a very excellent spitter. Jim hunched his shoulders. He nodded out to Howth and said, 'My da took me there once. I used think it was England, you see, when I was a kid. He brought me there and had me ask a fisherwoman was this still Ireland. She answered something very strange. She said, Not since the Chief passed over, nor yet till he come again.'

Doyler huffed a laugh. 'She meant Parnell.'

'I know that. The da was very angry. Queer old harp, he called her. He was always very set against Parnell.'

'Wouldn't surprise me your da sided with the priests.'

'Well, you're wrong actually. Had nothing to do with the priests. Parnell voted against the relief of Khartoum. The time General Gordon was under siege. The da never forgave him that. Gordon was his hero. He named me brother for him sure.'

For the first time that day Jim heard a genuine amusement in Doyler's voice. He let out a kink of laughter. 'He's the boyo, your da is. Parnell had the country torn asunder, and your da finds an argument nobody never heard of. There's original for you. More power to him, that's what Doyler says. – What the – what're yous doing down there?'

Not ten feet from them a gang of urchins had begun scaling the wall. They had lumps of mortar scattered about and tufts of valerian they'd tugged for a purchase. 'Would yous get down off of that wall,' said Doyler, 'before you have us all tumbled in the sea.'

'Want to get in, mister,' piped a crabby face.

Doyler reached down and heaved the creature up and over. 'What's wrong with the gate below?'

'Stuck.'

'Couldn't you see us here? All you had to do was ask, we'd open it for yous.' He brushed the kid down. 'Go on down by the gate,' he told the others. He marched the kid off, hauling him through the briers and in under the trees. Jim watched from the wall the other kids troop under his arm while he held the gate for them. One had a gash in his foot and Doyler bundled him down the rocks to bathe it. He had a rough kindness that way with children. 'There's Irish for you,' he said returning. 'No trouble too much save troubling the head.'

Jim nodded.

'Come and sit here with me,' Doyler said. 'I want to tell you something.'

'Can't you tell me here?'

'It's about schoolteaching.'

'What?'

'About being a schoolteacher.'

'What about it?'

'Come here and I'll tell you.'

Jim looked over his shoulder. Doyler was sitting up with his kilt pulled over his knees. He beckoned Jim and patted the grass beside. 'I want to talk is all.'

Jim dawdled over, pulling a face. He sat down. 'Well?'

'Have you thought at all what you'll do after college?'

'Sure that's miles off.'

'No it's not.'

'I need to be sure of an Exhibition first for the seniors.'

'No bother on you.' He began then talking about a King's scholarship and how it was the same course as the intermediate seniors. 'You'll be sitting the seniors anyway, may as well go up for the King's, what harm?' The King's was a scholarship to train for a teacher. What happened, you got the King's, then you went up to St Pat's in Dublin. St Pat's was the place to go. The boys at St Pat's would make a teacher of Jim. A bobby job was schoolteaching. A job with a collar and tie.

Jim had never given much thought to his future beyond that he'd somehow get away from the shop. The Post Office, he'd thought, a clerkship somewhere. But Doyler had it all worked out. Jim would go to St Pat's, he'd be a teacher, then maybe his friend would give him work at his school.

'Which friend?'

'Gaum you. His nibs from the Wolfe Tone. Don't you know he gives a school in Irish? Up Rathfarnham way.'

'He's a schoolteacher?'

'So he told me.'

'I didn't know you'd spoke with him.'

'An bhfuil tú schoolteacher, says I. Tá mé schoolteacher, says he.'

His cod-Gaelic wheedled the smile out of Jim. 'And you think I'd make a good teacher?'

'Never doubt it. And sure what better employment? Helping your fellow man to get on in the world – you'd be proud of a job like that. The only job for you, old pal.'

'I never thought,' said Jim.

'Well, now you have.'

'Yes, now I have.'

'You see, Jim, I think of these things. I think an awful lot of you, I do.'

Jim looked at him. He was lying on his front with a meadow grass sticking out from his mouth. How did Doyler do this? He could make Jim so angry with himself, so ashamed. The next minute, he was all alive, like a spark was inside, like the full of him was electric. How did Doyler do this to him? He really didn't know.

He stretched out in the grass too, leaning on his elbow, facing his friend, the pal of his heart, happy to watch him, fondly, his face. The grass was wonderfully cool in the shadows. It gave a fringy brush to his legs. Doyler grinned. He took the grass-stem from his mouth and tickled its ear under Jim's chin. 'You can tell does a fellow like you with a spear of grass, did you know that?'

'How do you tell?'

'You wave it under his chin, and if his face goes red at all, then you know.'

Jim laughed. The blush had risen, as of course it must, but for once he could be glad of it. He thought how lovely it would be to touch at this moment. The notion hadn't formed before Doyler's leg came to rest against his own. It pressed ever so lightly, and Jim pressed lightly back. He smiled with his bottom lip caught in his teeth, for it was wonderful to lie in the long grass, with just this tiny pressure of touch between.

Then Doyler said, 'I think I'm going to ask for a kiss.'

And Jim said, 'I think I hoped if you would.'

They neither of them moved. Until they heard voices approaching, and Jim quickly pulled away.

Butler, Courtney, Pigott. Butler had the cigarette, for his father had the tobacconist's.

'Clear off,' Doyler said. 'Yous aren't let in here.'

'Sure, boys, we're after interrupting the lovebirds.'

'Fuck off, Courtney.'

'Who're you telling – who's he telling to eff off?'

'Hark the college boy. Can't even fuck like a man.'

Butler said something about the ineffable Doyle. Courtney still looked shocked. Pigott leant against the wall. He had paper and tobacco for making a cigarette. He rolled it, watching Doyler. He licked the paper and said, 'Where's your badge?'

'Never you mind me badge.'

'You was sporting it earlier. Mighty proud you looked. Never had known we had a Larkinite in our midst.'

'Larrikinite,' said Butler.

'Stick it, Butler. You know where and all.'

'Had it whipped off pretty fly, all the same, when the priest was there.'

'You want to make something of that, Pigott?'

'Maybe you wouldn't want a certain somebody finding you out,' said Butler.

'Go on and smoke your gasper. We'll see about badges.'

'We'll see about feathers.'

'Butler, do you really want me to wallop you?'

'I'm a reasonable chap,' said Pigott, 'and I don't go for this baiting fellows less fortunate than meself. But you need to know I won't have a buttonman in my company. You need to understand that, Doyle.'

'It's a shame you'll be leaving the band so.'

'You make him see reason,' Pigott said to Jim. 'Tell your pal don't be making a parade of himself. Tell him I'm afraid he'll be properly licked else.'

'Aye will I,' said Doyler. Pigott raised a cautioning finger. He beckoned the others to follow him, and lumbered off. 'And if you lick me all over you won't miss me arse. Mawgabraw!' Doyler shouted. He turned to Jim. 'Do you mind the cheek of that?'

Jim said, 'He means what he says. His da's something in the Hibernians.'

'He looks the bully neck would have a da that way.'

He was panting a bit, out of his breath with anger. Jim said,

'We should go,' but Doyler paid no regard, just slumped in the grass. Jim knelt down. He felt jiddery in his legs and he had to hunker back on his heels. He was intimidated by the boys in a way he had not felt before. They had brought this on themselves and it was only right the boys should menace them. Through his fallen hair he stole a view of Doyler's face. There was doubt in his eyes, the way they squinted back at him. His forehead was frowning and his jaw chewed, ruminating, like he had trouble thinking. Some calculation, on the tip of Jim's nose, that would not add up.

He said, 'I seen them fists you had in your hands. You're a good pal. You was ready there to back me.'

'We'll go,' said Jim.

'Is that what they call us, the lovebirds?'

'No.'

'Why did he say it?'

'That's just Courtney.'

It was nearly chilly in the grass. The shadows of the trees reached beyond them and made crazy jags along the wall. From up the lawns came the groan of a warpipes.

'Lie down a moment.'

'No,' said Jim, 'we should go back.'

'A moment just.'

He pulled Jim down by the hands. Jim was looking about him, and Doyler said, 'They're gone. They won't be back. There's no one to see us here.' He pushed Jim's shoulders down, not roughly but firmly, and kept his hands there till Jim settled. 'It's all right,' he said. He lay beside, leaning over a little. He put his hand on Jim's leg.

The grass had nearly a smoky smell. Midges were rising. Jim felt a swamp of heat, though the sun was way behind the trees. His neck was straining as he tried to watch the hand.

The saffron of his kilt creased and contoured. The hand was moving upward. The saffron flower, he told himself, is either purple or white. It is the stigmas that are used for dye.

It didn't seem to be Doyler's hand at all, merely one of those things with which the world was furnished. It shifted the hem of Jim's kilt so that his thigh was revealed, gooselike and pale. The passage of the hand was mesmerizing. Doyler too watched it, darting betweenwhiles glances at Jim's face. Then very quietly he said, 'Did you ever hear tell of a place called Sparta?'

Jim felt the strain in his neck and a stiffening in his throat, and the impossible strangeness of moving things. The saffron flower is not yellow at all. It is the stigmas that give the dye. He swallowed. 'It was in ancient Greece. They fought Athens in the Peloponnesian War.'

'Did they win?'

'In the end they did.'

'I'm glad of that. Can I hold it now?'

'No,' said Jim, but he was already holding it.

'It's all right,' Doyler told him. 'You wanted this. It's what you wanted me to do.'

'No, I didn't. I don't.'

'Ask me to stop so, and I will.'

'Stop it, Doyler.'

He looked into Jim's face. Jim had to blink his eyes deep shut. The hand came away from his kilt but Jim couldn't look at it for fear of its being disfigured or discoloured some way. He couldn't look at Doyler at all, and he turned his head on the grass.

'We have to go now,' he said. 'They'll be wondering what's happened.'

'Won't you kiss me, Jim, even?'

'No.'

For a moment or two they lay side by side. Side by side they lay, then Doyler got up and walked away.

The shadows of evening were closing in and gathering about the sycamores, while MacMurrough wandered the fête's periphery, waiting for the drama to begin. He was thinking of Kettle. He was thinking of truth. The good and the true and that other one, the beautiful, whose presence in the triad, like the Holy Ghost's in the Trinity, he could never quite account for. It had always appeared a sop to the virtuous, those who had endured the joyless good and the starched truth and now, bless them, were entitled to a little entertainment. Bring on the beauty.

But as regards Kettle: why had MacMurrough spoken out in the library? It had seemed a manifesto. This is the truth and I will have it said. He had forced Kettle to an open repulse. The eyes had unhazed and for that moment MacMurrough stood revealed for the ugly sod he was. Tom-tom Kettle-drum. All the Home Rule in the world would not tarry that gentleman in the library then. Nor French brandy nor Spanish ale nor wine from the royal Pope.

MacMurrough, sneering, smiled. He found, flicked open, his grandfather's cigar-case. He viewed the contents as might a bully considering his victims. In a trice, the cigar-case was his aunt's travelling-glass, and he inquired of his brazen image, Am I truly such an ugly sod?

Yes, there was something altogether tantalizing about truth. One burnt to tell it, for it to be known. Dreaded it, too, that someone else should say it, their saying making it true, the truth true, unalterable. He thought of that phrase from Wilde: *What one has done in the secret chamber one has some day to cry on the housetop*. Wilde had meant in confession. Was it conceivable to cry out with pride? When Kettle had asked was there a flaw in his character, he had replied that he did not think it a flaw.

– Braggadocio is nothing to the point, said Scrotes.

No, agreed MacMurrough. He hadn't thought it would be.

Now warpipes summonsed the fugitive crowd; and rounding a shrubbery MacMurrough saw the declining sun had set the stage. Antic forms waited in the wings, but first, yes, of course – 'But first, my lords, reverend sirs, ladies and gentlemen' – the schoolmaster had words of introduction.

A crescent enclosure had been roped in front whereout the top-hats poked; birettas, a red among the black, peaked cowls of mendicants; ferny feathery whiskery toques. MacMurrough waited with the poor people at the back, bare-headed, his topper in his hand, wafting misty alps from a ripe maduro. The mobility muttered among themselves and he heard an old woman whisper, God bless your work, alannah. He turned, thinking absurdly of himself, but no, it was the schoolmaster she blessed.

'We of Na Fianna Eireann,' said he, 'address ourselves to the boys of Ireland.'

MacMurrough watched the tall rather awkward man who gazed with a calm unexpected confidence upon his audience. He was costumed in a uniform of heather green, military cap tucked under his elbow, a sword dangling at his thigh. Earlier, when they had met on the terrace, he had worn a frock-coat, old-fashioned, skirted. He had looked a minister then, something temperance or the Society of Friends. Now, for all his martial trappings, he presented the conscientious padre. His slight lisp his practised lips suppressed, as in measured cadences he addressed the nation's youth.

'We believe that the highest thing that a young man can do

is to serve well and truly, and we purpose to serve Ireland with all our fealty and with all our strength.'

He had come with his own blush of boys. All afternoon they had shimmered upon the lawns. MacMurrough had been attracted to them, naturally, but he found he hesitated to approach. How aloof they were, discrete from the mass. He had known the camaraderie of those who boarded together, the braggart bonds of public schoolboys. These were different. Their aloofness seemed not of their keeping but as though of their nature, unalloyable.

Now, they watched from the wings while their master spoke, mantled in antique cloth, in leather sandals shod, leaning on spears and broadswords, each boy with upturned face as he waited his part in the coming drama. And it seemed to MacMurrough their gaze would enray their master's face, that face the sun itself would glory, as it tipped in magnificent burst the darkling sycamores behind.

It was love, of course, that separated them. So clear it shone it hurt to see. A dozen boys who loved their master. In loving they became extraordinary. Embodiments of unattainable desire, fantastic as the man they served.

For the schoolmaster, MacMurrough had found, was indeed fantastic. His aunt's priest had made their introduction – Happy to, Servant, Yours to command – and shortly after had been called away. There was the least inquisition of a smile on the schoolmaster's face. Hair glistened with oil against a broad white forehead. Deep-set eyes, one of which had something of a cast, occasioning MacMurrough to avert his glance and peer at his shoes instead.

Might he help the schoolmaster to wine? The schoolmaster thanked him, but he would not. MacMurrough understood the schoolmaster was to give an oration on the morrow.

The schoolmaster had that honour, it was true. Was the departed a particular friend of the schoolmaster's? They were not personally acquainted, but the deceased had worked long in the public arena.

It was pinch and cramp to get any conversation at all. MacMurrough scraped his bals on the gravel. He had heard the schoolmaster was recently returned from Connemara. Gravely nodded the high-walled forehead. Was MacMurrough familiar with the west of Ireland? MacMurrough was ashamed to say, no; however, he entertained a notion of its being picturesque. The schoolmaster would assure him of that. And had the schoolmaster enjoyed his holiday? For his sins, the schoolmaster had been much engaged in the penning of his oration.

Which rather had them back where they'd started. And that, on the face of it, was that. Save there had been an undertone quite the obverse of these mundanities. There could not be so very much in their ages, but the schoolmaster had made MacMurrough feel himself a schoolboy.

Or, rather, he had not quelled the feeling. For MacMurrough often had a sense of his being younger. This was not a fancy, certainly it was not deliberate. His unconscious mind had not kept pace with the years. He did not know why and he had given up wondering, but just on that threshold before thought or action his sense of himself was of a burgeoning youth. He was on the verge of manhood, always the verge. So persistent was this notion that strangers he encountered, ontologically his junior, he would often consider his psychological senior. His immediate disposition was to defer to such were they of his caste, be fucked by them were they not. This notion could not survive the liminal step into consciousness. Consciousness pulled him up, sharp as a looking-glass, and told out his proper years. But there it was. Before he thought or he

323

acted, MacMurrough was a boy on the verge of manhood. Always, just.

And the schoolmaster, in his halting way, had not addressed himself *ad hominem* to MacMurrough. He had found out this youth, had found him out and drawn him on. For that little while on the terrace together, MacMurrough had consciously been a boy in the presence of his master. He had a schoolboy's itch to play practical jokes on this reverent character. Even more, a schoolboy's sense of fairness that it would be shabby to deceive so patently unworldly a man. He rather felt he wanted to please him. He wanted to overhear him say to another, Young MacMurrough is coming along well. We may expect great things of young MacMurrough.

It was all quite confusing and MacMurrough had been relieved to get away, to find Kettle in the library, and drink whiskey and soda with his urbane kind. Now, listening to the schoolmaster's speech from the stage, he wondered had many of us this child inside. It would explain the appeal of this curious man. For his sentiments, though he spoke them with dignity and with some passion, were commonplace enough: the local expression of a continental theme: Boy Scout mores and muscular worship, the Christ-like sacrifice of youth. The same had sung half Europe to the trenches. As ideal he proffered a legendary band of Gaels who had fought and died, as he put it, in the beauty of their boyhood. It was all very speech-day at school or any recruiting-meet where the cloth attended. Had the fellow been English, MacMurrough should have mocked him for the type of by-jingo bourgeois.

Yet he did appeal. And there was more to this appeal than the novelty of kilts and Gaelic. He found out the child in all who listened, and all who heard became their younger selves. MacMurrough could feel it now when he told of the Fianna of yore. How did they win their battles? Strength that was in their hands, Truth that was on their lips, Purity that was in their hearts.

Aye, there is manhood. MacMurrough closed his eyes. I am that boy on that manhood's verge. I yearn for magnificence, and my heart heaves for a tale of courage and high deeds. My face has not set, I know not yet what I have become. Precious is life, in my limbs, in my soul. Gladly will I spill it to a noble end.

MacMurrough took a step back. He blinked in the red of the sun. This man is dangerous.

But this man had finished. The speech was done. Applause clip-clapped from the crescent enclosure. The poor unknitted their brows and shuffled their feet, muttering once more among themselves. Behind the trees a bauble glowed whose rays were tinsel. Again a warpipe droned. Boys traversed the thumping boards. A torchlit tableau was formed. From the steps to the stage the schoolmaster watched. One saw his receding hairline, that he was a touch overweight, his somewhat of a stoop. The schoolmaster might have sensed MacMurrough's scrutiny, for his face turned to profile. The marred eye was concealed.

– A fascinating character, said Scrotes.

– Truly, agreed MacMurrough.

– In propinquity or while he orates, quite potent.

– Then how soon afterwards his words dissolve. Viewed dispassionately he becomes ridiculous.

Indeed, he presented an easy target for scoffing. His sword of rank adangle oddly, his puttees immaculately wound the wrong way round, was that a whistle he had hanging? Who hadn't known his ilk at school? Cadets, college OTC – adore the fandangles of soldiering, equipped with every last accoutrement, all things spruce and shiny. Two left feet when it comes to parade. The type who can't look at a gun without the thing blasting off, lethal near anything live. This man will take on the British Empire.

– Will he win? he asked Scrotes.

– He will certainly venture his life. The only doubt is the cause he will venture it in.

– Why, his country's freedom, I should think.

– Ah, said Scrotes, but which is his country? It is scarcely the tired old hag of the songs, nor yet the beautiful woman of the prophecies.

No, thought MacMurrough, that is not his Ireland.

– See, said Scrotes, his Ireland is on the stage.

Yes, there it was in the boys, those gossamery boys who thumped the stage. The soft barbarish Gaelic chanted his love to heaven and earth. By flaming torch the garden told it. A queer music hummed it to the sea. His steadfast gaze from the wings, their glances to him. Here was his Ireland, his drama his love.

MacMurrough thought of his own boys on their benches in the summerhouse. He dared not reach to them and they sensed his reserve. Their faces quickened if the priest or his aunt came, quickened if only in trepidation. Then sullened anew when those personages had left, giving back MacMurrough's distrust.

How did this schoolteacher do this? How did he make these boys love him so? Every glint of their eyes shot defiance to the world. Stooping stumbling fellow: he has shorn the curtains and entered the land of youth. See him reign, king of boys, master of all his desires.

And it seemed to MacMurrough that he, too, would make such love. And not a breath of a lip nor a hair of a brow should know of it. His gaze lifted to the purpling sky. May the heart be redeemed by renunciation? Are they not truly the good who, desiring evil, renounce their desires? Am I not also to love and be loved?

– Hush now, said Scrotes.

– Don't you get it, old man? I want to feel good. I never have that feeling. It's tiresome knowing oneself evil always. That man up there drips goodness like a sweat. I should just like a feel of it myself for once.

– MacMurrough, MacMurrough, said Scrotes, and his bony fingers turned gauntly him round. He led him to a seat far down the garden, where MacMurrough could hear the sea. He lowered his eyes and watched his button bals with patent golosh and the grass-blades that crazy-quilted them.

– It won't do, will it? he said. I can't pretend myself into acceptable shapes. His Majesty's Wandsworth has seen to that. Besides, it's not the doing, it's the being that's my offence. You could see that on Kettle's face. The doing is neither here nor there. Doing only offers an opportunity to be caught.

– You know, he continued, they make it so damned difficult. They make a thing so deeply wrong that no morality can afterward apply. It doesn't matter how we go about it, kindly or coldly. No good is so good as to mitigate; all further wrong is a feather's weight upon the deed itself. See it in the newspaper reports. One can be a gentleman thief. One can be a love-struck murderer. We're just unspeakable, we're sods.

– Who are we? asked Scrotes.

– People of my kind.

– You have a kind? said Scrotes.

– Yes, and we are easy to find. Under bridges, at the back-end of piers, in parks when parks are closed, in the shadows of others, in the night.

Far up the garden the boys of Erin mavroned and macree'd. Whish it whash, said the sea to the shore. By the summerhouse

327

MacMurrough saw the comfort for the troops who waited in a phalanx of tulips. Where was Doyle? The comfort might topple without his shoulder to slope to. There was Doyle far behind, on his own, in his kilt and sash and pinned to his sash, MacMurrough saw it, his Red Hand badge.

And he appeared at that moment beautiful to MacMurrough; proud, defiant, the way he watched the play like a wild animal considering food. He might be a badge himself, a golden crotchet that had pinned to the trees. The knowing of him, of his nasal whine, his feet that smelt, this did not take from his beauty. His beauty claimed his defects for the part of him that made it possible, made him true. MacMurrough saw the making of a man, of a fellow creature, of such who can say, boldly and freely, I do.

– When you told him of the Spartans, Scrotes asked, what did you intend?

– I don't know that I'm sure. One is sensible to his feelings for his friend. I thought it might cheer him to know those praised in his national song had felt the same.

– Not nearly the same, said Scrotes.

– I had rather gathered the Spartans were famed for it.

– The Spartans' desire was praiseworthy and good. Their world was shaped by that desire, as ours is shaped by man and wife.

MacMurrough pursed his lips. I want it to be all right for him, he said. For both of them.

– Help them.

– I have procured the one his suit. The other apparently can clothe himself. It should seem the extent of my capacity to assist.

– Help them make a nation, if not once again, then once for all.

– What possible nation can you mean?

– Like all nations, Scrotes answered, a nation of the heart. Look about you. See Irish Ireland find out its past. Only with a past can it claim a future. Watch it on tramcars thumbing its primers. Only a language its own can speak to it truly. What does this language say? It says you are a proud and ancient people. For a nation cannot prosper without it have pride. You and I, MacMurrough, may smile at the fabulous claims of the Celt. We may know that the modern Irishman as much resembles the Gael of old as he resembles the Esquimau or the Kafir on the Hindu Kush. And we may believe he is the better for that. But no matter. The struggle for Irish Ireland is not for truth against untruth. It is not for the good against the bad, for the beautiful against the unbeautiful. These things will take care of themselves. The struggle is for the heart, for its claim to stand in the light and cast a shadow its own in the sun.

– Help these boys build a nation their own. Ransack the histories for clues to their past. Plunder the literatures for words they can speak. And should you encounter an ancient tribe whose customs, however dimly, cast light on their hearts, tell them that tale; and you shall name the unspeakable names of your kind, and in that naming, in each such telling, they will falter a step to the light.

– For only with pride may a man prosper. With pride, all things follow. Without he have pride he is a shadowy skulk whose season is night. And now behold, the pageant is ending. The boys have fallen upon the stage and the splendour falls with the dying day. Soon there will be fireworks and the young must be led to their duty. You must go from this lofty place and tread again the trampled grass.

To his surprise MacMurrough found they had left the garden and climbed to Scrotes's turret room. It was full the night and

329

the pale moon that through the window shone had sketched an embrasure on the floor, sketched it half-way up the opposing wall. In this moonshaft they stood, Scrotes and he, and no shadow of theirs disturbed the dust that floated in the light behind.

Far, far below MacMurrough heard the crowd's applause. He would never speak with Scrotes again, this he knew, and he turned to him. Was I truly your friend? he asked. I believe I loved you. But I forget, you know.

– You were. You did. You do.

So spake Scrotes, and having spoke he smole a smile and home to raven regions lonely stole.

Leaving MacMurrough among the muttering poor. He made his way to the summerhouse where his boys were waiting.

'Are we ready?'

Yes, sir, they were. But there was a hemming and hawing and a shifting in their faces. MacMurrough took a breath.

'Look, that fellow Pearse, the gentleman I mean, has put up a good show. Let's see what we can do, will we? Not to better him. See if we can't somehow salute him.' Not a flicker of spirit. Was this nerves? 'Is Mr Mack with us?'

Two heels clicked behind. 'At your service, your honour.'

'You might march the boys out. Couple of turns round the lawn then up the steps to the stage. We'll give them what they want, this evening at least, which is A Nation Once Again.' Doyle. Where was Doyle? And others were missing too, the big drum brigade. 'What's happened with Doyle? Pigott. Fahy. Are we to have no drums?'

'Oh now, I'm sure now,' said Mr Mack, 'they won't be keeping us a minute longer than strictly.'

The friend looked up. 'He was called out by the father.'

'Whatever for?'

'Now now, quiet, Jim. Mr MacMurrough is talking. I'm certain they won't keep us a moment, your honour. Though, truth be told, young Doyle is no great shakes at the marching. With the game of a leg and all.'

The door opened. The priest strode the floor. Behind him, Fahy and Pigott. Between them, Doyle.

'What can you imagine is the meaning of this?' MacMurrough demanded. The two louts smirked, wearing the satisfied gloats of their master's bidding. 'Mister Taylor, can you explain yourself?'

'Mister MacMurrough, your aunt awaits you. I advise you speak with her immediately lest something be said you may after regret.'

'Nevertheless, I really must protest—'

'Then you will protest to your aunt who has vouchsafed your good conduct.' His two eyes cocked independently. 'I believe I need say no more.'

MacMurrough felt a crumple inside. He saw the friend on his feet, only his father restraining him. He saw the turned faces in the benches. The priest cracked his smile. He addressed the boys.

'The devil, we know, is omnipresent. As omnipresent as Our Lord and his seeing angels. Yet I had not expected to meet him in my own band of Irish boys. Look at the sorry cut of him, men.'

Doyler's head drooped in subjection. There was blood on his nose and his chin. His shirt was ripped where they must have torn his badge away. His nipple was exposed, a pathetic emblem.

'No God, no sin, no hell, no heaven, the black devil of socialism, hoof and horn, is among us. Do we want him?'

The silence told the boys did not.

'Do we say no to his works?'

Silence nodded its head.

'Do we cast him out?'

We do, said the tongueless faces and the priest signed to his henchmen to take Doyler away.

'Boys of Ireland,' he continued, 'you will join your hands in prayer with me now that our sainted isle will be protected and rendered strong against the manifold perils that beset her. For this once, lest there be any doubt, we will pray in the Saxon tongue. In the name of the Father, Son, and the Holy Ghost.'

In a hopeless stasis MacMurrough heard the praying, the braying versicles and hushed response. When he lifted his head he saw all faces lowered, save the friend's, whose gaze was on him. The boy's lips moved in suffrage, pleading with MacMurrough, begging him to do something. But MacMurrough could do nothing. He had crumpled inside, and his head lowered in shame.

There was an explosion outside, followed by another. The night through the windows burst into light. Star after star flared in the sky as the fireworks let off. Green, silver and gold the fragments glittered, then fluttered down like fabulous rain. And the air was rent by drumfire and shellblast and the surging cheers of the populace.

'Cushmawaunee,' he heard Mr Mack say, 'it looks as though we're after missing the grand finale.'

On and on the fireworks come and into the night are falling still. Across the rift of a continent they fall, bursting in stars and fountains of light. They crackle in a thousand squibs, in mad minutes of furious joy. In metal rain they shower to rise again

332

in scarlet flowers. Their dust like fairy dust descends, upon the brave, upon the coward.

They dart across the heavens of Greece, where Gordie watches the night sky. Beside him his chum remarks, Shower of lights tonight.

And Gordie says, Me da used say they was souls released from purgatory.

I never heard that before, says Gordie's chum. Gob, but there's enough of them.

They'd want to be, says Gordie.

Where y'off to now? asks Gordie's chum.

See if there ain't no water left on this tub.

When he comes back he says, Snacks, and hands the half-full of his can to his chum. The troopship gently rocks beneath them, at anchor in the bay.

Have you a sister at all? asks Gordie's chum.

I haven't, says Gordie. A brother only.

Shame that, says Gordie's chum. A man could settle with a sister of yours.

He could, Steerforth, he could, says Gordie. He lies back on the deck and watches the glittering sky. The glittering sky and the shimmering souls that minute by minute escape the dark.

Who's Steerforth? asks Gordie's chum.

Away with you, says Gordie, cuffing his neck.

In Ballygihen, in the tumbledown lodge, Mary Nights at last laid down her head. Oh, but it was the beautiful elegant lodge of the world. Upon the flawless stone she lay, and through the splendid loft she gazed. What cared she for falling stars? Oh God, that all the stars would fall and leave the thick black velvet cloth. Oh God above, of love and light, loan me the blanket of the night, till on the cold and grumpy ground, I'll warmly wrap it round me.

Her stiff old neck she turned on the stone. When might it end, she did not know. She did not know what end she pondered. But this she knew, and knew too well: the nights were drawing in.

CHAPTER TWELVE

H E WAS SWIMMING to the island, but the sea was slippery and thick, like a jelly that would set beneath him. Great guns he was going, but he wanted to try a kick in the legs. And it was true, it was better if he kicked. The push propelled him over the water, like flying, not flying but leaping, long horizontal leaps that skimmed the surface and he landed like an insect and kicked again. Strange to say, the water was uphill all the way.

He kicked through the crest of a wave and there was the Muglins before him. The water was warm now and shallow and emulsive. His feet felt sand underneath and he tiptoed through the ripples. He could hear her behind the rocks, she was singing or something, and the gulls moaned round and about, and flapped their wings. In a way he was annoyed and he wanted to know why had she been here all this while when she could have come home. Home was only a spit away. But when he came round the rocks, it wasn't his mother but Doyler who moaned, and his wrists were red in their chains while he writhed on the rock, and an old gander pecked at his eyes. Save it wasn't his eyes he pecked, but down down down below.

The dream dispersed and Jim lay awake in his settle-bed. The last turf slumped in the grate and the hag in the ashes leered blazily at him. He was damp in his shirt like truly he had swum in the sea, but the dream was fading and all he retained was a sensation of having flown, of having skittered through rain.

He thought it was mice in the shop, then rats in the yard. It came as no surprise when the scratching resolved to fingers on the window pane.

He climbed to his knees and pulled the blind. Doyler's face grinned ghostily through the glass. Jim eyed the ceiling. He tied the blind in place then levered the sash an inch. Doyler slipped his fingers under and together they shuddered it open.

'How'd you get in in the yard?'

'Shinned up the wall, of course.'

The breeze brushed the vigil flame and shadows swayed on the walls. Upstairs the bed moved and his father called down, 'Are you right there, Jim?'

'Fine, Da.'

'Go to sleep now, son.'

'Yes, Papa.'

They watched the ceiling till the bed-frame ceased complaining.

'You want to come in?'

'No.'

'I'll come out.'

'Stay.' He wore once more his blue-gone duds of old. He had a brown-paper parcel, tied up with packing thread, which he held up now. 'What cheer, eh?'

'You're leaving,' said Jim.

'Came to say goodbye.'

Words blurted out, admonitions, remonstrations. How Jim had warned him. Told him not to mind them fellows. Time and again he'd warned him against that. Would Doyler listen to him? No, Doyler would not listen.

The bed creaked above and Aunt Sawney coughed above and behind. In the quiet after, Doyler shook his head.

'Lookat, Jim, I'm going nowhere here. I came back for the mother, but the mother don't need me. There's things I have to do. And they won't be done in Glasthule.'

Jim mouthed the openings of different sentences. In the end they all amounted to the same and he said, 'I'll kiss you. I'd like to, I mean.'

Again the squeak of the bed above and their eyes lifted. Falling, they met. Doyler huffed his little laugh. The blood was crusting on the gash in his lip. His hand passed into the room and stroked Jim's chin. Jim knew the bone of his face through the fingers. Five times he knew it. Then the fingers fisted and gently pucked him. 'A chuck on the chin is worth two kisses, they say,' he said.

'The swimming,' said Jim.

'Sure you're the fine able swimmer. All's you need is the practice.'

'The Muglins, though.'

'Did you think I'd forget?'

He reached inside his shirt and tugged the string that held his medal. Between thumbs and fingers he twisted the tin till it split in two. Jim saw the proffered half of St Joseph.

'I'd give you me badge, only they stole that on me. Keep this instead while I'm away. It's my pledge to you. We'll have our Easter swim, my hand and heart on that. We'll make them rocks together, Jim. Are you straight so?'

'I'm straight as a rush,' Jim said. He sniffed. 'I am too.'

'Old pal o' me heart,' said Doyler.

'Come what may,' said Jim. 'Come what may.'

Doyler grinned. 'Come Easter sure. 1916.'

PART II

� decorative ornament✢

1916

ecce abstulisti dominem de hac vita,
cum vix explevisset annum in amicitia mea,
suavi mihi super omnes suavitates illius vitae meae.

– St Augustine

'C' COMPANY 7th R.D.F.,
30th Infantry Brigade,
British Mediterranean Force,
c/o G.P.O. London.

Dearest Father,

It is some while since last I wrote but you will know things
have 'hotted' up for us here. Indeed, we have seen *action* at
last! We landed but a week back and straight we were in on
the 'fun'. A boat of ours took a hit from the Turkish batteries
but our C.S.M. let a 'Come on my boyos!' and on we charged.
He was a regimental old sweat but truly the heart and soul of
the Company.

It was our objective a hill some way inland. We set off in
parade column at a good pace to make up after the beach. I
believe we presented a fearful sight for there was scarce sign
of Abdul, only the 'stay-behind' of snipers. The air whistled
with shells and great puffs of smoke. The excitement was
everywhere in the ranks. I need not dwell on the exhilaration
we felt as we sensed the coming of our first engagement. It was
hand-to-hand all the way after that. The Faughs on our left
gave out their war-cry, so we too let a roar from us. I cannot
tell how Abdul took it, but that roar is with me still. My hairs

341

are up on end to think of it. It was a race then between my
mob and the Toffs and I am happy to say your son's Company
'held the day' for we was first to raise the flag on the hill.
Round and round the cheers came from the men on the ships
and down by the beach.

The night we had only 'funk-firing' from Abdul. We
gathered our wounded and did what we could. Tired and
thirsty we were, but our spirits were high as I am sure you can
suppose. We had proved ourself for soldiers, so we felt. The
order came to regroup on the beach and we humped it back
for a well-deserved 'breather'. So these last days, I have swam
the Aegean blue and drank my fill of water that wasn't carted
three miles by a 'Dirty Shirt'. We all of us have smartened up
and we are ready for anything John Turk will throw at us.

Tomorrow is the Sunday and also the Feast of the
Assumption. Father Murphy will give Mass for us Old Toughs
on the beach. He is a saintly man and courageous with it. He
took great risks to aid the boys of whichever faith and after
there was no more stretchers, he had the bare arms of his
people to serve instead. He is greatly respected by all the men,
never mind he is a terror against games of chance and any
man that had a fondness of the 'devil's playthings'. Tomorrow
morning he will give absolution and after that we return up
the line.

Truly it is a comfort, for the swimming is grand but it is
not the best of bivveys. If you remember the fly-paper in the
shop here it is all fly-paper. The heat is something different.
Some of the boys is burnt to a toast, yet it can be cold by
night. You will know all this from your time East and it is only
'cabbage warmed up' coming from me.

But really it was a comfort when word came down of
action tomorrow. We have a saying that the sooner we fight,

the sooner we win. And we will win, Father, of that have no doubt. It is a grand body of men that I am with and the boys here are the grandest pals a fellow would wish for. I am proud to serve with them, as I am proud to be an Old Tough of the same regiment as my father.

Did I mention there is a Company in the Battalion that was formed from men at Trinity and the Bar? We call them the Old Toffs and there is much 'banter' between us mortals and they. My company is drawn mostly from the Coombe and the Liberties and the area of the docks. Scarce a man but he's a red-flag Larkinite. For all our talk there is one thing we all hold fast. We know that our fight is Ireland's fight. It is a 'long way to Tipperary' from the Aegean shore but Irishmen everywhere will hold their head high knowing the Irish regiments are 'doing their bit.' Father Murphy put it this way to us that we are fighting for Ireland through another like the French brigades of old.

As I write I see the hospital ship with all the lights shining. The air is thick with crickets. Amongst the odours one would expect, there is a particular one, of thyme which grows on the ridges here. Sometimes when I look at the headland over I think of the Hill of Howth.

I will wind up now for all the boys is writing this night. The officers will be cursing for the work we put them to. But let you know your son is well and the tummy I spoke of has all but gone in the do. No news for an age now. We are told this is to be expected with the distances. I hope the old mailer to England has not 'packed' it in.

It is curious how one can miss 'the old sod.' I often do contemplate those last months in Ireland. I recall our route marches along the lanes and the trees that were coming to leaf then. The clouds in the sky gave out their showers. I

343

remember the flowers that were coming up, yellow and blue, and the running of a stream at every turn. The air had a smell I cannot describe, but if I close my eyes it comes to me. It was awake in a way the land here is not awake, or not for me at any rate.

Our fight is Ireland's fight and the sooner we are 'stuck in' the sooner we bring this war to a speedy conclusion. It will be a proud day for Ireland when we parade through the streets of Dublin and I trust you will be proud of us too who kept the honour of your regiment.

Tell Jim to keep at his books and I will write him separate and that he is constant in my thoughts, as indeed are you, my dear father, and Aunt Sawney too, in my thoughts and prayers.

Your loving son,
Gordie

CHAPTER THIRTEEN

HE STEPS RACED on the street outside and into the lane
till the shop bell clanged. Mr Mack refolded the foxed and
crinkled pages of the letter, returned the letter to its place upon
the mantelshelf. The door flung wide and Jim was there, white
and breathless.

'They told me there was a telegram.'

'It's on the table, son.'

Mr Mack stared at the letter on its shelf, beside the framed
photograph of his son upon which his son had written, I trust
the cigarette does not offend. It does not offend, he told him.
You were mistaken to think it offended, nor anything you said
nor done offended. You were greatly mistaken in that.

Jim looked up from the telegram. 'Missing, Da?'

'That's right, missing.'

'What does it mean?'

Mr Mack fixed his face, then turned from the mantelshelf.
'Why, it means there's hope yet. Isn't that the best news?
Missing in action only. That's easy done. The muddle of war,
'tis surprising there isn't more goes missing. Where there's
hope there's, where there's hope there's—' But he could not
rightly recall what there was. 'Where there's hope there's a

way. They'll have him found soon enough, never doubt it. Then we'll have him home again and there'll be mafficking the length of the street. Don't doubt it, Jim. We'll be back the three of us together in no time. In time for Christmas even.'

'Christmas, Da?'

'Let that be the end of the lemoncholy now.'

The way the boy stood there holding the telegram, so mannishly determined against tears, it made Mr Mack finally to heave. He kept his face smiling but he could not stop the blubbers. He said, 'Now now, be a Briton. Turn off the main,' while the tears streamed down his cheeks.

'We'll say the Rosary, Da.'

'That's the spirit. If we pray every day and on the hour of every day, then. That's all we can do now, Jim. Did you come direct from school?'

'I did.'

'They had a right to tell you.'

He felt his son's hand on his shoulder and when he looked he saw how small were the hands of leaping boys. He put his great warty crawg on top and patted Jim's fingers. 'Fetch down the beads,' he said.

They prayed again that night after tea, himself and Aunt Sawney on either side of the range and Jim in the middle. Mr Mack saw the fire that reflected on coal-box and fender, and he had the notion of it grinning at the novelty and sharing the joke with its neighbours. He left Aunt Sawney do the calling, though he'd take his oath, for all her practice, she had the order wrong. After ten minutes of arguing the toss, he let her have her way. Besides the which, it wasn't the order Our Lady heard at all, but the intention behind it. When he rose from his knees he felt the ache in his back and his knees complained of the stony floor. He hung the beads on the shelf, avoiding Gordie's picture, then he put the kettle on the stove, saying, 'Cup of char suit us?'

''Tis easy knowing ye're not accustomed to prayer,' he got in return.

'Now now.'

'Great gammocks ye had to see me telling me beads. Great gas and gaiters ye had of it. 'Tis a changed story this day.'

'Now now, Aunt Sawney, there's no call for vexation.'

'The pity of it is ye left it so late.'

He turned sharply from the range and was about to let a return on her vinegar, when he saw she had her go-to-Mass hat on. 'Where are you off to this hour of night?'

'I'm away to get a stamp.'

'The post office is long closed.'

''Tisn't every soul from this house meets a closed door when they knocks.'

With that she was out, banging her stick on her passage through the shop. He stared glumly after her. His son had his nose dug in a book at the table. 'Is that reading for school?'

'Yes, Da.'

He took the tea-pot to rinse it and at the sink he said, 'At any rate, we'll be saying the Rosary in chapel next week. October is the Holy Month of the Rosary. The father has asked for help with the seating. Usher I'm to be. 'Tis quite a responsibility.'

The telegram had called him Corporal Gordon Mack. Wouldn't think to write to tell us, oh no. We might have celebrated that. But oh no, let the old man stew at home. God forgive me.

At last the kettle whistled. Clumsily the water poured. It was hard keeping his mind on things with the photograph behind on the shelf. He clumped the pot on the table, himself into a chair. 'There's been something I've been meaning to say, Jim.' He took a breath. 'The swimming you do.'

'What about it?'

''Tis getting on in the year.'

'The water's fine, Da. As warm in nor out now.'

'Winter's round the corner.'

'It's October only.'

'Getting dark these mornings. 'Tis dangerous a boy on his own.'

'I'm a fine able swimmer.'

Mr Mack heard a bang on the table. He felt the sting in his palm where his hand had slammed the board. The anger spilt from his tongue. 'Wouldn't you think of someone else for a change? Do you never think I might need you round the shop? Always out for yourself. I'm all right Jack, that's your motto.'

The miserables now to last till Christmas. Only shamming to be reading at all. After Gordie begging him to stick with his books. He passed the boy his tea. Species of nod was all he got. No use prinking me moustache, the thing is preened to death.

But things like this, you can't whip it out of them. 'Don't you see, son, it's yourself I'm thinking of?'

'Papa, don't ask me to stop swimming. I can't stop the swimming. Not now.'

'I'm not asking you, Jim.' He saw the hope flicker in his son's eyes that now he must snuff out. 'Not asking you, I'm telling you. No more swimming and that's the end of that.'

Oh, it was too much with the photograph on the shelf and Gordie's eyes on his back always, and the jaunty look of him from under his beaver, and his full dress kit that the photograph-johnnie would hire out for the occasion. And that cigarette, would he never have it finished? It was on his mind to take the picture there and then, whip it away upstairs, once for all, to the ledge above the prie-dieu where it belonged in the shadows with the photograph-portrait of his wife. God rest your soul and God forgive me, I've lost your son on you, so I have.

Chink-chink, stick-stick-stick, whiskery old chin poking in through the door. 'Aunt Sawney! You weren't long getting back.'

'No longer than ye was thieving me seat.'

How was this she wouldn't fail to catch him in her chair, yet he never could recall getting into it? He got up to let her sit, but she only grumbled away to the stairs. What was to be done with her at all? Has a genuine goatee on the grow there. Lips all chapped. Well, if 'tis chapped lips is her trouble, she oughtn't let the chaps to kiss them. He shook his head. Chapped lips. Chaps to kiss them. Sort of thing you could send in the papers.

It was curious to feel the scant mirth returning, even at the expense of a distracted old crone.

The nights were fast drawing in. Mary Nights, when asked, was emphatic about it. The fields were still in their ricks, and winter came. They had never known such storms. Even Aunt Sawney could not recall the like. People said it was the artillery barrages in France that disrupted the upper airs. Day after day the rain sheeted and grey lumbering clouds, like continents of night, heaved through the sky. The sea crashed on the sea-wall, shattering its waves in blizzards of foam. Seaweed lay everywhere. And when Jim went down there, in the howling wind, he felt the lawless solitude of weather too wild.

A sailing-ship struck by Sandycove Harbour. In the intervals of calm, in a pewter sea, tarnished and burnished by turns, bathers swam out to the wreck. But not Jim. Every morning before school, he climbed down the ladder at the Forty Foot cove, and there he clung while the waves surged and swayed him against the rock. But he did not let go the ladder, so it could not be said he swam. It was designing of him, what Brother Polycarp

349

would have called Jesuitical, and it troubled him, the deceit. Yet it was daunting to do and required a mighty determination: no thrashing your limbs, no release from your bounds, no reward at all, just the miserable freeze. He offered it up to the lost souls, in tenements of Dublin, in wastes of Gallipoli. It was all he could think to do. If he lost touch with the water, when spring came round, who could say would he know to swim at all?

The storms passed. Then the foggy nights looked in on the kitchen like shawlie ghosts at the window. In the morning the air had the taste of tin. Aunt Sawney added trimming upon trimming to her Rosary, and his father prayed to Our Lady of Lepanto who in 1571 had granted victory over the Turk. But the map on the wall that had recorded the progress of the war had stopped at Gallipoli, where a last red-topped pin signed Suvla Bay. In the shop one evening Jim snuck open a canister of thyme and sniffed the warm and arid scent. It told of dusty hills where shrubs took lightly in the dirt. A no man's land where Gordie had stumbled. He was missing now, presumed dead, but still Aunt Sawney would not let a card in the window. They too were in a no man's land.

Of all things unexpected, the canon returned, restored to health and vigour after his months in the West. He immediately set about overturning the curate's work. The Irish classes removed from the parish hall, the Volunteers no longer paraded after Mass, the plot in the Castlepark fields that had been marked for Gaelic games was turned over to allotments instead. Once more prayers were said for the King and votive Masses offered against the Turks. *Almighty and everlasting God, in Whose hand is all power and the right of all sovereignty, look to the help of Thy Christian people: that the heathen who trust in their own fierceness may be crushed by the power of Thy hand.* It was the same Mass Father Taylor would sometimes give, save the heathen then had been the English.

A while previous Jim's father had been promoted to the sixpenny-door at Mass. In the purge of the curate's appointments he was promptly demoted to the tuppenny-door again. Jim could see the dilemma it was for his father, as he brushed his moustache this way and that, trying to work out what course should he take. If he distanced himself from the curate might he get the sixpenny-door back? Or was it only the curate's patronage got him any door at all?

The flute band continued but the number of college boys dwindled. A new class joined, with whom Jim felt easier, whose fathers were known for their nationalism. The great debate was military compulsion, whether the British would introduce it to Ireland. Depending on that debate, so the fortunes of the band fluctuated. One week half a dozen boys would parade, another – if the papers had reported a particularly ominous speech – four times that number might show. But they were scarce a band at all now. They learnt no new music. Mr MacMurrough rarely came to the summerhouse. Jim met him down the Forty Foot and they would often chat a while. It was kind of him not to mention the odd way Jim bathed. He was a fine swimmer too. Jim liked to watch him dive.

In Glasthule when the band marched Jim felt the hurry of their feet, the way they were a little ashamed to be caught out of doors. Glasthule had dreamt a season, had dreamt an Irish nation. Now the cold light of day curled its lip at their foolery.

He recalled an evening in the unimaginable summer gone by when he went with Doyler to a hurling match at Blackrock. He heard them long before he saw them, a tinkling jingling frolicking chime, under the gruff calls of the hurlers and the quick cracks of their sticks. Then out of the haze on the far rise came the Lancers, jog-trotting along, a perfect line of rigid men that only the seat between man and mount seemed to move at all. The sun came out in curiosity of their metal and a breeze rose to flutter their flags.

Down they came. The spectators at the far end separated and one stumbled backward in the ditch. The game slowed in confusion till a player hopping with the ball, hopped slower and slower, and the ball rolled along on its own. Breast-high to the horses the hurlers stood. The eyes of the Lancers kept dead ahead. When they had traversed the field, they wheeled in perfect formation, with no word of command, traversed the opposite way. One or two of the horses made convenience of the slow measure to do their business on the grass. The last Lancer, with a deft lean from his saddle, swept up the ball and kept it. Then the jigging and jingling and fluttering pennants returned to the haze, faded on high, were gone.

Jim turned to Doyler, whose eyes shone with the brightness of tears. Had he said the word then, Jim would have followed. Aye, to be kicked and trampled and cursed and crippled, he would have followed his friend then. All the King's horse, nor all his men, would daunt the beat in his heart. On the tram home, while the trolley sparked and jerked in horrible masquerade of the cavalry's dance, he heard Doyler mutter, 'We will rise. We will.' And Jim had bit his lip to still the shiver in his spine. That day would come, sure as their Easter swim. And he too would rise with Doyler.

But where was Doyler? He had muzzy thoughts of tenements in Dublin. He might have gone down the Banks to ask of his people, but he didn't care to trouble them. Many evenings, after his deliveries, he pushed through the wind of the Point, down into the Forty Foot. In the dark, if he was certain of his solitude, he brought out his flute and played to the waves the music Doyler had learnt him there. Slipjigs mostly, those winding minor-keyed melodies, that seemed to say to him, *sleepily on and over, sleepily stop*

— and on again; sleepily slow but surely, steepily deepily sleepily down. He'd pull his collar up round his neck and watch the Muglins light. It seemed unlikely as sunshine that he'd swim to that island. That come the spring he'd go with Doyler and struggling against the stream they'd rise to those rocks, upon whose face they'd lie, and under the tumbling clouds all would be made clear.

All what would be made clear, he was not sure. There were words in the back of his mind, or in the sea that circled his mind, whose articulation, like his father with the Gaelic, his tongue could not get round. He sometimes felt if he would close his eyes and dip below, he might catch these words, they were drifting there in the flotsam, and he could say them now, if only to himself, and he would understand what it was that troubled him. Troubled and thrilled him, so that they were the same sensation to feel, trouble and thrill, a single trepidation. Yet it was not right he should understand now. He must wait till Doyler. Only when he was ready, when Doyler would bring him to the island, only then was the time for understanding.

But as soon as he got this far, he started over, like he was swimming in his mind and had touched the raft and now must head for the cove again, for indeed it was not clear what he should understand, or even that there was anything requiring his understanding. And why wouldn't he just look forward to the day instead of moidering in the deeps the while? For it might so be nothing would await him on the island. Yet the hurry of his heart told the lie of that. And there were words in the back of his mind or in the sea that circled his mind which, if only he would catch them, would tell the truth. And his heart didn't need to be told but knew already that Easter next, all would be clear.

Then the light of the Muglins recalled him and he sloped out of the Forty Foot and climbed on the shop bike, with its rusty chain and the mudflap that squeaked against the wheel, and cycled with the wind behind him home.

His father came in one evening, having been into Dublin, on what business he did not immediately say. He shook his coat at the yard door then hung it to dry before the range. The steam rose with the homely aroma of ironing. 'I went as far as the Coombe,' he said eventually. 'Coombe and the Liberties. Did you know they're away off beyond the Castle? I wasn't so sure at first.'

Jim smiled for his father was notorious for losing his way, especially in Dublin; though having been a Dublin Fusilier he refused to admit this and would never inquire directions. He brought his father cocoa and watched his hands engulf the mug. 'The Coombe, Da?' he said.

'Card after card after card,' he answered. 'Scarce a window but they has their card in the glass. Some of them, God help us, with two cards, three cards, to show for it. All of them edged in black. I read the names and regiments. Old Toughs or Blue Caps to a man. I thought I might recognize some of the names. But I did not. These were younger men. These would be Gordie's fellows. And all the young childer in the streets. I thought them is all orphans now.'

He finished his cocoa and the little grouts at the bottom he emptied on the fire. 'And do you know what it is? They had a shop there, no more than an old huckster's this was, and I saw in the window they had Turkish Delight on display. I was that shook. It was all I could do not to lob a brick through the glass. They have no respect some people, no cop-on at all.'

Next day the news came that the British had evacuated from Gallipoli. 'Without Single Loss of Life', the papers trumpeted. But Gordie they had left behind. Still Aunt Sawney would not hear of a card in the window. The black bordered the house instead.

*

It was Christmas week and they took down the mother hen from the kitchen shelf and smashed it on the yard flag. Jim watched his father search through the smithereens. His round face sagged, as it always did on these occasions, on account the cost of the hen and the scant coppers that chinkled out. But as he said, they would need less decorations this year. The usual festoons in the shop – there'd be mutterings from the customers else – but the kitchen would go bare, and only a candle in the parlour window to light the way.

They fetched down the box of Christmassings from the attic and replenished its unaccountable shrinkage, same every year, from the mother hen's savings. They got in the usual supply of tall red candles to give out among the customers on Christmas Eve. After many hours of fabulous sums on the kitchen table, Jim's father paid out the Christmas club savings, correct to the last farthing. They had puddings on the shelf in festive tins, which as usual no one would afford and Aunt Sawney would be serving them up at unlikely seasons in the coming year. Carollers sang in the street and pantomimes advertised on garish hoardings. And when a tiny snow fell, his father said to Jim, 'The old woman's picking her geese and selling the feathers penny apiece.' Then she hung them stiff from the poulterers' shutters.

'The army now was the place for Christmas,' he said while they were decorating the shop. He spoke more and more of his army days, the way remembering them would bring him closer to Gordie. 'Little balls of fluff that we'd tie with a thread and hang them from the ceiling. You'd come into the barrack and think the roof was after lifting off and there you was in the midst of a snowstorm. Great tuck-in you'd have on Christmas Day. Some regiments would have the officers to serve the men. The Dubs didn't go for any of that malarky. Behaviour unconductive. I regret to say there was considerable drink partook. Sergeants made themself scarce for the duration. Then when the festivities was over we'd take the men on a good twenty-mile march. Sweat old Christmas out of them.'

'What was Christmas like before the army?'

His father stroked his moustache. 'To tell the God's honest, I misbelieve I had any Christmas before I found the Dubs. If and I did, I don't recall it. Templemore was my first with the regiment. Mullingar, then Fermoy. It was England after that.'

Nothing was ever told of his father before the army. It was like he was born to the regiment. 'Did you mind leaving Ireland?'

'Sure I was only a nipper. Set sail for Southampton, not a cloud in the sky. What had I to mind anyway? The trouble of it was, I wasn't yet on the strength, not official-like. Had to beg them to take me. On me marrowbones I begged. Meself and young Mick, this was. Fearful fuss we must've put up for in the end the Adjutant took pity. Wasn't ulagoning from the stern I was, but gazing into the blue beyond.'

Jim pictured his father with his hands on the rail and the sun setting behind. His father without boots on, jags in his breeches, the orphan boy. 'How old would a nipper be?'

'Sure nobody took much note of your age in them days. If I was ten, I wasn't a day more. Four years out then, and 'twasn't the barrack rat but Bugler Mack what sailed with his regiment for the Rock. Proud as a peacock with my fusilier hackles. Blue facings that told the world the Dubs was a royal regiment.' The smile wavered on his face and he said, 'Though they wasn't the Dubs then. Was still the old 103rd. And I never did get the hang of the bugle.'

The details Jim already knew. HMS *Serapis* to Gibraltar; HMS *Devonshire* to Egypt; quartered in the Citadel in Cairo.

He wondered was Cairo near the somewhere-in-Egypt where Gordie had stayed.

'Egypt wasn't the worst,' his father continued. 'Imshee. Do you know what imshee means? 'Tis Gyppo that for go away. First thing you learns out East. Imshee! Imshee! With a smack of your cane on their b-t-m. Bamboo backsheesh they calls that. Terrible lads for the importuning.'

'But the Pyramids, Da, the Sphinx? Did you not see any the sights?'

'Would you get away with yourself and your sights. A regiment is too busy for any of that carry-on. Always something going forward, wedding or a funeral, any number of parades. And all the clobber and nick-nacks they give out. All to be kept spick and span. I doubt I'll ever forget it, the wonder of so many things to call my own. A poor lad who had only his Tipperary fortune before that. Do you know what's this is a Tipperary fortune?'

'The shirt on your back,' said Jim.

His father glanced down suspiciously from the steps. 'That and your wits,' he allowed. He had a pin in the corner of his mouth, which made it difficult for him to speak clearly. He took it out now and stabbed it through a streamer. Climbed down the steps which together they shifted the regulation three feet along the wall. Climbed again.

'Everything bright and coloured,' he said. 'Tunic to be pressed. Pouches and belts to be pipe-clayed. Five ration tins that you cleaned with bath-brick. Eight metal wash-basins. My very own knife, fork and spoon. All to be buffed four times daily with Globe Polish. And never touched but with a cloth. You kept any old makeshift yoke for use. Do you know how to be sure of a crease in a trousers?'

'Soap the inside, wet the outside, sleep on them under your mattress.'

'Did I happen to mention these things before?'

'Once or twice.'

'Ah sure well, that's how they teach in the army. By rote.'

Jim handed him the end of the streamer, retrieved the pin his father had dropped, reached that up to him. To be told,

'Head first, Jim. You don't never pass a pin that way. Where's this that streamer's got to?' After Jim had once more passed him its tail, he said, 'Sights now, let me see. Did I ever let on about the time I went down the casbah?'

'No,' said Jim, 'I don't think so.'

'With Mick this was. What it was, we heard tell of a padre, he was famous for it, he used go down the opium dens, on the scout, see, for swaddies what had been kidnapped. He'd have to brave his way out, carrying the poor lads on his back, some of them. Well, meself and Mick, we thought we'd have a twist at the rescuing lark ourself. Youthful high spirits, I suppose you'd call it. Officer we hit on wasn't at all grateful. Threatened to throw the book at us if we didn't clear out double-quick and let him alone with his hookah. Occifer, Mick used always pronounce it.'

Jim laughed obligingly. 'Mick would be Mick Doyle,' he said.

'What other Mick would I be talking of? 'Tis well known we was pals together. Mick and Mack the paddy-whacks. More than once he had me on the orderly's mat. Defaulters' book and regimental entries. Many's the scrape we had of it. Terrible to the world was Mick.'

His father a lad with a lad for his friend. His father cod-acting and getting into trouble. It made you blink twice to think of it.

'Then it was India. HMS *Serapis* again, trusty old sardine-can. Shocking voyage that was. Some of the men didn't make it at all. Fierce hot in the Arabian Ocean.'

Jim mimed Sea.

'What it was we hit a calm. Never known anything the like of it. Eerie to say the least. Ship steamed on but not a stir of a breeze gave out. And the heat like the insides of an oven. Poor old Mick. At death's door we all thought. Had to cradle him in me arms, I did, and drip the water on his tongue. Days on end I sponged his forehead, speaking the Brigid's Rosary in his ear. There was a fear of the water giving out but I scoured that tub upside-down till I had a source found from a sailor-johnnie. Time we reached port there was scarce a man left standing. Never bothered me. Never a day's sickness in me life. Got me first stripe out of that. Lance-jack Mack.'

'You must've been great together, Da.'

'Who?'

'You and Mr Doyle.'

'Didn't I say we was pals? That's the army way. Nothing you wouldn't do for a pal. Nor nothing he wouldn't do in return. End of the earth you'd go.'

On the deck of a boat in his scarlet tunic cradling his friend in his arms. What would you feel then? It was comical when you tried to picture it. Mr Doyle with his red hair and ashen face and his father's round face looking all concerned. His father with all his medals on and Mr Doyle sneaking glugs from a baby Powers. 'What happened with Mr Doyle?' he asked.

'What would you think happened him? He got better, sure.'

'I mean what happened your friendship?'

'Oh well you know,' his father said. 'The world has a way.'

He climbed down the steps to view his handiwork. Coloured tissue that swung in chains from printed mottoes. *Merry Christmas. Peace on Earth. Goodwill to All Men. Victory.*

'Gordie used love the decorations,' he said.

'He did that,' agreed Jim.

Jim fetched the dustpan and brush to tidy the mess his father

359

had left. His father watched a while then said, 'What happened I was made a sergeant of. Who said it first was a wise man that there's no friendship without you're equals. Might as well try be pals with a woman. This was up in Quetta. Do you know where Quetta is?'

'In the mountains.'

'Not in the mountains at all. Quetta is in the hills.' He looked pleased with himself and the nicety of his distinction. Then the smile went down and he continued, 'It was a shame the way it had to happen. I didn't wish to make anything of it. After all, he'd only come to congratulate me. But I couldn't but help notice his buttons the way they were. How would I know he'd take it so hard? But I had my three stripes on me and his buttons was greasy, whichever way you looked at it.'

'You said that to him?'

His father looked up sharp as if to have forgotten he was talking aloud. 'You needn't be glassing me, young fellow. I had my duties to perform and a sergeant can't be seen to have his favourites. What would become of discipline else? There's a burden to rank that one day you'll understand. But the bold Mick never forgave me, and God knows, I never blamed him for it. I doubt but he was ever the same man again.'

Jim knew his face was skewed and he tried to square it for his father's sake. But he could not accept his father behaving that way. He comes to shake your hand, your friend, the lad you grew up with. He wants to congratulate you on being made sergeant. And you reprimand him for his buttons. It was like your stripes would be sewn to your heart not your sleeve. Jim knew he would never play so false. No matter how the world divided them, he'd never let his pal down so. For friendship was a heartfelt thing. Its absence was an ache inside that no rank could ever assuage. He was certain he would never act so

– yet even as these assurances trundled on, the suspicion grew that in fact he already had.

How many times had Doyler invited him to his home and he made excuses not to go? Pop down and see the ma, Doyler would say, she does often be asking after you. But Jim had dreaded the squalor he would find. He saw no mother but a washerwoman at her skivvying and the dirt-faced children that would be clinging to her skirts. And when Doyler would ask the meaning of a word, in Latin say, or in the French of Madame MacMurrough, Jim would pretend not to know. And saying 'do be' and using 'was' for 'were' – as though he'd please a friend with his ignorance. What behaviour was that? He might have come out straight and told Doyler his buttons were too greasy to be seen in his company. Oh sure right enough, he'd follow Doyler to war, but he wouldn't stoop to visit his home. Was it he after all had sent Doyler away and not the Father Taylor at all?

And worse it got, for when Doyler had spoke of teaching, sure it was clear as day it was himself he meant. It was Doyler had wanted to be a schoolteacher. That was his secret wish. Why hadn't Jim said, We'll sit the King's together. He might have offered, it was so clear to him now, might have offered to help at least. He had most the books to share. And Doyler had better lights than ten college boys. How much he might have done. How much they might have done together. But no, Jim had his three stripes on his sleeve and Doyler had buttons far too greasy. Let Jim be the schoolteacher. It was good enough for Doyler if he was the dungman's lad the remainder of his days.

And God help me, he never asked anything of me, never ever a thing, save a kiss, and even that I refused him.

'Jim.'

'Yes, Da?'

'Turn back your cuffs if you're to brush the floor. You'll have your good shirt destroyed.'

He hadn't realized he was brushing the entire shop. His father was at the till. Quickly he said, 'Da, you could go down and see him.'

'Go down and see who is it?'

'Mr Doyle. Maybe it's not too late. You could explain what happened.'

'What's this you're on about? Why would I be knocking on Mick Doyle's door?'

'You were friends, Da.'

'Irrah, will you get on out of that. Mick and me ended years back. I left the army and 'twas only his jiggery-pokery had him follow me down to Glasthule.'

Clink, customer. Clink clink, customer customer. 'Now ladies,' his father said and his fingers tapped on the counter.

He held the door for the ladies' departure. The margarine smile showed he had drink detected on their breath. ''Tis fond of the rain,' he pronounced, looking out in the road. 'General Weatherall in command.' The door closed and he turned to take in the sweep of the shop. 'My my,' he said, 'but Gordie used love the old decorations.'

They both knew this wasn't so. Or if it was, it wasn't Gordie who had told them. What Gordie had loved was messing and scrapes and toss-ha'penny in the street. But the shop was how he would remember it. Shop, Christmas, home.

His father took off his hat that he had quickly put on when the customers came in. He looked inside its crown as though for corroboration and sighed. 'There's good news coming,' he said, his voice belying the words. 'I can feel it in my bones. There's good news on its way.'

*

Though it had to be said, when news came it did not appear to be tidings of joy. They came home from chapel after carols being sung, Mr Mack and his son, to find the parlour door ajar. Gas on inside and lady talk coming out that had squirks of amusement in it. Mr Mack could hardly persuade himself but he heard spoons kinking on saucers. He crept up to the jar and by the splay he saw Aunt Sawney with her go-to-Mass hat and the sugar tongues out. Her interlocutor he could not quite discover, but through the peep in the jamb she appeared a corpulent customer. And rather a sing-song voice for the avoirdupois she carried.

'Have ye enough of milk?'

'Thanks again, Miss Burke.'

'Call me Aunt Sawney, why wouldn't ye?'

'God increase you for that, mam.'

Two lumps of lump sugar were ferried with the sugar tongues to a china cup on outstretched saucer. 'Sugar for snap. Ye have the two of ye now to be thinking of. And when his lordship at the door has his fill of prying he may fetch a cup and join us himself.'

It took a moment for Mr Mack to apprehend who she intended. 'Is it you, Aunt Sawney? I didn't notice you were inside. Jim!' he called. 'I was only looking at this door and there's a fierce dust on the—Jim! Fetch a cloth like a good boy and give this door a rub-down. Hello, Aunt Sawney,' he said entering, chafing his hands against the chill of her look. 'Oh, forgive me now. Had I known you had company visiting, I wouldn't, why it's, well if it isn't, how are you, Nancy child?'

'Grand this day, thanks be to God, Mr Mack.'

His gaze took in the bay window of her front. ''Tis a long while now and we heard sight of you.' His gaze lifted to her still shining face. 'Anything strange?' he inquired.

363

'Strange enough,' she answered.

His fingers were tapping on his waistcoat pocket where long ago he had kept a fob. Up to his moustache, back to his fobless pocket. The room was sharp with secrets, with the mocking suspense of feminine eyes. 'I'll leave you at it so. You'll call, Aunt Sawney, should you require assistance?'

'Sit ye down,' Aunt Sawney answered.

'Well, I don't think as I will.'

'Ye'll do as ye're bid, Mr A. Mack Esquire, or if ye don't ye'll have the length of my tongue for your supper.'

'Will you have the goodness to get out of this, woman?'

Jim arrived at the door with a cloth. Mr Mack gestured for him to clear away out of that but Aunt Sawney beckoned him in.

'Fetch two cups for yourself and his lordship. We're to have this day a ponderation.'

'No no, not the boy.'

'The boy'll hear what's to be said.'

'But recollect yourself, Aunt Sawney.' He motioned to Nancy who bestrode her chair like something regal. 'He's only a lad.'

She near pounced on him at that. 'There was another boy was only a lad. Where is he this day? Get away, little man, and fetch them cups. We'll drink tea together as a family.'

Mr Mack saw, without consent, that his son obeyed. When he would be out of earshot, he said, 'Now this is nonsense, Aunt Sawney. You're evidently out of yourself. There's no family here.'

She said to Nancy, 'His lordship would have it his family ended with the regiment, so he would.'

'Leave the regiment out of this.'

'He sent him away, hunted him out of it, for the pennies he owed the publican. And d'ye know what my good boy did then?'

'What did he do, Aunt Sawney?'

The familiarity was scandalous to Mr Mack's ear.

'He did join his father's regiment. At age eighteen.'

'And didn't it make the man of him? Haven't you read his letters since?'

''Tisn't the letters we're reading now but the telegrams.' It was a cut which she made the best of by thrusting her chin where his face was. 'Ye have lost my good boy on me.' She threw a hand in Nancy's way. 'Will ye lose the grandchild with it?'

'What do you mean, grandchild? This really cannot be let go farther. This skit here has importuned on your kindness for long enough. I will not suffer these proceedings—'

She banged her stick on the floor. 'Ye'll sit down and suffer with the rest of us.'

He sat down, stared at his legs. 'She has no business calling at this house,' he told them. Then he broached the girl's face. 'You had no business returning here, Nancy. Madame MacMurrough did well to send you home. You ought be ashamed to show your face.'

''Twasn't home I went,' said Nancy.

'Wherever then.'

'She gave me money for England.'

'And wouldn't you be better off over, where nobody would know you? I cannot get over the out-and-out sauce of you. Strolling to my door on Christmas week.'

'Your son didn't mind me calling.'

'My son, is it? My son is likely dead or dying. He has done a brave deed for his King and Country. What manner of girl are you to come here and speak his name?'

'I'm the girl he loved.'

The one was close to blubbering now, so he turned his eyes to the other who chewed her tongue with toothless gums.

'She had no call coming,' he told her. 'You had no call letting her in.'

'She came for I bade her.'

'You bade her?'

'She wrote me, Mr Mack. Months back she wrote and told me the news.'

The girl was fumbling with a letter which Mr Mack waved aside. 'You have this hatched on me. You have it planned all the while. Behind my back to make a mockery of the house.' His son was at the door with the cups. 'Lookat, let the boy go only.'

'The boy'll stay.'

The tea was long stewed but his son poured with concentrated movements then sat down by the door. Mr Mack stared into his cup at the floating leaves. It was Jim who broke the silence.

'Where have you been staying, Nancy?'

'Up by the canal. Oh, it was dreadful, Mr Mack. Only for Aunt Sawncy gave hope, I don't know what to have done. They treated me something cruel. Like a common walker in off the street. And they had me doing laundry the day through. All day through, Mr Mack, without ever a smile or a kind word.'

'And what might you expect in the awkward state of you?' He tasted the bitter tea. In his mind's eye he saw a deeshy waif who gulped red-haired tea for there wasn't milk to be had in all that farming country. That farming country was Tipperary. Tipperary, the Yorkshire of Ireland. He washed the vision away and said, 'No no no, this won't do at all.'

Aunt Sawney banged her stick. 'I'll say this the once only. No blood of mine will be born in the Union.'

Mr Mack muttered, flecking his son with his eyes, 'How do we know whose blood is it at all?'

'Shame on you, Mr Mack, for thinking such a thing.'

'Is it shame on me? The strap of you to give such lip. I'm an honest man here. I try to do an honest labour. I tried to bring my sons up something decent. I looked to keep a good name to this house.' His hand beat on his breast with each argument. He turned to Aunt Sawney. 'God's sakes, woman, don't you know they have my name down for the Hibernians? I'm only clinging to the tuppenny-door as it is.'

'Pish,' she said, 'what sign of a fool are ye at all? If ye wanted to get on in the chapel, ye'd double your dues and be done with it. Ye're the careless man, Mr A. Mack Esquire. Careless enough to lose the half your name till we don't know is it MacThis or MacWhat-is-it. Careless enough to lose your woman bringing her home from Africa. You lost your son for to please the King of England. The little man here was a Presentationer only the black fellow saved him out of it.' Even Jim glanced up surprised at this. 'Will ye lose the infant to please the priesteen that's in it? I say again, 'tisn't born in the Union my good boy's child will be.'

The deeshy waif was back in his eye and the days he spent laying roads over the hills where the rain was a mist in the air. But never mind the deeshy waif. What about this coming one? 'And where's it to be born so?'

No one answered till Jim said, 'Papa?'

'Don't you be papping me.'

'Da, it was in the Union you were born. It was, wasn't it? Down Tipperary, Da?'

He swallowed. He took a long time answering. The waif in the evening used climb the ditch to peep at the world go by. 'What and I was? There's many a man better than me was born in the workhouse. I came into the world with nothing and what I have I have made myself.'

'But Da, was it not hard on you there?'

'It was hard enough.' Sat on the ditch and watched the world. 'Lookat, where would she sleep anyway?'

'She'll sleep in my bed with me.'

'She can have my bolster, Da. I'll have a coat instead of the blanket.'

'You have it all worked out behind my back. I'm not the man of this house at all.'

'I won't be staying, Mr Mack, only you ask me to.'

'For Gordie's sake, Da.'

On the ditch he sat till he saw them go by, the other boys no different from him, save they went by the middle of the road, and he waited on the ditch and watched the smoke in the sky from the houses. Then the red-coats came by with a rubbadub-dub, and when all the other boys had left off chasing, he carried on in the trail of the soldiers. That night they gave him biscuit that was hard as stone and bade him dance to the fifer. The cheery thin faces laughed in the firelight. The friendly fire with the hands about it in the homely camp of the red-coats.

He put his hand to his eyes and in a kind of blindness he stumbled to his feet.

'Lord have mercy, where's he at?'

'Leave him go,' said Aunt Sawney.

He maundered through to the kitchen and crabwise up the stairs. It was gloomy in the room and he ought have gone down again for a candle but he fumbled his hands along surfaces till he pooched out a match and lit the lamp. The chestnuts outside waved against the window. Twigs scratched the pane like the scraub of fingernails, like every targe in the parish would be scolding him for the house he kept. In the drawers of the prie-dieu he could find nothing. Where was it that he was looking for?

Her countenance stopped him. In the between-light of window and lamp he peered at her face. So often he had prayed here but he prayed with his eyes closed so that he had forgotten what her portrait told. She had the look of Aunt Sawney really.

Her face was in profile, the sharp nose and the thin lips, her eyes unseen but the one eyebrow brooding. The half of her hair that was visible was secured in a plait. She looked the competent wife, in charge of affairs, stern to the world.

Except the photographer had caught the full of her face in a looking-glass on a table beside. And in the oval of this glass she was altogether different. Her lips were not shut but had closed with a story. Her eyes shone wide and cryptic. While he watched he near could catch her laughter, mocking him for his lunacy.

They were like this were women. They could laugh and command without ever a contradiction. Suffer and smile with the same face.

He muttered something to her which he misbelieved had words to it. Then he took down the ring from its home on the ledge. He listened to his tread on the stairs and the creak of the box door as it closed behind him. Aunt Sawney was in the kitchen with her chin in his face.

'I'll say this the once only,' she told him. 'Ye're the good man, Mr Mack. 'Tis the way sometimes ye'd need coaxing to remind ye.'

Mr Mack said, 'When is the, when is the,' jerking his head to the parlour, 'when is the happy event?'

''Twill all be done by Christmas Day.'

Inside the parlour the young ones were gostering like it was an afternoon tea-party they were at. They hushed when he stood in the door. 'Put this on now,' he said. 'And if anyone should say anything, say you was coupled in Dublin. If they says anything more, send them to me. Or better still, send them round to your Aunt Sawney. But I'm warning you now, young lady—'

'Mr Mack, you won't regret it, I promise and you won't. And I'll soon have this place neat as ninepence.'

'What do you mean, neat?'

'Sure, the house is all colley and cobwebs. Leaping, so it is. But what would you expect with only men here and Aunt Sawney not current? I'll soon have it fit to be lived in again.' She put on the ring on her long finger. 'If only Gordie would be here to see it.' Then she burst into tears.

CHAPTER FOURTEEN

'QUARE FINE DAY, thanks be to God.'
          'Grand, thank the Lord.'
'A pet day for Christmas.'

'Breeze is a spanker, mind.'

'How was the water, gents?' asked the photographer.

'Wet.'

The photographer tinkered with his contraption while the men towelled down. 'Not too dry now, gents,' he called. 'We want it true to life for the readers at home.'

'Will someone tell that jasus to get on out of that. Catch our death waiting.'

Eventually the photographer was ready and he ushered the men to the spot he had selected, where the masts of the stricken barque in the background would lend a topical interest to the traditional scene. He looked out from his tripod. 'Tall gentleman at back. Could you maybe step forward?'

'Forward?'

'Maybe kneel in front.'

MacMurrough excused his way through the little throng. He took a pose like a sporting hero.

'You can caption it Our Newest Recruit,' someone quipped.

'Smile please.'

'Bejeesus,' said the men and the shutter snapped.

MacMurrough shrugged out of his clinging suit. Towelled quickly and leisurely dressed. Banter about him of men in the raw.

'Would you look at the hairy gorilla of John Mary Cruise.'

'Has he a clothes-brush for that pelt on him?'

'Shower of mermaids, the load of yous,' said John Mary Cruise and his towel flecked the blubber of buttocks. In due course the pimpled skin and sinewy limbs were restored to their clothy dignity, and the talk too put on its collar and tie.

'No use in football. All the good rugby men is in France. It's the Gaelic games I'm looking to now.'

'Damn the chance of that crowd enlisting.'

'Now gentlemen, politics.'

The photographer passed with his equipment stowed. 'Shame the sky wasn't colder-looking,' he said. He struck a match to a stubbed Woodbine. 'They prefer it at home if it's wintry.'

'When will that be in?'

'Might get the late editions Monday. Tuesday for definite.'

The men drifted away with handshakes for Christmas, and MacMurrough's hand too was shaken as the latest initiate to the Sandycove Bathers' Association. The puddles where the men had stood already were icing over and he gathered his roll and climbed to the rocks. He sat on an exposed ledge and smoked to the sea. Extraordinary blue. Flecks of white like a furry nap drifted across it. At ease with itself, a cat-creature somnolent after recent repast. Trust me not, said the blue-eyed smile.

A finger moved to his upper lip where the breeze abraded the tender smooth. That grim dread line: this morning he had shaved his 'tache off. Matter of an inch or so of hair, yet he felt positively airy for its going. The cigarette was exquisite, and left him unsatisfied. As Wilde had said, what more could one want?

In he patters now. Shy thing like a dog in slippers. Coast clear? Check behind walls. Undresses deep in the shelter, shirt and vest modestly last. Delightful how he folds his clothes, boots squared under the bench. That's right, turn round and let me see you in the sun.

Coming along nicely. Shoulders broadening, the chest separating, not the ribs and salt-cellars I remember only months back. Touch of a stiff if I'm not mistaken. Sensuality of the open air. A decent, hand-reared boy. Say hello. No, wait.

The boy padded to the cove. He reached for the ladder, but he stopped in half-stoop. A movement of his shoulders seemed to shrug the cold from him. He stood full upright in the strained sun, staring down at the water. Then slowly his arms began to rise. His fingers uncurled and his elbows bent. His arms rose, drawing him up, feet to his toes, toes to his tips. Up he rose, pulling his stomach in, stretching his torso, his armpits opening their downy nest. In a wide arc his arms rose, till high and forward of his head his hands prayer-like met. His head ducked down. So he stood, minutes it seemed.

Afterwards, MacMurrough could not decide what view he had of the boy, for he seemed to have seen all sides at once. His hair's shaven back and the flop of it over his forehead; those long shivery lashes and the freckles on his neck; how his spine grooved, how his nipples were pale and tight. He saw the deep cleft of his seat and the small stand of his front, the each shaped for the other. Water foamed below him and sky streaked above. His white body stood out sharply against the blur of stone and rock. Mica darted in the sun.

MacMurrough was certain the boy was aware of his presence. Certain too that he did not pry, but had been appointed

373

to see. A glimmering of fate told him he would know this boy. He would know him, perhaps, for all that he was and had been and should be. But he would never see him again so completely. He must look now and see all there was to see. The boy posed a practice dive, and not a very service-able one at that. But the animal within had willed its rev-elation.

At last MacMurrough let him go. He turned away. When next he looked, the boy had descended the ladder. He was in the frothing water, clinging to the rungs, his usual penance in the sea.

MacMurrough went to the shelter. The boy came huddling out. When he saw MacMurrough holding his towel he gave that extraordinary blink. Then he turned and MacMurrough wrapped the towel round his shoulders and began rubbing him dry. Rubbing all of him, all over his body, rubbing, it might be, a drenched puppy.

'Now dress,' he said.

He left him and returned to the ledge looking out on the sea, and smoked. After a time the boy joined him.

'I'm not allowed swim,' he said without prompting. 'I mean I promised my father I wouldn't till the spring. That's why I hold on the ladder. Because it's not really swimming.'

'I see,' said MacMurrough.

'Only I wouldn't like my father finding out.'

'Of course.'

It seemed faintly ridiculous their talking. Yet the boy needed to talk. They had come so close, so precipitantly. He needed to anchor his emotions. MacMurrough said, 'Fathers can be difficult at times.'

'Do you say so?'

So, said MacMurrough to himself, though he knew that this

time it could not be that way. 'How is the band these days?' he asked, filling in for the boy's awkwardness.

'The band is grand, thank you.'

'I don't hear much music coming from the summerhouse.'

'No, not music so much. They have us learning bandaging. I think we're to be an ambulance.'

'I'm told your father has resigned.'

'From the drilling? He has, yes.'

'How is she?'

'Who?'

'Forgive me, I've forgotten her name.'

'Is it Nancy?'

'She's all right, I hope?'

'Grand, I think.'

He had got the story from his aunt. Drill instructor of insufficient probity, nation's youth, curate's opinion not hers, regrettable all round. She had looked distressed rather; and not a little surprised at the man's having shown such ballast.

MacMurrough yawned. His eyes were tired from the glare and pinched in their corners with salt. They sat so close but he had no need to touch the boy, to pat his leg or stand up and, by adventure, brush his trousered stiff on his forehead. All that was given. It was settled and to come. He felt nearly sleepy: that luxurious sleepiness when slumber is certain, and one lies awake pondering trifles, till theftuous sleep drift one away.

'Yes, she's grand and fine,' the boy said.

'She must be coming due. A Christmas child.'

He was proud to be spoken to on such a subject, and studiedly he vouchsafed, 'We aren't sure the exact day, but I heard them mentioning it could be any time now.'

'And you'll be an uncle.'

'I will,' he said and smiled.

MacMurrough's fingers went to his pocket for a cigarette, but he willed them to wait. He suffered the exquisite delight of gratification delayed. So too with the boy, in not holding him, not touching him. But they were coming down now from that high place they had been. The moment of vision fast was fading. The after-glow of his bathe too was fading and MacMurrough felt the spanking breeze edging his appetite. Tiresome ceremony to go home to. Staff lined up at the pass door. Small token of one's appreciation. Little bob and the surreptitious fingering of the parcel, poker-faced estimation of content, of worth.

The boy held his cap in his hands. Its donning would mark an irreversible leave-taking. MacMurrough said, 'Did you get a Christmas box?'

'A book, I did. Kipling.'

'Let me guess. *Barrack-Room Ballads*.'

'*And Other Verses*. How did you know that?'

'Fathers are much the same, I suppose. Macaulay was my particular bugbear. "Lars Porsena of Clusium, by the nine gods he swore" – wretched stuff. My father would read chunks of it out loud after Christmas table. I could never understand, if he liked it so much, why he didn't buy himself the rotten books. I always wished for Shelley.'

He laughed at that. Schoolboy surprise at the masters maligned. Kind of relief, too, that they can be. 'I never read Shelley,' he said.

'You might like it.' Yes, bearding the pater in his den and quavering an interest in *Prometheus Unbound*. God-forsaken man. Having that obscenity in the house.

MacMurrough stroked the raw trace on his upper lip. The boy glancing saw this and his smile freshened, brightness itself.

'I knew there was something,' he said.

'Yes,' said MacMurrough. 'Moustache. Do you like it?'

'I do.'

'Shaved it off this very morning.'

'I was sure there was something, only I couldn't think what it was.'

'So you like me without?'

'I do so.'

'I'm pleased.'

'Yes, I like it.'

He coloured slightly. He stared down at the stone by his boots. How wonderful it was this coming to know, certain of the knowing to come. Every word was weighed and every glance an inquiry. Each gesture gave just that little too much away. As now when the boy fiddling with his cap let it slip and, they both reaching to retrieve it, their hands touched on the felt. Touched that little too long. With another glance, the boy relinquished his claim, leaving MacMurrough to hold the prize, that blue peter without which no departure was possible.

After an interval the boy asked, 'Was it because of Doyler you gave up the band?'

'Oh – partly, I suppose.' MacMurrough shrugged. 'I thought it most unseemly how the priest handled it.'

'You were close with him, I think.'

'We were friendly, yes, for a time.'

'I saw you together a few times all right.' His drying hair fell in his eyes. His tongue showed between parted teeth which themselves showed between pale sensual lips. 'I saw you once on the sea-wall. Doyler had the new suit on him that he started to wear. It was the first I saw him in it. I wouldn't have known him only I heard his voice. You were chatty together I thought.'

MacMurrough saw it from far off, coming, a wave over the sea, spraying the outlying rocks, unmindful, aimless, parting and merging, onward ever coming. And I thought that I –

377

'I used be jealous a touch that he'd be talking with you,' the boy went on. 'But I'm glad now if he did. I'm glad to be talking with you myself. I think you'd know what I was feeling. And I'm glad if Doyler was able to talk with you.'

On came the wave, and MacMurrough watched it, feeling the lumbering land's insignificance to the sea. The wave splashed carelessly on the rocks below, drenching him in the knowledge of his inconsequence. That I should have thought that I – How could I have thought that I –?

The boy's gaze was steadfast on the Muglins rock. He bit his lip. 'For I let him down.'

My gracious grief, thought MacMurrough. What on earth did I think I had done that I should ever dream that I – that of all people I – To have come to have imagined such a thing, I?

Still the boy continued, regardless of MacMurrough, berating himself for some negligence or lapse. Some private anguish that MacMurrough, should he live a thousand years, would not reach to. 'And all the time,' he said, 'I was telling him his buttons was greasy – were greasy, I mean.'

MacMurrough saw that his hand was patting the boy's knee. He might have been patting a wave, so insensate the leg. He let it drop and rest there; a fatuous five-fingered thing. 'You must miss him deeply.'

'I do that. I thought he might be home for the Christmas. But he didn't come yet.'

Of course, that was the present in all the world he hoped for. And I had thought to please him with a book of Shelley filched from my aunt. God, that I could be so insensible. 'I'm sure he'll be back.'

Now he turned. 'Will he?'

'Well, I'm sure he will.'

'Only I thought you might know where he was.'

'Why should he tell me?'

'It seemed to me he was close with you. I fancied you had talks together. Only he might have mentioned something.'

'I don't believe we talked that very much.'

'I used see you but.'

'Well, he never mentioned anything about going away.' And after all what had they talked about? The absorbing matter of MacMurrough and his dick. God, but I'm an egoistical bastard.

'I just hoped, really, he might have said.'

'He did tell me once that he was fond of you.'

'He did?'

'More than that. He said he loved you, actually.'

'He said that?'

'I'm sure he'll be back.'

'So am I sure.' He nodded to himself. His eyes went back, drawn to the Muglins. 'But I worry we'll be changed. How would we ever get back again? We were great that while together. Twice now we were great and twice he's left.'

MacMurrough made out, in the chiaroscuro of sun-blanched sea-drenched stones, Nanny Tremble's kind old face; and she was saying, The poor lovelorn lad, wouldn't he strike the heart out of you? And MacMurrough thought so too, and his heart in the shape of his hand lifted from the leg and wrapped about the sloping shoulders. He pulled the cap over the boy's head.

'Listen, young man, I can't do anything about that. But I can help with your swimming if you like. Ask your father would it be all right if I swam with you. He's bound to see sense. I could teach you a dive too.'

'You'd do that?'

'Yes, I would.'

'I'd be grateful if you did.'

MacMurrough stood up. He wanted quite desperately to get

away from this place now. He swapped his roll from one arm to the other. He held out his hand. 'Happy Christmas, Jim,' he said.

'A happy Christmas to you, Mr MacMurrough.'

'Here's a good one, Jim. "Boots, boots, boots, boots" – Do you know this one, Jim? About fighting the Boers this one is. "Boots, boots, boots, boots, There's no discharge in the war."' He peered out from his book. 'That's not entirely true,' he said. 'Mr Kipling got it wrong about that. They was still discharging time-expired men long after I got my papers.'

He looked over at his son the other side of the table, the pickings of their Christmas dinner between them. Capital T for Trouble on his face. 'Are we all right there, Jim?'

'Is she in pain?'

'Which?'

'Nancy upstairs.'

'What about Nancy?'

'Sure she's screaming out, Da.'

'Which?' Mr Mack turned a page of his book. 'Not screaming at all. Now, stopped. Told you she wasn't screaming.'

'Does it hurt?'

'Does what hurt?'

'Da, I don't know is it all going wrong or is she meant to be in pain that way.'

'Don't raise your voice.'

The box-stairs door opened and Mrs Tansy came in with the kettle. Mr Mack quickly rose to assist her, but she shoved him out of her way. He tapped his fingers on the table-edge. 'Everything up to the knocker above?' She shoved him again while she put the kettle to the hob. 'I could make the tea. Would that help?'

She clicked her tongue and up the stairs with her once more. The door closed snidely behind her.

'Womenfolk,' Mr Mack explained. 'At women's business.' His son's mouth was starting with questions, so he said, steering him towards the shop door, 'Are you finished eating?'

'I'm not hungry.'

He lit the gas-light in the shop. 'No pudding or nothing?'

'No.'

'You might risk a step outside so.' He opened the till, took out a half-crown, sized it up, put it back. 'Look son, here's two bob for you. There'll be something on at the Pavilion. You'd like that.'

'The Pavilion's burnt down.'

'Can't you find something to spend it on?'

'It's Christmas Day, Da. Everywhere's closed.'

He put the two bob in his son's hand, closed the hand. 'My treat,' he said.

'You want me to spend two shillings?'

'You don't have to spend it all. Come back with any change.'

'Change after what?'

'Matter a damn what.' His hand had banged on the counter, and to confute any sign of anger, he drummed his fingers merrily along. 'Go down the pier,' he said. 'You'd like a stroll down the pier.'

'Are you going, Da?'

'No no no, I'm wanted here.'

His son stared at the two coins like he'd be figuring out which reign it was. 'Can't you see, Jim, you're only in the way here?' A fearful howl came down from above and he saw the boy's face shudder. 'Don't worry your head about that. That's only a bit of old punishment for what Eve got up to.'

'Eve?'

He ushered his son to the street door. 'All quite natural and to be expected. Go on to the pier and don't come back till it's all over. That's the hookum.'

'How will I know when it's over?'

'Lookat, would you just get to hell out and enjoy yourself for once?' He pushed the boy into the lane and closed the door on his face. He turned off the gas again, returned to the kitchen.

The kettle was on the boil and he made the pot of tea. He had the ladies' cups ready for them when Mrs Rourke the handy-woman came down. 'Ye're the slatey man,' she said, waving aside the cup he offered, and she took the kettle to refill it. Half an hour later he was out on the road himself, having been told to find cold weather. But not before he had heard the new cry from above and had crept up the stairs to peek by the door. They had a fire lit in the high-barred grate. He felt the warmth of the room and the subdued air. Something holy had taken place there, a mystery was after happening, and the women bore with complacent looks their attendance on it. He saw the tub with its ruddy water. There was a smell, earthy and sweet, from where Nancy had got sick. The girl lay dozing, moaning lightly. In Aunt Sawney's arms the babe lay, Aunt Sawney hushoing quietly.

God bless the babe and spare the mother. And he had that. He had that indeed. Girl, said Mrs Tansy, closing the door on him. Glory be to God, he said tapping his breast.

He tapped it again outside in the night looking up at the light from Aunt Sawney's window. A girl. A darling dainty dote of a girl. A wee grandchild even. And a grandfather too. A mother and daughter. Uncle and niece. Great-aunt and great-niece. All the one go. It seemed an extraordinary abundance of creation. A great surging of life like a dam had broke. And there was the crying again, the tiny lungs that had called forth all this generation.

He hurried over to the chapel. At the back he knelt, with the humdrum women, and he stared at the host on its high throne and the twelve candles glimmering before it. A Forty Hours adoration was on. He heard the praying of the vigilants, way up by the altar. He crossed himself and left.

He was coming home, passing into Adelaide Road. The lights were on in Fennelly's. A private do it would be, friends and family. The empty streets echoed with the din that surged and shrunk in waves. Glancing up at the sky he saw a thin mist drifting to the sea, too thin to veil the teeming stars. There'll be a frost in the morning, he told himself. He tightened the scarf round his neck but not so tight it might be mistook for a muffler. Patted the crown of his Dunn's three-and-ninepenny. The occasion called for – he misbelieved he deceived himself – called for a small celebration. He knocked on Fennelly's door.

Regular ree-raw inside. Fug of the place and the free-and-easy way they had of pushing against you. Friends and family, my foot. Fennelly is only raking it in. He excused his way, wishing the season's greetings to any who looked likely to nod.

A wretched streel stopped in his path. 'Yous're I know what yous are. It's all very I know what it is. Yous'll know all about it an' I tell yous. Yous'll know the price of yous.' Terrible conviction in her voice. Nodding, smirking, Mr Mack greased past.

Counter a beery slew. 'Hello? No, soda. Hello? No, soda.' Faces registered with beastly familiarity. 'Soda, hello?'

Baby bottles of Powers on the shelf. Snuggled in the corner with soda beside. Baby and nurse they calls that. Buy a round for the house. Think of it. Nominate your poison, gents, the drinks is on me. Imagine that. To wet the infant's head. How much would that—? Say fourpence a head, how many heads, forty say, multiply by four, divide result by hundred and forty, twelve by twelve. How much we talking roughly?

'A soda when you're ready—Hello?'

Make it simpler. Four forties is hundred and sixty, minus hundred and forty, twelve from twenty is eight and carry one, one pound one and eightpence.

A terrific dig in the ribs brought Mr Mack round. The wretched streel was after tripping into him. Her wish of gin swayed before his face. He had to hold her by the shoulders to keep her upright.

'The Shah of Persia,' a mellifluous voice announced, 'contemplates an increment of his hareem.'

'Fill us up, y'oul fox.'

'Now now,' said Mr Mack, chucking a finger to his hat. A party was after gathering, he could feel them edging round him. Select, should have tried the select first.

'The General's on the ran-tan,' somebody called, and the phrase was taken up till Mr Mack heard it on every mouth in every tone and minor variation. On the ran-tan, on the razzle, on a batter, on a skite. The General's in liquor, he's langers, twisted, stocious, blue mouldy and cursing for soda. Chase me, ladies, I'm a fusilier. Take your washing in, Ma, old Macks is on the rampage. Call out the Silly Army.

Moments later and he was out in the road again, sucking in the crisp night air. Wretched place it was. Wretched gab off those fellows. Things they'd think. Names they'd call you. Not even behind your back, some of them. Wretched altogether. And not a one but his name in the tick book. It isn't a Christian country we live in at all.

In his pocket he had a half-bottle of Powers whiskey and a corona cigar. And he'd only gone in for a sober-water.

He stood on the street at a loss what to do with himself. Over the rooftops the chapel lights showed and Fennelly's echoed behind. He felt the miss of something, if only a hand

to shake. He wished now he hadn't sent Jim away. Precipitate that.

Out of the corner of his eye he saw the waif of a newsboy
mooching down. Bundle of white under his arm. What paper
is that on Christmas Day night? And who does he think to
sell it to?

Slower and slower the newsboy came till it seemed as close
as might be to an accident that he stopped and took his station
on the kerb beside Mr Mack. They spoke nothing for a time,
both of them watching the gutter below, then Mr Mack shook
the coins in his pocket. 'Well,' he said. 'What's the latest?'

'Constriptin.'

'Conscription,' Mr Mack corrected. 'There's a deal of trouble
in that.' A while, then he added, 'I wasn't aware there was papers
sold on Christmas Day.'

The boy shifted his sheaf, one arm to the other, importantly
to announce, '*Workers' Republic*.' He sniffed, then once again he
swapped the sheaf over, as though its substance was too great for
one thin arm to contain it long.

Mr Mack sniffed too. '*Workers' Republic*, is it?' There was a
ring of Larkinism to the name. 'And how did you come by that
in Glasthule?'

Carefully the boy explained. There was a young fella after
selling them, in Kingstown this was, yesday affnoon, he had
a uningform on him, all dark green, outside of the railway
station. The papers got thrun in the wind, after the polis
come, in the ruggy-up that follied, looking for his licence.
Then after the polis was gone, they took the young fella with
thcm, so he gathered them up the pages himself, and made
them at home into papers again. 'Worth penny each. Says so
on the front.'

He offered one in evidence and under the streetlamp Mr

385

Mack perused the page. 'And do you think to sell many of that outside of Fennelly's on Christmas Day night?'

The da had said to try it only. The da had said whatever got sold, he'd see that went where it was meant for. It was meant, the boy told him, for the Irish Citizen Army. Mr Mack made no doubt of that. 'And where's this your da is now?'

The boy jerked his head, indicating Fennelly's behind. Mr Mack nodded. Only for quick glances at the pub door to be sure of any customer, the boy hadn't looked his way at all. Now he asked of the gutter, 'Is it true you's not the general of the Fenians?'

'No more I am.'

'The da says you never was no Fenian.'

'Your da now would know all about that.'

'Says you's next or near a Positant now.'

'A Protestant?' said Mr Mack.

'Says they hunted you out the tuppenny-door at Mass. The ma says you keeps a strumpet at home with you, has her in the familiar way.'

'Now now.'

'What's a strumpet, mister?'

'Never you mind about that.'

Mr Mack viewed sideways the scrap of him and he wondered what on earth we had them for, to send them working this hour of night, to clothe them thinly and feed them poorly, and never a thought for impressionable young minds. Every day you see them, up and down the street, selling papers they can't read them or coals they can't burn them or cakes they'd never afford to eat. And their folks inside of Fennelly's knocking back the Christmas spirit. God send 'tis a kinder world for the wee one above.

'Listen, young shaper, how many of that rag have you there with you?'

'Thirteen.'

386

'How much is that all together?'

'One and three.'

'It is not,' said Mr Mack, though he counted out a shilling and thruppence for the boy. 'Get on home to your bed now. And don't be repeating things you oughtn't be listening to. Do you hear me now?'

The boy did not appear the least surprised by the exchange. As if it was a popular halt, Glasthule, for good Samaritans. Mr Mack stowed the sheaf under his arm. He wondered what was he to do with thirteen Larkinite papers. Knowing his luck now a constable would come along and he'd fetch up himself in the cells. Wasn't that the price of the police? Arrest the messenger and leave the message floating about for any young waif to pick it up again.

The boy without papers to shift flapped his arms instead. His tiny toes curled over the kerbstone. 'There'll be no rising so?'

Mr Mack shook his head. Wouldn't you think they'd find him a boots for the winter at least? 'No, son, there'll be no rising.'

'We was ready. Me and me pals was ready and willing.'

'I'm sure you were,' said Mr Mack. 'I'm sure you're good brave boys. But you'd do better thinking of school and getting your readamadaisy and your rickmatick right.'

He bade a good night and a happy Christmas to the boy who homeward trod. He turned round, then turned again. The sheeny light from the chapel was in his eye. His name had been down for the Forty Hours adoration. But the Forty Hours was too respectable for him now. He'd given a home to the mother of his grandchild and Christmas Eve he found his name struck off, for all to see, on the list inside of the door. Shine on, he told the church. A lighthouse in a bog would have no edge on you.

Mr Mack stared down the lane to the Banks.

*

They were a long time answering his knock so that in the end Mr Mack gave out, 'It's Quartermaster-Sergeant Mack only, come to inspect an old fusilier.'

A sound of shuffling then, and after a time the latch of the top-gate scraped from its catch. Mr Mack peered inside. He could make out little in the gloom, but he ventured, 'Is it himself?'

'It is,' said a voice by the fire. 'All that's left of me.'

Mr Mack entered the cabin. The smell wasn't the worst. Besides the which, it was a poor soldier who wouldn't bide his comrade's breath. They were wise all the same not to leave any candle burning, for the fire would be robbed of what glow remained. Like an old crone he huddled by the hearth, on his box with a blanket drawn round him. Mr Mack glimpsed the faded red of flannel legs and knew even the trousers was gone now.

Mr Doyle coughed, worrying the blanket. He kept his eyes on the ashes, and said, speaking with a strange old-time courtesy, 'I would bid you stay for a sup, but the woman is away at chapel yet.'

'Has she the youngsters with her?'

'And why wouldn't she? Warm there nor anywhere.'

Mr Mack left a parcel on what might be the table. Only the pickings of the goose from home, some old tarts, no more. 'I might take a heat off the fire, all the same.'

'Take an air of it and welcome. Whatever, there's little enough to sit on.'

'Had I the use of that bucket I might sit on that.'

'You might too.'

'Was I let.'

Mr Doyle nodded to the fire, as though in agreement with its ashes on some consequential point. 'Sure take it and welcome. 'Tis all we have bar the holes that are in it.'

That old cockiness, the jackeenism that so had disturbed Mr Mack when Mr Doyle had rolled up first in Glasthule, had dropped away like it had never been. In its place he heard the crabbed pride of a man with no farther to fall. But a countryman, thought Mr Mack, not any go-boy on the loose out of Dublin.

He turned the bucket upside-down. Another parcel he laid by the hearth. Before he would sit he took out the half-bottle of whiskey and pulled the stopper half-way. On the floor in front and between them he placed it, judging a finical equidistance. Mr Doyle turned his eyes till they took in the amberly gleaming bottle, then they swivelled home to the ashes.

'I was sorry to hear of your trouble,' said Mr Mack.

'I wasn't smiling hearing your own,' said Mr Doyle.

'Is herself over it at all?'

'You wouldn't know with women.'

Mr Mack lowered his voice. 'I thought you had a grand send-off for the weeshy thing.'

'We did our best sure.'

'Fine frisky horse. Grand plumes. Always sad to see the little coffin. The white brings it home somehow.'

'She left in better style than she lived, God bless the little Missy.'

'That goes for us all,' said Mr Mack. 'God willing. I would have gone myself but the shop and all. And my son had school that day.'

'A scholar you have there.'

'Something like it. What's the wind of your fellow?'

'No wind at all this way.'

'My young one was hoping to see him, I think.'

'They have a wish for one another.' The eyes darted up. 'That age and they know no better.' The quick flare brought on his coughing and had him spitting afterwards, copiously into the fire. Mr Mack saw it before it died, the pink tint of his phlegm.

'The old whiskey,' he said, 'would murder you altogether and you was to risk a sup.'

'`Twouldn't cure me at any rate.'

'A cigar would be the end of you entirely.'

'Not this side of Last Post and I'll taste again the smoke of a cigar.'

'Sure there's plenty smoke where we're headed,' said Mr Mack. He had the corona out of his coat and he was testing its end with the blade of his pocket-knife. 'Christmas box from the boy, but little the use it is to me. Is it this way you'd cut it, I don't know?'

'Ah sure give it here to me. Ballyhays you'll make of that.'

'You used have a fondness for the old cigar, I do recall.'

'I had me day.'

'You might light it now you've gone this far.'

'Throw me a spill and I will.' He blew on the spill, little whiffery breaths, till it took fire and he brought it to the cigar. In the flame Mr Mack saw his face, an old skin-and-bones of a thing. Deep furrows reached from his nose like tackles to hold his jaw in place. His hair was gone a shock of white, sticking out in startlement at the change. 'I'm not dead yet,' he said in disputatious tone. 'I might cheat the worms of me yet.'

'Why wouldn't you?' agreed Mr Mack. 'You have smoke enough and whiskey inside to be proof against all comers.'

'There's that.'

'Except they shoot us, we Old Toughs refuse to die.'

'The Dublin Refusiliers,' said Mr Doyle.

'You did always have a way with words,' said Mr Mack smiling and shaking his head. 'Would you take a sup of the creature now? If you had it to hand, say?'

'I wouldn't know to get any this hour.'

'There's a small drop I have with me.'

'I saw that. And you known to have the pledge taken.'

'Didn't we take it together sure?'

'Aye we did. There's many gone under the bridge since that.'

'Many and more,' agreed Mr Mack. 'We used always be pledging ourself after a night on the Billy Stink.'

'The old Billy Stink was a killer right enough.'

'That and the purge.'

'That and the purge.'

'And we did often share an old shock off a pipe together.'

'I did often have a red pipe put in my hand, 'tis no lie.'

'Sure the first pipe ever I smoked, we shared it.'

'People was known share a bit in them days, 'tis true.'

There was some old tinder in a nook in the hearth and Mr Mack, judging his station as old comrade would just about stretch to it, leant down and threw a stick or two on the fire. He opened the parcel he'd left beside him and one by one he placed the coals he'd brought. He dusted the coal-dust from his hands and held them over the blueing flame. They were talking the while, of the past still, Mr Mack asserting some friendly deed, Mr Doyle recognizing in a general way the possibility of such things occurring.

'The first time ever I scraped my chin,' said Mr Mack, ''twas yourself found me the razor. I can remember you now, stropping the blade on the sling of your hipe for me.'

'I wasn't the worst for doing a good turn. If I could see my way at all, God knows.'

Mr Mack stared into the flames, and sure what did he see but this fellow here, with his shoulders back, his chest blown, thighs that would grip a shilling bit. Red hair you'd think his head was on fire. Not a man but he was proud to step out with Red Doyle. He had the poor ladies fainting with the scarlet fever. Mick and Mack the paddy-whacks. Rang like bells.

'Till they gone and went and made a sergeant of you,' said Mr Doyle, 'and you turned like.'

And there it was, that old wound, done with as that fire and still with a heat at the heart of it. Mr Mack could see it now, in the flicker of flame, the queer look on the man's face that time, before he had snapped to attention. Yes, Sergeant, said he. Buttons greasy, said he. But his eyes were crooked the way they looked. Mr Mack could doubt but they were straight again since.

'You took the heart out of me that day, you did,' said Mr Doyle now. 'What you see before you is the close of that day's work.'

Oh and the rest, thought Mr Mack. All downhill after that, for sure. Tell a man his buttons is greasy and his pride is gone, his manhood broke, his life in tatters ever after. 'Do you know something?' he said. 'You was never any damned good for a soldier.'

'Nor you was any good for a sergeant.'

'We're snacks there then.'

'Snacks,' said Mr Doyle. 'And I'll tell you what else,' he said, more animated now and the blush on his cheek-tips deepening. 'There was nobody complaining me buttons was greasy at Talana Hill. No, nor at Glober's Koof. Tugela neither.'

'Grobler's Kloof,' said Mr Mack. 'Would you get it right.'

'I stood me ground, I did, with me fellow Toughs. I didn't turn tail the first shot was fired. I stood to them Bojers, I did. 'Twasn't me what ran for home.'

'To hades and back with you,' said Mr Mack. 'You've this story told up and down the street. We'll have this out once for all. I was time-expired. I had my discharge papers gave out me—'

'There's plenty men signed on again.'

'I had my passage booked. I had my young wife that was sickening. Sure the war was to be over by Christmas. How was I to know 'twould take three years? You think I had it rosy then, with my wife passed away on me and my two sons I didn't know what to do with them, coming into Southampton and the news everywhere of rout after rout after rout? You think there was many wanting to employ me then, a man come back from the Cape and a war on? Only for Aunt Sawney above I was on the dunghill, my two young sons with me. And not a night but I thought of the regiment.'

'Battalion,' said Mr Doyle.

'Ah, would you give it a rest, man.'

Mr Doyle began a cough that rumbled in his belly before it rose to his chest and made quick hacking barks in his throat, and only when he turned could Mr Mack see it wasn't coughing at all, but laughing he was at. 'God knows,' he said, 'I'd take me chances with old Piet any day, with General Bother himself, before I'd face that crosspatch above.'

Mr Mack granted him his laugh, and when the laughter was done the quiet that followed recalled him to the barracks at Quetta, high in the hills, when his sergeant's stripe was fresh on his sleeve. The sense he had of fun and fellowship retreating wherever he advanced, always a corridor's length away. 'And yet,' he said, ''tis true, you know. Them buttons of yours was greasy.'

'Sure what about it,' said Mr Doyle. 'I wouldn't know to get buttons now, leave out the grease to muck them. Bloody end to the lie in that.'

Mr Mack's fingers tapped on his knees. He watched the wispy

curls coming up from the cigar, which Mr Doyle had lit but would not yet smoke. 'Aren't we two very foolish old quilts,' he said, 'to be argufying the past? Whatever about buttons and time-expired, it isn't a sergeant at all I am now.'

'And what are you this night coming here to my hearth?'

Barmy old fool, thought Mr Mack. 'To tell the truth I'm a bit out of myself.'

'A child would tell you that.'

Mr Mack picked up the bottle and made as if to sip. He made as if to change his mind and offered the bottle over. 'For old time's sake itself?'

He had the bottle held out a long while before Mr Doyle nodded. He wiped his mouth and without looking accepted the whiskey. He drank his due of it, a good third, in slow slipping slugs, then wiped his lips again. He drew on the cigar till the smoke came out the sides of his mouth where the teeth were gone.

'Well, Arthur,' he said, after his cough had ended. 'Is it a grandfather you are this night?'

Mr Mack put his hand on the red-flannelled knee and he squeezed it gently where the bones beneath were the bones he knew that had aged and thinned with his memory of them. 'Well Mick,' he answered, 'I believe and I am.'

Jim had wandered as far as the West Pier where the *Helga* gunboat gleamed at its mooring. Now he walked back along the harbour front to the East Pier again. The yacht clubs had been shut up for the duration and on their terraces canteens had been erected. Yellow light hung about, like balloons, in the doorways, where groups of Tommies gathered round. He heard the accents of Dublin and Cork, of the West and the North. The soldiers' feet stamped in the cold, like horses'. Vapour drifted from their mouths and from the mugs they cupped in their hands.

The tide was high and the enclosed water of the harbour chopped and changed like an animal pacing its cage. He fancied the waves beyond the piers and felt queasy thinking of boats on the sea and the Tommies who must soon embark. It seemed a poor mouth that would forbid them decorations on their last night in Ireland.

Last Christmas they had all the decorations out. The trees along the front swung with lanterns, the Pavilion shone with all the lights of fairy. Last Christmas, if you went up Killiney Hill, you could sketch in jewels the arms of the piers as they reached to clutch their own from the sea. Last year the war would be over by Christmas. This year people said it might never be over.

He crossed the opening of the pier, whose high wall governed the wind, and passed along the road by the Crock's Garden, an exposed walk that straggled the shore. The wind here buffeted and blared, nicking his skin with an ice salt slice. He looked in through the railings where the bushes crowded the black-earth paths. He thought of the shelters down below that gave out on the sea. They were strange and eerie spaces, done out to be temples, with colonnaded fronts: they smelt of toilets. A match struck, startlingly close, and he saw the glows after of twin cigarettes. He hurried on.

He wondered might he go back and view the ruins of the Pavilion; but a train was approaching by the Metals, so he crossed the road to watch. Adventure of its coming, the clatter and rush, that climaxed in a billowing steam. Then lives flickering by in single snaps of light. That odd impulse to wave your cap at strangers. The train disappeared under the road, gathering its business behind it, and the night resumed.

Jim pressed against the wall that vibrated still with the train's rumble. He could feel his thing below, stiff and unmitigated. What sustained it he could not think, for nothing of the sort was on his mind. He heard a voice on the path which he thought might be Mr MacMurrough's. But no, there was a woman's voice too. An English officer passed, a girl on his arm.

He couldn't think what to do with himself. Had sufficient time elapsed for a child to be born? The screams back home had unsettled him, though it was a ridiculous notion to suppose it had anything to do with women's suffrage. Butler was all mouth. That time they were passing above the ladies' baths in Sandycove, and Butler was laughing and telling how you'd easy know by the higher pitch of the girls' squealing when the water reached the spot. 'Which spot?' 'Ask your ma.' And walking the lower tier of the pier so's you'd see up her legs if a girl was walking the upper. Why would you want to look there?

He ran his tongue along his upper lip, imagining the feel where a moustache had been shaved. He had a wish to do something, to shape by deed the confusion he felt inside. But no deed he could think of seemed remotely expedient. It was so cold. He turned the collar of his jacket up and pulled his scarf more tightly round. He crossed the road and descended into the Crock's Garden.

He was picking his way through the veronica bushes, down the sudden steps and winding paths, when he felt the company of a young man beside him. It was a soldier in his greatcoat and cap, who walked a while in silence, then remarked in a familiar way, 'Shame about the Christmas lights and all.'

'Yes,' said Jim. He had to shout to be heard above the wind. 'My brother brought me up the Hill last year.'

'That was decent of him.'

'Yes, he came home from the camp at Woodenbridge, he was

in his Kitchener blue, and Christmas Eve we walked up Killiney Hill together.'

'He'd have been fond of you, your brother.'

'I was never sure of his ragging but I liked him all the same.'

'Isn't that the way with brothers, sure?'

'When we got to the top we saw Kingstown below us and all the lights as far as Dublin. The city was like a fire and the Hill of Howth a dog at its hearth.'

'Did he mention anything to you that time?'

'Yes, he said it wouldn't be long now and he'd be out of this fucking kip.'

'Sure he was the devil's own. But that was his way only. He was fond of the old sod, I'll engage.'

'He's to be a father before this night is out.'

'Farther and farther away,' said his brother.

'Where're you going?' For his brother was cutting through the scrub to find his way to the sea.

'Must get back. I'll be ticked off for missing and I don't get back soon.'

'But they're not there any more. They've evacuated the beaches. You'll never find them now.'

'It's not this way you'll find what you're looking for.'

'What am I looking for?'

'So long, young 'un. Mind you keep to your books.'

Jim shook the phantasma from his head. A salt from the sea trickled on his face. The wind shivered up his jacket and his cold wet fingers drew the cuffs of his sleeves together. He had taken his cap off for fear of it flying. His hair flapped all ways.

He stood at the top of a steps. A blueish night light only just allowed the eyes to see. And he saw how the sea was truly wild. Waves dashed on the rocks, tumbling over in their hurry, creaming as far as the path below. Great gurgling sucks, like the sea drew breath, then roaring through chasms and spouting out in a froth of foam. It seemed to hang in the air, the foam, and shine of its own luminescence. The wind was boastful in his ear.

He closed his eyes and he saw himself in that sea, far far out, released from his bounds, riding the crest of billowing waves. He felt it in the pit of his stomach, the exhilaration of the deep, and the mystery of the deep reaching up to take him.

His eyes opened and he saw dimly the temples on the shoulder of the pier.

He edged along the path, judging the waves and darting between, till he came to the first of the temples. It was filthy dark inside but still he passed through the columns. The sudden quiet was enormous. He sat on a ledge at the back. Damp registered through his seat. He sensed the urinally smell. A drip from the roof dropped tip-tap. His mouth tasted of brine.

Before him in columned panorama the sea surged, grey with trouble and white with thrill. The same thrill and the same trouble boiled inside him. He felt a bursting to be known, to be born, that would no longer be delayed, but whose labour had come. He thought of that other birth at home and the child he soon would hold in his arms. Through his fingers he felt the wall behind and he was struck by the strangeness of concrete things: the ledge, the columns, the floor to his feet: things that did not move, while the sea never ceased.

He had not long to wait. A soldier had followed him. A match struck, a cigarette was lit. The red glow was offered in Jim's direction.

In his dark-green uniform Doyler lay, his slouch hat over his eyes, on the hard plank of his police-cell bed. There were steps outside and a rattle of keys. His cell door opened. It was the old sergeant who was at the desk last evening when the polis brought him in. He had a cup of tea with him which he held out to Doyler. 'Now,' he said. 'You have your tea. Drink it.'

Doyler caught the accent of Clare. West Clare, he thought: the fellows for football.

'Make the best of it, boy,' the sergeant advised, once more at the door. 'They'll let you out on the Monday, I'm told, with a caution only. You have your feed and sup till that. Do you want a read of an old newspaper?'

'You can give me back me *Workers' Republic*. I'll read that.'

'You have a mouth on you,' said the sergeant. 'I'm not wondering that it's bruised.'

Doyler lifted the tea to his mouth. 'I'd say you'd wish you was in West Clare tonight,' he said. 'Away out of Kingstown. The old Kate Mac home.'

The old sergeant nodded. 'Merry Christmas now,' he said.

'Merry Christmas, citizen,' said Doyler.

CHAPTER FIFTEEN

T HEY HAD MADE a kind of a cot for her, Mr Mack had and
Jim, out of, I don't know, an old oranges crate, and they'd
sanded it down and varnished it smooth, they were days at it,
should have heard them out in the yard, bickering over what
went where, and they'd taken the wheels from under the shop
cart, so it was a kind of a pram, suppose you'd call it, with a
handle at the end, which she pushed now, Nancy did, rocking it
gently to and fro. She had fetched the customer's chair from out
the shop, and she sat outside in the lane, under a fierce January
sun that wouldn't heat you one bit, save that it warmed the heart
to see. A couple old sparrows was chirping out of the chestnut
trees over, the way they'd be fooled by a sunny day into arguing
title. It was near enough her first steps out of the house, barring
the christening, and she still had trouble walking, though if she
thought to point to the pain, she couldn't rightly tell where was
it at. Up and down them stairs inside was murder altogether.

But God is good, and there wasn't pain but you was blessed
for it; and the little blessing lay asleep in her rickety pram. Every
few moments Nancy touched her hand to her cheek, checking
for chill, but everything was rosy yet. And she really was rosy,
was the little mite. That yellowy tinge, it had her in torments of

worry that first week, it was after lifting, like Aunt Sawney always said it would, and her skin now was soft and pink and, I don't know, velvety something. And you'd want to be bending down the while, to sniff her smell, that was all powdery-milkery. Oh it would put you in mind of eating her, so it would. 'I could eat you, gobble you right up,' she said, shaking her head into the oranges crate, and she was sure a smile was after fainting across the face, though the sleepy mite was dozing still, with her squoze-up eyes and her thumb just licking her mouth.

The truth of it was, she couldn't wait to be showing the little babba off. Oh not to the street, never mind the street, the street was only ignorant, so it was. And as for that curate, making her take off her ring for the christening, that was plain badness. No, but to show her off to the daylight and let her know there was a sun up there and a blue sky to shine out of, and she'd know, without even knowing she knew, the joy it was with the sun on your face. If only the hint of it, mind, for she kept her eyes out of the glare for fear it might wake the little mite and she'd go all dazzled.

Jim come out of the shop, with a rug in his arms, and she said, 'Did you bring that out for your niece?' He had. But wasn't the little mite smothered, near or next to, as it was. So she bade Jim wrap the rug round her own shoulders instead. You'd swear she was nettles or briars the way he wouldn't touch her, only let the cloth fall in place. 'Is that out of your bed?'

He said it was, colouring a touch. She drew it closer round her, the blanket Gordie had slept in under.

Poor old Jim. There was a cloud hanging over him, she didn't know what it was, only she hoped he wasn't jealous of all the attention. Night the babba was born, he comes home, but he's only hanging about the door. Say hello to your niece, says old Macks. And that's exactly what he does. Hello, says he, like he'd be shaking her hand next. Then at the christening when he was standing godfather and they came to that bit about the gentleman below, do you denounce his works and pomps? – it took a while for him to answer till they all turned to look. Then out he thunders, I do, and the blaze in his eyes you'd swear 'twas old Nick himself at the font, and the little man defying him heart and soul. Even that twister of a curate looked startled out of his stole.

Whatever it was, there was no touching him these days and he was for ever at the wash-bowl. He washed his face so hard, he rubbed the smiles away.

He was watching one time when she was changing the babba. She could tell he was checking off the anatomy and muddling out the parts in his head. 'See that,' she said, and of course he did, for he was gawping and blinking at it, the nubble out of the babba's belly. 'That goes down sure. We all had that, even you when you was little.' She breathed on a penny, placed it on the nubble, before wrapping the napkin round. 'That grows into your tummy button,' she told him. Oh I know, says he, colouring away. Knew that all along, he did of course. And sure God love the dote. At home she had all the beasts of the field, let alone her brothers and sisters. She pitied the townie children who'd know no better than they'd learn off the chickens in the yard. Declare to God, and I laid an egg, 'twould put no pass on Jim.

Not that Gordie was ever behind in catching on.

But where would you be without Aunt Sawney? You'd wonder how'd she know it all. Would swear she had a street of them raised, the little mites. And her parched old face when she watched you at nursing. She liked to see the child at her feed. Well, you'd go that way had you never gave milk. Smacking her gums, like she'd be tasting it herself. Hairy old chin she poked at the babba and her cheeks all sunk. You'd often wonder had she mistook the boot-blacking for rouge. But if ever a face told lies, Aunt Sawney's was the wickedest yet.

She woke in the night one time, without the babba crying, and she could just make out Aunt Sawney in her chair, rocking and rocking, slow-like and deliberate, over the drawer from the chest where the babba slept. Queer old fright she looked by the night-light. You couldn't but think of them withered old jugs and for a moment the fear came on that she'd take up the child and – you didn't know what with it.

But Nancy hadn't moved nor made any sound, and she was glad of that after, for Aunt Sawney only kept to her rocking, so slow and deliberate-like, nodding stiffly at each Jesus in her prayers. There was something the way she stared, something near fierce about it, the way with every rock of her chair she'd be willing her hopes inside the sleeping mite. Till a moan from the drawer broke the moment and soon enough the babba was looking for her feed. While the tiny mouth dribbled and the withered face watched, Nancy had prayed that Aunt Sawney would be spared to them, spared at least till the child would know her, and she'd love her Aunt Sawney for the true cause and source of her happiness, whatever share would come her way.

She sighed now, and smoothed her dress over her knees. To and fro she rocked the crate, the wheels on cobbles scraped. She sighed again, and rhymed a music-hall snatch.

It ain't all honey and it ain't all jam
Wheeling round the houses with a home-made pram.

It must be dinner-time for some boys came past, little tykes so they were, calling out 'Maggie! Maggie!' and pointing their dirty fingers down the lane. Sure let them point. Soon enough now and it won't be fingers they're pointing. She took up the song herself, and sang as she'd heard it off the girls by the canal.

O Maggie, hold your head up high
Walk tall and proud and strong.
You're worth twice twenty score and more
Than him that did this wrong.

Well, she didn't know what she was worth, not much she supposed, nor what Gordie was worth, little more now than a letter off the King. But you couldn't call it wrong what they done together, not when you saw the little mite here. Oh sure Gordie, Gordie, I've mourned and missed you longer than ever I loved you. I love you yet, but I can't be mourning for ever. Isn't it enough I'll never have my wedding-day nor never share your bed with you? Not once for my man to hold me in the night and wake with my man in my bed beside me. All that's gone. The beginning of that was the ending of it. They'll know me in years to come for the old maid does be watching at weddings. No, she never married, they'll say, though 'tis known she was pretty once. Going into a hugger-mugger then, to relish the shame of the tale.

She reached into the oranges crate and brought the bundle of sleep to her breast. Turning she saw the card in the shop window. Aunt Sawney had put it there after the babba was born. *Gordon Mack*, in thin black lettering inside of a thick black border. *Gallipoli 1915. RIP.* And he was a rip too. A rip and a bold particle. I was a girl then and he was a boy. You were after making a woman of me, Gordie, if you did but know. Though I doubt if ever I made a man of you. Is it only with men they can be made men of? Is it that why they rush to go?

At the bottom of the card, old Macks had added, *Corporal, 'C' Comp., 7th Royal Dublin Fusiliers. For King & Country.* Which last was a lie, but what harm, if it made old Macks happy.

Poor old Mr Mack. He has it harder than any of us, I sometimes think. There he is with his heart all set on being a gent. Will he never learn 'tis the mark of a gent, not that hats are lifted to him, but that he lifts his hat to others? And Mr Mack is a gent to the bone. To the crown of the bowler hat of him.

She went into the shop, where Jim looked up from the counter the way you'd be kind enough not to notice him there, and inside of the kitchen she heard Aunt Sawney giving a down-the-banks to Mr Mack. The babba gave an egg-shaped yawn while the shop door closed behind. Home, said the clink.

When the Dominican brother had called each boy privately to his room – this was on the last day of their retreat, two summers previous – he told them – or leastways he told Jim: Jim didn't know what he told the other boys, for no boy ever spoke of that confession – he told Jim of the sins of the flesh, the horror of impure thoughts, the terrible consequences of the solitary vice. No sins destroy a soul so utterly as this shameful sin, he said. It steals the sinner from the hands of God and leads him like a crawling thing into the mire of filth and corruption. Once steeped in this mire, he cannot get out. The more he struggles, the deeper must he sink: for he has lost the rock of faith. My Spirit does not dwell in you, the Lord hath said, if you are nothing but flesh and corruption. And so God gives up the impure to all the wicked inclinations of his heart. Hear him laugh at the truths of religion. Delightful to him the stench of corruption. In the mire of passions he wallows. Yet even so he will seek to hide his shame, even from his confessor, as if by darkness or solitude heaven were deceived. Will such a one at the last moment give a good confession, who has from his earliest youth heaped sacrilege on sacrilege? Will the tongue, which has been silent up to this day, be unloosed at the uttermost hour? No; God has abandoned him; heavy are the sins

405

that already weigh him down; he will add one other, and it will be the last.

This then was the spiritual sequel. The priest went on to tell the corporal sequelae, how God has set the mark of ignominy on the solitary sinner's face. The sickly pallor, the eyes darkened with the shadows of vice, the listless restless joyless posture. Where once the future shone brightly in his eyes, now but gleams the dark road to lunacy. In this life the asylum is his sole hope, in the next the fires of hell.

Jim had left that room, red-faced before the other boys who lined up outside waiting their turn, and he had walked the perimeter of the games field where other boys walked, each one alone, each with his head bowed down. He was burnt with shame and fear, but also he was scandalized. Why had no one warned him before this? Why wait till he was fifteen and he was confirmed in that vice? Indeed not confirmed only, but lost entircly, already abandoned by God. For the mark was on his face, plain to see, if he could bare to look, in his sallow skin, his dull eyes, in their maniacal blink. It was a scandal, and he had half a mind to go up to the national school now, burst in upon the classroom, cry it out to the young boys there, Don't do it! Don't think of it! Don't start or you're lost!

But horror, at such a pitch, required a frequent refuelling: his weekly confession attempted the task, but frequency of its nature makes horror tolerable. Time passed, and it was the discriminations and distinctions of sin, with regard to impure thoughts, that held Jim's mind. That the Church should see so far ahead, so deeply inside the soul, that no contingency was overlooked but she planned for all the twistings and quibblings of conscience: it was a majestic thing to contemplate, a structure built of thought and logic, magnificent and complex as the cathedrals the Protestants had stolen from her. In the end, whether his hand moved to that solitary vice was neither here nor there. For already there was the sin of *desiderium*, which was the desire for what is sinful; of *delectatio morosa*, the pleasure taken in a sinful thought; of *gaudium*, the dwelling with complacency on sins already committed.

It was round about that time when the notion first came on Jim that he might have a vocation for the Church.

Then his brother came home on his embarkation leave. He spoke about Nancy. He spoke about – fetching off, he called it. Jim had never encountered the expression and for a moment he couldn't think why his blood was rising. Then it hit him what his brother meant. It was worse, far worse, than confession. He felt his cheeks like coals.

'Or have you given that up for Lent?' said his brother.

'Shut up, you blackguard,' Jim told him.

'Ah, shut up yourself, young 'un. Did you think I never catched on what kept you in the privy? I only wanted to say it's all right, and don't mind what they says. There isn't much the army don't learn you. 'Tis going without will drive you doolally.'

'It's a sin.'

'Suit yourself. It does no harm. Better with a girl is all.'

Whatever about its sinfulness and harmfulness, this last was transpicuously absurd. Jim couldn't imagine doing it if a dog was in the room, let alone a girl. But living with a thing so long and so intimately could not but blunt the fear of its consequence. Besides, he was only half so wicked as he might be. His hand moved in actual sin, but his mind dwelt far away, far away from the efficacious sins of desire, perhaps on the sea, or on swimming there, or rocking amiably on the Forty Foot raft.

Sophistry! Cruel deluded casuistry! The Crock's Garden had been the end of that. He did not remember coming home, only lying in the dark later, in his settle-bed on his own. Even then he was not sufficiently steeped in the mire, but his hand must go below to the throb that was there, and moment by moment, touch by touch, he relived the scene, delighting in every strangeness, and the queer freedom he had felt in his submission, the relishing of his exposure, his bending to the seat and willing his vulnerableness, even of the pain savouring the memory, and hearing still the grunts of pleasure and his own compliant moans. And in his mind's touch when he reached behind, it was not a soldier's khaki he found, but a blue-gone shiny trousers.

A holy draught had come in then under the window to shake the holy Sacred Heart flame. And in that flicker he saw it, the fiend that was his soul. His monstrous heart, his vicious flesh, nothing escaped that searing flash. Flickered the flame like the kitchen walls had gaped and before him blazed the fires of hell, to which his bed was inching, dragging its length along, ever and downward, to tip him finally in the pit of damnation.

He leapt from the bed, giddy in flight, like he'd scut off a moving carriage. He found his Rosary beads. Quickly he prayed. So abandoned was he, the words would not come. He wound the beads round his hands. Let his beads now be the chains that bound him. Hindered in this way he dressed: he could not bear to be unclothed. He dug his fingernails into his palms. All night he prayed. On his knees by his bed, his elbows propped on the mattress, eyes held by the holy flame, smarting, stinging, watering, closing. And when they closed, his elbows slipped, shocking him awake, for he felt the bed itself had lurched. He had not thought a night could endure so long. While above strange noises he heard, a baby crying, a mother's voice, the boards creaking with untimely passage.

Next day was Sunday: there were no confessions to be had. Three Masses he heard, but without his receiving, there could be no solace. He thought to try St Michael's in Kingstown. It was St Stephen's day. He had never known the town so full with soldiers. He feared to look them in the face, yet hunted their profiles, as foundlings are said to, seeking their parents, though it was stray glances he sought, and feared to find them, cringing to think that any might know him. There were no confessions at St Michael's of course. He thought to stop a priest in the street. Father, I have sinned. But he dared not speak in the broad day. Another night he passed without sleep. The Monday, confessions were not till ten. He walked the streets while the shutters came down from the shops and the gas flared in the windows. Away on Howth dawn was only screaking. He heard early Mass, then did the Stations. In the second bench from the altar he told his Rosary. At last Father Taylor came in from the sacristy. A velvet shadow, he swept along the side passage. The door to his confessional latched home.

Jim joined the queue of penitents. It was impossible he should say these things to Father Taylor. He had no words for these things. His mind would not consider them, but physically, in a twinge of his head, jarred their notion away. Would Father Taylor know him? The lamp that lit the priest's profile would show his face if the priest turned. If the priest should turn and hunt him out of the confessional? There was a sin against the Holy Ghost that only a priest knew what it was. That sin could not be forgiven. If this were that sin? Was there truly such a sin?

The queue shuffled its few feet closer to grace. And he with it.

And now he was inside. The confessional evening closed round him. The crucifix glimmered in front. A woman's mutters sounded through the space. Forgiven, Latin, click. A moment when all awaits. With louder click his own slide opens. Through the cruciform gauze in the grating the bristling ear of the priest.

Jim told his sins that were commonplace and venial, hearing them for a national schoolboy's at his first confession. When he finished the priest said, 'Anything else, my son?' On Jim's hesitating, he prompted, as Jim had known he must, 'Sins of impurity?'

Jim took a breath and in its exhalation outspilt the story, all the horrid notes, in quavers and breves as he stuttered and paused, how the black bushes he threaded between, and the waves had splattered the pathway, till he came to the shelter, and there he waited while the sea in restless motion moved, on and on, unmanning himself with the awful truths, and in his nervousness and dread perhaps not entirely coherently, for the priest interrupted and asked, Was she a married woman?

Jim was startled for a moment, so that he answered, No. Was she a fallen woman? It wasn't a woman at all, Jim said. The priest paused. It was a girl, so. Jim began, but again the priest interrupted. Had he touched her? No, Father. He was certain he had not touched her? Father, it wasn't a girl at all. Was she a Protestant woman and she did lure him on? Jim had thought this worst was over, but no, he must suffer the scandal of speaking it again. Father, he was truly ashamed to tell it, but it was a soldier, Father. An English soldier? Jim didn't know. Was it the English soldier who lured him to the girl? It wasn't a girl, Father. With a testy shake of his head, which had Jim cowering lest he should turn, Father Taylor gave him to know it didn't matter her age but it was the sin he should mind. He should thank God and His Holy Mother that She had looked down on him then and prevented his touching the fallen Eve. Where did this take place? Jim answered the pier. The pier, the priest told him, was a perilous place. The pier was an occasion only begging for sin. The pier in fact was a Protestant intrigue where they paid fallen women to parade in their finery and lure Catholic boys to their peril. Was he sorry for his sin? He was, but there really was no girl involved. It didn't matter was she a girl or a woman, his guilt was the same, but if she was a married woman the sin was more grievous yet. Was he sure she was not married? Father, please, it was a soldier. The soldier must look to his own salvation. Father Taylor did not doubt he was a Saxon and a heretic and was most like lost to God. Either that or an Ulsterman. However, that he led Jim to the girl did not lighten one jot the blame attached to Jim. Did Jim promise never again to sin that way? It was a heinous sin even to speak to such a girl. Had he spoken? No, Father. Did he promise? He did. Would he promise never again to stray to the pier? He would promise that.

'How old are you?'

'Sixteen.'

Father Taylor then, continuing his forcefully whispered mode, discoursed upon chastity and marriage and think what his mother would say and letting down the good name of all Irish boys. With bleak dispassion Jim listened. He spoke of Our Lady and told how every impure thought, how every glance, was a thorn in Her sacred heart. Jim had had a narrow escape. He might have sinned deplorably had She not been watching over him. Accordingly, he gave penance of Rosaries and had already launched into his Latin, when Jim touched the grille and he said, 'Father?'

'What is it?'

'Am I truly absolved?'

'Have you told all your sins?'

'I have. Save, it was, it was a soldier, Father, not a girl.'

'Will you forget about the soldier. Forget about the girl. Pray for them in all charity by all means. But most important pray for your own soul that is in peril. And keep clear of the pier. Even for fishing.'

The slide clicked closed. Jim breathed in and out. He sniffed, and passed his sleeve across his eyes. He stood up and held a while the handle of the door, before he turned it and came out. The smell in the chapel had not changed. This was not the odour of sanctity, only of candles doused. Had he confessed at all? Sacrilege on sacrilege: the phrase came back from the Dominican retreat. Even then he thought he might go back in the box, have one more try, but some person shoved past and took his place. He looked round the chapel, wondering had he been long. Were the people watching? He returned to the bench two rows from the altar, said his penance.

It glimmered upon him, over the days that followed, why the priest had not understood his sin. He had not understood – how could he? – for no sin had been named that covered his wickedness. What he had done was so sinful, so unspeakably so, of such aberrance, to such unnatural degree, that the Church, for all her far-seeing and deep-searching, her vision and penetration, had not thought to provide against its happening. It was an extraordinary thing that he should have found this chink: he, the son of a Glasthule huckster, of a quakebuttock, a quakcbuttock himself, should in the majestic vault of Christendom a flaw have found. What had marked him for such villainy?

For the wickedness did not cease. Though he slept with his hands chained in his beads, nothing would bind him below, and often its throbbing woke him in the night. The cloudy shiny forms, which on his dreams attended, diffused in the shadows like ghosts themselves horrified. Or worse still, a pollution had wet his shirt. He would wash his shirt then, in the dark at the sink, and wear it clammy against his skin. He kept pebbles in his boots. If he walked anywhere and there were nettles, he was careful to pass his hand through the leaves. Not to be ostentatious, during the day he wore his beads as a bracelet, high up his right arm, under his sleeve. The crucifix drooped so he might finger it if needed.

He stopped eating, save bread, and drinking, save water. With the baby in the house all eyes were that way. It was a comfort to him for his mortifications might go unremarked. He pitied the infant whose birth he so had shamed. He dared not touch her. It was better after all she did not know him. The poor thing with no father, and now no uncle worth the name. Sacrilege on sacrilege: when he stood godfather to her.

One night Nancy came down for a drink of water from the sink. He had the Sacred Heart flame by his side and the light through the coloured glass made her face blotched and blooded. 'Still at it?' she asked. She sat down on the edge of his bed with her cup filled. He had to hide his rosaried hands under the covers.

'Is everything all right with you, Jim?' she asked. Oh sure everything was grand. Bobbing along nicely, thanks very much for asking but. He shifted his legs away from her under the covers. 'Does she keep you awake above?' Not at all, sure he liked to hear the baby giving vent. 'I suppose and they rag you at school?' Why would they rag him? 'They wouldn't be long looking for reasons.' He told her he paid no mind to coarse talk. 'You're fond of your niece though, aren't you?' It shook him she should ask that, and he answered he was more than fond, how could she doubt him, he loved his niece, of course he did. He was proud of Gordie's baby. 'Only you might hold her sometimes. She won't eat you.' He told her he was frightened of any harm coming. She smiled at him, sweetly, like a statue, full of grace. 'You're after growing thinner in the face,' she said, 'if thinner was possible. Your appetite is none too bright these days.' He was offering it up, he told her. 'Are you in practice for Lent?' He tried to smile for her, but his face wouldn't change, like it had lost the knack. 'I know what it is,' she said: 'you're missing your pal.'

No, she was wrong about that. He didn't miss Doyler at all.

413

Matter of fact he was only too glad if Doyler was away. 'Do you tell me?' Yes, that's what he told her.

She went to ruffle his hair but he shook his head out of the way. 'Cheer up, old trooper,' she said.

And it was true. He was only too thankful that Doyler was away. Doyler had been his friend, and if he had any feelings for him at all, he must be sure they never again were friendly. He no longer went to the Forty Foot. He did not think of the island. At school they were playing rugby. The scrum was torturous for him, a torment to be touched. One day when he ran he felt his feet lifting from the grass like the grass was liquid and he swam with the ball.

And that day, while play carried on far into the opponents' twenty-five, he saw walking the chalk on the field perimeter a familiar figure like an old crow. A black crow with a black umbrella, for the rain was sheeting down. He forgot about play entirely and he ran to greet him. 'Brother Polycarp!' he called, 'Brother Polycarp!'

He was out of his breath, hot and light-headed, when he caught the brother up. Brother Polycarp didn't stop or turn in his walk. 'It's Jim, Brother. Jim Mack.'

'Is that who it is,' the brother said.

He didn't sound very interested. 'Are you better again, Brother?'

'Better at what?'

Jim shook his head. The rain on his face was like a sweat. He felt very strange inside. The world felt strange, and looked it too, as though curtained by rain. In and out of the curtain boys ran. One charged into him and nearly knocked him over. He made out hooped jerseys with strange colours like tropical bees. They were playing football. In lovely toil they scrimmaged, the lofty goal to reach.

'May I talk with you, Brother?'

'Aren't you talking anyway?'

'Brother, I fear I made a mistake. About being a brother, Brother.'

'A brother Brother,' the brother mimicked. 'How is your pal?'

He seemed genuinely to want to know. Jim tried to frame responses. But he was so hot inside. For all it rained he felt hot and giddy, under the collar, so that his tie would strangle him if he did not loosen it. But when he went to his collar he found he was wearing a jersey. Fellows were calling his name. The ball rolled in a roily puddle. The turmoil of the game shoved about him, toiling and moiling. He believed he had a headache. But his head and its ache seemed miles separated.

'He's gone away, and he mustn't come back.'

'And so you think to be a brother.'

'Brother' – Jim did not know why, but he believed he might tell Brother Polycarp. Brother Polycarp would – 'Brother, I've done a terrible thing. Do you know what it is I've done? You do know, don't you?'

But Brother Polycarp had no interest in that. 'Publius Vergilius Maro,' he said: 'how's your Virgil these days?'

The brother was rambling; physically too, for his mouth moved in curious ways so that a dribble came out the corners, and his cheeks were caught in a crooked leer the way it was a stroke he had had. A stroke, as they said, of the hand of God.

Jim had to shake his head to clear the muzziness. For a moment he was running with a huge egg and his hands like balloons trying to hold it, then the ball was gone and he said, 'Brother Matthew takes us for Latin now.'

'"Sunt lacrimae rerum et mentem mortalia tangunt": translate.'

Distantly Jim recalled the phrase. 'You told us it could not be translated.'

'And I did, you could make a fist at it. Do you know when he died, Jim Mack, the Roman?' Jim didn't know. 'He died the first Christmas Day. Virgil and all his kind. The infant Jesus did that with the first pule out of his lungs. The infant Jesus wouldn't care much that the *Aeneid* was left unfinished. It was enough if Virgil was what he was, and all his kind must die.'

'It was Christmas Day, Brother when I – ' He was crying. 'It was on Christmas Day, Brother,' he cried.

'Tears there are of our doing and all that is mortal moves the heart.'

'Whose heart?'

Brother Polycarp lifted a finger from the handle of his umbrella and pointed it upward, indicating beyond the tented canvas. 'She's there, Jim.'

'I pray to Her,' Jim said. 'But She doesn't hear. Will you pray to Her for me, Brother Polycarp?'

'She hears you well enough. All of us She hears. Our every cry moves Her heart to breaking.' It was true. She heard them all. 'Think of Her pain, Jim, to hear our woes told and retold. It is the pain of a mother for her child that is sickening.'

'I am sick, brother,' said Jim.

'You have a fever,' said Brother Polycarp mundanely.

'I think I most probably do.'

'But they're gone, the others. Gone, or dead, or fast asleep. She alone remains, seeing and hearing and suffering our pain. Think of the anguish She must suffer, Jim, abandoned and powerless to help. Is it any wonder it rains so? She was made to be our intercessor, Jim, but there's none remains with whom to intercede.'

It was true. It did rain so.

'She is the vessel of life with no water in it,' the brother said. 'The bottle without the whiskey.'

The ball landed in Jim's hands and he was running with it, running with all his legs, and his ten hearts thumped and his three heads swam. In a moment of brilliant lucidity he knew why he never had trusted Brother Polycarp. When other brothers had put their hands between his legs he had never really minded. Only Brother Polycarp had put his hand round his neck. The ambiguity of that gesture had involved him in it, where the groping had left him untouched.

In lovely toil he neared the lofty goal. Try, they called. But he had tried and failed. A whistle blew. Fellows were cheering.

He stood astride the chalk line while the angled rain him keenly struck. His lank hair glued to his forehead. His forehead was burning. He shivered, but he felt the shivers as an elsewhere. A brother, looking curiously small and thin without his soutane on, dug his heel in the turf. He blew his whistle again and pointed at the kerf he had made in the ground. How grey was everything. The sheeting rain was frosted glass through which he viewed the world. He made out the dual spires of St Joseph's, a solid rain where all else fell. So light he felt and dizzy. Waves washed over him. He heard the calls of gulls. Insufferably hot.

His hand came out of the rain. He felt the crawl of it round his neck. At last it yanked and the chain came free. It seemed to shine before him, the dangling thing, like half a sun.

'Brother, Brother! It's Mack, Brother! He's fallen!'

He woke briefly in a darkened room whose strange furniture was crooked and mournful. Then a tall sheeny figure came in and pulled the curtains and the sash window, and all the crooked mournfulness flew out. He heard his father say, 'Is that the

modern way?' and he felt the breeze from the window, before
his eyes closed in sleep again.

The next time he woke, his father was at the washstand.
His braces hung down, his shoulders moved inside his vest.
Jim could see his face in the mirror, comically white, and he
watched fascinated the grins and grimaces he made, becoming
and unbecoming himself. The room smelt of pomade. He was
in his father's bed. They must have brought him here to be out
of the way. His father's mouth formed a dark oval.

'Ho ho ho! Is that an eye I see? Is that two eyes I see?'

'Hello, Da,' said Jim.

'Ho ho ho!' said his father again. He was at the door calling
to Aunt Sawney and dully he heard Aunt Sawney shishing him
back and that the boy wasn't out of it yet. His father came over
to the bed, patting his leg in excitement. He made an effort to
hush his voice. 'Let me look at you. Are you bright again?' The
big hand came over Jim's face and landed on his forehead. The
touch felt cool and enormously safe. 'You're fiery yet. But we're
on the mend. Ho ho ho!'

'I think I have a fever, Da.'

'Sure, you've had a fever these last four days.'

'What day is it?'

'Never you mind about that. You've only it broke in the
night. Rest now.'

The hand came over his eyes, closing them.

Later his father held his head while he fed him broth,
inconveniently really, from a huge wooden spoon into his mouth.
It must have been that evening when they had their first real
conversation. His father sat on a chair by the bed. He had been
reading from a book, but Jim could not recall what. His jaw
ached, as though it was worn out from speaking, and he still
heard echoes of voices in his head. Those monotonous phrases

and scenes that had repeated and repeated. It worried him now he had been talking through his fever.

'Oh sure ranting away you was.' His father swiped his nose significantly. 'We have all your secrets out now. There's no use hiding. We have you well taped, young man, so we have.'

But his father was laughing and Jim could see that he had no secrets told at all. He felt so happy looking at his father's face, all round and honest and pleased to see him.

'Belting out the hic haec hoc, you was. I never heard such Latin, 'twas better than a priest on Sunday. If I didn't know it before, I know it now, that I have a proper scriptuarian for a son.'

'I think I was dreaming of Brother Polycarp.' His eyes closed. 'Is Brother Polycarp dead, Da?'

'Don't you remember he was read out at Mass?'

'I remember something.'

'He died of a stroke, son. This was in Enniskillen. They say there's to be a month's mind at St Joseph's. We'll go to that.'

'Yes.'

His father closed his book. 'We oughtn't be talking sad things at all. The doctor says you'll be out of your strength a while yet.'

'You had a doctor in?'

'Half-crown doctor. White gloves, top hat, the works. Three-day fever, he calls it, which just goes to show.' Though what it showed he didn't say. 'A friend of yours was after recommending him.'

'Which friend was that?'

'I never knew you had such connections. Up there with the quality and you never let on.'

'Who was it, Da, tell me.'

'Mr MacMurrough of course.'

Jim felt confused, but the confusion did not distress him. His father leant over and kissed his forehead. 'Rest again now and I'll be up in an hour or two. You know there's the you-know under the bed. Well, you know that sure. Try to sleep now.'

It was the next morning before Jim had the story.

'What it was,' his father said, 'you was after making an appointment with Mr MacMurrough to swim with him. At the Forty Foot, this was.'

'Yes, I remember. He was to teach me a dive.'

'Then you never turned up.'

'I forgot all about it.'

'So he comes here looking for you. I was inside in the kitchen at the time. I heard the doorbell and I shouted, Presently, the way I do. Then, would you believe it, the bell on the counter gets a mighty wallop, and there's some joker calling Shop! Would you credit that? And if you only saw it, the stupid faction on your Aunt Sawney's face, when she tumbles who it is. I thought her gums would be sweeping the floor.'

Jim laughed, feebly, and it made him smile too, the wonderful way his father had with words he didn't know. Stupid faction and palatable nonsense and poppy lectric fits. 'What did he say, Da?'

'The short of it is he wanted your nibs here. But we'll come to that. What could we do only show him into the parlour, and he was after admiring that old brass tray of mine and your Aunt Sawney's firescreen.'

Jim saw them, the parrots, red and green, on the screen his great-aunt had embroidered, which his father complained wasn't embroidery at all but something he called Berlin-work and as such by rights ought not to be entertained during the current hostilities. And the brass tray from Benares that his father had kept by him all the way from India, which Aunt Sawney held was unfit for the parlour, such heathen ware, and she'd sneak it out for low use in the scullery where his father would have to be polishing it back up again. It near burst him with joy, thinking of his home, and the tangle of oddities that made it so special.

'Well, there was no holding Nancy and in she flounces with the baby and all. And Mr MacMurrough, he looks down at the little face, and do you know what he says? I'm glad to see, says he, there was room at the inn this Christmas.'

His father leant back in his chair and his eyebrows lifted.

'Isn't that the grand way of talking?'

'It's true too.'

He shrugged his head. 'Oh sure I wouldn't know about that. But I have to say, it shows the quality. He shook my hand, he did. Mr Mack, says he, you're a gentleman.'

Jim lay with smiles on his face that he felt could flutter away of themselves and fill the room with butterflies. He knew he was still feverish, for the smiling ached his muscles. It was so pleasant to lie there and know that sleep was coming, it was coming soon for his eyes were heavy, but sleep would be peaceful. All was safe, he was well. He saw round the room his father's things. The Staffordshire watch-holder with no watch to hold. The slats of wood and cloth by the door that his father called a prie-dieu. Above that, his mother's portrait. She looked surprised, but pleased, to see him there. This was a strange bed, in a room he wasn't used to, where the pillow and sheets were suffused with pomade. But it was home and he was not lost.

'Well?' said his father.

'Well what, Da?'

'Aren't you begging to know what Mr MacMurrough wanted with you?'

'To swim, I thought.'

'That's only the start of it. He has season tickets bought for the Kingstown Baths. Heated pool and sea-water pool, them both. Oh, sure he had some blarney about a gentleman expected and he never turned up. But ask me now, and I think he has them bought special. He has a wish for you, I do believe. Nothing would do but he came up to see you. Very modern ways he has. You couldn't say Hop but he had the window opened. Change of air, he called it.'

'I remember him, Da. I remember him coming in.'

'Well, and I hope you took your cap off to him. For he's a gentleman true and blue. Private lessons from Mr MacMurrough, what? Will that make you eat up your beef tea?'

'I have it finished.'

'So you have.' He took the bowl and with his other hand he touched and rubbed Jim's knee through the blankets. His face was out of the lamp, but still Jim saw his honest happiness which like soap shone on his cheeks. He picked up his book. 'I'll bring these down now.'

'What book were you reading?'

'Just some old thing out of Dickens. They gave it me to borrow from your school. Here's a good one for you. Who the Dickens was Boz? That came to me all on my own while I was sitting here. What do you think? Might send that in the papers. Do you catch on at all? Who the Dickens was Boz? They give a reward for items of interest like that.'

But Jim could see his father was already doubting if Who the Dickens wasn't a touch too choice for the newspapers. It was strange about Mr MacMurrough. In his fever, when he came in the room, he had seemed to Jim a silver knight, opening his window and banishing gloom. And he had looked so kind that last time they had met, his lip not checked by that moustache, and his eyes too that had lost the chill in their corners. His father

422

was telling how Nancy was stitching an old vest and a drawers together which she was to dye blue and he'd be a bathing beau in the Kingstown Baths.

'Da, I wouldn't have gone swimming without asking you.'

'Sure I know that, son.' He pulled a wry face. 'Leastways, if you did, you'd be holding on to the ladder.'

'You knew about that?'

'Where would your towel be going if it wasn't down the Forty Foot each morning? There's a twitter of wit in the old man yet. Ho ho ho, not totally queer in the attic.'

'And did you used follow me so?'

'If it was particular inclement I might stretch that far. Don't you know, son, you're my pride and joy. I wouldn't want to be holding you back always, but I couldn't bear any harm to come. Sure don't I know 'tis difficult with your brother, God bless him, and your mother, God rest her soul. But I missed you this last while. I don't know where was this you strayed to get all them pebbles in your boots. But we'll say no more about that. You're back with us now in the land of the living. She used have a saying, your mother did, the pulse of my heart. And you are that, to all of us.'

Jim saw his rosary beads hung on the post of the bedstead, and he saw that his father had hung his chain there too with his half a medal on it.

'Papa, he was right, Mr MacMurrough. You are a gentleman. I'm proud of you for a father.'

'Irrah now,' he answered, wagging his head. At the door, he said, 'I suppose 'tis a species of ridiculous to be calling me Papa. Do you hear that now? That's your niece is call-ing.'

'How is she?'

'Little Estella is grand sure. We didn't let Nancy in the room on account the fever and all. But little Estella is fine and dandy. Only she misses her Uncle Jim, I'd say.'

Estella. They had named her for his mother. He had never thought to ask what was his mother's name. Then the little thing had come and learnt it for him.

CHAPTER SIXTEEN

'THE PROBLEM IS, it's your' – MacMurrough slapped the side of his buttocks – 'you're letting them, it sink in the water. Think of your body as a balance.' He made a seesaw of his hands. 'Every time you lift your head, then' – one hand rose, the other descended – 'you push down instead of behind. Upshot is, your kick is wasted. Reason being you don't keep your' – another slap of his buttocks – 'up enough.'

'My legs is it?'

'Your arse,' said MacMurrough.

The boy peeked sideways, checking, then his face dimpled with cheek. MacMurrough slipped into the pool. 'I'll hold you.'

He got him into a swimming position, holding him by stomach and small of his back. Tickle the groin and we'd soon have that arse where we want it. 'Arching your neck again. Face in the water. Don't tense, I have you. Small kick will keep you balanced.'

Slowly, as he relaxed, the navy-clad hillocks rose to break the surface. Fondly lapped lagoony tides upon the tidal creek. One of the more agreeable ruts of life. 'Don't forget to breathe.' The boy sided his face, gulped, faced down again. 'Now. Forget about your arms. Roll and breathe. Roll and breathe. Head down and arse up.'

Too high now. MacMurrough lifted his hand from the boy's back and rested it on his bum, exerting a gentle pressure, at the same time lifting his shoulders, so that a straightish line was formed. They truly had come a long way together, and were getting along devilish well. Not so long ago, when these lessons had commenced, MacMurrough made no doubt the boy would be jumping ten feet from the water and banging his head on the diving-board, if his rear were so much as admitted to, let alone spoken of or, God help us, touched.

'Now do your stroke.'

He waded along with the boy swimming, releasing his hold till only his touch remained, and still the line held. The boy swam on, away from him, with fine leisurely crawls and unhectic flips of his feet. It was the only way. Anyone might dash a length. But to swim well, one must swim slow. MacMurrough pulled himself to the edge, where he sat with his feet in the sink, enjoying the contrary temperatures of tiles and water. The boy kept on, forgetting in his concentration to see where he was going, and swerving late to avoid oncomers. When he came back to the bar he asked had they finished and MacMurrough nodded they had.

'I'll get along to the other end so.'

Of course it was the cold pool at the open end the boy looked forward to, the freezing, sometimes wave-washed, sea-water pool, where he did his so many lengths, splashing in all directions, unfrustrated by MacMurrough's tuition. His moment had come the first week of their swimming together, that magical moment when the mind lets go and the body is released. You'll find it, MacMurrough had promised him, you'll feel it when you do. Then he slipped into the pool one time, and something the

426

way he moved, with an ease, almost a grace, MacMurrough could see he did not strive against the water. Rather, the water had received him and he joined a little in its fluency. The puzzle on his face when he looked back. 'I don't know, it's different today.'

'You're swimming,' MacMurrough told him.

He swallowed water, but he came up beaming. 'I think I am too!' He turned and plunged, thrashing his arms. 'It's easy sure!' Later, he said, still suffused with the wonder, 'I never knew. I never thought it could be like this. It's the most wonderful thing.' He stayed long in the water that day. He had found his element. He was in the swim.

Now, this afternoon six weeks on, MacMurrough came out into the crisp air to watch his dive. There he stood on the board. Not a von Gloeden study: the boy was too clad and the sky too dull: but reminiscent nevertheless. The unaware posture, the vital glow, limbs atop some ruined pilaster. He springs. Hands touch toes, but the knees are bent. Not so much a jack-knife as some brand of collapsible fork. We shall have to return to the diving. His arms the clear blue glass divide, ripples his body below. An Urning poem.

MacMurrough smiled. Anyone might know such a boy. But to know him best, one must know him slow. And these days, and most especially their afternoons, passed wondrous slow and leisurely. He went to his cubicle and dressed.

He smoked on a pool-side bench while the boy completed his lengths. Cold March day. It had drizzled earlier, but now the sun strained for a last shine. Over his shoulder stretched the Crock's Garden, but they did not walk there. No, to be sure, they did not walk the pier nor any part of it, and the boy even now could scarce bring himself to look that way. With impersonal eye MacMurrough viewed the sprawl of rocks, pretentious temples, scraggy veronica bushes, unlikely genus for the fruit of the knowledge of good and evil.

Bashful puzzled awkwardness – it had draped the boy like his home-made bathing suit when first these lessons had begun. But the boy was changing rapidly. He was shrugging that old skin; as his confidence grew, daily he shrugged it further. An adventurism pulsed inside, which every so often MacMurrough might trip, as when he asked the boy what had occurred in the Crock's Garden. Every so often it tripped into alarming ventures of its own, as when the boy asked MacMurrough – they were eating their ices on Doyle's Rock – would he ever kiss another man.

Would I kiss a man indeed. And what had the boy answered to the Crock's Garden? Sufficient for MacMurrough to tell him to stop. That he need not speak of it, nor dwell on it. That there was a difference between the dark and privacy. That the consequences of an action depended as much on the actors as on the deed. That the same deed, talking for instance, might be a chore or a delight, depending on the other. That if the other were special to him, the deed too might be special. In short, and unspoken, that with his friend he should feel differently.

For one might choose to leave the garden of Eden or one might dawdle there till expelled: either way, go one must. And the boy had said, quite simply, Yes, I know that now.

And now the boy had completed his lengths. He crawls to the bar, pulls upon the ladder, his bag of jewels shrunk in their cloth. Stands in that hunched way, blowing through the hands, which ever marks the swimmer returned to land. Shiveringly takes the towel MacMurrough proffers.

'How many lengths?'

'Thirteen each way.'

'How far is that?'

'Five hundred and twenty yards.'

'Not bad,' MacMurrough allowed. 'No resting?'

'None at all!'

Shocked that any should doubt him. 'You might try resting. On your back. You'll have to rest when you swim to the Muglins. Might as well practise it now.'

The boy considered and nodded. His half a medal dangled from his neck. It recalled to MacMurrough a ballad Nanny Tremble had used to sing. The lovelorn lass who spurns the sailor, not knowing him for her long-lost love, till he shows her the half of her ring he has worn these livelong salty years. Sometimes it was nearly too painful to have the boy close. Sometimes MacMurrough would need to smother him in his towel and chafe the gooseflesh out of him. Now he said, 'Hurry and dress. You'll perish me looking at you.'

He thought of Marlowe, while he smoked, that they were fools who did not love tobacco and boys. He thought of Aristophanes, and on a rock in the sea he foresaw two boys with two halves of a medal. See how they fit? We two are one.

And what did I answer when he asked would I kiss another man? I clipped him round the ear of course. Or at least I had thought to. Only his head had moved and I found I was stroking his hair. Lovely hair, the two textures together, razored behind and fingery-flop in front. He was quite nuzzling against my hand, like an animal, and when I looked I saw his long lashes were drawn over his eyes. I bent down and kissed his forehead. His eyes opened, and he gave that extraordinary blink. Big wide eyes which fixed you in memory, then the eyes squeezed, erasing what he saw.

'Ready?'

'Yes.'

His bright face flushed with health and vim. Grinning even. 'What's so amusing?' MacMurrough asked.

'The men over.'

'Well?'

'Doyler used always laugh when rich folk came down the Forty Foot. They wouldn't be used to walking out of their boots. The quality waddle, he called it.'

'I should hope you don't think I walk with a waddle.' His bare-faced denial. 'It's your turn to get the ices,' MacMurrough said severely and reached in his pocket for a coin.

'I have the money,' and the boy was off up the road.

Towards Newtown Smith and the sea MacMurrough ambled, then down the shore to a grey outcrop, licked by waves, happily named Doyle's Rock. The Pavilion was gone, and there was no place convenient to tea, save some bun-shop with trestle tables. It smelt of soup and biddies, and the first time they went there MacMurrough could think of no surer escape than two ices they might eat on the road. Strolling home, they had strayed to this rock. Schoolboys and their masters being creatures of habit, ices on Doyle's Rock were soon the necessary conclusion, the culmination even, of their afternoon swims together.

He had swum, before Jim had arrived for his lesson, his own quarter-mile dash to the pier and back. Now he felt the relax of his muscles, that ponderousness in the limbs that bespeaks their strength. A wonderful felicity of nature was this: that the employment of strength should strengthen one. For full a year he had immersed himself in the sea, that wondrous element, and he felt imbued now, a touch, with the sea's immensity. Coming to the shore, swimming: it was a kind of pilgrimage to our earliest beginnings. Before we slunk up the beach and – what? found our feet.

The boy came with his ices two. He sat down beside, brushing his shoulder against MacMurrough. He made a habit of these casual touches, and would often cover them with some artifice, as shifting his legs that one might rub against MacMurrough's or catching MacMurrough's attention with a hand on his shoulder, that remained there, its fingers patting. From the beginning there had been an assumption of friendship, even of close friendship. At times it seemed absurd, a fancy. It must be this way, MacMurrough thought, when hysterics claim a previous life, dementia praecox must be like this, déjà vu even. Yes, I had known him all my life – and then we met.

They gazed upon the glaucous sea where oily-necked birds floated and dived. Untimely intervals, unlikely places, they resurfaced, floated and dived again.

The boy said, 'You never told me you saved a man.'

'Who's been telling you that?'

'Sure it's all over the Forty Foot.'

'Well, I don't know that I saved him so much. He wasn't drowning, more floundering about.'

MacMurrough had been at the Forty Foot, where he liked to smoke his first cigarette of the day. At the boys' end some fellow was making for shore, making heavy weather of it, he could see. They called it the boys' end because boys might paddle on the sand there. But for swimming it was hardly recommended. Too many rocks, which at high tide, as then it was, made it positively dangerous. In particular a rounded reef called the Ring Rock, so notorious a hazard that an iron bar had been raised to mark its position. It was for this bar the swimmer was making. The surge washed him forward, then the backwash dragged him out again. He was clearly in trouble, though the danger was not so much his drowning as of his ripping his stomach on the rocks below. There was nothing for it. MacMurrough shrugged from his clothes and plunged.

'I can only wonder what it's like to save somebody,' Jim said.

'Do you know,' said MacMurrough, 'the strange thing was – I was in my underwear, obviously I had no towel – I had to ask the gentleman might I borrow his. Indeed you must, indeed I insist, said he. In the end it began to feel rather quits, my rescuing the man and his lending me his rotten towel.'

Jim laughed. 'Were you in your Jaegars?' he asked.

'Yes, I believe I was.'

'You look best in your Jaegars.'

He had made himself bright red and he shyly peeped up from his feet at MacMurrough's face. He made to cross his legs and their knees touched. MacMurrough recalled his own discovery of touch, the willing of it, its exploration: so very different from the being touched, the receiving into one's seclusion the touch of another. And so maddeningly sensual. Often, going home, MacMurrough ached of excitement unrelieved.

Across the bay in Sandycove, a last sun warmed the Martello tower. The whole of Sandycove looked warm, inviting, all tanned stone and water-washed fronts, as though a kinder climate would obtain there. It seemed absurd they should swim in Kingstown. How he had saved for those two season tickets. Yes, he had scrimped and scraped from his allowance, skimping on cigarettes even. Going then to the boy's home. Infant paraded for his benefit. They offered tea which he had declined. Funny really, quite happily hop in his bed, but drink their tea? One expects the best and can get by on the worst: it is the populars in between are beyond the pale. And the child Nancy looking so proud and womanly.

'You know,' he said, 'even if you get there you won't stay long on your island if it's this weather.'

The boy shrugged. 'What does it matter the weather?'

Even things he did not quite trust, MacMurrough took pleasure in seeing them in the boy. That loyalty which, given a cause, would be silently fanatic; the determination which, given a means, could be ruthless. They talked about the parade tomorrow, St Patrick's day, when the Dublin battalions of the Volunteers planned a demonstration in the centre of town. They might see Doyler there, MacMurrough suggested.

'I'd like to see him,' said Jim, 'though I don't know would it be right somehow so close before Easter.'

MacMurrough knew that one day soon, perhaps even tomorrow afternoon, he must trawl the Dublin slums for this famed Liberty Hall and find Doyler out. Roundly confront him with his, heartless was the only word, indifference. Not a tram-visit, not a letter, not even a Christmas card to his friend. What did Doyler imagine he was about?

Oh, it was all of it absurd, and MacMurrough could become positively angry with himself, could kick himself thinking of the fool he made. What did he imagine he was about? It all boiled down to his having no proper employment. By this rod I measure myself: that one should not drown on his swim to an island and that two should somehow get there. It was laughable – playing Mother Match to Erin's youth.

And yet he could think of nothing more grand than helping this boy to his happiness. A happiness whose consummation must inevitably dash any hope of his own. Absurd.

The boy's eyes were on the Point, beyond which lay the Forty Foot and the Muglins rock. His lips were pulled into his teeth. 'He asked me once, Doyler did – well, it doesn't matter what he asked. But I couldn't. I was just plain too frightened. I couldn't, even though I wanted to, sure I wanted to kiss him. There, I've told you now.'

MacMurrough laughed.

'I used always have this notion of being watched, you see. Not by other people. It was myself was watching me. Another me, a different fellow altogether. He never liked me. The way I behaved used truly annoy him. And I was scared of him too. It made me nervous, knowing he was watching me the while.'

'I should think it did.'

'Then after Christmas I fell in a terrible way. Well, you know about that. But all the while I knew this wasn't real, or that it wasn't the only real thing. There was this other me watching. He was a much stronger person, this other fellow. He wasn't frightened. And he was getting fed up now. He was really fed up waiting.'

'And then it all came to a head?'

'I don't know, but after my fever everything changed. I doubt I'd be scared now, not of anything. It's like that time in the water. I couldn't think what I was doing different. But I was swimming and I was sure of my strength. Maybe it's you, MacEmm, made the difference.'

Their ices were long eaten. Sandycove had drained the last flush of light and the sun was sinking fast. Soon the lamplighter would be trotting about. MacMurrough, wishing their time wouldn't be over, said, 'Well.' The boy felt this too, for he said, 'You could tell me about the Sacred Band again, of Thebes.'

MacMurrough laughed. 'It's caught your fancy, that, I believe.'

'I don't know. To fight with your friend beside you. That would be grand. There's grand things ahead. Can't you feel it?'

'Yes, I do feel grand things coming, sometimes.'

'Not a man but he fell with his face to the foe.' He quoted MacMurrough's telling. 'It makes you shiver to say it. Is it true you're to teach us the care of a rifle?'

'I have been asked. Not sure if I should really.'

'I'm sixteen.'

'Yes, I know you are.'

'Weren't you shooting at my age?'

Well, long before sixteen. He had been kept back at school one holiday, measles or something. He was bored and broke into the gun-cupboard. Took pot-shots at the gas-standards in the courts. His punishment had been, creative this, to join the senior OTC. 'Don't you see it's getting dangerous now, all this militarism?'

'We'll be asked to fight for Ireland, sure I know that.'

'But what is Ireland that you should want to fight for it?'

'Sure I know that too.' He raised a shoulder, his head inclined then turned: an attempt to shrug shake and nod, all the same time. When he was shy or self-conscious of something he would say, his body would often fail him. 'It's Doyler,' he said.

'Doyler is your country?'

'It's silly, I know. But that's how I feel. I know Doyler will be out, and where would I be but out beside him? I don't hate the English and I don't know do I love the Irish. But I love him. I'm sure of that now. And he's my country.'

Scrotes, my Scrotes, you should be here now.

The boy looked up from under his lashes. The colour had tipped his cheeks. 'I think a little bit of it too is yourself, MacEmm.'

'Me? My gracious.'

'Though I don't suppose you'd want me fighting about it. But I don't know anybody else I could talk these things with. I used think I'd burst with all the words in my head. I can talk things now. I don't know but it's like we have a language together. It's great with the swimming, but it's better again with the talking. You're a part of my country too now, MacEmm.'

They were speaking of patriots, Dublin associations of famous rebels, of battles ancient and modern. There Lord Edward had

435

lived, there the Danes had fled, on the left now the Ormond Camp when Cromwell held the city. The car through sober streets motored while the travellers made leaps and purlers in time.

MacMurrough leant forward from the back seat. 'We must be coming to Merrion Square.'

'Soon,' answered his aunt.

'Bagott Street,' said her priest. 'Up on the left now. Thomas Davis died there, a pneumonia brought on by ceaseless efforts for Young Ireland. "A Nation Once Again" – that was his. A tremendous poet, Madame MacMurrough, you will agree. An inspiration to us all, for all he was a heathen.'

'Merrion Square,' said Eveline.

They came into a bosky square of rose and russet terracing. Plates by the doors in close-lipped smiles told guinea fees for doctors, lawyers. Railings curved up steps, unfolding intricate shapes for lantern-holding, the snuffing of torches. The sun was seen to attend the upper windows.

'I don't believe I know,' the priest remarked, 'any patriot associated with Merrion Square. Though in course of time our new cathedral will rise here, and what truer monument to our country and her faith could a true-born patriot look for?'

Westland Row now and Trinity Fields to their left. 'The foreign college,' said Father Taylor.

A jam of jarveys toward the railway station slowed their pace to a crawl. MacMurrough leant forward again. 'There was one Irishman associated with Merrion Square,' he said. 'Yes, the English put him on trial.'

'It is ever the way,' the priest complacently affirmed.

'Three trials, in fact. On the first he had the wit to proclaim, I am the prosecutor in this case!'

'I see, yes, very good. For all his country's wrongs.'

'I need hardly tell you, Father Taylor, of the desertion by his friends, of witnesses bullied and corrupted, of the agitation against him got up by the newspapers.'

'It was ever the Saxon sneaking way.'

'They say the evening he was arrested the packet to France was filled to overflowing with like-minded gentlemen, fearing for their liberty.'

'Flight of the Earls,' said Father Taylor. 'The Wild Geese who chose to serve in exile than suffer the alien yoke at home. It is history in a nutshell. But you have not told me this gentleman's name?'

'His conviction was inevitable. But from the dock he gave a celebrated speech that defied to the heavens the traductions of his adversaries.'

'A speech from the dock! I have heard it said, and have said it myself, the speech from the dock is the only truly Irish drama. Three patriots may not gather but a rendition of Emmett or of Tone will edify the occasion. It is a form peculiarly suited to the Irish temperament. And what did this speech from the dock say?'

'The jury was unmoved, the judge called for order, but still the gallery cheered.'

'They may purchase however many juries, at whatever cost to their exchequer, but the honest man of the street they cannot touch. But I am surprised I have not guessed the gentleman's name. You must remind me now.'

Eveline interrupted. 'I fear, Father, I may come no closer to the station.'

'Madame, forgive me, I was talking with your nephew. This is fine for me now. Go raibh míle maith agat.'

'Irritating man,' she said, when MacMurrough had climbed

to the front and she was turning the car. 'He let the boys find their own way into town, just so he might have a motor ride.'

She made for St Stephen's Green and gave the car at the RIAC garage. They walked to the Shelbourne, where she had a day sitting-room arranged. MacMurrough watched out the window while she sat to repair her toilet.

'Are you really so lunatic,' she inquired, once the maid had left them, 'that you were about to give Oscar Wilde's name to the parish curate?'

'So you heard our little parlance?'

'I'm sure you think yourself most ingenious.'

'Well,' said MacMurrough, 'and was he not an Irishman? And did his speech not bring the gallery to its feet?'

'You refer to the eulogium on illicit love.'

'The love that dare not speak its name.'

'Its name,' she said, 'is buggery. As any soul in the three kingdoms might have told him.'

MacMurrough turned from the window and he looked with smiling admiration on his aunt. 'Do you know, at home we couldn't say Stomach to my mother without the vapours coming on. And here we are, discussing Wilde and buggery. You are a breath of air, Aunt Eva.'

Her lips narrowed, refusing the compliment. She said, 'The English behaved unforgivably with that man.' She saw him in her glass and said, 'Raise your eyebrows all you will, but it is true. They forgot what the Continent is for, and thought to replace it with Reading. They have attached a cachet to his name which to this day attracts the idle and dissolute. But then the English have always favoured punishment over sense. The man was a buffoon and ought to have been treated as such, green carnations and all.'

'I don't know that I agree,' said MacMurrough. 'Are green

438

carnations so very much more buffoonish than these?' He fingered the spray at his breast.

'These,' she answered, 'are shamrock leaves. They are the
emblem of our country, of its holiness and ancientry, which we
wear with pride on this day of each year. What is more, admit
I have never seen it, but we are told they grow naturally, which
cannot be said of a green carnation.'

'Then let us tolderol for nature and deck ourselves in tre-
foils.'

She was quiet after this tease, while some emollient she
smoothed in her face. 'Anthony, it is a year since you came
to me. I did not say then, but you frightened me. Your face
was quite stark and your tongue could be so cruel. I hated to
see you brooding and picking over your hurts. Yes, I pressed
you into activities. How else was I to help beyond feeding and
lodging you? Perhaps I was wrong. Perhaps it is the Forty Foot
that has helped you and I have done nothing at all. If so, I thank
the Forty Foot. But you have come through. Every day I see it,
your old confidence returning. Your face too has cleared and is
almost the face I loved so many years ago.'

'You loved?'

'I loved. It was a terrible punishment you suffered, I am not
the least deceived, but it is over. You know that it is over. You
have come through.'

'Yes,' said MacMurrough. 'I think you may be right. I think
I really may have come through.'

'You must put aside this fascination with Oscar Wilde. If you
cannot forget him, at the least regard the totality of the man. He
had a wife, he had children, he worked hard to support them. But
for that other buffoon, Queensberry, this would be all we knew of
the man, and we should all be very much the better for that.'

She rose from her seat. 'Such a pretty green, St Stephen's,' she remarked, looking out the window. 'I cannot think there is call for an umbrella.'

MacMurrough admired her from behind, with her beautiful hat that fell in lacy veils, cream and tan and umber, about her shoulders. What she needed, he decided, was some poor relative to keep company with her, and whom she might quietly terrify. With a start, he realized this was he. She turned. 'Boots,' she said and MacMurrough found a cloth.

While he polished, he said, 'Do you remember I mentioned I rescued a man?'

'At the Forty Foot, I do.'

'Shall I let you in who it was?'

'Do I know the gentleman?'

'I believe you may.' He looked up from his shoe-polishing. 'Sir Edward Carson.'

The mildest of surprises crossed her face. 'You are sure?'

'He gave me his card.' And MacMurrough had not needed his card, for he knew that face well, had studied with perverse fascination the vignettes, the caricatures, from the trial. And there he had stood before him, in the Forty Foot of all places, with his chewy lips and distended jaw, his slanting eyes and sloped-back forehead, he stood there, draggled in his drawers, insisting on MacMurrough's use of his towel, the brilliant instrument of Oscar Wilde's fall. The classmate who had performed his task, as Wilde had predicted, with all the added bitterness of an old friend. And who since that eminence of the forensic craft, Pelion upon Ossa, had been fomenting Orange trouble in his native sod.

His aunt said, 'It is wrong in me, I know, but I have never looked kindly on the Forty Foot. It attracts all conditions, which is always unfortunate.'

'But shall I tell you what I did?'

'You are decided that I wish to hear?'

'I'll tell you because you may pretend dismay but I know you'll find it amusing. I kissed him.'

'Sir Edward Carson?'

'Lavishly, on the lips.'

Yes he had kissed him, clamped his mouth on that awful mug, lips on rubbery lips he pressed, propelling his tongue inside the portals, kissed for all he was worth. And Carson had staggered away, spitting and spluttering as though all the Irish Sea had vomited into his mouth. And MacMurrough had laughed like a schoolboy, and he heard now his aunt was laughing too.

'You are a wicked, wicked boy,' she said, 'and the Lord knows what retribution may come. The Attorney-General. King Carson himself. You gave your name?'

'Naturally. I am a gentleman.'

'Oh, quel beau coup pour l'Irlande!' And she gazed upon her nephew with fondest affection. She took both his hands in hers. 'What a wonderful boy you are. And I did love you so and I do love you still.'

'Do you think he will make a stink?'

'The man is a cad and who can say what a cad may do? Let him utter a word, the country shall roar. Now let me look at you.'

In point of fact they were not boots MacMurrough wore, but stout toe-capped Oxfords. Puttees wrapped infallibly to his knees, cavalry breeches swished as he walked, then rather a plain, disappointing tunic, whose insignia on the sleeve, though he did not understand them, he was reliably informed, proclaimed him a captain of the Irish Volunteers. He even carried his very own swagger-stick.

'You look most becoming,' she pronounced. She settled once again the shamrock at his breast. She angled her elbow. 'I shall be proud to walk with my nephew through Dublin.'

441

*

This good favour in which MacMurrough currently stood had begun shortly before Christmas. His aunt invited him to accompany her on one of her motoring jaunts. 'Ferns,' she said.

'High Kinsella in this weather?'

'I thought we might shoot.'

Horrid drive in the freezing cold to that freezing tumble-down pile. Rough shooting with scatter guns, he had expected. But no, from a dirty oil-smeared covering his aunt produced a gleaming Lee-Enfield.

'How on earth did you lay your hands on this?' She did not immediately say. His hands ran along the barrel, bolt, trigger-guard. The stock was a touch loose. He would need to tighten the bolt. 'Short magazine modified,' he said. 'At college we had to make do with the Boer War originals.' He raised the rifle, trying the balance, sighted. 'You bribed a soldier, I expect.'

Her prim smile told indeed she had.

'Isn't that dangerous?'

But dangerousness, as a subject, did not interest her. She wished to know was it any good.

'Well, that very much depends what you want to shoot. If it's rabbits, it's useless. Thing was designed to stop a cavalry charge.'

But he knew how to shoot it? Well, of course he knew. He had shot for his college at Bisley. Service Rifle Team Event, he told her. And had he won? No, the team hadn't won – but MacMurrough was sufficiently proud of his musketry to lay the emphasis on team. So he was proficient? He could shoot a mark, yes.

'As I thought. You shall teach me.'

So all that day and the next he had taught his aunt to shoot rifle. The Sunday morning, even she could not disguise the pain in her shoulder. He advised a revolver. 'Yes,' she agreed. 'But that would mean bribing an officer, which would never do. I shall have to get one in liquor. Then he may mislay the thing.'

She had form, you had to give her that. Good or bad, it hardly mattered. She carried it off magnificently.

After Mass, groups of men and boys had come trudging up the avenue. At first MacMurrough had thought them retainers or tenants come to pay their respects. But not so. In the courtyard they lined up smartly in column of two files, and waited there, eyes forward, standing to attention. They carried pikes. They actually carried pikes. Intrigued, MacMurrough left the library where he had been browsing and came to the front steps. His aunt was already there, with an ancient gentleman attired, plausibly, in officer's rig. The gentleman addressed the men. Usual nationalist platitudes, save at the end MacMurrough heard his own name mentioned. His aunt produced the Lee-Enfield and announced that her nephew would be giving each man present a lesson in its use. They cheered.

Over sherry that evening, his aunt said, 'The men have elected you their captain.'

'The men?'

'They have elected you.'

'Those men who were outside?'

'I have already said.'

'Their captain?'

'Yes.'

'But it's preposterous. Why should they elect me?'

'You are a MacMurrough, what possible more could they

want? So tomorrow evening, Anthony, I really think you might wear your uniform. Pour encourager les autres, so to speak.'

'And now I have a uniform?'

'What sort of an officer would you present without a uniform? Really, you have the most modern ideas. You will find it in your dressing-room. In the pocket there is a membership card, which you might sign. The dues have been paid. Your commission will arrive by the post.'

'Might I just ask what it is I am a captain of?'

'Why, the Irish Volunteers.'

And that was how it came to be, on St Patrick's day morning, in the spring of 1916, MacMurrough walked his aunt through Dublin, in the three-starred tunic of a Volunteer captain. Of course, he was quite well aware the men had not elected him, no more than he had volunteered. But there was something pathetic about those men that Sunday morning. The awe in their faces when he aimed the rifle, the fragile way they touched it when given it to hold; he saw their shuffling looks when they took up their pikes afterwards to go home in the dark. A rifle – a thing that to any English countryman was familiar as vermin. It was not militarism and it was not nationalism: he did not know what it was, and he was sure he surprised his aunt even: but soon MacMurrough was training every weekend to Ferns, and looking forward to his visits.

He had little hope of any real musketry: ammunition was too precious. But he thought he might accustom the men to the handling of a weapon. Gradually, his OTC training was recalled, the pokey-drills and evolutions he had learnt as a boy. He had the men sight and fire, sight and fire, a spent cartridge-case in the bolt to guard the hammer, until they got some notion of a rifle's weight and balance. He taught its cleaning and oiling, gave lectures on deliquescent substances. He held little sergeant-major competitions in stripping and reassembling the action. Prizes he awarded of smiles and encouragement. That these serious-faced labourers and sons of small farmers, who God knows had toiled all day and all week, should give up their Sundays to him increased, according to their willingness to give, the value of what knowledge he could return. But he was not deceived. If patriotism had brought these men together, he doubted but it would leak under an enemy's fire: when they saw it was not their flag the enemy fired at, but their person. What is that thing which makes men go forward when every reason shrills their retreat? Not courage, but a kind of love, a bonding of disparate souls to the one company. He could not impart this. He had never felt it himself. I am not a trooper, he told himself. I am a sniper in the tree, a lone wolf.

But it was good to feel a rifle in his hands again, a good old Smellie too. He asked his aunt did she expect to procure many more.

'Perhaps not the same. Would that matter?'

'I don't know. I should think anything was better than pikes.'

'But you will be able to teach them?'

They were in the garden room in Ballygihen at the time. MacMurrough stood by the open doors, smoking and gazing at the lawns. He said, 'I don't know if I shall be here.'

'Where should you be?'

'You surely know I cannot delay in Ireland much longer. There is military compulsion now.'

'Not in Ireland there isn't. They would not dare introduce conscription into Ireland.'

'I am normally resident in England. Therefore I am liable.'

'I see. I had not thought.'

'Aunt Eva, I do not intend to sit in Ballygihen waiting for

the knock. And I will not have my conduct raked over by some jumped-up tribunal.'

'No, that would not do.'

'I have an appointment at Easter. After that, I shall cross to England and enlist at the first kiosk I find.'

'You have an appointment at Easter?'

'That is what I said.'

'And then you will cross to England?'

'Do not ask me to join an Irish regiment. I shall go some place where I know nothing and nobody knows anything of me.'

'But not till Easter?'

'Aunt Eva, what does it matter about Easter?'

'Nothing. Nothing at all. This martial spirit, it is all so sudden.'

'You hardly supposed I lacked conduct?'

'I should as well suppose you were a Smith or a Brown. But you will stay till Easter. And who knows what that may bring?'

MacMurrough smiled wanly, for he knew very well what Easter would bring. It would bring two boys to the Muglins and there would be nothing left in this country for him. He tossed his cigarette away. The war, which had seemed so tiresome with its petty news and thuggish holler, which all along had seemed the concern of other people, lesser people, stupider people, the exigencies of which seemed spiteful, and nowhere less spiteful than in the difficulty he began to experience in finding Turkish cigarettes – this war had opened its arms one night to him, one night as he lay in bed not sleeping, opened its arms like a warm night, inviting him through the doors and into the garden, but a garden where the paths did not lead to the sea, that aimless expanse, but led purposefully onward, marching onward, marching with a thousand men and each with a face and no name. There was, after all, something he could do. And

he could not think, for the life of him, why he had not thought
of it before.

In the meantime, it was St Patrick's day, a rare spring-blue morning. Through holiday crowds down Grafton Street he strolled,
his aunt upon his elbow. Soldiers on leave wore shamrock in
their lapels, officers too, some of them – a liberty granted by
Queen Victoria, if he remembered, in gratitude for the Irish
killed by the Boer. A constable on point wore a sprig in his
helmet. MacMurrough saw the eyes that narrowly followed him.
*I know every law and by-law you ever broke or thought of breaking. I
have all your crimes, me bucko.* Bloody great brutes, where do they
find them? Must breed them special, pig's fry three times daily.
MacMurrough had had an interesting brush with one of Dublin's
finest, just up there in the lavatory in Stephen's Green.

'The constable saluted me,' he said in surprise to his aunt.
'And I a captain of the Volunteers.'

'Yes,' she replied, 'you will find them full of pleasantries this
morning. The Irish constabulary has a keen appreciation of rifle
and gun, as many of our men today will carry. It is that which
has kept it so fond of the English.'

'We got some fine looks in the Shelbourne.'

'Didn't we indeed? We shall get them again over lunch.'

A flower-seller waved daffodils from a lane and Eveline
paused to admire the display. 'Daffydillies for the lady?' said
the flower-seller.

Behind her a younger woman, her hair matted and leaking
from her shawl, was staring at his aunt, and MacMurrough had
a feeling of tables being turned in her thoughts. Something very
sinister in her face. A boy too, maybe ten years old, in assorted
oversize and feminine rags. More than hunger in their eyes,

something like massacre, if ever the Church should lose its grip, massacre only a prayer away.

His aunt smiled kindly. 'You should be selling shamrock,' she told the weazen old face.

From alleyways the benisons of beggars came, from lanes they waved their precatory hands. Grafton Street sailed like a galleon between. In a sudden lull he heard the creak of his leather.

'I do so like Grafton Street,' his aunt said. 'There is nothing in Ferns the equal of it.'

And now they were coming into College Green and they must worm their way between stopped trams – trams delayed in Dublin, I ask you – motor-wagons, cabs with huffing horses and the cabbies standing up and calling to each other in consternation. Constables with whistles blew their faces red trying to make sense of the jam. The crowds were thick and MacMurrough felt the uncomfortable adjacency of the mob. He suggested a tram might afford their best vantage. But his aunt wished to press on. She tapped her umbrella on the setts, calling haughtily for way, and way miraculously appeared. At last they came through to the William III statue, where a reviewing stand had been raised, cunningly contrived to obscure his view, should ever King Billy choose to glance behind. 'Are we invited?' asked MacMurrough. 'Oh yes, I'm sure that we are.' He helped her up and willing hands above received her. She brushed herself down and he thought how handsome she looked amid the black and the green. Before them, in rank upon rank, stood the Dublin battalions of the Irish Volunteers. For that hour, on that day, Dublin was theirs.

And prettily they paraded. Up and down College Green, round and about the Grattan monument. The stiff face of Trinity was unmoved. The old parliament house turned its cold shoulder. If ever a building looked for a way out, that was it.

Some fellow MacMurrough could not see took the salute. Pikes glistened like a song.

MacMurrough thought of that other toyland up behind them, the Castle, seat of British administration, with its toy turrets and its toy court. This morning tin soldiers had trooped a Colour and this evening at the ball a toy lieutenant would play lords and ladies. It was a toy country.

He looked about at the buildings and streets and the people who crowded to see – good-humouredly now, while the spectacle recompensed the inconvenience it caused. The universality of things abstracted him. That, for instance, there should be smoothened surfaces for the use of traffic, and that these roads should come from the country and, meeting the city, should turn into streets. On both sides of these streets let there be pavings, set aside for the convenience of pedestrians, these pavings to be separated from the street by kerbing, ideally raised three inches from the surface, thus providing a gutter, which, through the street's cambering and a provident furnishing of drains, shall effect the disposal of rain and running sewage. But come, sir, enough of the paving: what of the people? Let the people be classified into sexes, of which there shall be two, male and female. The criterion shall be generative function, though please to note, this function is ideal and not actual: the prepubescent, the celibate, the emasculate, the nulliparous, the non-generative for whatever reason, shall yet be classified by sex. They shall be male or female. Female or male shall they be, though the greater shall be male. Come come, sir, enough about gender. The people shall further be graded according to wealth, and – humorous touch this – the more obviously a man labour, the more stinting shall be his reward; the more he work in the out-of-doors, the thinner his clothing shall be; the more his labour filthy him, the less water shall he have to wash. Typically, a home will consist of one male and one female, of roughly commensurate age, their immature offspring, other parasites, a peg from which to hang one's hat. Entry and exit are to be afforded by hinged arrangements in the walls, conventionally of wood. Let these arrangements be known as doors, whereof if one close, another shall open.

Given such overwhelming agreement, it was only natural that such quarrels as arose should hang on the colour of postboxes.

'I wonder,' said his aunt, 'if Casement has found shamrock for today.'

'Casement?'

She looked at him surprised, and he knew she had not intended to speak aloud. 'Sir Roger,' she said. 'He is in Germany, the soul.'

A definite note of romance in her voice. Casement. Kettle had mentioned that name. 'Is Sir Roger a prisoner of war?'

'How can you know so little?' she said with a quivering of irritation. 'He is raising an Irish Brigade from the Irish prisoners of war to fight not in England's but in Ireland's cause. When the time comes that brigade will sail to Ireland. With it he will raise the West and the South.'

'I see. Sir Roger is an attachment of yours?'

'He is an acquaintance.'

'Of long standing?' She did not care to answer. 'When may we expect Sir Roger?'

'Soon, I trust. Every day we delay brings the war closer to its end. And what is the use of a German victory if we have not risen to help it? These men before us will take Dublin and hold her in readiness for Casement's coming. Yes, dear old dirty Dublin, city of the foreigner, the Pale, the Castle city: she was ever the curse of Irish hopes. Now comes the time when she must redeem herself. Only these Dublin battalions may help her to that. Of their Irish blood they will make an

Irish capital. But that is none of our concern. Our concern is with Ferns.'

'Aunt Eva, will any of this help the poor, do you think?'

'The poor are patriotic as any other in Ireland.'

'No, I don't mean that. I mean there was a turn in the London halls, I can't remember who it was, but he got his great laugh when he said he never knew what the London beggars did with their cast-offs till he came to Dublin. But it isn't a joke really, is it. When you see boys without any trousers to wear and girls walking about in flour-sacks, you wonder what on earth is going on. I just wonder is any of this going to change that. Or is it just repainting the postboxes?'

'Postboxes?' she said. 'Yes, green – an inspired idea.'

'But my question, Aunt Eva.'

'Your question answers itself. That you should ask it is precisely why we must be to the fore. People of our standing have nothing to gain and all to give. If we leave it to the usual place-hunters and gombeen-men, we know already what a shambles the place will be. We need only look to the Parliamentary Party and any county council in the land.'

Now the march-past had ended. Notables came down to tour the ranks, among them, MacMurrough saw, the gentleman Pearse. Careful now, don't knock that sword.

Who does he remind me of? I really can't say. Or is it that others remind me of him? Someone in contemplation before a sculpture. A man bending to a child. The maiden curate greets his flock. Moments from other lives. A most unprepossessing vehicle for enthusiasm – until he speaks. At that Fenian's funeral, the day after Aunt Eva's fête, his command and suasion: in all the thousands listening not a face unstirred.

And here he is now, here is my boy. Pearse has found him out. This man Pearse has found him for me. He stops to talk.

He blushes, my boy, the only red in all that green. I can feel them as he looks, the lashes on his eyes, the shave of his hair on the back of his head, the very edge of soft, like brick-dust. I MacMurrough am part of his country. Pearse passes on, his light with him, losing my boy in the green again. And I'm not sure now have I seen him at all.

The crowd was growing restive. MacMurrough heard calls of Shirkers! Slackers! Avenge the Lusitania! The plight of poor little Belgium was widely bemoaned. Tram-men were banging their gongs, ever more insistently. An hour now they'd been stopped in their tracks. From his pedestal in Trinity, Burke raised his hand. *It is no inconsiderable part of wisdom,* he declared, *to know how much of an evil ought to be tolerated.* The guard at the bank, in their scarlet and busbies, looked impassively on. The police spies numbered in their notebooks. The Castle was right. Let the Volunteers make buffoons of themselves, pikes and all.

'Aunt Eva, may I ask what is to be done with the band?'

'I thought signalling,' she said. 'Signalling, I have heard, is an invaluable skill for boys.'

'You know I do not mean that.'

'You mean will they be sent to fight.' She stood very sternly, staring at the men and the women too with their Red Cross brassards. 'They will not. They will fight of their own will.'

'What little is left them. And you understand I will not be here?'

'I understand,' she said, 'that you have an appointment at Easter.'

They returned up Grafton Street. 'It's early yet for lunch,' Aunt Eva observed. 'Shall we take a turn in the Green?'

'Certainly,' said MacMurrough.

Young boys rambled along, touching what they passed with little-fingered hands. MacMurrough touched the bollards, as Dr

Johnson was said to have done, for luck. They entered Stephen's Green and the withdrawn world of laid-out gardens fell upon them. Voluminous ladies frou-frou'd past, titanics warded by tender husbands, each click of whose canes proclaimed, Behold the woman I fuck. A kid pushed a toddler in some box on wheels, wildly over the lawn. The doubtful fun on the toddler's face, the fierce joy on the boy's. Then the Dublin girls, their pale faces and glossy hair, the dark and the light, like fresh-poured stout, the leucomelanous complexion of Ireland.

'Do you know,' said his aunt, 'it really is a delightful day.'

And it was too. The daffodils opened in lakes of yellow beneath the trees. The japonica was coming to blossom, laburnum splashed in corners. A powdery blue sky sailed above the branches. The branches conceived the very merest imagining of green.

They crossed the lake by the humped bridge and rounded the George II block. 'Monumentally misplaced,' his aunt sniffed. Novices, a hush of them, hurried from the park to wait in the doorway to Newman's church. Something about Newman. Buried beside his life-long friend. Friend's name? Can't remember. The novices waited for their director, who came, his arms wide, herding them in, their bowed heads deprecating. Male hairy, bull of grace, the lard is with thee.

'Shall we sit?'

'We will.'

Though MacMurrough did not sit. He handed his aunt to the seat and stood beside. A few months back, he had stalked a likely-looking thing to this very bench. Chatted a while, then the thing had got up, gone on to the lavatory, just down the path there. MacMurrough had followed, only a big burly bumpkin of a policeman had come in and frightened the chase away. MacMurrough was still at the urinal when midnight blue bashed against him and he was propelled inside the closet. His trousers were down before he was scarcely aware of his buttons, his head thrust by the bowl. It was a brutish rutting, more of a flogging than a fuck, great baton of a dick poling his innards, his forehead chilling and bruising against the porcelain. Not the pleasantest of experiences, though in recall it did own a certain collywobbly titillation. When the bobby had done, he bade MacMurrough hitch his unmentionables. He yanked him by the hair and told him in his ear: 'And if I catch ya anywheres at it agin, y'ill be on tha boat ta England.'

'Not too cold, Aunt Eva?'

'Perhaps,' she replied. 'Let you finish your cigarette and we shall go in to lunch.'

Hello, what have we here? Rather a likely-looking thing himself. Fetching little bumfreezer, waiter or something. Do waiters have a lunch hour? I know you. Where do I know you from? Arseless thing, all legs, out of the bottomless pit where Dublin breeds. Got you. Clerk out of Lee's in Kingstown. Had fondled Doyler's flowers and frolics. There he goes, straight into the lats. And out again. Unforgivable to let it go waste.

'Aunt Eva, I shan't be a moment.'

'Anthony?'

'I must briefly – '

Make an arrangement at least. Yes, they had no swimming this afternoon. Take him to a Turkish baths. Would just fill the gap nicely, a little *plenum et obtabilem*, then catch the train to Ferns. Yes yes, MacMurrough was saying to himself, and he was just coming to the boy, he was just lifting his hand to tap the boy's shoulder, when he saw the boy was not alone. No, the boy had stopped, he was talking with another boy.

It can't be. Surely not.

'Well, Mr MacMurrough.'

But it was. 'What are you doing here?'

Doyler frowned. 'Now where would you want me to be?'

'Never mind that. What are you doing talking with this fellow?'

The clerk from Lee's, who might possibly now be a waiter, looked on bemused.

'I think I'll talk to any man I choose,' said Doyler.

'You'll talk to me now. I want a word with you.'

'You're talking, aren't you?'

'Get rid of this – Get rid of your piece of smut first.'

'Smut?' His frown deepened as his eyebrows lifted, cramping his forehead. His Adam's apple gave a little hop. 'Who the hell do you think you are?'

'Get rid of him.'

'Calling any man smut then ordering me about?'

'You get rid of him or I soon will.'

Doyler looked him up and down, taking in MacMurrough's uniform. He said to the clerk from Lee's, 'Go on over the bench there. I'll be with you a minute. Go on, now,' he told him. Then he turned to MacMurrough and he pushed him. He actually pushed him. 'I see you've taken it into your head to be a Volunteer,' he said. 'And I see some gobshite company was fuddled enough to make an officer of you. But you don't be ordering me about. The Volunteers might stop the traffic but they don't be running this country yet.'

MacMurrough could scarce persuade himself this was happening. Here was Doyler pushing him backward into a hedge. Doyler. And he had been talking with the clerk from Lee's. It was obvious they had made an appointment to meet. The clerk from Lee's who had fondled his flowers and his frolics.

Still Doyler went on. 'With your badge on your cap and three stars on your sleeve' – his fingers flipped the peak of

455

MacMurrough's cap, they flicked at his sleeve. 'Is it the spring fashions you was at?'

'Will you stop pushing, you damned fool. This has nothing to do with the Volunteers.'

'I'd say that's true and all. Devil the chance of yourself volunteering, but your aunt pushed you. I pity any men you lead, MacMurrough. Your kind never failed at nothing yet, for you never stopped at nothing long enough to find out.'

'Will you shut up and listen?'

'I'll listen when I'm good and ready.'

There was nothing for it but MacMurrough grabbed the boy's wrist and twisted it. 'This isn't about me, you little toe-rag, it's about Jim.'

'What about Jim?'

'Anthony?'

'I want you to go and see him.'

'What are you talking about?' He shrugged his arm free.

'He's with the band. They were at the parade, now they're visiting the pro-Cathedral. Go say hello.'

'Anthony?'

'What's Jim to do with you?'

'Tell him you'll be there at Easter. He's worried frantic. Jim, do you understand?'

'Anthony? What is this?'

'Oh, Aunt Eva, not now.'

'What's Jim been saying?'

'He hasn't said anything.'

'Have you laid a hand on him?'

'You, boy. Shoo, now. Go away.'

'If you laid a hand on Jim, I'll fucking murder you. I'll crucify you, you hear me.'

'Stop this. Go away. Shoo.'

'Aunt Eva, leave the umbrella down.'

'You hear me, MacMurrough? I don't know what I'll bloody do, but you'll wish you was never—'

'I shall fetch a constable and have you in charge.'

'You, lady, can fetch a fucking priest for I'm telling you now—'

But he did not tell, for MacMurrough caught him by the shoulders, pinning his arms with his elbows, and shook him against the railings. 'You will not talk to my aunt that way.' He had his hand over the boy's mouth and a knee poised in his groin. 'Do you hear me? Good. Now listen. Your friend is with the band and they are visiting the pro-Cathedral. He was hoping to see you at the parade. Give up your letch with the flowers and frolics here and go say hello. It's the least he deserves.'

MacMurrough lifted his hand from Doyler's mouth. The mouth was in a fleery grin like a horse's with the bit pulled. Doyler laughed. 'You never had him, had you. Oh but you're cursing to. Has you ate up. But you won't never have him, MacMurrough. You're nothing to Jim and you know that. Nothing at all while I'm there first.'

With no anger, with a feeling almost of its being foreordained, MacMurrough let his knee into the boy's groin, while the boy spat at him full in the face before the pain gripped and his bend began, into the groin where often by the sea in the summer gone he had enjoyed to let his mouth and his tongue.

It was a dismal lunch. MacMurrough pecked at his food. Aunt Eva soldierly knifed and forked her way through, her face in grim Dickensian way, an index to her mind. At length she said, 'I have been giving some thought to your problem with Turkish cigarettes. I have the address of a cigarist's who I believe will have what you want. You might visit there this afternoon before you train to Ferns.'

'Aunt Eva, don't let's pretend. I'm sorry about what happened. I was foolish and inept.'

'Oh, that is what you were. You were foolish and you were inept. I see. I have a foolish and inept nephew. And in what way is my nephew inept? Why, he cannot contain himself half an hour without dragging his corner-boy minions before his aunt.'

'Of course you are right. It was much worse than inept.'

'I say nothing of the vulgarity,' she continued, 'I believe that has spoken for itself. I say nothing of the exhibition: I have never cared for the general, nor ever will. But I had thought it was over. I had heartfully thought you had come to your senses.'

'But Aunt Eva, it's not ever going to be over.'

'Then I pity you.'

MacMurrough saw his cuffs, his links, the elegance of just this square foot about his plate. I have no human failings, none whatsoever. All my failings are animal.

'I pity you for you will never know what it is to be a man. As I have never known – '

'As you?'

'As I pity myself for the ingrate I have for a nephew. I had thought you would settle now, that you would wish to settle. Marriage and children, I should find you an employment even. I had thought this period would be something we would share, privately. We would come to laugh of it even, in happier times. I had thought it was finished. I was mistaken.'

He thought for a moment she was going to cry. That indeed she was crying, and was reaching now into her reticule for a mouchoir. What she brought out made her wrist look frail and old. He saw the veins where her coat had pulled back. Its weight was too much for her to brandish it successfully. Her arm wavered up and down. She did not point at MacMurrough, as he had half expected, but at a party of officers at a table beside. It had often flitted through his mind, but he had never given it any serious consideration, that his aunt was mad.

'What do you think?' she asked.

'A Webley. You must have got him very drunk, your officer.'

'We might go to the manager now. We could so easily take this building. It has a commanding presence, you will agree. With the Shelbourne, we should hold the entire Green.'

'Hadn't you better put it away now?'

'So soon?'

'Is it loaded, Aunt Eva?'

'I believe it may be.'

'Is the catch on?'

'I'm not sure if I can tell.'

'Please, Aunt Eva, will you give it to me now?'

Slowly the gun went down on to the table. 'We had as well put it to our heads,' she said. 'The fight is coming and we leave nothing behind us. We leave it all to penny-boys and clerks.'

CHAPTER SEVENTEEN

THE YOUNG MAN with Doyler, who indeed no longer worked at Lee's of Kingstown, but had advanced to a position of boots and bottle-washer at the Russell Hotel adjacent the Green, was looking uneasy. He had knelt beside Doyler. 'You all right now?' he asked.

Doyler pushed him away. 'I told you wait, didn't I?' He was still in agony. His groin felt it had kicked into his stomach. He had to bend tight and squeeze inside to hold the pain. And he was seething with anger. And now, Jesus, here was a peeler coming. That fucker sent him and all. He got to his feet, still bending and holding where it hurt. He felt a lightness in his head.

'You'll be all right in a minute. You need to stand and walk round.'

'Will you get your maulers off of me? Come on, get out of this place.'

He led the boots out by the Surgeons, and hurried up past the keeper's lodge into Harcourt Street. He stopped at the stable lane to the Russell Hotel. The weeds in the walls and crevices gave off a whiff of urine. He looked back to see was he followed. The pain was gone or bearable anyway. He sought his sensible workaday face. 'You sure now you can get me in? I don't want any trouble about it.'

The boots was sure. He went in the staff way, and after a time a coach-house door opened. He led Doyler through the dark and up narrow staircases that had a creak of worm and damp in their tread, up to the attic storey. Nobody had seen them. He opened a door into an odd-shaped bandboxy room. Three beds jammed inside. He pointed to one and said, 'That's where I sleep.'

Doyler was looking up at the skylight. 'How d'you get out?'

Well, you pulled the bed and if you balanced ever-so on the bedstead you could just with your fingers get a shove on the skylight. 'Give me an hour,' said Doyler. 'You'll have to be back again to let me out. You won't forget now?' He climbed on the bed, and the boots gave him his body for a ladder. The skylight eased open and he heard the clap of pigeon wings. Then he was out on the roof and all of the Green swam before him. He checked down again. That quilt of a boots had his face gawking. 'Put the bed back,' he told him, whispering now. 'And don't stand about looking to be catched.' He shifted the skylight back into place.

There was a parapet about two feet high where he lodged his feet and he leant back against the roof. Nobody would hardly see him up here. And people never looked up. Up was always the place to hide. He pulled some papers out of his pocket. One of them was a sketch he had made of the Green, its paths and ponds, bandstand, where would a thicket break the line of fire, that sort of thing. He judged it against what he saw, clearly now and entire for the first time. Not bad for a fellow had never made a map in his life. He began pencilling adjustments.

The pigeons trooped back. Little sideways steps they made along the ledge. They had the bricks white with their droppings. With a start he remembered what that fucker had done. He reached inside his trousers and felt about his groin. He spat.

There'd be another day and that man's time would come. He had work to do.

When he was satisfied with the Green, he looked about the surrounding rooftops. He began to make his way towards the railway station, crawling along and creeping over the intersecting walls. Every now and then he stopped to make a note of a problem in the way and its workaround, or of a particular vantage, say, for sniping. He'd write it up proper back at the Hall. You couldn't get all the way to the station, a lane cut in. But he'd known that anyway. Still, if you took a lep down on a wall there and shinned it up a drainpipe you might come close. That was another day's work. He started back for the Russell Hotel.

The boots was waiting for him under the skylight. He had a mug of tea ready. 'Now what did you go and do that for?'

'I only thought.'

Doyler took the tea, gruffly thanked him.

'That was your bloke, wasn't it?'

'Who was me bloke?'

'The gentleman.'

Doyler looked at him, not liking him at all, a sniffy sort of a face, would want to blow his nose. 'What do you mean, me bloke, anyway?'

'I thought you was with him, you know, that you went with him.'

'I never went anywheres with him bar Kingstown.'

'He got you them clothes.'

'He never bought me nothing and I don't know what you think you're saying. Here now and thanks for your tea.'

He held the door, then followed the boots through the back ways of the hotel and out into the stable lane. The quilt seemed to want to follow him into Harcourt Street. 'Was that any help to you?' he wanted to know.

'Help enough.'

'You can come again. I'll let you in.'

'I might then.'

'The architecture, isn't it. At the night classes.'

Doyler had a notion of clandestine activity which this lanky snuffles dogging him in the street didn't serve at all. He felt a pull on his sleeve and he turned impatiently. 'What is it you want?'

The boy leant his head sideways looking into Doyler's face. 'Don't you like me?'

'Ah now, what's this now? You don't want to be bothering your head if a man likes you. Don't you have work to do? You have it very easy here is all I can say. Go on now.'

He pushed him, not roughly, to send him on his way, then he crossed to Stephen's Green without looking back. Soft as shite that one was. A few weeks before, he was in the Green, trying to make sense of the paths, and that young quilt had come out of the gents there. He was all pally in an anxious sort of a way. Doyler thought he remembered him all right but he wasn't going to make any fuss about it. Only he happened to hear the Russell Hotel mentioned at training, and he let it drop that he might know the boots there. Would he be let on the roof, they wanted to know, and Doyler said he'd ask, what harm.

He made some quick turns in and out of alleyways to be sure of anyone following, then he headed down for the river. There was a Guinness barge tooting under the bridge and seagulls squalled above. He looked up O'Connell Street. Jim wouldn't be still at the pro-Cathedral. There was no good traipsing up there. What had he to say to Jim, anyway, that he couldn't write it in a letter? He was under orders. He hadn't time to be making calls.

He walked along the quay looking down at the lumpy green of the Liffey. Above the Customs House the Union Jack was flying. It had a way of flying, that flag, like the wind from the sea was made for it special. He turned the corner into Beresford Place, took the steps at a leap into Liberty Hall.

After the Glasthule feis, back last year, after he had packed his parcel and made his goodbye to his mother, and to Jim, Doyler had walked to Dublin of course. It was a Sunday morning and very quiet. Dawn was only breaking when he came into town. Not anything moved save the murk of the river. He sat against one of the supports of the Loop Line bridge, gazing at the grey drab building opposite. The windows were blinded and a lantern hung outside like it might be a kip or a police station. A band along the front read, *Irish Transport and General Workers' Union*. The letters above the fanlight said, *Liberty Hall*.

He had closed his eyes a while, when the high double doors opened and a man was sweeping dust from the lobby inside. He started to sweep the steps. He swept away while Doyler watched, then he leant on his broom. 'Busy?' he asked.

He was a Scotchman. Doyler gave a shrug.

'There you go,' he said, holding the broom in Doyler's direction. Doyler spat in a circumspect way. He left his parcel down and took the broom. He supposed it was the bruises on his face, for the caretaker said, 'You were fighting.'

Doyler answered, 'Not much.'

'He was a sight bigger than you.'

'Him and the other. Wasn't that but they had a priest for bottle-holder.'

'Foolhardy.' The man's moustache was thick and combed down over his mouth so you wouldn't know for sure was he smiling. 'What brings you here then?'

'I'm to join the Citizen Army.' Doyler was tired after his walk and no sleep that night, and he hadn't announced this with quite the dash he'd intended.

'You maybe like a fight so. You'll be a member of a union anyway?'

Doyler told him no – though he had wanted to be. He had a Red Hand badge that they wouldn't let him wear, but he wore it all the same inside of his collar.

'What work was that?' Doyler told him, adding that it didn't matter anyway, for he'd lost that work now. The priest had got him that work and the priest had told him he'd get him the kick too.

The caretaker wasn't so sure it didn't matter. 'Maybe there's others there looking to join the union.'

But Doyler could put the caretaker right about that. 'They're all of them yellow. Yellow to the last boy.'

'Yet you didn't join neither.'

'What does it matter if I joined? I put the badge on me once, which is the same thing, and the priest had the clothes ripped off of me. I knew he would and all, but I couldn't bear it any longer, hiding it.'

'If you were in the union, but, you might have fared different.'

'I'd have lost me job, man, amn't I after telling you?'

'But you did lose your job.'

Doyler frowned. 'I suppose if you wanted to look at it that way, you could.' He was irritable with his lack of sleep, and this caretaker irritated him too, hiding behind his moustache. 'I was a newsboy a long time in Kingstown,' he said. 'In the Lock-out the newsboys was the first to strike.'

'You were out in the Lock-out then?'

'No,' he said glumly. 'I was down in County Clare. But I

465

would have been out, God's oath on that. I would have been proud to be out.'

'You'd have been hungry, son,' said the caretaker. Again Doyler couldn't tell was he laughing or what. 'You'll want a cup of tea?'

'If you're making it, I will.'

'If I'm making it,' repeated the caretaker, shaking his head. He was a short thickset man with bandy legs. Doyler followed him into an office. 'Milk and sugar?' he asked.

'What about them?' said Doyler.

'What about them,' he repeated and he stamped off down a corridor, making noisy creaks on the boards.

Doyler looked round the room. There were maps on the wall. Paris, he read, Moscow, Cuba in the civil war. The building was startlingly quiet so that any little noise he made sounded grossly out of place. The caretaker returned with the tea. Doyler, looking at the maps still, said, 'Paris Commune.'

'You know of the Paris Commune then?'

'1871, aye. Sure they have a Carnegie library in Kingstown.'

'You can read and write then?'

Doyler took a step back and said scoffing, 'Can you?'

'Read I can, but there's many have doubts can I write.' It was confusing really, like talking with a ventriloquist, for under his moustache you couldn't see his mouth move hardly at all. He had a big round face above a neat collar and tie. 'So you think to join the Citizen Army. Wouldn't the boy scouts be better, young fellow like yourself?'

Doyler corrected him. 'It's not the boy scouts. It's na Fianna Éireann you mean.'

'You speak Irish?'

'Enough of it.'

The man sat down on the chair. There was a bed by the wall,

neatly made. Doyler wondered was this where he slept. He had a queer relaxed way for a caretaker. 'I'll tell you now,' he said, 'they had me locked up, a year since. They had me thinking I was there for a good long stretch, so I asked for an Irish grammar to be sent in. I hadn't the cover opened before the authorities had me out. They're a way feared of me learning Irish, I thought. But I hadn't the opportunity since.'

'What was you locked up for?'

'Sedition.'

Another man came down the corridor. He stopped at the door and the two men were talking. The door across was half ajar and Doyler ambled over with his tea. It looked like a meeting-hall inside. He peeked round the jamb. And there it was. It was hanging on the wall. He just stopped in the door staring at it. The truest blue he had ever seen, like the bluest deepest calmest ocean. The plough wasn't at all how he had imagined, something you would have to guess at, like the shapes in the sky, but it was a real plough, a manifest thing, you might nearly step up to the flag and pull it away to do work in a field. The stars were done in silver and the plough was done in gold. The gold and silver had a motion, they seemed to swish with movement, like a breeze through the blue. It was surely the most beautiful thing in the world.

He said, hardly aware if he was speaking, 'The Plough and the Stars. It's the Starry Plough of the Citizen Army.'

The man had come behind. 'What're you here for, son?'

'I want to serve my country.'

'How'll you serve your country in Liberty Hall?'

'The working class is the only class that never betrayed Ireland.'

'Did you hear that, Bill? We have a theoretician with us.'

'No,' said Doyler. 'But I've read *Labour in Irish History*, by

Mr James Connolly. And if I wasn't such a ludamawn, I'd have known all along it was Mr Connolly I was speaking with.'

That day Doyler joined the crowds that trooped behind the coffin of O'Donovan Rossa, the dead Fenian. He was told afterwards that a fine speech was given at the graveside, but back where he was standing he could hear nothing. What was the use of fine speeches when the thousands who were there wouldn't catch a word? He didn't give a curse for speeches anyway, nor for dead Fenians, come to that. He slept a few hours under a hedge in Glasnevin. The evening then he was back at Liberty Hall. He asked could he see Mr Connolly, and after a deal of waiting he was shown to a door where he knocked.

'Here he is,' said Mr Connolly when he entered. 'Do you know at all where South Lotts is?'

'I can find out for you.'

'He's a comedian this one,' he said to the other man who was with him at the table. 'I know where South Lotts is. Do you, is the question. You'll never be much use for a messenger if you can't find your way about Dublin.'

'I can learn it. I'll learn it tomorrow. I won't stop till I know.'

'He's willing anyway,' said the other man.

'You have no work?' said Mr Connolly.

'Not yet I haven't. I'll try for hand-carting tomorrow.'

'You have a busy day. You'll join the union?'

'I'll be proud to.'

'That's one and thruppence. You think to be a Citizen soldier? That's sixpence a week for the uniform fund. You're in debt to one and ninepence already and you haven't a stroke of work done.'

'I have a suit I'm to pawn. It's nearly new.'

Mr Connolly laughed and the other man laughed, then Mr

Connolly said to the other man, 'Well, Kane, is he any use to you?'

'I don't know now. Won't look too handsome running messages with that leg.'

'Ah get him an old bicycle, for God's sake. There's any the God number of men will risk their lives for Ireland. Few enough these days will risk their jobs. He's sharp enough too. Put him in with a couple of the other lads. And find him something to eat. He's not winked at food all day to look at him.'

He was already busy with the papers on the table. Doyler asked Kane in the corridor outside, 'How did he know if I risked my job?'

'Inquiries confirmed your story, son. That'll do you for now.'

They had an entertainment that night in the Hall. Doyler waited at the back, till a woman in the benches beckoned him forward. It was cheap sitting as standing, she told him. Bottoms squashed up till room was found. A man patted his back as he sat down. By nod and wink he was welcomed. He saw their laughing faces. He laughed a little with them. Then he nodded off, leaning upon his neighbour's shoulder.

Two lads took him to where they lodged, a widow woman's room at the very top of a tenement building. She bade him welcome, regretting if the welcome was bigger than the feast. In their curtained-off corner the lads showed him to side-step where the boards were rotten. There was a tiny paper-mended window and a mattress on the floor with little enough space for one. It didn't signify. Nothing extraneous signified any more. Home now would be Liberty Hall.

It made him laugh in the months after, that the Hall had been so quiet that first morning. For never again, though he came there all hours of the day, and the night too, and he came to master the topsy-turvy of its corridors and stairs, never again did he find the remotest chance of peace in the place. People were ever rushing in and out, men and women on union business, boys of the Fianna and girls too, Citizen soldiers. The printing-press would be clacking away, musical instruments were blaring, somewhere deep in the recesses a mysterious hammering would be going on, you wouldn't know what was preparing. Plays were rehearsed and put on, and God forgive him, he even acted in the chorus of one. And the trains all day rattled over the Loop Line bridge. He had never known a place like it.

Days on frost when no work was to be had, and whatever hour he had to himself, he spent there. He lent his hand to anything. Simple things at first, like carting coal or helping in the kitchen. He took messages on an old yoke of a bike, and he'd deliberately shine no light and cycle on the footpath, careless of any peeler. He went nowhere without a sheaf of the *Workers' Republic* to hawk it in the street. Any reading that came his way, he devoured it.

With the other lads he'd go heckling the recruiting meetings of the British Army, while the Fianna boys – little newsboy gurriers, right larkers, right scrawls – crept in under the legs of the speakers, throwing up the booths till everything was mayhem. There was a strike at the docks, and he helped out there, standing picket if called on. He was a buttonman at last, with the pride of a buttonman, his red-hand badge stuck out from his lapel.

As time passed he was let in deeper to the secrets of the Hall. A munitions factory in the basement where explosives were devised: grenades of condensed-milk cans, bombs stuffed in cocoa-tins. He spent days filling shotgun cartridges, then nights bricking them away behind false walls. He helped in the workshop where bayonets and crowbars were made. There was even a miniature rifle range where he was let practise with a saloon-pistol. He was sharp and he was useful. And when there was nothing useful to be doing, which was rare but not unknown, he argued tactics with whoever was there to argue him back.

The army drilled in the late evening. A talk would be given after on a military subject. Saturday nights they camped at Croydon Park and drilled in the good green fields. He had no gun of course and wouldn't be trusted with one a while yet. But he trained like the other youngsters with a solid pick-axe handle, shoed at one end with metal. It was just that bit longer than a peeler's baton, just that bit heavier, so that the peelers had learnt to stand clear of their road. Days when the breweries were malting, when every oven in the city must have a cake it was baking, they marched with the hop of hunger in their bellies. November came and they marched through the fall of leaves. The rain fell in sheets and still they marched, with a cold hope of broth on the boil. The children laughed and aped them with sticks in the street. And they passed with the Plough and the Stars before them, shoulder to shoulder each man to his neighbour, marching to the drum of their feet. It was grand. It was very grand.

Days hurtled one into the next. He didn't lie down but he was fast asleep. He didn't wake but he was down to the Hall. He had never imagined a time like it. The world was made a wind to rush him. His hair flew in that wind when he took at a leap the steps to the Hall. Its roar was in his ears when he sang with the men, the words that Connolly had penned for them,

Send it aloft on the breeze, boys
That watchword the grandest known
That Labour will rise from its knees, boys
And claim the earth for its own.

Some weeks he earned enough out of carting to send a little home to his mother. Most weeks he went hungry. It was so cold that winter, in the widow's garret they took it in turns to sleep in the middle of the bed. They had to take their boots in under the blanket with them, for fear the rats would get at them. One night they got the knock. They scrambled into their clothes, which had been their pillows, stumbling into each other in their hurry. They were down at the Hall at the kick of time, the widow woman hobbling after with a can of tea. Doyler grabbed his sheaf of mobilization orders, biked like a maniac to the cottages and tenements that were his watch. They were a muddled and edgy army that formed in the dark before the Hall. Then Connolly came down the steps. 'City Battalion of the Irish Citizen Army, by the right, quick march!'

They marched that night on Dublin Castle. 'We'll be back,' said Connolly to the startled peeler on point behind the gates.

Shortly after this, each man was called individually into Connolly's office. When it came Doyler's turn, he saluted his commandant and stood at ease.

'I want to know this,' said Mr Connolly. 'If it comes to a fight, and we know it will, sooner than later: if the Volunteers won't fight, are you willing to go on without them?'

Doyler had no trouble answering that. 'I'd prefer it even.'

When you got to know him, you could tell from his eyes when Mr Connolly would be smiling. 'I liked you. I liked you the first I saw you. Doyle, isn't it?'

'Yes sir.'

'Did the night manoeuvre alarm you, son?'

'I'd better have liked it with a gun.'

Mr Connolly nodded. 'Dismissed, Private Doyle.'

He had a problem with his Ss. Dih-mit, it sounded like.

Doyler had his uniform then. It had belonged to another man who had died or dropped out. He would have to sew it and fit it himself. But he was proud to stand in the army hall, with the dark green on him, and the Red Hand in his hat, standing before the Plough and the Stars. He was a Citizen soldier. The Citizen

Army was the guard and guide of labour. It was an arm round labour's shoulder, you could say. The workers were with them. They could not fail. He lifted his hand and saluted his flag.

Afterwards, this was a moment he kept deep in his heart, for it was the last of his undisturbed love for Liberty Hall.

He was back again at the Russell Hotel the next day after St Patrick's. He sent a note for the boots and soon enough he was up on the roof. This time he worked his way towards Earlsfort Terrace, noting as before the skylights, drainpipes, the sneak-ups and grease-downs.

He enjoyed this kind of work. It made sense to him. The kind of fighting it supposed made sense too. Snipe from the rooftops, a round or two, then powder away to be lost in the crowds. Drilling and parading was well and good, but column advance, feint, enfilade and defilade – lot of use was that against the British Empire. No, first bring the workers out. All the workers, a general strike. Bring the country to its knees. Then snipe and run, a bomb here, a grenade tossed there. Angry mobs where the military could be trusted to lose their nerve. Soon have the country ungovernable.

It wasn't himself had thought any that up. Connolly's teaching was that. Yet these days he heard no talk of a general strike. The talk was all of them joining with the Volunteers. That together they'd take over Dublin. It was mad talk, mad as their sham attacks on Dublin Castle. It made him spit to hear it, and his forehead to frown like a ploughed field.

He heard something, and turning quick, he saw that quilt of a boots had climbed all the way along the rooftops carrying two mugs of tea. He put away the notes he was writing. 'Mary and Joseph,' he said, 'I don't know but you're a resourceful fellow. How'd you get them mugs through that skylight?'

He managed it some way or other, he wasn't sure now.

'Did you put back the skylight after you?'

He had. They were in the dip between two pitches of roof, quite out of sight except of any pigeons passing. Doyler took a sup from his tea. 'Get a job here meself, I think. They don't give you hardly nothing to do.'

The boots sat down. He wasn't chatty so much as anxious to talk. He was from Lucan, he said, he didn't know anyone in Dublin. He nodded to Doyler's badge and said he had a brother was a buttonman and his uncle too. Good for them, Doyler told him. He supposed Doyler was wondering why had he left his employment in Kingstown. He didn't like to say, but he'd tell Doyler if Doyler wanted to know. Did Doyler want to know?

Doyler couldn't give a tuppenny curse either way, but he chucked his head and the boots said, 'D'you remember the walker was in Lee's that time?' Doyler recollected a walker all right. Well, the walker had got his cards. He was away in England now. The boots hadn't liked the walker anyhow. Only . . . Only . . .

'Only what?' asked Doyler.

'We was found out.'

'Found out about what sure?'

'Found out together like, me and him.'

Doyler felt his lip was curling. He didn't like this. He didn't want to be hearing any more of this. But the boy was telling away, his eyes on Doyler's cup, only looking him in the face if Doyler brought his cup to his lips. There was a drip forming out of his nose.

'They had the polis called and they bate me up a bit. The walker had it worse. But anyway they sent to the parish priest at home. I can't go back there now. I didn't dare go back to me lodgings even. I came into Dublin but I didn't know anyone here. I was a couple nights walking round. I was dreading the polis'd stop me and they'd find out then from the polis in Kingstown. Then I met a fellow in the Green, down where I met you, and he got me this position I have now. I was lucky that way, without any references. Except I don't think I like him either.'

'All this happened you?'

He looked briefly up. 'That's right.'

'Can't you get out of this and find a decent job?'

'Doing what?'

'Anything at all, man. Carting even.'

'Don't want to do carting.'

'You can't stop here if that's going on. Does he take a liberty with you, this man?'

'I only wanted to have a friend. That's all.'

'You have to do something. What about your folks?'

'They won't write me. I thought you might be a friend.'

'What if they catch you with this new fellow, what'll you do then?'

'I don't care about that. I just wanted to be with somebody I liked. Just to go for a walk even.'

'They give you time to go walking? Mary and Joseph, I don't believe you do a tap of work.'

'What's it matter to you what time I have?' he said colouring. 'If I have it easy at work, what's that to you?'

'Nothing,' said Doyler. 'Nothing. You're right. Every man should have leisure to go walking.'

'Well then.'

'Well then.' The boots was looking sulkily at his knees. The colour was draining. 'Are you scared now?' Doyler asked.

He looked up, an angashore of a face. 'I am scared.' He sniffed. 'I was happy to see you. I thought I might talk with you.'

'Sure we are talking.'

'I suppose we are.'

'Lookat, maybe we'll go for a ramble. I don't know when I'll have time, but I'll call on you. That do you?'

'I'd like that.'

'Back with you now, while I finish what I'm at.'

'Is it work for the Citizen Army?'

'What do you know about the Citizen Army?'

'I often seen you in your uniform. Up in O'Connell Street and outside of Liberty Hall.'

'You haven't been following me about?'

'No. No. And all my family is buttonmen. You've nothing to fear from me.'

Doyler looked into his face. He wished to God if he might find a rag to blow his nose. 'I better not have,' he said. 'Go on.'

Back at the Hall Doyler wandered along the corridors. He was hungry, he didn't know was he feeding at all. His feet were bealing from chilblains he had on his heels. He had chilblains on his fingers too.

They were rehearsing a play in the concert room. He watched a while. Connolly had written this play. It had a young fellow, he didn't know to fight for Ireland or take his shilling with the British Army. In the end he joined the Volunteers. Doyler walked out, stomping on the boards and letting the doors clatter behind him. If Connolly wanted to be writing plays, why wouldn't he have the fellow join the Citizen Army? He left the Hall, shaking his head. He couldn't work out what had happened with Connolly.

At drill now there were Volunteer officers let watch their evolutions. They were let sit in on their talks and demonstrations. One time after drill, his captain called him out. He wasn't satisfied with Doyler's attitude. Did Doyler think himself above army discipline? Did he think it hilarious to go whacking Volunteer officers on the head?

'I was at me drill. He was in the way.'

His captain gave him the speech on the Volunteers. On true nationalist movements, on working in harmony, on common purposes. Doyler wanted to spit. The Volunteers were a contamination. What did they care for the rights of labour? Was they born Englishmen, they'd be all for King and Empire. Their thinking was wool and dreams, whereas his was hard and severe, hard and severe as the lives of the people.

'You're getting above yourself, Doyle,' his captain told him. He told him go careful, he had his eye on him now.

Doyler walked along the river, past the Customs House, and along the docks where men were hard at their work still. He nodded to some he knew. One asked was he looking for work, there was something going by the canal he'd heard. Doyler said no, he wasn't interested tonight.

How many ships had docked at the Liffey? Thousands, he supposed, sure hundreds of thousands, countless. Only one had docked that signified anything to him. That was the foodship *Hare* that had carried food from the workers of England to the starved and locked-out workers of Dublin. That was a day all right, when she pulled into the quay, all decked with flags and her siren whooping. He could see the crowds so clearly, the faces laughing and cheering and the little children clapping their hands for food. He could not pass along the Dublin quays without thinking of that ship. Imagine it, a ship to bring food where families was starving. Was ever there such a thing? He felt a great tearful love for the people of England that they'd defy everyone, their union bosses even, and come to the aid of their Irish fellows. He would give ten years of his life and gladly to be here that day. Anything at all to be in Dublin for the Lock-out.

But he was already down in Clare that time. Sometimes he would day-dream that he wasn't in Clare, was a newsboy still. He'd let on he got the bad of a leg that way, out of a baton charge of the peelers. He wouldn't mind an odd limp getting it some way useful like that. Instead of himself at home beating the leg from under him with the leg of a chair he broke in his temper. And all for the price of him wanting to go to the college. That night he crept out the Banks and he never looked back till he came to Clare. They said then the leg would never mend. They were right too.

He wandered along till it was gone dark. Past yard and mill and warehouse, where men still laboured under lights and flares, and boys still pushed their barrows. He heard in the holds of ships that were moored the horrible distress of cattle. He looked up at the sky but he saw no stars to shine. They had the earth to plough all right, but no hope of any stars, no hope at all so far as he could see.

Then, when he was dead on his feet, he made his way back to his tenement kip. The two lads looked at him strange at times. They said his hands moved about in his sleep. More than once he was woke by a thump from one of them.

It turned April and Lent already was half-way gone. They had moved into town, his mother and the shrimpses and himself, bolting the moon out of Glasthule. They'd hunted out a cottage by King Street where they let out the back room. Himself was very poorly now, and when Doyler visited he could see the change that had come about. They had cups to drink out of, the shrimpses each had boots and there was a supply of turf by the fire. His army pension might actually go to some good, with himself on his back and unable to drink it.

His mother sat him by the fire and gave him tea and bread. She was worried the way he looked, was he feeding himself, why wouldn't he take his meals with them. He wasn't hardly listening, just looking at the flame of the turf. Then he heard her asking, 'What happened with your friend?'

'Nothing, so far as I know.'

'I did at times see him in the street in Glasthule. He looked lonely to me there.' Doyler said nothing. 'Wouldn't you go out a day and swim with him?' his mother went on. He told her he had his duties. 'And he the friend of your heart itself?'

'I have no friends now, Ma, beyond the army and the workers that come behind it.'

'Is it that they teach you at Liberty Hall?'

He stared into his Lenten red-headed tea. The shrimpses were crowded round a smoky lamp, the eldest showing the others something in a copy-book. They'd hung an old sheet for a screen. Himself was coughing quietly behind, almost decently, like he didn't want to be disturbing the visitor. 'How is he?' he asked.

'He's not great.'

'Will I tell you, Ma, what they teach at Liberty Hall? Calvary is what. They have Connolly spouting nonsense about blood and sacrifice. Them poets out of the Volunteers has got to him. I wish to God Jim Larkin would come back.'

'Hasn't God been good to give you one Jim?'

'Ah, ma, I'm in the army. Aren't we training for war sure.'

'A whisper, son – if there's others unhappy, they won't be happier for your sorrow. You'd want a long arm and you putting it round an army. You're lonely to the world I think.'

He came out of the Hall one evening and that quilt of a boots was waiting for him. 'Ah no,' said Doyler, 'this won't do at all.'

'Only you said we'd walk together.'

'Lookat, I can't be dropping everything. Didn't I say I'd leave word? How d'you know I'm not busy tonight?'

The boots would wait, he didn't mind waiting. He was happy to wait.

Doyler looked up and down the quay. 'All right. I'll step back with you as far as the Green. That's all, mind.'

The boots chatted away in his nervy manner. He seemed to want to please with his talk. There had been an attempted raid on Liberty Hall some weeks previous, and the boots was full of the stir of it. 'Is it true there was two hundred armed polis?' he asked. Doyler just chucked his head. 'They say Mr Connolly himself stood at the steps with his gun aimed. They say he told the polis the first man moved was a dead man.'

It was true enough. The Hall had been left unguarded for some reason. The peelers came. Connolly kept them at bay while the word went out for mobilization.

'They say all over Dublin there was strange sights of men running through the streets with their bandoliers and rifles on them. You'd have a bandolier,' he said to Doyler. 'I'd say you'd have one.'

'Never you mind,' Doyler told him. The boots was obviously after reading it up in a *Workers' Republic*.

'The polis soon found they had no business with Liberty Hall,' he went on. 'The Citizen Army had them downfaced for sure.'

'For sure,' said Doyler.

'I'd say you was there too, well in the thick.'

Aye he was, and he remembered how the men had come running, in twos and threes at first, then by their tens and dozens, all in a sweat and filthy from work, some of them wringing wet that had swam the canal in their hurry. The Fianna boys were there already and they were holding hands to form a line, perfectly fearless, between the peelers and the Hall. Then came the Women's Corps, some of them with their children with them that had no place else to leave them. They didn't mind the lost wages or the jobs they put at risk. They came to defend their Hall, the one place in all that city they might call their own. He remembered the strange mishmash of weapons they carried – iron bars, hammers, clubs, the odd rifle and bandolier. Shoulder to shoulder they stood before the blue-black mass of peelers. And Doyler had stood with them with his shoed handle of a pick. The pride he felt that day near pained him. Near pained him still. There was a lump in his throat he thought he'd never have it swallowed. These were his people. He was a Citizen soldier.

And Connolly would throw them away. He would give them all, hand and gun, to the Volunteers. They were too right not to trust Doyler with a gun, though he had waited these months for a rifle his own. He might shoot Connolly himself.

The boots said, 'The Citizen Army are the boys. They're the ones put manners on the polis.'

They had come to the Green. Beyond was the Russell Hotel. Doyler said, 'Listen, if you're that fond of them, wouldn't you think to join?'

The boots sniffed. 'He won't let me.'

'This man that got you the employment, do you mean?'

'That's right. He's the manager inside.'

At a lane by the Surgeons Doyler stopped and pulled him aside. 'What does he make you do?' he asked. The boy looked dismayed by the question. His head leant down into his chest. 'He take you into his bed, does he?'

'No. Not that.'

'What does he do then?'

'There's a cupboard,' said the boy.

He wouldn't look at Doyler now. For a moment Doyler had a thought of putting his arm round his shoulder, try to cheer the chappie up. But he shook that nonsense out of his head. 'Don't come looking for me no more,' he told him. 'If you've time to

481

go walking, you've time to go looking for a decent employment.'
He turned on his heels.

He was hawking the paper outside the GPO one day, and who came by only Mr Mack, mooching along in a daze and staring up at the tops of the buildings. 'Mr Mack,' he said.

'My my, it's Doyler Doyle. Well, I wouldn't have known you. How's this you're keeping?'

'Grand, Mr Mack, and how's yourself?'

'Bobbing along, sure, bobbing along. We don't see you out our way at all this weather. Sure I know what it is, the big smoke here. Poor old Glasthule is in the ha'penny place altogether.'

'Something like it, Mr Mack.'

He wanted to know what was this Doyler was selling, and Doyler showed him the *Workers' Republic*. Paper of Liberty Hall, he told him. But Mr Mack could give him the story on that, and he was off telling about some poor young fellow was nabbed in Kingstown for peddling the self-same sheet. Mr Mack didn't know but he had to eat his Christmas dinner off His Majesty's plate. He swung back on his heels. 'You want to be careful with that rag, Doyler. I don't know how much is this they pay you, I won't ask neither, but keep an eye out for them constables on the beat. You'd be wiser selling the *Evening Mail*. The *Herald* even.'

Doyler was grinning away. He was very pleased to meet Mr Mack. It was something from a long-lost past, something from his childhood even. 'You're a long way from home,' he said.

'I'm here on – well, I'm not here on business at all. Well, it is business actually, important business. What it is, I'm on my way to the Castle.'

'Are you sure about that?'

'Oh yes, my mind is made up.'

'But, Mr Mack, the Castle is down the opposite way.'

'Dublin Castle?'

'Back over the bridge and up Dame Street.'

He gave a look north and south like he thought they might have moved. 'I knew that,' he said, 'I knew that. Only I thought to take a stroll past the bank here.' He was indicating the post office. 'Fine building, with the columns and things. I was just thinking how Dublin has a wealth of fine buildings to boast of.'

'What would have you calling on the Castle though?'

'What it is, I'm to sign up for the Georgius Rex.'

'Them old crocks?'

'Now now, fair's fair. They may be old but the heart's in the right place. I was thinking if it wasn't time we put some beef into the home defences. Enter stage right, an old sweat of the Old Toughs.' He laughed at his humour and Doyler nodded his head. 'Hasn't the Castle called me in special to discuss the matter. Down this way you say?'

'Over the river and right by the bank.' A group of cavalry officers was strolling up with their judies on their arms. It wasn't only peelers Doyler had to look out for. He'd often be dodging the canes of the military.

'Jim will be delighted now that I met you. Have you any message at all?'

The officers passed under the portico. Doyler held up his paper for them to read. The canes swaggered. One of the lady-friends looked back amused. 'I don't know now, Mr Mack.'

'Will I say you're looking fine and smart, and that'll do?'

He stared after the officers. 'Tell him I'm a Citizen soldier.'

'Citizen soldier,' repeated Mr Mack. Doyler felt him, in girth and circumstance like a peeler himself, looking gravely down at him. 'Is that what this uniform is about?'

'That I'm in the Citizen Army and I'm under orders.'

'I was wondering what was this you was caught up in. Are you sure now you know what you're about, young man?'

483

'Mr Mack, I tell no lie, but I've known since before I can remember that this was what I wanted.'

'Well now.' There was a genuine concern in his big round face. He had his hand in his pocket.

'Ah no,' said Doyler, 'I couldn't take that.'

'Take heed of an old soldier now. You won't never fill a tunic without a good feed first. Get along and get something to eat. Something with peas. You're not getting your greens at all, by the looks. I know you're a sound man for a lend.'

'All right, Mr Mack, I will so, and I'll have it back—'

'Don't be in any hurry about that.' Doyler was looking down at the money. He felt Mr Mack's hand on his shoulder. 'You know now with your folks gone and all, you might kip down the night at home with us. If you wanted to get out of this, a moment even. Jim would go crackers to see you.'

'That's kind of you, Mr Mack.'

'Mind now, I mean it.'

'Thanks for that, Mr Mack.'

'Not a word.'

Doyler wandered back to Liberty Hall. A couple of kidgers, seeing him in uniform, play-marched beside him. He felt lonely in himself, very lonely in the tenement-shadowed streets. The guard at the door told him he was wanted above. It was his captain. 'I hear you were trying to get yourself arrested again, Private Doyle.'

'I was trying to sell the paper, sir.' He'd sometimes get this off the officers, a carpeting for selling in the main thoroughfares. But Doyler couldn't see much use selling to people who wanted to read the paper. It was the people who didn't, or didn't know they wanted, you had to catch. Else you was talking to yourself.

'When will you learn, Doyle, that there is such a thing as a revolutionary moment. And that moment will not be decided by a harum-scarum hothead getting himself arrested for selling without a licence and answering the police in Irish.'

'Yes, sir.'

'Good. They tell me you've been looking for a gun.'

'I believe I've paid up regular as the next man.'

The captain was writing on a slip of paper. 'We had a shout from one of our people. Volunteers are shifting pieces down Ferns way. Our man thinks there might be one goes missing first. You up for that?'

'From under the nose of the Volunteers? Too right I am.'

The paper slid over the table. Doyler picked it up, but before he could read the captain had it plucked away again.

'You're a puzzle to me, son. I think you'd prefer a rifle off the Volunteers than off the constabulary. Or off of the British Army even.'

'Maybe I would.'

'The Volunteers are our friends now. You want to remember that.'

'Then why am I pinching a gun from them?'

His captain watched him a moment. He gave the paper back. 'Could be some of them are more friendly than others. Dismissed.'

MacMurrough rapped on the door of a shed. An inquiry was hailed and he answered his name. Hurried movement inside, nails hammering into wood. Eventually bolts withdrew and the door opened a pinch. It was daylight outside, but whoever it was shone a hard torch in his face.

'All right.'

MacMurrough squeezed in the door. 'I understand you have a consignment for Ferns.'

'You're early.'

'Yes, we are rather. Less difficulty finding the place than anticipated.'

'We?'

'Yes, my aunt. She's waiting in her motor-car. Eveline MacMurrough.' He still had a hand at his head, shielding his eyes. 'Look here, is that light necessary?'

The torch flicked off, and MacMurrough saw it was indeed a gloomy interior. Sort of railway sort of shed. He believed he recognized the man. He had been one of the customers in that peculiar tobacconist's his aunt had recommended. With sly humour they had watched him, and with that same humour the man watched him now.

'I have the order checked for you,' he said. 'Glad to say everything present and accounted for.'

'Well, if you would point me to it, I shall be off.'

The man shone his torch on a bench at the back. There were three wooden boxes, long boxes marked crudely in red, *Piping*. It was evidently the lid of one of these MacMurrough had heard being hammered. 'Are they heavy?'

'I think you'll manage.'

MacMurrough humped them to the car, one at a time, lifting them over the Stepney wheel, and on to the rear seat.

'Do be careful, Anthony. If you only knew the bother they have caused getting them.'

'What are they, Aunt Eva? As though one couldn't guess.'

The man held the door while he returned for the last box. He was leaning to lift when he heard the distinct catch of a bolt pulled back. He quickly glanced. Poking from some crates, point blank, a rifle, aimed at him.

It was a situation in which only the rifle was familiar. A Mauser, MacMurrough noted, and an ancient one at that. He had frozen in mid-hump. He could make out hands, fingers, arms in the shadows, but no face. He saw the bolt lifted and pushed home. Snatch. The finger cocked. MacMurrough was thinking how extraordinary to be lured to this out-of-the-way place when she might have had him shot anywhere. The finger pressed. His eyes were closing. The finger pressed, till – crack. Fired dry. Nothing. The face lifted from the sights. White teeth, a chip off the middle, Doyler grinning from the dark.

MacMurrough threw the box in the back of the car. 'Drive,' he told his aunt.

'I had every intention.'

'Now. Get us out of here.'

They were out of the docks area and its wretched slums, and people in the streets had ceased pointing at the lovely motor. MacMurrough's fright communicated in a resentment toward his aunt. 'Really, Aunt Eva, you cannot continue in this way. I will not tolerate any more these manipulations. If you wish me to run guns with you, have the decency to ask. You must surely know by now I am entirely under your thumb.'

'I really don't think—'

'No, you really do not think. When will you learn that rifles are dangerous toys? Most especially in the hands of children.'

'I really don't think,' Eveline repeated, 'those constables ahead are directing traffic.'

MacMurrough looked. They had crossed the river and were coming towards Trinity. The flow of traffic had slowed almost to a standstill. Four policemen advanced down the line. They carried carbines. 'No,' he agreed. 'They are checking the vehicles.'

'We have been betrayed.'

'How can you know that?' But already he was thinking: Doyler. Stupid vindictive renter. I'll wring his neck for him.

'Perhaps now you will understand the need for secrecy.' She

pulled out her travelling-glass and actually checked her face powder.

'Turn the car,' said MacMurrough.

'There are more behind. And if I judge by their absurd hats, two plain-clothes government men.'

MacMurrough turned. They were there. The traffic was stopped both directions. Hopefully he threw a rug over the boxes. They looked like three boxes of rifles with a rug on top. The traffic inched them to discovery.

'You must take this.'

'I don't want it. What is it?' It was her Webley of course. 'Aunt Eva, I can't start shooting people.'

'Whatever happens, they must not get the rifles. I have bartered half my jewels and all of my influence for these rifles. I accepted nothing shoddy or made-in-Birmingham. These are German rifles.' Bloody vintage ones at that, MacMurrough might have told her. 'They must go to Ferns. They are nine, which minus the one the Citizen Army will have filched makes eight. We cannot proceed without them.'

'We cannot proceed at all.'

She put her glass away. 'Hold tight,' she said. 'If I am hit, you may need to take the wheel.'

'Be careful! What are you doing?'

'The back of my hand to caution.'

The engine raced, she loosed the clutch, the car slammed into the motor in front. Reverse now, and she smashed into the lorry behind. MacMurrough put a hand to his face, smirking behind it, more in shame than in fear. Slam into the front again, smash behind, till she made a clearance. The police were running. The Webley slipped to the floor. He bent to retrieve it and heard a singing noise pass where his head had been. Now they were wildly into the middle road where they slithered

488

over the tram-lines. The policemen in front were kneeling to fire. 'Shoot!' she called. 'Before they shoot us, damn you!' He fired aimlessly, but it scattered the men. They veered crazily between two trams. She flung the car into a dizzy turn while sliding along the seat, virtually into MacMurrough's lap. They scraped through the opposing traffic. Stalls were overturned, he caught the briefest whiff of oranges. Shots fired after them. They were down some side street, up another, safe.

'Where are we?'

'Temple Bar.'

'Aunt Eva, you are indisputably a wonder.'

'We must thank goodness for the Wide Street Commissioners. Except my poor Prince Henry—'

Some bowler-hatted ass stepped into the road. He looked for all the world to be studying the tops of buildings.

'My God,' she said. She swerved, but to avoid him she must mount the pavement. She rounded the corner and, watching it coming, smashed into the corner lamppost.

She shook herself. But she could not shake herself free. She heard the tramp of boots behind. Her nephew stupidly talking to her.

'Go,' she said.

'I can't without you.'

'I cannot shift my legs.'

'I must fetch an ambulance.'

'I don't need an ambulance. I need my nephew to go. Go to Ferns. Everything is prepared for you.' In her agitation she was thumping the horn. 'Will you go! Please, for my sake.'

He was walking backwards from the car. The pain was in her back. She was passing out but she could not afford to fall yet. Go, you fool. The police were nearly upon her. She pushed on the horn. Go, Anthony, go. He turned on his heels, running, and her eyes in redness closed.

Mr Mack arrived seconds before the constabulary men. 'Officers, officers, I saw everything. I was only looking for the street name—'

'Did you see a man get out?'

'I did, officer. He went off towards Trinity. I can explain all. I was only looking for the street name. I never heard a whisper till—Why, I do believe it's Madame MacMurrough it is.'

'You know this woman?'

Mr Mack watched the posse of officers charging entirely the opposite direction for Trinity. 'Where are they going?' he asked.

'You said Trinity. Now do you know this lady?'

Mr Mack's eyes skewed east and west. 'Which way, your honour, would you say Trinity was?'

It took the better part of three hours, but Mr Mack at last found his way, courtesy of the Dublin Metropolitan Police, to Dublin Castle. While he was being led through the courtyard to the DMP office, there to explain why he had aided a fugitive in escaping the law, from a window above two splendid officers of the crown, in scarlet undress and blue undress, contemplated the scene.

'Hmm,' said the lieutenant in blue.

'Well, it doesn't look as if our man will show,' said the captain. He sat down, angling his chair on its two back legs

'Hmm,' said the lieutenant again. 'What is this Georgius Rex anyway?'

'Load of codgers. Make tea mostly for the troops.'

'What's a Sinn Feiner want joining that for?'

'Rifle,' said the captain. 'We let them march with Martinis once a month.'

'Oh,' said the lieutenant blandly. 'Dublins, wasn't he?'

'Quartermaster-Sergeant, it says. Turned tail in the Boer War.'

'What sort of a rotter leaves his regiment in a wartime?'

'Yes, I thought we'd have some fun with that.'

'I was chatting with one of these Dublins. Do you know, he actually considered there was a history attached to the Irish regiments.'

'Mercenaries, weren't they, out in India. John Company.'

'Chap actually believed they had some claim to honour.'

'Interesting.'

'I thought it damnable strange. I say, here's a poser. Which is better for officer training: polo or hunting?'

'That is a poser. Polo or hunting. Very good indeed. I'll have to think that one out.'

The lieutenant looked at his finger nails. 'It is a bore.'

The captain, whose scarlet was just that shade too noisy for the lieutenant's liking, clapped the four legs of his chair on the floor. 'You can come to enjoy it after a while. Keeping a tab on the buggers.'

'They're all pro-German. We should shoot the leaders, pack the rest off to France. In my opinion, there is too much kid-gloving in this country.'

'Oh, it won't come to shooting people. And if it does, we can leave that safely to the Irish. You surely know the one thing they hate more than us English.'

'Well, it ain't porter and it ain't German gold.'

'It's an Irishman with the pluck to stand up to us.'

The captain laughed and the lieutenant eyed him with distaste. He did not rate the man's tailor at all.

*

491

Doyler woke with a start. His rifle had slipped from his hands. He looked about him. For a moment he couldn't work out where he was. The stars gleamed above. Liberty Hall of course, on the roof, on guard detail. He picked up his rifle. He pulled the bolt back and fingered the chamber. But of course there was no cartridge inside. He blessed himself, despising the urge. It was the night of Good Friday.

The week had run with rumour. The British were to raid all centres. The British were to seize all arms. Any name on the nationalist side was to be taken and imprisoned. The Archbishop himself was to be imprisoned. The guard at Liberty Hall was doubled, then trebled, round the clock. It was known the Volunteers had manoeuvres planned for Easter Sunday. Their leaders were every day and night at the Hall, the lights in Connolly's office burnt late. It was joked they were promoting each other to generals and admirals. Then Doyler received his orders. Special mobilization – all ranks with equipment and two days' rations – Liberty Hall, Sunday at three. So it was settled. Easter Sunday it was. He went to his officers and asked for extra duties. They gave him guard detail at the Hall, thankful enough for his offer. He was not sure could he trust himself without keeping busy.

He smelt a cigarette smoke from over the roof. If he listened, he could hear the other lads chatting. Those things you talked about on guard detail, Mr Mack sort of things. What's this is the Latin for candle. Name the states of America. They hadn't ought to be chatting at all. He sat down with his rifle on his lap.

Muster at three at Liberty Hall. There was an unreal quality to the words. Muster, liberty. Two days' rations – were they mad? Where was he supposed to find two days' rations? Easter Sunday – on this day she rose again, Ireland. It was too far-stretched. Far too stretched to be frightened about it.

But there it was: he was frightened. And it had come as such a revelation, he had wanted to stop people he knew in the street. You'll never guess – I'm not brave at all. Now he hugged his rifle while away behind a Protestant bell struck midnight. Easter Saturday already. The cold metal of his gun warmed where he touched. When he touched again it had chilled.

He remembered how Connolly had addressed the army. Any man with doubts should leave now, he told them. Let another stand in his place. There would be no recriminations. Only let him go now. Not a man had moved.

But in the pause, Doyler had imagined himself to leave. He dropped his rifle, he tossed his hat. Out the door and his tunic shrugged from him, down the steps and he shook from his boots and his trousers. Then he ran, naked he ran, where to? The river, he leapt from the quay to the river. The tide carried him, the darkly-going green, where did it carry him? To the blue, to the sea, swimming to the sea.

He slept late the Saturday morning. He had no duties, but he dressed in his uniform and made a parcel of his working clothes. He must go see his mother. He set off for King Street. The city was half alive again after the grim and shuttered Friday. Then he thought he'd please her by getting confession first. Any number of chapels beckoned, but he couldn't make up his mind. In the end he met his mother in the street. She took him home through the markets where the knowledge and sight and stink of death assaulted him. She gave him red tea and he gave her what he had, which was his working clothes and one and fourpence.

'You'll be going to Glasthule,' she said. He didn't answer and she looked bothered at him. 'And you with swimming for Easter?'

'I have me duties tomorrow.'

'Don't we all have duties?'

493

'I'm not talking about making the tea, Ma. This is my country.'

'What country is that without a friend in it? When you go to Glasthule say to Mr Mack he might come in soon.'

'Himself?'

She nodded. 'Go in now,' she said, 'and make your peace with your father.'

'What father is that?'

'He gave you a name, son, when there was no call on him. He gave you a name and a home when you had none before. For no better than I married him, speak your peace.'

He threw the dregs of his cup in the back of the fire. 'Wasn't I intending to anyway?' he said. But he didn't move, and he said, 'Ma, do you remember, Ma, when I stole the pig's cheek?'

'I don't.'

'Out of the butcher's barrel. Do you not remember that? I had it hid under me coat running home. The brine was dripping and it took the dye out of the coat where I hid it. You must remember that, Ma?'

'I don't, son.'

'You took it off me then and you cooked it. You had me sit to table with this pig's cheek in front of me. And I kept telling you, Ma, I got it for all of us, yourself and the girls and himself even. You wouldn't hear of it. Sat me down with the knife and a fork to eat it by meself. Himself came home and you hid it away. He was angry smelling meat and no dinner. He left in a black rage and you brung it out again, the pig's cheek. I wasn't let go till I had it ate, the plate of it. I remember the girls was looking at me. But you said I was hungry, I must eat it all.'

'You was often hungry, son.'

'Then you took me down the butcher's after, and I waited while you paid for it. Paid for it. I watched the coppers going in

494

the butcher's hand. I remember how thirsty I was. And I knew then you'd have no supper that night. The girls would have no supper. I was so thirsty after the brine and me mouth all greasy from me eating. And them coppers going one upon the other into the butcher's hand. Don't you remember that, Ma?'

'I remember you did always come home with the pennies you earned. I don't remember any pig's cheek.'

'Oh, Ma, I wanted to do some good always. I never did it the right way, sure I didn't?'

'You were a great good to me, son. You are yet.'

'But I wanted to be needed, Ma. You would never let on you needed me. You don't need me now, sure you don't, Ma?'

She put her hand to his head. 'A cheann dubh dhílis,' she said, 'my black-headed boy. Don't you know 'tis loving I have, not needing. God send one day you'll be happy with that.'

He had fallen forward from the chair, and he laid his head on her breast, wrapping his arms tightly round her waist.

'Aren't you desperate scared?' she said. 'My Lady of the Wayside, for the sake of the child You hold in Your arms, take hold the hand of my boy and he going.'

He left soon after. Still dragged the day. He could not think what to do with it. At the pro-Cathedral he looked in at the confessions. The lines snaking from the confessionals were close-packed with uniformed men. The light green and the dark green intermingled, Volunteers and Citizen soldiers, already in prayer the one army. It made him think of laughing, the first in a while. What need had the Castle of spies and informers? In Ireland, if you would know was a rising due, look no farther than the Saturday confessions.

He had stopped inside the door. Now the voices gathered about him, male voices groaning their sins to their beads in their hands. The votary candles flickered, yellow and blue and red,

495

shedding no light only telling the dark about them. The statues all were draped still. A finger poked starkly out of one of them.

He thought of himself at home, when he had looked in on him behind his screen, his stepfather. He was more dead than living now, but still he clung on. Doyler had opened his hand and placed a plug of tobacco there. To chew, he told him, then pointed to his mouth, Chew. The fingers closed on his own fingers, and Doyler had felt them pulling him down. Sweet Jesus, but that man clung to life. And Doyler understood that. He too would cling to life. That life which all his thinking years he had dreamt to spend in a magnificent cause. He'd take this miserable existence instead. He would too. He'd never live with himself, but he'd take it, and hate himself ever on. Jesus, I'm too coward to turn back even.

He turned on his heel. He must go to Jim. Even while he thought this, he did not believe it. He was making for the Russell Hotel. Across the river, past Trinity, up Grafton Street to the Green. He sent in a note. It seemed he must wait an age before the coach-house door would open. He followed the boots up the stairs. He stood on the bed-frame and slid the skylight open. He stepped back. He hadn't spoken a word to the boots. Now he just nodded for him to go first. The boots did as told. Then Doyler pulled himself out and replaced the skylight. He led the boots creeping along to the pit where two roofs pitched. The boots kept his back to him. Doyler didn't know was he shy or ashamed. He didn't care. He pressed up behind, he had his hands at the boy's buttons undoing them. The black trousers came down, he tugged at the drawers. He had himself unbuttoned now. He lifted the tail of the boy's shirt. He kept one hand on his back pushing down, the other round his waist. The boots staggered to his hands and knees. Doyler too went down on his knees where the surface scraped his skin. He spat and rubbed his spittle in. He pushed. He pushed till it hurt but he could gain no way. He took a hand to aim but still he could do nothing. He rammed against the stupid flesh. He took hold of the boots with his hands on his thighs and tugged him backward. He could do nothing. He could not even do this.

'Christ almighty,' he cursed, 'ain't you use for nothing?'

He gave a mighty shove at the boots who tottered forward. He leant back on his hunkers. The boots was sniffing back his sobs. His fingers pulled at his drawers, his trousers. Crouching the way he was he couldn't get his shirt tucked in.

'What are you snivelling for anyway? Isn't that what you wanted?'

'You didn't need to be so rough.'

'You want to see me rough? Throw you off the roof, then you'll know me rough all right.'

'You didn't have to be rough with me.'

'Ah will you shut your snivel. What manner of a man are you I don't know. Right sheela.'

He still hadn't turned round. He was still kneeling, fumbling with his shirt and holding his trousers up the same time.

'Ah lookat here,' said Doyler exasperated. 'Turn round for God's sake till I sort you out.'

He didn't turn but he let Doyler coax him round. Doyler pulled the trousers down. He straightened the shirt tail, then pulled the trousers up properly, buttoning the waistband. 'You can do the rest for yourself,' he told him. 'Have you a handkerchief?' Not looking he nodded. Doyler found it in his pocket. 'Go on now, blow your nose.'

He blew his nose, but he didn't wipe his eyes, which were red and sore-looking.

'I'm sorry, all right? I've said I'm sorry now.'

Again the boy nodded.

'I didn't do nothing anyway. I didn't hurt you.'

'I thought you'd be friendly.'

'Lookat I have a friend already.'

'You didn't do that to him.'

'No I didn't.'

'You did it to me though.'

'I said I'm sorry. You can hit me if you want.'

'Don't want to hit you.'

'You can sit down anyway, can't you?'

The boots sat down, sliding against the tiles till he was hunched like Doyler.

'Listen to me,' said Doyler. 'I have me friend. Least I think I do. And I wanted to be with him.'

'Why wouldn't you go there then?'

'I don't know why.'

'You're scared to,' the boots said and sniffed.

'Blow your nose,' said Doyler. He watched him blow his nose. 'That's better, isn't it? It's better when you blow your nose.'

'You're scared he won't be your friend no more.'

Yes, he was scared. He was scared to be with Jim. And he wanted to hold him. He wanted so much just his arm round his neck. But he didn't know could he be trusted. If he made Jim do what he made this boy do. And worse if Jim would let him.

'Do you miss him?'

Doyler sighed, and with that breath spilt all the tide of his loneliness and fears. 'I miss him, aye,' he said. 'He was pal o' me heart, so he was. I try not to think of him, only I can't get him off my mind. He's with me always day and night. I do see him places he's never been, in the middle of a crowd I see him. His face looks out from the top of a tram, a schoolboy wouldn't pass but I'm thinking it's him. I try to make him go away, for I'm a soldier now and I'm under orders. But he's always there and I'm desperate to hold him. I doubt I'm a man except he's by me.'

'Maybe he misses you too. I'd miss you was you my friend.'

Doyler patted his knee, that could never be more than bones to him.

'What scares me most,' said the boots, 'is not that I'll be hit or they'll hate me. I'm scared if I wouldn't find anyone. I can't help looking, can I?'

'No, you do right to look.' Doyler stood up. 'I'm going to Kingstown.'

'Good luck,' he said.

'You know now you can still hit me if you want?'

'I never wanted to hit you.'

'Sure I know you didn't. If I thought you did, I wouldn't offer it.' He held out his hand to give the boots a pull up.

'I still like you,' he said.

'Ah come here to me,' said Doyler, 'you old wirrasthrue thing.'

He went back to the widow woman's room and took his rifle from the rafters. He'd take that in case, but his equipment could wait till tomorrow. To hell with his guard duty. They'd get some other jasus to guard their Hall for them. It was a long journey on foot, seven miles. It was raining hard when he got to Kingstown. He had his rifle in a brown-paper parcelling. By Glasthule the paper was sogging away. He passed between chapel and college. He found he was walking more briskly. He had a spring in his step. He turned up Adelaide Road. He was running now. Sprinting and scarce a falter of his leg. The months fell with his feet till it was only a day since last they swam. He spun into the lane, splashing in puddles. The door pushed and the bell clinked. Jim was behind the counter. He looked up. His smile had been practising all day. Doyler held out his rifle in one hand and his bush-hat in the other. 'What cheer, eh?' he said.

CHAPTER EIGHTEEN

D OYLER HAD THE salt and he was offering it round the table. 'Salt?' he said to Jim. The words wouldn't form on Jim's lips. He felt his face stupid with smiles, but his face wouldn't brook their interruption. 'Will I leave a pinch of it anyway?' Jim nodded and a white scruple formed on his plate.

'Elbows, Jim,' said his father. 'You don't see Doyler with his elbows on the table.'

His father sat with the bread before him, his face significant, sleeves hitched up, slicing. Jim heard Nancy laughing into Doyler's ear, 'Would think 'twas the Christmas goose to be carved.' He watched Doyler dip in his egg. The spoon paused before his mouth and he glanced over, the way Jim had called him to look. The dark gleamed in his eyes, and they collusive, full of meaning. Jim felt his own quicken in response. Doyler grinned, the spoon in his mouth. A boot reached under the table and rubbed Jim's shin. He thought his smile then would leap the plates to hit Doyler smack on the cheek. It had been this way since he arrived. Scarce a word between them, what conversation they had in gestures – a shake, a shrug, the cock of a query; smiles, their thieving eyes.

Meanwhile Jim's father made talk and Doyler politely earned

his tea. No, Mr Mack, he had never stepped inside of the Castle. True to be sure, Dublin was notorious for losing your way in it. Italy joins Austria? No, he hadn't heard that. Certainly, that was a grave development. Oh yes, he saw it now. On the map, yes. That was a good one, Mr Mack. Italy joins Austria. No, he never thought of that. Sure why not, send it in, the papers might publish it.

The tea things came and went, sparingly with Lent. At last the table was cleared and Jim might leave his elbows legitimately there. He rested his chin in the crook of his hands, watchful and listening. The fire spat at the hearthrug. Long time ago he would used curl on that rug, a ball of pinky heat, while the furniture winked and tall shadows peopled the walls. Then, like now, though he had not then the words to describe it, he was aware of his detachment, of his being a witness to the moment, witness not participant. Now, in a lazy way, he was pleased to remain so, these last few hours, a time yet. His feet pressed against the bench he sat on which later they'd pull out for their bed.

Doyler had little Estella on his lap, and he was dandling her up and down, asking her, riddling, 'Will I tell you a story of Johnny Magorey? Will I begin it? That's all that's in it.'

Jim's father said, 'I believe there are two flutes here some-wheres about. Are you with us at all there, Jim?'

'What, Da?'

'I said we have two flutes here somewheres.'

'Yes,' said Jim. 'I kept your flute for you.'

'Sure I knew you would.'

Jim showed it down from the press, casually, and busied himself with his own, piecing the sections. Hours of work that flute had cost him. Cleaning the years of use from the finger-holes, new-twining the tenons, oiling the brittle from the wood, shining away till he found its yellow gleam; and all the while testing to be sure of the tone, bright and near silvery in the high Ds, dark and warm in the low. Doyler gave out a scale. He said something. Jim shied his head. 'Oh well sure,' he muttered.

'Slipjigs,' called Doyler. He rapped on the floor, one two three, and off they flew, spattering the dew. Nancy tapped on the tiles, Estella jogged on her lap. His father called up the stairs, 'Are you all right with the rattle, Aunt Sawney?' 'Way with you!' they heard her back. They had the dew nicely spattered: on they played. It was a puzzle how they agreed the tunes, but a glance to Doyler and Doyler would nod, and their fingers leapt to the change. The night came down and the fire gathered them round. They slowed to airs. Doyler's eyes glimmered in their corners, watching him. Jim closed his own and he heard the notes, how they found themselves, as once Doyler had told they would. He heard them drifting above, their harmonies, shifting in the draughts of the fire; with the smoke they lifted, up up above, in modes he did not know the names of them, aloft and adrift in the night and the stars.

'You been practising,' said Doyler.

Jim nodded.

Nancy said, 'Now then, Mr Mack, will we leave these two dotes to themself a while?'

'Already?' said his father. 'And I was only thinking I'd fetch the spoons.'

''Tis Lent a while yet,' she said, 'and Our Lord still in the tomb.'

There was admonishment in her tone and Jim saw his father glance to the walls the way he'd hear the neighbours malavoguing his house. 'Bed so,' he said.

Nancy was away up the stairs. His father went out the yard – 'The inconvenience,' he said with a wink to Doyler. They were alone a moment. Doyler bent down for a heat off the fire. He looked over at Jim. 'You've a spot on your chin,' he said.

'So have you. You have three growing.'

He laughed and Jim laughed too. Jim finished with the flutes, running a cloth through the sections. He said, 'I didn't expect you'd be in a uniform.'

Doyler stood straight and squared his shoulders. 'Am I handsome or what?'

'Throwing shapes, so you are.'

'And yourself in your breeches. They're gone too small for you now.'

Jim lowered his head, feeling the passage of Doyler's eyes. His hand smoothed the crease of his knee, wet from the flute. Doyler said, 'But I always preferred you in your breeches.'

Jim peeked up through the strands of his hair. 'You never told me that before.'

'Did I not? I might have.' Doyler rubbed his nose, finger and thumb, like a snuffers. 'Lookat, I'll go back into town. I'll be out again tomorrow, promise.'

'You said you'd be staying.'

'I'm saying I could go back. If you wanted like.'

'Don't be saying that, Doyler. You wouldn't leave now.'

'No.' Again he fretted with his nose. 'Where'd you stow me rifle anyway?'

'It's safe,' said Jim. 'Help me out with the bed.'

His father returned, making low inward mouth-music. He played with lighting his candle while they undressed to their shirts. They climbed in the bed, head and toe, and his father said, 'What's this, no prayers?' They had to climb out again and kneel on the floor. Doyler hid a claub of laughing behind his hands. Jim blessed himself and they clambered once more in the bed.

'Goodnight so, boys. Sure you won't stay awake gostering all hours?'

'No, Da.'

'Goodnight, Mr Mack, and thanks now.'

'Not a word.'

The gas came down, the stairs door closed. Jim heard the steady tramp above, the weary grievance of his father's bed. The legs beside him stretched and he squinched up by the wall to make room. Out from the dark Doyler said, 'Your feet'll froze me. And you know what? They smell and all.'

'Yours are no soap.'

The covers threw back and Doyler's shirt was shimmering by the window. The blind eased up. 'There's no moon,' he said, 'but it's better open.' He knelt there a moment. He appeared to rise in the air: it was his shirt pulling off. 'Shift over,' he said. Feet travelled Jim's legs in drifts of warm and ice, then Doyler lay beside. He pinched Jim's shirt. 'Take it off.'

Jim pulled the shirt over his head. When he lay back, Doyler's arm was waiting on the pillow. It turned him in its hold. 'Now we're settled,' Doyler said.

'We are too.'

'You don't mind?'

'No, it's lovely.'

He cuddled over Doyler's chest. His head lifted and dropped with each breath. He listened to the pump of the heart. His hand had fallen on Doyler's side. Now he strayed it up his arm, fingering the hairs in the sneak of his armpit, then up along the shoulder. There was a feeling in this touch, yellow and soft, that was very like the colour of candle-light. He found the leather string round Doyler's neck, and he traced it along, on past his scapular, till he touched the half of a medal.

'It's there,' said Doyler, 'never fear.'

'Sure I knew that.'

Then Jim was telling, he didn't know why, about the flag he had made. A green flag, he had it stitched himself out of an old cloth. And he'd fashioned a kind of a strap to carry it on his back with. He'd tried it swimming and you wouldn't hardly notice it in the way. Had Doyler forgot? The flag was for the patriots Gidley and MacKinley. To claim the Muglins for Ireland.

Doyler was huffing away. 'What's funny?' asked Jim.

'I know a pole too we can hang it from.'

Jim felt a tug on him below and his breath came murmuring out. He had to take another breath the further to let it murmur.

Doyler creaked round to face him. 'It's a tiny bed,' he said.

'I can make more room.'

'No, it's a tiny bed not to be friendly in it.' He pulled Jim closer and pressed against him. 'Sure you don't mind?'

'It's lovely, Doyler.'

'I wouldn't want you having any doubts.'

It streamed out of Jim then. Oh sure he knew that, he had no doubt about that, all along he never doubted, leastways he believed he knew, save he couldn't see it back last summer, he was scared then, but he wasn't scared now, he had longed for it to be this way, and how could it be any different, it was never a case of whether, only of when or who first, weren't they made to be this way—

'Shut up,' said Doyler. 'Case of whether—You're giving me earache.' He pulled Jim closer again. And it was strange being there, not strange with Doyler, but with this other thing that shared their bed and bumped against Jim at times, expected of course, but in physicality an astonishing event. Doyler laughed into his ear, 'You know, with your pole and mine, never mind a flag, we could hang our washing out.'

Jim turned on his belly.

'No use turning your back, Jim Mack. Your back's as good as your front is to me.'

'I'm not shy,' said Jim. 'Only if you touch me again—'

'Come here to me, you gaum.'

'No,' said Jim. 'No,' he said again. 'I mean, Doyler, don't.' The shape that had crouched above him stiffened. 'No?'

'We can't.'

A moment. 'Will they hear us above?'

'It's not that.'

A moment again. 'Don't you want me, Jim?'

Jim reached his hands to Doyler's shoulders. 'Don't you know we have to wait till the island?'

A long while then while Doyler arched over him. The thin light of night, and of vigil and embers, found the outline of his face. Then he lay down stiff in the space beside. He took a breath.

'Lookat Jim, I never swum to the Muglins that time. What happened I was swept out one day. I was struggling like mad to keep afloat even. Only for a launch chancing by I don't doubt I'd be drownded. I'm sorry for leading you on. I did it by reason I wanted to swim with you. I wanted to be with you that way. Do you hear me?'

'Yes.'

'And about them fellows with the flag. They was never patriots. They was robbers and murderers. They was no better than pirates. And me leg too, Jim. I never hurt that in the Lock-out. That was himself at home did that.'

'Is that it?'

'That's it. I'm sorry now. But you can't swim to the Muglins. It's too tough a stretch.'

'You can so swim there,' said Jim. 'I know for I swum half-way and back.'

'You did?'

'I did, last week. And I had enough in me to swim it again the same time.'

Doyler let a low whistle. 'Me life on you, Jim, but you're the man if you did.'

'And I know about the pirates for I spoke with men at the Forty Foot and they only laughed at my story. That doesn't signify. We still have the Muglins to claim for Ireland and that's why I made the flag. About the leg I guessed, for you was either in Clare or in Dublin, you couldn't be both. Now listen to me. We'll swim to the island tomorrow. We have that pledged and we can't go back on a pledge. You're not forgetting we spat on it?'

'I'm not forgetting we spat on it.'

'Well then. If you never been there, that's all the better. It was a thing that muddled me that you swum there already. It's clearer now. It'll be us two together, out there in the sea. We have to go, because in a way, you see, we'll always be there.'

'We will?'

'No one will take it from us. Even you can't nor I can't. That's why we'll swim.'

'When did you work this out?'

Jim heard the tone in Doyler's voice. He heard himself sound strangely too. 'I've been thinking is all.'

'You been talking to MacMurrough?'

'We go swimming all right.'

Doyler scratched his arm. 'You like him?'

'I do.'

'I suppose and he told you about them Spartans?'

'A thousand and one things he told me. You wouldn't know where he was coming from half the time. Spartans, Alexander the Great, the Sacred Band of Thebes. Even the Gaels, that they had a ceremony, two men if they loved each other.'

'What ceremony?'

'A blessing. Before a priest and all. Christian priest.'

'I wouldn't fancy the blessing we'd get off that curate if he catched us now.'

'MacEmm says there's more things happened already than ever you'd dream of to come. MacMurrough: I call him MacEmm.'

'I don't like him.'

'You had a barney is all. Friends can't fall out that way. You'll make up, you'll see.'

'Has he been saying things about me?'

'Only things I asked him. Don't worry about that now. Haven't you me with you now?'

'I think I have.'

'Hold me so,' said Jim. He lifted Doyler's arm and snook in under it. He bundled himself small the closer to be held. He felt a great emulsive flow of love, all the truer for his needing no arm to hold him. The parts had shifted. He felt the marvel of his will that had brought Doyler to him this night. Doyler had not understood about the island. But that would come. Doyler had nothing to fear. Jim would swim him to the Muglins, he would swim him home again. There was no end to the swimming they would do.

He was coming on to yawn. His breath sucked in the draught from the window. His shoulders hunched, his legs stretched to their toes, he made claws of his fingers in his hands – a fierce pandiculation of his limbs. This is my body. See how it fits. Everything fits. I am a finely tailored flesh. He arched his groin. Feel this, my stand. Its throb alone would fetch it. His breath streamed out. The magnificence of my chest.

'You yawning?' asked Doyler.

Jim flung himself on top like a coil released. He crushed his body upon Doyler's, each muscle straining to bear and be known. He caught Doyler's arms and reached them wide, spreading his legs with his own between. He pressed his groin, flesh upon flesh, upon Doyler's groin, hub of their wheel.

'Whoa,' said Doyler. 'What's brought this on now?'

'Tell me if you love me.'

'All right, I love you.'

'Tell me again. Keep telling me.'

'I love you, Jim.'

'And why wouldn't you love me? Amn't I all you wanted? Amn't I all of it yours?'

He nuzzled his head in the pillow. He had released Doyler's hands and they enfolded him now. They seemed so big of a sudden. 'Doyler,' he said, and of that same sudden his voice sounded small and quavery. 'Doyler . . . what and we don't make the island?'

'But we will sure. That spit of a swim, we'll easy make it.'

'I know we will. We can't drown anyway. The wars are coming and we need to be fighting for Ireland.'

Doyler said nothing, only patted his shoulder, and after a time, Jim said, 'I'm sleepy.'

'Sleep so,' Doyler told him. Jim turned on his side, pulling an arm with him so that Doyler spooned beside, holding the arm to him, while his eyes closed, surely and immaterially to sink him in sleep.

But Doyler did not sleep. He lay on his lump of pillow, watching the night that gaped at the window. His arm moved up and down with Jim's breathing, wisps of Jim's hair tickled his face. Old pal o' me heart. Indeed it was true, the wars were coming, and already far over the seas where the world turned, the sun was creeping up the sky.

And high and bright and clear it shone, early next morning

509

when they stepped out to Mass. Outside the chapel, all along the railings, newspaper placards had been posted. 'What does it mean?' asked Jim.

'Manoeuvres cancelled, it says,' said Doyler.

'I know, but what does that mean?'

'I don't know for sure.' Two young Volunteers were standing about reading an *Independent*. Doyler wandered up. 'What's going on?' he asked.

They looked him over in his Citizen rig. 'Manoeuvres cancelled,' they said.

'You telling me the Volunteers has funked it?'

'We haven't funked nothing, pal. Orders came in the night.'

'That's right,' said the other. 'We'll be off to the races now.'

These were Volunteers out of Dalkey. They wouldn't know much about any rising planned. 'Can I have a read of it?' Doyler took the paper. 'No Parades!' said the headline. 'Volunteer Marches Cancelled. A Sudden Order'.

'What does it mean?' said Jim, coming impatient.

'I'll tell you what it means. It means we're free.'

'Ireland?'

'Where would you go with Ireland? We are, you and me.' He still couldn't believe it. They had cancelled the rising. The last minute the Volunteers had lost their nerve. Didn't he know them for shapers? He was free of it all. He clapped Jim on the shoulders. 'We're in the swim!' he was saying.

Jim smiled uncertainly and the Volunteers looked on indulgently at this mad Citizen soldier who laughed out loud for liberty.

Saturday afternoon MacMurrough visited his aunt. She was kept under detention at the military hospital in Dublin Castle. Oddly enough he had not been questioned himself about the guns. A policeman had called to inform him of a regrettable accident involving his aunt. The next, a detective arrived inquiring about his residency in Ireland. So that was how they would play it. With that ball in the air, even if the swim had not been tomorrow, he should be leaving on the Monday. Gruesome to travel on a bank holiday, but such were the exigencies of wartime. Mailboat to Holyhead, train to somewhere in the Midlands. Nottingham, he thought. Is Nottingham in the Midlands? Fuck my way to France.

While he waited to be shown to his aunt's ward, he became aware of the corridor's collection of war-wounded. Avoiding their faces, he glanced the more on their injuries. The different lengths of leg that might be cut off, how neat the tucks in armless tunics, in wheelchairs feet that pointed askew. He heard their unearthly banter: the races, the rain, Nurse O'Hara. He had a notion of his being naked in their presence, an urge to cover his exposure with his hands. How very much more precious was the body than the life. A ward door opened, a nurse came out: a glimpse beyond of unsayable distress. His hands in his pockets of their own accord moved to cover his balls. This too in France. The ward door creaked home, saying whyee, whyee, why.

Unlucky bastards. Unlucky to be in their presence.

At last his ticket was accepted and he was directed to his aunt's ward. He found her on a verandah overlooking the Castle gardens, arranged in a wicker bath-chair. The cuts to her face had all but healed, though a nasty bruising still showed at her forehead. She did not complain, but her posture told the pain of her back. A sergeant in scarlet attended her. One of his aunt's *coups de maîtresse*, so characteristic, had transformed this keeper into a family retainer. Shorty, she called him, on the grounds presumably of his being tall and burly. She conducted their relations in something of a music-hall turn.

MacMurrough kissed her. She said, 'Shorty, you will remember my nephew.'

'Yes, mum. Nephew, mum.'

'Did I mention he was a captain in the Volunteers?'

'Indominatably, mum.'

'He has resigned his commission.'

'Wise, mum.'

'It was hoped once upon a time he would lead the men of Ferns. Yes, in the rising that was to come. But there will be no rising, will there, Shorty?'

'Couldn't say so, mum.'

'Because they have taken Casement.'

MacMurrough asked for a private word, but this was not possible, indominatably not. He found a chair and brought it close. 'Aunt Eva, I am told they will put you under a ban from Ireland. You will have to remove to England.'

'Is that what you are told?' she said. 'I have been telling Shorty about Casement. Shorty never knew he was Irish, sure you didn't, Shorty?'

'Sir Roger, mum? English as roast beef.'

'There. Even our heroes must be English.'

'Aunt Eva, there are arrangements to be made.'

'They'll hang him,' she said. 'Won't they, Shorty, hang Casement?'

'Traitor, mum. Indominatably.'

MacMurrough sighed. He had as well ask or she might never drop it. 'Tell Aunt Eva, what is the news of Sir Roger?'

'Casement,' she corrected him. 'He has never liked to be Sir Rogered.' She waved at a newspaper, which told, blandly he thought, of an arms seizure in Kerry. But apparently Shorty had assured her it was all to do with Casement. Casement had been captured with the arms, he had been spirited through the Castle and already lay in chains in London. MacMurrough eyed Shorty, who might be on parade so inscrutable his demeanour. It occurred to him there might after all be a logic behind this tiresome double-turn.

Casement had brought an arms ship through the blockade, she told him, through the teeth of the British navy even, all the way from Germany he had brought it, to the coast of Kerry. 'He does this wonderful thing, this incredible thing for them. And what do the fools of Volunteers do? What do they do, Shorty?'

'Muck up, mum.'

'They muck bloody up. They couldn't get the arms to the beach even. These are the men who refused any assistance. A woman's use is a nurse and typewriter. Have they never looked at their wives? Have they not seen their mothers? They might try managing a household on these novel lines. We should have lunch for supper and come home without the kiddies. One wonders what they hope to do with the Poor Old Woman, after they have toasted her in exotic beverage. Throw her to the kitchens with the praties?'

'So the plans' – MacMurrough glanced to the sergeant – 'the plans are off?'

'He means the rising,' she told Shorty. 'How can there be a rising without arms? We shall be lucky if they riot. Certainly it will never come to a peace conference. Sure it will not, Shorty?'

'Couldn't say so, mum.'

'He can't say,' she said, 'but I know he agrees. You do, Shorty, I know you do.'

Shorty remained mum.

'Aunt Eva, this really is getting us nowhere.'

'No,' she agreed, 'it has got us nowhere at all. And now poor Casement must hang for it.'

She was gazing beyond the Castle walls at the soft-turned Dublin hills. It was raining there and soon the rain would fall on Dublin. Her chin was trembling and her lips quivered with words. He saw how creased and pale they were. 'He is the only man I ever thought was beautiful.'

MacMurrough was struck by her tone. 'Aunt Eva, I believe . . .' He took her hand, which felt cold in his. He believed there might be a tear in her eye.

'A beautiful man, Shorty, no?'

'Pleasant face, mum. Say so myself.'

'Never a mean turn in his heart. An utterly selfless man. The first I saw him, I was struck. I knew immediately I was in the presence of something extraordinary in our land. Something we had not seen in Ireland in the centuries. The soul shone through his face. Though you are to remember,' she said, aside to Shorty, 'he was not raised a Romanist.'

'Protestant, mum,' Shorty averred.

'It shone in his face, his soul, his rare and natural face. And I thought, there indeed stands an Irish gentleman.'

MacMurrough was overcome with compassion. 'I'm so sorry, Aunt Eva. You must fear so dreadfully for him.' He saw her mouth puckering, her eyes veiled with tears. Her hand was so cold. He stroked it. He could not bear to see her so wretched, nor suffer her heart, that proud thing, to be bared before this English yokel. 'Come, Aunt Eva, bid your man to leave us a moment. We'll talk alone. Truly I had no conception of your sensibilities in this matter.'

'No more you had. They teach little of the heart in the gutter.'

He was stung. He loosed her hand. She took it away.

'Well, the English have him now,' she said, 'and they will tear him to pieces. Hanging is the least they will do.'

'Now, mum,' said Shorty. MacMurrough watched him pat her shawl closer round her shoulders. 'Nip in the air, mum. Best turn in.'

He sought in the man's eye some collusion, a notice that they both were dealing with a woman distracted. Nothing. MacMurrough was excluded, entirely.

Still his aunt stared at the mountains. It might be her portrait she sat for. Then, in defiance, her hand flung out. 'Hang us and be damned,' she cried. 'It is too absurd to die of an influenza. Or of a Tuesday. Don't you think, Shorty?'

Shorty wheeled her round. 'Tricky business, 'flu, mum.'

MacMurrough said, 'Aunt Eva, you sting me and provoke me. I do not protest. I am too conscious of your pain. But you are misinformed, I find, of the gutter.'

'And what will you pretend to teach me?'

'Perhaps that, gutter or mountain, the heart breaks as surely.'

'Indeed. And now we discover your heart to be broken.'

'Perhaps it is. But it is proud too. There is a boy I love and his soul too shines in his face. Though it never may be, I am proud to love him.'

The bath-chair had stopped at the glass doors to the ward. His aunt did not look his way, only nodded her head. 'Well, Shorty,' she said at length, 'what do you make of that?'

'Smitten, mum. Happens.'

'And so you will go to the Front?'

'I will.'

How very old she did look, without powder or preparation. 'I think indeed you may begin to love. The heart must be proud to love. You shall have High Kinsella,' she added. 'I

515

have arranged that with your father. You may yet be The MacMurrough, and a poor MacMurrough you'd be without High Kinsella behind you.'

'It seems unlikely,' he answered, 'the world the way it is.'

'No,' she agreed. She said, with the merest interrogation, 'You shall be brave.'

'I hope to. I wasn't very brave with you in the car.'

She nodded. 'You will be brave. Sure he will, Shorty?'

'Indominatably, mum. A MacMurrough.'

That was the Saturday, a most dismal parting. MacMurrough made his way to Trinity, waited there for his tram. It came; he sat on the open upper tier, with the pipe-smokers and the spit. The fender grated on the setts, the trolley hissed above. Snatches of his interview with his aunt repeated, inducing involuntary musculations. *Conception of your sensibilities in this matter* – could he truly have said that? Words of a stiff. His hand went to his pocket, it came away empty: naturally he had forgotten the tobacconist's. The garish shine on his good brogues caught his eye: and he sighed. It was one of the trials of Dublin, that one mightn't stand still a second for the accostment of her shoeshines. At Ballsbridge a boy ran skipping with his hoop. For a moment MacMurrough thought of cliffs, of gulls that soared on island airs. His buttocks clenched on the seat. *I am proud to love him* – tell me I didn't say that, please tell me I didn't say that to my aunt.

And if it is love, it is a curiously inefficient force, urge and halt, the both at the same time. I want, but nothing I can propose would satisfy this wanting. I can't say what it is I want, not anything much, not even to fuck him particularly, if at all. Simply I want. Earnestly, most hurriedly, wretchedly want. God, let it be true they make a man of you in the army.

The conductor called out the stops: Sandymount, Blackrock, Monkstown. Kingstown, he called, and MacMurrough on an impulse whipped down the stair. He no sooner dismounted than the rain fell, that particularly Irish rain which soaked without apparently wetting. He sloped down to the sea. He realized he was looking at places for the last time, the Crock's Garden, the swimming-baths, over there at Doyle's Rock. And he had hoped to avoid all this; or rather to hoard this see-ing for one final gulp from the mailboat rail. Now he had blundered into it. He heard the rain's whisper on the tide: through pearly clouds the sun still shone. He looked beyond at Sandycove harbour, the Martello above on its modest cliff; at the walls that seemed to rock and tumble in the light. It was a strange land, of rainshine and sunpour; and it was true there was a spirit in this land that called to freedom, a singularly Irish freedom with which really there was nothing in the world to do.

He pushed through the gate to Ballygihen House. The staff had been paid off, save for old Moore who would act for caretaker. He stared a while at the grey facade, watching through a gauze of rain that softly from the mountains came. Somebody was waiting.

'My gosh, what are you doing out here in the wet?'

'I was hoping I'd find you.'

'I thought you'd be busy today.'

'Oh sure Doyler won't be here till the evening.'

'You sound very sure. Come in, come in. Are you wet?'

'I was sheltering.'

'Come in, please.' He led him through the garden room. The boy was looking at the furnishings, white-sheeted now. 'I forgot, you haven't seen inside before.'

'Will I take off my boots?'

'Not at all.'

'I think Doyler was inside before though.'

MacMurrough stopped. He turned. 'Yes, he was, actually. Do you mind waiting? I must find something dry.'

'Can't I come up with you?'

'Do, by all means.'

The boy followed MacMurrough into his bedroom. MacMurrough took off his coat. He noted an exaggeration in his movements. This is my towel – see? I dry myself. He must have changed a hundred times before the boy. Difference a bed in a room could make. 'Why did you want to see me?'

He was worried. MacMurrough had left him worried after Thursday – Thursday being the last they had swum together. He had got to thinking that night that MacMurrough was leaving. He didn't know what it was, something the way MacMurrough was talking. Then he looked for him all Good Friday and no sign of him and the house shut up.

'I had business in Ferns,' MacMurrough said.

'Oh, you did.'

MacMurrough had undressed to his combination shorts, his Jaegars. He was towelling his legs. The boy had his head bowed. From out of the veil of his hair, he said, 'My, you're a handsome man.'

MacMurrough wasn't sure he had heard him. 'Good grief,' he said.

'Oughtn't I say that?'

'No—'

'I'm sorry, I didn't know. Only I thought—'

'No, I mean, of course you should say it. I don't mean that. I mean it's a surprise. A very pleasant one. Truly.'

'MacEmm, you wouldn't leave that way without saying anything, sure you wouldn't?'

'I shall have to be leaving some day soon.' Even now MacMurrough could not state plainly his intention. It would be too much to have the boy waving while the boat sailed. Far rather dismay him a day or two till he read it in a letter.

'Some day is all right, though I'm not sure about soon.'

MacMurrough slipped thankfully into a trousers.

'Doyler was in this bed, wasn't he?'

Again the boy had stopped him. 'Jim, are you sure you want to be asking these questions?'

'It doesn't matter, MacEmm. I'm glad if you were with Doyler. I am. I'm glad.'

MacMurrough turned from him, into his closet to choose a tie. The big fawn one, he heard called after. 'This one is it?'

'Can I tie it for you?'

'Of course you may.'

He stood before him, a most solemn face, his jaw working with the twining of his hands. It was a while before he spoke. Even then it was MacMurrough's shirt stud he addressed. 'MacEmm – when Doyler comes, it will be all right, won't it?' He gave a glance at MacMurrough's face.

'My goodness,' said MacMurrough, 'it has you worried out of your mind.'

'I know it'll be all right. Only I think I needed you to tell me it will.'

He put his hands square on the boy's shoulders. 'It's your friend who's coming, Jim, not some stranger. Didn't you tell me you loved him? Don't you know when you love someone you don't need to do anything at all?'

'You don't?'

'You just look in his eyes and smile.'

'Oh,' said Jim. He was biting his lip. His chin lifted and he was forcing his narrow shrinking face into the semblance of a smile. His eyes fluttering looked into MacMurrough's. 'Oh,' he said again.

MacMurrough's arms flung about him and pressed the boy to his body. His fingers raked through his hair, near pulling it. The face crushed against his shoulder and, muffled, the boy said, 'I do love you, MacEmm.'

'Oh Jim,' said MacMurrough. His arms in their strength would hold him more tightly still, would crumple the slender frame, grunt the breath from its lungs. And still tighter they would hold him, hurting him, willing the hurt, rather to experience than to express, in this pain they would give, the extremity of the passion he felt. He saw them reflected in the body-glass: the tumbled hair, the jacket skewed in his grip, the boy's arms that languid reached to his neck. A corner of the bed peeked into view. 'Come now,' he said. He took Jim by the shoulders again. 'You mustn't leave him waiting.'

He walked him to the gates and watched him down the road to Glasthule. A terrible fear shook him, a fear for his boy and what the future might hold. Lest he should stumble and the crowd should find him. For we live as angels among the Sodomites. And every day the crowd finds some one of us out. I know their lewd calls and their obscene gestures. I know their mockery that bides their temper's loss. I have seen in lanes and alleys of Piccadilly faces streaked with their spit and piss, and mouths they have bloodied with boots and blows. For rarely an angel finds a Lot to house him. And I would not my boy should suffer so.

You had it wrong, old man, my Scrotes. There is no grand mistake. Aristotle wrote something that Augustine got wrong that Aquinas codified in law. It's so much fustian, mere philosophastering. What hates is madness. There's no reason, only madness. All your laws and fulminations are not the agent, but the event. Who but a madman could revile this boy? It's all of it mad, a madness to fill the spaces, lovely and comfortable as hating a Hun. Do you hear me, old man? Your pages are not worth the ink.

But he heard not the rustle of one sere page.

That evening, he took Scrotes's papers from the drawers of his desk, bundled there any old how, months back, and forgotten since Christmas and before. The foxed corners and their yellowing hue recalled the nightmarish quality of those hours, his feverish lucubration, searching for their order, for their signification. Not theirs alone but his own too, his justification. Now pages slipped to the floor; he retrieved them: the crabbed hand on the cramped paper, in the scant light the thin moan . . .

Some things are by nature pleasant . . . Great Thou art, O Lord, of praise most worthy . . . others are not pleasant by nature . . . Whether the unnatural vice is the greatest sin among the species of lust? . . . To Carthage I came . . . I answer that . . . for these arise in some by nature . . . On the contrary, Augustine says . . . corrupting and perverting their nature . . . I answer that . . . and in addition to these, paederasty . . . which Thou hast made and ordained . . . Now those in whom nature is the cause of this state . . . in ways forbidden burning to that use . . . On the contrary, the Philosopher says . . . no one would call such intemperant . . . And therefore are shameless acts . . . I answer that . . . Nature does nothing . . . being against nature . . . without purpose . . . We speak of that as being natural . . . everywhere and always to be detested . . . which is in accord with nature . . . Nor is there a nature in anything . . . or uselessly . . . but Thou knowest it . . . I answer that . . . I came to Carthage . . . On the contrary . . . BEHOLD! YOU TOOK THAT MAN FROM MY LIFE, WHEN NEVER A YEAR OUR LOVE HAD GROWN – AND HE SWEETER TO ME THAN ALL THINGS SWEET!

This suffices for the answers to the objections.

Fustian, so much foolosophy. And what in the end did it

amount to, beyond an aged gent, bemused of his wits, exposing himself in a gents in Oxford – and who paid the price in Wandsworth Gaol? MacMurrough gathered the papers and carried them to the kitchen, where old Moore kept the range, and he fed them, sheaf by sheaf, into the fire. The angels danced in the flickering flames. *We shall now begin, over again, anew.*

He slept that night thinking of loves and lighthouses. That one love might shine to bring all loves home. What more was the meaning of Easter?

Easter Sunday then and morning found him in the side rows at early Mass. He must never have caught a low Mass at Easter before, because the vapidity surprised him. No asperges, no waft of incense; couple of altar boys chirping alleluias, then the oddest of sermons. The words trumpeted resurrection and renewal, but the curate's delivery was all to pot, jitters and stutters and losing his place. MacMurrough had a distinct impression of a complication in the night. Something with the door to the tomb, mechanism had jammed. Saviour hasn't quite risen yet, but we're working on it. We'll keep you informed. In the meantime, let us, um, pray.

It had all to do with the Casement business, he supposed, and the placards outside cancelling the Volunteer parades. At least Jim was safe out of that. But Jim would never be safe. Nor could he wish safety on the boy. Again he sat at a café in Artois. On the table the letter stained, while the guns growled in the distance. *I write to tell you, who had a wish for the boy, the sad news concerning my son* . . . I must be released. I must yield decision to another. O Lord, grant not the Kaiser victory before I come to France.

The stale sniff of adulterated frankincense oppressed him. He left before the last Gospel, avoiding the spill of cooks and maids in the glory of their bonnets. He walked briskly to Bullock, where he had a boat waiting in the harbour.

'Everything ready?' he asked.

'Ready, sor,' said the boatman, and he and second oar pushed off. They passed under the steep neck of the pier. A chop of curiosity as the sea met them, then out into the bay.

It truly was the morning of the world. The sky blued above to shade and silver in the sea. What was it, eight o' clock? Already he felt stuffy in his coat and tie. He had risen very early. All had remained night within while outside morning screaked in the garden. At his window he listened to the birds. He sniffed the new-mown lawns and later watched squirrels, like writing, loop across them. The dandelions were in their first clocks; already bluebells, some. The sycamores were coming to leaf, a green stubble after the hard night. And he had thought on a whim to hear Mass.

'Where to, sor?'

'Out a bit, I should think.'

'Out where, sor?'

'Wales.'

He had even received the Host, and had enjoyed the accident of its acrid taste. It had carried him to school mornings when entire love-makings were conducted by smile and nod between communicants and choir. He remembered the cornering eyes of the boys and their singing oval mouths. Oh, but I was a god then. Even more, I was one with the crowd.

'A hard row to Wales, sor.'

'Here will do so. Only bring the boat about so I can see the shore.'

The bells had returned from Rome and he heard now their revelry, that rowdy way they sounded after Lent. And just as he noticed them, he saw the boys, rounding along the rocky shore from the Forty Foot. How was he swimming? He was swimming fine. Rushing it a bit? No, he was taking his time. The other too swam well. Yes, he did swim well, actually. Curious that: he has no kick, and still he keeps up. Inconsiderate, really; MacMurrough thought it rather a cheek.

But he must not stare or attract attention. He took up a fishing-line he had arranged for. He was wearing a hat of his grandfather's. They should not notice him.

He had no great fear for the boys till they were past Bullock and coming to Dalkey. He had marked rather a nanny route and gone over it thoroughly with Jim. Swim along the shore with the tide, then swerve across the tide and come to seaward of Maiden Rock. Come to landward, and the tide would sweep them into Dalkey Sound and they might give up any hope of the Muglins. A short hop by Clare Rock. Then the final leg, and quite a challenge it was. MacMurrough had essayed it himself. One had to aim more or less for Scotland to arrive more or less at Wales. He had managed it, but his muscles ached and a knot of pain lodged below his breast-bone. He floated by, seeing the rock for the bird-shitten desolation it was. He hadn't liked to come ashore, nor even to hold by its crags, feeling his touch an infringement of sorts. He had crawled back across Muglins Sound to Dalkey Island, and rested on the decent grass.

He watched the boys under the brim of his hat. On an impulse he dipped his hand over the side. Icy cold, but they would be over that pain by now. They were swimming naked. Well, he had known they would. He waited while they passed Bullock. That damned flag. I told him not to bring that flag. Senseless drag, let alone the weight. Something in the boatmen's mutters: he realized they were watching the boys, had been discussing them even. He snapped at them to mind what they were about. He moved along till he sat in the stem. He glanced over his shoulder at the Muglins. Perhaps a mile, mile and a half. It was a hard swim in the open sea for sixteen-year-old boys. Would I come to him in time? Listen to me, Nanny Trembling in a boat.

He had never questioned the swim or sought any explanation for it. It was a boyhood test, so far as he considered it, of endurance, togetherness, whatever. Then, on Maundy Thursday, at Doyle's Rock, he had shaken Jim's hand. This was the end of his lessons and, so he had intended, their last meeting. He said, not even thinking of the words, 'I wish you luck and I hope you won't be disappointed. I hope you both pass the test.'

And Jim had said, 'Oh no, it's not a test.'

'What is it then?'

'It's nothing like a test.'

'Do you know what it is?'

'I think I do.' He paused, ordering his thoughts. He looked up through his hair, then swept it out of the way. 'You see, MacEmm, we're extraordinary people. We must do extraordinary things.'

'How we,' said Doyler, 'how we doing?'

'Near,' said Jim, 'near there.'

'We easy make it.'

'Easy,' said Jim.

The shiver gripped his jaw. He had to duck his head to be gone of it. They were by Clare Rock, treading water. Between the heaves and the pants and the shivery-shakes it was hard talking at all. The flag in its yoke tossed over to him.

'Your bags,' called Doyler.

Jim noosed his neck. Doyler paddled closer till their faces met on the skin of the swell. 'Not beat at all,' he said, 'you.'

'Amn't I, amn't I knocked up?'

Doyler reached his hands to Jim's shoulders, sending them both down. He held Jim under and rubbed their faces, a class of kissing. Jim came up spluttering and flung back his hair. 'You soft?' he cried.

'Happy,' said Doyler, 'in sea again.'

'Want to save your breath.'

'No more 'n a spit now.'

'Save your breath,' said Jim, slicing a splash, 'when we get there.' He looked about him, feeling a spasm of giddiness. Whatever course MacMurrough had plotted, he couldn't find the Forty Foot now. Up and down they bobbed, making hectic doggy-paddles, so strange after the concentrated stroke of their swimming.

After a time, Doyler said, 'Old shoes – up again.'

Jim nodded. His eyes narrowed on the Muglins. The rock had grown as they neared it, but the channel they must cross had widened too. Even in this tide with little or no carry, the current flowed grey-green.

'We risk it so?'

'Time all right.'

Doyler smiled and Jim smiled too. He nodded and they pushed out. Soon as Jim found his stroke, the ache was back in his arms. Only it was doubled now or trebled, the way the hurt had been storing all the while he rested. And for all he strove, such small return: the Muglins refused to budge. He gave up looking and centred on his stroke, till gradually he found that state where exertion became timeless. The moments no longer heaped the one upon the other. He felt the water, its living run along his body. He lost his sense of the sea's resistance and felt instead its acceptance of him. It was the sea's ache in his chest and limbs, the sea's toil that crawled him on. He had been doing this for ever and surely he must go on doing this for ever more.

Then a seaweed came in his mouth. It wouldn't spit out, he had to tread water to take his fingers to it. He saw Doyler had halted a little way off. He looked up and it was there, the Muglins, no more than a good stone's throw. There was a landing-deck and reefs jutting out and individual crevices. It was a place all of a sudden. The beacon stood high on its rock.

He looked at Doyler and saw the same notion had struck him. He slipped off the flag yoke and flung it clumsily toward the rocks. 'Steady?' he called.

'Go!' cried Doyler. And they plunged headlong, tore through the waves. Well, it wasn't gala form, and he doubted he'd win any prize for style, nor for speed neither. He was thrashing wildly and a breath wouldn't last more than two strokes. It was a mystery this last spurt where it came from but it was always there waiting, if you knew how to reach for it. He saw the flash of Doyler's arm. He made a stab for a landing, but his wrist was grabbed by Doyler who held it aloft in champion style while their bodies glided on.

'We made it!'

'We did and all!'

'Aren't we mad?'

'Delirious.'

The ground was giddy and dream-like after the sea. Jim's hands seemed to sink into it. He collapsed on the landing-deck. The sun beat down, but it was cold. From out the stone the shivers came, like the rock itself would be jittering.

'Get up,' said Doyler. 'You'll catch a founder. Ten times round the beacon.'

'Ten times round your head.'

'Tig,' said Doyler. He gave a swipe at Jim's balls. 'You're it.'

'I'm not it, I'm dead.'

But Doyler was off round the beacon. Out let his yahoo yell. 'Chase me,' he called. Wearily Jim rose. He bunched his toes against the rocks. He felt light-headed. 'Come on and chase me,' called Doyler. The sunlight was terrifically fierce. Mica glittered in the rock. Doyler looked so queer you couldn't but smile. He was dancing in some Mohawk fashion. His lad was leaping up and down. It was a kind of giggling when you smiled and shivered the same time. Jim took a step or two. He found indeed he could shift his legs. Indeed he might have something to yell even. 'Catch me,' shouted Doyler, insistently, slapping his behind. Jim followed him round. He followed, he chased, his frame unknotted, he hared ahead. Round and round the beacon they raced, yahooing and roaring the hoarse of their voice. Till all in a heap they fell, heaving and blowing, the sweat dripping from them.

Doyler's eyes, like black crystals, were looking him in the face. A steam rose from his shoulders. His arm went up round Jim's neck, drawing him down. Still their chests heaved.

'That was some chase you put me through.'

Jim nodded. His eyes closed as he came down to Doyler's mouth.

'What is it?'

'It's a ship it sounds like.'

They clambered round the rock. It was a ship all right, low in the water, a small grey-hulked vessel. The ensign flew, a squat gun poked.

'The *Helga*.'

'Aye, HMS *Helga* all right. Submarine patrol. Don't wave.'

'No.'

'I mean they'll think we want rescuing.'

Then Jim said, 'The flag, quick.'

So they hauled out the flag, Jim holding the bottom corner

and Doyler, standing a little above him, the top, while he kept
an arm about Jim's neck. The breeze took the green and flapped
it mildly. A sailor was leaning over the rail. He watched them
a while, then another sailor came. Jim thought they might be
laughing. Then both sailors came to attention and brought their
hands to salute. And so the King's ship passed and the green flag
flew from the Muglins.

'Well, we have that done.'

'We have.'

'We'll be heading back now, I suppose.'

'We will not,' said Jim. 'We have the tide to turn first.'

There was a dip in the rock out of the wind. There was even
a slab they might lie on, with a seaweed growing which a mind
unfussy to these things might take for moss. 'Didn't I tell you?'
crowed Doyler. He scraped off the winkles and spread the green
flag over. There they stretched. The air had a hazy look. There
was the very slightest sniff of ammonia.

Jim listened to the sea-sounds, wave and gull, till these sounds
no longer obtruded on his mind, and an immense sea-quiet
settled about him. He looked out to seaward, to the vastness
of ocean, blue and deep-blue and green-blue, a little awed by
its immediacy, that feeling of infinity, that here it begins. There
was no horizon, only a shimmering haze, and this intensified the
sense of boundless expanse. And then to landward, and the shore
so stunningly close, quite toppling in its rush towards them.

Doyler might have followed his thoughts, for he said, 'It looks
amazing near, don't it?'

'It does too.'

'You wouldn't credit all that trouble of getting here.'

A year near enough, thought Jim. Doyler lay on his belly, his
face on his folded arms. Jim turned that way too. The sun beat
down. He said, 'Was it today it was planned for, Doyler?'

'Was what planned?'

'The rising.'

'Oh that. I think so.'

'You would have told me.'

'I didn't know if I would. I'd tell you now of course.'

'Yes of course.'

'I have parade this afternoon. I can't miss that. But nothing will happen.'

'I see. But you would tell me?'

He didn't say anything for a while. Then he said, 'You know, I was scared with the rising. Would you believe that?'

'No.' Another pause, and Jim asked, 'Would you be scared now?'

'There's nothing to be scared of now.'

He had turned on his side and Jim had turned too to face him. Doyler kept glancing up, his eyes checking, each move his fingers made, glancing back at Jim's face. 'They're like toadstools,' he said.

'They are a bit, all right.'

'Do you mind what I'm doing?'

'It's nice sure.' But there was still this business not absolutely cleared up, and so as there could be no misunderstandings between them, of whatsoever nature or cause, Jim stated plain as he might, 'You'd only be making a muddle not telling me.'

'Telling you what?'

'The rising of course.' Doyler let a laugh. 'Don't you see,' Jim reasoned, 'I'd be running from billy to jack and who's to say would I find you at all?'

'All right, honour bright, cross me heart and hope to die. I'll send it in a telegram, urgent. A night letter, a marconigram, a pigeongram even. I'll send smoke signals out of the Sugarloaf. That do you?'

'I only want to be with you.'

'I know you do.'

Doyler's hand had removed. He fetched a phlegm and a gobshell splashed in the bladderwrack. He had turned on his belly again. He looked disappointed, and Jim reached a hand to his shoulder. 'It's all right, Jim,' he said. 'We've come this far. I can wait.' Another spurt jetted through his teeth. A moment, then he said, 'You see the Martello beyond on Dalkey Island? Do you know the story with that? What it was—'

'Is this true now?'

'Go way, would I lie to you? Back I don't know when, after the British gave up them towers, well, that one on the island over, don't ask me why, it got forgot.'

'No,' said Jim. 'That was the Sandycove tower.'

'It was not. You know so much, do you know what happened?'

'The sergeant and two swaddies kept at their duties, twenty years they kept at them. Me da told me all about it.'

'Your da's a decent skin, and I wouldn't go against him save he's not within the bawl of an ass of it. 'Twas a corporal with two gunners. And never mind their duties, they didn't do spit the week long save blow their bunce in the Dalkey shebeens. Now that corporal's name was Reilly. And it's after him you get it, living the life of Reilly. Now.'

'Is that true?'

'True as I'm lying here holding your lad in me hand, it is.' Jim felt a laughter burst from him. Then Doyler said, 'Can I kiss you now?'

'You know better than to ask.'

'Why wouldn't I ask?'

'You know you can kiss me.'

'I'll kiss you all over.'

But it was Jim who kissed first. He lay atop Doyler, pinning his shoulders, and kissed his forehead and his cheeks, his chin, his throat, kissing the apple in his throat. He kissed the bruise on his shoulder and the seven hairs, counting them, on his chest where the half a medal lay. He watched Doyler's face through the strands of his hair while he snuck down, still watching, and kissed the very tip of his horn which bounced up against Jim's nose and his chin making him blink, till he kissed it again on the hop. He felt his face like a red velvet. He was charged with the wonder of desire and delay. He pulled up again and made a hold of Doyler's arm.

'I'm not shy, you know,' he said.

'You don't be acting very shy.'

'But you understand we had to come?'

'I know I wouldn't miss it.'

Jim nodded. He said, 'I suppose it's soft wanting to cuddle always.'

'It is not. I'd hate you and you didn't.'

'Gordie used bring his arm round me in bed sometimes. I used love it then. I'd wake in the night and his arm would be there. One time then, he was lying awake and I think he twigged that I was awake too. He gave the hell of a shove and kicked me down the bottom of the bed. We were sleeping head and toe after that.'

'Is it hard with him gone?'

'I dream of him.'

'You would too.'

'I don't know if you ever dreamt of anyone was close to you and he's dead. It's terrible strange. He's always walking, I don't know, some hill or other. He's not walking fast or anything, save it's hard catching up with him, hard to keep up even. He won't turn to look at you, just keeps walking on. And you're saying,

What're you doing here? After they told us you was dead? You're shocked like and all annoyed. You can't get any talk out of him. And you're crying really and saying, Why're you doing this? Won't you come home now? He's not looking at you, he's just walking on and on. I try to hold his arm, I try to turn him round. Don't you know we miss you? Don't you know you can come home out of this and we'll forget all about it? There's everything so weary with him. And he just says, Oh well you know. And he keeps on walking.

'I hate it when I dream like that. I wake up and I'm so angry. I'm really angry with him.'

'I'm sorry, Jim.'

Jim felt Doyler bring his head round, he felt him kiss his eyes, his eyes feeling wet after. He said, 'Oh well.'

Doyler said nothing.

Then Jim said, 'I don't know what's it called. Will you do it with me? If I lie down, will you lie on top of me?'

'I'd like to. It'll maybe hurt a bit.'

Jim hunched his shoulders, making him feel skinny of a sudden. He felt his bottom lip caught in his teeth. It did that if he smiled feeling awkward.

For a moment or two, he was aware of the hardness of the stone beneath him. He heard them come back again, the seaside sounds of waves and birds. Behind his eyelids the sun had its red glare. There was a sweat on his back which the air traced. He felt it far away, the intimate search of foreign fingers. Then Doyler pushed against him. His eyes squeezed and all sensation shook.

It was a moment when he scarcely existed but to suffer pain. Then Doyler's weight came down on top of him. His hair fell on Jim's cheek, reawaking the sense of his face.

'You all right?'

He rubbed his cheek against Doyler's. He opened his lips

and felt with his tongue along Doyler's teeth, searching out the chip off the middle one. He tasted a salt of the sea where the lips creased at the side. Doyler was upon him and inside him, on his breath even, all about him. His body strained the more to meet the body above. He did not think of anything, but his thoughts were there in the back of his mind or in the sea that circled his mind. They had this together now. They had their island. Whenever a thought crossed or a look met, if a hair but brushed a finger, this was where they would be. No one could take it from them, chance what might, nor he couldn't nor Doyler. He had to bring Doyler here because Doyler didn't know to come of his own. This was the light the Muglins had shone all those years. It was here was their home, it was in the sea, an island.

Doyler whispered in his ear, 'It's my turn next.' It had Jim smiling to think of that. He felt lazy and free. 'There's all the time,' he said.

'Throw a line over, sor?'

'Do, by all means. And let me know when the tide turns.'

MacMurrough took off his coat and folded it behind his head, pulled down his hat over his eyes; closed his eyes, tired after the glaring water, to drowse the while. And drowsing he saw but waves and beacon and rock. But in the dip of that rock he knew there formed a primal unity, which was not, as Aristophanes had thought, an egg-shaped being, rather a twin-backed flapping seal; that unity the jealous gods had thought to sunder, not reckoning the human heart.

It was the boatman who woke him, plucking his trousers. 'Only they looks to be harrished, sor,' he was saying.

'What is it?'

'Shwimmers, sor. Only they's in trouble, could be.'

'Where?' He pointed. 'Row,' MacMurrough said; then bellowed, 'Row, man, damn you!'

He shoved the man, near upsetting the boat. He could make out one head in the water. There was a slick on the surface, a spill of something – never oil? The glare was bewildering. He had to throw water in his eyes. One head, yes. Down it ducked. Not oil: that wretched flag. He shouted to the men, 'Row, row', as he pulled at his clothes. The head came up. It was Jim. A breath, then down again. The flag was sinking, had sunk. But Jim was safe. He registered no relief. A kind of training took over, that his mind and dreaming body these months had rehearsed. Training judged the boat's speed, their distance, his balance on the gunwale; it dived him to the water. The cold hit, near gasping his breath. He skimmed to the surface; air gulped in his throat. He pulled on the waves, tugging on them, willing a purchase, laddering them almost. Jim was ducking again and he charged into him, grabbed his hair, savagely wrenched him away. 'Boat,' he yelled, then plunged below. He kicked with the current. His eyes still smarted, but the water was clear. He saw the cloth, a dark jelly-fish below. Beneath it, the boy had stopped struggling. In silence, dreamily, MacMurrough unwound the cords that had wrapped themselves round, propelled the imponderable weight to the surface. Jim was still there and he roared at him, 'Boat!' He dragged the boy to the stern and Jim, inside now, helped pull the body over.

'MacEmm,' Jim was saying, 'MacEmm.'

'Tongue. Check his tongue.' He turned the boy on his front, straddled his back. Push, one thousand. All cramped in the well of the boat, water swilling about. Push, two thousand, his hands on the small of the boy's back. Up, three thousand. He saw Jim open the mouth, search his fingers inside. 'Pulse,' he shouted. Wait, four thousand. The boy's face was turned on his elbow: his face livid, so very nearly lifelike. Wait, five thousand. Jim's fingers fiddled with his wrist. Push, one thousand. 'I think so,' he heard. Up, three thousand. 'Pulse, yes!' Wait, five thousand. He felt a shudder under his hands. 'Tongue,' he called again. Push, two thousand. Water trickled out of the mouth. Up, three thousand. 'He's not breathing.' Wait, four thousand. 'MacEmm, he's not breathing.' Wait, five thousand. 'Please, MacEmm.' He glimpsed the red faces of the men rowing. Push, one thousand. The horizon pitched and sended. Wait, five thousand. Jim shivering watching. 'My shirt on,' he told him. The shirt absurdly wrapping round his own shoulders. Still push one thousand and up three thousand and wait five thousand and push. A freak wave buffeted the boat as MacMurrough came down, one thousand, to push. The boy choked and he made to turn his face to cough or to vomit. 'Tongue,' shouted MacMurrough. 'Breathing!' shouted Jim. 'He's breathing, MacEmm!' Still MacMurrough pushed and upped and waited till there could be no doubting. The boy moaned, and to moan he must breathe.

He wrapped his coat over the boy's back, then turned him round. 'Put my shirt on,' he snapped at Jim. He held his hand on the chest, gauging the strength of the breathing. 'My watch,' he said. Jim had it ready. He timed the breaths. He felt for the boy's pulse: thready, but undeniable. He lifted the boy's legs into his trousers. Jim was on the stern bench dripping, juddering. He clambered over and slapped him hard on the cheek. 'I warned you about that flag.' Biting his lip, disbelief in his eyes: a little colour returned. 'Where are we?' MacMurrough called to the men.

'Bullock rocks, sor.'

'Don't let up.' To Jim again. 'You know the doctor's house?' Nod. 'You must run. If the doctor is away, you must find from his people where there's another. Give my name and have them use the telephone.'

'He'll be all right now?'

'He's breathing well. But you must fetch a doctor. Don't panic now, Jim. I need you with your wits.'

MacMurrough attended to the boy, buttoning his coat on him and checking his pulse and his breathing. He opened an eyelid where the eye was dull. But it flinched against the light and the eyelid blinked. The body convulsed with shivers.

He glanced over his shoulder. Jim's face would repent a judge. 'Come here, Jim.' The boy crept over. 'Take his hand now. He's fine. A little shock, that's all. Try keep him warm.'

'MacEmm, I wasn't panicking.'

'All right.'

'But you did right to hit me if you thought I was.'

MacMurrough turned his head. 'Keep him warm now.'

At last she heard him, his brisk boots on the tiled floor, Shorty stepping through the hospital ward. With a tenderly soldierliness he took up his station behind her. 'Mum,' said he, turning about the bath-chair, 'the motor-car awaits.'

Which meant no more, Eveline was not deceived, than that her permit had been approved to hear public Easter Mass. They passed along corridors, where walking wounded sidled by the walls, into the Castle grounds. The motor waited by the steps, and with Shorty's efficient bracing she slipped into the leather lap of the rear. All the courtesies. Motor and driver, her personal attendant, a cornered space in the officers' ladies' ward: the London influence of her brother of course.

The sentry at the gates saluted, the constable peeked his helmet. Under the gate-arch now, with its figure of Justice atop, her back turned significantly on the city. Shorty, in acknowledgment of the weather, hurrumphed and passed a white-gloved hand to his mouth. Eva responded in like vein, primming her face so that she stared impassively ahead: it truly was a most pretty morning.

The motor-car purred to its halt outside a blank façade, dead to a lane, a chapel whose sole recommendation, so Eveline perceived, was the absence of any side exit: this prisoner *de luxe* should not through faith be tempted to her liberty. The pilgrim crowd, discomposed by their passage, reformed by the chapel steps. Urchin eyes spilt on the coachwork, breaths gaped on the glass. She saw the pinched and mesquin faces of the women. Beyond, on a tenement sill, flowers waved in a window-box like weeds on a cliff. Shorty, in full stepping-out rig, soon made way and handed Eveline to the chapel porch. He eyed her a little doubtfully. 'Thank you, Shorty,' she said, dismissing him. 'Perhaps an hour. You shan't forget me now?' And she stepped through the portal unaided.

The usher was abashed to receive her. He asked only a ha'pence and she understood then why the chapel should hum so exclusively of the Lord's unwashed. He guided her to a forward seat where she knelt awkwardly, a veiled island of dignity beyond the promiscuous shawls.

Poor people, yet buoyant with it. There was a murmur from the benches almost of chatting. Forty days they had mortified their wants: now they feasted on the expectation of meat, a pipe of tobacco, alleluia. A youth in soutane came to light the candles. So very few candles, a begrudgement of flowers. Her back ached, so too her neck. Escape: the notion of course had crossed her mind. But where to go, what to do? History had finished with her generation. Better surely exile than to remain here, in this land of taint and squalor, among a people who saw no further than their pipes, hoped for no better than bacon at table. Twice four hundred years had Ireland famished in Lent. What cared this *racaille* for that?

Oh lah, but this was too unfair, and immediately she repented her *dureté*. Lent must have fallen very hard this year. Fish was grown so expensive in the war, it was rather a treat for the rich than any penance of the poor to be fasting on it.

A hand-bell rang. The susurration ceased, quiet came down in a fust of incense. A shock of white as entered the priest.

An elderly gentleman, quite alone save for the soutaned young man, now surpliced, his server: a well-looking youth whom presently Eva believed she must recognize. Surely I have met that young man? The priest bowed, genuflected to the altar, signed the cross. That quaint unsongful intoning, *Introibo ad altare Dei.* Low Mass in a slum chapel at half before noon.

The server's responses came reasoned and clear – so very much more fitting than the rote-learnt gabble of the usual altar boys. A college student, Eva considered: an act of charity to serve in this *quartier*. So simply he stood and so surely he spoke, they were true, she was certain, the words that he said, that he would go unto the altar of God, unto God who gave joy to his youth.

And yes, there was a joy in this server's youth, a joy to look at him even, so fresh of face in this dowdy scene. The vestments he wore did not shroud him entirely, and she made out, though her veil blurred a little her view, the collar of a tunic at his neck: at the cuffs and legs the heather green of a uniform. So, a Volunteer lad – had she inspected him, perhaps, at a parade?

The priest made his confession to the server, and in the people's name the server begged God's mercy on the priest. After, the young man made his own confession, in the name of all gathered, striking his breast for their fault, their fault, their most grievous fault. Perhaps it was this chapel and its sanctuary so very bare: the scene imposed its drama on Eva. The youth bows to the venerable priest: it might be Ireland's sins he confesses, that she has not risen, she has not risen, most grievously has not risen.

How it must anguish them, she thought, the young, to know once more their hopes are deceived. How shall we ever expect their pardon? This lad would go out alone, she made no slightest doubt, with his bare hands to fight, were but one good man to lead the way. That one good man lay in chains in London. Now when she saw them joined in prayer, how white and fine were his fingers: a virile delicacy that carried her to Casement. How he had delighted, that noble-hearted man, in the upright spirit of the young.

Poor dear Casement. Yet one other uncrowned king in this land of kings uncrowned. This foolish bungling land, where the sole occasion they came to a coronation, it was the baker's boy from Oxford they must light upon, Lambert Simnel, the creature. The shame of it all. Was it anywhere but in Ireland that a rebellion could be cancelled by a notice in the press? Nothing could be salvaged. Now the English would confiscate all arms. The leaders would be imprisoned or banished. Conscription would be enforced, what manhood remained to be bled in France. Let her go, let her go with what grace was left her, into exile in England. She might come to see Casement there. A personal recompense after this national disgrace.

The mountains, the mountains, they called to her now. The Mass continued in a kind of dumb-show, while in her mind she motored away from this city, beyond its clustering villages, till the road began its climb to the moors. Dublin lay behind, and before and about her were the great shoulders of hills, the heather and gorse and bog-grass, green and pink and gold.

There was a spirit in those hills which the foreigner had

never touched. Cities they had raised and walls against it. The cities reached their roads to trample it. Nothing dismayed that spirit: neither kindness nor crowbars swayed it a jot. That spirit, it could drive the foreigner mad for freedom, or wicked to stamp that freedom out. It was deep in the land. In the mist it hung, it seeped below in the suck of turf.

Eveline needed but think of those mountains and she felt it within her, that spirit, a flame in her breast. She could not reason it. Nothing would it benefit her, Ireland free or subject. For all she cared, nothing would it benefit Ireland. Ireland might go forward, she might go better forward and faster to freedom, by ballot, committee, constitutional reform. She might be richer for it, more blessed, her people content, her industries prosperous, the miserable drain of emigration staunched. But nothing suchlike would assuage that spirit. The hurts were ancient, they were deep in the land. That spirit was a flame whose tallow was blood. War was its cry: no hand-fed Home Rule, but liberty asserted by right of arms.

My name is MacMurrough, my patrimony the mountains. Over the hills would I go, over the military road.

Her eyes closed and she felt the soreness behind them. She would go nowhere now save into exile in England. And every day her body healed brought exile that day closer. They would take her under guard to London and place her there in her brother's keeping. That meddlesome woman. Harridan, harpie. She used be seen motoring in the hills. They say she had a hand in gun-running and such. Making a spectacle of her name and sex. Had ought to wear a cap and sew at home. It's easy known why no man would have her. Would live in mortal fear for his trousers.

Christe elaison! In glad confident voice the server called down a saviour's blessing. *Kyrie elaison*, the priest agreed.

Eva rewoke to the Mass before her. Something had changed, the impression was distinct upon her, while her mind had wandered. He seemed to have grown in this interlude, the serving lad, and the space between altar and nave, contrarily, to have gulfed. She saw his bare white throat and the hair on his forehead damp and a little blown. His hair was black, so very black. As she watched, she was aware of an inexplicable exhilaration – there, she felt it, patter, in her heart. He glanced to her, and she caught the shine in his eyes. His head lifted, proud and joyous, with a smile almost of amusement, that seemed to say, It is a little thing that I shall do.

Strength that is in his hands, truth that is on his lips, purity that is in his heart: the words returned of the schoolmaster Pearse, spoken in her garden so long ago. This serving lad, so dazzling he stood, might be such as they of the Fianna of old.

It no longer seemed any ordinary Mass: no common rubric was told. The priest took a book whereof was read some circumstance regarding a tomb. The server listened with an interested curiosity. There was a sense of his waiting, of his being long prepared for this coming event. A god would be brought down to the altar. An extraordinary notion: a god to come down before Eva's eyes. Though it seemed to Eva it was the server now, not the priest, who was the centre of this mystery.

She sensed the hush from the benches behind, their occupants tilted forward so that her neck bristled with suspected touch. The suspense, a crowded silent bating, told rather pity and wonder than any approval of the boy. Who was he? What was this little thing he would do?

Casement and Pearse: now came, unseemingly, the image of her nephew, his languorous vigour roused while he knelt beside her, this women's aisle of the nave, watching this lad. She recalled his face upon their last interview, soul-pained and doomed, there too a shade of Casement. And then, this love he had not blushed to avow: some bathing boy, he too perhaps in the joy of his youth; a love which tomorrow would send him, her nephew, to the trenches.

And it seemed of a sudden inevitable that his love should be so. Inevitable that such love should send him to war. Inevitable as war was inevitably male. It was a preserve she had struggled all her life to touch, yet never had reached. Nor had any woman touched it, Kathleen nor Rosaleen nor the Shan Van Vocht, for all their summons and goad. They knelt beside her, Casement and Pearse and her nephew, each feasting upon this lad, and this lad performing with a significance secret to their eyes: and she felt a little ashamed, feminine, a folly.

Came the Offertory, and a heathen withershin rite it presented. A silver plate, a gold cup, cruets of wine and water she watched astonished as the server surrendered these treasures to the priest. And now he had nothing left in this world to give, and he knelt again to pray. His face was offered full to the window, whose light in glory round him shone. How frail the linen that pulled upon the tough green cloth.

The air dinned in Eva's ears while the priest obscurely muttered. There was something very wrong about this, altogether wrong that this child should fascinate so. But she could not bear to remove her eyes. A sacrifice, she thought: a chosen lad. So intense was her gaze, his eyes turned a second time in response. They flashed again, and in that flash she glimpsed the ferocious wish of his courage. A hand-bell sounded: in his hands the priest some nick-nack elevated. Abruptly the youth bowed his head. With a shine on his neck the window-light played, with a glint of metal on the soft bared skin. She felt a tear in her heart. She believed she cried out. Outside, the bells tolled from every steeple. Every steeple in the land tolled noon high Mass.

Later, she knelt at the rail waiting for communion. She felt her age in her hands that trembled to join; in their tiny form she remembered her beauty. Her heart heaved on the hollow air, as though physically they had torn it from her, that spirit, that flame. And what more, bar shriek, might she have done? A woman could not shame men to arms who every day saw women subject. Nor Kathleen nor Rosaleen nor the Shan Van Vocht. Now came the golden youth. And when he came, holding the paten, she felt his breath when she lifted her veil, a nothing, the brush of a tassel, his given life, Ireland.

She waited at her place while the people left. Soon she was alone in the chapel. She waited, certain of his coming, as she was certain now of the rising to come. But a rising not as Eva had hoped nor any sane person would hope. Rather black Good Friday than Easter triumphant: not the opened tomb but the cross on the hill. He would go out, this young Ireland, he and a necessary few. In the beauty of his boyhood he would offer his life, by the overwhelming sword to die: a ravishment really: and Irishmen everywhere would shake for shame.

The sacristy door opened. She saw him plainer now, in his Volunteer green, quietly ashimmer, enthused still but muted, a trace fatigued, dazed even, and perhaps with a falter in his step on this earthly ground. At the aisle he genuflected to the altar. She reached, before he turned to leave, her hand to his elbow.

'Young man, forgive me,' she said, hearing her voice come whispered and awed. 'You must tell me. The sword of light, it will yet shine. Tell me now.'

He looked at her at gaze a moment. Her fingers fretted the cloth of his sleeve, feeling for the scorch of that flame which these years had blazed in her breast. She searched his face through the gauze of her veil.

'Not today,' she said, 'but tomorrow, surely?'

His eyes flecked down the aisle, where she knew Shorty watched for her. The eyes flashed back. That smile, almost of amusement, had reformed on his face. Curtly, deliberately, he nodded. He strode down the aisle. Turning, she saw Shorty had moved from his way and the young man thrust through the chapel doors to the shiver of day beyond.

Her face too formed the grim appearance of a smile. So let it be. Tomorrow.

In the end the doctor was no more useful than his motor which ferried them through a clapping, even cheering, crowd up the road from Bullock to Ballygihen. A spoon of arrow-root in a port wine, Parrish's nerve tonic was not to be despised, beef tea had its place in the pharmacopoeia, a draught of chlorodyne towards evening maybe: these sanatives the doctor recommended. And so, all afternoon Doyler had groaned while Jim plied teaspoon and invalid cup. Until MacMurrough intervened. The doctor was only earning his fee, he assured him: all Doyler needed was rest, a window open and the pot handy.

Even Mr Mack had called with his particular corrective, a bottle of something extra A1 against the – pantomime – 'keeping it regular, if you'll pardon the expression'.

MacMurrough had mentioned Jim might stay up with Doyle the night.

'Did you hear that, Jim? Mr MacMurrough says you're to stay with Doyle the night. Is it here in Ballygihen you mean, Mr MacMurrough?'

'Oh yes, doctor's orders, mayn't be moved.'

The evening then, while Doyler drowsed under the chlorodyne, they fetched a sofa into MacMurrough's room and arranged it by the window where just they could hear the sea. They talked of old times, things that had happened weeks, sometimes months, before; their old chats on Doyle's Rock, the Saturdays they swam with a Blackrock priest to the pier and back, their ice-creams. Jim talked of the plans he had made. That he would go for the King's scholarship in June. Yes, he would try for a schoolteacher. He would need to get a digs then in Dublin. Doyler would share that digs with him. In the night, they'd go over the books together. Himself, he had the makings maybe, but Doyler was promised for a teacher. The world knew the teacher Doyler would be and it was the pity of the world if he didn't try. Jim wouldn't rest till Doyler had the scholarship too. They would be schoolteachers together. It was only right.

He was a kind boy and rarely unthoughtful, and he paused now and then in the rehearsal of these schemes to intrude MacMurrough's lumping presence: a chair at his table, an hour of his evening, holidays all three to the West. Their low voices in the falling light invited an intimacy. MacMurrough rested against the sofa's shoulder and Jim rested upon his lap and MacMurrough played his hand through Jim's hair. Across the room where a night-light burnt, Doyler dozed in MacMurrough's bed.

'Do you know what it is, MacEmm?' Jim said. 'It's having to thank you more than any drowning has him exhausted.'

'I shouldn't be at all surprised.'

MacMurrough reached for his wine, a good claret, '93, which he had come upon during the boy's hunt for an invalid port. He had no more cigarettes and he had rather go without than smoke Woodbines, what other delights Glasthule had to offer. He might rumble out a cigar before bed.

'I don't know but, if you hadn't been there, would I have managed it at all.'

'Managed what exactly?' MacMurrough inquired.

'I could easy get him back to the Muglins. But I wouldn't

know much about the pumping thing. You'll have to teach me that.'

Absurd youth. The shock was long erased: a tremor in a boat: no conception now of the horror a minute might have wrought. Even with the boy breathing MacMurrough had feared, as he had encountered before after a near-drowning, a comatose state. It was hard to be sure by the mouth, but he doubted Doyler had stopped breathing at all. His recovery was too swift and certain. Already when MacMurrough carried him up the harbour steps, he was complaining the trousers weren't his and what had happened his uniform. The devil's own luck: and no worse for it than gripes, the sicks, and a light feverishness: his due anyway after the water he had drunk.

He reached his wine to the floor. The boy stretched his shoulders, tame upon MacMurrough's bosom. 'You oughtn't have been there at all,' he said. 'Out in your boat looking over us. By rights I should be annoyed, but you know, I'm not at all annoyed with you.'

And so I am absolved.

'You were in your Jaegars too. When I'll be a teacher I'll wear Jaegar drawers.' He turned his head to see MacMurrough's face. 'Won't I be handsome?'

If MacMurrough hadn't surmised before, he might be certain now how swimmingly things had gone on the Muglins. The boy was glowing, MacMurrough could feel it on the palm of his hand, positively glowing with knowledge, animal and sexual. He had felt this once himself, but he could not recall the incident nor the other with whom it had been shared; and when he tried, the memory that came was of his face bruised and his arm held high after a schools' boxing tournament.

'But you know, it's strange,' the boy continued, 'I did think of you out there on the island and I knew you were thinking of me.

547

And I knew you knew how happy I was. You was so happy for me too, I knew that.' A pause, recapitulating, then: 'Were happy, I mean.' He twisted round on the sofa. 'I never asked—'

'The curse and flames!' cried MacMurrough.

'Did I hurt you? I never hurt you there, MacEmm?'

The imp had elbowed him exactly on his horn. 'Don't pretend you don't know what you're about. And you may take that fool's grin off your face. I won't desire you to rub it, no nor to kiss it better.'

The smile, at such wickedry, quite bulged from his face.

'Lie back now where I was comfortable.'

He lay back and MacMurrough once again stroked his fingers through his hair, beautiful hair, without tangle or scrag, you could play with it all ways and always it found itself with the merest shake of his head. He washed it in rainwater. Why in rainwater? The boy didn't know, but it was something his father had taught him to do. What a wonderful father to have.

'I was going to ask you, how did you come to be so good in the sea?'

'Oh, the sea,' said MacMurrough. He touched his wine, then recited in his most elegant Hibernian,

'My grief on the sea,
How the waves of it roll.
For they heave between me
And the love of my soul.'

'That's lovely,' said Jim.

'Yes, I got it out of a book of my aunt's. It goes on:

'And my love came behind me,
He came from the south;
His breast to my bosom,
His mouth to my mouth.'

'A lovely warm feel. I'd say wine was like that.'

'So we often hope,' said MacMurrough. 'The sea,' he reiter-ated. 'I'm not sure I can remember how it started. Well I do, I suppose. I was holidaying at some dreary resort, might have put my name down for anything, but I opted for swimming. Actually, I was in a boating accident some while before that. The others, there were two others, well they drowned. I didn't.' He waited. 'Perhaps we're drawn to what frightens us.'

'Are we?'

Yes, that horror drew him still. He screaming in the waves and his brother coming back for him. Then his other brother coming back. He patted the boy's head as to comfort his own. Wine.

'Did you swim at school?'

'I did, relays and dash. After college, I even worked at a London pool. What they call a life-saver. Had to hide the work from my people, of course. I just liked to be by the water.'

'So do I.'

'Yes, I know you do.'

'I don't fear it though.'

'You ought to, Jim. And you will need to be careful with other things too.'

'I couldn't give a tip for being careful.'

'You will have to be, and that fellow with you.'

That fellow gave a snort in his sleep. 'I'll check his tempera-ture,' said Jim. He went to refresh the bowl, came back, flannelled Doyler's face. It was very beautiful to see his unselfconscious care. One boy caring for another boy. It was very beautiful.

He came back to the sofa. He lifted MacMurrough's wine and silently gave it into his hand. They listened to the night sounds through the window, while the mood recouped, repos-sessed them.

'MacEmm, can I ask you? I don't know does it mean . . .

does it mean anything with marrying, MacEmm? Doyler and me.'

'No Jim, you can't ask me that.'

'I don't know, you see.'

'I haven't cigarettes to be answering questions like that.'

'I can get you cigarettes out of FitzGerald's.'

'FitzGerald's is closed.'

'I never thought of it before and then I wondered, is it this way you'd be with a wife? You see, I don't know.'

'Wouldn't you be wiser waiting and see?'

He turned, carefully. 'MacEmm, you haven't this brought from England with you, you know. It was here anyway. I wasn't the first in the Crock's Garden and I doubt I'll be the last. I'm sorry for the soldier for I doubt I was much comfort to him and I hope he found better joy where he went. But you know I wouldn't live that way. I have to make it different. It will be different. Won't it?'

'I hope it will, my dear.'

'Say it will.'

'It will, so.'

'I know people don't like us. Boys at school and in the band, Fahy for instance – from the start they never liked seeing us together. Strange, for when I was alone nobody ever noticed me even. It makes me think did they know before we did. But how would they know?'

He broke off. A squeak outside, a scringe on the window-pane. 'Bats,' he said.

'Yes,' said MacMurrough. 'There's an owl too sometimes. And there's a blackbird in the morning. He'll wake you if the crows don't. You can tell the time from the tree he's singing from.'

'And the sea too. It's a wonderful house.' He gave that blink which had a feeling of velvet when the lashes came down. He yawned and MacMurrough too felt tiredness come upon him. 'I keep thinking how lucky I was meeting you, MacEmm. It's a gift you've gave me. It might have been so different. How empty it would be if we didn't know – it's like a secret really – didn't know how we could be.'

'You'll have me tearful soon, young man.' He pecked him on the forehead. 'Come, we'll make up your bed.'

A little of his fine-pretty-fellow returned and he said, 'Anyway, why would I want to be careful? Won't I have you to be looking over me, in your grand house too?'

You shall not, thought MacMurrough. And the lease on this house will not be renewed.

They shifted the sofa to Doyler's bedside. MacMurrough found rugs and pillows while Jim refilled the warming-pan at the fire – yes, fire in the room and the windows ajar, the extravagance. The boy went out with the pot and returned, maidenly, with it cleaned. Doyler was deep asleep with an interrupted, minor, snore, like a dog's.

'He'll be fine,' said Jim.

'He will of course. Do you need a pyjamas?'

'Do you wear pyjamas?'

'No.'

'I don't so.'

'Goodnight then, Jim.'

'Wait a moment. Wait till I'm in bed.'

He was undressing. He had his shirt pulled out and underneath its folds MacMurrough watched his fingers unbuckle his belt. The boy watched too, as though unsure of the procedure, darting upward glances at MacMurrough. The trousers unbuttoned and they slipped to the floor. He stepped out of them. His shoulder lifted, and he rubbed it along his neck and chin, before he pulled his shirt over his head. The drawers he had recently taken to wearing ridged at his pelvis. It was an outline MacMurrough was familiar with from time out of mind, but this was the first it had been presented proud and blooded. He pulled the string of the drawers, they slipped, and his stand sprang out.

He stood in his oval of candleshine, his slight blush tinting his face. He reached his hands behind his neck and stretched mightily, languorously, sumptuously. He held his stretch while his chest swelled and his nipples paled. His hands came down, and in their coming down, the god left him; and he was smiling that way he often smiled, a little wonderingly, with his bottom lip caught in his teeth.

'I won't let you go, you know.'

MacMurrough nodded. 'Don't catch cold now.'

'I won't,' he said.

CHAPTER NINETEEN

E ASTER MONDAY, and another God-sent day, sky blue and
the grass green, wedding bells tripping over themself to be
heard, any turn you took, wedding processions trooping to their
breakfasts, and the people chirpy and nodding in the streets and
the streets with a closed look, but not staunchly closed, as who
should say in a Sunday manner, but rather sportingly shuttered as
befitted a bank holiday when shopmen, according as the maggot
bit, might choose or choose not to vend their wares. Mr Mack, no
misery-moper he, had opted for holiday; and so it was among the
gay citizenry of Dublin's fair city he was that morning to be found,
tipping his how-d'ye-dos like a native-born, and smiling with the
full intense joy of the beaming sun above. Mind, there wasn't
much of any sun in these misfortunate streets where his direction
took him, away from the fashionable thoroughfares, nothing at all
bar the shadows, keen as knives, that cut the corners. And looking
up betwixt impending tenement walls and the rags of washing
that stretched between, he saw the sky for a pale faraway streak.
Grass, you could go kick for it, green or otherwise. Terrible
depressing environs to be traipsing of a spring morning.

But Mr Mack was off to do his duty by an ailing comrade
and matter a damn the solicitudes of the journey. He passed a

tom-fiddler at a corner pitch, scratching out dance music of our own devil-may-care variety, and he added a pleasing percussion of his own when he dropped a copper in the tramp's hat. Corner-boy eyes squinted at him. Little mothers of the doorstep bounced cheery baby on their laps. Boots rolled over idle pebbles – penny-boys laid off for the holiday, penniless. The streets grew quieter, the sounds of children faded that swung from lampstands. A decently clad woman quite startled him coming out of a stables, and it was a pleasure to lift his hat to her and feel the shadowy air on the crown of his head. The tenemented buildings descended by degrees to poky lanes and humble whitewashed cottages. And sure he didn't need young Doyler's directions then, had only to look for the door in poorest repair.

'It's Fusilier Doyle,' he let out before he could choke it. 'I mean, 'tis Sergeant-Major Doyle. Not at all, 'tis Quartermaster-Sergeant—'

'Is it you, Mr Mack?'

'It is, Mrs Doyle, come to visit an ailing fusilier.'

Sure he wouldn't delay, he was only passing, but he'd have a taste of tea whatever, but not to mind that tin of milk, he'd drink it red. Oh well sure, if 'twas open, missus, go on so. He patted conscientiously each of the girls on the head while they watched his parcel that he deposited by the hearth. Was that himself inside of the curtain? It was. He'd been inside in his bed now six weeks since the giving under him of his legs. The fever had took him then. Mr Mack nodded gravely. Would Mr Mack have a peek inside whatever? It might cheer him out of it, seeing an old friend like. Mr Mack would of course, he'd be happy to sit with an old comrade.

And God knows, thought Mr Mack while he finished his tea, wouldn't it take old Doyle to sniff out a hovel likes of this. Who would credit it, this day and age, that Dublin could boast an earthen floor? Leave out now the unrendered walls, the slats of wood that did for the door. To top it all, hadn't they found a family in worse condition than themself to out-let the back room of it to. True, she kept it tidy enough. A blow of air wouldn't hurt the old conk, however.

He stooped in under the rag that hung for a curtain. His old comrade made no sound or movement. Well he did, but that was only his breathing, very short-coming and laborious, more rattle than breath. He lay with his head sideways. His eyes were open and the one eye that showed seemed huge in his face, sunken, the way it saw from deep inside. Uncanny really, what you'd call unearthly. A hand lay out of the bedding, massive-looking by comparison with the spindle of his arm. The relics of a man, no more.

Mr Mack bent down and said some words. Now the eye stirred. He didn't know was he recognized, but something lit in that face. The hand lifted from the blanket and Mr Mack took it in his own. Surprising heavy it weighed. The rosary beads shook on his wrist and the head nid-nodded. Some important information he had to say, it seemed the entire skin and bones must tremble to tell it. Mr Mack put his ear to the lips. It took a while till he understood. 'That's right,' he said, 'the Colonel gave you a cane.'

The head lay back on the bedding. Mr Mack kept hold the hand. 'A malacca cane,' he told him, 'with a gold-embossed top, sure you remember that.' The eyes still shifted, but it seemed to Mr Mack the violence of the trembling had eased a touch. He patted his old pal's hand. He believed he knew what that sinking mind wished to hear, and what harm, wasn't it the good truth anyhow? He hitched his knees and sat down on the bed. He told him the tale of his cane. How Fusilier Doyle had paraded the smartest man in the battalion, by far and away the smartest. How he'd won the stick, five times he won it, five times in a row, mind. Bombay, Karachi, Quetta, not a maidan in all India but

555

Fusilier Doyle had stood the smartest. Begod, he had that stick won so many damned times, men cursed their luck. Sure they'd never get nowhere with Red Doyle to the fore.

His own head nodded too now, recalling, and he looked up suddenly, saying, 'Do you remember, Mick, the time—' But that old head knew nothing more than what it wished to hear, and Mr Mack sighed, returned to his telling. How the Colonel had thought to get Doyle a stick of his own. Lieutenant-Colonel Holmes that was, an officerly gentleman. 'Not any old stick neither,' he told him, 'but a cane. Had to send to Malacca special. Swankiest yoke you'd think of. Wouldn't see the better of it from here to Donegal. The better? You wouldn't see the like. A gold-topped malacca cane.'

All rich it was in colour and what's this they call it, mottled. Had the Bengal tiger leaping out from the knob. Indeed Mr Mack could picture it still, going wallop on a lazar's bum or clickety-click under the awnings of the street. Clickety-clack, slinging the bat, as arm-in-arm they strolled. 'It was a gold-topped malacca cane,' he repeated, tapping the hand with each stress, 'and a fine grand smart handsome fellow you was with it.' The eyes no longer stirred. Only for a sweat that glistened on his temple, he was gone already. Mr Mack replaced the hand on the bedding, rethreaded the beads through its fingers. He saw his own hand was trembling now. He brought a finger under his nose and sniffed.

'And your buttons too would shame the sun. They would too. They would too.'

In the room the girls were nibbling the crubeens he'd brought. They eyed him with something less than trust, the way he might be thinking of taking them back again. He had a quiet word with Mrs Doyle inquiring, discreetly as he might, of the arrangements, and she said they had the insure paid, thank God, himself was always up to his time with that, and it was good of Mr Mack to ask, thank you for that, he was very good altogether and the crubeens too.

He put on his hat. 'You'll let me know?'

She would.

He came out in the street. The Angelus bell was ringing. He lifted his hat and crossed himself, still with a wet on his finger from the Doyles' font. He stood by a wall muttering the words. The people at the wall opposite had the look of a frieze, stopped there too and muttering their prayers. Behind rose the bleak black blocks of malt-houses, distilleries. There was a house at the corner, not overly dowdy-looking; he went in. He drank a whiskey choking and smoked the half of a cigar, coughing in stifled whoops. He stared at the rows of glasses and bottles, gauging how much capital would be tied up in stock. It was a question that often exercised him, the comparative worth of a corner-grocery's stock. He went out to the pisser at back, and returning he saw another whiskey waiting for him. He drank it slowly, disremembering having ordered it. He felt very old. He was altogether sad.

Sad, and yet cheated too. He felt his youth to be stolen, so it was. That fellow above thieving the happy times from his past. What were they only young fellows together with never a thought in the world? By rights, they would have remained that, a thing of the memory, something fond and scarlet in the mists, you'd look behind on it and smile. But no, this fellow had to burst back in his life. Right into his shop he burst with his smilery and his clothery. You'd have to see him then and know your old pal for the chancer he'd made of himself, with his jokery and his fakery and his Dublin jackeenery. You'd have to be stepping over him in the street, the drunken gutter-singing rowdy. You'd hear it from biddies how he battered his woman and famished his care. And now this wheezing old skin, you'd have to smell him and take his hand and sit in his miserable hut and drink his germs with his miserable tea and his aimless pernickety wife. It was bloody, so it was, it was bloody. It would drive a man to drink – and Mr Mack held out his glass to the curate – wouldn't it take him to choose a house with a freckle-faced flame-haired lad for a curate – 'Put the other half in that, when you're ready. Only a nipperkin now. And a ginger beer for yourself.'

He was a touch light in the head leaving that pub, and considerably lighter in his pocket, having stood treat, for some very practical reason that escaped him now, a round or was it two for the house. He had lost Doyler's street-directions but he held in his hand an infallible nod for the Irish National, though how he was expected to find his way to Fairyhouse he did not know. What time was it at all?

He came out at a crossroads, King Street said the sign. He stood at the corner. High and low he stared, puzzled to an amplush. He couldn't make it out at all. It seemed to him there were evictions up and down the street. Bedsteads coming out of the little houses, mattresses, a settee even. You'd think all the bailiffs in Ireland had suddenly descended this day. And a rum set of bailiffs they looked too, no more than boys the most of them. Out of every house they came, lugging some old goods or other and piling them in the street. Children were bawling, women were tugging at their belongings, beseeching, all manner of language, dog's abuse at the shrill of their voice. And the piles extending right across the street, sticks of furniture, any old thing. Now what sense was there in that? Only blocking the public highway.

Mr Mack took a step towards them. The street crunched under his boot. Everywhere he looked, broken glass. Broken glass everywhere, bits of bottles and plate glass smashed. How long was this he was on the skite in that lushery? He didn't know but a riot was after taking place in the meantime. And never a constable in sight.

A cart was jolting towards the crossroads and Mr Mack ran out. 'Halt,' he called. 'Don't come down. There's glass in the road, she'll slip and hurt, the beast.'

One of the bailiffs stepped out. He had a gun. He had a gun pulled on the carter. 'This cart is commandeered,' he said.

'Take the gun, take it off him,' a woman shrilled. 'Shirkers, they's only cowards.'

Mr Mack said, 'What's going on here?'

The woman turned to him. 'They took me bed, they took me only bed they did.'

'The republic will repay you, missus,' said the fellow with the gun.

'What republic?' said Mr Mack.

'Get down off that cart,' said the gunman.

They took the cart. They turned it endways up with the bedsteads and mattresses. The woman was explaining to Mr Mack, as a man of some authority in a bowler hat, that it was the bed her mother had left her, her poor mother, God rest her soul, she died in that bed.

The carter's cob whisked its tail. The carter looked round the circle of people. 'Ye saw that. Ye won't deny it. He had a gun on me.'

'Daylight robbery,' said a man at the door of his shop.

'Ye'll back me up. He had a gun.'

Suddenly, down the street, came the sound of gunfire. Holy Mother of God! Screaming and shoving, the people scattered, Mr Mack with them, dodging into doorways. Mr Mack peeked out: nothing in the road save three girls who stood in a row with their aprons hitched up at their mouths, gaping, and a curious weazen man who hopped about – he had lost a boot – hopped about, bleeding from the glass and dodging bullets the same time. Making an extraordinary stookawn of himself for there were no bullets to dodge. Nothing at all was happening, and gingerly following the lead of the bolder class of urchin, Mr Mack came out in the street again. Another crackle of musketry and they were all scarpering anew, but the fire was sustained now, and clearly from down by the river; way down by the Four Courts, Mr Mack heard. He had received a fierce dig in the ribs and he was looking about for the culprit, saying 'Now now' with his finger raised, when a cry went up. Lancers! The Lancers! The Lancers is coming! Some dashed ahead only to hurry back, rejoining the mass that generally surged forward, sweeping Mr Mack along. 'Now we'll see the fun,' said a man in his ear. 'The Lancers is the boyos will sort them blackguards.'

But that musketry came from no Lancer's carbine. Mr Mack recognized that barking discharge, inconceivable though it was in the streets of Dublin. Mausers without a doubt, great blunderbussy yokes of things the Boers had always favoured. But what would the Boers be doing in Dublin? A hurry of hooves ahead; a screaming avenue formed in the crowd; terror big in its eyes, a riderless horse bolted through.

Up side streets surged the crowd, searching, anywhere, to centre its alarm. Dumbly Mr Mack was carried along. His head he found was somewhat obfusticated in drink: he could form no very clear understanding of what was happening and the natural malignity of streets worked on him so that he had no notion at all where he was in this maze of back alleys and cuts. Horse-clops echoed everywhere, many many horse, or a few gone galloping wild. The Boer War Mausers growled still, and it would scarce surprise him now if de Wet himself appeared at the head of a

commando – wasn't it always whispered de Wet was none but
Parnell returned?

But who came in the end was only two bewildered troopers.
They hunched over their mounts, evidently lost, and the mounts,
their reins trailing, snorted and blew. Someone shouted the rebels
were at the barricade. And yes, it did look like a barricade, now
Mr Mack came to regard it. The Lancers fired quick cracks off
their carbines. 'There's a child down!' someone shouted. Mother
of God, we'll all be slaughtered. The barricade returned a broken
blustering volley. Chunks of masonry showered off the walls. The
crowd had scattered, losing Mr Mack his hat. The two horses
bucked and tossed, going at a strange diagonal gait, sparks firing
off the cobbles, till they reared wildly, bucketed up another side
street. 'A child is down!' the call kept going round. Mr Mack
darted out to retrieve his hat. And the crowd, that stupid poking
gawping mass, heaved behind him again, pushed him down once
more to the barricade, breached the rickety thing and flooded
through, tumbling it down behind them. Mr Mack glimpsed a
face bloodied below, not a child's thank God, trampled over.

A group of men from the barricade – some had green sort
of uniforms on them – were advancing with rifles up the farther
street. 'Who are they supposed to be?' said Mr Mack.

'Them're the Sinn Feiners,' said his neighbour.

'Oh, they're Sinn Feiners,' said Mr Mack, peering the better
to see these queer near-fabled specimens.

'They'll be thinking to cut the troopers off at the corner.'

Mr Mack saw them kneel and ready their aim. He crossed
himself. 'If them fellows know to shoot at all them Lancers'll be
slaughtered,' said his neighbour, 'King's men and all.' Mother
of God, we'll all be slaughtered. Some in the crowd yelled a
warning, but no horseman would hope to hear above those
cobbles. The troopers came. The rebel guns fired. Snarling

they fired. The troopers slumped from their saddles, thumped in the road.

The people stood stunned. Murderers! someone called, but the cry was not taken up. Stunned, disbelieving, appalled – and fearful. Slowly the people moved back, separating from the deed-doers. A Sinn Feiner lad ran down the road waving a trooper's lance. In the quiet of the fading hooves he waved it. He had a flag attached. A queer flag, in equal divisions, green white and orange. He lodged the lance in a manhole plate in the middle of the street, and there the flag flew, green white and orange. 'Murderers, murderers,' came that voice again, all alone in the quiet. The lad's face flushed with a ferocious courage. He raised his rifle and fired in the air. Only then did his comrades cheer, and they too fired off their guns, that furious joy of blooding.

Mr Mack turned and blundered through the crowd. He blundered by the dead child and the woman who Murderers! Murderers! wailed. Along the lively inquisitive streets he lurched. He must find his tram. He must be home.

Nelson's Pillar fingered from out the housetops. He fixed its direction in his eye, and for once his eye did not deceive his feet. Indeed, a hard push and a scrape it would be, avoiding O'Connell Street that holiday afternoon. Every tenement, every fever-nest, every rookery in Dublin was spilling its contents in the road and it seemed to Mr Mack all slumdom must reel its way to his tram-stop. Every shawlie and shabaroon, every larrikin and scut, every slut, daggle-tail, trollop and streel, frowsy old bowsies and loitering corner-boy sprawlers in caps, every farthing-face and ha'penny-boy, every gutty, gouger, louser, glugger, nudger, sharper, shloother, head, every whore's melt of them, mister-me-friend and go-by-the-wall, the dogs in the street themself – all rascaldom was making for Mr Mack's tram-stop; and he must pinch and shove to gain any headway at all.

At last he stood on the Pillar steps. The great wide splendid thoroughfare – O'Connell Street was you a Catholic, Sackville Street was you at all in the Protestant way (was it any wonder if a man went astray in this town?) – swarmed with a wild ree-raw mindless throng. Every now and then the shout would go up: Troopers! or The military! or The polis is coming! or They's shooting wild! and the crowd would stampede him by, leaving Mr Mack to cling to the pedestal, as to a cliff, to keep any footing. Tricksters was all, hoaxsters, for no polis came, no military. Loot was master. By him sailed the most fanciful apparitions. A slum-boy in three top-hats swinging golf-clubs. Dirty-faced girls with boas and high-heeled shoes on. The mess of life veered and shifted. Another plate window crashed.

Across the way where the crowd thinned was the General Post Office. The Sinn Feiners held it. He could see nothing of the Sinn Feiners themself bar the muzzles of guns that poked from the windows and crouching forms behind the parapet on the roof. That same strange unaccountable flag, green white and orange, flapped above them. What on earth would Sinn Feiners want with a post office? It crossed his mind in a daft way that they, like him before, had mistook it for a bank.

Handbills were posted all about. Slap-dash affairs with shoddy spacing and type. Something in Erse. Some further flim-flam in English. The Provisional Government of the Irish Republic. To the People of Ireland. Signed then by a poweration of names nor he nor anyone else had heard of.

The Lancers had charged here too, it was told. There was a dead horse down the way. All about the steps, flowers were strewn and trampled, where the flower-sellers' stalls had been toppled. Barricades blocked the side streets, erected of particular things: bicycles jumbled and piled in one, hunks of marble for another, bales of newsprint – the work of disparate guilds whimsically chosen. Trams had been overturned. There were no trams running. No juice, the tram-man told him. Even trains: the Sinn Feiners had dug up the lines. And no polis. No polis anywhere. Withdrawn to barracks. Every last pigeon-hearted lily-livered chicken-gutted sneak of them. It was pandemonium. It was Donnybrook Fair. It was all ballyhooly let loose.

Naming calls: and he did not dare put words to his fear. But he knew the green uniform Doyler would always be wearing; and he had seen the wish of that Sinn Feiner boy's face. Jim's age, no older. He must get home.

He lurched down the steps and plunged into the push. He shoved carelessly, in a dream nearly – he had long since lost his hat. The rebels had shot three priests in their vestments. The British had hung the Archbishop. The South was up. The West was up. The Germans had landed in Tralee. Carson was marching on Dublin with forty thousand Orangemen. The Lord Lieutenant was raising the Curragh. The Lord Lieutenant was dead.

The unaccustomed whiskey dulled his intelligence. He felt the golden shine of the sun that had not diminished all afternoon: it seemed a timeless day. And it was tiring, all this excitement and the rumours that bandied about, the all of it a strain on his dignity. He looked at the grinning chomping children's faces. Down this end it was the sweet shops that had been looted, and each slum-boy and girl had a sudden rich child's Lenten hoard.

The Liffey breeze revived him a somewhat, and he asked of a respectable man in spats was there any news of Kingstown, was it held for the King yet? To be told the German High Seas fleet was this moment shelling the harbour. Zeppelins were travelling up the Wicklow coast and two U-boats had been spotted in the mouth of the Liffey. Mr Mack nodded his head. But worse news than this, the rebels had fired on the old gentlemen of the Georgius Rex. The Georgius Rex, Mr Mack repeated. Mown down in the street they were. Marching home off an exercise, down by the canal this was: murdered. This was shocking altogether, and Mr Mack said, 'I only thought to join them myself. Matter of weeks back, I'm only waiting to hear.' The gentleman viewed him, and under his lidded gaze Mr Mack was acutely aware of his hatless undress and the drink on his breath. 'Indeed,' said the gentleman. And the poor Pope has committed suicide, a young lady added in all earnestness.

Mr Mack went with the tram-lines, following where the shamrock tram-stops led. The general confluence was against him, but enough were walking his direction for him not to feel entirely lunatic. Musketry could still be heard. Nothing dangerous or anything, only spurts of it that he took to be the military. Mausers growled then in response, two or three streets away always. At the canal he spoke with a whey-faced man, who gripped a child by the wrist and pointed out the different houses held by the rebels. They had shot at a man in his own motor. In his own motor they had shot at him. And was it here they killed the Georgius Rex? asked Mr Mack. The whey-faced man didn't know about that, indeed by his quizzical look he found Mr Mack disappointing. His own motor, he repeated. Shot at a man in his very own motor. 'And this gallows here' – pulling the boy round – 'was seen to be talking to them.'

'Did you talk with the Sinn Feiners now?' asked Mr Mack. The boy wore a crabby adult expression that disguised a little the hurt of the man's grip. 'Don't you know that's aiding and abetting the King's enemies?'

'But it's Mr Ronan from the two-pair back,' the boy insisted in a squeaking breaking voice.

'You're only digging your grave,' the whey-faced man told

him. 'I'm waiting on a constable coming by for to take him in charge.'

Begod, you'll be waiting, thought Mr Mack. Then of all people, strolling along the canal, his shadow rolling on the low canal wall, came Father O'Toiler. 'Father, Father,' called Mr Mack advancing across the bridge. He felt exposed there with the Sinn Feiners watching from the houses, and concerned for the curate's dignity, he said, 'Holy be, is it safe at all, your reverence?'

'Safe?' repeated the priest. 'As to that, Mr Mack, we are not out of the woods yet, not by a chalk long as my ashplant here. A day delayed, nevertheless a start has been made which is half the answer and I believe we may venture a small halloo.'

'Oh indeed,' said Mr Mack, 'hello.' A curious gruntling noise the priest was making, not at all dissimilar to a certain domestic animal, and an expression slipped about his face that might conceivably be smiling – a transformation of his habitual austerity shocking as any of the day's events.

'Safe, that is, for any Irishman,' he said.

He stepped along, and Mr Mack stepped beside and a little behind him, along the tended imperturbable terraced street. The lawns in the gardens had been mown; a slight tingling sensation irritated Mr Mack's nose. Last week's blossom drifted in the gutters, this week's fluttered above them. Mr Mack hemmed. He did not wish to importune his reverence, but his reverence would understand it was his son he was worried for. Was there anything with the flute band in this terrible business? The Father would understand he did not mean to be casting astertions of any type or any sort. The Father had only the boys' best interest at heart. But boys would often be getting the wrong end of the stick. The Father would understand he spoke as a father himself. It was with a parent's concern he spoke, all considerations aside.

'Mr Mack,' the priest replied, 'if but one of my boys be out this glorious day, my labour with that band is well done.'

'But Father dear, you cannot intend what you say. These are ruffians. There's talk of Larkinites with them – Germans, I don't know what else. It's murder and mayhem it is. And there's worse will come of it, I know that, I know.'

There were no Germans, the curate was pleased to inform him, Germany being second only to England for the cradle of heresy. And what Larkinites there were were not Larkinites now, but good brave Catholic sons of Ireland, who in this final hour had repented their former impieties. Together they stood now, the staunch and the prodigal returned, as the Army of the Irish Republic. Mr Mack might remark the republican flag which was a third of it orange in generous acknowledgment to the Protestant north. Mr Mack might consider that generosity misplaced and an unfortunate lapse in so Catholic a cause. But Father O'Toiler would assure him that a little Irish weather would soon fade that orange to Vatican yellow. For Mr Mack was to consider this was indeed a Catholic rising and therefore a blessed one too. Holy Mother Church, despairing at last of the English recanting, turned to her first-loved children. The Saxon tide must trouble no more the sacred shore. Again must Ireland rise, isle of saints and scholars, to shine a lamp among the nations. And her spiritual empire, that empire of the soul, which stretched to the world's imagined corners, wherever had preached her missionary sons or wandered in exile her children lamenting, this empire she would lay at the feet of the Cross, the humblest fief, and the jewel in the crown, of the Holy Father of the Holy See.

'But the people,' said Mr Mack, 'they're not for this carry-on at all.'

The Irish people, Father O'Toiler assured him, most happily assured him, had not the right to be wrong. The people might quibble and fiddle with Home Rule. But it was written: 'the Erne shall rise rude in torrents and the hills be rent and the sea in red waves shall roll.' And it was scarcely to be supposed the poet of the Roisín Dubh had in mind the coming of a shoneen talking-house, a gombeen legislature scrounged and cadged for by whiskey-swilling fixers in the imperial Parliament across the sea. No, the curate continued, drawing breath and swinging his ashplant before him, freedom was never to be given or argued for: it might only be taken. And so it was, in fulfilment of the prophecies, the few Irish men and boys had risen this day.

'Blood and death and tears,' he said. 'Who don't fall in battle will hang from the Saxon tree. Many the mother will mourn and many the hearth will be lonely. And they will be reviled, Mr Mack, as was Our Saviour. But Ireland will rise again, as did Our Lord. She will waken and look upon herself as one from a dream. And she will wonder at the magnificence of her sons. Pray, Mr Mack, pray God your son may so be exalted as with these joyful martyrs to die. For already in heaven the saints prepare the welcoming feast.

'And now, Mr Mack, I believe I must leave you. I am on a mission of mercy to the sisters at St Mary's. I was at Boland's mills with Commandant de Valera, a rigorous man and pious, and would you believe we ran plumb out of the Holy Sacrament.'

It would scarce have surprised Mr Mack now if the priest had lifted his frock-coat and floated across the road, so strange and elated his countenance. Mr Mack shook his head; and he was shaking it still when he traipsed at last into Kingstown. The sleepy town was sleepy yet. Invalids and convalescents pushed in their chairs. Weary children walked with balloons. The mailboat siren wailed, dead to its time by the Findlater's clock. Constables stood their point immemorial. The gunfire, wild rumours, all that riot and rumpus lay far behind, a rumour itself. Perhaps there was more of a crowd in the streets than was normal, and they remonstrating against the trains and the trams, the qualified things, never on time and the least sign of trouble, banjaxed. Respectable people; and their indignation worked on Mr Mack till he wondered might it not be true, that it was all a little local madness, nothing strange in Ireland, every second week sure, hotheads and firebrands, demonstrations in the streets, parading with arms, an imitation of violence, a longing even, but never realized, shrunk from at the brink.

Then at the cab-rank he watched two gentlemen come to blows, bidding for the sole jarvey. And it was eerie the streets with so little traffic, only people walking, trudging, their jaded faces; entire families, well-to-do and with their maids some of them, who had been bathing at Killiney or taking the ozone down in Bray. He felt the truth had not made up its mind: the signs were contrary everywhere.

At the People's Park, would you credit it, that runt of a newsboy latched on to him, and he was dogging Mr Mack all along Glasthule Road, piping out his little news or his want of news, making a holy show of Mr Mack in the street. Until Mr Mack turned, flailing at him, not intending to strike, but striking nonetheless his nails on his lip so that it bled.

It bled, and Mr Mack said, 'Oh dear me, no.' The boy took no more regard of his cut than of a fly, and he was still piping away his idiotic questions. Mr Mack had his handkerchief out, and he wet the corner to dab it on the boy's chin. 'You're not hurt,' he told him.

'But mister, what about the papers, mister?'

'Well, what about them?' said Mr Mack, still dabbing.

'The even papers. What's happened the even papers, mister?'

'There are no evening papers,' Mr Mack explained. 'Don't you know now there's a rising in Dublin?'

'But what am I to sell so?'

'You won't be selling anything sure.'

'But they can't do that, mister. I'll be bate now.'

'No you won't now.'

'I'll be bate, mister, and I don't have nothing brung home.'

'Is it your da you mean?' The boy nodded. 'Sure he'll know it's not your fault.' Mr Mack put away his handkerchief. Where he had dabbed was the only clean in the wee scrap's face. He stood wobble-kneed and his toes turned in. His squinting eyes, misbelieving, peered up at Mr Mack. Terrible slight he looked. 'Don't you see now,' Mr Mack told him, not unkindly, 'where your talk of Fenians and fighting and nation-once-again has got you?'

'Nobody never said about the even papers, mister.'

'Here now,' said Mr Mack. Here we go again, he thought. 'Sixpence, that's all I have. Off you go. It'll all be over tomorrow, never fear, and you'll be back with your *Herald* and *Mail*.'

And now who was this only Mary Nights. Mary Nights not to her hour and her direction into Dublin, a thing never known in weal nor woe, come wind nor weather, in hail rain nor shine. Her determined old head bent to her course. 'They's drawing out,' said she, 'the nights.'

The bell clinked. Lord save us, he was home at last. Nancy was at the kitchen door. She had a bowl in her elbow, mixing something. 'Why, Mr Mack, you haven't your hat.'

Mr Mack wiped the back of his hand across his forehead. 'Never mind that. Is Jim about?'

'Sure he was moping about the shop till I told him go out and play.'

'When was this?'

'I don't know now. He was back again then and he called out to me. He's to eat his dinner at MacMurrough's.'

'Mr MacMurrough's? Was Doyler with him?'

'Doyler's in his bed still, poorly. You look took yourself, Mr Mack. Is there anything the matter?'

'Oh sure Nancy, the most terrible thing has happened, you wouldn't believe.'

'Don't I know, Mr Mack. And where would you find another hat the size of you?'

Before Mr Mack had left for town that morning, he had told Jim – not to keep shop, exactly: it was a holiday and the shop was firmly shut for the holiday – but to keep by, with an ear for the bell, in case of a customer would be caught sudden and they'd need a goods in an emergency. For a corner-grocery, he said, his hand braced in the air against any contraposition, was as much a service to the community as a shop in the strict sense. Jim had mentioned Doyler above at MacMurrough's. Tush, his father had replied. Hadn't Jim only now told him that Doyler was right as rain? Was he saying now there was any imminent danger of a relax? Was Doyler about to be drownded in his bed, was he? Fine bobbish fellow likes of Doyler, he didn't want Jim to be mollycoddling. Let Jim read a book at home, hadn't he examinations this summer? His father might wish he had leisure for reading a book, so he might.

His father was gone then, and Jim settled with his tome, *From Crécy to Tel el-Kebir*, the very article for a blue sky in the morning. Mollycoddle, he thought – milksop too: he had fed Doyler bread dipped in milk when he woke. There were other names he could think of: miss boy, molly mop, molly maguire – though the Molly Maguires were agrarian banditti who had dressed, he did not know why, in women's clothing. By noon, the brightness outside had deepened nearly to night the apparent evening within. Drake

571

had circumnavigated the globe and Spain approached her acme; while Nancy up in Aunt Sawney's room was calling for him to fetch water. He made his noisy tread on the stairs and waited in the door.

'You can come in,' she said.

'Will I leave it here?'

Nancy tipped a look at Aunt Sawney, who was sitting up in bed with her bed-jacket on and her day-cap, and the big bolster behind. 'He hangs about the door for fear he'll catch something prejudicial.'

'I do not,' said Jim, walking boldly in. Immediately he was aware of the smell, a woman's room smell, of toilet soap and bodily things, cleansing and motions. Of sickness too, or rather the things against sickness, ointments and creams. He nearly could touch the warmth, a stuff of lavender and camphor balls, stale the way they had it hoarded through the winter. It was a strangely self-contained room: he never saw anything purchased for it, yet it had a share of jars and bottles that must surely run out.

'And what is the little man at today?' asked Aunt Sawney.

'Reading a book,' he answered.

Nancy rolled up the soiled napkin and dropped it in the pan of water. Things changed when they left this room. He would pick that up now and carry it down the stairs to the range. It would be hideous then, but here you wouldn't mind it at all. He watched Nancy blow on a penny before she placed it on the baby's belly-button. She did up the napkin guggling in the baby's face, and asking it, singingly, 'How many miles to Dubellin town? Three score and ten.'

'Why wouldn't the little man go out?' Aunt Sawney said.

'Old Macks has him minding shop,' Nancy told her. 'Would you credit it? Minding shop and the shop closed itself.'

Aunt Sawney smacked her gums. She looked nice in her bed with her bed-jacket on. Nancy had knitted her that. 'Are you well, Aunt Sawney?' he asked.

'Come here, little man,' she said. A shilling she had for him. 'Is it the black fellow?' she wanted to know then.

He laughed. 'Is what the black fellow sure?'

Nancy stood up with the babe in her arms, heaving her. 'Go on out with you,' she said, 'and I'll listen for the bell.'

'All right so, I will.'

He found MacEmm smoking in the garden room in Ballygihen. He had his towel roll on the table and a carton of Player's cigarettes. Jim couldn't say exactly why, but he thought the Player's a very good sign. The patient – Hygeia's darling, so MacEmm called him – was doing nicely above, no sicks now, only the gripes and the grumps. Mrs Moore had him eating broth quite tame. Himself, he was tired playing sick-nurse and was off down the Forty Foot. If Jim had his swimmers and any sense he'd come bathing with him.

'I have my swimmers.'

'Come then.'

But he would just pop up and see Doyler first. He found him dozing still. Jim pulled the covers and let his hand on the forehead. It wasn't a fever at all, only a temperature. 'Hello there,' said Doyler.

'You're awake so.'

'I don't know but I'm groggy all over.'

'It's the doctor's draught he gave you.'

'Have I missed me parade?'

'Don't mind that,' said Jim, settling him back on the pillow. 'Are you hungry at all?'

He wasn't. He was already dropping away. Jim looked at him a while, sensible of a niggly disappointment. He bent over and kissed him on the glisten of his temple. He tiptoed out of the dimmed rayed room. Old Mrs Moore on her chair beyond the door smiled so kindly. Yes, she told him, he was bravely now and the broth on the boil whenever.

Oh but it was grand at the Forty Foot and swell to swim. He dived and cut his dash before the regulars' benevolent appraisal. 'Was you one of them madcaps swum to the Muglins?' He was indeed. 'Gob, but I held the pair of yous in me glass. Pegging away like blazes. I said to meself, I says, God help Wales if it gets in them fellas' way. Won me two bob out of that.' Jim hoped he hadn't bet on them coming back. 'Gob, but I didn't. How's the other fella?' The other fellow was fine sure. Jim glided through the nugatory holiday throng and dived again from the high board. He floated on his back and gazed at the vast heavenly dome above, infinity. Over there the Muglins, and close by, watching from his ledge, MacEmm, reposing, admiring him.

They dried in the sun on the slabs with their towels under. Jim said, 'I thought of entering in the Gala this year.'

'So you should.'

'You'd train me of course.'

MacEmm laughed. He dressed, saying he had one or two commissions in Kingstown. Jim followed him along the road past Sandycove Harbour. He was going to Kingstown to buy his ticket. Jim knew this for certain, and he said, 'Don't do it, MacEmm, please don't go.'

They were passing through the little Otranto gardens, and MacEmm stopped now at a bench that overlooked the bay. He said, 'It's not how I should have wished it, my dear. I should be long gone by now, but your pal has screwed my plans rather. Drowning, I mean. They say Easter longed for is gone in a day. And now it has gone, and I—My gosh, look at that!'

'Yes,' said Jim, 'I've seen it before.'

'So graceful.'

'It's from out Drumcondra way. They have an aerodrome.'

'Extraordinary.'

'But MacEmm, you can't leave with Doyler sick.'

'Doyler has an upset tummy. If he's not better tomorrow he must try for a hospital. – Do you see him climb? How wonderful it must be.'

'I'll steal your ticket. I won't steal it, I'll tear it up.'

'All alone up there. Such terrific solitude.'

'You won't listen to me.'

'Oh Jim, I am listening to you. But I don't belong here now. You must surely understand that. – Look, he dives, the vol plané!'

'It's not true, you do so belong.'

Jim had tried to bring his arm round the high faraway neck, with clumsy inadequacy, and he could only leave his fingers latched on the shoulder, while the neck strained to follow the puttering engine above. Puttering which repeated now in his own chest as his breath unwilling sobbed.

'Oh Jim, don't cry on me now.' The big arm came wrapping round, shrugging his paltry fingers from the shoulder, and pulling him close to the creamy soft cloth of his suit. 'Aren't you the beautiful boy of the world? And don't you know I love you too much? Far too much to interfere between you and your pal. But I couldn't bear to watch you with another always. It's too much for me.'

'I don't know what difference that makes.'

'If you don't know that, my dear, you should never have swum to your Muglins at all.'

There was some shiloo on the sea-wall. Fellows weren't watching the skies any more, but were gathering about some news. A startling intelligence, to tell by their faces. 'Fairyhouse,'

MacEmm said. 'Apparently an outsider won the National.' He told Jim to go back to the house and mind after Doyler, that he'd see him this evening, they'd have that together. Then he got up and made his way to the road. Jim watched his walk, a strong leisurely stride, and his windy clothes billowing behind him. Then after a while, Jim got up too and went down by the sea-wall where the little men were big with faces.

Moments later, mad and tumultuous, he was haring through the garden gate. Up the lawns, through the garden doors, skidding on the polished wood, into the hall where he paused, panting, his hand upon the swirling knob of the baluster. His head brimmed with the news. His heart positively had leapt to his mouth. He must collect himself. There were too many things. He heard Mrs Moore below in the kitchen. He went down. Yes, he said. Broth, he said. Sitting up, yes, that was good. He'd bring it, yes, himself, he would. And thanks now, Mrs Moore.

He climbed the stairs, judicious of each step. His hurry of spirits transferred to the tray: the spoon that rattled, broth that spilt on the bread and the good napkin. The door yawned. 'Doyler?' He wasn't sitting up at all. 'Doyler, are you all right?' Groaning and his breath at a gasp. The poor fingers shook and picked at the bedding. A dread turn he had took. 'Doyler?' He must fetch the doctor. The tray had set down: Jim found the flannel seized in his hand. He swabbed the forehead, saying, 'Doyler, Doyler, can't you hear me at all?'

His hand was nabbed, a strength jerked him down: great big slobber on his face, and Doyler saying, 'Gaum you.'

'Eejit you!' shouted Jim with stunning ferocity. 'The fear of God in me, you did.'

'Serves you right and all. Leaving me here to me fate.'

'You wasn't left. You was sleeping sure.'

'All over me one minute, and I close me eyes, you're off. Poor old Doyler can fetch for himself.'

'You had Mrs Moore outside the door.'

'Any excuse to be gone of me.'

'A rotten low trick to play.'

Jim flung the curtains and day gushed in. What time was it, he wanted to know, what day was it even. Was that broth he smelt? His belly thought his throat was cut. Did Jim know at all what a horrible big house was this to be abandoned in it? And where was his clothes?

'It's two, maybe three in the afternoon.'

'Give us here that tray. I've the hungry staggers whiffing it.'

Jim considered him while he ate or, better, slurped the broth. A fright he looked with his hair tussled and the pillow-creases on his face. He still looked pasty and his eyes lacked glister. 'Easy,' he said, 'you're not the better of it yet.'

Doyler snorted a look. There was nothing ever the wrong with him. He was maybe tired, was all. He was maybe after neglecting himself a trifle in Dublin. Neglecting the inner man, he elaborated, patting his stomach. Patting it a touch too hard, for he let a groan, 'Mary and Joseph, the cramp in me belly.'

'You got a bug out of the water,' said Jim complacently, taking the bowl before he had it bolted. 'You might have known not to go guzzling the Irish Sea. Truthfully now, how poorly do you feel?'

'I'm grand. Grand total. Who was the biddy outside? Was it she made the broth? Listen and I tell you. I went out looking for the flush-down article—'

'There's a pot under the bed sure.'

'Never mind that. Hello now, says she. Hello missus, says I. How're you coming up? says she. Fine now missus, thanks.

You're rallying anyway, she says, looking me up and down. And there I was, the full of the door, stark mother naked.'

'Never,' said Jim. 'Oh gosh, you weren't?'

'God's truth. And you know that way you are when you wake up?' He made a size with his hands. 'There's no aiming at a po with that.'

'Don't, Doyler.'

'And there she was, calm as clocks, getting her eyeful up and down. You're rallying, says she. I nearly bursted. Oh, laugh away. I tell you, I was back in bed before you'd cry crack. She had me all of a heap thinking she might be getting notions.'

'You ought never be let out,' said Jim. 'And your shirt only on the rail where you flung it.'

'Where? Sure I didn't think, the house so quiet. Pass us over that now and I'll be making me move.'

'You won't be making any move,' said Jim. 'You're stopping here. Two days' bed, the doctor was decided.'

'Aye aye. Suppose he left a note excusing me work and all. Better, a draft on his bankers to tide me over. A decent set, these half-crown medicals.'

'He was a guinea doctor, matter of fact.'

'A guinea doctor! Kiss me pink. I'm not rallying at all, I'm resurrected. Get on now, Jim.' He made motions of getting up, but the pain gripped him. It wasn't sudden, you could see on his face it was coming round. He arched forward clasping his belly. Seconds and it was gone, and he flumped on the pillow. But he looked harrowed after, and a little surprised.

'Is it very bad?'

'I don't know, it rolls round. Actually, it is. I'm at death's door if you did but know. It isn't upright I'll be leaving this premises. Oh Jim, won't you pray for your pal? And won't you promise me, Jim, you'll cry at me funeral? Tell them, 'twas of a broken heart and the colic he died.'

'Shut up,' said Jim. 'I don't know anyone would cry over you.'

'Serious now, they'll be wondering in town what's happened me. I didn't say, but I skipped a guard detail Sunday morning, then the evening I missed parade. I have me officers, you know. Year and a day I'll be peeling spuds and the revolution nowhere the nearer.'

'What revolution?'

'Gaum you. Just give us me shirt and find me me uniform.'

'I can't.'

'Why can't you?'

'It got flung in the sea.'

'Ah no, Jim, not me uniform.'

Yes, Jim was sorry, his uniform got soaked, flung in the sea in the muddle. Jim had took it home to get the salt out and he didn't know would it be dry again till morning. Doyler wouldn't mind stopping the night, would he? MacEmm had said it was all right. And Doyler wasn't fit, need only look at him. 'You're delicate still,' he said, easing him back in the bed.

'Will you get your hands off me, Jim. I've a pain, I'm not an invalid.' He reached behind his head, plumping the pillow. 'Well I'm stuck here so.'

He didn't look too entirely put out. Jim pulled off his boots and sat up on the bed. 'Listen,' he began, 'there was a paper inside your tunic. I didn't like to look but it got dropped out. Some sort of a street plan.'

'That,' said Doyler, 'is me pride and joy. Do you know what it is? I drew it meself. It's what you could call the opposite of a street plan. Give us here that bread and I'll tell you.'

'No, it's too heavy on your stomach.'

'I need me strength is all.' He reached anyway and the remains of the broth to dip it in. 'Now what it does,' he said, indistinctly through the slop in his mouth, 'instead of the streets, it shows the ways above the streets – the rooftops of course. All round Stephen's Green.'

'So Stephen's Green would be an important place?'

'Any number of roads coming into Dublin, they meet there. If I had it here I'd show you plain. Snipe and run.' He made the motion of a rifle with his arm and elbow. Pow, the arm shot up, the elbow recoiled and broth spilt on the sheet. 'That's all right, scrape of soda'll sort that out. Snipe and run,' he repeated. 'Never mind your slope-and-port, your form-fours. Snipe and run. What's up with you?'

Jim was staring at the bruise on Doyler's shoulder. It was just where the recoil of his gun would have hit, had his gun been real and not play. But his gun was real. It was hiding this minute in the broom-cupboard at Jim's home. He believed for the first time he understood that Doyler was a soldier, that he really had been in training, that Doyler in a very real sense was under orders. He wondered was it entirely sane what he was about.

'Oh that,' said Doyler, following his look. 'That's all you get for your pains.'

'Does it hurt that bad shooting a gun?'

'Hurts worse getting shot, I believe.'

Jim tried to think and make sense of his thoughts. Was he depriving the army of a trained soldier? It was only for one night, mind. And Doyler might be trained, but he really wasn't fit. And wouldn't Jim be there anyway to stand in his place? 'Doyler,' he said, 'they would want me, wouldn't they, in the Citizen Army?'

'Ah no now, Jim, you'll steer clear of that lot. You're grand now and you don't want any messing in Dublin. Your da's in the right of that. He does right to be lost in town. A fool would be home there.'

That decided it. Doyler would never let him in with him. Far better to have Doyler come find him. No, the Citizen Army would do fine. Tomorrow they'd have three, where they only had one before, and MacEmm a crack shot. He commanded his face. 'And do you think,' he asked, 'is it St Stephen's Green that Mr Pearse would be? If ever there was to be a rising, I mean.'

'Don't ask me where that crowd'd be. Abbey Theatre most like, giving a reading. Have I got this straight now? We're to spend the night together here?'

'Oh gosh no,' said Jim. 'I have deliveries all evening.'

'He never has you doing deliveries the bank holiday?' Jim shrugged: the unaccountable quirks of fathers. 'You're saying I'm to be stuck in this house on me own the night? Ah Jim, it's an awful big house. There's noises.'

'That's the wind.'

'It's creepy on your own.'

'MacEmm'll be here. He'll stay up with you sure.'

'You and your bloody MacEmm. You won't be happy till you have us the three in a bed. I'll show you what I think of his nobs.' He made a grab for Jim's arms, twisting them. Jim let him wrestle away, exerting only a token opposition. His arms were pinioned under and Doyler sat him astride, naked as Adam and as flawless. 'James Mack, is that what I think it is? It is and all. You're worser than a he-goat, Jim Mack. You'd take advantage of a poor sick man to have your dirty end away.'

'I won't,' said Jim, 'today.' He gazed fondly into Doyler's eyes till Doyler rolled over on a pillow and was quiet. 'Penny for them,' he said. 'I have a shilling even.'

'Sure sorrow the shilling they're worth,' said Doyler.

'Tell me anyway.'

'I was thinking earlier lying here what you said about the schoolteaching. I don't know, it's a mad idea, but I can't think why I wouldn't give it a twist.'

'Of course you will,' said Jim. 'You'll sit the scholarship. Maybe not this year, but next. We'll do the books together.'

'And I was thinking, wouldn't it be gas if we did get a digs. Now I know we won't now. Pie in the sky, I know that. But wouldn't it be a gas if we did manage it? I can picture it even.'

'So can I.'

'No you can't. You never lived anywheres poor.'

'I can too. It's poky and damp and there's a torn wallpaper and the fire won't draw.'

'There's no fire. We can't afford a fire to keep. And there's bugs in the wallpaper.'

'We'll have a box for our table and an old newspaper for a cloth.'

'We'll have nix to eat and nuppence to buy it with.'

'We'll eat bread and onions.'

'Bread and onions, bread and onions, bread and onions,' said Doyler. 'Because you know onions repeat.'

'And every time we sit to table, we'll be reading that same old paper, tenth time the same column. We'll curse it, so we will.'

'We'll have no light to read by.'

'We'll shake the lamp to find any oil left.'

'There's no lamp sure.'

'And you know,' said Jim, exploring his fingers along Doyler's arm, along the scrapes and grazes of the elbow, their mesmeric tactility, 'you know, things won't be like this then.'

'Why wouldn't they?'

'Listen to me. When you'd touch me, I won't be jumping, I won't be startled, won't hardly show if I felt it even.'

'What about it?'

'I'm just thinking that would be pleasant. To be reading, say, out of a book, and you to come up and touch me – my neck, say, or my knee – and I'd carry on reading, I might let a smile, no more, wouldn't lose my place on the page. It would be pleasant to come to that. We'd come so close, do you see, that I wouldn't be surprised out of myself every time you touched.'

'And wouldn't you better like it if I touched you, say, down here, say? And if I was to go down, say, like this, say?'

'Don't bend, you'll bring on the cramp.'

'And, say now, I took hold your buttons and undone them, say, like this, say, and I fetched out your lad, what would you say to that?'

'Don't, Doyler. Stop it.'

'And say I was to lick my, say my tongue, say? Only the tip of my tongue, like this, say?'

'Oh my goodness,' whispered Jim. 'Oh my gracious me.'

He didn't need to ask where Doyler had learnt this. In this same bed – oh my gosh. The love he felt was extraordinary. The sense of its power astounded him. That all this should happen, and then Ireland to rise! that he should not be separated from any he loved. He felt humbled, and a little awed. The little hairs curled through Doyler's fingers as up and down the fingers stroked. This very bed. The eyes closed and the mouth wide and the thick lips on the pink thing. My gosh.

After, while they lay, Jim said, 'Will I tell you now about the Sacred Band of Thebes?'

'Tell me anything you like.'

'They was an army,' Jim began. Yes, an army. They stood three hundred strong. And each man stood with his friend by his side. They fought that way, friend and friend, side by side. They were famed the world over, the ancient world over, for their courage and loyalty. They never once broke or ran. 'For you know,' said Jim, 'it would be awful hard to do anything dishonourable with your friend by your side.'

'So they was never bate?'

'Well, they was,' said Jim. At Chaeronea they fell. But not a man but he had his face to the foe and his friend beside him, dead too. Sometimes it could make Jim cry picturing this. The victor too had cried to see them on the battlefield, when all else had broke and run, the Sacred Band of Lovers, each man so brave and true to the end.

'So that's what they was,' said Doyler, 'lovers?' Jim nodded. 'The sergeants too? Did they have their chaps?'

'They were all of them lovers,' Jim said firmly.

'Was they not worried they'd be thought partial? Giving out guard detail and that, a sergeant might be accused of favouring his own chap.'

'I don't know,' said Jim, 'but the sergeants had only sergeants for their friend.'

'I'm with you now,' said Doyler. 'So was the general's chap a general also? That was two generals. Two generals is a very chancy business. Could lead to any manner of confusion.'

'I know what you're doing,' said Jim, 'and you're only wasting your breath. You know it's the most wonderful thing.'

'Tell me this, Jim: what happened if one of them died?'

'What do you mean?'

'What happened the other fellow then? Did he fall on his sword or what? Did he hunt round quick to catch another chap? Maybe they had him excused drill till he found another fellow.'

'You're no use at all,' said Jim, 'and I don't know why I bother with you.' Doyler was making to rib-tickle his belly, and Jim just thumped him on the shoulder. He got up and was dressing. Doyler stretched in the sheets.

'I don't believe a bed and Doyler was ever this long

acquainted. Reminds me of himself at home. When he used take to his bed till me ma found the money for his trousers to get back from the pawn. Like father, like son, eh?'

'Father? said Jim.

'Something like it, I suppose. When's your man due back?'

'Any time.'

'You positive now he don't mind me being here?'

'No, he's glad. He's glad if I'm happy.' Jim sat down on the bed, tying his boots. 'He's going tomorrow. He's to join the army in England. Only he wanted to be sure we were all right before he left.'

'What's it have to do with him anyway?'

'He's a complicated man. I think the way it is, he wanted to leave something behind. He's got it into his head he'll be killed in the war. I have to stop that. I have to stop him leaving.'

'You sound like him sometimes.' Jim looked up. 'Goodness gracious,' Doyler mimicked.

'Do I say that?'

'My golly gosh.'

'I don't say that.' The pillow flung at him. He flung it back. 'The state of this bed,' he said. He tugged the sheets, tucking them under.

'How you going to stop him?'

'We'll see.' Jim's thoughts ran on and he said, 'It makes sense too. If there's fighting to be done, or dying even, it's only sensible it's an Irish war, not an English. That way, we'll all be fighting together.'

'Mary and Joseph, but you're the bloodthirsty animal.'

'I am not. Did you know the English had him in gaol?'

'Sure the Irish would gallows him, only for the scandal of naming what he done.'

'Not in my country they won't. Listen now, you'll sleep some more?'

'I'll have sores on me bum and I sleep any more.'

Jim felt his forehead. 'There's still a temperature. We'll have a big day tomorrow. You can show me round the Green.'

'Jim?' It was funny but he knew what Doyler would ask. 'Jim, did you go with him, Jim?'

He smiled, partly in reassurance, but there was more to it, he knew, and he said, 'There were times all right we might have.'

'You wouldn't let him though?'

'Sure he wouldn't let himself.'

'Proper gent.'

It was comical seeing Doyler looking round for somewhere to spit in that elegant polished space, the only house Jim had known that didn't smell of food, only furniture. 'The pot's under the bed,' he told him. He went over and pulled the curtains to. At the door he said, 'You know there's nothing to fear, don't you? If only you might have come swimming today you'd know it for sure. The Muglins there and the great sky above – we're immortal. We're no more than filling in now.'

He waited outside the door a moment to be sure of Doyler's resting. Satisfied, he gathered the bundle of Doyler's clothes and skimmed down the stairs. In one of the recesses in the hall he hurried out of his jacket and trousers and into the dark-green uniform. Nothing really fitted. The chafe of the trousers, a thick coarse cloth, prickled the inside of his thighs, the sort of an irritation you'd offer up for the Holy Souls. The mirror glanced him passing, a green stranger, and he paused for a more formal inspection. The tunic was too big and the trousers too long. He saw his inquisitive face poking out from under the brim of the slouch hat. He thought of his brother. Yes, he did look a soldier, he truly did. Too much the soldier in fact. He took off the tunic and hat again. He'd be better carrying them till he was surer of Dublin, how things stood. He might be stopped and questioned, there might be military checks, he didn't know what else.

He left his clothes by the hall stand, where they wouldn't be noticed but they would be found. He couldn't leave Doyler go to war with only MacEmm's linens to wear. He pulled the heavy front door and he was away up the drive. A moment's unease coming into the shop, for his father might be home and he'd be nosing about the strange trousers. But there was no sign of him yet. He went immediately to the broom-cupboard, shifted round inside till he came on Doyler's rifle. 'Is that you, Jim?' called Nancy. He looked sharply: she was out the yard. She was saying something about the weather and he answered, Yes. The rifle was still in its brown paper covering. He stared at it a while considering, then he poked the sticks of three brushes down the top. He was going in his shirtsleeves: let people think he was a working man.

'What's that?' he said. Something about his dinner. 'I'm to eat at MacMurrough's,' he called. He was looking about to see was there anything else. His rosary beads. He reached up quickly to the shelf, and touching them, he glanced on the wall beside where his father's best coat hung on its hook. It looked so exactly like the back view of his father, it stopped him in his reach. He smiled. It really was like his father, shaped to the exact slope of his shoulders. He looked about the room. There were correspondences everywhere. He knew these things so very well, the fittings and furnishings of his boyhood, yet each particular object appeared clearer and fresher than ever he had known it before, as though they all had been very recently painted, but with a strange and vivid paint that applied no colours but memories. This is my home, he thought. Or rather, as after an absence, This was the home where I grew up. He saw, and necessarily touched, the table and his bench, where he had sat these countless meals. He saw the ghost of him on the match-boarding behind where the varnish had rubbed away. Another ghost showed beside, bigger a bit, where his brother had sat. On the press were his schoolbooks and prizes – *The Sieges of Gibraltar*, he read – all covered in brown paper and his father's neat stencil on the spines. He saw the dark disc round the gas-lamp that would widen and deepen till again his father whitewashed the ceiling, for the disc to form and grow and deepen again. Out in the scullery was the sink where his father had scrubbed him, scrubbed him pink with a hard brush, while he sat and shivered on that perilous height. It was all here. He sniffed, catching the smell of his home, cabbagy same like any kitchen in the world, save with something sweeter in it, apples maybe, mouldering in a box. He went to the mantelshelf and lifted the lid off the Huntley and Palmer's biscuit tin. He looked happily at its contents, pleased they had never changed, all manner of scrip-scrap his father had saved: pins, buttons, bands, three foreign coins passed for sixpences, a Danish safety-pin. Nothing had changed. And he thought of his father who too had never changed. With his significant looks and his consequential airs, desperate lest any should think him soft. He had left the regiment that was his life to bring his sons home when their mother was dying. Such unselfish love, and oh such bravery. How he loved his father. It was the same huge love he felt for all, for Doyler and MacEmm, for Aunt Sawney and Nancy and Gordie's baby: how very much he loved them all. How very much indeed.

In the summer of long ago he had heard of Wolfe Tone who gallantly and gay had gone about his deed. He too had loved so well. He too had been so loved.

He went out in the shop. He passed between the narrow shelves and the dusted finicky wares. On the wall he saw the advertisement card for Robin Starch, the *new* starch, the robin still told – sparrow-dull now so long it had hung. He picked up the rifle and bundled the tunic and hat under his arm. He pulled the door and the bell clinked, and he had the strangest notion standing there that the door had pulled itself.

The door had pulled itself and the bell of its own discretion had clinked. And now it clinked again as the door swung home behind him, and he turned towards Sallynoggin and the unfrequented road to town.

With the last bundle of washing, Nancy heaved backwards in from the yard: through the scullery and into the kitchen where she hefted the washing on the table. 'Now,' she said. She took a moment to wipe her forehead, listening to the peevish cries above, then up the box-stairs door, aware of the climb of each stair in her calves. 'Well Aunt Sawney,' she said, coming in the room. Aunt Sawney sat in her chair by the window, the babba on her lap. Nancy took the mite in her arms. 'What's this now?' she asked, poking a finger at the screwed-up face, 'what's this has you complaining to your Aunt Sawney about?'

Aunt Sawney thought the way the child was hungering.

'Sure that's only good complaints.'

She humped the babba, easing the strain afterwards with a hand to her back. She took a corner of the bed to sit on. 'Now,' she said, while she loosened her blouse. A lovely evening light was in the room, all glimmery after the glare outside. 'It's buttered eggs for tea,' she told Aunt Sawney, 'and I've a mind to try a custard after.' The babba nuzzled her mouth to her breast.

Aunt Sawney said nothing, only rocked to and fro. She had her beads already in her hands, but there was something in her face, worrisome a touch, the way the mysteries she told this evening would be unusually doleful. 'Are you right there, Aunt Sawney?'

She didn't answer, only stared out the window.

'There you are now,' said Nancy, as the little mouth dribbled its surfeit. In a glance of the swing-glass on the bedroom table, she caught a peek of her reflection. I have a face, she told herself, the colour and texture of a turnip. She rebuttoned her blouse. The mite was looking for hiccupping then, and she said to Aunt Sawney, 'Will you take her again for a quarter of a mo while I see to them sheets below?'

Aunt Sawney nodded and reached the bundle to her arms. But still she said nothing, only stared her face out the window, that same window on that same strip of lane where these years she had watched her good boy go, come and go, come and go, till he never came no more. And now she had watched the little man too with the black fellow's gun to his shoulder.

'Are you sure you're all right in yourself?' she heard Nancy say. The glitter formed in the opaque of her eyes while still she stared, rocking in her chair, with the bundle of babe held close to her shoulder, and her hand tapped on the babe's back, the whole of her hand, in determined solacing pats.

'You want to play?'

'Play what?'

'Nap,' said Doyler. He was sprawled on the saraband rug by MacMurrough's hearth, dealing a kind of demon patience with Aunt Eva's reserved écarté cards. The evening long their conversation had not risen from the inquisitorial. Feel better? – Aye. Hungry? – No. MacMurrough had roamed the scattered appointments of his bedroom, packing his case, while Doyler hung grimly to hearth and bedlands, a parcelling of their space. Silly really. 'Oh very well,' said MacMurrough.

'I've no money,' said Doyler, 'so we'll play for noses instead.'

'Whatever you say. What are noses?'

'Things, you find them usually on your face.'

He gathered the cards and snappily shuffled them. MacMurrough creaked to the floor to sit. He felt a general disgruntlement, a sense of a damper. It was too bad of Jim, he had expected better. This evening, his last in Ireland – a coda to the action, when properly ordered it should have provided the climax, well perhaps not climax, but a generous envoi. The Titian-glow of fire and candles, their voices quieting, his soothing wine: the evening previous repeated in fact, save with the added piquancy of tickets in his pocket, of the imminent and ineluctable tide. Instead he had this fellow parked on his rug the night. The state of the room too displeased him that evinced Jim's absence more than any maid's: yesterday's grate, the cigarette-blue air, the slop and jumble of the sick-bedside.

Fellow wasn't even sick, merely trouserless.

But MacMurrough took his cards and played the game. And noses, so he found, answered his mood to a turn. Whenever he made his nap, which he made invariably and far too unluckily for his heart, he got to rap Doyler with his winning cards: rap on the nose per point staked. How brave the boy bode, how meek he suffered: it did the soul good to see. They changed to brag, but brag the boy might, MacMurrough had aces. Aces went low, and MacMurrough had kings. The boy's pugnacious nose reddened to a geranium. 'My dear,' said MacMurrough, gathering the pack, 'you cannot conceive how it becomes you, a little trouncing.'

'You play a lot at cards, do you?'

'No,' said MacMurrough. 'But then I've always been,' he

began, and finished, 'unlucky in love.' Here was a rival's compliment and Doyler received it grinning, touchingly with his lips closed to contain his laugh. 'You're doyling,' said MacMurrough. 'Yes, you're doyling. I used so to like it when you doyled.'

'Aye aye, and what's doyling?'

'Doyling, if you didn't know, is that brazen discourteous vainglorious smirk which commonly distorts your face: the giving of it.' And he clipped once again the boy's rubious conk.

'I'll get you back,' said Doyler, but not vindictively, and once or twice indeed he did, making a comedy of adjusting MacMurrough's head just so, for the neatest crack at his nose. It was child's play, parlour-game stuff, and it held just that sufficience of malice to excuse their enjoyment, encourage it even. The gas was up, they fell about, a rorty time was had by all. MacMurrough broke off to fetch barley water and a pale ale, a plate of biscuits.

'My poor aunt,' he said returning. 'If she could see the state of her playing-cards.'

Doyler pounced on the biscuits. He sat on the floor cross-legged, in his shirt only, no drawers. MacMurrough had thought to throw him an old trousers, but there was that delicacy between them of clothes. Every now and then, slipping out from his shirt-tail, came the hint of a hair of his sex. A proposition which once propounded MacMurrough found hard to ignore, and yet whose advancement, let alone its achievement, would surely be indescribably banal.

'Funny thing about your aunt,' Doyler said, munching. 'Did you know she was well thought of down Liberty Hall?'

'Liberty Hall, my aunt?'

Doyler shrugged. 'Back in the Lock-out she helped out in the soup-kitchen there.'

'You're pulling my leg.'

'God's truth. There's a painting even. She has an apron on and her sleeves rolled up. Enormous big cauldron on the boil beside her.'

'But this is extraordinary.' He pictured his aunt in the steaming frame with the hungry masses huddled behind: in Parisian pinny she plies the ladle.

'Beats me,' said Doyler, 'with half Dublin out of work, why they has to get rich folks to cook the soup. But there you are.'

'Yes,' said MacMurrough, 'there you are.' Truly she was a remarkable woman. He remembered how she had chastened him once for his unguarded assertion of female practicalism. He regarded women as practical, she told him, because he never saw the sex but it was tending to his needs: bringing his tea, making his fire, paying his cigarist's bills. Yes, he would miss his aunt. All very large and fine having boys in and out of the house, but his aunt had been a good sport. And now she must retire, *hors de combat*. How it must pain her. Really, the English had grown too high: to presume to exile Irish men and women from their own country. Their own country – the thought repeated, and he looked at Doyler, whom Jim had once spoken of as his country. 'What happened us at all, Doyler,' he asked, 'that we should have fallen so out of sympathy?'

'Matter of a knee in the balls.'

'Oh yes, that.' MacMurrough conceded a moral homer, a hit not by virtue of the boy's being right but of his being wronged that morning in St Stephen's Green.

'You was after that young chap Paddy's day.'

'Yes, him.'

'Piece of smut, you called him.'

'Yes, we shan't require the exhaustive history.'

'You made out as I was after him too.'

'Yes.' Thank you Doyler, nicely pilloried. He took a Player's, lit it. 'And were you?'

'Was I what?' For a moment the glowers returned. 'Did you put a peeler on me in the park?'

'Grief no.'

'I didn't know if you did. No, I wasn't after that chap. Not that time anyway. Not that way. Another time, maybe I was.'

'You were?'

'Does it matter?'

'No.' A sense of symmetry had MacMurrough inquire was it Doyler who informed the Castle of his aunt's rifles. But of course Doyler hadn't. 'You did put the wind up me though, that rifle, finding it bang in my face.' Doyler grinned. MacMurrough inspired the rough virginia of his Player's, reluctantly admitting an accustomation. 'I never thought to ask – have you started smoking?'

'I don't, but thanks now for offering.'

'Not at all.'

They smiled daftly at each other. Reluctantly MacMurrough admitted a contentment with the evening. In its own unparticular way, it brought a close to this Irish episode, back where it had all begun with the boy from the Forty Foot who hobbled and spat. Rum fellow he was, but he wasn't a bad old hat. It was good to have things cleared up between them, if cleared up they were. He might almost thank Jim, though it was absurd to imagine the boy had intended it this way.

Looking at him now MacMurrough felt again the attractions of Doyle. Bold breezy insouciance that had made of him such worthy game. But he saw better the bitterness in the eyes, on his shoulder the chip, and he remembered the shrug, carelessly given, but which at heart he gave for he held himself not worth a care. So much MacMurrough might recognize in himself. Oh, other things too: a damnable honesty, the penchant for misery, a yearning for magnificence but a spirit unwinged.

'You know,' said Doyler, 'you don't have to go, you know.'

'Why thank you, Doyler. I shall stay so.'

'I mean, not on my account you needn't. Jim says you're to join the British Army. I'd hate to think I drove any man to taking the Saxon shilling.'

And so should I, young man, hate to think you had driven me anywhere. 'My aunt once told me that nothing is gained by clinging to life save more life to cling to. The world I find is embarked on a grand adventure. I find I choose to play.' He had stood up saying this, ruffling his hand in Doyler's scraggy thick hair. 'You know where everything is, don't you?'

'You leaving me?'

'Yes, I'm going to bed.'

'You leaving me here on me own?'

'What did you expect?'

'Nothing. Wasn't sure was all.'

But there was a haunt in his face, like a maid new-arrived, of the big night in the big room in the big creak of a house. 'Hope you don't mind the dark?'

He did not, most definitely not, what did MacMurrough take him for, he had no fear of the dark whatsoever, guaranteed.

'Good,' said MacMurrough, lowering the lamp. The night and its draughts inhaled the light, and he left the boy to fret alone. He thought about it while he undressed in his appropriated cupboard across the hall. Earlier, the way one does, it was ravishment and rampage, a forcible entry, his hurting the boy face-down on the leafy pile, the punishment of piss, other debasements, idly he had meditated. But when it all boiled down, a cuddle would nearly do. Yes it would; and it surprised how quickly the door knob was in his hand.

'Who is it?' came the small voice.

'Move over,' said MacMurrough. He climbed in the bed. 'Lift up,' he said, nudging under the shoulders. He turned the body, a sack, in his arm. 'It's silly,' he said, 'pretending we're strangers.'

The sack lumpily reposed. 'I want to fuck you,' MacMurrough said. There was no response. MacMurrough sighed. He patted the body where his hand had fallen. 'I just want to,' he said. 'I want to,' he elaborated, 'but I won't mind if you don't choose to.'

'Now there's a lie with a lid on it.' Doyler's hand, in a casual way, had fingered below and found out MacMurrough's stand. 'You like this?'

It wasn't the most imaginative ploy, but MacMurrough answered, Yes, for a tease, he did.

'How much will you pay me so?'

Little toe-rag. 'Must we bring that up?'

'You know that suit, MacMurrough? I sold that suit.'

'My dear, it was yours to do with as you pleased. I'm glad you sold it. I never liked it.'

'Why'd you buy it me so?'

'I thought it made you happy. You surely knew I was fond of you. You were a cussed bloody-minded sod, and I admired you for it.'

The hand below had cupped MacMurrough's balls. Now a tentative ambivalent pressure exerted, exciting really, exquisite even; until Doyler said, 'You'd pay Jim so, would you?'

Oh dear oh dear, MacMurrough thought; Doyler Doyler, my dear.

'I used see them in Dublin, MacMurrough, the girls in their glad-necks. Up and down the street they'd go. I wanted to burn that suit. I knew what that suit made of me. But I needed the brass, so I sold it instead. Didn't pawn it, sold it.'

MacMurrough brought his own hand down to cover the boy's grip, and he squeezed a little so that his groin hurt, nothing nauseating, just a little manageable penance. He said, 'I'm sorry, Doyler, if you feel badly about that.'

'You never lifted a finger.'

MacMurrough believed he knew what the boy meant. It was a scene whose recall could torment him still, so that physically he would need to flinch the memory away: the garden fête, the summerhouse, the boy's shirt ripped, his nipple bared, that pathetic emblem, his bowed head. And MacMurrough rooted to the floor while the priest smiled, the priest barked.

'Not a finger,' the boy repeated. 'After you leading me on to believe we was friendly. You had me going and all, MacMurrough. You told me wear that badge. You told me. I knew then all I meant to you.'

'Doyler, I am sorry. You must try to understand I wasn't myself back then.'

'Sure I don't mind.'

The balls were loosed, MacMurrough reprieved. Doyler turned away, and MacMurrough turned with him, not to be ultimately estranged. Even so he could feel himself hard by the boy's bum. God damn me for an arrogant whoreson pimp.

'Listen to me now.'

'You can't tell me nothing.'

'Listen to me, Doyler. Whatever passed between us, you must understand it was only me paying you. It made something of me, not of you. You never sold anything.' He reached an arm round and held it on his chest. 'Won't you say you forgive me now?'

'Sure I told you I don't mind. There was a time I had the blue murders thinking of you. I don't no more.'

They lay that way a while, MacMurrough embracing the boy,

and Doyler embraced but rigidly untouched. Then MacMurrough said, 'You will look after him, won't you?'

'He don't need looking after.'

'He has no notion of being careful.'

'He's a rare plucked one, ain't he.'

'He is, yes.'

'Will I tell you?'

To MacMurrough's confusion, the boy turned round. He turned round and rested, even insisted, his head on MacMurrough's chest. They were back as MacMurrough had started, and his hand patted once more the boy's side.

'Will I tell you?' he repeated. 'We went to Mass on Easter Sunday. We were at the back with the men and when it came to communion he stood up. He gave such a look at me and said, Come on. I thought, you know, after the night we'd spent. But he was so sure of things. We went up together. I snuck me eyes at him kneeling there. The priest was beside and he had his tongue out waiting. He was so sure everything was right and square. I don't know but I loved him that minute. He frightened me a bit too. He'll be a great leader of men one day.'

'Yes, I believe he will.' MacMurrough heard a doom in his voice, and to dispel it he added, 'Lead them a merry old dance.' He became aware of Doyler's hand again on his stand. He had the strangest sensation of Jim's watching, of his willing this. 'We still might, you know,' he said, 'if you'd a mind to.'

The hand maintained its impartial progress up and down. 'What and I was to do you?'

Yes he was, a cussed bloody-minded sodomitical object. 'That's sweet of you, my dear, and don't think I shouldn't enjoy it, except you're of that age, you'd imagine you'd put one over upon me.'

'Fair's fair,' said Doyler.

'Believe me, nature knows best in these matters.'

'That's the way it is, MacMurrough. Take it or leave it.'

'Oh very well,' MacMurrough said. 'Only Doyler, not as a punishment.'

Doyler hawked his throat. The hand removed from MacMurrough's stand. He hawked again and spat twice in the hand. That old unction, MacMurrough thought, by arse or by tarse once more to balm us.

They slept cuddling, the each the other, though it seemed to MacMurrough he but dozed, when the bells were clanging to shake the windows and waken the sleep of the just.

CHAPTER TWENTY

THE RAIN HAD begun to fall, drizzling upon Jim's sleep. He blinked awake. He was sensible of an urgency, though not immediately of its cause. One by one his body told its complaints: the cold, the stiffness, the hunger, and now the wet. A church bell was striking the hour somewhere over the city, ringing once, ringing twice. He made out his neighbour in the grey light, shifting too in the narrow trench. Three bells the church rang. The rain fell on his face and he peered at the sky. Four bells, and a clattering chaos shattered the quiet.

The earth splattered before him. Branches snapped from trees, scattered on the grass. Stunned, Jim watched the lawn squirm in a scythe, like a snake. 'Keep down, ye bleddy fool!' he heard. Something ssssinged past him, sssinged again. Clay spurted up, battered his face. A terrific jab in his shoulder and he was thrust headlong into the trench. 'Can't ye stay down?'

'What is it?'

'Machine-bleddy-gun. Maybe two.'

Gung, the man pronounced it. It made Jim want to giggle. 'Where are they?' he asked, whispering. That too made him gigglish.

'Shelbourne Hotel.'

Jim had his rifle though he wasn't sure was it Doyler's still. They had taken the one he came with and it was a while before he had them persuaded into giving him one back. The British machine-guns chattered away, churning up the grass. There were sharper cracks between: rifles, he was told. A boy was down by the gates – was he down or lying low? He could see other figures hunched along the trenches. He pulled on the bolt, but he had forgotten the safety. He flipped it over and drew the bolt back, feeling for the cartridge inside. The trench was only shallow: he had to crouch sideways to fix the butt to his shoulder. He recalled cryptic comments MacEmm had let drop. You didn't aim a rifle, your position aimed it. You didn't shoot a gun, you allowed it to shoot. He gripped the barrel and fondled the guard. He had forgotten to bless himself: it didn't matter. He took a breath, then swung out over the low-banked earth and aimed in a wide arc along the range of buildings. Endless buildings, with four, five, six storeys to them, windows staggered up and down, countless windows, a precipice of brick and glass. He had not thought to ask which was the Shelbourne.

It was surprise enough that the bell should be pulled at all. But earth-shattering, a preliminary of jacobin terror to come, when MacMurrough finally had the bolts pulled and the great door yawned wide, to find it was a tradesman-like fellow in a butcher's boater who at this ungodly hour the godly portal steps disturbed.

'Why, Mr Mack,' he said.

'My apologies, a thousand apologies,' said Mr Mack. The unwonted boater lifted and dropped, discharging its wet upon Mr Mack's nose. MacMurrough looked beyond him at the drizzle-hued world. A magpie raucously gnattered in the trees.

Perhaps four, a quarter after, in the morning. The boater was evidently a size or several too small, for it tilted on Mr Mack's head, in jaunty disavowal of his face where anxiety, effusion, exhaustion, the misery of weather, all jostled for command. His apologies again, only it was his son, his son James, he hadn't come home in the night.

'Jim?'

Mr Mack had waited up for the boy, only he nodded off, pray God forgive him, in Aunt Sawney's chair – Mr MacMurrough would remember Aunt Sawney, Miss Alexandra Burke, he should say – woke up in her chair—

'Won't you step in?' said MacMurrough.

'I won't now,' said Mr Mack, stepping into the hall, 'delay now and the terrible hour to be calling, but after the dreadful occurrences in Dublin—'

'Dublin? A train strike, I understood.'

'If only,' said Mr Mack, 'if only.' But the entire city was up, the rebels were out, Sinn Feiners were out. Lancers – he saw two killed himself, murdered in the street. Rioting. Destruction. Looting of premises. Barricades. 'Barricades,' he repeated, 'with mattresses in them.'

'Mattresses,' MacMurrough said, he too grasping this detail as peculiarly cogent and distressing.

'And no sign of Jim at home and no word left. I have it in my head—Doyler!'

MacMurrough turned. Doyler stood at the half-pace leaning over the baluster rail.

'Good morning now, Mr Mack.'

'Doyler, thank all that's good and holy, you're here. I thought it might be the way you was mixed up—But no, sure you're the sensible lad. Jim is here with you so?'

'He was, Mr Mack. Only he went out for an early dip.'

'A dip, is it?'

'I'll go fetch him, Mr Mack. I'll send him home to you.'

'Not to trouble yourself. Are you well again?'

'Grand, and it's no trouble at all.'

'Sure what am I saying?' said Mr Mack, his hand springing to his damp forehead. 'The events has left me all to seek. And his coat only staring me in the face.'

Indeed it was: on a low hook on the hall stand, Jim's Norfolk jacket, among the whips and canes. MacMurrough looked with puzzlement at Doyler.

'Rest easy, Mr Mack,' said Doyler lightly, 'I'll fetch him home direct.'

'Well, if you're sure now.' The boater straw returned to his head, his expression better tallying with its rake. It lifted in farewell and another thousand of apologies, the door closing behind him.

'Bring me up that jacket,' said Doyler.

MacMurrough came into his dressing-closet where Doyler was ransacking the wardrobe. He had pulled on a pair of MacMurrough's trousers, the corrugate folds of the legs giving him a clown's look, one who had mislaid his stilts. 'Is there never a braces or a belt?' he cried, coat-hangers flinging on the floor.

MacMurrough tossed him Jim's trousers. 'I found them in the hall.'

'Scheming bloody monkey. I'll pay him out for this. I'll murder him, so I will, bloody massacre him.'

'You knew nothing of this?'

'Answer me, would I be here and I did? He knew I'd stop him. He knew I'd never let him a hand in this.'

He knew more than that, thought MacMurrough.

'Can't think why I didn't catch on. Staring me in the bleeding face. Stephen's Green this, Stephen's Green that. You and your train strike. I knew there was more to it, I knew—What do you want getting dressed for?'

'I'll be coming along.'

'Oh no you don't, mister. This is between me and Jim.'

In his consternation Doyler had snapped the lace of his boot. He was making rather a camel of it, rethreading the sucked ends through the eyes. MacMurrough threw him an ironed pair. He unhooked a smart check Newmarket vest. 'It's damp out,' he said: 'put this on inside the jacket.' For himself he chose tweed and a hunting jerkin underneath, forgoing for once his linens and creams. From a cabinet he produced his aunt's Webley. He revolved the chamber, counting the cartridges remaining.

'Is that thing loaded?'

'Yes,' MacMurrough replied, it rather pointing than aiming at the boy's good leg. 'So don't let's argue who's coming.'

Doyler went back to his boots. 'Do what you want, MacMurrough, only don't get in my way.'

MacMurrough pulled on his socks. Of course there could be no real danger in Dublin. But equally there could be no thought of his leaving without he first made sure. Once again, the mailboat receded into the Irish Sea. It was becoming exhausting, this not going. He glanced at Doyler, who frowned back. Yes, Jim had outwitted them all ways, tickled them to his purpose, in their very rumping manipulating them. He could only marvel at the boy's mastery of the world – that same world which tossed MacMurrough, upped sided and downed him, and over which he had no more influence than the choosing of the socks he wore while it tossed. He pulled on his boots.

'Ready?'

'Aye, ready.'

The sun no doubt had risen, but it was a dreary lightless morning, with a rain that never entirely ceased, but dripped from trees and mizzled between the showers. MacMurrough had thought they might take a cab or an outside car. Doyler asserted, as a soldier of the Irish Republic, he had the right to seize any vehicle he chose. But they passed not a postman's bike. At Kingstown MacMurrough roused the stables – to find the stabler had no notion of his mounts riding to Dublin. Did the gentleman not know the ruccus was in Dublin? The Larkinites held the town for the Kaiser. They was shooting horses and sharing the meat.

Hens pecked in the yard, sparrows fluttered on the walls. Kingstown wore its conventional slumberous air. MacMurrough fingered the Webley in his pocket, considering the puissance of its persuasion. He turned to Doyler whose only guidance was, 'Don't think you're getting me up on one of them yokes.' When he turned back he saw the gates were swinging, the stable door had shut in his face. 'I don't think,' he said, 'we make very effective revolutionaries.'

'Will you stow that thing down the back of your pants,' said Doyler. 'Any thick of an eejit can spot you're carrying a piece.'

Doyler persisted in this knowing, lording-it manner as on they tramped to Blackrock. It was MacMurrough's fault. He blamed MacMurrough. MacMurrough had filled Jim's head with notions. Did a man MacMurrough's age not know he was dealing with a kid?

'Wait a minute here. Are you saying I encouraged Jim?'

'Well, who the hell else did?'

'Well, you're the one who struts about in a uniform.'

'What are you allegating now? You saying I packed him off to Stephen's Green?'

'Well, I certainly didn't.'

'Of course I wear a uniform. I'm supposed to wear a uniform. Amn't I a Citizen soldier?'

'And now Jim's gone off to be one too.'

'That's nothing to the point. And I don't strut neither. Leg like mine, you'd want to strut.' His leg, which had largely been forgotten in their hurry, now made stiff semi-circles for a pace or two, knocking into MacMurrough's shins.

'You'll find,' said MacMurrough, 'you'll get along faster if you rest your tongue.'

'I'm not saying nothing.'

'Good.'

'Fine by me.'

They tramped in silence. They passed, briefly, through the Kingstown slums, then on to the broad avenues of Monkstown. It was a strain, with the streets so empty, maintaining any sense of urgency. It was cherry week: all along the road and down the side roads, an exotic snow had pinked the gardens. Chestnuts were new-clothed and on the tip of candling, their loose green shawls picked with cream. But mostly the trees were bare yet, affording little shelter from the weather.

For no very good reason, MacMurrough fell to pondering his funeral. Like so many things in life, he had missed his moment for death. That last year at school, had I topped it then, the splendour of it, my apotheosis. Cowled monks sanctus chanting. A squealer I favoured once with a smile, his wispy treble, pie Jesu. At the back, bowed, awed, scrubbed, combed, urchins from the local boxing club; one, his stubby face, agnus dei, my protégé. Dear Father and dearest Mother, comforted, a little surprised even, as they glimpse in the candled gloom that lux aeternum the boy choir sings. He will be especially remembered for his many kindnesses to his younger fellows. Libera me. A look, a smile, a chink in the Sunday faces: a message slips in a pocket. *Tonight at eight by the lats.* In paradisium.

Sometimes I wonder does anything in the world exist for me

606

at all, beyond the horizontal refreshment. Well, all quite natural: one is walking, after all, to war. Please to note, no dies irae.

Movement at last: a milk van round a corner came clopping, colloping, collopaling to a stop clop. As they drew near, the driver threw them a wary nod. Maids were queuing at the churn, tattling over their half-gallon cans. 'Yez off to town, boys? – Don't Maggie! – I hope yez aren't Sinn Feiners, boys? – Maggie don't!'

'Well,' said MacMurrough, 'do we take it?'

'Crawl there faster than that old nag.'

It dawned on MacMurrough that Doyler was rather the dull insurrectionist. That brief exchange had launched him again on his gripes. MacMurrough never thought things through. A round table would have the edge on MacMurrough. Was MacMurrough demented altogether to be telling Jim them tales?

'Which tales are these now?'

'Don't ask me. The Holy Band of Thesbians.'

'Of Thebes,' said MacMurrough. 'The Sacred Band.'

'All lovey-dovey dying together. Don't you know he's dippy over you? He takes anything you say at face. That's a kid you're telling that to. He don't know it's stories.'

'Doyler, he's the same age as you. Besides, I grew up on tales like that.'

'Aye and you're some example.'

'What are you talking about? The entire world grows up on those stories. Only difference is, I told him the truth, that they were lovers, humping physical fellows.' Yes, and Jim had grasped instinctively that significance: that more than stories, they were patterns of the possible. And I think, how happier my boyhood should have been, had somebody – Listen, boy, listen to my tale – thought to tell me the truth. Listen while I tell you, boy, these men loved and yet were noble. You too shall love, body and soul, as they; and there shall be a place for you, boy, noble and magnificent as any. Hold true to your love: these things shall be.

Instead of finding out for yourself, with a dictionary in a dark corner, by which time it's just one other lie you've nailed them in on the sallady path of youth.

But MacMurrough was talking to himself. Doyler carried on. 'Will I tell you what he says to me yesterday, he says, There's nothing to fear, says he. We're immortal. His very words – We're immortal. The sky had told him so.'

Yes, MacMurrough allowed, it was certainly of a piece. It had all rather gone to his head, the Muglins, uncovering himself, rumpty-tumpty with this bugger here.

'Can't believe I listened a word he said. He's a kid sure. He never strayed farther than the Dalkey tram. Mary and Joseph, the nonsense he talked about schoolteaching. A digs, by Jesus. And I listened him.'

And really it was inconsiderate. MacMurrough had the right to leave, it was necessary that he should leave. And now this wretched squabble in Dublin – what if he should be caught in it? Oh God oh no, if by some chance he were shot, bloody stuck here in a hospital. Or worse, he were arrested, wound up in gaol. Good grief, they'd take me for a rebel. Oh no no no, this really is not good enough.

'I'll find him, I'll fetch him out,' said Doyler, 'I'll clatter him something he'll never forget. That's right,' he continued, working himself up as he spoke, 'you'll hold him while I'll hit him. I'll blister him, I will, bleeding bate him good-looking. Then you'll bring him home out of that. That's your job. You understand that now?'

'Who are we kidding?' said MacMurrough.

The breath huffed out of Doyler. Visibly he sagged. 'I don't know, but if he's anyway hurt at all.'

'Come on,' MacMurrough said. He took Doyler by the arm. 'We're coming to Blackrock. There'll be news there. There'll be something.'

The Shelbourne was the stately cream and orange building that towered upon the left. What it did was to dominate their flank. The British had snuck in in the night and garrisoned it. Their own trenches now were useless for trenches: they were dug too shallow. The machine-gunners and snipers in the hotel bedrooms had them pinned down, but they might not return the fire. Elevation was the word used to describe this situation, a problem of it. Elevation. The boy at the park gates was dead still.

Most the men had scattered from the trenches. They had taken cover in the bushes round about. But it was the wrong time of year really, for the trees weren't half in leaf yet, and the shrubberies too were thin and bare. The women had left, hitching their skirts and trotting with the wounded. Whistles blew here and there. Guns could be heard over the house-tops, and pot-shots now and then nearer to hand. But mostly in the Green there was a kind of a hush. The ducks settled again on the ponds, huffily quacking. You could hear the voices of the soldiers down Merrion Row. Then a movement somewhere, and the mad clatter would start over, entire Shelbourne, from each its windows, blazing at the one square foot.

There had been talk of bombs. A bicycle would fly past the hotel, lob bombs through the windows. They'd rush it then. 'I can cycle,' Jim said, but it was a talent in no very short supply, and no one paid him much attention, save the comedian who asked, 'Who's the firecracker, Bill?'

'Never bleddy mind this one,' Bill replied. 'This one's from the Southside.' Bill was a sergeant. He had a grey moustache and a face harassed and father-like. He had taken it into his head to keep Jim in hand. Jim mightn't look at the Shelbourne without a dig in his legs and the sergeant bawling him down out of that.

In the hushes between the firing, Jim found his mind strangely wandered. He wrote a letter to Gordie. Well, here we are, he told him, in the trenches in Stephen's Green. He discussed with the inner man the breakfast he'd most enjoy. He tried to describe a triangle that would demonstrate this problem of elevation. Enormously steep hypotenuses he proposed, yet still he could not satisfactorily prove the difficulty. It had ought to be the same trouble firing down as firing up. Yet the incessant rattling gave the lie to that. It wasn't the worst, he believed. There'd be no more of trig if trig had fell the first casualty of war.

Not literally the first, of course, for the boy was still dead at the park gates.

The sergeant wanted to know was he all right there. Southside, he called him. 'You keeping out of trouble there, Southside?'

'I'm keeping fine,' Jim answered him. He heard himself sounding unnaturally loud. 'I'm fine sure,' he repeated more composedly.

It was this sergeant last evening who took Jim's rifle from him. It was dark when Jim got to the Green and the streets about were all but deserted. There were barricades across the junctions, carts and motor-cars, but they were loosely thrown, obstacles more than barriers. They too seemed deserted. He approached the park gates to find them locked. People moved against the shadows inside, figures only. It took a while to catch anyone's attention. Even then they were dubious of him, though he told them about Doyler, that he was ill under doctor's orders, that he'd be in tomorrow for definite; in the meantime Jim was here to stand in his place. The sergeant was called, this man Bill, and he took one look at Jim, demanded his rifle and told

Jim go home out of that, they had sufficient of bleddy chisselurs already.

It had been on the cards all along that appearance might disfavour Jim – folk had a disposition to finding him young-looking and inadequate. It was against this eventuality he had borrowed Doyler's uniform in the first place. To no avail. He had to keep following them round the outside of the park, calling through the railings his knowledge of semaphore and bandaging and to strip a rifle. It was an astonishingly trying time. The worse for he could see other lads his own age, sure some of them positively infants.

One of these lads asked him was he hungry, and he brought a custard pie. 'Sure why don't you hop the railings anyway?' he suggested.

'Can I do that?' asked Jim.

'You there,' came a bark behind. A short fellow pointing at him, clipping along the street. 'What do you mean, leaving your post?'

Jim said, 'I don't know, sir.'

'This barricade is to be manned at all times. And where's your rifle?'

'It's inside in the park, sir.'

The man told off the lad to fetch it. 'Don't you know that's a military offence,' he said to Jim, 'to leave your equipment behind you?'

He spoke with a thorough conviction, such that Jim could nearly feel shamefaced for his dereliction. He said, 'It won't happen again, sir.'

'Be sure of that. Are you hungry?'

'I'm not, sir.'

'Stay there now till you're relieved.'

The lad came back with a rifle and a bandoleer of cartridges.

That was the Commandant, he told him. He gave Jim another custard pie. They shook hands through the railings.

That lad was dead now. In a way, he was still dead, lying by the park gates. But another boy had fallen since and the Commandant himself dashed out to fetch him. He heaved him home to cheers from the men, and the bullets spurting about him, one through his hat even. It was the bravest thing, a conspicuous bravery, and Jim had stood out, loading and bolting and shooting, fast as his fingers would fumble, to give a covering fire. Till the sergeant again had him ditched in the trench. That time Jim had turned. 'I'm not here to be cowering,' he said.

'Ye'll bleddy obey yer elders. D'ye know at all the pains we had getting of them bullets? Firing them off at the bleddy masonry, snip of ye.'

At last word came of action. Action at last, for it was mad holed up in these slobby trenches. It was not a retreat. It was a withdrawal. They were to make a tactical withdrawal to the far corner of the Green where a hump in the ground would better give cover. They would gather their forces there. Jim nodded his head listening to this, encouraging agreement among the men. 'And then we'll charge,' he said, still nodding.

'Ye can stow that, Southside.'

'Who's the ball?'

'This one's with me.'

'Lord have mercy on our souls.'

'Stow that and all.'

Over and over the sergeant told Jim what he was to do. He wasn't to move till the word was gave. Then he'd crawl out behind the sergeant. He was to follow the sergeant exactly what he did. He'd keep his head down in the daisies. They'd get out of this safe, Jim would see.

Still that boy by the park gates. There were other bodies

about, but his looked so very much apart. It seemed nearly wicked to be carrying on without him. Jim wondered what had he done to be lying there alone, for he had seemed a friendly chap. A goner, somebody had called him. Jim swallowed, finding a difficulty in the action. He brought his hand to feel about his throat. He had a scarf round his neck that he woke up in the night to find the sergeant had wrapped there. His shoulder was hurting a bit now.

Last night, when they had relieved him from the barricade at last, he had joined a group of men in the dark in the park. He'd thought they might be talking tactics or making bombs, and he was a little disappointed to find it was only the Rosary they were at. But he took out his beads and knelt beside. This sergeant shook his head at him, but presently he gave Jim the calling of a gaudious mystery. After, when they took their places in the trenches, he bade Jim stay near. Commandant Mallin made a tour of the posts and he told them the news, how the country was up. Cork was taken, Limerick was taken, the West was awake and marching for Dublin, the boys of Wexford were on the march once more. – They had only to hold out till help came. And Jim had thought while he lay in his trench and the moon only risen and clouding over, had thought of Doyler and MacEmm in the big house together. Boy, they was in for some waking up.

Now all of a sudden a woman appeared on the sward before him. She took her aim – it was hard to say, a giant pistol or a miniature rifle – calmly stood there and took her aim. She fired. A machine-gun was silenced, actually silenced. She returned, waving her arms, directing the withdrawal. She saw Jim gulping. 'Can't have the rotters have all the running,' she said.

Oh boy, my gracious, good grief – they better come soon,

Doyler and MacEmm. There wouldn't be nothing left them to do.

Blackrock, and the world awake. Knots of workmen gathered about the tram-stops, unwilling to walk but uncertain of holiday. The church doors were open, chapel as they still insisted in Ireland, and the hour drew its chain of pilgrims. Every passenger was pumped for his news, and that smidgen added to the general murmur. The soldiers, the rebels, the men of the north, the mountainy men, all of them up, marching all, the Prussians indeed on the Naas road.

It was disconcerting to be told such startling truths and never a hint of the teller's opinion. They had as well been gabbling of Poland or Salonika, such little consequence these rumours bore. The news itself was the marvel and the faces told the marvel of telling it.

Doyler went among the men, asking was anyone on strike, was any man of them here present called out on strike. He insisted on this point, and some of the men did look sheepish a touch, as though they believed they had ought to be on strike. But rumour soon had the better of that. Dundalk was known to be agitating. Galway was worse. Belfast for gospel was brung to a standstill. And did MacMurrough know three bishops had been shot dead in their mitres?

Who was it was out, Doyler asked, was it the Volunteers were out in Dublin? Sinn Feiners, he was told. The Sinn Feiners hadn't any arms, Doyler told them, did they mean the Volunteers? What the heck did it matter their name, weren't they out anyway? Then a young chap said, My brother's a Volunteer and he's not out. So's mine and me cousin, said another.

'Well, who is it out?' said Doyler. He was becoming angry,

and MacMurrough too was sensible of a rising animus, a want to separate from all by-standers and fire his Webley at their hats. See how I shoot? Make rumour of me. 'Have yous a bicycle even to lend a man?'

'We'll go on,' said MacMurrough.

'God damn yous for Irishmen,' Doyler cursed and spat.

Out on the road again, they discussed what could be made of it. 'I'm telling no secrets,' Doyler said, 'if I tell you now it was due on Sunday. Something went wrong then, and they called it off. I thought for good. Turns out now they only delayed it a day. But if I didn't know, how many others in the same boat? Looks to me there was a split in the Volunteers and it's only the madcaps gone out. Whatever about that, it's gone off half-cock.'

Well, of course it has, MacMurrough thought to himself. It wouldn't be an Irish rebellion else. There had always been something whimsical, even Punch-like, about Ireland at war. One thought of Emmett, the handsome romantic, and his long-laid plans confused by a riot. Of the Young Irelanders whose Tyrtaean anthems and Philippic gush could rise no further, push coming to shove, than the Battle of Widow McCormack's Cabbage Patch. Of the Fenians, when the rebel force, numbering some hundreds, finding itself lost in the fog, surrendered to a dozen astonished constabulary; their captors then precluding any escape by the ingenious expedient of removing the men's braces. A nation so famously seditious in song, so conspicuously inefficient in deed: it was only the comic that redeemed her. 'You don't really suppose Dublin can be in the hands of rebels?' he asked.

Doyler spat. 'If they wasn't arrested by the peeler on point.' MacMurrough nodded. Presently he added, 'Maybe it's true, there's German aid.'

'There's no German aid,' MacMurrough told him. 'An arms

ship was seized off Kerry. Sir Roger Casement is in prison in London.'

'Casement?'

'You've heard of him?'

'Everyone's heard of Casement. You know that for sure now? They have him in London?'

'Yes.'

He didn't say anything for a while. He shrugged. 'Could be like they say, the country is up.'

'Yes,' MacMurrough agreed. Because really, the alternative was too awful. A few hundred madcaps in arms in Dublin, and the British Empire ranging to strike.

The hedges chirped their hungry news, crows barracked above them. The fat contented cows munched their post-emulgial cud. The fields passed them by. Green they passed, and lushly green they stretched to the hills, whence mildly came the mizzling rain. The turf-smoke rose in rakes from the cottages. The air had a flatulent reek of earth. MacMurrough felt his pace had quickened. He heard Doyler's breath coming harder by his side. This country was not up. A fool would tell you this country was up.

Ballsbridge at last, the lip of the city; and here the rumours grew circumstantial. The OTC held Trinity for the Crown. The Castle had beat off a rebel attack. St Stephen's Green was barricaded and the Tommies drawn up in Merrion Row. And now they heard it. Crack. Crack. And then a score of cracks that scrunched together. 'Volleying,' said Doyler. 'That's the military.'

It's happening, MacMurrough told himself. I walk towards it. And yet, it was not happening. The Royal Spring Show was on. Tweedy hats, prize bulls, hobbled madams waited by the entrance. God damn this country, would it never make up its mind?

They turned towards Baggot Street. Way down from the canal, a lone figure cycled the middle of the road. 'Peeler,' said Doyler.

Yes, one of Dublin's famed giants in blue, a rain-caped spike-topped copper. 'I understood they were recalled to barracks.'

'Maybe only inside of the canals.'

'How far is the Green now?'

'Beyond over the bridge.'

'We need some momentum,' MacMurrough said. 'It grates on the nerves, this walking to war.'

'It's the dead that walk,' said Doyler.

Ghoulish thing to say. 'Why the dead?'

'Something Jim told me. Dream he had of his brother.'

His white-gloved hand waving, the policeman was calling to the people to remain in their homes. He might have been the barker for some fairground attraction. The people crowded the road behind to find out the advertised peril.

'Remind me now,' said MacMurrough, 'the police are the enemy?'

'Them lot's always the enemy. Wait now, you're not going to shoot him?'

'Of course I'm not going to shoot him.'

MacMurrough flagged the constable down. He scooted to a halt on the pedal, his kindly face raised. 'Now sir.'

MacMurrough said, 'My name is MacMurrough, of Ballygihen House and of High Kinsella, County Wexford. Do you understand?'

The constable nodded and brought his hand to salute. MacMurrough continued, 'Now, this fellow here, he fucked me last night. Isn't he the handsome rake? Yes, he fucked me something divine, then after he fetched up my arse, he turned me over and brought me off in his mouth. Glorious, constable, words cannot describe, you'd want to try it yourself. Or perhaps you have? In the meantime, you'll be so good as to lend me your bike for I find we're running late for the revolution.'

The constable followed but imperfectly the thrust of this communication, for in the act of his saluting, MacMurrough had punched him in the stomach. Punched so hard the constable doubled, and MacMurrough, still holding forth, boxed his face, a left upper-cut to the jaw and a right just under his nose. It was troublesome with the helmet and cape, so dispensing with the ring, he booted the man in the groin and kneed him upwards on the chin. He held him by the cape while he reeled. 'You want a go?'

'No,' said Doyler, shaking his head.

He let go the policeman, who crumpled to the road.

'Why'd you do that?'

'Oh I don't know.' MacMurrough picked up the bike. He was short of breath. The violence still trembled in his legs. 'The boot was by way of apology, I suppose.'

'Apology accepted.'

People were gathering. An elderly woman had fainted. 'I say,' came a man's voice.

Doyler knelt down to the policeman and was undoing his collar. 'You'll be all right, lay still.' The constable reached a hand to grab his ankle, and Doyler told him, in a very grown-up and reasoned voice, 'Be sensible, man. I won't mind shooting you at all and you must think of your wife and home.' His ankle was let go.

'They're robbing that poor man,' a lady said. 'Common thuggery, I call it,' pronounced a gentleman.

MacMurrough said, 'Well, we're in it now.'

Doyler stood up. 'Was that true about last night?' he wanted to know.

'Glorious, every minute. We'll do it again, I hope. Soon.'

A smile slanted across his face, half-doyler. 'You know, MacMurrough, I never disliked that side of it with you. It was always the 'tache I could never get beyond of.'

MacMurrough laughed. 'Cross-bar, or sit up behind?'

'Sit up behind'll do.'

MacMurrough plunged on the pedal. He splashed through puddles. The bike wobbled till he found his momentum. Wind at last. Yahoo, he heard Doyler call behind. The gunfire grew louder and the volleys imperative, ever more imperious. He heard the garrulous natter of machine-guns. Here we go, our mad minute of glory, charging towards it. And it was true, the dead it was that walked. See them mutter and stare from the pavements. His aunt was right. It was far too absurd to die of a Tuesday.

A tingling in his arse told him it was today Tuesday, and he laughed out loud. 'We'll all be dead by tonight,' he called to Doyler.

'Sure I know that,' Doyler called back. 'Yahoo!'

The sergeant whispered Jim the word, and Jim leapt from the trench. He careered it over the lawn, dodging and ducking behind tree trunks, weaving in and out, skipping the branches that had fallen, other debris he didn't know what it was, the lawn-rail. He heard the sergeant calling him back, but he was damned if he was cowering any longer nor crawling behind them pudding posteriors. The bullets came amazing close, ssshooting past. The noise quite shocked at times. But he reckoned he had the gauge of them now. They had no wish to hit him or hurt him, only to be the same place as he. It was fool's play really. All he needed was to keep one step ahead. The corner of his eye he saw the swerving skew of their impact, sure miles off aim the most of them. The land rose for the bridge over the pond. He resisted the lure of the parapet's shelter. The machine-guns tore up the water and the ducks again quackled and fled. Now his stamp on the wet sand path. Lawn-rail again and the slippery, whoops, slithery grass. He was there but for the mound to climb. There were trees up above and he saw flashes between of returning fire. He wanted to cheer. He was gallant and gay. It crossed his mind to stop now, kneel and take careful aim.

A shout. He looked round. The sergeant had followed him. He was down. Jim's feet carried on, teetering a bit, before he had command of them. He turned back. The sergeant was waving him away, cursing him. Jim shook his head, trying to think why the man had followed him at all. Couldn't he see it was dangerous? It was only his ankle, his bleddy ankle, twisted it. Jim took his arm but he couldn't shift his weight. It was all very awkward with his gun in one hand and the clutch of cartridges he kept in the other. The sergeant carried on cursing in his bleddy way, telling Jim he had hold the wrong arm, was he born defective. Jim thought quickly. He took the man's rifle and ran up the mound, flung both their guns into the keeping of hands there and ran back down the slope. The sergeant had hobbled to his feet. Jim saw them floatingly, a line of dancing raindrops, tracing their lenient curve towards him. The sergeant was a goner. There was only the one way to save him, and he threw himself on top, hurling the man to the ground. He lay covering his corporation with as much as his body and limbs would allow. The bullets veered as he had known they must, though it was astonishing how close they would come and still not hit you. He had felt their wind even. Can you walk at all? Bleddy lunatic.

At last they woke up on the mound. Fellows were coming

out, reaching their hands down. 'Will you hurry up,' said Jim. It was vexing beyond belief. They hopped the sergeant one way or another round the bank of elm trees and down behind the hump in the ground. Jim lay with his head against the slope, breathing, luxuriating in breath. Suddenly, he was shivering cold.

'Is he all right?' a girl asked. 'He's shocking pale.'

'Leave him stew,' said a man.

'Ankle,' uttered Jim. 'He got it twisted.'

'That's right,' said the girl, 'heave it up now, you'll be fine.'

'What's up with him?' said a boy's voice piping.

'He's after getting his sergeant near killed.'

'Oh,' said the boy's voice piping.

Jim wiped his mouth on the back of his hand. He swallowed, his throat bitter and raw. The flush receded. He took off his bush-hat. He was sweating and cold and hot.

The boy said, 'You want a custard pie?'

Jim's eyes focused. 'How old are you supposed to be?' he asked.

'Jeez,' said the boy and walked away.

Twice now Mr Mack had returned to Ballygihen, but no sign of anyone, nor Doyler nor Mr MacMurrough, only that chappie of a gardener who wished it be known he was caretaker now and who did Mr Mack think he was, agitating this here bell of the big house. No luck at the Forty Foot: nobody swimming and no sight of Jim, the only news on any man's tongue was Dublin, Dublin, Dublin. Wearily, traipsily, Mr Mack set his face in the rain toward Kingstown.

The streets were awake now. Already George's Street crawled with traffic. At the junction with Marine Road he saw the why of that: a kind of a picket had formed, manned by respectable gentleman of the Georgius Rex with brassards on their sleeves, and a couple Baden-Poweller boys in uniforms and hats. They were stopping drivers and asking questions. Nothing what you would call official, they assured Mr Mack, but still something had to be done to put a halt to these Sinn Feiner rascals; and Mr Mack, saluting with a tip of his boater, agreed, saying it was a shocking state of affairs altogether, and only for he was stepping into town himself he would stop to lend a hand.

'What business would that be on?' asked one of the gentlemen, and Mr Mack, taking a breath to reply, had the breath taken from him by the sound that now approached from the harbour below. Soldiers, hundreds of them, sure what was he saying, half a battalion at the very least, and the scrunch of their boots on the road, all in step, at a marching gait, in column of two files, coming up from the mailboat pier. And louder still they came, rank upon rank, there seemed no end to them, battalion, half a brigade, and he shook his head in wonder. Holy God, his lips muttered and he blessed himself with a slow-moving hand. Has it come to this already?

He heard their voices now, the more likely lads calling out Parley-voo or Bonjour mamselle to the feminine gender that gathered to look, the way they had it mistook for some place foreign where they'd landed: their accents of the English Midlands queer as Russian in this fashionable town. He saw their faces, haggard and sick-looking some of them, after the crossing they had of it, young fellows of Gordie's age, no more, all weighed down with equipment, with rifle and pack and the accoutrements of war, their officers looking warily about them, distrusting. Though the populace was doing its best now, with cups of tea and plates of bread, distributing them, and a school had opened its gates for a billet.

Up the rebels! some fool of a youngster was heard to cry, but the crowd descended so quick, Mr Mack could see no face, only the boots kicking before the lad was trundled away. Holy Mother of God, he thought to himself. And this is only the beginning of it. This is only the very beginning.

The traffic had been stopped this while, and Mr Mack had grown aware, on the back of his head, of the intimidation of unfriendly stares. He turned to catch a young Baden-Poweller watching from under his Boy Scout hat. Now he heard this pipsqueak say, 'Granddadda,' pulling on a gentleman's sleeve, 'he's one of them, I'm sure of it, Granddadda.'

'What's this now?' said Mr Mack.

'Glasthule, Granddadda, remember? He was in the papers about it. The recruitment posters.'

'Now now,' said Mr Mack sternly, 'don't you be talking things you know nothing about. Now look here,' he added to the men who closed about him, 'will you have the goodness to take your hands off of me?'

'Fetch a constable,' said a gentlemen.

'Put him in charge,' said another.

Mr Mack shrugged his arms but the grip of the men, for all their respectability, was surprising tight. One had produced a musket even. Some of the folks watching made mutter about the King's Highway and the liberty to walk thereon, but most said nothing at all, only the louts in the crowd who set up that curious Irish jeer of a cheer while they waited on the peelers' coming. But Mr Mack did not think of the crowd while he stood there in the gentlemen's grip; not of the crowd, nor of the papers nor his customers nor shop. When the constables came, all six of them, wiping their bakes of their grinny breakfasts, he gave them no thought, whoreson oafs though they were who, given their day, would drive the entire nation into the arms of the Fenians. No thought to the constables nor any to the Georgius Rex: the people had the right of that, gentlemen my backside, gorgeous wrecks was all they were. He did not think of canon nor curate, of doors, tuppenny nor sixpenny. Not of Ireland nor Dublin, which both must surely be brought to ruin. His years with the Colours were nothing to him, his regiment might never have been. While the constables marched him away, he stared back up the road where the soldiers had gone, the first of thousands to come, thinking only, helplessly, Jim, my son James, my son, my Jim.

The rebel officer – though they were not to be called rebels: this was a rising, not a rebellion and the officer stickled for the distinction – pointed out the areas of interest. 'We have posts in Leeson Street and Harcourt Street. We had the railway station too, but with so few turned out, that was more a liability than much else. We hold the Green itself, or we did hold it till this morning. Headquarters is currently removing to the College of Surgeons.' He indicated a grey façade across the far western end of the park, just visible through a tracery of elms, where the Republican flag breezed above.

'Commandant MacDonagh holds Jacob's mills up the way. Commandant de la Vera holds Boland's mills down the way. No shortage of tucker for us. You probably know the general headquarters is up at the General Post Office. That is where the Republic was declared and Commandant-General Pearse read the proclamation.'

Post office! MacMurrough repeated to himself. At last, the Republic of Letters!

'The British,' the young man continued, 'insofar as they bear on our forces in the Green, hold the Shelbourne Hotel with, we believe, two machine-gun crews, any number of sharp-shooters and they have a barricade manned in Merrion Row. Portobello barracks is kept pretty brisk and Beggars Bush too. The Castle, there's fighting still. If you listen you can hear it. That other you can hear is Trinity where the West Brits is playing Old Harry with our communications.'

The Green was laid out as a rectangle with broad avenues running the length of each side, these then terraced with banks, hotels, gentlemen's clubs, meeting-houses, more hotels, one or two churches to relieve the eye, the like. They had cycled slap bang into the military at the Baggott Street end, so MacMurrough had doubled round to the Leeson Street entry, where Doyler had hailed this rebel officer. He had been on a scouting mission and was now returning, with his two companions, to rejoin the main rebel force. The Shelbourne rose just across the park from them, a matter of three hundred yards, and they were strolling, this officer in full rebel rig plus sombrero, in blatant view of its serried windows.

'I don't mind now,' said Doyler, in a carefully neutral tone, 'but is it supposed to be safe walking here?'

'From the British? Safe enough. For the moment they have game in plenty with our men retreating to the Surgeons. You'll see it now in a minute. It sounds to me there's one of their machine-guns down. That'll be only temporary, of course. Madame got one of them earlier.'

'Did she too?'

'Stepped out calm as a clock, and as cold.'

MacMurrough said, 'What about casualties?'

'Ask yourself this,' the officer replied: 'three-foot trenches and the crack of dawn machine-guns spewing from above.'

MacMurrough exchanged glances with Doyler, each asking of the other the solution to this conundrum. 'Have you heard tell at all,' said Doyler, 'of a young chap, name of Jim Mack?'

'Not I,' said the officer. 'Volunteer, is he?'

'Don't know rightly what he'd be.'

'You can make all the inquiries you want, Doyle, after you report to Section. You missed parade on Sunday. You skipped your guard detail too. Now you're telling me another man has your rifle. By rights, you'd be thrown in the guardhouse.'

'Is it Connolly in charge here?'

'Commandant-General Connolly is at the GPO. Commandant-General Connolly has been promoted commander-in-chief of all Republican forces in Dublin.'

Doyler whistled between his teeth. 'So that's what they gave him. Command of the Volunteers.'

'You know I don't like you, Doyle, so you can button your lip. There are no Volunteers any more, nor citizen soldiers. There is only the Irish Republican Army now.'

'Who's in charge here, so? – sir,' he added.

'Commandant Mallin.'

How many commandants did they need? MacMurrough wondered. He wondered too what might be his station in life, this satisfied Republican soldier. Clerk, copyist, pen-repairer, some blind alley his talents would never be recognized. One saw it best at country fairs: the organizational zeal of stewards who the remainder of the year bushelled along as grocer's assistants, sacristans, the like. Or am I being a scintilla unfair? Who am I, MacMurrough, to impugn another man's motives?

The wind of their bike-ride had flagged. A shame, but they walked again deadly-lively with the crowd. That bloody machine-gun – like a very loud typewriter. Some old bugger in the Shelbourne firing off a complaint to the manager. He listened to the distinctive report of the rebels' Mausers. He had shot Mausers himself, and he knew them for good guns, even

these vintage single-loaders. Shot straight, shot far, shot hard –
just didn't shoot very often.

Of course Jim's all right. I should know, the world should
blast it, were anything the slightest wrong.

'No,' the officer expanded, 'this side of the Green we have
little to fear of the British. It's them hussies behind are the
menace here.'

Yes, they were trailing something of a mêlée in their wake.
Fishwives, slatterns, the usual Dublin viragos, hurled abuse
at their backs for filthy rebels, dirty Sinn Feiners, fly-boys,
fire-siders, pop-gunners, together with some general remarks
touching the male anatomy. Their leader and sense-carrier, a
stout specimen with a wonderful, though perhaps accidental,
décolletage, carried the handle of a pick which she slapped in her
hand in a manner that quite overthreatened the meagre elephant-
guns of the insurgents. She took notice of MacMurrough's
admiring look and unleashed a stream of invective that cast
his ancestry, vaunted these centuries, in a wholly new and
uncertain light.

'Separation women,' the officer said, 'paid off by the British.'
He turned of a sudden and boomed, 'If you are Irish women at
all, you will return to your kitchens and mind your spinning.'

An utterance nicely gauged to disperse the viraginous mob.
Even his companions raised eyebrows. 'Spinning,' said Doyler
in MacMurrough's ear, 'where does he think they're out of?'

'Tell him about Baggot Street, the soldiers.'

'There's military round the corner in Baggot Street, sir,'
Doyler said. 'Maybe three or four hundred. We cycled straight
into them.'

'What are they at?'

'Drinking tea mostly. People in the houses is bringing it out
to them.'

'Devil the tea they'd bring us.'

There had been a traffic accident at the end of the street which closer inspection proved a barricade. They passed through and of a sudden, there they were, behind the rebel line. Some few rebels were ranged upon a shady hump inside the Green, sprawled in regulation firing-pose; others sat on the slope behind, breakfasting it seemed. Whistles blew; and every so often a party jumped the park railings and dashed the street to the College of Surgeons, a grim cold columned edifice whose pavement and roof were periodically swept by machine-gunfire from the Shelbourne. Rifle-shots skipped off the far cobbles, twanged off the bollards. How very differently, MacMurrough noted, a bullet sounded at the unfavourable end of the barrel. Saving ricochets, they were safe enough on this side of the street. But who were these others—

'Who are those people there supposed to be?' he asked.

'Them?' said the officer. 'That's the gallery.'

Citizens, for the most part men, in doorways, on the steps of a church, in the maws of alleys and lanes, in far more obvious danger than any of the rebels, spectating. Here was that quintessence of Dublin, the epitome of the quidnunc, that quarter-moon, man-in-the-moon face, with the chin jutting to meet the nose and the mouth slanting some neat aperçu to its neighbour, cheekiest face in Europe, and the nosiest. MacMurrough heard, or fancied he heard, the commentary kept up: the accuracy of fire debated, the different weaponry compared, alternative venues cried up or down, the better vantages disputed.

The disappointment, which had swelled all during their walk by the Green, now lumped in MacMurrough's throat. There was nothing going to be splendid here. The stupid wonder of these people, their excitable unconcern when – ooh! – a rebel was nearly downed crossing the street, it really was too much. It was unconscionable. And now, it wanted but this, here came the

fishwives again, and wouldn't you know, with cabbages this time
to hurl with their abuse. He hurried out of range and there was
some small stir when a rebel lad aimed his rifle at their ringleader.
Shoot her by all means, MacMurrough enjoined, flicking bloody
filth from his trousers, but don't let's spare the men with their
mealy-mouthed mean-eyed gawping and never a one with the
courage of his derision.

He felt a nudge from Doyler. He followed his nod. And there
he was, Jim Mack.

He was acting as a kind of rebel policeman, standing in the
street, waving the groups to cross to the Surgeons – no wait a
minute, halt, yes quickly now, safely now, don't trip. It was quite
possible his job was important. It was even possible he was doing
it well. What was undeniable was, a foot or so closer to the park
and he should perform the same duty in absolute safety – but
no, he must venture this further foot where the military could
just bother the brim of his hat.

In a flash MacMurrough knew the morning he had spent.
Nothing beyond him, nothing the equal of him, his earnest
noddings, his half-baked suggestions, retreating from the trenches
three or four times till he was satisfied he got it right. There he
stood in his baggy drapes and his outsize hat. Behold, he goes
to war, my boy.

It was a moment too glorious meanly to keep and he turned
to Doyler as Doyler turned, their faces brimming, to share the
delight. They nodded to each other, an agreement at last: not
as prize-fighters will agree, or barristers, after their bout: an
acknowledgment of what they shared, of two who had been led
a merry old dance.

'I better report,' said Doyler.

'Yes, I suppose I had best make myself known.'

'You sure you're staying?'

'Wild horses,' said MacMurrough.

'I'll tell them you's a Volunteer captain. It's no lie anyway. I'll tell them you was caught on the hop in Dublin and you can't get down into Wexford. That's no lie neither.'

Yes, his poor Wexford boys. MacMurrough wondered how they fared. It was a rotten shame, but he was not a man to lead other men. He could not give courage as great men do, as a comical kid could even. But he did not lack conduct, his aunt had reminded him that. He recalled now the small boy who had played along the sea-wall. By night he had dreamt of magnificence and on the wings of its tales he flew. Well, it was more miserable here than magnificent, he supposed. But he believed he might reach across the years to that boy and lift him up on his high shoulders. See, I come to war because I love that boy. See how beautiful he is, see how fine. Here is his friend: he too is fine and beautiful. They go to war because they love, each his country. And I too love my country. Do you feel the wind that is rising, the magnificent wind? These things will come, my dear. Let you dream of this.

He returned the little boy to his rocks by the sea where too the drizzle fell. He thought now of Aunt Eva as they wandered, he and Doyler, down the road to Jim. She'd have taken the Shelbourne, yes she would, with just her Webley a-wobble in her hand, and there'd be none of this nonsense of entrenching a park. Her verve, her dash, her bottom, her form – of all the misfortunes, Ireland's too, to be incarcerated this week in the Castle.

Doyler was frowning. He was gazing beyond Jim at the terrace of buildings that fronted the end of the street. Gentlemen's clubs, officers' clubs, where the Union flag flew above. MacMurrough wasn't sure, but he believed he too had seen something. Doyler said, 'Them windows just opened.'

'Yes, I thought so too.'

'That second machine-gun, I wonder now what happened it?'

'Yes, I wonder,' said MacMurrough.

'Did you ever hear of a raking fire?'

An enfilade, MacMurrough was going to reply, but he was stung by something in the hand. He heard Doyler shouting. He was shouting Jim's name. MacMurrough brought his hand to look at it. He found he was kneeling in the road. He looked at the blood dripping from his palm. While he looked, blood clouded his eyes.

Jim turned smiling at the shout. Doyler was running for him, that funny run he had. He saw his clothes on him, all wrists and ankles. He was just saying something, something like, Here you are at last, and Doyler flung into him. The breath thumped out of Jim. He fell flump on the road with Doyler on top. Doyler said something that sounded like Oh-oh.

Jim lifted his shoulders. The head hung limp. 'Doyler?' he said, turning him over. He saw MacEmm sitting in the road with his handkerchief out. There was blood on his face. 'Doyler?' he said again.

Feet were rushing across the street. There was some screaming. Pebbles kicked up off the setts. The second machine-gun had opened fire. But where? He shook Doyler's shoulders. No no no, he had saved the sergeant. 'MacEmm!' he cried.

Up along the street the trace of bullets came. Jim flattened on top of Doyler and the blast veered short. He sprang up and reached his arms under Doyler's shoulders. He hefted him up. 'MacEmm!' he cried. He was dragging Doyler toward the Surgeons. A burst of fire riddled the street and Doyler's body jerked. His shirt was, his shirt was ripped, and his belly was, his belly was ripped too. Jim turned the other way, himself between Doyler and harm, dragging him against the fire, but the bullets zipped from the other gun now, and again the body jerked, just jerked. No no no, I saved the sergeant. 'I saved the sergeant!' he screamed. Even as Doyler slipped from his arms, another fire ripped through him. Jim stood bestride his body, his rifle aimed. A body blundered by. The rifle was snatched from his hands. 'MacEmm,' he said, 'I can't see where they are.'

MacMurrough aimed the rifle. His head teetered with ponderables: windage, distance, sighting, all useless. He could not hold his hand still. He lowered the gun. The fingers were gripped in his hand and he forced them to loose. The pain shot through and blood blinked in his eye again. Then all of one movement, he swung the gun up where it aimed and fired.

The near rattering ceased.

Jim was cradling Doyler's head. He seemed in a shock. He was telling of some incident with a sergeant, most persistently telling it. 'Yes,' MacMurrough said, 'that's good.' He took off his coat and he laid it over the maul of Doyler's wounds. He slewed the rifle over his shoulder and pushed his Webley into Jim's hand. 'Guard me,' he said, knowing his words could have no meaning.

'You're hit,' said Jim.

MacMurrough said, 'My hand, nothing.'

'No, your head, hit in the head.'

He bent down and lifted Doyler in his arms. It seemed the very edge of madness, for they were talking in the middle of a street that whizzed with bullets and ricochets. Fire was returned from the Surgeons roof. Symbolic, like his own with the machine-gun that already had started again.

'Come now,' he said to Jim. He carried the body to the

far pavement, Jim treading beside. The bollards twanged about them, the cobbles rebounded. In the sanctuary of a lane by the Surgeons, he laid Doyler down.

Already a man was at his side, whispering into his ear, Confiteor Deo omnipotenti, beatae Mariae semper Virgini . . .

MacMurrough looked at Jim's face. The eyes were blinking with a strange period. His chin trembled. The whispered prayer stuttered on his lips. He lifted his face. 'I saved the sergeant,' he said to MacMurrough.

. . . nimis cogitatione, verbo et opere . . . Of all things fatuous, MacMurrough noted the man's pronunciation. A European Latin, as though it were a language.

'Volunteer Mack.' A hand touched on Jim's shoulder. 'Volunteer Mack, there.'

It was an officer. MacMurrough saw Jim snap to attention. His blinking had ceased.

'Is this a civilian death, do you know?'

Jim answered, 'Doyle, sir. Citizen Army.'

'So it is,' said the officer. 'May God rest his soul. He would best be removed to a hospital. I'll detail two men.'

MacMurrough said, 'No. He's a soldier. He'll be coming inside.'

The officer looked him up and down. 'Do you say so?'

'So,' said MacMurrough. He bent down again to Doyler. His hand passed through the scrag of his hair and under his head. The man with the prayer had closed his eyes. Gently again he lifted his body. The pain seared up his arm to sway his head. He looked at Jim, who cold and unseeing stared. 'Come now, my dear,' he said. 'We'll bring him in now.'

CHAPTER TWENTY-ONE

T HEY WERE WALKING as they had often walked, dosey-doe together, with his arm round Jim's neck and Jim's head bending to his shoulder. He said, Will I tell you a story of Johnny Magorey? Tell so, said Jim. But he didn't tell. His arm squeezed a pinch and he danced out ahead. Jim had a notion of his shirt loose in the wind and his black hair flowing. Then he dipped below the sand dunes. Come on, Jim heard him calling – Slow as a wet week, so y'are. Amn't I coming, said Jim.

It was a place they knew very well, where they always came to swim, though when Jim tried he could not think the name. Doyler was already tugging off his clothes. Jim was far too fond to watch. He just smiled in the direction the shirt dazzled, where the gleaming black hair coursed in the wind. Are you straight, Jim Mack? Straight as a rush, Jim told him. Come on with me so. He was out in the waves where the breakers rolled and the sound came like far away. Will I tell you a story of Johnny Magorey? There isn't any story, Jim told him laughing. Not much, said Doyler. His hand held out, and Jim reached for it, but he tricked it away and Jim pushed through a wave.

He dived under his legs and came back on the surface with his feet on the sand. Doyler was gone, and for a moment

Jim couldn't find him. Then he saw him back over by the dunes and he ran out of the water shouting, Doyler! Where you going?

It was hard work climbing them dunes and when Jim got to the brim he saw that Doyler was gone even farther away. He was walking up this slope, just walking up this slope, and Jim didn't think if he'd ever catch him. Doyler! he called. Doyler, will you wait a minute! He was getting angry now and he called out, I'm not following you any more! But Doyler kept to his walking. Please stop, Jim cried. Won't you stop it now? Doyler, please, you can't leave me! Don't leave me here!

'Doyler!'

He sat up bolt on the floor. His breath drew fast and shallow. Men coughed in the dark, they moved in their sleep. By the door the sentry horse-like stamped. He smelt the reek of slop-pails. From very close behind, MacEmm said, 'Are you all right, Jim?'

Jim nodded. He felt the miss of something in his hand, and he started, checking for his Webley. But the British of course had that taken from him. He leant back on MacMurrough's shoulder and MacMurrough's arm came round his side. They seemed alone in the vaulting barrack hall: a curtain of dark removed the other prisoners. He had that way, did MacEmm, of finding a place apart, or just by being there making it apart.

'MacEmm, I'm frightened,' Jim said.

'Yes, my dear,' said MacMurrough, sounding tired and low, 'we're all a bit frightened now that it's over.'

'No, I'm frightened if they don't shoot us.'

MacEmm's arm gave a squeeze of his side. 'Nobody's going to be shot now.'

'They will too be shot,' said Jim. 'But I'm worried they won't shoot me. They'll say I'm too young or something and I'll be left out.'

'You're being silly, Jim. We're prisoners of war. There's nothing like shooting going to happen.'

'You don't understand.'

'Well, what is it so?'

'I know what I'll become if they let me go. And I don't know can I bear to be that.'

'You'll be a schoolteacher, of course.'

Jim thought of that a while, trying to make sense of the sound of the word. A school, a teacher, schoolteachering. 'I suppose there will be such things,' he said. 'All that will go on, I suppose. But it won't for me.'

He leant on his elbow, looking up at MacMurrough's face. 'You know, don't you, MacEmm, what I'll be. I'll be ruthless with them. I'll shoot them easy as stones. I won't never give up. I'll be a stone myself. Tell me you know that.' MacMurrough's hand just patted him. 'If you loved me, you'd tell me.'

'You're tired, Jim. You'll feel better in the morning.'

Jim weighed his head again on the shoulder. 'I don't know why you won't tell me.'

MacMurrough's hand come round his chest. It fiddled with his shirt buttons, doing them up. 'You'll be a schoolteacher,' he said. 'I'll find an island where we'll live. A small island all to ourselves. There'll be sand and dunes and cliffs. We shall call it Noman. Do you know why we shall call it Noman?'

'Go on so.'

'Because no man is an island. Listen to me now. We'll have a cow and a pig and hens. We'll go swimming every day. The weather will be atrocious. I shall smoke a pipe.'

'And who'll I teach on an island all to ourselves?'

'There'll be other islands convenient with whole families of gurriers crying out for pandies.'

Jim smiled, feeling the crack in his face. He was kind was MacEmm to think of these things. And he would try to be with him on his island when he could. But he wouldn't be swimming no more. He would be a stone and he would sink. He knew it annoyed MacEmm, him speaking this way, but he could not help it, and he said, 'You know I'll be a stone. Why won't you tell me you know, if you love me?'

'Shush now, Jim. There's men trying to sleep.'

'You don't love me at all.'

The arm came tightly round and the hand pressed upon his heart. MacEmm's breath was in his ear, telling him it would pass, it would all pass, it would one day be over. 'You won't forget any of it, my dear, I promise you that. But you'll swim again and smile. I swear it.'

But no, it would never be over, Jim knew. This was only the beginning. They had to do this to learn how to hate. They had forgotten to hate the British. Now they'd learn. And they wouldn't be playing soldiers no more. Next time would be murder. And he'd murder every last one till they were gone of his country. That he would. 'Every last one,' he told MacMurrough. 'And still I'll kill them. I'll kill them for fun if there was any fun to be had.'

'Stop it, Jim. You'll get no comfort thinking that way. It's not what anyone would have wanted. Not anyone,' MacMurrough repeated, holding Jim tightly still.

'Sure don't I know,' said Jim, and he heard his voice flinty and frail. 'He'd never want me this way. Nor you too, MacEmm. That's why I hope they'll shoot us all. I don't know can I bear to become what I'll be.'

'You'll be my lovely boy,' said MacMurrough, 'and you'll

grow to be my lovely man. That's all now. You must try get some sleep.' He bent down and kissed Jim's head, pulling his fingers through the drag of his hair. Then he laid back his own head against the wall.

The smell of smoke and burning oils wafted in the window draughts. He would murder this minute for a cigarette. A Rosary was being told by some of the men and he listened a while to the soft-spoke rhyme. Every now and then his hand lifted of itself and patted the boy's side. He was scttling at last, curled inside MacMurrough's shoulder.

Distantly, intermittently, a Mauser barked – some kid on the roofs who had not heard, or would not heed, the general surrender. It was told Pearse and Connolly yet lived, though it was difficult to conceive anyone's surviving the GPO. Those last nights the conflagration had helled all Dublin.

'Think of it,' the woman they called Madam had said to him while they watched the fires from the Surgeons roof: 'that's not Rome burning, that's Dublin.'

And yes, there was a certain grandeur to it. 'When this is over,' MacMurrough had murmured, 'they'll crucify us.'

'Won't they!' Madam replied.

And MacMurrough had quizzed her face, under the blue startling light of a British flare, this incongruous banditta who was officer second-in-command of their troop: like no one so much as his aunt, but his aunt corrected, unfettered to the past.

'Will they see this from Glasthule?' Jim had broke in.

'They will, my dear.' Yes, they would be crowding Killiney Hill for their view.

'My poor father.'

MacMurrough had seen him then, Mr Mack in his straw boater, up on the Hill, among the crowd but not of it, an eavesdrop on the general consternation, his eyes never shifting from the flickering sky; and the words muttered on his great fatherful face, *Jim, my son James,* while the fires burnt, the fires of Dublin, Dublin burning. MacMurrough had felt the terrible onus to survive.

Though in its way, a childish Irish way, it had proved a civil enough fight for them at the Surgeons. Unofficial lulls thrice daily for the Angelus; the decided ceasefire every morning, eleven sharp, when the park-keeper fed the ducks in the Green. Childish too the caprice of their rations: finest plum jam but no bread to scrape it on, tea brewed of cabbage water, cake. And a kid-soldier who stopped MacMurrough to inquire were they winning: 'Only,' said he, 'I never been in a revolution before.' The bombardment of the GPO had fascinated MacMurrough: the annunciatory puffs of smoke and the flames that roared to greet them; then the crashing gun's report, the shell's eruption – an illogical sequence, effect before cause, an object lesson in the madness of war. In the incomparable weather of that week, under that bluest of skies after the Tuesday rain, the domes and spires of the city's soul had seemed curious idlers watching a quarrel.

And they too had seemed idlers who watched from the Surgeons roof. All week had grown a sense of disengagement. The occasional firefight, bloody at times, but mostly the hours of waiting, of pot-shots and Rosaries. Typical to find oneself in the unfashionable end of a rising. For one by one the British had cut off the rebel outposts. Surrounded them, and more or less disregarded them; to concentrate their ire on the GPO, where the flag flew over Connolly and Pearse, the genius perhaps and certainly the heart of the fight.

The order to surrender came on the Sunday morning. There was some rankling among a part of the men who fabulously all week had sustained the persuasion that all was well.

MacMurrough found Jim in the makeshift chapel in the college anatomy-room, where the rebel dead were laid out on slabs. He was staring with that unblinking gaze that newly had come upon his face. A dust of rubble powdered his cheeks, and he stony and still the way a tear would crack him. 'Come, my dear,' MacMurrough said. 'We must leave him now.'

'What will happen?'

'He'll be treated with respect, I'm sure. They're soldiers.'

'I mean with us.'

'Well, we'll be prisoners.'

'I see.'

His rosary beads had dropped by his side and MacMurrough crouched to pick them up.

'You can keep them,' the boy said. 'I won't be needing beads no more.'

The British marched them through the streets. All hungry Dublin crowded the way. In all that taunting spitting mob one man gravely had lifted his hat. That little, lovely, silent act recalled MacMurrough to Wilde, when Wilde too had been paraded for the crowd. And MacMurrough had wondered could there truly be something to this business – that stooping so utterly low one should rise again to gain all.

Now the British held them prisoner, in their temporary gaol, a barracks hall. MacMurrough lay against the wall and Jim lay sleeping on his chest. They stretched ahead, the years, of military confinement, convict labour. How many, he wondered, would the British shoot? If yet they lived, Connolly and Pearse, they were walking dead. They said his aunt was dead. Caught in a crossfire at the Castle, they said. MacMurrough reached his hand in his pocket where he kept Jim's beads. There was a comfort in the childhood shapes, the aves and gauds that rolled in his fingers.

He remembered the moment in the street with a dreamlike vividity. He had grabbed Jim's rifle and fumbled to fire it. The bullets everywhere zipped driftingly by. He had taken a breath, and in its inspiration he heard his aunt's voice telling him again and again to be brave, to be proud. Then he had felt it, all about him, the wind of the beat of magnificent wings. Here was splendour at last, splendour indeed, splendour enough for a lifetime. In that confusion of senses, it was no wonder if the rifle sighted by ear. He picked up the boy's body in his arms and the shreds of a heart walked beside him.

When later in the week they brought him news of his aunt, he had not needed to be told, for the scene had revealed itself while about him that wind had beat. She was slumped on a Castle balcony, her death-face grim and ghosted still with exhilaration. Shorty lay beside her, though whether he had given his pistol for her to fire, or she had seized it from him, he was now too mum to tell, indominatably . . .

MacMurrough brought his hand to his head where the ache all week had not ceased. He closed his eyes, and wove through the pain till he summoned the form of an island home. He would build that home for Jim. Brick by brick he would build it. He had never built before, but now he would begin. He wished to God it would all be over. It was tedious of the British to delay him this way. He wanted to be making a start, to build.

It was true what Jim said, this wasn't the end but the beginning. But the wars would end one day and Jim would come there then, to the island they would share. One day surely the wars would end, and Jim would come home, if only to lie broken in MacMurrough's arms, he would come to his island home. And MacMurrough would have it built for him, brick by brick, washed by the rain and the reckless sea. In the living stream they'd swim a season. For maybe it was true that no man is an island: but he believed that two very well might be.

Jim's eyes had fallen closed, and when he opened them again morning already blew through the curtains. Will I tell you a story of Johnny Magorey? Jim looked from the bed and there he was, sitting on the window-sill. What are you doing here? Jim said. Get up out of that, Doyler told him, sure it's a grand day out.

It was too. A bluey smoky morning where the dew on the grass looked live and lovely. Doyler dropped on the lawn and Jim slipped out through the window behind him.

Who's that, your man inside with you? Oh sure you know, said Jim shyly. Doyler grinned, but Jim didn't look at him grinning. He didn't need to, the grin was all round him. Will I tell you a story of Johnny Magorey? Tell me so, said Jim.

Will I begin it? said Doyler laughing. That's all that's in it, he laughing said.

Oh sure that grin. Oh sure that wonderful saucerful grin. Jim sat on the grass and he plucked at the blades. He knew for certain sure that Doyler would be turning from him again. He said, You'll be walking away from me soon, won't you now? There was no answer. Jim plucked the grass and stared beyond where the waves broke on the island shore. He said, I wish if you wouldn't, Doyler. It does break my heart when you walk away.

Old pal o' me heart, said Doyler.

But already he had turned, and he was walking away. Walking that slow dreadful slope with never a leaf or a stone. Walking; and though Jim tried to keep pace, he could not, and sometimes he called out, Doyler! Doyler! but he never heard or he did not heed, only farther and farther he walked away. And when Jim woke from these dreams, if he did not remember, he knew he had dreamt, for the feeling inside him of not feeling at all. And it was hard then to make his day, hard to make anything much save war; and those years that followed had plenty war.

After a time he learnt to harbour the share of his heart was left him, and he did not look for Doyler, not in crowds nor the tops of trams, nor in the sudden faces of lads he trained and led to fight. Even in his dreams he did not look for him, but stared at the sea while behind him he knew Doyler so dreadfully walked away; and after he woke he stayed where he lay, fingering the revolver he kept by his side.

He never looked again for his friend, until one time, though it was years to come, years that spilt with hurt and death and closed in bitter most bitter defeat, one time when he lay broken and fevered and the Free State troopers were hounding the fields, when he lay the last time in MacMurrough's arms, and MacEmm so tightly held him close: his eyes closed as he drifted away, and that last time he did look for his friend. Doyler was far far away on his slope, and his cap waving in the air. 'What cheer, eh?' he called.